classics omnibus

D.H. Lawrence

2 Books in 1

Sons and Lovers

&

Women in Love

A Wilco Book

Outstanding works of universal interest

© WILCO PUBLISHING HOUSE 2004

This Omnibus edition printed in 2007

ISBN NO.: 81-8252-284-6

D.H. Lawrence
Sons and Lovers &
Women in Love

Complete and Unabridged

Published by
WILCO PUBLISHING HOUSE
33, Sri Saibaba Marg, Kalaghoda,
Mumbai – 400 023. INDIA
Tel: (91-22) 22041420 / 22842574
Fax: (91-22) 22041429
E mail: wilcos@vsnl.com

About the Author

D. H. LAWRENCE
(1885-1930)

Famed novelist, poet, essayist, and author of short stories, David Herbert Lawrence was born in a small colliery village of Eastwood in Nottinghamshire, in the U.K.

Lawrence's maiden novel *The White Peacock* appeared in the newspaper *English Review* in 1911, but it was his enchanting poems that were first published six years later. He expressed his utter dismay at the hypocritical Anglo-Saxon mindset in a harsh satire; had radical ideas on relationships between the sexes, and held a burlesque view of the rapidly industrializing world. No wonder the works of Lawrence led to heated controversies and invited censorship for 'fescennine indecency'.

During the tense period of WW-I, his wife Frieda's alleged sympathies with the Germans added further woes to the lives of the couple, forcing them to leave England and migrate in search of a new homeland – in Italy, Germany, Ceylon, Australia, and the United States – never returning to England.

The poems of D.H. Lawrence revolved around the nature and the inner lives of animals, flowers, and plants. He is however best remembered for his novels; the most popular among them: *Sons and Lovers* (1913), *Women in Love* (1916), and, *Lady Chatterley's Lover* (1928) which was among the several of his works that were banned as obscene on account of their intensely erotic content.

A chronic victim of tuberculosis, Lawrence died at the young age of 44, in France.

SONS AND LOVERS

CONTENTS

PART ONE

CHAPTER 1

The Early Married Life of the Morels

'THE BOTTOMS' succeeded to 'Hell Row.' Hell Row was a block of thatched, bulging cottages that stood by the brook-side on Greenhill Lane. There lived the colliers who worked in the little gin-pits* two fields away. The brook ran under the alder-trees, scarcely soiled by these small mines, whose coal was drawn to the surface by donkeys that plodded wearily in a circle round a gin. And all over the countryside were these some pits, some of which had been worked in the time of Charles II, the few colliers and the donkeys burrowing down like ants into the earth, making queer mounds and little black places among the corn-fields and the meadows. And the cottages of these coal-miners, in blocks and pairs here and there, together with odd Farms and homes of the stockingers, straying over the parish, formed the village of Bestwood.

Then, some sixty years ago, a sudden change took place. The gin-pits were elbowed aside by the large mines of the financiers. The coal and iron field of Nottinghamshire and Derbyshire was discovered. Carston, Waite and Co. appeared. Amid tremendous excitement, Lord Palmerston formally opened the company's first mine at Spinney Park, on the edge of Sherwood Forest.

About this time the notorious Hell Row, which through growing old had acquired an evil reputation, was burned down, and much dirt was cleansed away.

Carston, Waite and Co. found they had struck on a good thing, so, down the valleys of the brooks from Selby and Nuttall,

---

* Coal mines of shallow depths, enabling the mules to haul the extracted coal.

new mines were sunk, until soon there were six pits working. From Nuttall, high up on the sandstone among the woods, the railway ran, past the ruined priory of the Carthusians and past Robin Hood's Well, down to Spinney Park then on to Minton, a large mine among corn-fields; from Minton across the farm-lands of the valleyside to Bunker's Hill, branching off there, and running north to Beggarlee and Selby, that looks over at Crich and the hills of Derbyshire; six mines like black studs on the countryside, linked by a loop of fine chain, the railway.

To accommodate the regiments of miners, Carston, Waite and Co. built the Squares, great quadrangles of dwellings on the hillside of Bestwood, and then, in the brook valley, on the site of Hell Row, they erected the Bottoms.

The Bottoms consisted of six blocks of miners' dwellings, two rows of three, like the dots on a blank-six domino, and twelve houses in a block. This double row of dwellings sat at the foot of the rather sharp slope from Bestwood, and looked out, from the attic windows at least, on the slow climb of the valley towards Selby.

The houses themselves were substantial and very decent. One could walk all round, seeing little front gardens with auriculas and saxifrage in the shadow of the bottom block, sweet-williams and pinks in the sunny top block; seeing neat front windows, little porches, little privet hedges, and dormer windows for the attics. But that was outside; that was the view on to the uninhabited parlours of all the colliers' wives. The dwelling-room, the kitchen, was at the back of the house, facing inward between the blocks, looking at a scrubby back garden, and then at the ash-pits. And between the rows, between the long lines of ash-pits, went the alley, where the children played and the women gossiped and the men smoked. So, the actual conditions of living in the Bottoms, that was so well built and that looked so nice, were quite unsavoury because people must live in the kitchen, and the kitchens opened on to that nasty alley of ash-pits.

Mrs. Morel was not anxious to move into the Bottoms, which was already twelve years old and on the downward path, when she descended to it from Bestwood. But it was the best she could do. Moreover she had an end house in one of the top blocks, and thus had only one neighbour; on the other side an extra strip of garden. And, having an end house, she enjoyed a kind of aristocracy among the other women of the 'between' houses, because her rent was five shillings and sixpence instead of five shillings a week. But this superiority in station was not much consolation to Mrs. Morel.

She was thirty-one years old, and had been married eight years. A rather small woman, of delicate mould but resolute bearing, she shrank a little from the first contact with the Bottoms women. She came down in the July, and in the September expected her third baby.

Her husband was a miner. They had only been in their new home three weeks when the wakes, or fair, began. Morel she knew, was sure to make a holiday of it. He went off early on the Monday morning, the day of the fair. The two children were highly excited. William, a boy of seven, fled off immediately after breakfast, to prowl round the wakes ground, leaving Annie, who was only five, to whine all morning to go also. Mrs. Morel did her work. She scarcely knew her neighbours yet, and knew no one with whom to trust the little girl. So she promised to take her to the wakes after dinner.

William appeared at half-past twelve. He was a very active lad, fair-haired, freckled, with a touch of the Dane or Norwegian about him.

'Can I have my dinner, mother?' he cried, rushing in with his cap on. "Cause it begins at half-past one, the man says so.'

'You can have your dinner as soon as it's done,' replied the mother.

'Isn't it done?' he cried, his blue eyes staring at her in indignation. 'Then I'm goin' be-out it.'

'You'll do nothing of the sort. It will be done in five minutes. It is only half-past twelve.'

'They'll be beginnin',' the boy half cried, half shouted.

'You won't die if they do,' said the mother. 'Besides, it's only half-past twelve, so you've a full hour.'

The lad began hastily to lay the table, and directly the three sat down. They were eating batter-pudding and jam, when the boy jumped off his chair and stood perfectly still. Some distance away could be heard the first small braying of a merry-go-round, and the tooting of a horn. His face quivered as he looked at his mother.

'I told you!' he said, running to the dresser for his cap.

'Take your pudding in your hand – and it's only five past one, so you were wrong – you haven't got your twopence,' cried the mother in a breath.

The boy came back, bitterly disappointed, for his twopence; then went off without a word.

'I want to go, I want to go,' said Annie, beginning to cry.

'Well, and you shall go, whining, wizening little stick!' said the mother. And later in the afternoon she trudged up the hill under the tall hedge with her child. The hay was gathered from the fields, and cattle were turned on to the eddish. It was warm, peaceful.

Mrs. Morel did not like the wakes. There were two sets of horses, one going by steam, one pulled round by a pony; three organs were grinding, and there came odd cracks of pistol-shots, fearful screeching of the cocoanut man's rattle, shouts of the Aunt Sally man, screeches from the peepshow lady. The mother perceived her son gazing enraptured outside the Lion Wallace booth, at the pictures of this famous lion that had killed a negro and maimed for life two white men. She left him alone, and went to get Annie a spin of toffee. Presently the lad stood in front of her, wildly excited.

'You never said you was coming – isn't the' a lot of things?
– that lion's killed three men – I've spent my tuppence – an'
look here.'

He pulled from his pocket two egg-cups, with pink moss
roses on them.

'I got these from that stall where y'ave ter get them marbles
in them holes. An' I got these two in two gocs – 'acpenny a go –
they've got moss-roses on, look here. I wanted these.'

She knew he wanted them for her.

'H'm!' she said, pleased. 'They *are* pretty!'

'Shall you carry 'em, 'cause I'm frightened o' breakin' em?'

He was tipful of excitement now she had come, led her about
the ground, showed her everything. Then, at the peep-show, she
explained the pictures, in a sort of story, to which he listened as
if spellbound. He would not leave her. All the time he stuck close
to her, bristling with a small boy's pride of her. For no other
woman looked such a lady as she did, in her little black bonnet
and her cloak, She smiled when she saw women she knew. When
she was tired she said to her son:

'Well, are you coming now, or later?'

'Are you goin 'a'ready?' he cried, his face full of reproach.

Already? It is past four, *I* know.'

'What are you goin' a'ready for?' he lamented.

'You needn't come if you don't want,' she said.

And she went slowly away with her little girl, whilst her son
stood watching her, cut to the heart to let her go, and yet unable
to leave the wakes. As she crossed the open ground in front of
the Moon and Stars she heard men shouting, and smelled the
beer, and hurried a little, thinking her husband was probably in
the bar.

At about half-past six her son came home, tired now, rather
pale, and somewhat wretched. He was miserable, though he did

not know it, because he had let her go alone. Since she had gone, he had not enjoyed his wakes.

'Has my dad been?' he asked.

'No,' said the mother.

'He's helping to wait at the Moon and Stars. I seed him through that black tin stuff wi' holes in, on the window, wi' his sleeves rolled up.'

'Ha!' exclaimed the mother shortly. 'He's got no money. An' he'll be satisfied if he gets his 'lowance, whether they give him more or not.'

When the light was fading, and Mrs. Morel could see no more to sew, she rose and went to the door. Everywhere was the sound of excitement, the restlessness of the holiday that at last infected her. She went out into the side garden. Women were coming home from the wakes, the children hugging a white lamb with green legs, or a wooden horse. Occasionally a man lurched past, almost as full as he could carry. Sometimes a good husband came along with his family, peacefully. But usually the women and children were alone. The stay-at-home mothers stood gossiping at the corners of the alley, as the twilight sank, folding their arms under their white aprons.

Mrs Morel was alone, but she was used to it. Her son and her little girl slept upstairs; so, it seemed, her home was there behind her, fixed and stable. But she felt wretched with the coming child. The world seemed a dreary place, where nothing else would happen for her – at least until William grew up. But for herself, nothing but this dreary endurance – till the children grew up. And the children! She could not afford to have this third. She did not want it. The father was serving beer in a public house, swilling himself drunk. She despised him, and was tied to him. This coming child was too much for her. If it were not for William and Annie, she was sick of it, the struggle with poverty and ugliness and meanness.

She went into the front garden, feeling too heavy to take herself out, yet unable to stay indoors. The heat suffocated her. And looking ahead, the prospect of her life made her feel as if she were buried alive.

The front garden was a small square with a privet hedge. There she stood, trying to soothe herself with the scent of flowers and the fading, beautiful evening. Opposite her small gate was the stile that led uphill, under the tall hedge, between the burning glow of the cut pastures. The sky overhead throbbed and pulsed with light. The glow sank quickly off the field; the earth and the hedges smoked dusk. As it grew dark, a ruddy glare came out on the hilltop, and out of the glare the diminished commotion of the fair.

Sometimes, down the trough of darkness formed by the path under the hedges, men came lurching home. One young man lapsed into a run down the steep bit that ended the hill, and went with a crash into the stile. Mrs. Morel shuddered. He picked himself up, swearing viciously, rather pathetically, as if he thought the stile had wanted to hurt him.

She went indoors, wondering if things were never going to alter. She was beginning by now to realise that they would not. She seemed so far away from her girlhood, she wondered if it were the same person walking heavily up the back garden at the Bottoms as had run so lightly on the breakwater at Sheerness ten years before.

'What have *I* to do with it?' she said to herself. 'What have I to do with all this? Even the child I am going to have! It doesn't seem as if *I* were taken into account.'

Sometimes life takes hold of one, carries the body along, accomplishes one's history, and yet is not real, but leaves oneself as it were slurred over.

'I wait,' Mrs. Morel said to herself – 'I wait, and what I wait for can never come.'

Then she straightened the kitchen, lit the lamp, mended the fire, looked out the washing for the next day, and put it to soak. After which she sat down to her sewing. Through the long hours her needle flashed regularly through the stuff. Occasionally she sighed, moving to relieve herself. And all the time she was thinking how to make the most of what she had, for the children's sakes.

At half-past eleven her husband came. His cheeks were very red and very shiny above his black moustache. His head nodded slightly. He was pleased with himself.

'Oh! Oh! waitin' for me, lass? I've bin 'elpin' Anthony, an' what's think he's gen me? Nowt b'r a lousy hae'fcrown, an' that's ivry penny – '

'He thinks you've made the rest up in beer,' she said shortly.

'An' I 'aven't – that I 'aven't. You b'lieve me, I've 'ad very little this day, I have an' all.' His voice went tender. 'Here, an' I browt thee a bit o' brandy-snap, an' a cocoanut for th' children.' He laid the gingerbread and the cocoanut, a hairy object, on the table. 'Nay, tha niver said thankyer for nowt i' thy life, did ter?'

As a compromise, she picked up the cocoanut and shook it, to see if it had any milk.

'It's a good 'un, you may back yer life o' that. I got it fra' Bill Hodgkisson. "Bill," I says, "tha non wants them three nuts, does ter? Arena ter for gi'ein' me one for my bit of a lad an' wench?" "I ham, Walter, my lad,." 'e says; "ta'e which on 'em ter's a mind." An' so I took one, an' thanked 'im. I didn't like ter shake it afore 'is eyes, but 'e says, "Tha'd better ma'e sure it's a good un, Walt." An' so, yer see, I knowed it was. He's a nice chap, is Bill Hodgkisson, 'e's a nice chap!'

'A man will part with anything so long as he's drunk, and you're drunk along with him,' said Mrs. Morel.

'Eh, tha mucky little 'ussy, who's drunk, I sh'd like ter know?'

said Morel. He was extraordinarily pleased with himself, because of his day's helping to wait in the Moon and Stars. He chattered on.

Mrs Morel, very tired, and sick of his babble, went to bed as quickly as possible, while he raked the fire.

Mrs Morel came of a good old burgher family, famous independents who had fought with Colonel Hutchinson, and who remained stout Congregationalists. Her grandfather had gone bankrupt in the lace-market at a time when so many lace manufacturers were ruined in Nottingham. Her father, George Coppard, was an engineer – a large, handsome, haughty man, proud of his fair skin and blue eyes, but more proud still of his integrity. Gertrude resembled her mother in her small build. But her temper, proud and unyielding, she had from the Coppards.

George Coppard was bitterly galled by his own poverty. He became foreman of the engineers in the dockyard at Sheerness. Mrs Morel – Gertrude – was the second daughter. She favoured her mother, loved her mother best of all; but she had the Coppards' clear, defiant blue eyes and their broad brow. She remembered to have hated her father's overbearing manner towards her gentle, humorous, kindly-souled mother. She remembered running over the breakwater at Sheerness and finding the boat. She remembered to have been petted and flattered by all the men when she had gone to the dockyard, for she was a delicate, rather proud child. She remembered the funny old mistress, whose assistant she had become, whom she had loved to help in the private school. And she still had the Bible that John Field had given her. She used to walk home from chapel with John Field when she was nineteen. He was the son of a well-to-do tradesman, had been to college in London, and was to devote himself to business.

She could always recall in detail a September Sunday afternoon, when they had sat under the vine at the back of her father's house. The sun came through the chinks in the vine-leaves and made beautiful patterns, like a lace scarf, falling on her and on him. Some of the leaves were clean yellow, like yellow flat flowers.

'Now sit still,' he had cried. 'Now your hair, I don't know what it is like! It's as bright as copper and gold, as red as burnt copper, and it has gold threads where the sun shines on it. Fancy their saying it's brown. Your mother calls it mouse-colour.' She had met his brilliant eyes, but her clear face scarcely showed the elation which rose within her.

'But you say you don't like business,' she pursued.

'I don't. I hate it!' he cried hotly.

'And you would like to go into the ministry,' she half implored.

'I should. I should love it, if I thought I could make a first-rate preacher.'

'Then why don't you – why *don't you?*' Her voice rang with defiance.

'If I were a man, nothing would stop me.'

She held her head erect. He was rather timid before her.

'But my father's so stiff-necked. He means to put me into the business, and I know he'll do it.'

'But if you're a *man?*' she had cried.

'Being a man isn't everything,' he replied, frowning with puzzled helplessness.

Now, as she moved about her work at the Bottoms, with some experience of what being a man meant, she knew that it was *not* everything.

At twenty, owing to her health, she had left Sheerness. Her father had retired home to Nottingham. John Field's father had been ruined; the son had gone as a teacher in Norwood. She did not hear of him until, two years later, she made determined inquiry. He had married his landlady, a woman of forty, a widow with property.

And still Mrs Morel preserved John Field's Bible. She did not now believe him to be – Well, she understood pretty well what he might or might not have been. So she preserved his Bible, and kept his memory intact in her heart, for her own sake. To her dying day, for thirty-five years, she did not speak of him.

When she was twenty-three years old, she met, at a Christmas party, a young man from the Erewash Valley. Morel was then twenty-seven years old. He was well set-up, erect, and very smart. He had wavy black hair that shone again, and a vigorous black beard that had never been shaved. His cheeks were ruddy, and his red, moist mouth was noticeable because he laughed so often and so heartily. He had that rare thing, a rich, ringing laugh. Gertrude Coppard had watched him, fascinated. He was so full of colour and animation, his voice ran so easily into comic grotesque, he was so ready and so pleasant with everybody. Her own father had a rich fund of humour, but it was satiric. This man's was different: soft, non-intellectual, warm, a kind of gambolling.

She herself was opposite. She had a curious, receptive mind, which found much pleasure and amusement in listening to other folk. She was clever in leading folk on to talk. She loved ideas, and was considered very intellectual. What she liked most of all was an argument on religion or philosophy or politics with some educated man. This she did not often enjoy. So she always had people tell her about themselves, finding her pleasure so.

In her person she was rather small and delicate, with a large brow, and dropping bunches of brown silk curls. Her blue eyes were very straight, honest, and searching. She had the beautiful hands of the Coppards. Her dress was always subdued. She wore dark blue silk, with a peculiar silver chain of silver scallops. This, and a heavy brooch of twisted gold, was her only ornament. She was still perfectly intact, deeply religious, and full of beautiful candour.

Walter Morel seemed melted away before her. She was to the miner that thing of mystery and fascination, a lady. When she spoke to him, it was with a southern pronunciation and a purity of English which thrilled him to hear. She watched him. He danced well, as if it were natural and joyous in him to dance. His grandfather was a French refugee who had married an English barmaid – if it had been a marriage. Gertrude Coppard watched the young miner as he danced a certain subtle exultation like glamour in his movement, and his face the flower of his body, ruddy, with tumbled black hair, and laughing alike whatever partner he bowed above. She thought him rather wonderful, never having met anyone like him. Her father was to her the type of all men. And George Coppard, proud in his bearing, handsome, and rather bitter; who preferred theology in reading, and who drew near in sympathy only to one man, the Apostle Paul; who was harsh in government, and in familiarity ironic; who ignored all sensuous pleasure; – he was very different from the miner. Gertrude herself was rather contemptuous of dancing; she had not the slightest inclination towards that accomplishment, and had never learned even a Roger de Coverley[*]. She was a puritan, like her father, high-minded, and really stern. Therefore the dusky, golden softness of this man's sensuous flame of life, that flowed off his flesh like the flame from a candle, not baffled and gripped into incandescence by thought and spirit as her life was, seemed to her something wonderful, beyond her.

He came and bowed above her. A warmth radiated through her as if she had drunk wine.

'Now do come and have this one wi' me,' he said caressingly. 'It's easy, you know. I'm pining to see you dance.'

She had told him before she could not dance. She glanced at his humility and smiled. Her smile was very beautiful. It moved the man so that he forgot everything.

'No, I won't dance,' she said softly. Her words came clean and ringing.

Not knowing what he was doing – he often did the right

---

* A type of dance.

thing by instinct – he sat beside her, inclining reverentially.

'But you mustn't miss your dance,' she reproved.

'Nay, I don't want to dance that – it's not one as I care about.'

'Yet you invited me to it.'

He laughed very heartily at this.

'I never thought o' that. Tha'rt not long in taking the curl out of me.'

It was her turn to laugh quickly.

'You don't look as if you'd come much uncurled,' she said.

'I'm like a pig's tail, I curl because I canna help it,' he laughed, rather boisterously.

'And you are a miner!' she exclaimed in surprise.

'Yes. I went down when I was ten.'

She looked at him in wondering dismay.

'When you were ten! And wasn't it very hard?' she asked.

'You soon get used to it. You live like th' mice, an' you pop out at night to see what's going on.'

'It makes me feel blind,' she frowned.

'Like a moudiwarp[*]!' he laughed. 'Yi, an' there's some chaps as does go round like moudiwarps.' He thrust his face forward in the blind, snout-like way of a mole, seeming to sniff and peer for direction. 'They dun though!' he protested naively; 'Tha niver seed such a way they get in. But tha mun let me ta'e thee down some time, an' tha can see for thysen.'

She looked at him, startled. This was a new tract of life suddenly opened before her. She realised the life of the miners, hundreds of them toiling below earth and coming up at evening. He seemed to her noble. He risked his life daily, and with gaiety. She looked at him, with 'a touch of appeal in her pure humility.

'Shouldn't ter like it?' he asked tenderly. ' 'Appen not, it 'ud dirty thee.'

She had never been 'thee'd' and 'thou'd' before.

---

* Like a mole.

The next Christmas they were married, and for three months she was perfectly happy: for six months she was very happy.

He had signed the pledge, and wore the, blue ribbon of a teetotaller: he was nothing if not showy. They lived, she thought, in his own house. It was small, but convenient enough, and quite nicely furnished, with solid, worthy stuff that suited her honest soul. The women, her neighbours, were rather foreign to her, and Morel's mother and sisters were apt to sneer at her ladylike ways. But she could perfectly well live by herself, so long as she had her husband close.

Sometimes, when she herself wearied of love-talk, she tried to open her heart seriously to him. She saw him listen deferentially, but without understanding. This killed her efforts at a finer intimacy, and she had flashes of fear. Sometimes he was restless of an evening: it was not enough for him just to be near her, she realised. She was glad when he set himself to little jobs.

He was a remarkably handy man – could make or mend anything. So she would say:

'I do like that coal-rake of your mother's – it is small and natty.'

'Does ter, my wench? Well, I made that, so I can make thee one.'

'What! why, it's a steel one!'

'An' what if it is! Tha s'lt ha'e one very similar, if not exactly same.'

She did not mind the mess, nor the hammering and noise. He was busy and happy.

But in the seventh month, when she was brushing his Sunday coat, she felt papers in the breast-pocket, and, seized with a sudden curiosity, took them out to read. He very rarely wore the frock-coat he was married in: and it had not occurred to her before to feel curious concerning the papers. They were the bills of the household furniture, still unpaid.

'Look here,' she said at night, after he was washed and had had his dinner. 'I found these in the pocket of your wedding-coat. Haven't you settled the bills yet?'

'No. I haven't had a chance.'

'But you told me all was paid. I had better go into Nottingham on Saturday and settle them. I don't like sitting on another man's chairs and eating from an unpaid table.'

He did not answer.

'I can have your bank-book, can't I?'

'Tha can ha'e it, for what good it'll be to thee.'

'I thought –' she began. He had told her he had a good bit of money left over. But she realised it was no use asking questions. She sat rigid with bitterness and indignation.

The next day she went down to see his mother.

'Didn't you buy the furniture for Walter?' she asked.

'Yes, I did,' tartly retorted the elder woman.

'And how much did he give you to pay for it?'

The elder woman was stung with fine indignation.

'Eighty pound, if you're so keen on knowin',' she replied.

'Eighty pounds! But there are forty-two pounds still owing!'

'I can't help that.'

'But where has it all gone?'

'You'll find all the papers, I think, if you look – beside ten pound as he owed me, an' six pound as the wedding cost down here.'

'Six pounds!' echoed Gertrude Morel. It seemed to her monstrous that, after her own father had paid so heavily for her wedding, six pounds more should have been squandered in eating and drinking at Walter's parents' house, at his expense.

'And how much has he sunk in his houses?' she asked.

'His houses – which houses?'

Gertrude Morel went white to the lips. He had told her the house he lived in, and the next one, was his own.

'I thought the house we live in –' she began.

'They're my houses, those two,' said the mother-in-law. 'And not clear either. It's as much as I can do to keep the mortgage interest paid.'

Gertrude sat white and silent. She was her father now.

'Then we ought to be paying you rent,' she said coldly.

'Walter is paying me rent,' replied the mother.

'And what rent?' asked Gertrude.

'Six-and-six a week,' retorted the mother.

It was more than the house was worth. Gertrude held her head erect, looked straight before her.

'It is lucky to be you,' said the elder woman, bitingly, 'to have a husband as takes all the worry of the money, and leaves you a free hand.'

The young wife was silent.

She said very little to her husband, but her manner had changed towards him. Something in her proud, honourable soul had crystallised out hard as rock.

When October came in, she thought only of Christmas. Two years ago, at Christmas, she had met him. Last Christmas she had married him. This Christmas she would bear him a child.

'You don't' dance yourself, do you, missis?' asked her nearest neighbour, in October, when there was great talk of opening a dancing-class over the Brick and Tile Inn at Bestwood.

'No – I never had the least inclination to,' Mrs Morel replied.

'Fancy! An' how funny as you should ha' married your Mester. You know he's quite a famous one for dancing.'

'I didn't know he was famous,' laughed Mrs Morel.

'Yea, he is though! Why, he run that dancing-class in the Miners' Arms club-room for over five year.'

'Did he?'

'Yes, he did.' The other woman was defiant. 'An' it was thronged every Tuesday, and Thursday, an' Sat' day – an' there was carryin's-on, accordin' to all accounts.'

This kind of thing was gall and bitterness to Mrs Morel and she had a fair share of it. The women did not spare her, at first; for she was superior, though she could not help it.

He began to be rather late in coming home.

'They're working very late now, aren't they?' she said to her washer-woman.

'No later than they allers do, I don't think. But they stop to have their pint at Ellen's, an' they get talkin'. an' there you are! Dinner stone cold an' it serves 'em right.'

'But Mr Morel does not take any drink.'

The woman dropped the clothes, looked at Mrs Morel, then went on with her work, saying nothing.

Gertrude Morel was very ill when the boy was born. Morel was good to her, as good as gold. But she felt very lonely, miles away from her own people. She felt lonely with him now, and his presence only made it more intense.

The boy was small and frail at first, but he came on quickly. He was a beautiful child, with dark gold ringlets, and dark blue eyes which changed gradually to a clear grey. His mother loved him passionately. He came just when her own bitterness of disillusion was hardest to bear; when her faith in life was shaken, and her soul felt dreary and lonely. She made much of the child, and the father was jealous.

At last Mrs Morel despised her husband. She turned to the child; she turned from the father. He had begun to neglect her, the novelty of his own home was gone. He had no grit, she said bitterly to herself. What he felt just at the minute, that was all to him. He could not abide by anything. There was nothing at the back of all his show.

There began a battle between the husband and wife – a fearful, bloody battle that ended only with the death of one. She fought to make him undertake his own responsibilities, to make him fulfil his obligations. But he was too different from her. His nature was purely sensuous, and she strove to make him moral, religious. She tried to force him to face things. He could not endure it – it drove him out of his mind.

While the baby was still tiny, the father's temper had become so irritable that it was not to be trusted. The child had only to give a little trouble when the man began to bully. A little more, and the hard hands of the collier hit the baby. Then Mrs Morel loathed her husband, loathed him for days; and he went out and drank; and she cared very little what he did. Only, on his return, she scathed him with her satire.

The estrangement between them caused him, knowingly or unknowingly, grossly to offend her where he would not have done.

William was only one year old, and his mother was proud of him, he was so pretty. She was not well off now, but her sisters kept the boy in clothes. Then, with his little white hat curled with an ostrich feather, and his white coat, he was a joy to her, the twining wisps of hair clustering round his head. Mrs Morel lay listening, one Sunday morning, to the chatter of the father and child downstairs. Then she dozed off. When she came downstairs, a great fire glowed in the grate, the room was hot, the breakfast was roughly laid, and seated in his armchair, against the chimney-piece, sat Morel, rather timid; and standing between his legs, the child – cropped like a sheep, with such an odd round poll – looking wondering at her; and on a newspaper spread out upon the hearthrug, a myriad of crescent-shaped curls, like the petals of a marigold scattered in the reddening firelight.

Mrs Morel stood still. It was her first baby. She went very white, and was unable to speak.

'What dost think o' 'im?' Morel laughed uneasily.

She gripped her two fists, lifted them, and came forward. Morel shrank back.

'I could kill you, I could!' she said. She choked with rage, her two fists uplifted.

'Yer non want ter make a wench on' im,' Morel said, in a frightened tone, bending his head to shield his eyes from hers. His attempt at laughter had vanished.

The mother looked down at the jagged, close-clipped head of her child. She put her hands on his hair, and stroked and fondled his head.

'Oh – my boy!' she faltered. Her lip trembled, her face broke, and, snitching up the child, she buried her face in his shoulder and cried painfully. She was one of those women who cannot cry; whom it hurts as it hurts a man. It was like ripping something out of her, her sobbing.

Morel sat with his elbows on his knees, his hands gripped together till the knuckles were white. He gazed in the fire, feeling almost stunned, as if he could not breathe.

Presently she came to an end, soothed the child and cleared away the breakfast-table. She left the newspaper, littered with curls, spread upon the hearthrug. At last her husband gathered it up and put it at the back of the fire. She went about her work with closed mouth and very quiet.

Morel was subdued. He crept about wretchedly, and his meals were a misery that day. She spoke to him civilly, and never alluded to what he had done. But he felt something final had happened.

Afterwards she said she had been silly, that the boy's hair would have had to be cut, sooner or later. In the end, she even brought herself to say to her husband it was just as well he had played barber when he did. But she knew, and Morel knew, that that act had caused something momentous to take place in her soul. She remembered the scene all her life, as one in which she had suffered the most intensely.

This act of masculine clumsiness was the spear through the side of her love for Morel. Before, while she had striven against him bitterly, she had fretted after him, as if he had gone astray from her. Now she ceased to fret for his love: he was an outsider to her. This made life much more bearable.

Nevertheless, she still continued to strive with him. She still had her high moral sense inherited from generations of Puritans. It was now a religious instinct, and she was almost a fanatic with him, because she loved him, or had loved him. If he sinned, she tortured him. If he drank, and lied, was often a poltroon, sometimes a knave, she wielded the lash unmercifully.

The pity was, she was too much his opposite. She could not be content with the little he might be; she would have him the much that he ought to be. So, in seeking to make him nobler than he could be she destroyed him. She injured and hurt and scarred herself, but she lost none of her worth. She also had the children.

He drank rather heavily, though not more than many miners, and always beer, so that whilst his health was affected it was never injured. The week-end was his chief carouse. He sat in the Miners' Arms until turning-out time every Friday, every Saturday, and every Sunday evening. On Monday and Tuesday he had to get up and reluctantly leave towards ten o'clock. Sometimes he stayed at home on Wednesday and Thursday evenings, or was only out for an hour. He practically never had to miss work owing to his drinking.

But although he was very steady at work, his wages fell off. He was blab-mouthed, a tongue-wagger. Authority was hateful to him, therefore he could only abuse the pit-managers. He would say, in the Palmerston:

'Th' gaffer come down to our stall this morning, an' 'e says, "You know, Walter, this 'ere'll not do. What about these props?" An' I says to him, "Why, what art talkin' about? What d'st mean about th' props?"

"It'll never do, this 'ere," 'e says. "You'll be havin' th' roof in, one o' these days." An' I says, "Tha'd better stan' on a bit o' clunch, then, an' hold it up wi' thy 'ead." So 'e wor that mad, 'e cossed an' 'e swore, an' t'other chaps they did laugh." Morel was a good mimic. He imitated the manager's fat, squeaky voice, with its attempt at good English.

"I shan't have it, Walter. Who knows more about it, me or you?" So I says, "I've niver fun out how much tha' knows, Alfred. It'll' 'appen carry thee ter bed an' back."

So Morel would go on to the amusement of his boon companions. And some of this would be true. The pit-manager was not an educated man. He had been a boy along with Morel, so that, while the two disliked each other, they more or less took each other for granted. But Alfred Charlesworth did not forgive the butty these public-house sayings. Consequently, although Morel was a good miner, sometimes earning as much as five pounds a week when he married, he came gradually to have worse and worse stalls, where the coal was thin, and hard to get, and unprofitable.

Also, in summer, the pits are slack. Often, on bright sunny mornings, the men are seen trooping home again at ten, eleven, or twelve o'clock. No empty trucks stand at the pit-mouth. 'The women on the hillside look across as they shake the hearthrug against the fence, and count the waggons the engine is taking along the line up the valley. And the children, as they come from school at dinner-time, looking down the fields and seeing the wheels on the headstocks* standing, say:

'Minton's knocked off. My dad'll be at home.'

And there is a sort of shadow over all, women and children and men, because money will be short at the end of the week.

* The large wheels on the pit-heads of mines that wind the coal hauling gear.

Morel was supposed to give his wife thirty shillings a week, to provide everything – rent, food, clothes, clubs, insurance, doctors. Occasionally, if he were flush, he gave her thirty-five. But these occasions by no means balanced those when he gave her twenty-five. In winter, with a decent stall, the miner might earn fifty or fifty-five shillings a week. Then he was happy. On Friday night, Saturday, and Sunday, he spent royally, getting rid of his sovereign or thereabouts. And out of so much, he scarcely spared the children an extra penny or bought them a pound of apples. It all went in drink. In the bad times, matters were more worrying, but he was not so often drunk, so that Mrs Morel used to say:

'I'm not sure I wouldn't rather be short, for when he's flush, there isn't a minute of peace.'

If he earned forty shillings he kept ten; from thirty-five he kept five; from thirty-two he kept four, from twenty-eight he kept three; from twenty-four he kept two; from twenty he kept one-and-six; from eighteen he kept a shilling; from sixteen he kept sixpence. He never saved a penny, and he gave his wife no opportunity of saving; instead, she had occasionally to pay his debts; not public-house debts, for those never were passed on to the women, but debts when he had bought a canary, or a fancy walking-stick.

At the wakes time, Morel was working badly, and Mrs Morel was trying to save against her confinement. So it galled her bitterly to think he should be out taking his pleasure and spending money, whilst she remained at home, harassed. There were two days holiday. On the Tuesday morning Morel rose early. He was in good spirits. Quite early, before six o'clock, she heard him whistling away to himself downstairs. He had a pleasant way of whistling, lively and musical. He nearly always whistled hymns. He had been a choir-boy with a beautiful voice, and had taken solos in Southwell cathedral. His morning whistling alone betrayed it.

His wife lay listening to him tinkering away in the garden, his whistling ringing out as he sawed and hammered away. It always gave her a sense of warmth and peace to hear him thus as she lay in bed, the children not yet awake, in the bright early morning, happy in his man's fashion.

At nine o'clock, while the children with bare legs and feet were sitting playing an the sofa, and the mother was washing up, he came in from his carpentry, his sleeves rolled up, his waistcoat hanging open. He was still a good-looking man with black, wavy hair, and a large black moustache. His face was perhaps too much inflamed, and there was about him a look almost of peevishness. But now he was jolly. He went straight to the sink where his wife was washing up.

'What, are thee there!' he said boisterously. 'Sluther off an' let me wesh mysen.'

'You may wait till I've finished,' said his wife.

'Oh, mun I? An' what if I shonna?'

'This good-humoured threat amused Mrs Morel.

'Then you can go and wash yourself in the soft-water tub.'

'Ha! I can an' a', tha mucky little 'ussy.'

With which he stood watching her a moment, then went away to wait for her.

When he chose he could still make himself again a real gallant. Usually he preferred to go out with a scarf round his neck.

Now, however, he made a toilet. There seemed so much gusto in the way he puffed and swilled as he washed himself, so much alacrity with which he hurried to the mirror in the kitchen, and, bending because it was too low for him, scrupulously parted his wet black hair, that it irritated Mrs Morel. He put on a turn-down collar, a black bow, and ware his Sunday tall-coat. As such, he looked spruce, and what his clothes would not do, his instinct for making the most of his good looks would.

At half-past nine Jerry Purdy came to call for his pal. Jerry was Morel's bosom friend, and Mrs Morel disliked him. He was a tall, thin man. With a rather foxy face, the kind of face that seems to lack eyelashes. He walked with a stiff brittle dignity, as if his head were on a wooden spring. His nature was cold and shrewd. Generous where he intended to be generous, he seemed to be very fond of Morel, and more or less to take charge of him.

Mrs Morel hated him. She had known his wife, who had died of consumption, and who had, at the end, conceived such a violent dislike of her husband, that if he came into her room it caused her to haemorrhage. None of which Jerry had seemed to mind. And now his eldest daughter, a girl of fifteen, kept a poor house for him, and looked after the two younger children.

'A mean, wizen-hearted stick!' Mrs Morel said of him.

'I've never known Jerry mean in *my* life,' protested Morel: 'A opener-handed and more freer chap you couldn't find anywhere, accordin' to my knowledge.'

'Open-handed to you,' retorted Mrs Morel. 'But his fist is shut tight enough to his children, poor things.'

'Poor things! And what for are they poor things, I should like to know.'

But Mrs Morel would not be appeased on Jerry's score.

The subject of argument was seen, craning his thin neck over the scullery curtain. He caught Mrs Morel's eye.

'Mornin', missis! Mester in?'

'Yes – he is.'

Jerry entered unasked, and stood by the kitchen doorway. He was not invited to sit down, but stood there, coolly asserting the rights of men and husbands.

'A nice day,' he said to Mrs Morel.

'Yes.'

'Grand out this morning – grand for a walk.'

'Do you mean *you're* going for a walk?' she asked.

'Yes. We mean walkin' to Nottingham,' he replied.

'H'm!'

The two men greeted each other, both glad: Jerry, however, full of assurance, Morel rather subdued, afraid to seem too jubilant in presence of his wife. But he laced his boots quickly, with spirit. They were going for a ten-mile walk across the fields to Nottingham. Climbing the hillside from the Bottoms, they mounted gaily into the morning. At the Moon and Stars they had their first drink, then on to the Old Spot. Then a long five miles of drought to carry them into Bulwell to a glorious pint of bitter. But they stayed in a field with some haymakers whose gallon bottle was full, so that, when they came in sight if the city, Morel was sleepy. The town spread upwards before them, smoking vaguely in the midday glare, fridging the crest away to the south with spires and factory bulks and chimneys. In the last field Morel lay down under an oak-tree and slept soundly for over an hour. When he rose to go forward he felt queer.

The two had dinner in the Meadows, with Jerry's sister, then repaired to the Punch Bowl, where they mixed in the excitement of pigeon racing. Morel never in his life played cards, considering them as having some occult, malevolent power – 'the devil's pictures,' he called them! But he was a master of skittles and of dominoes. He took a challenge from a Newark man, on skittles. All the men in the old, long bar took sides, betting either one way or the other. Morel took off his coat. Jerry held the hat containing the money. The men at the tables watched. Some stood with their mugs in their hands. Morel felt his big wooden ball carefully, then launched it. He played havoc among the nine-pins, and won half-a-crown, which restored him to solvency.

By seven o'clock the two were in good condition. They caught the 7.30 train home.

In the afternoon the Bottoms was intolerable. Every inhabitant remaining was out of doors. The women, in twos and threes, bareheaded and in white aprons, gossiped in the alley between the blocks. Men, having a rest between drinks sat on their heels and talked. The place smelled stole; the slate roofs glistered in the arid heat.

Mrs Morel took the little girl down to the brook in the meadows, which were not more than two hundred yards away. The water ran quickly over stones and broken pots. Mother and child leaned on the rail of the old sheep-bridge, watching. Up at the dipping-hole, at the other end of the meadow, Mrs Morel could see the naked forms of boys flashing round the deep yellow water, or an occasional bright figure dart glittering over the blackish stagnant meadow. She knew William was at the dipping-hole, and it was the dread of her life lest he should get drowned. Annie played under the tall old hedge picking up alder cones, that she called currants. The child required much attention, and the flies were teasing.

The children were put to bed at seven o'clock. Then she worked awhile.

When Walter Morel and Jerry arrived at Bestwood they felt a load off their minds; a railway journey no longer impended so they could put the finishing touches to a glorious day.

They entered the Nelson with the satisfaction of returned travellers. The next day was a work-day, and the thought of it put a damper on the men's spirits. Most of them, moreover, had spent their money. Some were already rolling dismally home, to sleep in preparation for the morrow. Mrs Morel, listening to their mournful singing, went indoors.

Nine o'clock passed and ten, and still 'the pair' had not returned. On a doorstep somewhere a man was singing loudly, in a drawl, 'Lead, kindly Light. Mrs Morel was always indignant with the drunken men that they must sing that hymn when they got maudlin.

'As if "Genevieve" weren't good enough,' she said.

The kitchen was full of the scent of boiled herbs and hops. On the hob a large black saucepan steamed slowly. Mrs Morel took a panchion, a great bowl of thick red earth, streamed a heap of white sugar into the bottom, and then, straining herself to the weight, was pouring in the liquor.

Just then Morel came in. He had been very jolly in the Nelson, but coming home had grown irritable. He had not quite got over the feeling of irritability and pain, after having slept on the ground when he was so hot; and a bad conscience afflicted him as he neared the house. He did not know he was angry. But when the garden-gate resisted his attempts to open it, he kicked it and broke the latch. He entered just as Mrs Morel was pouring the infusion of herbs out of the saucepan. Swaying slightly, he lurched against the table. The boiling liquor pitched. Mrs Morel started back.

'Good gracious,' she cried, 'coming home in his drunkenness!'

'Comin' home in his what?' he snarled, his hat over his eye.

Suddenly her blood rose in a jet.

'Say you're *not* drunk!' she flashed.

She had put down her saucepan, and was stirring the sugar into the beer. He dropped his two hands heavily on the table; and thrust his face forward at her.

"Say you're not drunk," he repeated. 'Why, nobody but a nasty little bitch like you 'ud 'ave such a thought.'

He thrust his face forward at her.

'There's money to bezzle with, if there's money for nothing else.'

'I've not spent a two-shillin' bit this day,' he said.

'You don't get as drunk as a lord on nothing,' she replied. 'And,' she cried, flashing into sudden fury, 'if you've been sponging on your beloved Jerry, why, let him look after his children, for they need it.'

'It's a lie, it's a lie. Shut your face, woman.'

They were now at battle-pitch. Each forgot everything save the hatred of the other and the battle between them. She was fiery and furious as he. They went on till he called her a liar

'No,' she cried, starting up, scarce able to breathe 'Don't call me that – you, the most despicable liar that ever walked in shoe-leather.' She forced the last words out of suffocated lungs.

'You're a liar!' he yelled, banging the table with his fist. 'You're a liar, you're a liar.'

She stiffened herself, with clenched fists.

'The house is filthy with you,' she cried.

'Then get out on it – it's mine. Get out on it!' he shouted. 'It's me as brings th' money whoam*, not thee. It's my house, not thine. Then ger out on't – ger out on't!'

'And I would,' she cried, suddenly shaken into tears of impotence. 'Ah, wouldn't I, wouldn't I have gone long ago, but for those children. Ay, haven't I repented not going years ago, when I'd only the one' – suddenly drying into rage. 'Do you think it's for *you* I stop – do you think I'd stop one minute for *you?*'

'Go, then,' he shouted, beside himself 'Go!'

'No!' she faced round. 'No,' she cried loudly, 'you shan't have it *all* your own way; you shan't do *all* you like. I've got those children to see to. My word,' she laughed, 'I should look well to leave them to you.

'Go,' he cried thickly, lifting his fist. He was afraid of her. 'Go!'

'I should be only too glad. I should laugh, laugh, my lord, if I could get away from you,' she replied.

He came up to her, his red face, with its bloodshot eyes, thrust forward, and gripped her arms. She cried in fear of him, struggled to be free. Coming slightly to himself, panting, he pushed her roughly to the outer door, and thrust her forth, slotting the

* home.

bolt behind her with a bang. Then he went back into the kitchen, dropped into his armchair, his head, bursting, full of blood, sinking between his knees. Thus he dipped gradually into a stupor, from exhaustion and intoxication.

The moon was high and magnificent in the August night. Mrs Morel, seared with passion, shivered to find herself out there in a great white light, that fell cold on her, and gave a shock to her inflamed soul. She stood for a few moments helplessly staring at the glistening great rhubarb leaves near the door. Then she got the air into her breast. She walked down the garden path, trembling in every limb, while the child boiled within her. For a while she could not control her consciousness; mechanically she went over the last scene, then over it again, certain phrases, certain moments coming each time like a brand red-hot down on her soul; and each time she enacted again the past hour, each time the brand came down at the same points, till the mark was burnt in and the pain burnt out, and at last she came to herself She must have been half an hour in this delirious condition. Then the presence of the night came again to her. She glanced round in fear. She had wandered to the side garden, where she was walking up and down the path beside the currant bushes under the long wall. The garden was a narrow strip, bounded from the road that cut transversely between the blocks, by a thick thorn hedge.

She hurried out of the side garden to the front, where she could stand as if in an immense gulf of white light, the moon streaming high in face of her, the moonlight standing up from the hills in front, and filling the valley where the Bottoms crouched, almost blindingly. There, panting and half weeping in reaction from the stress, she murmured to herself over and over again: 'The nuisance! the nuisance!'

She became aware of something about her. With an effort she roused herself to, see what it was that penetrated her consciousness. The tall white lilies were reeling in the moonlight and the air was charged with their perfume, as with a presence.

Mrs Morel gasped slightly in fear. She touched the big, pallid flowers on their petals, then shivered. They seemed to be stretching in the moonlight. She put her hand into one white bin: the gold scarcely showed on her fingers by moonlight. She bent down to look at the binful of yellow pollen; but it only appeared dusky. Then she drank a deep draught of the scent. It almost made her dizzy.

Mrs Morel leaned on the garden gate, looking out, and she lost herself awhile. She did not know what she thought. Except for a slight feeling of sickness, and her consciousness in the child, herself melted out like scent into the shiny, pale air. After a time the child, too, melted with her in the mixing-pot of moonlight, and she rested with the hills and lilies and houses, all swum together in a kind of swoon.

When she came to herself she was tired for sleep. Languidly she looked about her; the clumps of white phlox seemed like bushes spread with linen; a moth ricochetted over them and right across the garden. Following it with her eye roused her. A few whiffs of the raw, strong scent of phlox invigorated her. She passed along the path, hesitating at the white rosebush. It smelled sweet and simple. She touched the white ruffles of the roses. Their fresh scent and cool, soft leaves reminded her of the morning-time and sunshine. She was very fond of them. But she was tired, and wanted to sleep. In the mysterious out-of-doors she felt forlorn.

There was no noise anywhere. Evidently the children had not been wakened, or had gone to sleep again. A train, three miles away, roared across the valley. The night was very large, and very strange, stretching its hoary distances infinitely. And out of the silver-grey fog of darkness came sounds vague and hoarse: a corncrake not far off, sound of a train like a sigh, and distant shouts of men.

Her quietened heart beginning to beat quickly again, she hurried down the side garden to the back of the house. Softly she lifted the latch; the door was still bolted, shut hard against her. She rapped gently, waited, then rapped again. She must not rouse the children, nor the neighbours. He must be asleep, and he would not wake easily. Her heart began to burn to be indoors. She clung to the door-handle. Now it was cold; she would take a chill, and in her present condition!

Putting her apron over her head and her arms, she hurried again to the side garden, to the window of the kitchen. Leaning on the sill, she could just see, under the blind, her husband's arms spread out on the table, and his black head on the board. He was sleeping with his face lying on the table. Something in his attitude made her feel tired of things. The lamp was burning smokily; she could tell by the copper colour of the light. She topped at the window more and more noisily.

Almost it seemed as if the glass would break. Still he did not wake up.

After vain efforts, she began to shiver, partly from contact with the stone, and from exhaustion. Fearful always for the unborn child, she wondered what she could do for warmth. She went down to the coal house, where there was an old hearthrug she had kept for the rag man the day before. This she wrapped over her shoulders. It was warm, if grimy. Then she walked up and down the garden path, peeping every now and then under the blind, knocking, and telling herself that in the end the very strain of his position must wake him.

At last, after about an hour, she rapped long and low at the window. Gradually the sound penetrated to him. When, in despair, she had ceased to top, she saw him stir, then lift his face blindly. The labouring of his heart hurt him into consciousness. She rapped imperatively at the window. He started awake. Instantly she saw his fists set and his eyes glare. He had not a grain of physical fear. If it had been twenty burglars, he would have gone blindly for them. He glared round, bewildered, but prepared to fight.

'Open the door, Walter,' she said coldly.

His hands relaxed. It dawned on him what he had done. His head drooped, sullen and dogged. She saw him hurry to the door, heard the bolt chock. He tried the latch. It opened – and there stood the silver grey night, fearful to him, after the tawny light of the lamp. He hurried back

When Mrs Morel entered, she saw him almost running through the door to the stairs. He had ripped the collar off his neck in his haste to be gone ere she came in, and there it lay with bursten button-holes. It made her angry.

She warmed and soothed herself. In her weariness forgetting every thing, she moved about at the little tasks that remained to be done, set his breakfast, rinsed his pit-bottle, put his pit-clothes on the hearth to warm, set his pit-boots beside them, put him out a clean scarf and snap bag and two apples, raked the fire, and went to bed. He was already dead asleep. His narrow black eyebrows were drawn up in a sort of peevish misery into his forehead, while his cheeks' downstrokes, and his sulky mouth, seemed to be saying: 'I don't care who you are nor what you are, I shall have my own way.'

Mrs Morel knew him too well to look at him. As she unfastened her brooch at the mirror, she smiled faintly to see her face all smeared with the yellow dust of lilies. She brushed it off, and at last lay down. For some time her mind continued snapping and jetting sparks, but she was asleep before her husband awoke from the first sleep of his drunkenness.

CHAPTER 2

The Birth of Paul, and Another Battle

AFTER SUCH a scene as the last, Walter Morel was for some days abashed and ashamed, but he soon regained his old bullying indifference. Yet there was a slight shrinking, a diminishing in his assurance. Physically even, he shrank, and his fine full presence waned. He never grew in the least stout, so that, as he sank from his erect, assertive bearing, his physique seemed to contract along with his pride and moral strength.

But now he realised how hard it was for his wife to drag about at her work, and, his sympathy quickened by penitence, hastened forward with his help. He came straight home from the pit, and stayed in at evening till Friday, and then he could not remain at home. But he was back again by ten o'clock, almost quite sober.

He always made his own breakfast. Being a man who rose early and had plenty of time he did not, as some miners do drag his wife out of bed at six o'clock. At five, sometimes earlier, he woke, got straight out of bed, and went downstairs. When she could not sleep, his wife lay waiting for this time, as for a period of peace. The only real rest seemed to be when he was out of the house.

He went downstairs in his shirt and then struggled into his pit-trousers, which were left on the hearth to warm all night. There was always a fire, because Mrs Morel raked. And the first sound in the house was the bang, bang of the poker against the raker, as Morel smashed the remainder of the coal to make the kettle, which was filled and left on the hob, finally boil. His cup and knife and fork, all he wanted except just the food, was laid ready on the table on a newspaper. Then he got his breakfast, made the tea, packed the bottom of the doors with rugs to shut out the draught, piled a big fire, and sat down to an hour of joy. He toasted his bacon on a fork and caught the drops of fat on his bread; then he put the rasher on his thick slice of bread, and cut off chunks with a clasp-knife, poured his tea into his saucer, and was happy. With his family about, meals were never so pleasant. He loathed a fork; it is a modern introduction which has still scarcely reached common people. What Morel preferred was a clasp-knife. Then, in solitude, he ate and drank, often sitting, in cold weather, on a little stool with his back to the warm chimney-piece, his food on the fender, his cup on the hearth. And then he read the last night's newspaper – what of it he could – spelling it over laboriously. He preferred to keep the blinds down and the candle lit even when it was daylight; it was the habit of the mine.

At a quarter to six he rose, cut two thick slices of bread and butter, and put them in the white calico snap-bag. He filled his tin bottle with tea. Cold tea without milk or sugar was the drink he preferred for the pit. Then he pulled off his shirt, and put on his pit-singlet, a vest of thick flannel cut low round the neck, and with short sleeves like a chemise.

Then he went upstairs to his wife with a cup of tea because she was ill, and because it occurred to him.

'I've brought thee a cup o' tea, lass,' he said.

'Well, you needn't, for you know I don't like it,' she replied.

'Drink it up; it'll pop thee off to sleep again.'

She accepted the tea. It pleased him to see her take it and sip it.

'I'll back my life there's no sugar in,' she said.

'Yi – there's one big un,' he replied, injured.

'It's a wonder,' she said, sipping again.

She had a winsome face when her hair was loose. He loved her to grumble at him in this manner. He looked at her again, and went, without any sort of leave-taking. He never took more than two slices of bread and butter to eat in the pit, so an apple or an orange was a treat to him. He always liked it when she put one out for him. He tied a scarf round his neck, put on his great, heavy boots, his coat, with the big pocket, that carried his snap-bag and his bottle of tea, and went forth into the fresh morning air, closing, without locking, the door behind him. He loved the early morning, and the walk across the fields. So he appeared at the pit-top, often with a stalk from the hedge between his teeth, which he chewed all day to keep his mouth moist, down the mine, feeling quite as happy as when he was in the field.

Later, when the time for the baby grew nearer, he would bustle round in his slovenly fashion, poking out the ashes, rubbing the fireplace, sweeping the house before he went to work. Then, feeling very self righteous, he went upstairs.

'Now I'm cleaned up for thee; tha's no 'casions ter stir a peg all day, but sit and read thy books.'

Which made her laugh, in spite of her indignation.

'And the dinner cooks itself?' she answered.

'Eh, I know nowt about th' dinner.'

'You'd know if there weren't any.'

'Ay, 'appen so,' he answered, departing.

When she got downstairs, she would find the house tidy, but dirty. She could not rest until she had thoroughly cleaned; so she went down to the ash-pit with her dust-pan. Mrs Kirk, spying her, would contrive to have to go to her own coal-place at that minute. Then, across the wooden fence, she would call:

'So you keep wagging on, then?'

'Ay,' answered Mrs Morel deprecatingly. 'There's nothing else for it'

'Have you seen Hose?' called a very small woman from across the road. It was Mrs Anthony, a black-haired, strange little body, who always wore a brown velvet dress, tight fitting.

'I haven't,' said Mrs Morel.

'Eh, I wish he'd come. I've got a copperful of clothes an' I'm sure I heered his bell.'

'Hark! He's at the end.'

The two women looked down the alley. At the end of the Bottoms a man stood in a sort of old-fashioned trap*, bending over bundles of cream-coloured stuff; while a cluster of women held up their arms to him, some with bundles. Mrs Anthony herself had a heap of creamy, undyed stockings hanging over her arm.

'I've done ten dozen this week,' she said proudly to Mrs Morel.

'T-t-t!' went the other. 'I don't know how you can find time.'

'Eh!' said Mrs Anthony. 'You can find time if you make time.'

'I don't know how you do it,' said Mrs Morel. 'And how much shall you get for those many? '

'Tuppence-ha'penny a dozen,' replied the other.

'Well,' said Mrs Morel, 'I'd starve before I'd sit down and seam twenty-four stockings for twopence ha'penny.

'Oh, I don't know,' said Mrs Anthony. 'You can rip along with 'em.'

Hose was coming along, ringing his bell. Women were waiting at the yard-ends with their seamed stockings hanging over their arms. The man, a common fellow, made jokes with them, tried to swindle them, and bullied them. Mrs Morel went up her yard disdainfully.

It was an understood thing that if one woman wanted her neighbour, she should put the poker in the fire and bang at the back of the fireplace, which, as the fires were back to back, would make a great noise in the adjoining house. One morning Mrs Kirk, mixing a pudding, nearly started out of her skin as she heard the thud, thud, in her grate. With her hands all floury, she rushed to the fence.

'Did you knock, Mrs Morel?'

---

* a light, two-wheeled, cart.

'If you wouldn't mind, Mrs Kirk'

Mrs Kirk climbed on to her copper, got over the wall on to Mrs Morel's copper, and ran in to her neighbour.

'Eh, dear, how are you feeling?' she cried in concern.

'You might fetch Mrs Bower,' said Mrs Morel.

Mrs Kirk went into the yard, lifted up her strong, shrill voice, and called:

'Ag-gie – Ag-gie!'

The sound was heard from one end of the Bottoms to the other. At last Aggie came running up, and was sent for Mrs Bower, whilst Mrs Kirk left her pudding and stayed with her neighbour.

Mrs Morel went to bed. Mrs Kirk had Annie and William for dinner. Mrs Bower, fat and waddling, bossed the house.

'Hash some cold meat up for the master's dinner, and make him an apple-charlotte pudding,' said Mrs Morel.

'He may go without pudding *this* day,' said Mrs Bower.

Morel was not as a rule one of the first to appear at the bottom of the pit, ready to come up. Some men were there before four o'clock, when the whistle blew loose-all; but Morel, whose stall, a poor one, was at this time about a mile and a half away from the bottom, worked usually till the first mate stopped, then he finished also. This day, however, the miner was sick of the work. At two o'clock he looked at his watch, by the light of the green candle – he was in a safe working – and again at half-past two. He was hewing at a piece of rock that was in the way for the next day's work. As he sat on his heels, or kneeled, giving hard blows with his pick, 'Uszza – uszza!' he went.

'Shall ter finish, Sorry?'* cried Barker, his fellow butty.

'Finish? Niver while the world stands!' growled Morel.

And he went on striking. He was tired.

'It's a heart-breaking job,' said Barker.

* 'Sorry' is commonly used to address; perhaps a corruption of 'sirrah'.

But Morel was too exasperated, at the end of his tether, to answer. Still he struck and hacked with all his might.

'Tha might as well leave it, Walter,' said Barker. 'It'll do tomorrow, without thee hackin' thy guts out.'

'I'll lay no b– finger on this tomorrow, Isr'el!' cried Morel.

'Oh, well, if tha wunna, someb'dy else'll ha'e to,' said Israel.

Then Morel continued to strike.

'Hey-up there – *loose-a!*' cried the men, leaving the next stall.

Morel continued to strike.

'Tha'll happen catch me up,' said Barker, departing.

When he had gone, Morel, left alone, felt savage. He had not finished his job. He had overworked himself into a frenzy. Rising, wet with sweat, he threw his tool down, pulled on his coat, blew out his candle, took his lamp, and went. Down the main road the lights of the other men went swinging. There was a hollow sound of many voices. It was a long, heavy tramp underground.

He sat at the bottom of the pit, where the great drops of water fell plash. Many colliers were waiting their turns to go up, talking noisily. Morel gave his answers short and disagreeable.

'It's rainin', Sorry,' said old Giles, who had had the news from the top.

Morel found one comfort. He had his old umbrella, which he loved, in the lamp cabin. At last he took his stand on the chair, and was at the top in a moment. Then he handed in his lamp and got his umbrella, which he had bought at on auction for one-and-six. He stood on the edge of the pit-bank for a moment, looking out over the fields; grey rain was falling. The trucks stood full of wet, bright coal. Water ran down the sides of the waggons, over the white 'C.W. and Co.' Colliers, walking indifferent to the rain, were streaming down the line and up the field, a grey, dismal host. Morel put up his umbrella, and took pleasure from the peppering of the drops thereon.

All along the road to Bestwood the miners tramped, wet and grey and dirty, but their red mouths talking with animation. Morel also walked with a gang, but he said nothing. He frowned peevishly as he went. Many men passed into the Prince of Wales or into Ellen's. Morel, feeling sufficiently disagreeable to resist temptation, trudged along under the dripping trees that overhung the park wall, and down the mud of Greenhill Lane.

Mrs Morel lay in bed; listening to the rain, and the feet of the colliers from Minton, their voices, and the bang, bang of the gates as they went through the stile up the field.

'There's some herb beer behind the pantry-door,' she said. 'Th' master'll want a drink, if he doesn't stop.'

But he was late, so she concluded he had called for a drink, since it was raining. What did he care about the child or her?

She was very ill when her children were born.

'What is it?' she asked, feeling sick to-death.

'A boy.'

And she took consolation in that. The thought of being the mother of men was warming to her heart. She looked at the child. It had blue eyes, and a lot of fair hair and was bonny. Her love came up hot, in spite of everything. She had it in bed with her.

Morel, thinking nothing, dragged his way up the garden path, wearily and angrily. He closed his umbrella, and stood it in the sink; then he sluthered his heavy boots into the kitchen. Mrs Bower appeared in the Inner doorway.

'Well,' she said, 'she's about as bad as she can be. It's a boy childt.'

The miner grunted, put his empty snap-bag and his tin bottle on the dresser, went back into the scullery and hung up his coat, then came and dropped into his chair.

'Han yer got a drink?' he asked.

The woman went into the pantry. There was heard the pop of a cork. She set the mug, with a little, disgusted rap, on the table before Morel. He drank, gasped, wiped his big moustache on the end of his scarf, drank, gasped, and lay back in his chair. The woman would not speak to him again. She set his dinner before him, and went upstairs.

'Was that the master?' asked Mrs Morel.

'I've gave him his dinner,' replied Mrs Bower.

After he had sat with his arms on the table – he resented the fact that Mrs Bower put no cloth on for him, and gave him a little plate, instead of a full-sized dinner-plate – he began to eat. The fact that his wife was ill; that he had another boy, was nothing to him at that moment. He was too tired; he wanted his dinner; he wanted to sit with his arms lying on the board; he did not like having Mrs Bower about. The fire was too small to please him.

After he had finished his meal, he sat for twenty minutes; then he stoked up a big fire. Then, in his stockinged feet, he went reluctantly upstairs. It was a struggle to face his wife at this moment, and he was tired. His face was black, and smeared with sweat. His singlet had dried again, soaking the dirt in. He had a dirty woollen scarf round his throat. So he stood at the foot of the bed.

'Well, how are ter, then?' he asked.

'I s'll be all right,' she answered.

'H'm!'

He stood at a loss what to say next. He was tired, and this bother was rather a nuisance to him, and he didn't quite know where he was.

'A lad, tha says,' he stammered.

She turned down the sheet and showed the child.

'Bless him!' he murmured: Which made her laugh, because he blessed by rote – pretending paternal emotion, which he did not feel just then.

'Go now,' she said.

'I will, my lass,' he answered, turning away.

Dismissed, he wanted to kiss her, but he dared not. She half wanted him to kiss her, but could not bring herself to give any sign. She only breathed freely when he was gone out of the room again, leaving behind him a faint smell of pit-dirt.

Mrs Morel had a visit every day from the Congregational clergyman. Mr Heaton was young, and very poor. His wife had died at the birth of his first baby, so he remained alone in the manse. He was a Bachelor of Arts of Cambridge, very shy, and no preacher. Mrs Morel was fond of him, and he depended on her. For hours he talked to her, when she was well. He became the god-parent of the child.

Occasionally the minister stayed to tea with Mrs Morel. Then she laid the cloth early, got out her best cups, with a little green rim, and hoped Morel would not come too soon; indeed, if he stayed for a pint, she would not mind this day. She had always two dinners to cook because she believed children should have their chief meal at midday, whereas Morel needed his at five o'clock. So Mr Heaton would hold the baby, whilst Mrs Morel beat up a batter-pudding or peeled the potatoes, and he, watching her all the time, would discuss his next sermon. His ideas were quaint and fantastic. She brought him judiciously to earth. It was a discussion of the wedding at Cana.

'When He changed the water into wine at Cana,' he said, 'that is a symbol that the ordinary life, even the blood, of the married husband and wife, which had before been uninspired, like water, became filled with the Spirit, and was as wine because, when love enters, the whole spiritual constitution of a man changes, is filled with the Holy Ghost, and almost his form is altered.'

Mrs Morel thought to herself:

'Yes, poor fellow, his young wife is dead; that is why he makes his love into the Holy Ghost.'

They were halfway down their first cup of tea when they heard the sluther of pit-boots.

'Good gracious!' exclaimed Mrs Morel, in spite of herself.

The minister looked rather scared. Morel entered. He was feeling rather savage. He nodded a 'How d'yer do' to the clergyman, who rose to shake hands with him.

'Nay,' said Morel, showing his hand, 'look thee at it! Tha niver wants ter shake hands wi' a hand like that, does ter? There's too much pickhaft and shovel-dirt on it.'

The minister flushed with confusion, and sat down again. Mrs Morel rose, carried out the steaming saucepan. Morel took off his coat, dragged his armchair to table, and sat down heavily.

'Are you tired?' asked the clergyman.

'Tired? I ham that,' replied Morel. '*You* don't know what it is to be tired, as *I'm* tired.'

'No,' replied the clergyman.

'Why, look yer 'ere,' said the miner, showing the shoulders of his singlet. 'It's a bit dry now, but it's wet as a clout with sweat even yet. Feel it.'

'Goodness!' cried Mrs Morel. 'Mr Heaton doesn't want to fell your nasty singlet.'

The clergyman put out his hand gingerly.

'No, perhaps he doesn't,' said Morel; 'but it's all come out of *me*, whether or not. An' iv'ry day alike my singlet's wringin' wet. 'Aven't you got a drink, Missis, for a man when he comes home barkled up from the pit.

'You know you drank all the beer,' said Mrs Morel, pouring out his tea.

'An' was there no more to be got?' Turning to the clergyman – 'A man gets that caked up wi' th' dust, you know, – that clogged up down a coalmine, he *needs* a drink when he comes home.'

'I am sure he does,' said the clergyman.

'But it's ten to one if there's owt for him.'

'There's water – and there's tea,' said Mrs Morel.

'Water! It's not water as'll clear his throat.'

He poured out a saucerful of tea, blew it, and sucked it up through his great black moustache, sighing afterwards. Then he poured out another saucerful, and stood his cup on the table.

'My cloth!' said Mrs Morel, putting it on a plate.

'A man as comes home as I do's too tired to care about cloths,' said Morel.

'Pity!' exclaimed his wife, sarcastically.

The room was full of the smell of meat and vegetables and pit-clothes.

He leaned over to the minister, his great moustache thrust forward, his mouth very red in his black face.

'Mr Heaton,' he said, 'a man as has been down the black hole all day, dingin' away* at a coal face, yi, a sight harder than that wall – '

'Needn't make a moan of it,' put in Mrs Morel.

She hated her husband because, whenever he had an audience, he whined and played for sympathy. William, sitting nursing the baby, hated him, with a boy's hatred for false sentiment, and for the stupid treatment of his mother. Annie had never liked him; she merely avoided him.

When the minister had gone, Mrs Morel looked at her cloth.

'A fine mess!' she said.

'Dos't think I'm goin' to sit wi' my arms danglin', cos tha's got a parson for tea wi' thee?' he bawled.

They were both angry, but she said nothing. The baby began to cry, and Mrs Morel, picking up a saucepan from the hearth, accidentally knocked Annie on the head, whereupon the girl began to whine, and Morel to shout at her. In the midst of this pandemonium, William looked up at the big glazed text over the mantelpiece and read distinctly:

* pounding away.

'God Bless Our Home!'

Whereupon Mrs Morel, trying to soothe the baby, jumped up, rushed at him, boxed his ears, saying:

'What are you putting in for?'

And then she sat down and laughed, till tears ran over her cheeks, while William kicked the stool he had been sitting on, and Morel growled:

'I canna see what there is so much to laugh at.'

One evening, directly after the parson's visit, feeling unable to bear herself after another display from her husband, she took Annie and the baby and went out. Morel had kicked William, and the mother would never forgive him.

She went over the sheep-bridge and across a corner of the meadow to the cricket-ground. The meadows seemed one space of ripe, evening light, whispering with the distant mill-race. She sat on a seat under the alders in the cricket-ground, and fronted the evening. Before her, level and solid, spread the big green cricket-field, like the bed of a sea of light. Children played in the bluish shadow of the pavilion. Many rooks, high up, came cawing home across the softly-woven sky. They stooped in a long curve down into the golden glow, concentrating, cawing, wheeling, like black flakes on a slow vortex, over a tree-clump that made a dark boss among the pasture.

A few gentlemen were practising, and Mrs Morel could hear the chock of the ball, and the voices of men suddenly roused; could see the white forms of men shifting silently over the green, upon which already the under shadows were smouldering. Away at the grange, one side of the haystacks was lit up, the other sides blue-grey. A waggon of sheaves rocked small across the melting yellow light.

The sun was going down. Every open evening, the hills of Derbyshire were blazed over with red sunset. Mrs Morel watched the sun sink from the glistening sky, leaving a soft flower-blue overhead, while the western space went red, as if all the fire had swum down there, leaving the bell cast flawless blue. The mountain-ash berries across the field stood fierily out from the dark leaves, for a moment. A few shocks of corn in a corner of the fallow stood up as if alive; she imagined them bowing, perhaps her son would be a Joseph. In the east, a mirrored sunset floated pink opposite the west's scarlet. The big haystacks on the hillside that butted into the glare went cold.

With Mrs Morel it was one of those still moments when the small frets vanish, and the beauty of things stands out, and she had the peace and the strength to see herself. Now and again, a swallow cut close to her. Now and again, Annie came up with a handful of alder-currants. The baby was restless on his mother's knee, clambering with his hands at the light.

Mrs Morel looked down at him. She had dreaded this baby like a catastrophe, because of her feeling for her husband. And now she felt strangely towards the infant. Her heart was heavy because of the child, almost as if it were unhealthy, or malformed. Yet it seemed quite well. But she noticed the peculiar knitting of the baby's brows, and the peculiar heaviness of its eyes, as if it were trying to understand something that was pain. She felt, when she looked at her child's dark, brooding pupils, as if a burden were on her heart.

'He looks as if he was thinking about something – quite sorrowful,' said Mrs Kirk.

Suddenly, looking at him, the heavy feeling at the mother's heart melted into passionate grief. She bowed over him, and a few tears shook swiftly out of her very heart. The baby lifted his fingers.

'My lamb!' she cried softly.

And at that moment she felt, in some far inner place of her soul, that she and her husband were guilty.

The baby was looking up at her. It had blue eyes like her

own, but its look was heavy, steady, as if it had realised something that had stunned some point of its soul.

In her arms lay the delicate baby. Its deep blue eyes, always looking up at her unblinking, seemed to draw her innermost thoughts out of her.

She no longer loved her husband; she had not wanted this child to come, and there it lay in her arms and pulled at her heart. She felt as if the navel string that had connected its trail little body with hers had not been broken. A wave of hot love went over her to the infant. She held it close to her face and breast. With all her force, with all her soul she would make up to it for having brought it into the world unloved. She would love it all the more now it was here; carry it in her love. Its clear, knowing eyes gave her pain and fear. Did it know all about her? When it lay under her heart, had it been listening then? Was there a reproach in the look? She felt the marrow melt in her bones, with fear and pain.

Once more she was aware of the sun lying red on the rim of the hill opposite. She suddenly held up the child in her hands.

'Look!' she said. 'Look, my pretty!'

She thrust the infant forward to the crimson, throbbing sun, almost with relief. She saw him lift his little fist. Then she put him to her bosom again, ashamed almost of her impulse to give him back again whence he came.

'If he lives,' she thought to herself 'what will become of him – what will he be?'

Her heart was anxious.

'I will call him "Paul," ' she said suddenly; she knew not why.

After a while she went home. A fine shadow was flung over the deep green meadow, darkening all.

As she expected, she found the house empty. But Morel was home by ten o'clock, and that day, at least, ended peacefully.

Walter Morel was, at this time, exceedingly irritable. His work seemed to exhaust him. When he came home he did not speak civilly to anybody. If the fire were rather low he bullied about that – he grumbled about his dinner; if the children made a chatter he shouted at them in a way that made their mother's blood boil, and made them hate him.

On the Friday, he was not home by eleven o'clock. The baby was unwell, and was restless, crying if he were put down. Mrs Morel, tired to death, and still weak, was scarcely under control.

'I wish the nuisance would come,' she said wearily to herself.

The child at last sank down to sleep in her arms. She was too tired to carry him to the cradle.

'But I'll say nothing, whatever time he comes,' she said. 'It only works me up; I won't say anything. But I know if he does anything it'll make my blood boil,' she added to herself.

She sighed, hearing him coming, as if it were something she could not bear. He, taking his revenge, was nearly drunk. She kept her head bent over the child as he entered, not wishing to see him. But it went through her like a flash of hot fire when, in passing, he lurched against the dresser setting the tins rattling, and clutched at the white pot knobs for support. He hung up his hat and coat, then returned, stood glowering from a distance at her, as she sat bowed over the child.

'Is there nothing to eat in the house?' he asked, insolently, as if to a servant. In certain stages of his intoxication he affected the clipped, mincing speech of the towns. Mrs Morel hated him most in this condition.

'You know what there is in the house,' she said, so coldly, it sounded impersonal.

He stood and glared at her without moving a muscle.

'I asked a civil question, and I expect a civil answer,' he said affectedly. 'And you got it,' she said, still ignoring him.

He glowered again. Then he came unsteadily forward. He leaned on the table with one hand, and with the other jerked at the table drawer to get a knife to cut bread. The drawer stuck because he pulled sideways. In a temper he dragged it, so that it flew out bodily, and spoons, forks, knives, a hundred metallic things, splashed with a clatter and a clang upon the brick floor. The baby gave a little convulsed start.

'What are you doing, clumsy, drunken fool?' the mother cried.

'Then tha should get the flamin' thing thysen. Tha should get up, like other women have to, an' wait on a man.'

'Wait on you – wait on you?' she cried. 'Yes, I see myself.'

'Yis, an' I'll learn thee tha's got to. Wait on me, yes, tha sh'lt wait on me.'

'Never, milord. I'd wait on a dog at the door first.'

'What – what?'

He was trying to fit in the drawer. At her last speech he turned round. His face was crimson, his eyes bloodshot. He stared at her one silent second in threat.

'P-h!' she went quickly, in contempt.

He jerked at the drawer in his excitement. It fell, cut sharply on his shin, and on the reflex he flung it at her.

One of the corners caught her brow as the shallow drawer crashed into the fireplace. She swayed, almost fell stunned from her chair. To her very soul she was sick; she clasped the child tightly to her bosom. A few moments elapsed; then, with an effort, she brought herself to. The baby was crying plaintively. Her left brow was bleeding rather profusely. As she glanced down at the child, her brain reeling, some drops of blood soaked into its white shawl; but the baby was at least not hurt. She balanced her head to keep equilibrium, so that the blood ran into her eye.

Walter Morel remained as he had stood, leaning on the table with one hand, looking blank. When he was sufficiently sure of his balance, he went across to her, swayed, caught hold of the back of her rocking-chair, almost tipping her out; then, leaning forward over her, and swaying as he spoke, he said, in tone of wondering concern:

'Did it catch thee?'

He swayed again, as if he would pitch on to the child. With the catastrophe he had lost all balance.

'Go away,' she said, struggling to keep her presence of mind.

He hiccoughed. 'Let's – let's look at it,' he said, hiccoughing again.

'Go away!' she cried.

'Lemme – lemme look at it, lass.'

She smelled him of drink, felt the unequal pull of his swaying grasp on the back of her rocking-chair.

'Go away,' she said, and weakly she pushed him off.

He stood, uncertain in balance, gazing upon her. Summoning all her strength she rose, the baby on one arm. By a cruel effort of will, moving as if in sleep, she went across to the scullery, where she bathed her eye for a minute in cold water; but she was too dizzy. Afraid lest she should swoon, she returned to her rocking-chair, trembling in every fibre. By instinct, she kept the baby clasped.

Morel, bothered, had succeeded in pushing the drawer back into its cavity, and was on his knees, groping, with numb paws, for the scattered spoons.

Her brow was still bleeding. Presently Morel got up and came craning his neck towards her.

'What has it done to thee, lass?' he asked, in a very wretched, humble tone.

'You can see what it's done,' she answered.

He stood, bending forward, supported on his hands, which grasped his legs just above the knee. He peered to look at the wound. She drew away from the thrust of his face with its great moustache, averting her own face as much as possible. As he looked at her, who was cold and impassive as stone, with mouth shut tight, he sickened with feebleness and hopelessness of spirit. He was turning drearily away, when he saw a drop of blood fall from the averted wound into the baby's fragile, glistening hair. Fascinated, he watched the heavy dark drop hang in the glistening cloud, and pull down the gossamer. Another drop fell. It would soak through to the baby's scalp. He watched, fascinated, feeling it soak in; then, finally, his manhood broke.

'What of this child?' was all his wife said to him. But her low, intense tones brought his head lower. She softened: 'Get me some wadding out of the middle drawer,' she said.

He stumbled away very obediently, presently returning with a pad, which she singed before the fire, then put on her forehead, as she sat with the baby on her lap.

'Now that clean pit-scarf.'

Again he rummaged and fumbled in the drawer, returning presently with a red, narrow scarf. She took it, and with trembling fingers proceeded to bind it round her head.

'Let me tie it for thee,' he said humbly.

'I can do it myself,' she replied. When it was done she went upstairs, telling him to rake the fire and lock the door.

In the morning Mrs Morel said:

'I knocked against the latch of the coal-place, when I was getting a raker in the dark, because the candle blew out.' Her two small children looked up at her with wide, dismayed eyes. They said nothing, but their parted lips seemed to express the unconscious tragedy they felt.

Walter Morel lay in bed next day until nearly dinner-time.

He did not think of the previous evening's work. He scarcely thought of anything, but he would not think of that. He lay and suffered like a sulking dog. He had hurt himself most; and he was the more damaged because he would never say a word to her, or express his sorrow. He tried to wriggle out of it. 'It was her own fault,' he said to himself. Nothing, however, could prevent his inner consciousness inflicting on him the punishment which ate into his spirit like rust, and which he could only alleviate by drinking.

He felt as if he had not the initiative to get up, or to say a word, or to move, but could only lie like a log. Moreover, he had himself violent pains in the head. It was Saturday. Towards noon he rose, cut himself food in the pantry, ate it with his head dropped, then pulled on his boots, and went out, to return at three o'clock slightly tipsy and relieved; then once more straight to bed. He rose again at six in the evening, had tea and went straight out.

Sunday was the same: bed till noon, the Palmerston Arms till 2.30, dinner, and bed; scarcely a word spoken. When Mrs Morel went upstairs, towards four o'clock, to put on her Sunday dress, he was fast asleep. She would have felt sorry for him, if he had once said, 'Wife, I'm sorry.' But no; he insisted to himself it was her fault. And so he broke himself. So she merely left him alone. There was this deadlock of passion between them, and she was stronger.

The family began tea. Sunday was the only day when all sat down to meals together.

'Isn't my father going to get up?' asked William.

'Let him lie,' the mother replied.

There was a feeling of misery over all the house. The children breathed the air that was poisoned, and they felt dreary. They were rather disconsolate, did not know what to do, what to play at.

Immediately Morel woke he got straight out of bed. That was characteristic of him all his life. He was all for activity. The prostrated inactivity of two mornings was stifling him.

It was near six o'clock when he got down. This time he entered without hesitation, his wincing sensitiveness having hardened again. He did not care any longer what the family thought or felt.

The tea-things were on the table. William was reading aloud from 'The Child's Own,' Annie listening and asking eternally 'Why?' Both children hushed into silence as they heard the approaching thud of their father's stockinged feet, and shrank as he entered. Yet he was usually indulgent to them.

Morel made the meal alone, brutally. He ate and drank more noisily than he had need. No one spoke to him. The family life withdrew, shrank away, and became hushed as he entered. But he cared no longer about his alienation.

Immediately he had finished tea he rose with alacrity to go out. It was this alacrity, this haste to be gone, which so sickened Mrs Morel. As she heard him sousing heartily in cold water, heard the eager scratch of the steel comb on the side of the bowl, as he wetted his hair, she closed her eyes in disgust. As he bent over, lacing his boots, there was a certain vulgar gusto in his movement that divided him from the reserved, watchful rest of the family. He always ran away from the battle with himself. Even in his own heart's privacy, he excused himself, saying, 'If she hadn't said so-and-so, it would never have happened. She asked for what she's got.' The children waited in restraint during his preparations. When he had gone, they sighed with relief.

He closed the door behind him, and was glad. It was a rainy evening. The Palmerston would be the cosier. He hastened forward in anticipation. All the slate roofs of the Bottoms shone black with wet. The roads, always dark with coal-dust, were full of blackish mud. He hastened along. The Palmerston windows were steamed over. The passage was paddled with wet feet. But the air was warm, if foul, and full of the sound of voices and the smell of beer and smoke.

'What shollt ha'e, Walter?' cried a voice, as soon as Morel appeared in the doorway.

'Oh, Jim, my lad, wheriver has thee sprung frae?'

The men made a seat for him, and took him in warmly. He

was glad. In a minute or two they had thawed all responsibility out of him, all shame, all trouble, and he was clear as a bell for a jolly night.

On the Wednesday following, Morel was penniless. He dreaded his wife. Having hurt her, he hated her. He did not know what to do with himself that evening, having not even twopence with which to go to the Palmerston, and being already rather deeply in debt. So, while his wife was down the garden with the child, he hunted in the top drawer of the dresser where she kept her purse, found it, and looked inside. It contained a half-crown, two halfpennies, and a sixpence. So he took the sixpence, put the purse carefully back, and went out.

The next day, when she wanted to pay the greengrocer, she looked in the purse for her sixpence, and her heart sank to her shoes. Then she sat down and thought: 'Was there a sixpence? I hadn't spent it, had I? And I hadn't left it anywhere else?'

She was much put about. She hunted round everywhere for it. And, as she sought, the conviction came into her heart that her husband had taken it. What she had in her purse was all the money she possessed. But that he should sneak it from her thus was unbearable. He had done so twice before. The first time she had not accused him, and at the weekend he had put the shilling again into her purse. So that was how she had known he had taken it. The second time he had not paid back.

This time she felt it was too much. When he had had his dinner – he came home early that day – she said to him coldly:

'Did you take sixpence out of my purse last night?'

'Me!' he said, looking up in an offended way. 'No, I didna! I niver clapped eyes on your purse.'

But she could detect the lie.

Why, you know you did,' she said quietly.

'I tell you I didna,' he shouted. 'Yer at me again, are yer? I've had a out enough on't.'

'So you filch sixpence out of my purse while I'm taking the clothes in.'

'I'll may yer pay for this,' he said, pushing back his chair in desperation. He bustled and got washed, then went determinedly upstairs. Presently he came down dressed, and with a big bundle in a blue-checked, enormous handkerchief.

'And now,' he said, 'you'll see me again when you do.'

'It'll be before I want to,' she replied; and at that he marched out of the house with his bundle. She sat trembling slightly, but her heart brimming with contempt. What would she do if he went to some other pit, obtained work, and got in with another woman? But she knew him too well – he couldn't. She was dead sure of him. Nevertheless her heart was gnawed inside her.

'Where's my dad?' said William, coming in from school.

'He says he's run away,' replied the mother.

'Where to?'

'Eh, I don't know. He's taken a bundle in the blue handkerchief, and says he's not coming back.'

'What shall we do?' cried the boy.

'Eh, never trouble, he won't go far.'

'But if he doesn't come back,' wailed Annie.

And she and William retired to the sofa and wept. Mrs Morel sat and laughed.

'You pair of gabeys!' she exclaimed. 'You'll see him before the night's out.'

But the children were not to be consoled. Twilight came on. Mrs Morel grew anxious from very weariness. One part of her said, it would be a relief to see the last of him, another part fretted because of keeping the children, and inside her, as yet, she could not quite let him go. At the bottom, she knew very well he could *not* go.

When she went down to the coal place at the end of the garden, however, she felt something behind the door. So she looked. And there in the dark lay the big blue bundle. She sat on a piece of coal in front of the bundle and laughed. Every time she saw it, so fat and yet so ignominious, slunk into its corner in the dark, with its ends flopping like dejected ears from the knots, she laughed again. She was relieved.

Mrs Morel sat waiting. He had not any money, she knew, so if he stopped he was running up a bill. She was very tired of him – tired to death. He had not even the courage to carry his bundle beyond the yard-end.

As she meditated at about nine o'clock, he opened the door and came in, slinking, and yet sulky. She said not a word. He took off his coat, and slunk to his armchair, where he began to take off his boots.

'You'd better fetch your bundle before you take your boots off,' she said quietly.

'You may thank your stars I've come back tonight,' he said, looking up from under his dropped head, sulkily, trying to be impressive.

'Why, where should you have gone? You daren't even get your parcel through the yard-end,' she said.

He looked such a fool she was not even angry with him. He continued to take his boots off and prepare for bed.

'I don't know what's in your blue handkerchief,' she said. 'But if you leave it the children shall fetch it in the morning.'

Whereupon he got up and went out of the house, returning presently and crossing the kitchen with averted face, hurrying upstairs. As Mrs Morel saw him slink quickly through the inner doorway, holding his bundle, she laughed to herself; but her heart was bitter, because she had loved him.

CHAPTER 3

The Casting Off of Morel –
the Taking On of William

DURING THE next week Morel's temper was almost unbearable. Like all miners, he was a great lover of medicines, which, strangely enough, he would often pay for himself.

'You mun get me a drop o' laxy vitral,' he said. 'It's a winder as we canna ha'e a sup i' th' 'ouse.'

So Mrs Morel bought him elixir of vitriol, his favourite first medicine. And he made himself a jug of wormwood tea. He had hanging in the attic great bunches of dried herbs: wormwood, rue, horehound, elder flowers, parsley-purt, marshmallow, hyssop, dandelion, and century. Usually there was a jug of one or other decoction standing on the hob, from which he drank largely.

'Grand!' he said, smacking his lips after wormwood. 'Grand!' And he exhorted the children to try.

'It's better than any of your tea or your cocoa stews,' he vowed. But they were not to be tempted.

This time, however, neither pills nor vitriol nor all his herbs would shift the 'nasty peens in his head.' He was sickening for on attack of an Inflammation of the brain. He had never been well since his sleeping on the ground when he went with Jerry to Nottingham. Since then he had drunk and stormed. Now he fell seriously ill, and Mrs Morel had him to nurse. He was one of the worst patients imaginable. But, in spite of all, and putting aside the fact that he was breadwinner, she never quite wanted him to die. Still there was one part of her wanted him for herself.

The neighbours were very good to her: occasionally some had the children in to meals, occasionally some would do the downstairs work for her, one would mind the baby for a day. But it was a great drag, nevertheless. It was not every day the neighbours helped. Then she had nursing of baby and husband, cleaning and cooking, everything to do. She was quite worn out, but she did what was wanted of her.

And the money was just sufficient. She had seventeen shillings a week from clubs, and every Friday Barker and the other butty put by a portion of the stall's profits for Morel's wife. And the neighbours made broths, and gave eggs, and such invalids' trifles. If they had not helped her so generously in those times, Mrs Morel would never have pulled through, without incurring debts that would have dragged her down.

The weeks passed. Morel, almost against hope, grew better. He had a fine constitution, so that, once on the mend, he went straight forward to recovery. Soon he was pottering about downstairs. During his illness his wife had spoilt him a little. Now he wanted her to continue. He often put his hand to his head, pulled down the corners of his mouth, and shammed pains he did not feel. But there was no deceiving her. At first she merely smiled to herself. Then she scolded him sharply.

'Goodness, man, don't be so lachrymose.'

That wounded him slightly, but still he continued to feign sickness.

'I wouldn't be such a mardy baby,' said his wife shortly.

Then he was indignant, and cursed under his breath, like a boy. He was forced to resume a normal tone, and to cease to whine.

Nevertheless, there was a state of peace in the house for some time. Mrs Morel was more tolerant of him, and he, depending on her almost like a child, was rather happy. Neither knew that she was more tolerant because she loved him less. Up till this time, in spite of all, he had been her husband and her man. She had felt that, more or less, what he did to himself he did to her. Her living depended on him. There were many, many stages in the ebbing of her love for him, but it was always ebbing.

Now, with the birth of this third baby, her self no longer set towards him, helplessly, but was like a tide that scarcely rose, standing off from him. After this she scarcely desired him. And, standing more aloof from him, not feeling him so much part of herself, but merely part of her circumstances, she did not mind so much what he did, could leave him alone.

There was the halt, the wistfulness about the ensuing year, which is like autumn in a man's life. His wife was casting him off, half regretfully, but relentlessly; casting him off and turning now for love and life to the children. Henceforward he was more or less a husk. And he half acquiesced, as so many men do, yielding their place to their children.

During his recuperation, when it was really over between them, both made an effort to come back somewhat to the old relationship of the first months of their marriage. He sat at home and, when the children were in bed, and she was sewing – she did all her sewing by hand, made all shirts and children's clothing – he would read to her from the news paper, slowly pronouncing and delivering the words like a man pitching quoits. Often she hurried him on, giving him a phrase in anticipation.

And then he took her words humbly.

The silences between them were peculiar. There would be the swift, slight 'cluck' of her needle, the sharp 'pop' of his lips as he let out the smoke, the warmth, the sizzle on the bars as he spat in the fire. Then her thoughts turned to William. Already he was getting a big boy. Already he was top of the class, and the master said he was the smartest lad in the school. She saw him a man, young, full of vigour, making the world glow again for her.

And Morel sitting there, quite alone, and having nothing to think about, would be feeling vaguely uncomfortable. His soul would reach out in its blind way to her and find her gone. He felt a sort of emptiness, almost like a vacuum in his soul. He was unsettled and restless. Soon he could not live in that atmosphere, and he affected his wife. Both felt an oppression on their breathing when they were left together for some time. Then he went to bed and she settled down to enjoy herself alone, working, thinking, living.

Meanwhile another infant was coming, fruit of this little peace and tenderness between the separating parents. Paul was seventeen months old when the new baby was born. He was then a plump, pale child, quiet, with heavy blue eyes, and still the peculiar slight knitting of the brows. The last child was also a boy, fair and bonny. Mrs Morel was sorry when she knew she was with child, both for economic reasons and because she did not love her husband; but not for the sake of the infant.

They called the baby Arthur. He was very pretty, with a mop of gold curls, and he loved his father from the first. Mrs Morel was glad this child loved the father. Hearing the miner's footsteps, the baby would put up his arms and crow.

And if Morel were in a good temper, he called back immediately, in his hearty, mellow voice:

'What then, my beauty? I sh'll come to thee in a minute.'

And as soon as he had taken off his pit-coat, Mrs Morel would put an apron round the child, and give him to his father.

What a sight the lad looks!' she would exclaim sometimes, taking back the baby, that was smutted on the face from his father's kisses and play. Then Morel laughed joyfully.

'He's a little collier, bless his bit o' mutton!' he exclaimed.

And these were the happy moments of her life now, when the children included the father in her heart.

Meanwhile William grew bigger and stronger and more active, while Paul, always rather delicate and quiet, got slimmer, and trotted after his mother like her shadow. He was usually active and interested, but sometimes he would have fits of depression. Then the mother would find the boy of three or four crying on the sofa.

'What's the matter?' she asked, and got no answer.

'What's the matter?' she insisted, getting cross.

'I don't know,' sobbed the child.

So she tried to reason him out of it, or to amuse him, but without effect. It made her feel beside herself. Then the father, always impatient, would jump from his chair and shout:

'If he doesn't stop, I'll smack him till he does.'

'You'll do nothing of the sort,' said the mother coldly. And then she carried the child into the yard, plumped him into his little chair, and said: 'Now cry there, Misery!'

And then a butterfly on the rhubarb-leaves perhaps caught his eye, or at last he cried himself to sleep. These fits were not often, but they caused a shadow in Mrs Morel's heart, and her treatment of Paul was different from that of the other children.

Suddenly one morning as she was looking down the alley of the Bottoms for the barm-man[*], she heard a voice calling her. It was the thin little Mrs Anthony in brown velvet.

'Here, Mrs Morel, I want to tell you about your Willie.'

'Oh, do you?' replied Mrs Morel. 'Why, what's the matter?'

'A lad as gets 'old of another an' rips his clothes off'n 'is back,' Mrs Anthony said, 'wants showing something.'

'Your Alfred's as old as my William,' said Mrs Morel.

' 'Appen 'e is, but that doesn't give him a right to get hold of the boy's collar, an' fair rip it clean off his back.'

'Well,' said Mrs Morel, 'I don't thrash my children and even if I did, I should want to hear their side of the tale.'

'They'd happen be a bit better if they did get a good hiding,' retorted Mrs Anthony. 'When it comes ter rippin' a lad's clean collar own 'is back a-purpose – '

'I'm sure he didn't do it on purpose,' said Mrs Morel.

'Make me a liar!' shouted Mrs Anthony.

---

[*] a yeast-seller.

Mrs Morel moved away and closed her gate. Her hand trembled as she held her mug of barm.

'But I s'll let your mester know,' Mrs Anthony cried after her.

At dinner-time, when William had finished his meal and wanted to be off again – he was then eleven years old – his mother said to him:

'What did you tear Alfred Anthony's collar for?'

'When did I tear his collar?'

'I don't know when, but his mother says you did.'

'Why – it was yesterday – an' it was torn a'ready.'

'But you tore it more.'

'Well, I'd got a cobbler as 'ad licked seventeen – an' Alfy Ant'ny 'e says:

> "Adam an' Eve an' pinch-me,
> Went down to a river to bade.
> Adam an' Eve got drownded,
> Who do yer think got saved?"

'An' so I'says, "Oh, Pinch-*you*," an' so I pinched 'im, an' 'e was mad, an' so he snatched my cobbler an' run off with it. An' so I run after 'im, an' when I was gettin' hold of him, 'e dodged, an' it ripped 'is collar. But I got my cobbler – '

He pulled from his pocket a black old horse-chestnut hanging on a string. This old cobbler had 'cobbled' – hit and smashed – seventeen other cobblers on similar strings. So the boy was proud of his veteran.

'Well,' said Mrs Morel, 'you know you've got no right to rip his collar.'

'Well, our mother!' he answered. 'I never meant tr'a done it – an' it was on'y an old indirrubber collar as was torn a'ready.'

'Next time,' said his mother, '*you* be more careful. I shouldn't like it if you came home with *your* collar torn off.'

'I don't care, our mother; I never did it a-purpose.'

The boy was rather miserable at being reprimanded.

'No – well, you be more careful.'

William fled away, glad to be exonerated. And Mrs Morel who hated any bother with the neighbours, thought she would explain to Mrs Anthony, and the business would be over.

But that evening Morel came in from the pit looking very sour. He stood in the kitchen and glared round, but did not speak for some minutes. Then:

'Wheer's' that Willy?' he asked

'What do you want *him* for?' asked Mrs Morel, who had guessed.

'I'll let 'im know when I get him,' said Morel, banging his pit-bottle On to the dresser.

'I suppose Mrs Anthony's got hold of you and been yarning to you about their Alfy's collar,' said Mrs Morel, rather sneering.

'Niver mind who's got hold of me,' said Morel. 'When I get hold of '*im* I'll make his bones rattle.'

'It's a poor tale,' said Mrs Morel, 'that you're so ready to side with any snipey vixen who likes to come telling toles against your own children,'

'I'll learn 'im!' said Morel. 'It none matters to me whose lad 'e is; 'e's none goin' rippin' an' tearin' about just as he's a mind.'

' "Ripping and tearing about!" repeated Mrs Morel. 'He was running after that Alfy, who'd taken his cobbler, and he accidentally got hold of his collar, because the other dodged – as on Anthony would.'

'I know!' shouted Morel threateningly.

'You would, before you're told,' replied his wife bitingly.

'Niver you mind,' stormed Morel. 'I know my business.'

'That's more than doubtful,' said Mrs Morel, 'supposing some loud mouthed creature had been getting you to thrash your own children.'

'I know,' repeated Morel.

And he said no more, but sat and nursed his bad temper. Suddenly William ran in, saying:

'Can I have my tea, mother?'

'Tha can ha' e more than that!' shouted Morel.

'Hold your noise, man,' said Mrs Morel; 'and don't look so ridiculous.'

'He'll look ridiculous before I've done wi' him!' shouted Morel, rising from his chair and glaring at his son.

William, who was a tall lad for his years, but very sensitive, had gone pale, and was looking in a sort of horror at his father.

'Go out!' Mrs Morel commanded her son.

William had not the wit to move. Suddenly Morel clenched his fist, and crouched.

'I'll *gi'e* him "go out!" ' he shouted like an insane thing.

"What!' cried Mrs Morel, panting with rage. 'You shall not touch him for *her* telling, you shall not!'

'Shonna I?' shouted Morel. 'Shonna I?'

And, glaring at the boy, he ran forward. Mrs Morel sprang in between them, with her fist lifted.

'Don't you *dare!*' she cried.

'What!' he shouted, baffled for the moment. 'What!'

She spun round to her son.

'Go out of the house!' she commanded him in fury.

The boy, as if hypnotised by her, turned suddenly and was gone. Morel rushed to the door, but was too late. He returned, pale under his pit-dirt with fury. But now his wife was fully roused.

'Only dare!' she said in a loud, ringing voice. 'Only dare, milord, to lay a finger on that child! You'll regret it for ever.'

He was afraid of her. In a towering rage, he sat down.

When the children were old enough to be left, Mrs Morel joined the Women's Guild. It was a little club of women attached to the Co-operative Wholesale Society, which met on Monday night in the long room over the grocery shop of the Bestwood 'Co-op.' The women were supposed to discuss the benefits to be derived from co-operation, and other social questions. Sometimes Mrs Morel read a paper. It seemed queer to the children to see their mother, who was always busy about the house, sitting writing in her rapid fashion, thinking, referring to books, and writing again. They felt for her on such occasions the deepest respect.

But they loved the Guild. It was the only thing to which they did not grudge their mother – and that partly because she enjoyed it, partly because of the treats they derived from it. The Guild was called by some hostile husbands, who found their wives getting too independent, the 'clat-fart' shop – that is, the gossip-shop. It is true, from off the basis of the Guild, the women could look at their homes, at the conditions of their own lives, and find fault. So the colliers found their women had a new standard of their own, rather disconcerting. And also, Mrs Morel always had a lot of news on Monday nights, so that the children liked William to be in when their mother came home, because she told him things.

Then, when the lad was thirteen, she got him a job in the 'Co-op.' office. He was a very clever boy, frank, with rather rough features and real viking blue eyes.

'What dost want ter ma'e a stool-harsed* Jack on 'im for?' said Morel. 'All he'll do is to wear his britches behind out, an' earn nowt. What's 'e startin' wi'?'

'It doesn't matter what he's starting with,' said Mrs Morel.

'It wouldna! Put 'im i' th' pit we me, an' 'e'll earn a easy ten shillin' a wik from th' start. But six shillin' wearin' his truck-end out on a stool's better than ten shillin' i' th' pit wi' me, I know.'

---

* Stool-*arsed*. A weak, chair-borne, office-goer.

'He is not going in the pit,' said Mrs Morel, 'and there's an end of it.'

'It wor good enough for me, but it's non good enough for 'im.'

'If your mother put you in the pit at twelve, it's no reason why I should do the same with my lad.'

'Twelve! It wor a sight afore that!'

'Whenever it was,' said Mrs Morel.

She was very proud of her son. He went to the night-school, and learned shorthand, so that by the time he was sixteen he was the best shorthand clerk and book-keeper on the place, except one. Then he taught in the night-schools. But he was so fiery that only his good nature and his size protected him.

All the things that men do – the decent things – William did. He could run like the wind. When he was twelve he won a first prize in a race; an inkstand of glass, shaped like on anvil. It stood proudly on the dresser, and gave Mrs Morel a keen pleasure. The boy only ran for her. He flew home with his anvil, breathless, with a 'Look, mother!'

That was the first real tribute to herself. She took it like a queen.

'How pretty!' she exclaimed.

Then he began to get ambitious. He gave all his money to his mother. When he earned fourteen shillings a week, she gave him back two for himself and, as he never drank, he felt himself rich. He went about with the bourgeois of Bestwood. The townlet contained nothing higher than the clergyman. Then came the bank manager, then the doctors, then the tradespeople, and after that the hosts of colliers. William began to consort with the sons of the chemist, the schoolmaster, and the tradesmen. He played billiards in the Mechanics Hall. Also he danced this in spite of his mother. All the life that Bestwood offered he enjoyed, from the sixpenny-hops down Church Street, to sports and billiards.

Paul was treated to dazzling descriptions of all kinds of flower-like ladies, most of whom lived like cut blooms in William's heart for a brief fortnight.

Occasionally some flame would come in pursuit of her errant swain. Mrs Morel would find a strange girl at the door, and immediately she sniffed the air.

'Is Mr Morel in?' the damsel would ask appealingly.

'My husband is at home,' Mrs Morel replied.

'I – I mean *young* Mr Morel,' repeated the maiden painfully.

'Which one? There are several.'

Whereupon much blushing and stammering from the fair one.

'I – I met Mr Morel – at Ripley,' she explained.

'Oh – at a dance!'

'Yes.'

'I don't approve of the girls my son meets at dances. And he is *not* at home.'

Then he came home angry with his mother for having turned the girl away so rudely. He was a careless, yet eager-looking fellow, who walked with long strides, sometimes frowning, often with his cap pushed jollily to the back of his head. Now he came in frowning. He threw his cap on to the sofa, and took his strong jaw in his hand, and glared down at his mother. She was small, with her hair taken straight back from her forehead. She had a quiet air of authority, and yet of rare warmth. Knowing her son was angry, she trembled inwardly.

'Did a lady call for me yesterday, mother?' he asked.

'I don't know about a lady. There was a girl came.'

'And why didn't you tell me?'

'Because I forgot, simply.'

He fumed a little.

'A good-looking girl – seemed a lady?'

'I didn't look at her.'

'Big brown eyes?'

'I did *not* look. And tell your girls, my son, that when they're running after you, they're not to come and ask your mother for you. Tell them that – brazen baggages you meet at dancing-classes.'

'I'm sure she was a nice girl.'

'And I'm sure she wasn't.'

There ended the altercation. Over the dancing there was a great strife between the mother and the son. The grievance reached its height when William said he was going to Hucknall Torkard – considered a low town – to a fancy-dress ball. He was to be a Highlander. There was a dress he could hire, which one of his friends had had, and which fitted him perfectly. The Highland suit came home. Mrs Morel received it coldly and would not unpack it.

'My suit come?' cried William.

'There's a parcel in the front-room.'

He rushed in and cut the string.

'How do you fancy your son in this!' he said, enraptured, showing her the suit.

'You know I don't want to fancy you in it.'

On the evening of the dance, when he had come home to dress, Mrs Morel put on her coat and bonnet.

'Aren't you going to stop and see me, mother?' he asked.

'No; I don't want to see you,' she replied.

She was rather pale, and her face was closed and hard. She was afraid of her son's going the same way as his father. He hesitated a moment, and his heart stood still with anxiety. Then he caught sight of the Highland bonnet with its ribbons. He picked it up gleefully, forgetting her. She went out.

When he was nineteen he suddenly left the Co-op. office and got a situation in Nottingham. In his new place he had thirty shillings a week instead of eighteen. This was indeed a rise. His mother and his father were brimmed up with pride. Everybody praised William. It seemed he was going to get on rapidly. Mrs Morel hoped, with his aid, to help her younger sons. Annie was now studying to be a teacher. Paul, also very clever, was getting on well, having lessons in French and German from his godfather, the clergyman who was still a friend to Mrs Morel. Arthur, a spoilt and very good-looking boy, was at the Board-school, but there was talk of his trying to get a scholarship for the High School In Nottingham.

William remained a year at his new post in Nottingham. He was studying hard, and growing serious. Something seemed to be fretting him. Still he went out to the dances and the river parties. He did not drink. The children were all rabid teetotallers. He came home very late at night, and sat yet longer studying. His mother implored him to take more care, to do one thing or another.

'Dance, if you want to dance, my son; but don't think you can work in the office, and then amuse yourself, and then study on top of all. You can't; the human frame won't stand it. Do one thing or the other amuse yourself or learn Latin; but don't try to do both.'

Then he got a place in London, at a hundred and twenty a year. This seemed a fabulous sum. His mother doubted almost whether to rejoice or to grieve.

'They want me in Lime Street on Monday week, mother,' he cried, his eyes blazing as he read the letter. Mrs Morel felt everything go silent inside her. He read the letter: ' "And will you reply by Thursday whether you accept. Yours faithfully – " They want me, mother, at a hundred and twenty a year, and don't even ask to see me. Didn't I tell you I could do it! Think of me in London! And I can give you twenty pounds a year, mater.' We s'll all be rolling in money.'

'We shall, my son,' she answered sadly.

It never occurred to him that she might be more hurt at his going away than glad of his success. Indeed, as the days drew near for his departure, her heart began to close and grow dreary with despair. She loved him so much! More than that, she hoped in him so much. Almost she lived by him. She liked to do things for him: she liked to put a cup for his tea and to iron his collars, of which he was so proud. It was a joy to her to have him proud of his collars. There was no laundry. So she used to rub away at them with her little convex iron, to polish them, till they shone from the sheer pressure of her arm. Now she would not do it for him. Now he was going away. She felt almost as if he were going as well out of her heart. He did not seem to leave her inhabited with himself. That was the grief and the pain to her. He took nearly all himself away.

A few days before his departure – he was just twenty – he burned his love-letters. They had hung on a file at the top of the kitchen cupboard. From some of them he had read extracts to his mother. Some of them she had taken the trouble to read herself. But most were too trivial.

Now, on the Saturday morning he said:

'Come on, Postle, let's go through my letters, and you can have the birds and flowers.'

Mrs Morel had done her Saturday's work on the Friday, because he was having a last day's holiday. She was making him a rice cake, which he loved, to take with him. He was scarcely conscious that she was so miserable.

He took the first letter off the file. It was mauve-tinted, and had purple and green thistles. William sniffed the page.

'Nice scent! Smell.'

And he thrust the sheet under Paul's nose.

'Um!' said Paul, breathing in. 'What d'you call it? Smell, mother.'

His mother ducked her small, fine nose down to the paper.

'I don't want to smell their rubbish,' she said, sniffing.

'This girl's father,' said William, 'is as rich as Croesus. He owns property without end. She calls me Lafayette, because I know French. "You will see, I've forgiven you" – I like *her* forgiving me. "I told mother about you this morning, and she will have much pleasure if you come to tea on Sunday, but she will have to get father's consent also. I sincerely hope he will agree. I will let you know how it transpires. If, however, you – " '

'Let you know how it what?' interrupted Mrs Morel.

' "Transpires" – oh yes!'

' "Transpires!" ' repeated Mrs Morel mockingly. 'I thought she was so well educated!'

William felt slightly uncomfortable, and abandoned this maiden, giving Paul the corner with the thistles. He continued to read extracts from his letters, some of which amused his mother, some of which saddened her and made her anxious for him.

'My lad,' she said, 'they're very wise. They know they've only got to flatter your vanity, and you press up to them like a dog that has its head scratched.'

'Well, they can't go on scratching for ever,' he replied. 'And when they've done, I trot away.'

'But one day you'll find a string round your neck that you can't pull off,' she answered.

'Not me! I'm equal to any of 'em, mater, they needn't flatter themselves.'

'You flatter *yourself*,' she said quietly.

Soon there was a heap of twisted black pages, all that remained of the file of scented letters, except that Paul had thirty or forty pretty tickets from the corners of the notepaper – swallows and forget-me-nots and ivy sprays. And William went to London, to start a new file.

CHAPTER 4

The Young Life of Paul

PAUL WOULD be built like his mother, slightly and rather small. His fair hair went reddish, and then dark brown; his eyes were grey. He was a pale, quiet child, with eyes that seemed to listen, and with a full, dropping underlip.

As a rule he seemed old for his years. He was so conscious of what other people felt, particularly his mother. When she fretted he understood, and could have no peace. His soul seemed always attentive to her.

As he grew older he became stronger. William was too far removed from him to accept him as a companion. So the smaller boy belonged at first almost entirely to Annie. She was a tomboy and a 'flybie-skybie'*, as her mother called her. But she was intensely fond of her second brother. So Paul was towed round at the heels of Annie, sharing her game. She raced wildly at lerky with the other young wild-cats of the Bottoms. And always Paul flew beside her, living her share of the game, having as yet no part of his own. He was quiet and not noticeable. But his sister adored him. He always seemed to care for things if she wanted him to.

She had a big doll of which she was fearfully proud, though not so fond. So she laid the doll on the sofa, and covered it with on antimacassar, to sleep. Then she forgot it. Meantime Paul must practise jumping off the sofa arm. So he jumped crash into the face of the hidden doll. Annie rushed up, uttered a loud wail, and sat down to weep a dirge. Paul remained quite still.

'You couldn't tell it was there, mother; you couldn't tell it was there,' he repeated over and over. So long as Annie wept for the doll he sat helpless with misery. Her grief wore itself out. She forgave her brother – he was so much upset. But a day or two afterwards she was shocked.

* whimsical.

'Let's make a sacrifice of Arabella,' he said. 'Let's burn her.'

She was horrified, yet rather fascinated. She wanted to see what the boy would do. He made on altar of bricks, pulled some of the shavings out of Arabella's body, put the waxen fragments into the hollow face, poured on a little paraffin, and set the whole thing alight. He watched with wicked satisfaction the drops of wax melt off the broken forehead of Arabella, and drop like sweat into the flame. So long as the stupid big doll burned he rejoiced in silence. At the end he poked among the embers with a stick, fished out the arms and legs, all blackened, and smashed them under stones.

'That's the sacrifice of Missis Arabella,' he said. 'An' I'm glad there's nothing left of her.'

Which disturbed Annie inwardly, although she could say nothing. He seemed to hate the doll so intensely, because he had broken it.

All the children, but particularly Paul, were peculiarly *against* their father, along with their mother. Morel continued to bully and to drink. He had periods, months at a time, when he made the whole life of the family a misery. Paul never forgot coming home from the Band of Hope one Monday evening and finding his mother with her eye swollen and discoloured, his father standing on the hearthrug, feet astride, his head down, and William, just home from work, glaring at his father. There was a silence as the young children entered, but none of the elders looked round.

William was white to the lips, and his fists were clenched. He waited until the children were silent, watching with children's rage and hate; then he said:

'You coward, you daren't do it when I was in.'

But Morel's blood was up. He swung round on his son. William was bigger, but Morel was hard-muscled, and mad with fury.

'Dossn't I?' he shouted. 'Dossn't I? Ha'e much more o' thy

chelp*, my young jockey, an' I'll rattle my fist about thee. Ay, an' I sholl that, dost see.'

Morel crouched at the knees and showed his fist in an ugly, almost beast-like fashion. William was white with rage.

'Will yer?' he said, quiet and intense. 'It 'ud be the last time, though.' Morel danced a little nearer, crouching, drawing back his fist to strike. William put his fists ready. A light came into his blue eyes, almost like a laugh. He watched his father. Another word, and the men would have begun to fight. Paul hoped they would. The three children sat pale on the sofa.

'Stop it, both of you,' cried Mrs Morel in a hard voice.

'We've had enough for *one* night. And *you,*' she said, turning on to her husband, 'look at your children!'

Morel glanced at the sofa.

'Look at the children, you nasty little bitch!' he sneered. 'Why, what have *I* done to the children, I should like to know? But they're like yourself; you've put 'em up to your own tricks and nasty ways – you've learned 'em in it, you 'ave.'

She refused to answer him. No one spoke. After a while he threw his boots under the table and went to bed.

'Why didn't you let me have a go at him?' said William, when his father was upstairs. 'I could easily have beaten him.'

'A nice thing – you're own father,' she replied.

'*Father!*' repeated William. 'Call *him my* father?'

'Well, he is – and so – '

'But why don't you let me settle him? I could do, easily.'

'The idea!' she cried. 'It hasn't come to *that* yet.'

'No,' he said, 'it's come to worse. Look at yourself. *Why* didn't you let me give it him?'

'Because I couldn't bear it, so never think of it,' she cried quickly.

And the children went to bed, miserably.

* insolence.

When William was growing up, the family moved from the Bottoms to a house on the brow of the hill, commanding a view of the valley, which spread out like a convex cockleshell, or a clamp-shell, before it. In front of the house was a huge old ash-tree. The west wind, sweeping from Derbyshire, caught the houses with full force, and the tree shrieked again. Morel liked it.

'It's music,' he said. 'It sends me to sleep.'

But Paul and Arthur and Annie hated it. To Paul it became almost a demoniacal noise. The winter of their first year in the new house their father was very bad. The children played in the street, on the brim of the wide, dark valley, until eight o'clock. Then they went to bed. Their mother sat sewing below. Having such a great space in front of the house gave the children a feeling of night, of vastness, and of terror. This terror came in from the shrieking of the tree and the anguish of the home discord. Often Paul would wake up, after he had been asleep a long time, aware of thuds downstairs. Instantly he was wide awake. Then he heard the booming shouts of his father, come home nearly drunk, then the sharp replies of his mother, then the bang, bang of his father's fist on the table, and the nasty snarling shout as the man's voice got higher. And then the whole was drowned in a piercing medley of shrieks and cries from the great, windswept ash-tree. The children lay silent in suspense, waiting for a lull in the wind to hear what their father was doing. He might hit their mother again. There was a feeling of horror, a kind of bristling in the darkness, and a sense of blood. They lay with their hearts in the grip of an intense anguish. The wind came through the tree fiercer and fiercer. All the cords of the great harp hummed, whistled, and shrieked. And then came the horror of the sudden silence, silence everywhere, outside and downstairs. What was it? Was it a silence of blood? What had he done?

The children lay and breathed the darkness. And then, at last, they heard their father throw down his boots and tramp upstairs in his stockinged feet. Still they listened. Then at last, if the wind allowed, they heard the water of the top drumming into the kettle, which their mother was filling for morning, and they could go to sleep in peace.

So they were happy in the morning – happy, very happy playing, dancing at night round the lonely lamp-post in the midst of the darkness. But they had one tight place of anxiety in their hearts, one darkness in their eyes, which showed all their lives.

Paul hated his father. As a boy he had a fervent private religion.

'Make him stop drinking,' he prayed every night. 'Lord, let my father die,' he prayed very often. 'Let him not be killed at pit,' he prayed when, after tea, the father did not come home from work.

That was another time when the family suffered intensely. The children came from school and had their teas. On the hob the big black saucepan was simmering, the stew-jar was in the oven, ready for Morel's dinner. He was expected at five o'clock. But for months he would stop and drink every night on his way from work.

In the winter nights, when it was cold, and grew dark early, Mrs Morel would put a brass candlestick on the table, light a tallow candle to save the gas. The children finished their bread-and-butter, or dripping, and were ready to go out to play. But if Morel had not come they faltered. The sense of his sitting in all his pit-dirt, drinking, after a long day's work, not coming home and eating and washing, but sitting, getting drunk, on an empty stomach, made Mrs Morel unable to bear herself. From her the feeling was transmitted to the other children. She never suffered alone any more: the children suffered with her.

Paul went out to play with the rest. Down in the great trough of twilight, tiny clusters of lights burned where the pits were. A few last colliers straggled up the dim field-path. The lamp-lighter came along. No more colliers came. Darkness shut down over the valley; work was gone. It was night.

Then Paul ran anxiously into the kitchen. The one candle still burned on the table, the big fire glowed red. Mrs Morel sat alone. On the hob the saucepan steamed; the dinner-plate lay waiting on the table. All the room was full of the sense of waiting, waiting for the man who was sitting in his pit-dirt, dinnerless, some mile away from home, across the darkness, drinking himself drunk. Paul stood in the doorway.

'Has my dad come?' he asked.

'You can see he hasn't,' said Mrs Morel, cross with the futility of the question.

Then the boy dawdled about near his mother. They shared the same anxiety. Presently Mrs Morel went out and strained the potatoes.

'They're ruined and black,' she said; 'but what do I care?'

Not many words were spoken. Paul almost hated his mother for suffering because his father did not come home from work.

'What do you bother yourself for?' he said. 'If he wants to stop and get drunk, why don't you let him?'

'Let him!' flashed Mrs Morel. 'You may well say "let him."'

She knew that the man who stops on the way home from work is on a quick way to ruining himself and his home. The children were yet young, and depended on the breadwinner. William gave her the sense of relief, providing her at last with someone to turn to if Morel failed. But the tense atmosphere of the room on these waiting evenings was the same.

The minutes ticked away. At six o'clock still the cloth lay on the table, still the dinner stood waiting, still the same sense of anxiety and expectation in the room. The boy could not stand it any longer. He could not go out and play. So he ran in to Mrs Inger, next door but one, for her to talk to him. She had no children. Her husband was good to her, but was in a shop, and came home late. So, when she saw the head at the door, she called:

'Come in, Paul.'

The two sat talking for some time, when suddenly the boy rose, saying:

'Well, I'll be going and seeing if my mother wants an errand doing.' He pretended to be perfectly cheerful, and did not tell his friend what ailed him. Then he ran indoors.

Morel at these times came in churlish and hateful.

'This is a nice time to come home,' said Mrs Morel.

'Wha's it matter to yo' what time I come whoam?' he shouted.

And everybody in the house was still, because he was dangerous. He ate his food in the most brutal manner possible, and, when he had done, pushed all the pots in a heap away from him, to lay his arms on the table. Then he went to sleep.

Paul hated his father so. The collier's small, mean head, with its black hair slightly soiled with grey, lay on the bare arms, and the face, dirty and inflamed, with a fleshy nose and thin, paltry brows, was turned sideways, asleep with beer and weariness and nasty temper. If anyone entered suddenly, or a noise were made, the man looked up and shouted:

'I'll lay my fist about thy y' ead, I'm tellin' thee, if tha doesna stop that clatter! Dost hear?'

And the two last words, shouted in a bullying fashion, usually at Annie, made the family writhe with hate of the man.

He was shut out from all family affairs. No one told him anything. The children, alone with their mother, told her all about the day's happenings, everything. Nothing had really taken place in them until it was told to their mother. But as soon as the father came in, everything stopped. He was like the scotch in the smooth, happy machinery of the home. And he was always aware of this fall of silence on his entry, the shutting off of life, the unwelcome. But now it was gone too far to alter.

He would dearly have liked the children to talk to him, but they could not. Sometimes Mrs Morel would say:

'You ought to tell your father.'

Paul won a prize in a competition in a child's paper. Everybody was highly jubilant.

'Now you'd better tell your father when he comes in,' said Mrs Morel. 'You know how he carries on and says he's never told anything.'

'All right,' said Paul. But he would almost rather have forfeited the prize than have to tell his father.

'I've won a prize in a competition, dad,' he said.

Morel turned round to him.

'Have you, my boy? What sort of a competition?'

'Oh, nothing – about famous women.'

'And how much is the prize, then, as you've got?'

'It's a book.'

'Oh, indeed!'

'About birds.'

'Hm – hm!'

And that was all. Conversation was impossible between the father and any other member of the family. He was an outsider. He had denied the God in him.

The only times when he entered again into the life of his own people was when he worked, and was happy at work. Sometimes, in the evening, he cobbled the boots or mended the kettle or his pit-bottle. Then he always wanted several attendants, and the children enjoyed it. They united with him in the work, in the actual doing of something, when he was his real self again.

He was a good workman, dexterous, and one who, when he was in a good humour, always sang. He had whole periods, months, almost years, of friction and nasty temper. Then sometimes he was jolly again. It was nice to see him run with a piece of red-hot iron into the scullery, crying:

'Out of my road – out of my road!'

Then he hammered the soft, red-glowing stuff on his iron goose, and made the shape he wanted. Or he sat absorbed for a moment, soldering. Then the children watched with joy as the metal sank suddenly molten, and was shoved about against the nose of the soldering-iron, while the room was full of a scent of burnt resin and hot tin, and Morel was silent and intent for a minute. He always sang when he mended boots because of the jolly sound of hammering. And he was rather happy when he sat putting great patches on his moleskin pit-trousers, which he would often do, considering them too dirty, and the stuff too hard, for his wife to mend.

But the best time for the young children was when he made fuses. Morel fetched a sheaf of long sound wheat-straws from the attic. These he cleaned with his hand, till each one gleamed like a stalk of gold, after which he cut the straws into lengths of about six inches, leaving, if he could, a notch at the bottom of each piece. He always had a beautifully sharp knife that could cut a straw clean without hurting it. Then he set in the middle of the table a heap of gunpowder, a little pile of black grains upon the white-scrubbed board. He made and trimmed the straws while Paul and Annie filled and plugged them. Paul loved to see the black grains trickle down a crack in his palm into the mouth of the straw, peppering jollily downwards till the straw was full. Then he bunged up the mouth with a bit of soap – which he got on his thumbnail from a pat in a saucer – and the straw was finished.

'Look dad!' he said.

'That's right, my beauty,' replied Morel, who was peculiarly lavish of endearments to his second son. Paul popped the fuse into the powdertin, ready for the morning, when Morel would take it to the pit, and use it to fire a shot that would blast the coal down.

Meantime Arthur, still fond of his father, would lean on the arm of Morel's chair, and say:

'Tell us about down pit, daddy.'

This Morel loved to do.

'Well, there's, one little 'oss – we call 'im Taffy,' he would begin. 'An' he's a fawce un!'

Morel had a warm way of telling a story. He made one feel Taffy's cunning.

'He's a brown un,' he would answer, 'an' not very high. Well, he comes i' th' stall wi' a rattle, an' then yo' 'ear 'im sneeze.

' " 'Ello, Taff," you say, "what art sneezin' for? Bin ta'ein' some snuff?"

'An' 'e sneezes again. Then he slives[1] up an' shoves 'is 'ead on yer, that cadin'[2].

' "What's want, Taff?" yo' say.'

'And what does he?' Arthur always asked.

'He wants a bit o' bacca, my duckey.'

This story of Taffy would go on interminably, and everybody loved it. Or sometimes it was a new tale.

'An' what dost think, my darlin'? When I went to put my coat on at snap-time, what should go runnin' up my arm but a mouse.

'"Hey up, theer!" I shouts.

'An' I wor just in time ter get 'im by th' tall.'

'And did you kill it?'

'I did, for they're a nuisance. The place is fair snied wi, 'em.'[3]

'An' what do they live on?'

'The com as the 'osses drops – an' they'll get in your pocket an' eat your snap, if you'll let 'em – no matter where yo' hing your coat – the slivin', nibblin' little nuisances, for they are.'

These happy evenings could not take place unless Morel had some job to do. And then he always went to bed very early, often before the children. There was nothing remaining for him to stay up for, when he had finished tinkering, and had skimmed the headlines of the newspaper.

And the children felt secure when their father was in bed. They lay and talked softly awhile. Then they started as the lights

---

1 sneaks.
2 tame.
3 infested with them.

went suddenly sprawling over the ceiling from the lamps that swung in the hands of the colliers tramping by outside, going to take the nine o'clock shift. They listened to the voices of the men, imagined them dipping down into the dark valley. Sometimes they went to the window and watched the three or four lamps growing tinier and tinier, swaying down the fields in the darkness. Then it was a joy to rush back to bed and cuddle closely in the warmth.

Paul was rather a delicate boy, subject to bronchitis. The others were all quite strong; so this was another reason for his mother's difference in feeling for him. One day he came home at dinner-time feeling ill. But it was not a family to make any fuss.

'What's the matter with *you?*' his mother asked sharply.

'Nothing,' he replied.

But he ate no dinner.

'If you eat no dinner, you're not going to school,' she said.

'Why? ' he asked.

'That's why.'

So after dinner he lay down on the sofa, on the warm chintz cushions the children loved. Then he fell into a kind of doze. That afternoon Mrs Morel was ironing. She listened to the small, restless noise the boy made in his throat as she worked. Again rose in her heart the old, almost weary feeling towards him. She had never expected him to live. And yet he had a great vitality in his young body. Perhaps it would have been a little relief to her if he had died. She always felt a mixture of anguish in her love for him.

He, in his semi-conscious sleep, was vaguely aware of the clatter of the iron on the iron-stand, of the faint thud, thud on the ironing-board. Once roused, he opened his eyes to see his mother standing on the hearthrug with the hot iron near her cheek, listening, as it were, to the heat. Her still face, with the mouth closed tight from suffering and disillusion and self-denial, and her nose the smallest bit on one side, and her blue eyes so young, quick, and warm, made his heart contract with love. When she was quiet, so, she looked brave and rich with life, but as if she had been done out of her rights. It hurt the boy keenly, this feeling about her that she had never had her life's fulfilment: and his own incapability to make up to her hurt him with a sense of impotence, yet made him patiently dogged inside. It was his childish aim.

She spat on the iron, and a little ball of spit bounded, raced off the dark, glossy surface. Then, kneeling, she rubbed the iron on the sock lining of the hearthrug vigorously. She was warm in the ruddy firelight. Paul loved the way she crouched and put her head on one side. Her movements were light and quick. It was always a pleasure to watch her. Nothing she ever did, no movement she ever made, could have been found fault with by her children. The room was warm and full of the scent of hot linen. Later on the clergyman came and talked softly with her.

Paul was laid up with on attack of bronchitis. He did not mind much. What happened happened, and it was no good kicking against the pricks. He loved the evenings, after eight o'clock, when the light was put out, and he could watch the fire-flames spring over the darkness of the walls and ceiling; could watch huge shadows waving and tossing, till the room seemed full of men who battled silently.

On retiring to bed, the father would come into the sick-room. He was always very gentle if anyone were ill. But he disturbed the atmosphere for the boy.

'Are ter asleep, my darlin'?' Morel asked softly.

'No; is my mother comin'?'

'She's just finishin' foldin' the clothes. Do you want anything?' Morel rarely 'thee'd' his son.

'I don't want nothing. But how long will she be?'

'Not long, my duckie.'

The father waited undecidedly on the hearthrug for a moment or two. He felt his son did not want him. Then he went to the top of the stairs and said to his wife:

'This childt's axin' for thee; how long art goin' to be?'

'Until I've finished, good gracious! Tell him to go to sleep.'

'She says you're to go to sleep,' the father repeated gently to Paul. 'Well, I want *her* to come,' insisted the boy.

'He says he can't go off till you come,' Morel called downstairs.

'Eh, dear! I shan't be long. And do stop shouting downstairs. There's the other children – '

Then Morel came again, and crouched before the bedroom fire. He loved a fire dearly.

'She says she won't be long,' he said.

He loitered about indefinitely. The boy began to get feverish with irritation. His father's presence seemed to aggravate all his sick impatience. At last Morel, after having stood looking at his son awhile, said softly:

'Good-night, my darling.'

'Good-night,' Paul replied, turning round in relief to be alone.

Paul loved to sleep with his mother. Sleep is still most perfect, in spite of hygienists, when it is shared with a beloved. The warmth, the security and peace of soul, the utter comfort from the touch of the other, knits the sleep, so that it takes the body and soul completely in its healing. Paul lay against her and slept, and got better; whilst she, always a bad sleeper, fell later on into a profound sleep that seemed to give her faith.

In convalescence he would sit up in bed, see the fluffy horses feeding at the troughs in the field, scattering their hay on the trodden yellow snow; watch the miners troop home – small, black figures trailing slowly in gongs across the white field.

Then the night came up in dark blue vapour from the snow.

In convalescence everything was wonderful. The snowflakes, suddenly arriving on the window-pane, clung there a moment like swallows, then were gone, and a drop of water was crawling down the glass. The snowflakes whirled round the corner of the house, like pigeons dashing by. Away across the valley the little black train crawled doubtfully over the great whiteness.

While they were so poor, the children were delighted if they could do anything to help economically. Annie and Paul and Arthur went out early in the morning, in summer, looking for mushrooms, hunting through the wet grass, from which the larks were rising, for the white-skinned, wonderful naked bodies crouched secretly in the green. And if they got half a pound they felt exceedingly happy: there was the joy of finding something, the joy of accepting something straight from the hand of Nature, and the joy of contributing to the family exchequer.

But the most important harvest, after gleaning for frumenty, was the blackberries. Mrs Morel must buy fruit for puddings on the Saturdays; also she liked blackberries. So Paul and Arthur scoured the coppices and woods and old quarries, so long as a blackberry was to be found, every weekend going on their search. In that region of mining villages blackberries became a comparative rarity. But Paul hunted far and wide. He loved being out in the country, among the bushes. But he also could not bear to go home to his mother empty. That, he felt, would disappoint her, and he would have died rather.

'Good gracious!' she would exclaim as the lads came in late, and tired to death, and hungry, 'wherever have you been?'

'Well,' replied Paul, 'there wasn't any, so we went over Misk Hills. And look here, our mother!'

She peeped into the basket.

'Now, those are fine ones!' she exclaimed.

'And there's over two pounds – isn't there over two pounds?'

She tried the basket.

'Yes,' she answered doubtfully.

Then Paul fished out a little spray. He always brought her one spray, the best he could find.

'Pretty!' she said, in a curious tone, of a woman accepting a love token.

The boy walked all day, went miles and miles, rather than own himself beaten and come home to her empty-handed. She never realised this, whilst he was young. She was a woman who waited for her children to grow up. And William occupied her chiefly.

But when William went to Nottingham, and was not so much at home, the mother made a companion of Paul. The latter was unconsciously jealous of his brother, and William was jealous of him. At the same time, they were good friends.

Mrs Morel's intimacy with her second son was more subtle and fine, perhaps not so passionate as with her eldest. It was the rule that Paul should fetch the money on Friday afternoons. The colliers of the five pits were paid on Fridays, but not individually. All the earnings of each stall were put down to the chief butty, as contractor, and he divided the wages again, either in the public-house or in his own home. So that the children could fetch the money, school closed early on Friday afternoons. Each of the Morel children – William, then Annie, then Paul had fetched the money on Friday afternoons, until they went themselves to work. Paul used to set off at half-past three, with a little calico bag in his pocket. Down all the paths, women, girls, children, and men were seen trooping to the offices.

These offices were quite handsome: a new, red-brick building, almost like a mansion, standing in its own well-kept grounds at the end of Greenhill Lane. The waiting-room was the hall, a long, bare room paved with blue brick, and having a seat all round, against the wall. Here sat the colliers in their pit-dirt. They had come up early. The women and children usually loitered about on the red gravel paths. Paul always examined the grass border, and the big grass bank, because in it grew tiny pansies and tiny forget-me-nots. There was a sound of many voices. The women had on their Sunday hats. The girls chattered loudly. Little dogs ran here and there. The green shrubs were silent all around.

Then from inside came the cry 'Spinney Park – Spinney Park.' All the folk for Spinney Park trooped inside. When it was time for Bretty to be paid, Paul went in among the crowd. The pay-room was quite small. A counter went across, dividing it into half. Behind the counter stood two men – Mr Braithwaite and his clerk," Mr Winterbottom. Mr Braithwaite was large, somewhat of the stern patriarch in appearance, having a rather thin white beard. He was usually muffled in an enormous silk neckerchief, and right up to the hot summer a huge fire burned in the open grate. No window was open. Sometimes in winter the air scorched the throats of the people, coming in from the freshness. Mr Winterbottom was rather small and fat, and very bald. He made remarks that were not witty, whilst his chief launched forth patriarchal admonitions against the colliers.

The room was crowded with miners in their pit-dirt, men who had been home and changed, and women, and one or two children, and usually a dog. Paul was quite small, so it was often his fate to be jammed behind the legs of the men, near the fire which scorched him. He knew the order of the names – they went according to stall number.

'Holliday,' came the ringing voice of Mr Braithwaite. Then Mrs Holliday stepped silently forward, was paid, drew aside.

'Bower – John Bower.'

A boy stepped to the counter. Mr Braithwaite, large and irascible, glowered at him over his spectacles.

'John Bower!' he repeated.

'It's me,' said the boy.

'Why, you used to 'ave a different nose than that,' said glossy Mr Winterbottom, peering over the counter. The people tittered, thinking of John Bower senior.

'How is it your father's not come?' said Mr Braithwaite, in a large and magisterial voice.

'He's badly,' piped the boy.

'You should tell him to keep off the drink,' pronounced the great cashier:

'An' niver mind if he puts his foot through yer,' said a mocking voice from behind.

All the men laughed. The large and important cashier looked down at his next sheet.

'Fred Pilkington!' he called, quite indifferent.

Mr Braithwaite was an important shareholder in the firm.

Paul knew his turn was next but one, and his heart began to beat. He was pushed against the chimney-piece. His calves were burning. But he did not hope to get through the wall of men.

'Walter Morel!' came the ringing voice.

'Here!' piped Paul, small and inadequate.

'Morel – Walter Morel!' the cashier repeated, his finger and thumb on the invoice, ready to pass on.

Paul was suffering convulsions of self-consciousness, and could not or would not shout. The backs of the men obliterated him. Then Mr Winterbottom came to the rescue.

'He's here. Where is he? Morel's lad?'

The fat, red, bald little man peered round with keen eyes. He pointed at the fireplace. The colliers looked round, moved aside, and disclosed the boy.

'Here he is!' said Mr Winterbottom.

Paul went to the counter.

'Seventeen pounds eleven and fivepence. Why don't you shout up when you're called?' said Mr Braithwaite. He banged on to the invoice a five-pound bag of silver, then, in a delicate and pretty movement, picked up a little ten-pound column of gold, and plumped it beside the silver. The gold slid in a bright stream over the paper. The cashier finished counting off the money; the boy dragged the whole down the counter to Mr Winterbottom, to whom the stoppages for rent and tools must be paid. Here he suffered again.

'Sixteen an' six,' said Mr Winterbottom.

The lad was too much upset to count. He pushed forward some loose silver and half a sovereign.

'How much do you think you've given me?' asked Mr Winterbottom. The boy looked at him, but said nothing. He had not the faintest notion.

'Haven't you got a tongue in your head?'

Paul bit his lip, and pushed forward some more silver.

'Don't they teach you to count at the Board-school?' he asked.

'Nowt but Algibbra an' French,' said a collier.

'An' cheek an' impidence,' said another.

Paul was keeping someone waiting. With trembling fingers he got his money into the bag and slid out. He suffered the tortures of the damned on these occasions.

His relief, when he got outside, and was walking along the Mansfield Road, was infinite. On the park wall the mosses were green. There were some gold and some white fowls pecking under the apple-trees of an orchard. The colliers were walking home in a stream. The boy went near the wall, self-consciously. He knew many of the men, but could not recognise them in their dirt. And this was a new torture to him.

When he got down to the New Inn, at Bretty, his father was not yet come. Mrs Wharmby, the landlady, knew him. His grandmother, Morel's mother, had been Mrs Wharmby's friend.

'Your father's not come yet,' said the landlady, in the peculiar halfscornful, half-patronising voice of a woman who talks chiefly to grown men. 'Sit you down.'

Paul sat down on the edge of the bench in the bar. Some colliers were 'reckoning' – sharing out their money – in a corner; others came in. They all glanced at the boy without speaking. At last Morel came; brisk, and with something of on air, even in his blackness.

'Hello!' he said rather tenderly to his son. 'Have you bested me? Shall you have a drink of something?'

Paul and all the children were bred up fierce anti-alcoholists, and he would have suffered more in drinking a lemonade before all the men than in having a tooth drawn.

'The landlady looked at him *de hout en bas,** rather pitying, and at the same time, resenting his clear, fierce morality. Paul went home, glowering. He entered the house silently. Friday was baking day, and there was usually a hot bun. His mother put it before him.

Suddenly he turned on her in a fury, his eyes flashing:

'I'm *not* going to the office any more,' he said.

'Why, what's the matter?' his mother asked in surprise. His sudden rages rather amused her.

'I'm *not* going any more,' he declared.

'Oh, very well, tell your father so.'

He chewed his bun as if he hated it.

'I'm not – I'm not going to fetch the money.'

'Then one of Carlin's children can go; they'd be glad enough of the sixpence,' said Mrs Morel.

This sixpence was Paul's only income. It mostly went in buying birthday presents; but it was an income, and he treasured it. But –

'They can have it, then!' he said. 'I don't want it.'

'Oh, very well,' said his mother. 'But you needn't bully me about it.'

'They're hateful, and common, and hateful, they are, and I'm not going any more. Mr Braithwaite drops his "h's," an' Mr Winterbottom says "You was." '

'And is that why you won't go any more?' smiled Mrs Morel.

The boy was silent for some time. His face was pale, his

* with utter disdain.

eyes dark and furious. His mother moved about at her work, taking no notice of him.

'They always stan' in front of me, so's I can't get out,' he said.

'Well, my lad, you've only to ask them,' she replied.

'An' then Alfred Winterbottom says, "What do they teach you at the Board-school?" '

'They never taught *him* much,' said Mrs Morel, 'that is a fact – neither manners nor wit – and his cunning he was born with.'

So, in her own way, she soothed him. His ridiculous hypersensitiveness made her heart ache. And sometimes the fury in his eyes roused her, made her sleeping soul lift up its head a moment, surprised.

'What was the cheque?' she asked.

'Seventeen pounds eleven and fivepence, and sixteen and six stop pages,' replied the boy. 'It's a good week; and only five shillings stoppages for my father.'

So she was able to calculate how much her husband had earned, and could call him to account if he gave her short money. Morel always kept to himself the secret of the week's amount.

Friday was the baking night and market night. It was the rule that Paul should stay at home and bake. He loved to stop in and draw or read; he was very fond of drawing. Annie always 'gallivanted' on Friday nights; Arthur was enjoying himself as usual. So the boy remained alone.

Mrs Morel loved her marketing. In the tiny market-place on the top of the hill, where four roads, from Nottingham and Derby, Ilkeston and Mansfield, meet, many stalls were erected. Brakes[1] ran in from surrounding villages. The market-place was full of women, the streets packed with men. It was amazing to see so many men everywhere in the streets.

Mrs Morel usually quarrelled with her lace woman, sympathised with her fruit man – who was a gabey[2], but his wife

1 Four-wheeled carts.
2 talkative and full of gossip.

was a bad un – laughed with the fish man – who was a scamp but so droll – put the linoleum man in his place, was cold with the odd-wares man, and only went to the crockery man when she was driven – or drawn by the cornflowers on a little dish; then she was coldly polite.

'I wondered how much that little dish was,' she said.

'Sevenpence to you.'

'Thank you.'

She put the dish down and walked away; but she could not leave the market-place without it. Again she went by where the pots lay coldly on the floor, and she glanced at the dish furtively, pretending not to.

She was a little woman, in a bonnet and a black costume. Her bonnet was in its third year; it was a great grievance to Annie.

'Mother!' the girl implored, 'don't wear that nubbly little bonnet.'

'Then what else shall I wear,' replied the mother tartly. 'And I'm sure it's right enough.'

It had started with a tip; then had had flowers; now was reduced to black lace and a bit of jet.

'It looks rather come down,' said Paul 'Couldn't you give it a pick me-up?'

'I'll jowl your head for impudence,' said Mrs Morel, and she tied the strings of the black bonnet valiantly under her chin.

She glanced at the dish again. Both she and her enemy, the not man, had an uncomfortable feeling, as if there were something between them. Suddenly he shouted:

'Do you want it for fivepence?'

She started. Her heart hardened; but then she stooped and took up her dish.

'I'll have it,' she said.

'Yer'll do me the favour, like?' he said. 'Yer'd better spit in it, like yer do when y'ave something give yer.'

Mrs Morel paid him the fivepence in a cold manner.

'I don't see you give it me,' she said. 'You wouldn't let me have it for fivepence if you didn't want to.'

'In this flamin', scrattlin' place you may count yerself lucky if you can give your things away,' he growled.

'Yes; there are bad times, and good,' said Mrs Morel.

But she had forgiven the pot man. They were friends. She dare now finger his pots. So she was happy.

Paul was waiting for her. He loved her home-coming. She was always her best so – triumphant, tired, laden with parcels, feeling rich in spirit. He heard her quick, light step in the entry and looked up from his drawing.

'Oh!' she sighed, smiling at him from the doorway.

'My word, you *are* loaded!' he exclaimed, putting down his brush.

'I am!' she gasped. 'That brazen Annie said she'd meet me. *Such* a weight!'

She dropped her string bag and her packages on the table.

'Is the bread done?' she asked, going to the oven.

'The last one is soaking,' he replied. 'You needn't look, I've not forgotten it.'

'Oh, that pot man!' she said, closing the oven door. 'You know what a wretch I've said he was? Well, I don't think he's quite so bad.'

'Don't you?'

The boy was attentive to her. She took off her little black bonnet.

'No. I think he can't make any money – well, it's everybody's cry alike nowadays – and it makes him disagreeable.'

'It would *me,*' said Paul.

'Well, one can't wonder at it. And he let me have – how much do you think he let me have *this* for?'

She took the dish out of its rag of newspaper, and stood looking on it with joy.

'Show me!' said Paul.

The two stood together gloating over the dish.

'I *love* cornflowers on things,' said Paul.

'Yes, and I thought of the teapot you bought me – '

'One and three,' said Paul.

'Fivepence!'

'It's not enough, mother.'

'No. Do you know, I fairly sneaked off with it. But I'd been extravagant, I couldn't afford any more. And he needn't have let me have it if he hadn't wanted to.'

'No, he needn't, need he,' said Paul, and the two comforted each other from the fear of having robbed the not man.

'We c'n have stewed fruit in it,' said Paul.

'Or custard, or a jelly,' said his mother.

'Or radishes and lettuce,' said he.

'Don't forget that bread,' she said, her voice bright with glee.

Paul looked in the oven; topped the loaf on the base.

'It's done,' he said, giving it to her.

She topped it also.

'Yes,' she replied, going to unpack her bag. 'Oh, and I'm a wicked, extravagant woman. I know I s'll come to want.'

He hopped to her side eagerly, to see her latest extravagance. She unfolded another lump of newspaper and disclosed some roots of pansies and of crimson daisies.

'Four penn'orth!' she moaned.

'How *cheap!*' he cried.

'Yes, but I couldn't afford it *this* week of all weeks.'

'But lovely!' he cried.

'Aren't they!' she exclaimed, giving way to pure joy. 'Paul, look at this yellow one, isn't it – and a face just like an old man!'

'Just!' cried Paul, stooping to sniff. 'And smells that nice! But he's a bit splashed.'

He ran in the scullery, came back with the flannel, and carefully washed the pansy.

'*Now* look at him now he's wet!' he said.

'Yes!' she exclaimed, brimful of satisfaction.

The children of Scargill Street felt quite select. At the end where the Morels lived there were not many young things. So the few were more united. Boys and girls played together, the girls joining in the fights and the rough games, the boys taking part in the dancing games and rings and make-belief of the girls.

Annie and Paul and Arthur loved the winter evenings, when it was not wet. They stayed indoors till the colliers were all gone home, till it was thick dark, and the street would be deserted. Then they tied their scarves round their necks, for they scorned overcoats, as all the colliers' children did, and went out. The entry was very dark, and at the end the whole great night opened out, in a hollow, with a little tangle of lights below where Minton pit lay, and another far away opposite for Selby. The farthest tiny lights seemed to stretch out the darkness for ever. The children looked anxiously down the road at the one lamp-post which stood at the end of the field-path. If the little, luminous space were deserted; the two boys felt genuine desolation. They stood with their hands in their pockets under the lamp, turning their backs on the night, quite miserable, watching the dark houses. Suddenly a pinafore under a short coat was seen, and a long-legged girl came flying up.

'Where's Billy Pillins an' your Annie an' Eddie Dakin?'

'I don't know.'

But it did not matter so much – there were three now. They set up a game round the lamp-post, till the others rushed up, yelling. Then the play went fast and furious.

There was only this one lamp-post. Behind was the great scoop of darkness, as if all the night were there. In front, another wide, dark way opened over the hill brow. Occasionally somebody came out of this way and went into the field down the path. In a dozen yards the night had swallowed them. The children played on.

They were brought exceedingly close together owing to their isolation. If a quarrel took place, the whole play was spoilt. Arthur was very touchy, and Billy Pillins – really Philips – was worse. Then Paul had to side with Arthur, and on Paul's side went Alice, while Billy Pillins always had Emmie Limb and Eddie Dakin to back him up. Then the six would fight, hate with a fury of hatred, and flee home in terror. Paul never forgot, after one of these fierce internecine fights, seeing a big red moon lift itself up, slowly, between the waste road over the hill-top, steadily, like a great bird. And he thought of the Bible, that the moon should be turned to blood. And the next day he made haste to be friends with Billy Pillins. And then the wild, intense games went on again under the lamppost, surrounded by so much darkness. Mrs Morel, going into her parlour, would hear the children singing away:

> 'My shoes are made of Spanish leather
> My socks are made of silk
> I wear a ring on every finger
> I wash myself in milk.'

They sounded so perfectly absorbed in the game as their voices came out of the night, that they had the feel of wild creatures singing. It stirred the mother; and she understood when they came in at eight o'clock, ruddy, with brilliant eyes, and quick, passionate speech.

They all loved the Scargill Street house for its openness, for the great scallop of the world it had in view. On summer evenings the women would stand against the field fence, gossiping, facing the west, watching the sunsets flare quickly out, till the Derbyshire hills ridged across the crimson far away, like the black crest of a newt.

In this summer season the pits never turned full time, particularly the soft coal. Mrs Dakin, who lived next door to Mrs Morel, going to the field fence to shake her hearthrug, would spy men coming slowly up the hill. She saw at once they were colliers. Then she waited, a tall, thin, shrew-faced woman, standing on the hill brow, almost like a menace to the poor colliers who were toiling up. It was only eleven o'clock. From the far-off wooded hills the haze that hangs like fine black crape at the back of a summer morning had not yet dissipated. The first man came to the stile. 'Chock-chock!' went the gate under his thrust.

'What, han' yer knocked oft?' cried Mrs Dakin.

'We han missis.'

'It's a pity as they letn yer goo,' she said sarcastically.

'It is that,' replied the man.

'Nay, you know you're flig* to come up again,' she said.

And the man went on. Mrs Dakin, going up her yard, spied Mrs Morel taking the ashes to the ash-pit.

'I reckon Minton's knocked off, missis,' she cried.

'Isn't it sickenin'!' exclaimed Mrs Morel in wrath.

'Ha! But I'n just seed Jont Hutchby.'

'They might as well have saved their shoe-leather,' said Mrs Morel. And both women went indoors disgusted.

The colliers, their faces scarcely blackened, were trooping home again. Morel hated to go back. He loved the sunny morning. But he had gone to pit to work, and to be sent home again spoilt his temper.

'Good gracious, at this time!' exclaimed his wife, as he entered.

'Can I help it, woman?' he shouted.

---

* eager.

'And I've not done half enough dinner.'

'Then I'll eat my bit o' snap as I took with me,' he bowled pathetically. He felt ignominious and sore.

And the children, coming home from school, would wonder to see their father eating with his dinner the two thick slices of rather dry and dirty bread-and-butter that had been to pit and back.

'What's my dad eating his snap for now?' asked Arthur.

'I should ha'e it holled at me if I didna,' snorted Morel.

'What a story!' exclaimed his wife.

'An' is it goin' to be wasted?' said Morel. 'I'm not such a extravagant mortal as you lot, with your waste. If I drop a bit of bread at pit, in all the dust an' dirt, I pick it up an' eat it.'

'The mice would eat it,' said Paul. 'It wouldn't be wasted.'

'Good bread-an'-butter's not for mice, either,' said Morel. 'Dirty or not dirty, I'd eat it rather than it should be wasted.'

'You might leave it for the mice and pay for it out of your next pint,' said Mrs Morel.

'Oh, might I?' he exclaimed.

They were very poor that autumn. William had just gone away to London, and his mother missed his money. He sent ten shillings once or twice, but he had many things to pay for at first. His letters came regularly once a week. He wrote a good deal to his mother, telling her all his life, how he made friends, and was exchanging lessons with a Frenchman, how he enjoyed London. His mother felt again he was remaining to her just as when he was at home. She wrote to him every week her direct, rather witty letters. All day long, as she cleaned the house, she thought of him. He was in London: he would do well. Almost, he was like her knight who wore *her* favour in the battle.

He was coming at Christmas for five days. There had never been such preparations. Paul and Arthur scoured the land for holly and evergreens. Annie made the pretty paper loops in the old-fashioned way. And there was unheard-of extravagance in the larder. Mrs Morel made a big and magnificent cake. Then, feeling queenly, she showed Paul how to blanche almonds. He skinned the long nuts reverently, counting them all, to see not one was lost. It was said that eggs whisked better in a cold place. So the boy stood in the scullery, where the temperature was nearly at freezing-point, and whisked and whisked, and flew in excitement to his mother as the white of egg grew stiffer and more snowy.

'Just look, mother! Isn't it lovely?'

And he balanced a bit on his nose, then blew it in the air.

'Now, don't waste it,' said the mother.

Everybody was mad with excitement. William was coming on Christmas Eve. Mrs Morel surveyed her pantry. There was a big plum cake; and a rice cake, jam tarts, lemon tarts, and mince-pies – two enormous dishes. She was finishing cooking spanish tarts and cheese-cakes. Everywhere was decorated. The kissing bunch of berried holly hung with bright and glittering things, spun slowly over Mrs Morel's head as she trimmed her little tarts in the kitchen. A great fire roared. There was a scent of cooked pastry. He was due at seven o'clock, but he would be late. The three children had gone to meet him. She was alone. But at a quarter to seven Morel came in again. Neither wife nor husband spoke.

He sat in his armchair, quite awkward with excitement, and she quietly went on with her baking. Only by the careful way in which she did things could it be told how much moved she was. The clock ticked on.

'What time dost say he's coming?' Morel asked for the fifth time. 'The train gets in at half past six,' she replied emphatically.

'Then he'll be here at ten past seven.'

'Eh, bless you, it'll be hours late on the Midland,' she said indifferently. But she hoped, by expecting him late, to bring him early. Morel went down the entry to look for him. Then he came back.

'Goodness, man!' she said. 'You're like an ill-sitting hen.'

'Hadna you better be gettin' him summat t'eat ready?' asked the father.

'There's plenty of time,' she answered.

'There's not so much as I can see on,' he answered, turning crossly in his chair. She began to clear her table. The kettle was singing. They waited and waited.

Meantime the three children were on the platform at Sethley Bridge, on the Midland main line, two miles from home. They waited one hour. A train came – he was not there. Down the line the red and green lights shone. It was very dark and very cold.

'Ask him if the London train's come,' said Paul to Annie, when they saw a man in a tip cap.

'I'm not,' said Annie. 'You be quiet – he might send us off.'

But Paul was dying for the man to know they were expecting someone by the London train: it sounded so grand. Yet he was much too much scored of broaching any man, let alone one in a peaked cap, to dare to ask. The three children could scarcely go into the waiting-room for fear of being sent away, and for fear something should happen whilst they were off the platform. Still they waited in the dark and cold.

'It's an hour an' a half late,' said Arthur pathetically.

'Well,' said Annie, 'it's Christmas Eve.'

They all grew silent. He wasn't coming. They looked down the darkness of the railway. There was London! It seemed the uttermost of distance. They thought anything might happen if one came from London. They were all too troubled to talk. Cold, and unhappy, and silent, they huddled together on the platform.

At last, after more than two hours, they saw the lights of an engine peering round, away down the darkness. A porter ran out. The children drew back with beating hearts. A great train bound for Manchester drew up. Two doors opened, and from one of them, William. They flew to him. He handed parcels to them cheerily, and immediately began to explain that this great train had stopped for *his* sake at such a small station as Sethley Bridge: it was not booked to stop.

Meanwhile the parents were getting anxious. The table was set, the chop was cooked, everything was ready. Mrs Morel put on her black apron. She was wearing her best dress. Then she sat, pretending to read. The minutes were a torture to her.

'H'm!' said Morel. 'It's an hour an' a ha'ef.'

'And those children waiting!' she said.

'Th' train canna ha' come in yet,' he said.

'I tell you, on Christmas Eve they're *hours* wrong.'

They were both a bit cross with each other, so gnawed with anxiety. The ash-tree moaned outside in a cold, raw wind.

And all that space of night from London home! Mrs Morel suffered. The slight click of the works inside the clock irritated her. It was getting so late; it was getting unbearable.

At last there was a sound of voices, and a footstep in the entry.

'Ha's here!' cried Morel, jumping up.

Then he stood back. The mother ran a few steps towards the door and waited. There was a rush and a patter of feet, the door burst open. William was there. He dropped his Gladstone bag and took his mother in his arms.

'Mater!' he said.

'My boy!' she cried.

And for two seconds, no longer, she clasped him and kissed him. Then she withdrew and said, trying to be quite normal:

'But how late you are!'

'Aren't I!' he cried, turning to his father. 'Well, dad!'

The two men shook hands.

'Well, my lad!'

Morel's eyes were wet.

'We thought tha'd niver be commin',' he said.

'Oh, I'd come!' exclaimed William.

Then the son turned round to his mother.

'But you look well,' she said proudly, laughing.

'Well!' he exclaimed. 'I should think so – coming home!'

He was a fine fellow, big, straight, and fearless-looking. He looked round at the evergreens and the kissing bunch, and the little tarts that lay in their tins on the hearth.

'By Jove! mother, it's not different!' he said, as if in relief.

Everybody was still for a second. Then he suddenly sprang forward, picked a tort from the hearth, and pushed it whole into his mouth.

'Well, did iver you see such a parish oven!' the father exclaimed.

He had brought them endless presents. Every penny he had he had spent on them. There was a sense of luxury overflowing in the house. For his mother there was an umbrella with gold on the pale handle. She kept it to her dying day, and would have lost anything rather than that. Everybody had something gorgeous, and besides, there were pounds of unknown sweets: Turkish delight, crystallised pineapple, and such-like things which, the children thought, only the splendour of London could provide. And Paul boasted of these sweets among his friends.

'Real pineapple, cut off in slices, and then turned into crystal – fair grand!'

Everybody was mad with happiness in the family. Home was home, and they loved it with a passion of love, whatever the suffering had been. There were parties, there were rejoicings. People came in to see William, to see what difference London had made to him. And they all found him 'such a gentleman, and such a fine fellow, my word!'

When he went away again the children retired to various places to weep alone. Morel went to bed in misery, and Mrs Morel felt as if she were numbed by some drug, as if her feelings were paralysed. She loved him passionately.

He was in the office of a lawyer connected with a large shipping firm, and at the midsummer his chief offered him a trip in the Mediterranean on one of the boats, for quite a small cost. Mrs Morel wrote: 'Go, go, my boy. You may never have a chance again, and I should love to think of you cruising there in the Mediterranean almost better than to have you at home.' But William came home for his fortnight's holiday. Not even the Mediterranean, which pulled at all his young man's desire to travel, and at his poor man's wonder at the glamorous south, could take him away when he might come home. That compensated his mother for much.

CHAPTER 5

Paul Launches into Life

MOREL WAS rather a heedless man, careless of danger. So he had endless accidents. Now, when Mrs Morel heard the rattle of an empty coal-cart cease at her entry-end, she ran into the parlour to look, expecting almost to see her husband seated in the waggon, his face grey under his dirt, his body limp and sick with some hurt or other. If it were he, she would run out to help.

About a year after William went to London, and just after Paul had left school, before he got work, Mrs Morel was upstairs and her son was painting in the kitchen – he was very clever with his brush – when there came a knock at the door. Crossly he put down his brush to go. At the same moment his mother opened a window upstairs and looked down.

A pit-lad in his dirt stood on the threshold.

'Is this Walter Morel's?' he asked.

'Yes,' said Mrs Morel. 'What is it?'

But she had guessed already.

'Your mester's got hurt,' he said.

'Eh, dear me!' she exclaimed. 'It's a wonder if he hadn't, lad. And what's he done this time?'

'I don't know for sure, but it's 'is leg somewhere. They ta'ein' 'im ter th' 'ospital.'

'Good gracious me!' she exclaimed. 'Eh, dear, what a one he is! There's not five minutes of peace, I'll be hanged if there is! His thumb's nearly better, and now – Did you see him?'

'I seed him at th' bottom. An' I seed 'em bring 'im up in a tub, an' 'e war in a dead faint. But he shouted like anythink when Doctor Fraser examined him i' th' lamp cabin – an' cossed an' swore, an' said as 'e war goin' to be ta'en whoam – 'e worn't goin' ter th' 'ospital.'

The boy faltered to an end.

'He *would* want to come home, so that I can have all the bother. Thank you, my lad. Eh, dear, if I'm not sick – sick and surfeited, I am!'

She came downstairs. Paul had mechanically resumed his painting.

'And it must be pretty bad if they've taken him to the hospital,' she went on. 'But what a *careless* creature he is! *Other* men don't have all these accidents. Yes, he *would* want to put all the burden on me. Eh, dear, just as we *were* getting easy a bit at last. Put those things away, there's no time to be painting now. What time is there a train? I know I s'll have to go trailling to Keston. I s'll have to leave that bedroom.'

'I can finish it,' said Paul.

'You needn't. I shall catch the seven o'clock back, I should think. Oh, my blessed heart, the fuss and commotion he'll make! And those granite setts at Tinder Hill – he might well call them kidney pebbles – they'll jolt him almost to bits. I wonder why they can't mend them, the state they're in, an' all the men as go across in that ambulance. You'd think they'd have a hospital here. The men bought the ground, and, my sirs, there'd be accidents enough to keep it going. But no, they must trail them ten miles in a slow ambulance to Nottingham. It's a crying shame! Oh, and the fuss he'll make! I know he will! I wonder who's with him. Barker, I s'd think. Poor beggar he'll wish himself anywhere rather. But he'll look after him, I know. Now there's no telling how long he'll be stuck in that hospital – and won't he hate it! But if it's only his leg it's not so bad.'

All the time she was getting ready. Hurriedly taking off her bodice, she crouched at the boiler while the water rim slowly into her lading-can.

'I wish this boiler was at the bottom of the sea!' she exclaimed, wriggling the handle impatiently. She had very handsome, strong arms, rather surprising on a smallish woman.

Paul cleared away, put on the kettle, and set the table.

'There isn't a train till four-twenty,' he said. 'You've time enough.'

'Oh no I haven't!' she cried, blinking at him over the towel as she wiped her face.

'Yes you have. You must drink a cup of tea at any rate. Should I come with you to Keston?'

'Come with me? What for, I should like to know? Now, what have I to take him? Eh, dear! His clean shirt – and it's a blessing it is clean. But it had better be aired. And stockings – he won't want them – and a towel, I suppose; and handkerchiefs. Now what else?'

'A comb, a knife and fork and spoon,' said Paul. His father had been in the hospital before.

'Goodness knows what sort of state his feet were in,' continued Mrs Morel, as she combed her long brown hair, that was fine as silk, and was touched now with grey. 'He's very particular to wash himself to the waist, but below he thinks doesn't matter. But there, I suppose they see plenty like it.'

Paul had laid the table. He cut his mother one or two pieces of very thin bread-and-butter.

'Here you are,' he said, putting her cup of tea in her place.

'I can't be bothered!' she exclaimed crossly.

'Well, you've got to, so there, now it's put out ready,' he insisted.

So she sat down and sipped her tea, and ate a little, in silence. She was thinking.

In a few minutes she was gone, to walk the two and a half miles to Keston Station. All the things she was taking him she had in her bulging string bag. Paul watched her go up the road between the hedges – a little, quick-stepping figure, and his heart ached for her, that she was thrust forward again into pain and trouble. And she, tripping so quickly in her anxiety, felt at the back of her, her son's heart waiting on her, felt him bearing what part of the burden he could, even supporting her. And when she was at the hospital, she thought: 'It *will* upset that lad when I tell him how bad it is. I'd better be careful.' And when she was trudging home again, she felt he was coming to share her burden.

'Is it bad?' asked Paul, as soon as she entered the house.

'It's bad enough,' she replied.

'What?'

She sighed and sat down, undoing her bonnet-strings. Her son watched her face as it was lifted, and her small, work-hardened hands fingering at the bow under her chin.

'Well,' she answered, 'it's not really dangerous, but the nurse says it's a dreadful smash. You see, a great piece of rock fell on his leg – here – and it's a compound fracture. There are pieces of bone sticking through – '

'Ugh – how horrid!' exclaimed the children.

'And,' she continued, 'of course he says he's going to die – it wouldn't be him if he didn't. "I'm done for, my lass!" he said, looking at me. "Don't be so silly," I said to him. "You're not going to die of a broken leg, however badly it's smashed." "I s'll niver come out of 'ere but in a wooden box," he groaned. "Well," I said, "if you want them to carry you into the garden in a wooden box, when you're better, I've no doubt they will." "If we think it's good for him," said the Sister. She's on awfully nice Sister, but rather strict.'

Mrs Morel took off her bonnet. The children waited in silence.

'Of course, he is bad,' she continued, 'and he will be. It's a great shock, and he's lost a lot of blood; and, of course, it is a very dangerous smash. It's not at all sure that it will mend so easily. And then there's the fever and the mortification – if it took bad ways he'd quickly be gone. But there, he's a clean-blooded man, with wonderful healing flesh, and so I see no reason why it *should* take bad ways. Of course there's a wound – '

She was pale now with emotion and anxiety. The three children realised that it was very bad for their father, and the house was silent, anxious.

'But he always gets better,' said Paul after a while.

'That's what I tell him,' said the mother.

Everybody moved about in silence.

'And he really looked nearly done for,' she said. 'But the Sister says that is the pain.'

Annie took away her mother's coat and bonnet.

'And he looked at me when I came away! I said: "I s'll have to go now, Walter, because of the train – and the children." And he looked at me. It seems hard.'

Paul took up his brush again and went on painting. Arthur went outside for some coal. Annie sat looking dismal. And Mrs Morel, in her little rocking-chair that her husband had made for her when the first baby was coming, remained motionless, brooding. She was grieved, and bitterly sorry for the man who was hurt so much. But still, in her heart of hearts, where the love should have burned, there was a blank. Now, when all her woman's pity was roused to its full extent, when she would have slaved herself to death to nurse him and to save him, when she would have taken the pain herself, if she could, somewhere far away inside her, she felt indifferent to him and to his suffering. It hurt her most of all, this failure to love him, even when he roused her strong emotions. She brooded awhile.

'And there,' she said suddenly, 'when I'd got half-way to Keston, I found I'd come out in my working boots – and *look* at them.' They were an old pair of Paul's, brown and rubbed through at the toes. 'I didn't know what to do with myself, for shame,' she added.

In the morning, when Annie and Arthur were at school, Mrs Morel talked again to her son, who was helping her with her housework.

'I found Barker at the hospital. He did look bad, poor little fellow! "Well," I said to him, "what sort of a journey did you have with him?"

"Dunna ax me, missis!" he said. "Ay" I said, "I know what he'd be."

"But it *wor* bad for him Mrs Morel, it *wor* that!" he said. "I know," I said. "At ivry jolt I thought my 'eart would ha' flown clean out o' my mouth," he said. "An' the scream 'e gives sometimes! Missis, not for a fortune would I go through wi' it again."

"I can quite understand it," I said. "It's a nasty job though," he said, "an' one as'll be along while afore it's right again." "I'm afraid it will," I said. I like Mr Barker – I *do* like him. There's something so manly about him.'

Paul resumed his task silently.

'And of course,' Mrs Morel continued, 'for a man like your father, the hospital is hard. He *can't* understand rules and regulations. And he won't let anybody else touch him, not if he can help it. When he smashed the muscles of his thigh, and it had to be dressed four times a day, *would* he let anybody but me or his mother do it? He wouldn't. So, of course, he'll suffer in there with the nurses. And I didn't like leaving him. I'm sure, when I kissed him an' came away, it seemed a shame.'

So she talked to her son, almost as if she were thinking aloud to him, and he took it in as best he could, by sharing her trouble to lighten it. And in the end she shared almost everything with him without knowing.

Morel had a very bad time. For a week he was in a critical condition. Then he began to mend. And then, knowing he was going to get better, the whole family sighed with relief, and proceeded to live happily.

They were not badly off whilst Morel was in the hospital. There were fourteen shillings a week from the pit, ten shillings from the sick club, and five shillings from the Disability Fund; and then every week the butties had something for Mrs Morel – five or seven shillings – so that she was quite well to do. And whilst Morel was progressing favourably in the hospital, the family was extraordinarily happy and peaceful. On Saturdays and Wednesdays Mrs Morel went to Nottingham to see her husband. Then she always brought back some little thing: a small tube of paints for Paul, or some thick paper; a couple of postcards for Annie, that the whole family rejoiced over for days before the girl was allowed to send them away; or a fret-saw for Arthur, or a bit of pretty wood. She described her adventures into the big shops with joy. Soon the folk in the picture-shop knew her and knew about Paul. The girl in the bookshop took a keen interest in her. Mrs Morel was full of information when she got home from Nottingham. The three sat round till bedtime, listening, putting in, arguing. Then Paul often raked the fire.

'I'm the man in the house now,' he used to say to his mother with joy. They learned how perfectly peaceful the home could be. And they almost regretted – though none of them would have owned to such callousness – that their father was soon coming back.

Paul was now fourteen, and was looking for work. He was a rather small and rather finely-made boy, with dark brown hair and light blue eyes. His face had already lost its youthful chubbiness, and was becoming somewhat like William's – rough-featured, almost rugged – and it was extraordinarily mobile. Usually he looked as if he saw things, was full of life, and warm; then his smile, like his mother's, came suddenly and was very lovable; and then, when there was any clog in his soul's quick running, his face went stupid and ugly. He was the sort of boy that becomes a clown and a lout as soon as he is not understood, or feels himself held cheap; and, again, is adorable at the first touch of warmth.

He suffered very much from the first contact with anything. When he was seven, the starting school had been a nightmare and a torture to him. But afterwards he liked it. And now that he felt he had to go out into life, he went through agonies of shrinking self-consciousness. He was quite a clever painter for a boy of his years, and he knew some French and German and mathematics that Mr Heaton had taught him. But nothing he had was of any commercial value. He was not strong enough for heavy manual work, his mother said. He did not care for making things with his hands, preferred racing about, or making excursions into the country, or reading, or painting.

'What do you want to be?' his mother asked.

'Anything.'

'That is no answer,' said Mrs Morel.

But it was quite truthfully the only answer he could give. His ambition as far as this world's gear went, was quietly to earn his thirty or thirty-five shillings a week somewhere near home, and then, when his father died, have a cottage with his mother, paint and go out as he liked, and live happy ever after. That was his programme as far as doing things went. But he was proud within himself, measuring people against himself, and placing them, inexorably. And he thought that *perhaps* he might also make a painter, the real thing. But that he left alone.

'Then,' said his mother, 'you must look in the paper for the advertisements.'

He looked at her. It seemed to him a bitter humiliation and on anguish to go through. But he said nothing. When he got up in the morning, his whole being was knotted up over this one thought:

'I've got to go and look for advertisements for a job.'

It stood in front of the morning, that thought, killing all joy and even life, for him. His heart felt like a tight knot.

And then, at ten o'clock, he set off. He was supposed to be a queer, quiet child. Going up the sunny street of the little town, he felt as if all the folk he met said to themselves: 'He's going to the Co-op reading room to look in the papers for a place. He can't get a job. I suppose he's living on his mother.' Then he crept up the stone stairs behind the drapery shop at the Co-op, and peeped in the reading-room. Usually one or two men were there, either old, useless fellows, or colliers 'on the club.' So he entered, full of shrinking and suffering when they looked up, seated himself at the table, and pretended to scan the news. He knew they would think, 'What does a lad of thirteen want in a reading-room with a newspaper?' and he suffered.

Then he looked wistfully out of the window. Already he was a prisoner of industrialism. Large sunflowers stored over the old red wall of the garden opposite, looking in their jolly way down on the women who were hurrying with something for dinner. The valley was full of corn, brightening in the sun. Two collieries, among the fields, waved their small white plumes of steam. For off on the hills were the woods of Annesley, dark and fascinating. Already his heart went down. He was being taken into bondage. His freedom in the beloved home valley was going now.

The brewers' waggons came rolling up from Keston with enormous barrels, four a side, like beans in a burst bean-pod. The waggoner, throned aloft, rolling massively in his seat, was not so much below Paul's eye. The man's hair on his small, bullet head, was bleached almost white by the sun, and on his thick red arms, rocking idly on his sock apron, the white hairs glistened. His red face shone and was almost asleep with sunshine. The horses, handsome and brown, went on by themselves, looking by for the masters of the show.

Paul wished he were stupid. 'I wish,' he thought to himself, 'I was fat like him, and like a dog in the sun. I wish I was a pig and a brewer's waggoner.'

Then, the room being at last empty, he would hastily copy on advertisement on a scrap of paper, then another, and slip out in immense relief. His mother would scan over his copies.

'Yes,' she said, 'you may try.'

William had written out a letter of application, couched in admirable business language, which Paul copied, with variations. The boy's handwriting was execrable, so that William, who did all things well, got into a fever of impatience.

The elder brother was becoming quite swanky. In London he found that he could associate with men far above his Bestwood friends in station. Some of the clerks in the office had studied for the law, and were more or less going through a kind of apprenticeship. William always made friends among men wherever he went, he was so jolly. Therefore he was soon visiting and staying in houses of men who in Bestwood, would have looked down on the unapproachable bank manager, and would merely have called indifferently on the Rector. So he began to fancy himself as a great gun. He was, indeed, rather surprised at the ease with which he became a gentleman.

His mother was glad, he seemed so pleased. And his lodging in Walthamstow was so dreary. But now there seemed to come a kind of fever into the young man's letters. He was unsettled by all the change, he did not stand firm on his own feet, but seemed to spin rather giddily on the quick current of the new life. His mother was anxious for him. She could feel him losing himself. He had danced and gone to the theatre, boated on the river, been out with friends; and she knew he sat up afterwards in his cold bedroom grinding away at Latin, because he intended to get on in his office, and in the law as much as he could. He never sent his mother any money now. It was all taken, the little he had, for his own life. And she did not want any, except sometimes, when she was in a tight corner, and when ten shillings would have saved her much worry. She still dreamed of William, and of what he would do, with herself behind him. Never for a minute would she admit to herself how heavy and anxious her heart was because of him.

Also he talked a good deal now of a girl he had met at a dance, a handsome brunette, quite young, and a lady, after whom the men were running thick and fast.

'I wonder if you would run, my boy,' his mother wrote to him, 'unless you saw all the other men chasing her too. You feel safe enough and vain enough in a crowd. But take care, and see how you feel when you find yourself alone, and in triumph.'

William resented these things, and continued the chose. He had taken the girl on the river. 'If you saw her, mother, you would know how I feel. Tall and elegant, with the clearest of clear, transparent olive complexions, hair as black as jet, and such grey eyes – bright, mocking, like lights on water at night. It is all very well to be a bit satirical till you see her. And she dresses as well as any woman in London. I tell you your son doesn't half put his head up when she goes walking down Piccadilly with him.'

Mrs Morel wondered, in her heart, if her son did not go walking down Piccadilly with an elegant figure and fine clothes, rather than with a woman who was near to him. But she congratulated him in her doubtful fashion. And, as she stood over the washing-tub, the mother brooded over her son. She saw him saddled with an elegant and expensive wife, earning little money, dragging along and getting draggled in some small, ugly house in a suburb. 'But there,' she told herself, 'I am very likely a silly – meeting trouble half-way.' Nevertheless, the load of anxiety scarcely ever left her heart lest William should do the wrong thing by himself.

Presently, Paul was bidden call upon Thomas Jordan, Manufacturer of Surgical Appliances, at 21, Spaniel Row, Nottingham. Mrs Morel was all joy.

'There, you see!' she cried, her eyes shining. 'You've only written four letters, and the third is answered. You're lucky, my boy, as I always said you were.'

Paul looked at the picture of a wooden leg, adorned with elastic stockings and other appliances, that figured on Mr Jordan's notepaper, and he felt alarmed. He had not known that elastic stockings existed. And he seemed to feel the business world, with its regulated system of values, and its impersonality, and he dreaded it. It seemed monstrous also that a business could be run on wooden legs.

Mother and son set off together one Tuesday morning. It was August and blazing hot. Paul walked with something screwed up tight inside him. He would have suffered much physical pain rather than this unreasonable suffering at being exposed to strangers, to be accepted or rejected. Yet he chattered away with his mother. He would never have confessed to her how he suffered over these things, and she only partly guessed. She was gay, like a sweetheart. She stood in front of the ticket-office at Bestwood, and Paul watched her take from her purse the money for the tickets. As he saw her hands in their old black kid gloves getting the silver out of the worn purse, his heart contracted with pain of love of her.

She was quite excited, and quite gay. He suffered because she *would* talk aloud in presence of the other travelers.

'Now look at that silly cow!' she said, 'careering round as if it thought it was a circus.'

'It's most likely a bottfly,' he said very low.

'A what?' she asked brightly and unashamed.

They thought awhile. He was sensible all the time of having her opposite him. Suddenly their eyes met, and she smiled to him – a rare, intimate smile, beautiful with brightness and love. Then each looked out of the window.

The sixteen slow miles of railway journey passed. The mother and son walked down Station Street, feeling the excitement of lovers having on adventure together. In Carrington Street they stopped to hang over the parapet and look at the barges on the canal below.

'It's just like Venice,' he said, seeing the sunshine on the water that lay between high factory walls.

'Perhaps,' she answered, smiling.

They enjoyed the shops immensely.

'Now you see that blouse,' she would say, 'wouldn't that just suit our Annie? And for one-and-eleven-three. Isn't that cheap?'

'And made of needlework as well,' he said.

'Yes.'

They had plenty of time, so they did not hurry. The town was strange and delightful to them. But the boy was tied up inside in a knot of apprehension. He dreaded the interview with Thomas Jordan.

It was nearly eleven o'clock by St Peter's Church. They turned up a narrow street that led to the Castle. It was gloomy and old-fashioned, having low dark shops and dark green house-doors with brass knockers, and yellow-ochred doorsteps projecting on to the pavement; then another old shop whose small window looked like a cunning, half-shut eye. Mother and son went cautiously, looking everywhere for 'Thomas Jordan and Son.' It was like hunting in some wild place. They were on tiptoe of excitement.

Suddenly they spied a big, dark archway, in which were names of various firms, Thomas Jordan among them.

'Here it is!' said Mrs Morel. 'But now where is it?'

They looked round. On one side was a queer, dark, cardboard factory, on the other a Commercial Hotel.

'It's up the entry,' said Paul.

And they ventured under the archway, as into the jaws of the dragon. They emerged into a wide yard, like a well, with buildings all round. It was littered with straw and boxes, and cardboard. The sunshine actually caught one crate whose straw was streaming on to the yard like gold. But elsewhere the place was like a pit. There were several doors, and two flights of steps. Straight in front, on a dirty glass door at the top of a staircase, loomed the ominous words 'Thomas Jordan and Son Surgical Appliances.' Mrs Morel went first, her son followed her. Charles I mounted his scaffold with a lighter heart than had Paul Morel as he followed his mother up the dirty steps to the dirty door.

She pushed open the door, and stood in pleased surprise. In front of her was a big warehouse, with creamy paper parcels everywhere, and clerks, with their shirt-sleeves rolled back, were going about in on at home sort of way. The light was subdued, the glossy cream parcels seemed luminous, the counters were of dark brown wood. All was quiet and very homely. Mrs Morel took two steps forward, then waited. Paul stood behind her. She had on her Sunday bonnet and a black veil; he wore a boy's broad white collar and a Norfolk suit.

One of the clerks looked up. He was thin and tall, with a small face. His way of looking was alert. Then he glanced round to the other end of the room, where was a glass office. And then he came forward. He did not say anything, but leaned in a gentle, inquiring fashion towards Mrs Morel.

'Can I see Mr Jordan?' she asked.

'I'll fetch him,' answered the young man.

He went down to the glass office. A red-faced, white-whiskered old man looked up. He reminded Paul of a pomeranian dog. Then the same little man came up the room. He had short legs, was rather stout, and wore on alpaca jacket. So, with one ear up, as it were, he came stoutly and inquiringly down the room.

'Good-morning!' he said, hesitating before Mrs Morel, in doubt as to whether she were a customer or not.

'Good-morning. I came with my son, Paul Morel. You asked him to call this morning.'

'Come this way,' said Mr Jordan, in a rather snappy little manner intended to be business-like.

They followed the manufacturer into a grubby little room, upholstered in black American leather, glossy with the rubbing of many customers. On the table was a pile of trusses, yellow wash-leather hoops tangled together. They looked new and living. Paul sniffed the odour of new wash-leather. He wondered what the things were. By this time he was so much stunned that he only noticed the outside things.

'Sit down!' said Mr Jordan, irritably pointing Mrs Morel to a horsehair chair. She sat on the edge in an uncertain fashion. Then the little old man fidgeted and found a paper.

'Did you write this letter?' he snapped, thrusting what Paul recognized as his own notepaper in front of him.

'Yes,' he answered.

At that moment he was occupied in two ways: first, in feeling guilty for telling a lie, since William had composed the letter; second, in wondering why his letter seemed so strange and different, in the fat, red hand of the man, from what it had been when it lay on the kitchen table. It was like part of himself, gone astray. He resented the way the man held it.

'Where did you learn to write?' said the old man crossly.

Paul merely looked at him shamedly, and did not answer.

'He is a bad writer,' put in Mrs Morel apologetically. Then she pushed up her veil. Paul hated her for not being prouder with this common little man, and he loved her face clear of the veil.

'And you say you know French?' inquired the little man, still sharply.

'Yes,' said Paul.

'What school did you go to?'

'The Board-school.'

'And did you learn it there?'

'No – I – ' The boy went crimson and got no further.

'His godfather gave him lessons,' said Mrs Morel, half-pleading and rather distant.

Mr Jordan hesitated. Then, in his irritable manner – he always seemed to keep his hands ready for action – he pulled another sheet of paper from his pocket, unfolded it. The paper made a crackling noise. He handed it to Paul.

'Read that,' he said.

It was a note in French, in thin, flimsy foreign handwriting that the boy could not decipher. He stored blankly at the paper.

' "Monsieur," ' he began; then he looked in great confusion at Mr Jordan. 'It's the – it's the – '

He wanted to say 'handwriting,' but his wits would no longer work even sufficiently to supply him with the word. Feeling an utter fool, and hating Mr Jordan, he turned desperately to the paper again.

' "Sir, – Please send me" – er – er – I can't tell the – er – "two pairs – *gris fil bas* – grey thread stockings" – er – er – "*sans* – without" – er – I can't tell the words – er – "*doigts* – fingers" – er – I can't tell the – '

He wanted to say 'handwriting,' but the word still refused to come. Seeing him stuck, Mr Jordan snatched the paper from him.

' "Please send by return two pairs grey thread stockings without *toes*," "Well,' flashed Paul, '*doigts*' means "fingers" – as well – as a rule – ' The little man looked at him. He did not know whether '*doigts*' meant 'fingers'; he knew that for all *his* purposes it meant 'toes.'

'Fingers to stockings!' he snapped.

'Well, it *does* mean fingers,' the boy persisted.

He hated the little man, who made such a clod of him. Mr Jordan looked at the pale, stupid, defiant boy, then at the mother, who sat quiet and with that peculiar shut-off look of the poor who have to depend on the favour of others.

'And when could he come?' he asked.

'Well,' said Mrs Morel, 'as soon as you wish. He has finished school now.'

'He would live in Bestwood?'

'Yes; but he could be in – at the station – at quarter to eight.'

'H'm!'

It ended by Paul's being engaged as junior spiral clerk at eight shillings a week. The boy did not open his mouth to say another word, after having insisted that '*doigts*' meant 'fingers.'

He followed his mother down the stairs. She looked at him with her bright blue eyes full of love and joy.

'I think you'll like it,' she said.

' *"Doigts"* does mean "fingers," mother, and it was the writing. I couldn't read the writing.'

'Never mind, my boy. I'm sure he'll be all right, and you won't see much of him. Wasn't that first young fellow nice? I'm sure you'll like them.'

'But wasn't Mr Jordan common, mother? Does he own it all?'

'I suppose he was a workman who has got on,' she said. 'You mustn't mind people so much. They're not being disagreeable to *you* – it's their way. *You* always think people are meaning things for you. But they don't.'

It was very sunny. Over the big desolate space of the market-place the blue sky shimmered, and the granite cobbles of the paving glistened. Shops down the Long Row were deep in obscurity, and the shadow was full of colour. Just where the horse trams trundled across the market was a row of fruit stalls, with fruit blazing in the sun – apples and piles of reddish oranges, small greengage plums and bananas. There was a warm scent of fruit as mother and son passed. Gradually his feeling of ignominy and of rage sank.

'Where should we go for dinner?' asked the mother.

It was felt to be a reckless extravagance. Paul had only been in an eating-house once or twice in his life, and then only to have a cup of tea and a bun. Most of the people of Bestwood considered that tea and bread-and-butter, and perhaps potted-beef, was all they could afford to eat in Nottingham. Real cooked dinner was considered great extravagance. Paul felt rather guilty.

They found a place that looked quite cheap. But when Mrs Morel scanned the bill of fare, her heart was heavy, things were so dear. So she ordered kidney pies and potatoes as the cheapest available dish.

'We oughtn't to have come here, mother,' said Paul.

'Never mind,' she said. 'We won't come again.'

She insisted on his having a small currant tort, because he liked sweets.

'I don't want it, mother,' he pleaded.

'Yes,' she insisted; 'you'll have it.'

And she looked round for the waitress. But the waitress was busy, and Mrs Morel did not like to bother her then. So the mother and son waited for the girl's pleasure, whilst she flirted among the men.

'Brazen hussy!' said Mrs Morel to Paul. 'Look now, she's taking that man his pudding, and he came long after us.'

'It doesn't matter, mother,' said Paul.

Mrs Morel was angry. But she was too poor, and her orders were too meagre, so that she had not the courage to insist on her rights just then. They waited and waited.

'Should we go, mother?' he said.

Then Mrs Morel stood up. The girl was passing near.

'Will you bring one currant tort?' said Mrs Morel clearly.

The girl looked round insolently.

'Directly,' she said.

'We have waited quite long enough,' said Mrs Morel.

In a moment the girl came back with the tort. Mrs Morel asked coldly for the bill. Paul wanted to sink through the floor. He marvelled at his mother's hardness. He knew that only years of battling had taught her to insist even so little on her rights. She shrank as much as he.

'It's, the last time I go *there* for anything!' she declared, when they were outside the place, thankful to be clear.

'We'll go,' she said, 'and look at Keep's and Boot's, and one or two places, shall we?'

They had discussions over the pictures, and Mrs Morel wanted to buy him a little sable brush that he hankered after. But this indulgence he refused. He stood in front of milliners' shops and drapers' shops almost bored, but content for her to be interested. They wandered on.

'Now, just look at those black grapes!' she said. 'They make your mouth water. I've wanted some of those for years, but I s'll have to wait a bit before I get them.'

Then she rejoiced in the florists, standing in the doorway sniffing.

'Oh! oh! Isn't it simply lovely!'

Paul saw, in the darkness of the shop, an elegant young lady in black peering over the counter curiously.

'They're looking at you,' he said, trying to draw his mother away.

'But what is it?' she exclaimed, refusing to be moved.

'Stocks!' he answered, sniffing hastily. 'Look, there's a tubful.'

'So there is – red and white. But really, I never knew stocks to smell like it!' And, to his great relief, she moved out of the doorway, but only to stand in front of the window.

'Paul!' she cried to him, who was trying to get out of sight of the elegant young lady in black – the shop-girl. 'Paul! Just look here!'

He came reluctantly back.

'Now, just look at that fuchsia!' she exclaimed, pointing.

'H'm!' He made a curious, interested sound. 'You'd think every second as the flowers was going to fall off, they hang so big an' heavy.'

'And such an 'abundance!' she cried.

'And the way they drop downwards with their threads and knots!'

'Yes!' she exclaimed. 'Lovely!'

'I wonder who'll buy it!' he said.

'I wonder!' she answered. 'Not us.'

'It would die in our parlour.'

'Yes, beastly cold, sunless hole; it kills every bit of a plant you put in, and the kitchen chokes them to death.'

They bought a few things, and set off towards the station. Looking up the canal, through the dark pass of the buildings, they saw the Castle on its bluff of brown, green-bushed rock, in a positive miracle of delicate sunshine.

'Won't it be nice for me to come out at dinner-times?' said Paul. 'I can go all round here and see everything. I s'll love it.'

'You will,' assented his mother.

He had spent a perfect afternoon with his mother. They arrived home in the mellow evening, happy, and glowing, and tired.

In the morning he filled in the form for his season-ticket and took it to the station. When he got back, his mother was just beginning to wash the floor. He sat crouched up on the sofa.

'He says it'll be here by Saturday,' he said.

'And how much will it be?'

'About one pound eleven,' he said.

She went on washing her floor in silence.

'Is it a lot?' he asked.

'It's no more than I thought,' she answered.

'An' I s'll earn eight shillings a week,' he said.

She did not answer, but went on with her work. At last she said:

'That William promised me, when he went to London, as he'd give me a pound a month. He has given me ten shillings – twice; and now I know he hasn't a farthing if I asked him. Not that I want it. Only just now you'd think he might be able to help with this ticket, which I'd never expected.'

'He earns a lot,' said Paul.

'He earns a hundred and thirty pounds. But they're all alike. They're large in promises, but it's precious little fulfilment you get.'

'He spends over fifty shillings a week on himself,' said Paul.

'And I keep this house on less than thirty,' she replied; 'and am supposed to find money for extras. But they don't care about helping you, once they've gone. He'd rather spend it on that dressed-up creature.'

'She should have her own money if she's so grand,' said Paul.

'She should, but she hasn't. I asked him. And I know he doesn't buy her a gold bangle for nothing. I wonder whoever bought *me* a gold bangle.'

William was succeeding with his 'Gypsy,' as he called her. He asked the girl – her name was Louisa Lily Denys Western – for a photograph to send to his mother. The photo came – a handsome brunette, taken in profile, smirking slightly – and, it might be, quite naked, for on the photograph not a scrap of clothing was to be seen, only a naked bust.

'Yes,' wrote Mrs Morel to her son, 'the photograph of Louisa is very striking, and I can see she must be attractive. But do you think, my boy, it was very good taste of a girl to give her young man that photo to send to his mother – the first? Certainly the shoulders are beautiful, as you say. But I hardly expected to see so much of them at the first view.'

Morel found the photograph standing on the chiffonier in the parlour. He came out with it between his thick thumb and finger.

'Who dost reckon this is?' he asked of his wife.

'It's the girl our William is going with,' replied Mrs Morel.

'H'm! 'Er's a bright spark, from th' look on 'er, an' one as wunna do him owermuch good neither. Who is she?'

'Her name is Louisa Lily Denys Western.'

'An' come again to-morrer!' exclaimed the miner. 'An' is 'er on actress?'

'She is not. She's supposed to be a lady.'

'I'll bet!' he exclaimed, still staring at the photo. 'A lady, is she? An' how much does she reckon ter keep up this sort o' game on?'

'On nothing. She lives with an old aunt, whom she hates, and takes what bit of money's given her.'

'H'm!' said Morel, laying down the photograph. 'Then he's a fool to ha' ta'en up wi' such a one as that.'

'Dear Mater,' William replied. 'I'm sorry you didn't like the photograph. It never occurred to me when I sent it, that you mightn't think it decent However, I told Gyp that it didn't quite suit your prim and proper notions, so she's going to send you another, that I hope will please you better. She's always being photographed; in fact, the photographers *ask* her if they may take her for nothing.'

Presently the new photograph came, with a little silly note from the girl. This time the young lady was seen in a black satin evening bodice, cut square, with little puff sleeves, and black lace hanging down her beautiful arms.

'I wonder if she ever wears anything except evening clothes,' said Mrs Morel sarcastically. 'I'm sure I ought to be impressed.'

'You are disagreeable, mother,' said Paul. 'I think the first one with bare shoulders is lovely.'

'Do you?' answered his mother. 'Well, I don't.'

On the Monday morning the boy got up at six to start work. He had the season-ticket, which had cost such bitterness, in his waistcoatpocket. He loved it with its bars of yellow across. His mother packed his dinner in a small, shut-up basket, and he set off at a quarter to seven to catch the 7:15 train. Mrs Morel came to the entry-end to see him off.

It was a perfect morning. From the ash-tree the slender green fruits that the children call 'pidgeons' were twinkling gaily down on a little breeze, into the front gardens of the houses. The valley was full of a lustrous dark haze, through which the ripe corn shimmered, and in which the steam from Minton pit melted swiftly. Puffs of wind came. Paul looked over the high woods of Aldersley, where the country gleamed, and home had never pulled at him so powerfully.

'Good-morning, mother,' he said, smiling, but feeling very unhappy.

'Good-morning,' she replied cheerfully and tenderly.

She stood in her white apron on the open road, watching him as he crossed the field. He had a small, compact body that looked full of life. She felt, as she saw him trudging over the field, that where he determined to go he would get. She thought of William. He would have leaped the fence instead of going round to the stile. He was away in London, doing well. Paul would be working in Nottingham. Now she had two sons in the world. She could think of two places, great centers of industry, and feel that she had put a man into each of them, that these men would work out what she wanted; they were derived from her, they were of her, and their works also would be hers. All the morning long she thought of Paul.

At eight o'clock he climbed the dismal stairs of Jordan's Surgical Appliance Factory, and stood helplessly against the first great parcel-rack, waiting for somebody to pick him up. The place was still not awake. Over the counters were great dust sheets. Two men only had arrived, and were heard talking in a corner, as they took off their coats and rolled up their shirt-sleeves. It was ten past eight. Evidently there was no rush of punctuality. Paul listened to the voices of the two clerks. Then he heard someone cough, and saw in the office at the end of the room an old decaying clerk, in a round smoking-cap of black velvet embroidered with red and green, opening letters. He waited and waited. One of the junior clerks went to the old man, greeted him cheerily and loudly. Evidently the old 'chief' was deaf. Then the young fellow came striding importantly down to his counter. He spied Paul.

'Hello!' he said. 'You the new lad?'

'Yes,' said Paul.

'H'm! What's your name?'

'Paul Morel'

'Paul Morel? All right, you come on round here.'

Paul followed him round the rectangle of counters. The room was second storey. It had a great hole in the middle of the floor, fenced as with a wall of counters, and down this wide shaft the lifts went, and the light for the bottom storey. Also there was a corresponding big, oblong hole in the ceiling, and one could see above, over the fence of the top floor, some machinery; and right away overhead was the glass roof, and all light for the three storeys came downwards, getting dimmer, so that it was always night on the ground floor and rather gloomy on the second floor. The factory was the top floor, the warehouse the second, the storehouse the ground floor. It was an insanitary, ancient place.

Paul was led round to a very dark corner.

'This is the "Spiral" corner,' said the clerk. 'You're Spiral, with Pappleworth. He's your boss, – but he's not come yet. He doesn't get here till half-past eight. So you can fetch the letters, if you like, from Mr Melling down there.'

The young man pointed to the old clerk in the office.

'All right,' said Paul.

'Here's a peg to hang your cap on. Here are your entry ledgers. Mr Pappleworth won't be long.'

And the thin young man stalked away with long, busy strides over the hollow wooden floor.

After a minute or two Paul went down and stood in the door of the glass office. The old clerk in the smoking-cap looked down over the rim of his spectacles.

'Good-morning,' he said, kindly and impressively. 'You want the letters for the Spiral department, Thomas?'

Paul resented being called 'Thomas.' But he took the letters and returned to his dark place, where the counter made on angle, where the great parcel-rack came to an end, and where there were three doors in the corner. He sat on a high stool and read the letters – those whose handwriting was not too difficult. They ran as follows:

'Will you please send me at once a pair of lady's silk spiral thigh-hose, without feet, such as I had from you last year; length, thigh to knee, etc.' Or, 'Major Chamberlain wishes to repeat his previous order for a silk non-elastic suspensory bandage.'

Many of these letters, some of them in French or Norwegian, were a great puzzle to the boy. He sat on his stool nervously awaiting the arrival of his 'boss.' He suffered tortures of shyness when, at half-past eight, the factory girls for upstairs trooped past him.

Mr Pappleworth arrived, chewing a chlorodyne gum, at about twenty to nine, when all the other men were at work. He was a thin, sallow man with a red nose, quick, staccato, and smartly but stiffly dressed. He was about thirty-six years old. There was something rather 'doggy,' rather smart, rather cute and shrewd, and something warm, and something slightly contemptible about him.

'You my new lad?' he said.

Paul stood up and said he was.

'Fetched the letters?'

Mr Pappleworth gave a chew to his gum.

'Yes.'

'Copied 'em?'

'No.'

'Well, come on then, let's look slippy. Changed your coat?'

'No.'

'You want to bring an old coat and leave it here.' He pronounced the last words with the chlorodyne gum between his side teeth. He vanished into darkness behind the great parcel-rack, reappeared coatless, turning up a smart striped shirt-cuff over a thin and hairy arm. Then he slipped into his coat. Paul noticed how thin he was, and that his trousers were in folds behind. He seized a stool, dragged it beside the boy's, and sat down.

'Sit down,' he said.

Paul took a seat.

Mr Pappleworth was very close to him. The man seized the letters, snatched a long entry-book out of a rack in front of him, flung it open, seized a pen, and said:

'Now look here. You want to copy these letters in here.' He sniffed twice, gave a quick chew at his gum, stored fixedly at a letter, then went very still and absorbed, and wrote the entry rapidly, in a beautiful flourishing hand. He glanced quickly at Paul.

'See that?'

'Yes.'

'Think you can do it all right?'

'Yes.'

'All right then, let's see you.'

He sprang off his stool. Paul took a pen. Mr Pappleworth disappeared. Paul rather liked copying the letters but he wrote slowly, laboriously, and exceedingly badly. He was doing the fourth letter, and feeling quite busy and happy, when Mr Pappleworth reappeared.

'Now then, how'r' yer getting on? Done 'em?'

He leaned over the boy's shoulder, chewing, and smelling of chlorodyne.

'Strike my bob, lad, but you're a beautiful writer!' he exclaimed satirically. 'Ne'er mind, how many h'yer done? Only three! I'd 'a eaten 'em. Get on, my lad, an' put numbers on 'em. Here, look! Get on!'

Paul ground away at the letters, whilst Mr Pappleworth fussed over various jobs. Suddenly the boy started as a shrill whistle sounded near his ear. Mr Pappleworth came, took a plug out of a pipe, and said, in on amazingly cross and bossy voice:

'Yes?'

Paul heard a faint voice, like a woman's, out of the mouth of the tube. He gazed in wonder, never having seen a speaking-tube before.

'Well,' said Mr Pappleworth disagreeably into the tube, 'you'd better get some of your back work done, then.'

Again the woman's tiny voice was heard, sounding pretty and cross.

'I've not time to stand here while you talk,' said Mr Pappleworth, and he pushed the plug into the tube.

'Come, my lad,' he said imploringly to Paul, 'there's Polly crying out for them orders. Can't you buck up a bit? Here, come out!'

He took the book, to Paul's immense chagrin, and began the copying himself. He worked quickly and well. This done, he seized some strips of long yellow paper, about three inches wide, and made out the day's orders for the workgirls.

'You'd better watch me,' he said to Paul, working all the while rapidly. Paul watched the weird little drawings of legs, and thighs, and ankles, with the strokes across and the numbers, and the few brief directions which his chief made upon the yellow paper. Then Mr Pappleworth finished and jumped up.

'Come on with me,' he said, and the yellow papers flying in his hands, he dashed through a door and down some stairs, into the basement where the gas was burning. They crossed the cold, damp storeroom, then a long, dreary room with a long table on trestles, into a smaller, cosy apartment, not very high, which had been built on to the main building. In this room a small woman with a red serge blouse, and her black hair done on top of her head, was waiting like a proud little bantam.

'Here y'are!' said Pappleworth.

'I think it is "here you are!" ' exclaimed Polly. 'The girls have been here nearly half an hour waiting. Just think of the time wasted!'

'*You* think of getting your work done and not talking so much,' said Mr Pappleworth. 'You could ha' been finishing off.'

'You know quite well we finished everything off on Saturday!' cried Polly, flying at him, her dark eyes flashing.

'Tu-tu-tu-tu-terterter!' he mocked. 'Here's your new lad. Don't ruin him as you did the last.'

' "As we did the last!" ' repeated Polly. 'Yes, *we* do a lot of ruining, we do. My word, a lad would *take* some ruining after he'd been with you.'

'It's time for work now, not for talk,' said Mr Pappleworth severely and coldly.

'It was time for work some time back,' said Polly, marching away with her head in the air. She was an erect little body of forty.

In that room were two round spiral machines on the bench under the window. Through the inner doorway was another longer room, with six more machines. A little group of girls, nicely dressed and in white aprons, stood talking together.

'Have you nothing else to do but talk?' said Mr Pappleworth.

'Only wait for you,' said one handsome girl, laughing.

'Well, get on, get on,' he said. 'Come on, my lad. You'll know your road down here again.'

And Paul ran upstairs after his chief. He was given some checking and invoicing to do. He stood at the desk, labouring in his execrable handwriting. Presently Mr Jordan came strutting down from the glass office and stood behind him to the boy's great discomfort. Suddenly a red and fat finger was thrust on the form he was filling in.

'*Mr* J. A Bates, Esquire!' exclaimed the cross voice just behind his ear.

Paul looked at 'Mr J. A Bates, Esquire' in his own vile writing, and wondered what was the matter now.

'Didn't they teach you any better than *that* while they were at it? If you put "Mr" you don't put "Esquire" – a man can't be both at once.'

The boy regretted his too-much generosity in disposing of honours, hesitated, and with trembling fingers, scratched out the 'Mr' Then all at once Mr Jordan snatched away the invoice.

'Make another! Are you going to send *that* to a gentleman?' And he tore up the blue form irritably.

Paul, his ears red with shame, began again. Still Mr Jordan watched.

'I don't know what they *do* teach in school. You'll have to write better than that. Lads learn nothing nowadays, but how to recite poetry and play the fiddle. Have you seen his writing?' he asked of Mr Pappleworth.

'Yes; prime, isn't it?' replied Mr Pappleworth indifferently.

Mr Jordan gave a lime grunt, not unamiable. Paul divined that his master's bark was worse than his bite. Indeed, the lime manufacturer, although he spoke bad English, was quite gentleman enough to leave his men alone and to take no notice of trifles. But he knew he did not look like the boss and owner of the show, so he had to play his role of proprietor at first, to put things on a right footing.

'Let's see, *what's* your name?' asked Mr Pappleworth of the boy.

'Paul Morel'

It is curious that children suffer so much at having to pronounce their own names.

'Paul Morel, is it? All right, you Paul-Morel through them things there, and then – '

Mr Pappleworth subsided on to a stool, and began writing. A girl came up from out of a door just behind, put some newly pressed elastic web appliances on the counter, and returned. Mr Pappleworth picked up the whitey-blue knee-band, examined it, and its yellow order-paper quickly, and put it on one side. Next was a flesh-pink 'leg.' He went through the few things, wrote out a couple of orders, and called to Paul to accompany him.

This time they went through the door whence the girl had emerged. There Paul found himself at the top of a lime wooden flight of steps, and below him saw a room with windows round two sides, and at the farther end half a dozen girls sitting bending over the benches in the light from the window, sewing. They were singing together 'Two' Lillie Girls in Blue.' Hearing the door opened, they all turned round, to see Mr Pappleworth and Paul looking down on them from the far end of the room. They stopped singing.

'Can't you make a bit less row?' said Mr Pappleworth. 'Folk'll think we keep cats.'

A hunchback woman on a high stool turned her long, rather heavy face towards Mr Pappleworth, and said, in a contralto voice:

'They're all tom-cats then.'

In vain Mr Pappleworth tried to be impressive for Paul's benefit. He descended the steps into the finishing-off room, and went to the hunchback Fanny. She had such a short body on her high stool that her head, with its great bands of bright brown hair, seemed over large, as did her pale, heavy face. She wore a dress of green-black cashmere, and her wrists, coming out of the narrow cuffs, were thin and flat, as she put down her work nervously. He showed her something that was wrong with a knee-cap.

Well,' she said, 'you needn't come blaming it on to me. It's not my fault.' Her colour mounted to her cheek.

'I never said it *was* your fault. Will you do as I tell you?' replied Mr Pappleworth shortly.

'You don't say it's my fault, but you'd like to make out as it was,' the hunchback woman cried, almost in tears. Then she snatched the kneecap from her 'boss,' saying: 'Yes, I'll do it for you, but you needn't be snappy.'

'Here's your new lad,' said Mr Pappleworth.

Fanny turned, smiling very gently on Paul.

'Oh!' she said.

'Yes; don't make a softy of him between you.'

'It's not us as 'ud make a softy of him,' she said indignantly.

'Come on then, Paul,' said Mr Pappleworth.

'*Au revoy,* Paul,' said one of the girls.

There was a titter of laughter. Paul went out, blushing deeply, not having spoken a word.

The day was very long. All morning the work-people were coming to speak to Mr Pappleworth. Paul was writing or learning to make up parcels, ready for the midday post. At one o'clock, or, rather, at a quarter to one, Mr Pappleworth disappeared to catch his train: he lived in the suburbs. At one o'clock, Paul, feeling very lost, took his dinner-basket down into the stockroom in the basement, that had the long table on trestles, and ate his meal hurriedly, alone in that cellar of gloom and desolation. Then he went out of doors. The brightness and the freedom of the streets made him feel adventurous and happy. But at two o'clock he was back in the corner of the big room. Soon the work-girls went trooping past, making remarks. It was the commoner girls who worked upstairs at the heavy tasks of truss-making and the finishing of artificial limbs. He waited for Mr Pappleworth, not knowing what to do, sitting scribbling on the yellow order paper. Mr Pappleworth came at twenty minutes to three. Then he sat and gossiped with Paul, treating the boy entirely as an equal, even in age.

In the afternoon there was never very much to do, unless it were near the week-end, and the accounts had to be made up. At five o'clock all the men went down into the dungeon with the table on trestles, and there they had tea, eating bread-and-butter on the bare, dirty boards, talking with the same kind of ugly haste and slovenliness with which they ate their meal. And yet upstairs the atmosphere among them was always jolly and clear. The cellar and the trestles affected them.

After tea, when all the gases were lighted, *work* went more briskly. There was the big evening post to get off. The hose came up warm and newly pressed from the workrooms. Paul had made out the invoices. Now he had the packing up and addressing to do, then he had to weigh his stock of parcels on the scales. Everywhere voices were calling weights, there was the chink of metal, the rapid snapping of string, the hurrying to old Mr Melling for stamps. And at last the postman came with his sock, laughing and jolly. Then everything slacked off, and Paul took his dinner-basket and ran to the station to catch the eight-twenty train. The day in the factory was just twelve hours long.

His mother sat waiting for him rather anxiously. He had to walk from Keston, so was not home until about twenty past nine. And he left the house before seven in the morning. Mrs Morel was rather anxious about his health. But she herself had had to put up with so much that she expected her children to take the same odds. They must go through with what came. And Paul stayed at Jordans, although all the time he was there his health suffered from the darkness and lack of air and the long hours.

He came in pale and tired. His mother looked at him. She saw he was rather pleased, and her anxiety all went.

Well, and how was it?' she asked.

'Ever so funny, mother,' he replied. 'You don't have to work a bit hard, and they're nice with you.'

'And did you get on all right?'

'Yes; they only say my writing's bad. But Mr Pappleworth – he's my man – said to Mr Jordan I should be all right. I'm Spiral, mother; you must come and see. It's ever so nice.'

Soon he liked Jordan's. Mr Pappleworth, who had a certain 'saloon bar' flavour about him, was always natural, and treated him as if he had been a comrade. Sometimes the 'Spiral boss' was irritable, and chewed more lozenges than ever. Even then, however, he was not offensive, but one of those people who hurt themselves by their own irritable more than they hurt other people.

'Haven't you done that *yet*?' he would cry. 'Go on, be a month of Sundays.'

Again, and Paul could understand him least then, he was jocular and in high spirits.

'I'm going to bring my little Yorkshire terrier bitch tomorrow,' he said jubilantly to Paul.

What's a Yorkshire terrier?'

'*Don't* know what a Yorkshire terrier is? *Don't know a Yorkshire* – Mr Pappleworth was aghast.

'Is it a little silky one – colours of iron and rusty silver?'

'That's it, my lad. She's a gem. She's had five pounds' worth of pups already, and she's worth over seven pounds herself; and she doesn't weigh twenty ounces.'

The next day the bitch came. She was a shivering, miserable morsel. Paul did not care for her; she seemed so like a wet rag that would never dry. Then a man called for her, and began to make coarse jokes. But Mr Pappleworth nodded his head in the direction of the boy, and the talk went on *satto voce*.

Mr Jordan only made one more excursion to watch Paul, and then the only fault he found was seeing the boy lay his pen on the counter.

'Put your pen in your ear, if you're going to be a clerk. Pen in your ear!' And one day he said to the lad, 'Why don't you hold your shoulders straighter? Come down here,' when he took him into the glass office and fitted him with special braces for keeping the shoulders square.

But Paul liked the girls best. The men seemed common and rather dull. He liked them all, but they were uninteresting. Polly, the little brisk overseer downstairs, finding Paul eating in the cellar, asked him if she could cook him anything on her little stove. Next day his mother gave him a dish that could be heated up. He took it into the pleasant, clean room to Polly. And very soon it grew to be an established custom that he should have dinner with her. When he came in at eight in the morning he took his basket to her, and when he came down at one o'clock she had his dinner ready.

He was not very tall, and pale, with thick chestnut hair, irregular features, and a wide, full mouth. She was like a small bird. He often called her a 'robinet.' Though naturally rather quiet, he would sit and chatter with her for hours telling her about his home. The girls all liked to hear him talk. They often gathered in a little circle while he sat on a bench, and held forth to them, laughing. Some of them regarded him as a curious little creature, so serious, yet so bright and jolly, and always so delicate in his way with them. They all liked him, and he adored them. Polly he felt he belonged to. Then Connie, with her mane of red hair, her face of apple-blossom, her murmuring voice, such a lady in her shabby black frock, appealed to his romantic side.

When you sit winding,' he said, 'it looks as if you were spinning at a spinning-wheel – it looks ever so nice. You remind me of Elaine in the "Idylls of the King." I'd draw you if I could.'

And she glanced at him blushing shyly. And later on he had a sketch he prized very much: Connie sitting on the stool before the wheel, her flowing mane of red hair on her rusty black frock, her red mouth shut and serious, running the scarlet thread off the hank on to the reel.

With Louisa, handsome and brazen, who always seemed to thrust her hip at him, he usually joked.

Emma was rather plain, rather old, and condescending. But to condescend to him made her happy, and he did not mind.

'How do you put needles in?' he asked.

'Go away and don't bother.'

'But I ought to know how to put needles in.'

She ground at her machine all the while steadily.

'There are many things you ought to know,' she replied.

'Tell me, then, how to stick needles in the machine.'

'Oh, the boy, what a nuisance he is! Why, *this* is how you do it.' He watched her attentively. Suddenly a whistle piped. Then Polly appeared, and said in a clear voice:

'Mr Pappleworth wants to know how much longer you're going to be down here playing with the girls, Paul.'

Paul flew upstairs, calling 'Goodbye!' and Emma drew herself up.

'It wasn't *me* who wanted him to play with the machine,' she said.

As a rule, when all the girls came back at two o'clock he ran upstairs to Fanny, the hunchback, in the finishing-off room. Mr Pappleworth did not appear till twenty to three and he often found his boy sitting beside Fanny, talking, or drawing, or singing with the girls.

Often, after a minute's hesitation, Fanny would begin to sing. She had a fine contralto voice. Everybody joined in the chorus, and it went well. Paul was not at all embarrassed, after a while, sitting in the room with the half a dozen workgirls.

At the end of the song Fanny would say:

'I know you've been laughing at me.'

'Don't be so soft, Fanny!' cried one of the girls.

Once there was mention of Connie's red hair.

'Fanny's is better, to my fancy,' said Emma.

'You needn't try to make a fool of me,' said Fanny, flushing deeply.

'No, but she has, Paul; she's got beautiful hair.'

'It's a treat of a colour,' said he. 'That coldish colour like earth, and yet shiny. It's like bog-water.'

'Goodness me!' exclaimed one girl, laughing.

'How I do but get criticised,' said Fanny.

'But you should see it down, Paul,' cried Emma earnestly. 'It's simply beautiful. Put it down for him, Fanny, if he wants something to paint.'

Fanny would not, and yet she wanted to.

'Then I'll take it down myself,' said the lad.

Well, you can if you like,' said Fanny.

And he carefully took the pins out of the knot, and the rush of hair, of uniform dark brown, slid over the humped back.

What a lovely lot!' he exclaimed.

The girls watched. There was silence. The youth shook the hair loose from the coil.

'It's splendid!' he said, smelling its perfume. 'I'll bet it's worth pounds.'

'I'll leave it you when I die, Paul,' said Fanny, half joking.

'You look just like anybody else, sitting drying their hair,' said one of the girls to the long-legged hunchback.

Poor Fanny was morbidly sensitive, always imagining insults. Polly was curt and business-like. The two departments were for ever at war, and Paul was always finding Fanny in tears. Then he was made the recipient of all her woes, and he had to plead her cause with Polly.

So the time went along happily enough. The factory had a homely feel. No one was rushed or driven. Paul always enjoyed it when the work got faster, towards post-time, and all the men united in labour. He liked to watch his fellow clerks at work. The man was the work and the work was the man, one thing, for the time being. It was different with the girls. The real woman never seemed to be there at the task, but as if left out, waiting.

From the train going home at night he used to watch the lights of the town, sprinkled thick on the hills, fusing together in a blaze in the valleys. He felt rich in life and happy. Drawing farther off, there was a patch of lights at Bulwell like myriad petals shaken to the ground from the shed stars; and beyond was the red glare of the furnaces, playing like hot breath on the clouds.

He had to walk two and more miles from Keston home, up two long hills, down two short hills. He was often tired, and he counted the lamps climbing the hill above him, how many more to pass. And from the hilltop, on pitch-dark nights, he looked round on the villages five or six miles away, that shone like swarms of glittering living things, almost a heaven against his feet. Marlpool and Heanor scattered the far-off darkness with brilliance. And occasionally the black valley space between was traced, violated by a great train rushing south to London or north to Scotland. The trains roared by like projectiles level on the darkness, fuming and burning, making the valley clang with their passage. They were gone, and the lights of the towns and villages glittered in silence.

And then he came to the corner at home, which faced the other side of the night. The ash-tree seemed a friend now.

His mother rose with gladness as he entered. He put his eight shillings proudly on the table.

'It'll help, mother?' he asked wistfully.

'There's precious little left,' she answered, 'after your ticket and dinners and such are taken off.'

Then he told her the budget of the day. His life-story, like an Arabian Nights, was told night after night to his mother. It was almost as if it were her own life.

CHAPTER 6

Death in the Family

ARTHUR MOREL was growing up. He was a quick, careless, impulsive boy, a good deal like his father. He hated study, made a great moan if he had to work, and escaped as soon as possible to his sport again.

In appearance he remained the flower of the family, being well made, graceful, and full of life. His dark brown hair and fresh colouring, and his exquisite dark blue eyes shaded with long lashes, together with his generous manner and fiery temper, made him a favourite. But as he grew older his temper became uncertain. He flew into rages over nothing, seemed unbearably raw and irritable.

His mother, whom he loved, wearied of him sometimes. He thought only of himself. When he wanted amusement, all that stood in his way he hated, even if it were she. When he was in trouble he moaned to her ceaselessly.

'Goodness, boy!' she said, when he groaned about a master who, he said, hated him, 'if you don't like it, alter it, and if you can't alter it, put up with it.'

And his father, whom he had loved and who had worshipped him, he came to detest. As he grew older Morel fell into a slow ruin. His body, which had been beautiful in movement and in being, shrank, did not seem to ripen with the years, but to get mean and rather despicable. There came over him a look of meanness and of paltriness. And when the mean-looking elderly man bullied or ordered the boy about, Arthur was furious. Moreover, Morel's manners got worse and worse, his habits somewhat disgusting. When the children were growing up and in the crucial stage of adolescence, the father was like some ugly irritant to their souls. His manners in the house were the same as he used among the colliers down pit.

'Dirty nuisance!' Arthur would cry, jumping up and going straight out of the house when his father disgusted him. And Morel persisted the more because his children hated it. He seemed to take a kind of satisfaction in disgusting them, and driving them nearly mad, while they were so irritably sensitive at the age of fourteen or fifteen. So that Arthur, who was growing up when his father was degenerate and elderly, hated him worst of all.

Then, sometimes, the father would seem to feel the contemptuous hatred of his children.

'There's not a man tries harder for his family!' he would shout. 'He does his best for them, and then gets treated like a dog. But I'm not going to stand it, I tell you!'

But for the threat and the fact that he did not try so hard as he imagined, they would have felt sorry. As it was, the battle now went on nearly all between father and children, he persisting in his dirty and disgusting ways, just to assert his independence. They loathed him.

Arthur was so inflamed and irritable at last, that when he won a scholarship for the Grammar School in Nottingham, his mother decided to let him live in town, with one of her sisters, and only come home at week-ends.

Annie was still a junior teacher in the Board-school, earning about four shillings a week. But soon she would have fifteen shillings, since she had passed her examination, and there would be financial peace in the house.

Mrs Morel clung now to Paul. He was quiet and not brilliant. But still he stuck to his painting, and still he stuck to his mother. Everything he did was for her. She waited for his coming home in the evening, and then she unburdened herself of all she had pondered, or of all that had occurred to her during the day. He sat and listened with his earnestness. The two shared lives.

William was engaged now to his brunette, and had bought her an engagement ring that cost eight guineas. The children gasped at such a fabulous price.

'Eight guineas!' said Morel. 'More fool him! If he'd gen me some on't, it 'ud ha' looked better on 'im.'

'Given *you* some of it!' cried Mrs Morel. 'Why give *you* some of it!'

She remembered *he* had bought no engagement ring at all, and she preferred William, who was not mean, if he were foolish. But now the young man talked only of the dances to which he went with his betrothed, and the different resplendent clothes she wore; or he told his mother with glee how they went to the theatre like great swells.

He wanted to bring the girl home. Mrs Morel said she should come at the Christmas. This time William arrived with a lady, but with no presents. Mrs Morel had prepared supper. Hearing footsteps, she rose and went to the door. William entered.

'Hello, mother!' he kissed her hastily, then stood aside to present a tall, handsome girl, who was wearing a costume of fine black-and-white check, and furs.

'Here's Gyp!'

Miss Western held out her hand and showed her teeth in a small smile.

'Oh, how do you do, Mrs Morel!' she exclaimed.

'I am afraid you will be hungry,' said Mrs Morel.

'Oh no, we had dinner in the train. Have you got my gloves Chubby?'

William Morel, big and raw-boned, looked at her quickly.

'How should I?' he said.

'Then I've lost them. Don't be cross with me.'

A frown went over his face, but he said nothing. She glanced round the kitchen. It was small and curious to her, with its glittering kissing-bunch, its evergreens behind the pictures, its wooden chairs and little deal table. At that moment Morel came in.

'Hello, dad!'

'Hello, my son! Tha's let on me!'

The two shook hands, and William presented the lady. She gave the same smile that showed her teeth.

'How do you do, Mr Morel?'

Morel bowed obsequiously.

'I'm very well, and I hope so are you. You must make yourself very welcome.'

'Oh, thank you,' she replied, rather amused.

'You will like to go upstairs,' said Mrs Morel.

'If you don't mind; but not if it is any trouble to you.'

'It is no trouble. Annie will take you. Walter, carry up this box.'

'And don't be an hour dressing yourself up,' said William to his betrothed.

Annie took a brass candlestick, and, too shy almost to speak, preceded the young lady to the front bedroom, which Mr and Mrs Morel had vacated for her. It, too, was small and cold by candle-light. The colliers' wives only lit fires in bedrooms in case of extreme illness.

'Shall I unstrap the box?' asked Annie.

'Oh, thank you very much!'

Annie played the part of maid, then went downstairs for hot water.

'I think she's rather tired, mother,' said William. 'It's a beastly journey, and we had such a rush.'

'Is there anything I can give her?' asked Mrs Morel.

'Oh no, she'll be all right.'

But there was a chill in the atmosphere. After half an hour Miss Western came down, having put on a purplish coloured dress, very fine for the collier's kitchen.

'I told you you'd no need to change,' said William to her.

'Oh, Chubby!' Then she turned with that sweetish smile to Mrs Morel. 'Don't you think he's always grumbling, Mrs Morel?'

'Is he?' said Mrs Morel. 'That's not very nice of him.'

'It isn't, really!'

'You are cold,' said the mother. 'Won't you come near the fire?'

Morel jumped out of his armchair.

'Come and sit you here!' he cried. 'Come and sit you here!'

'No, dad, keep your own chair. Sit on the sofa, Gyp,' said William.

'No, no!' cried Morel. 'This cheer's warmest. Come and sit here, Miss Wesson.'

'Thank you so much,' said the girl, seating herself in the collier's armchair, the place of honour. She shivered, feeling the warmth of the kitchen penetrate her.

'Fetch me a hanky, Chubby dear!' she said, putting up her mouth to him, and using the same intimate tone as if they were alone; which made the rest of the family feel as if they ought not to be present. The young lady evidently did not realise them as people: they were creatures to her for the present. William winced.

In such a household, in Streatham, Miss Western would have been a lady condescending to her inferiors. These people were, to her, certainly clownish – in short, the working classes. How was she to adjust herself?

'I'll go,' said Annie.

Miss Western took no notice, as if a servant had spoken. But when the girl came downstairs again with the handkerchief, she said, 'Oh, thank you!' in a gracious way.

She sat and talked about the dinner on the train, which had been so poor; about London, about dances. She was really very nervous, and chattered from fear. Morel sat all the time smoking his thick twist tobacco, watching her, and listening to her glib

London speech, as he puffed. Mrs Morel, dressed up in her best black silk blouse, answered quietly and rather briefly. The three children sat round in silence and admiration. Miss Western was the princess. Everything of the best was got out for her: the best cups, the best spoons, the best tablecloth, the best coffee-jug. The children thought she must find it quite grand. She felt strange, not able to realise the people, not knowing how to treat them. William joked, and was slightly uncomfortable.

At about ten o'clock he said to her:

'Aren't you tired, Gyp?'

'Rather, Chubby,' she answered, at once in the intimate tones and putting her head slightly on one side.

'I'll light her the candle, mother,' he said.

'Very well,' replied the mother.

Miss Western stood up, held out her hand to Mrs Morel.

'Good-night, Mrs Morel,' she said.

Paul sat at the boiler, letting the water run from the tap into a stone beer-bottle. Annie swathed the bottle in an old flannel pit-singlet, and kissed her mother good-night. She was to share the room with the lady, because the house was full.

'You wait a minute,' said Mrs Morel to Annie. And Annie sat nursing the hot-water bottle. Miss Western shook hands all round, to everybody's discomfort, and took her departure, preceded by William. In five minutes he was downstairs again. His heart was rather sore; he did not know why. He talked very little till everybody had gone to bed, but himself and his mother. Then he stood with his legs apart, in his old attitude on the hearthrug, and said hesitatingly:

Well, mother?'

'Well, my son?'

She sat in the rocking-chair, feeling somehow hurt and humiliated, for his sake.

'Do you like her?'

'Yes,' came the slow answer.

'She's shy yet, mother. She's not used to it. It's different from her aunt's house, you know.'

'Of course it is, my boy; and she must find it difficult.'

'She does.' Then he frowned swiftly. 'If only she wouldn't put on her *blessed* airs!'

'It's only her first awkwardness, my boy. She'll be all right.'

'That's it, mother,' he replied gratefully. But his brow was gloomy. 'You know, she's not like you, mother. She's not serious, and she can't think.'

'She's young, my boy.'

'Yes; and she's had no sort of show. Her mother died when she was a child. Since then she's lived with her aunt, whom she can't bear. And her father was a rake. She's had no love.'

'No! Well, you must make up to her.'

'And so – you have to forgive her a lot of things.'

'*What* do you have to forgive her, my boy?'

'I dunno. When she seems shallow, you have to remember she's never had anybody to bring her deeper side out. And she's *fearfully* fond of me.'

'Anybody can see that.'

'But you know, mother – she's – she's different from us. Those sort of people, like those she lives amongst, they don't seem to have the same principles.'

'You mustn't judge too hastily,' said Mrs Morel.

But he seemed uneasy within himself.

In the morning, however, he was up singing and larking round the house.

'Hello!' he called, sitting on the stairs. 'Are you getting up?'

'Yes,' her voice called faintly.

'Merry Christmas!' he shouted to her.

Her laugh, pretty and tinkling, was heard in the bedroom. She did not come down in half an hour.

'Was she *really* getting up when she said she was?' he asked of Annie.

'Yes, she was,' replied Annie.

He waited awhile, then went to the stairs again.

'Happy New Year,' he called.

'Thank you, Chubby dear!' came the laughing voice, far away.

'Buck up!' he implored.

It was nearly an hour, and still he was waiting for her. Morel, who always rose before six, looked at the clock.

'Well, it's a winder!' he exclaimed.

The family had breakfasted, all but William. He went to the foot of the stairs.

'Shall I have to send you an Easter egg up there?' he called, rather crossly. She only laughed. The family expected, after that time of preparation, something like magic. At last she came, looking very nice in a blouse and skirt.

'Have you *really* been all this time getting ready?' he asked.

'Chubby dear! That question is not permitted, is it, Mrs Morel?'

She played the grand lady at first. When she went with William to chapel, he in his frock coat and silk hat, she in her furs and London-made costume, Paul and Arthur and Annie expected everybody to bow to the ground in admiration. And Morel, standing in his Sunday suit at the end of the road, watching the gallant pair go, felt he was the father of princes and princesses.

And yet she was not so grand. For a year now she had been a sort of secretary or clerk in a London office. But while she was with the Morels she queened it. She sat and let Annie or Paul wait on her as if they were her servants. She treated Mrs Morel with a certain glibness and Morel with patronage. But after a day or so she began to change her tune.

William always wanted Paul or Annie to go along with them on their walks. It was so much more interesting. And Paul really *did* admire 'Gypsy' whole-heartedly; in fact, his mother scarcely forgave the boy for the adulation with which he treated the girl.

On the second day, when Lily said, 'Oh, Annie, do you know where I left my muff?' William replied:

'You know it is in your bedroom. Why do you ask Annie?'

And Lily went upstairs with a cross, shut mouth. But it angered the young man that she made a servant of his sister.

On the third evening William and Lily were sitting together in the parlour by the fire in the dark. At a quarter to eleven Mrs Morel was heard raking the fire. William came out to the kitchen, followed by his beloved.

'Is it as late as that, mother?' he said. She had been sitting alone.

'It is not late, my boy, but it is as late as I usually sit up.'

'Won't you go to bed, then?' he asked.

'And leave you two? No, my boy, I don't believe in it.'

'Can't you trust us, mother?'

'Whether I can or not, I won't do it. You can stay till eleven if you like, and I can read.'

'Go to bed, Gyp,' he said to his girl. 'We won't keep mater waiting.'

'"Annie has left the candle burning, Lily,' said Mrs Morel; 'I think you will see.'

'Yes, thank you. Good-night, Mrs Morel.'

William kissed his sweetheart at the foot of the stairs, and she went. He returned to the kitchen.

'Can't you trust us, mother?' he repeated, rather offended.

'My boy, I tell you I don't *believe* in leaving two young things like you alone downstairs when everyone else is in bed.'

And he was forced to take this answer. He kissed his mother good-night.

At Easter he came over alone. And then he discussed his sweetheart endlessly with his mother.

'You know, mother, when I'm away from her I don't care for her a bit. I shouldn't care if I never saw her again. But, then, when I'm with her in the evenings I am awfully fond of her.'

'It's a queer sort of love to marry on,' said Mrs Morel, 'if she holds you no more than that!'

'It is funny!' he exclaimed. It worried and perplexed him. 'But yet there's so much between us now I couldn't give her up.'

'You know best,' said Mrs Morel. 'But if it is as you say, I wouldn't call it *love* – at any rate, it doesn't look much like it.'

'Oh, I don't know, mother. She's an orphan, and – '

They never came to any sort of conclusion. He seemed puzzled and rather fretted. She was rather reserved. All his strength and money went in keeping this girl. He could scarcely afford to take his mother to Nottingham when he came over.

Paul's wages had been raised at Christmas to ten shillings, to his great joy. He was quite happy at Jordan's, but his health suffered from the long hours and the confinement. His mother, to whom he became more and more significant, thought how to help.

His half-day holiday was on Monday afternoon. On a Monday morning in May, as the two sat alone at breakfast, she said:

'I think it will be a fine day.'

He looked up in surprise. This meant something.

'You know Mr Leivers has gone to live on a new farm. Well, he asked me last week if I wouldn't go and see Mrs Leivers, and I promised to bring you on Monday if it's fine. Shall we go?'

'I say, little woman, how lovely!' he cried. 'And we'll go this afternoon?'

Paul hurried off to the station jubilant. Down Derby Road was a cherry-tree that glistened. The old brick wall by the Statutes ground burned scarlet, spring was a very flame of green. And the steep swoop of highroad lay, in its cool morning dust, splendid with patterns of sunshine and shadow, perfectly still. The trees sloped their great green shoulders proudly; and inside the warehouse all the morning, the boy had a vision of spring outside.

When he came home at dinner-time his mother was rather excited.

'Are we going?' he asked.

'When I'm ready,' she replied.

Presently he got up.

'Go and get dressed while I wash up,' he said.

She did so. He washed the pots, straightened, and then took her boots. They were quite clean. Mrs Morel was one of those naturally exquisite people who can walk in mud without dirtying their shoes. But Paul had to clean them for her. They were kid boots at eight shillings a pair. He, however, thought them the most dainty boots in the world, and he cleaned them with as much reverence as if they had been flowers.

Suddenly she appeared in the inner doorway rather shyly.

She had got a new cotton blouse on. Paul jumped up and went forward.

'Oh, my stars!' he exclaimed. 'What a bobby-dazzler!'

She sniffed in a little haughty way, and put her head up.

'It's not a bobby-dazzler at all!' she replied. 'It's very quiet.'

She walked forward, whilst he hovered round her.

'Well,' she asked, quite shy, but pretending to be high and mighty, 'do you like it?'

'Awfully! You *are* a fine little woman to go jaunting out with!'

He went and surveyed her from the back

'Well,' he said, 'if I was walking down the street behind you, I should say, "Doesn't that little person fancy herself!" '

'Well, she doesn't,' replied Mrs Morel. 'She's not sure it suits her.'

'Oh no! she wants to be in dirty black, looking as if she was wrapped in burnt paper. It *does* suit you, and *I* say you look nice.'

She sniffed in her little way, pleased, but pretending to know better.

'Well,' she said, 'it's cost me just three shillings. You couldn't have got it ready-made for that price, could you?'

'I should think you couldn't,' he replied.

'And, you know, it's good stuff.'

'Awfully pretty,' he said.

The blouse was white, with a little sprig of heliotrope and black.

'Too young for me, though, I'm afraid,' she said.

'Too young for you!' he exclaimed in disgust. 'Why don't you buy some false white hair and stick it on your head.'

'I s'll soon have no need,' she replied. 'I'm going white fast enough.' Well you've no business to,' he said. 'What do I want with a white haired mother?'

'I'm afraid you'll have to put up with one, my lad.,' she said rather strangely.

They set off in great style, she carrying the umbrella William had given her, because of the sun. Paul was considerably taller than she, though he was not big. He fancied himself.

On the fallow land the young wheat shone silkily. Minton pit waved its plumes of white steam, coughed, and rattled hoarsely.

'Now look at that!' said Mrs Morel. Mother and son stood on the road to watch. Along the ridge of the great pit-hill crawled a little group in silhouette against the sky, a horse, a small truck, and a man. They climbed the incline against the heavens. At the end the man tipped the waggon. There was an undue rattle as the waste fell down the sheer slope of the enormous bank.

'You sit a minute, mother,' he said, and she took a seat on a bank, whilst he sketched rapidly. She was silent whilst he worked, looking round at the afternoon the red cottages shining among their greenness.

'The world is a wonderful place,' she said, 'and wonderfully beautiful.'

'And so's the pit,' he said. 'Look how it heaps together, like something alive almost – a big creature that you don't know.'

'Yes,' she said. 'Perhaps!'

'And all the trucks standing waiting, like a string of beasts to be fed,' he said.

'And very thankful I am they *are* standing,' she said, 'for that means they'll turn middling time this week.'

'But I like the feel of men on things, while they're alive. There's a feel of men about trucks, because they've been handled with men's hands, all of them.'

'Yes,' said Mrs Morel.

They went along under the trees of the highroad. He was constantly informing her, but she was interested. They passed the end of Nethermere, that was tossing its sunshine like petals lightly in its lap. Then they turned on a private road, and in some trepidation approached a big Farm. A dog barked furiously. A woman came out to see.

'Is this the way to Willey Farm?' Mrs Morel asked.

Paul hung behind in terror of being sent back. But the woman was amiable, and directed them. The mother and son went through the wheat and oats, over a little bridge into a wild meadow. Peewits, with their white breasts glistening, wheeled and screamed about them. The lake was still and blue. High overhead a heron floated. Opposite, the wood heaped on the hill, green and still.

'It's a wild road, mother,' said Paul. 'Just like Canada.'

'Isn't it beautiful!' said Mrs Morel looking round.

'See that heron – see – see her legs?'

He directed his mother, what she must see and what not. And she was quite content.

'But now,' she said, 'which way? He told me through the wood.'

The wood, fenced and dark, lay on their left.

'I can feel a bit of a path this road,' said Paul. 'You've got town feet, somehow or other, you have.'

They found a little gate, and soon were in a broad green alley of the wood, with a new thicket of fir and pine on one hand, an old oak glade dipping down on the other. And among the oaks the bluebells stood in pools of azure, under the new green hazels, upon a pale fawn floor of oak-leaves. He found flowers for her.

'Here's a bit of new-mown hay,' he said; then, again, he brought her forget-me-nots. And again, his heart hurt with love, seeing her hand, used with work, holding the little bunch of flowers he gave her. She was perfectly happy.

But at the end of the riding was a fence to climb. Paul was over in a second.

'Come,' he said, 'let me help you.'

'No, go away. I will do it in my own way.'

He stood below with his hands up ready to help her. She climbed cautiously.

What a way to climb!' he exclaimed scornfully, when she was safely to earth again.

'Hateful stiles!' she cried.

'Duffer of a little woman,' he replied, 'who can't get over 'em.'

In front, along the edge of the wood, was a cluster of low red farm buildings. The two hastened forward. Flush with the wood was the apple orchard, where blossom was falling on the grindstone. The pond was deep under a hedge and overhanging oak-trees. Some cows stood in the shade. The farm and buildings, three sides of a quadrangle, embraced the sunshine towards the wood. It was very still.

Mother and son went into the small railed garden, where was a scent of red gillivers. By the open door were some floury loaves, put out to cool. A hen was just coming to peck them. Then, in the doorway suddenly appeared a girl in a dirty apron. She was about fourteen years old, had a rosy dark face, a bunch of short black curls, very fine and free, and dark eyes; shy, questioning, a little resentful of the strangers, she disappeared. In a minute another figure appeared, a small, frail woman, rosy, with great dark brown eyes.

'Oh!' she exclaimed, smiling with a little glow, 'you've come, then. I *am* glad to see you.' Her voice was intimate and rather sad.

The two women shook hands.

'Now are you sure we're not a bother to you?' said Mrs Morel. 'I know what a farming life is.'

'Oh no! We're only too thankful to see a new face, it's so lost up here.'

'I suppose so,' said Mrs Morel.

They were taken through into the parlour – a long, low room, with a great bunch of guelder-roses in the fireplace. There the women talked, whilst Paul went out to survey the land. He was in the garden smelling the gillivers and looking at the plants, when the girl came out quickly to the heap of coal which stood by the fence.

'I suppose these are cabbage-roses?' he said to her, pointing to the bushes along the fence.

She looked at him with startled, big brown eyes.

'I suppose they are cabbage-roses when they come out?' he said.

'I don't know,' she faltered. 'They're white with pink middles'

'Then they're maiden-blush.'

Miriam flushed. She had a beautiful warm colouring.

'I don't know,' she said.

'You don't have *much* in your garden,' he said.

'This is our first year here,' she answered, in a distant, rather superior way, drawing back and going indoors. He did not notice, but went his round of exploration. Presently his mother came out, and they went through the buildings. Paul was hugely delighted.

'And I suppose you have the fowls and calves and pigs to look after?' said Mrs Morel to Mrs Leivers.

'No,' replied the little woman. 'I can't find time to look after cattle, and I'm not used to it. It's as much as I can do to keep going in the house.'

'Well, I suppose it is,' said Mrs Morel.

Presently the girl came out.

'Tea is ready, mother,' she said in a musical, quiet voice.

'Oh, thank you, Miriam, then we'll come,' replied her mother, almost ingratiatingly. 'Would you *care* to have tea now, Mrs Morel?'

'Of course,' said Mrs Morel. 'Whenever it's ready.'

Paul and his mother and Mrs Leivers had tea together. Then they went out into the wood that was flooded with bluebells, while furry forget-me-nots were in the paths. The mother and son were in ecstasy together.

When they got back to the house, Mr Leivers and Edgar, the eldest son, were in the kitchen. Edgar was about eighteen. Then Geoffrey and Maurice, big lads of twelve and thirteen, were in from school. Mr Leivers was a good-looking man in the prime of life, with a golden-brown moustache, and blue eyes screwed up against the weather.

The boys were condescending, but Paul scarcely observed it. They went round for eggs, scrambling into all sorts of places. As they were feeding the fowls Miriam came out. The boys took no notice of her. One hen, with her yellow chickens, was in a coop. Maurice took his hand full of corn and let the hen peck from it.

'Durst you do it?' he asked of Paul.

'Let's see,' said Paul.

He had a small hand, warm, and rather capable-looking. Miriam watched. He held the corn to the hen. The bird eyed it with her hard, bright eye, and suddenly made a peck into his hand. He started, and laughed. 'Rap, rap, rap!' went the bird's beak in his palm. He laughed again, and the other boys joined.

'She knocks you, and nips you, but she never hurts,' said Paul, when the last corn had gone.

'Now, Miriam,' said Maurice, 'you come an' 'ave a go.'

'No,' she cried, shrinking back.

'Ha! baby. The mardy-kid!' said her brothers.

'It doesn't hurt a bit,' said Paul. 'It only just nips rather nicely.'

No,' she still cried, shaking her black curls and shrinking.

'She doesn't,' said Geoffrey. 'She niver durst do anything except recite poitry.'

'Dursn't jump off a gate, dursn't tweedle, dursn't go on a slide, dursn't stop a girl hittin' her. She can do nowt but go about thinkin' herself somebody. "The Lady of the Lake.' Yah!' cried Maurice.

Miriam was crimson with shame and misery.

'I dare do more than you,' she cried. 'You're never anything but cowards and bullies.'

'Oh, cowards and bullies!' they repeated, mincingly, mocking her speech.

> 'Not such a clown shall anger me,
>   A boor is answered silently'

he quoted against her, shouting with laughter.

She went indoors. Paul went with the boys into the orchard, where they had rigged up a parallel bar. They did feats of strength. He was more agile than strong, but it served. He fingered a piece of appleblossom that hung low on a swinging bough.

'I wouldn't get the apple-blossom,' said Edgar, the eldest brother. 'There'll be no apples next year.'

'I wasn't going to get it,' replied Paul, going away.

The boys felt hostile to him; they were more interested in their own pursuits. He wandered back to the house to look for his mother. As he went round the back, he saw Miriam kneeling in front of the hen-coop, some maize in her hand, biting her lip, and crouching in an intense attitude. The hen was eyeing her wickedly. Very gingerly she put forward her hand. The hen bobbed for her. She drew back quickly with a cry, half of fear, half of chagrin.

'It won't hurt you,' said Paul.

She flushed crimson and started up.

'I only wanted to try,' she said in a low voice.

'See, it doesn't hurt,' he said, and, putting only two corns in his palm, he let the hen peck, peck, peck at his bare hand. 'It only makes you laugh,' he said.

She put her hand forward, and dragged it away, tried again, and started back with a cry. He frowned.

Why, I'd let her take corn from my face,' said Paul, 'only she bumps a bit. She's ever so neat. If she wasn't look how much ground she'd peck up every day.'

He waited grimly, and watched. At last Miriam let the bird peck from her hand. She gave a little cry – fear, and pain because of fear – rather pathetic. But she had done it, and she did it again.

'There, you see,' said the boy. 'It doesn't hurt, does it?'

She looked at him with dilated dark eyes.

'No,' she laughed, trembling.

Then she rose and went indoors. She seemed to be in some way resentful of the boy.

'He thinks I'm only a common girl,' she thought, and she wanted to prove she was a grand person like the 'Lady of the Lake.'

Paul found his mother ready to go home. She smiled on her son. He took the great bunch of flowers. Mr and Mrs Leivers walked down the fields with them. The hills were golden with evening; deep in the wood showed the darkening purple of bluebells. It was everywhere perfectly still, save for the rustling of leaves and birds.

'But it is a beautiful place,' said Mrs Morel.

'Yes,' answered Mr Leivers; 'it's a nice little place, if only it weren't for the rabbits. The pasture's bitten down to nothing. I dunno if ever I s'll get the rent off it.'

He clapped his hands, and the field broke into motion near the woods, brown rabbits hopping everywhere.

Would you believe it!' exclaimed Mrs Morel.

She and Paul went on alone together.

Wasn't it lovely, mother?' he said quietly.

A thin moon was coming out. His heart was full of happiness till it hurt. His mother had to chatter, because she, too, wanted to cry with happiness.

'Now *wouldn't* I help that man!' she said. '*Wouldn't* I see to the fowls and the young stock! And *I'd* learn to milk, and *I'd* talk with him, and *I'd* plan with him. My word, if I were his wife, the farm would be run, I know! But there, she hasn't the strength – she simply hasn't the strength. She ought never to have been burdened like it, you know. I'm sorry for her, and I'm sorry for him too. My word, if *I'd* had him, I shouldn't have thought him a bad husband! Not that she does either; and she's very lovable.'

William came home again with his sweetheart at the Whitsuntide. He had one week of his holidays then. It was beautiful weather. As a rule, William and Lily and Paul went out in the morning together for a walk. William did not talk to his beloved much, except to tell her things from his boyhood. Paul talked endlessly to both of them. They lay down, all three, in a meadow by Minton Church. On one side, by the Castle Farm, was a beautiful quivering screen of poplars. Hawthorn was dropping from the hedges; penny daisies and ragged robin were in the field, like laughter. William, a big fellow of twenty-three, thinner now and even a bit gaunt, lay back in the sunshine and dreamed, while she fingered with his hair. Paul went gathering the big daisies. She had taken off her hat; her hair was black as a horse's mane. Paul came back and threaded daisies in her jet-black hair – big spangles of white and yellow, and just a pink touch of ragged robin.

'Now you look like a young witch-woman,' the boy said to her. 'Doesn't she, William?'

Lily laughed. William opened his eyes and looked at her. In his gaze was a certain baffled look of misery and fierce appreciation.

'Has he made a sight of me?' she asked, laughing down on her lover.

'That he has!' said William, smiling.

He looked at her. Her beauty seemed to hurt him. He glanced at her flower-decked head and frowned.

'You look nice enough, if that's what you want to know,' he said.

And she walked without her hat. In a little while William recovered, and was rather tender to her. Coming to a bridge, he carved her initials and his in a heart.

L. L. W.
W.M.

She watched his strong, nervous hand, with its glistening hairs and freckles, as he carved, and she seemed fascinated by it.

All the time there was a feeling of sadness and warmth, and a certain tenderness in the house, whilst William and Lily were at home. But often he got irritable. She had brought, for an eight-days' stay, five dresses and six blouses.

'Oh, would you mind,' she said to Annie, 'washing me these two blouses, and these things?'

And Annie stood washing when William and Lily went out

the next morning. Mrs Morel was furious. And sometimes the young man, catching a glimpse of his sweetheart's attitude towards his sister, hated her.

On Sunday morning she looked very beautiful in a dress of foulard, silky and sweeping, and blue as a jay-bird's feather, and in a large cream hat covered with many roses, mostly crimson. Nobody could admire her enough. But in the evening, when she was going out, she asked again:

'Chubby, have you got my gloves?'

Which?' asked William.

'My new black *suede*.'

'No.'

There was a hunt. She had lost them.

'Look here, mother,' said William, 'that's the fourth pair she's lost since Christmas at five shillings a pair!'

'You only gave me *two* of them,' she remonstrated.

And in the evening, after supper, he stood on the hearthrug whilst she sat on the sofa, and he seemed to hate her. In the afternoon he had left her whilst he went to see some old friend. She had sat looking at a book. After supper William wanted to write a letter.

'Here is your book, Lily,' said Mrs Morel. 'Would you care to go on with it for a few minutes?'

'No, thank you,' said the girl. 'I will sit still.'

'But it is so dull.'

William scribbled irritably at a great rate. As he sealed the envelope he said:

'Read a book! Why, she's never read a book in her life.'

'Oh, go along!' said Mrs Morel, cross with the exaggeration.

'It's true, mother – she hasn't,' he cried, jumping up and taking his old position on the hearthrug. 'She's never read a book in her life.'

"Er's like me,' chimed in Morel. "Er canna see what there is i' books, ter sit borin' your nose in '*em* for, nor more can I.'

'But you shouldn't saw these things,' said Mrs Morel to her son.

'But it's true, mother – she *can't* read. What did you give her?'

Well, I gave her a lime thing of Annie Swan's. Nobody wants to read dry stuff on Sunday afternoon.'

Well, I'll bet she didn't read ten lines of it.'

'You are mistaken,' said his mother.

All the time Lily sat miserably on the sofa. He turned to her swiftly.

'*Did* you read any?' he asked.

'Yes, I did,' she replied.

'How much?'

'I don't know how many pages.'

'Tell me *one thing* you read.'

She could not.

She never got beyond the second page. He read a great deal, and had a quick, active intelligence. She could understand nothing but lovemaking and chatter. He was accustomed to having all his thoughts sifted through his mother's mind; so, when he wanted companionship, and was asked in reply to be the billing and twittering lover, he hated his betrothed.

'You know, mother,' he said, when he was alone with her at night, 'she's no idea of money, she's so wessel-brained[1] When she's paid, she'll suddenly buy such rot as *marrons glacés*[2] and then *I* have to buy her season-ticket, and her extras, even her underclothing. And she wants to get married, and I think myself we might as well get married next year. But at this rate – '

'A fine mess of a marriage it would be,' replied his mother. 'I should consider it again, my boy.'

'Oh, well, I've gone too far to break off now,' he said, 'and so I shall get married as soon as I can.'

1 hare-brained.
2 (Fr.) sugar-coated chestnuts.

'Very well, my boy. If you will, you will, and there's no stopping you; but I tell you, I can't sleep when I think about it.'

'Oh, she'll be all right, mother. We shall manage.'

'And she lets you buy her underclothing?' asked the mother.

'Well,' he began apologetically,' she didn't ask me; but one morning – and it *was* cold – I found her on the station shivering, not able to keep still; so I asked her if she was well wrapped up. She said: "I think so." So I said: "Have you got warm underthings on?" And she said: "No, they were cotton." I asked her why on earth she hadn't got something thicker on in weather like that, and she said because she *had* nothing. And there she is – a bronchial subject! I *had* to take her and get some warm things. Well, mother, I shouldn't mind the money if we had any. And, you know, she *ought* to keep enough to pay for her season-ticket; but no, she comes to me about that, and I have to find the money.'

'It's a poor lookout,' said Mrs Morel bitterly.

He was pale, and his rugged face, that used to be so perfectly careless and laughing, was stamped with conflict and despair.

'But I can't give her up now; it's gone too far,' he said. 'And, besides, for *some* things I couldn't do without her.'

'My boy, remember you're taking your life in your hands,' said Mrs Morel. '*Nothing* is as bad as a marriage that's a hopeless failure. Mine was bad enough, God knows, and ought to teach you something; but it might have been worse by a long chalk'

He leaned with his back against the side of the chimney-piece, his hands in his pockets. He was a big, raw-boned man, who looked as if he would go to the world's end if he wanted to. But she saw the despair on his face.

'I couldn't give her up now,' he said.

Well,' she said, 'remember there are worse wrongs than breaking off an engagement.'

'I can't give her up *now,'* he said.

The clock ticked on; mother and son remained in silence, a conflict between them; but he would saw no more. At last she said:

Well, go to bed, my son. You'll feel better in the morning, and perhaps you'll know better.'

He kissed her, and went. She raked the fire. Her heart was heavy now as it had never been. Before, with her husband, things had seemed to be breaking down in her, but they did not destroy her power to live. Now her soul felt lamed in itself. It was her hope that was struck.

And so often William manifested the same hatred towards his betrothed. On the last evening at home he was railing against her.

Well,' he said, 'if you don't believe me, what she's like, would you believe she has been confirmed three times?'

'Nonsense!' laughed Mrs Morel.

'Nonsense or not, she has! That's what confirmation means for her – a bit of a theatrical show where she can cut a figure.'

'I haven't, Mrs Morel!' cried the girl – 'I haven't! it is not true!'

What!' he cried, flashing round on her. 'Once in Bromley, once in Beckenham, and once somewhere else.'

'Nowhere else!' she said, in tears – 'nowhere else!'

'It *was!* And if it wasn't, why were you confirmed *twice?*'

'Once I was only fourteen, Mrs Morel,' she pleaded, tears in her eyes. 'Yes,' said Mrs Morel; 'I can quite understand it, child take no notice of him. You ought to be ashamed, William, saying such things.'

'But it's true. She's religious – she had blue velvet Prayer-Books – and she's not as much religion, or anything else, in her than that table-leg. Gets confirmed three times for show, to show herself off, and that's how she is in *everything – everything!*'

The girl sat on the sofa, crying. She was not strong.

'As for *love!*' he cried, 'you might as well ask a fly to love you! It'll love settling on you – '

'Now, say no more,' commanded Mrs Morel. 'If you want to say these things, you must find another place than this. I am ashamed of you, William! Why don't you be more manly. To do nothing but find fault with a girl, and then pretend you're engaged to her!'

Mrs Morel subsided in wrath and indignation.

William was silent, and later he repented, kissed and comforted the girl. Yet it was true, what he had said. He hated her.

When they were going away, Mrs Morel accompanied them as far as Nottingham. It was a long way to Keston station.

'You know, mother,' he said to her, 'Gyp's shallow. Nothing goes deep with her.'

William, I *wish* you wouldn't say these things,' said Mrs Morel, very uncomfortable for the girl who walked beside her.

'But it doesn't, mother. She's very much in love with me *now,* but if I died she'd have forgotten me in three months.'

Mrs Morel was afraid. Her heart beat furiously, hearing the quiet bitterness of her son's last speech.

'How do you know?' she replied. 'You *don't* know, and therefore you've no right to say such a thing.'

'He's always saying these things!' cried the girl.

'In three months after I was buried you'd have somebody else, and I should be forgotten,' he said. 'And that's your love!'

Mrs Morel saw them into the train in Nottingham, then she returned home.

'There's one comfort,' she said to Paul – 'he'll never have any money to marry on, that I *am* sure of. And so she'll save him that way.'

So she took cheer. Matters were not yet very desperate. She firmly believed William would never marry his Gypsy. She waited, and she kept Paul near to her.

All summer long William's letters had a feverish tone; he

seemed unnatural and intense. Sometimes he was exaggeratedly jolly, usually he was flat and bitter in his letter.

'Ay,' his mother said, 'I'm afraid he's ruining himself against that creature, who isn't worthy of his love – no, no more than a rag doll.'

He wanted to come home. The midsummer holiday was gone; it was a long while to Christmas. He wrote in wild excitement, saved he could come for Saturday and Sunday at Goose Fair, the first week in October.

'You are not well, my boy,' said his mother, when she saw him.

She was almost in tears at having him to herself again.

'No, I've not been well,' he said. 'I've seemed to have a dragging cold all the last month, but it's going, I think.'

It was sunny October weather. He seemed wild with joy, like a schoolboy escaped; then again he was silent and reserved. He was more gaunt than ever, and there was a haggard look in his eyes.

'You are doing too much,' said his mother to him.

He was doing extra work, trying to make some money to marry on, he said. He only talked to his mother once on the Saturday night, then he was sad and tender about his beloved.

'And yet, you know, mother, for all that, if I died she'd be broken-hearted for two months, and then she'd start to forget me. You'd see, she'd never come home here to look at my grave, not even once.'

'Why, William,' said his mother, 'you're not going to die, so why talk about it?'

'But whether or not – ' he replied.

'And she can't help it. She is like that, and if you choose her – well, you can't grumble,' said his mother.

On the Sunday morning, as he was putting his collar on:

'Look,' he said to his mother, holding up his chin, 'what a rash my collar's made under my chin!'

Just at the junction of chin and throat was a big red inflammation.

'It ought not to do that,' said his mother. 'Here, put a bit of this soothing ointment on. You should wear different collars.'

He went away on Sunday midnight, seeming better and more solid for his two days at home.

On Tuesday morning came a telegram from London that he was ill. Mrs Morel got off her knees from washing the floor, read the telegram, called a neighbour, went to her landlady and borrowed a sovereign, put on her things, and set off. She hurried to Keston, caught an express for London in Nottingham. She had to wait in Nottingham nearly an hour. A small figure in her black bonnet, she was anxiously asking the porters if they knew how to get to Elmers End. The journey was three hours. She sat in her corner in a kind of stupor, never moving. At King's Cross still no one could tell her how to get to Elmers End. Carrying her string bag, that contained her nightdress, comb and brush, she went from person to person. At last they sent her underground to Cannon Street.

It was six o'clock when she arrived at William's lodging. The blinds were not down.

'How is he?' she asked.

'No better,' said the landlady.

She followed the woman upstairs. William lay on the bed, with bloodshot eyes, his face rather discoloured. The clothes were tossed about, there was no fire in the room, a glass of milk stood on the stand at his bedside. No one had been with him.

'Why, my son!' said the mother bravely.

He did not answer. He looked at her, but did not see her. Then he began to say, in a dull voice, as if repeating a letter from dictation:

'Owing to a leakage in the hold of this vessel, the sugar had set, and become converted into rock. It needed hacking – '

He was quite unconscious. It had been his business to examine some such cargo of sugar in the Port of London.

'How long has he been like this?' the mother asked the landlady.

'He got home at six o'clock on Monday morning, and he seemed to sleep all day; then in the night we heard him talking, and this morning he asked for you. So I wired, and we fetched the doctor.'

Will you have a fire made?'

Mrs Morel tried to soothe her son, to keep him still.

The doctor came. It was pneumonia, and, he said, a peculiar erysipelas*, which had started under the chin where the collar chafed, and was spreading over the face. He hoped it would not get to the brain.

Mrs Morel settled down to nurse. She prayed for William, prayed that he would recognise her. But the young man's face grew more discoloured. In the night she struggled with him. He raved, and raved, and would not come to consciousness. At two o'clock, in a dreadful paroxysm, he died.

Mrs Morel sat perfectly still for an hour in the lodging bedroom; then she roused the household.

At six o'clock, with the aid of the charwoman, she laid him out; then she went round the dreary London village to the registrar and the doctor.

At nine o'clock to the cottage on Scargill Street came another wire:

William died last night. Let father come, bring money.'

Annie, Paul, and Arthur were at home; Mr Morel was gone to work. The three children said not a word. Annie began to whimper with fear; Paul set off for his father.

It was a beautiful day. At Brinsley pit the white steam melted slowly in the sunshine of a soft blue sky; the wheels of the headstocks twinkled high up; the screen, shuffling its coal into the trucks, made a busy noise.

'I want my father; he's got to go to London,' said the boy to the first man he met on the bank.

'Tha wants Walter Morel? Go in theer an' tell Joe Ward.'

* an infectious skin disease.

Paul went into the little top office.

'I want my father; he's got to go to London.'

'Thy feyther? Is he down? What's his name?'

'Mr Morel.'

What, Walter? Is owt amiss?'

'He's got to go to London.'

The man went to the telephone and rang up the bottom office.

Walter Morel's wanted. Number 42, Hard. Summat's amiss; there's his lad here.'

Then he turned round to Paul.

'He'll be up in a few minutes,' he said.

Paul wandered out to the pit-top. He watched the chair come up, with its waggon of coal. The great iron cage sank back on its rest, a full carfle* was hauled off, an empty tram run on to the chair, a bell ting'ed somewhere, the chair heaved, then dropped like a stone.

Paul did not realise William was dead; it was impossible, with such a bustle going on. The puller-off swung the small truck on to the turntable, another man ran with it along the bank down the curving lines.

'And William is dead and my mother's in London, and what will she be doing?' the boy asked himself, as if it were a conundrum.

He watched, chair after chair come up, and still no father. At last, standing beside a waggon, a man's form! The chair sank on its rests, Morel stepped off. He was slightly lame from on accident.

'Is it thee, Paul? Is 'e worse?'

'You've got to go to London.'

The two walked off the pit-bank, where men were watching curiously. As they came out and went along the railway, with the sunny autumn field on one side and a wall of trucks on the other, Morel said in a frightened voice:

"E's niver gone, child?'

---

* a coal wagon.

'Yes.'

'When wor't?'

The miner's voice was terrified.

'Last night. We had a telegram from my mother.'

Morel walked on a few strides, then leaned up against a truck side, his hand over his eyes. He was not crying. Paul stood looking round, waiting. On the weighing-machine a truck trundled slowly. Paul saw everything, except his father leaning against the truck as if he were tired.

Morel had only once before been to London. He set off, scored and peaked, to help his wife. That was on Tuesday. The children were left alone in the house. Paul went to work, Arthur went to school, and Annie had in a friend to be with her.

On Saturday night, as Paul was turning the corner, coming home from Keston, he saw his mother and father, who had come to Sethley Bridge Station. They were walking in silence in the dark, tired, straggling apart. The boy waited.

'Mother!' he said, in the darkness.

Mrs Morel's small figure seemed not to observe. He spoke again.

'Paul!' she said, uninterestedly.

She let him kiss her, but she seemed unaware of him.

In the house she was the same – small, white, and mute. She noticed nothing, she said nothing, only:

'The coffin will be here tonight, Walter. You'd better see about some help.' Then, turning to the children: 'We're bringing him home.'

Then she relapsed into the same mute looking into space, her hands folded on her lap. Paul, looking at her, felt he could not breathe. The house was dead silent.

'I went to work, mother,' he said plaintively.

'Did you?' she answered, dully.

After half an hour Morel, troubled and bewildered, came in again.

'Wheer s'll we ha'e him when he *does* come?' he asked his wife.

'In the front-room.'

'Then I'd better shift th' table?'

'Yes.'

'An' ha'e him across th' chairs?'

'You know there – Yes, I suppose so;'

Morel and Paul went, with a candle, into the parlour. There was no gas there. The father unscrewed the top of the big mahogany oval table, and cleared the middle of the room; then he arranged six chairs opposite each other, so that the coffin could stand on their beds.

'You niver seed such a length as he is!' said the miner, and watching anxiously as he worked.

Paul went to the bay window and looked out. The ash-tree stood monstrous and black in front of the wide darkness.

It was a faintly luminous night. Paul went back to his mother.

At ten o'clock Morel called:

'He's here!'

Everyone started. There was a noise of unbarring and unlocking the front door, which opened straight from the night into the room.

'Bring another candle,' called Morel.

Annie and Arthur went. Paul followed with his mother. He stood with his arm round her waist in the inner doorway. Down the middle of the cleared room waited six chairs, face to face. In the window, against the lace curtains, Arthur held up one candle, and by the open door, against the night, Annie stood leaning forward, her brass candlestick glittering.

There was the noise of wheels. Outside in the darkness of the street below Paul could see horses and a black vehicle, one lamp, and a few pale faces; then some men, miners, all in their shirt-sleeves, seemed to struggle in the obscurity. Presently two men appeared, bowed beneath a great weight. It was Morel and his neighbour.

'Steady!' called Morel, out of breath.

He and his fellow mounted the steep garden step, heaved into the candle-light with their gleaming coffin-end. Limbs of other men were seen struggling behind. Morel and Burns, in front, staggered, the great dark weight swayed.

'Steady, steady!' cried Morel, as if in pain.

All the six bearers were up in the small garden, holding the great coffin aloft. There were three more steps to the door. The yellow lamp of the carriage shone alone down in the black road.

'Now then!' said Morel.

The coffin swayed, the men began to mount the three steps with their load. Annie's candle flickered, and she whimpered as the first men appeared, and the limbs and bowed heads of six men struggled to climb into the room, bearing the coffin that rode like sorrow on their living flesh.

'Oh, my son – my son!' Mrs Morel sang softly, and each time the coffin swung to the unequal climbing of the men: 'Oh, my son – my son – my son!'

'Mother!' Paul whimpered, his hand round her waist. 'Mother!'

She did not hear.

'Oh, my son – my son!' she repeated.

Paul saw drops of sweat fall from his father's brow. Six men were in the room – six coatless men, with yielding, struggling limbs, filling the room and knocking against the furniture. The coffin veered, and was gently lowered on to the chairs. The sweat fell from Morel's face on its boards.

'My word, he's a weight!' said a man, and the five miners sighed, bowed, and, trembling with the struggle, descended the steps again, closing the door behind them.

The family was alone in the parlour with the great polished box. William, when laid out, was six feet four inches long. Like a monument lay the bright brown, ponderous coffin. Paul thought it would never be got out of the room again. His mother was stroking the polished wood.

They buried him on the Monday in the little cemetery on the hillside that looks over the fields at the big church and the houses. It was sunny, and the white chrysanthemums frilled themselves in the warmth.

Mrs Morel could not be persuaded, after this, to talk and take her old bright interest in life. She remained shut off. All the way home in the train she had said to herself: 'If only it could have been me!'

When Paul came home at night he found his mother sitting, her day's work done, with hands folded in her lap upon her coarse apron. She always used to have changed her dress and put on a black apron, before. Now Annie set his supper, and his mother sat looking blankly in front of her, her mouth shut tight. Then he beat his brains for news to tell her.

'Mother, Miss Jordan was down today, and she said my sketch of a colliery at work was beautiful.'

But Mrs Morel took no notice. Night after night he forced himself to tell her things, although she did not listen. It drove him almost insane to have her thus. At last:

What's a-matter, mother?' he asked.

She did not hear.

What's a-matter?' he persisted. 'Mother, what's a-matter?'

'You know what's the matter,' she said irritably, turning away.

The lad – he was sixteen years old – went to bed drearily. He was cut off and wretched through October, November, and December. His mother tried, but she could not rouse herself. She could only brood on her dead son; he had been let to die so cruelly.

At last, on December 23, with his five shillings Christmas-box in his pocket, Paul wandered blindly home. His mother looked at him, and her heart stood still.

What's the matter?' she asked.

'I'm badly, mother!' he replied. 'Mr Jordan gave me five shillings for a Christmas-box!'

He handed it to her with trembling hands. She put it on the table.

'You aren't glad!' he reproached her; but he trembled violently.

Where hurts you?' she said, unbuttoning his overcoat.

It was the old question.

'I feel badly, mother.'

She undressed him and put him to bed. He had pneumonia dangerously, the doctor said.

'Might he never have had it if I'd kept him at home, not let him go to Nottingham?' was one of the first things she asked.

'He might not have been so bad,' said the doctor.

Mrs Morel stood condemned on her own ground.

'I should have watched the living, not the dead,' she told herself.

Paul was very ill. His mother lay in bed at nights with him; they could not afford a nurse. He grew worse, and the crisis approached. One night he tossed into consciousness in the ghastly, sickly feeling of dissolution, when all the cells in the body seem in intense irritable to be breaking down, and consciousness makes a last flare of struggle, like madness.

'I s'll die, mother!' he cried, heaving for breath on the pillow.

She lifted him up, crying in a small voice:

'Oh, my son – my son!'

That brought him to. He realised her. His whole will rose up and arrested him. He put his head on her breast, and took ease of her for love.

'For some things,' said his aunt, 'it was a good thing Paul was ill that Christmas. I believe it saved his mother.'

Paul was in bed for seven weeks. He got up white and fragile. His father had bought him a pot of scarlet and gold tulips. They used to flame in the window in the March sunshine as he sat on the sofa chattering to his mother. The two knitted together in perfect intimacy. Mrs Morel's life now rooted itself in Paul.

William had been a prophet. Mrs Morel had a little present and a letter from Lily at Christmas. Mrs Morel's sister had a letter at the New Year.

'I was at a ball last night. Some delightful people were there, and I enjoyed myself thoroughly,' said the letter. 'I had every dance – did not sit out one.'

Mrs Morel never heard any more of her.

Morel and his wife were gentle with each other for sometime after the death of their son. He would go into a kind of daze, staring wide-eyed and blank across the room. Then he got up suddenly and hurried out to the Three Spots, returning in his normal state. But never in his life would he go for a walk up Shepstone, past the office where his son had worked, and he always avoided the cemetery.

CHAPTER 7

Lad-and-Girl Love

PAUL HAD been many times up to Willey Farm during the autumn. He was friends with the two youngest boys. Edgar the eldest, would not condescend at first. And Miriam also refused to be approached. She was afraid of being set at nought, as by her own brothers. The girl was romantic in her soul. Everywhere was a Walter Scott heroine being loved by men with helmets or with plumes in their caps. She herself was something of a princess turned into a swine-girl in her own imagination. And she was afraid lest this boy, who, nevertheless, looked something like a Walter Scott hero, who could paint and speak French, and knew what algebra meant, and who went by train to Nottingham every day, might consider her simply as the swine-girl, unable to perceive the princess beneath; so she held aloof.

Her great companion was her mother. They were both brown-eyed and inclined to be mystical, such women as treasure religion inside them, breathe it in their nostrils, and see the whole of life in a mist thereof. So to Miriam, Christ and God made one great figure, which she loved tremblingly and passionately when a tremendous sunset burned out the western sky, and Ediths, and Lucys, and Rowenas, Brian de Bois Guilberts, Rob Roys, and Guy Mannerings, rustled the sunny leaves in the morning, or sat in her bedroom aloft, alone, when it snowed. That was life to her. For the rest, she drudged in the house, which work she would not have minded had not her clean red floor been mucked up immediately by the trampling farm-boots of her brothers. She madly wanted her little brother of four to let her swathe him and stifle him in her love; she went to church reverently, with bowed head, and quivered in anguish from the vulgarity of the other choir-girls and from the common-sounding voice of the curate; she fought with her brothers, whom she considered brutal louts; and she held not her father in too high esteem because he did not carry any mystical ideals cherished in his heart, but only wanted to have as easy a time as he could, and his meals when he was ready for them.

She hated her position as swine-girl. She wanted to be considered. She wanted to learn, thinking that if she could read, as Paul said he could read, 'Colomba,' or the 'Voyage outour de ma Chambre,' the world would have a different face for her and a deepened respect. She could not be princess by wealth or standing. So she was mad to have learning whereon to pride herself. For she was different from other folk, and must not be scooped up among the common fry. Learning was the only distinction to which she thought to aspire.

Her beauty – that of a shy, wild, quiveringly sensitive thing – seemed nothing to her. Even her soul, so strong for rhapsody, was not enough. She must have something to reinforce her pride, because she felt different from other people. Paul she eyed rather wistfully. On the whole, she scorned the male sex. But here was a new specimen, quick, light, graceful, who could be gentle and who could be sad, and who was clever, and who knew a lot, and who had a death in the family. The boy's poor morsel of learning exalted him almost sky-high in her esteem. Yet she tried hard to scorn him, because he would not see in her the princess but only the swine-girl. And he scarcely observed her.

Then he was so ill, and she felt he would be weak. Then she would be stronger than he. Then she could love him. If she could be mistress of him in his weakness, take care of him, if he could depend on her, if she could, as it were, have him in her arms, how she would love him!

As soon as the skies brightened and plum-blossom was out, Paul drove off in the milkman's heavy float up to Willey Farm. Mr Leivers shouted in a kindly fashion at the boy, then clicked to the horse as they climbed the hill slowly, in the freshness of the morning. White clouds went on their way, crowding to the back of the hills that were rousing in the springtime. The water of Nethermere lay below, very blue against the seared meadows and the thorn trees.

It was four arid a half miles' drive. Tiny buds on the hedges, vivid as copper-green, were opening into rosettes; and thrushes called, and blackbirds shrieked and scolded. It was a new, glamorous world.

Miriam, peeping through the kitchen window, saw the horse walk through the big white gate into the farmyard that was backed by the oakwood, still bare. Then a youth in a heavy overcoat climbed down. He put up his hands for the whip and the rug that the good-looking, ruddy farmer handed down to him.

Miriam appeared in the doorway. She was nearly sixteen, very beautiful, with her warm colouring, her gravity, her eyes dilating suddenly like an ecstasy.

'I say,' said Paul, turning shyly aside, 'your daffodils are nearly out. Isn't it early? But don't they look cold?'

'Cold!' said Miriam, in her musical, caressing voice.

'The green on their buds – ' and he faltered into silence timidly.

'Let me take the rug,' said Miriam over-gently.

'I can carry it,' he answered, rather injured. But he yielded it to her.

Then Mrs Leivers appeared.

'I'm sure you're tired and cold,' she said. 'Let me take your coat. It is heavy. You mustn't walk far in it.'

She helped him off with his coat. He was quite unused to such attention. She was almost smothered under its weight.

'Why, mother,' laughed the farmer as he passed through the kitchen, swinging the great milk-churns, 'you've got almost more than you can manage there.'

She beat up the sofa cushions for the youth.

The kitchen was very small and irregular. The farm had been originally a labourer's cottage. And the furniture was old and battered. But Paul loved it – loved the sock-bag that formed the hearthrug, and the funny little corner under the stairs, and the small window deep in the corner, through which, bending a little, he could see the plum-trees in the back-garden and the lovely round hills beyond.

Won't you lie down?' said Mrs Leivers.

'Oh no, I'm not tired,' he said. 'Isn't it lovely coming out, don't you think? I saw a sloe-bush in blossom and a lot of celandines. I'm glad it's sunny.'

'Can I give you anything to eat or to drink?'

'No, thank you.'

'How's your mother?'

'I think she's tired now. I think she's had too much to do. Perhaps in a little while she'll go to Skegness with me. Then she'll be able to rest. I s'll be glad if she can.'

'Yes,' replied Mrs Leivers. 'It's a wonder she isn't ill herself.'

Miriam was moving about preparing dinner. Paul watched everything that happened. His face was pale and thin, but his eyes were quick and bright with life as ever. He watched the strange, almost rhapsodic way in which the girl moved about, carrying a great stew-jar to the oven, or looking in the saucepan. The atmosphere was different from that of his own home, where everything seemed so ordinary. When Mr Leivers called loudly outside to the horse, that was reaching over to feed on the rose-bushes in the garden, the girl started, looked round with dark eyes, as if something had come breaking in on her world. There was a sense of silence inside the house and out. Miriam seemed as in some dreamy tale, a maiden in bondage, her spirit dreaming in a land for away and magical. And her discoloured old blue frock and her broken boots seemed only like the romantic rags of King Cophetua's beggar-maid.

She suddenly became aware of his keen blue eyes upon her, taking her all in. Instantly her broken boots and her frayed old frock hurt her. She resented his seeing everything. Even he knew that her stocking was not pulled up. She went into the scullery, blushing deeply. And afterwards her hands trembled slightly at her work. She nearly dropped all she handled. When her inside dream was shaken, her body quivered with trepidation. She resented that he saw so much.

Mrs Leivers sat for some time talking to the boy, although she was needed at her work. She was too polite to leave him. Presently she excused herself and rose. After a while she looked into the tin saucepan.

'Oh *dear,* Miriam,' she cried, 'these potatoes have boiled dry!'

Miriam started as if she had been stung.

'*Have* they, mother?' she cried.

'I shouldn't care, Miriam,' said the mother, 'if I hadn't trusted them to you.' She peered into the pan.

The girl stiffened as if from a blow. Her dark eyes dilated; she remained standing in the same spot.

'Well,' she answered, gripped tight in self-conscious shame, 'I'm sure I looked at them five minutes since.'

'Yes,' said the mother, 'I know it's easily done.'

'They're not much burned,' said Paul. 'It doesn't matter, does it?' Mrs Leivers looked at the youth with her brown, hurt eyes.

'It wouldn't matter but for the boys,' she said to him. 'Only Miriam knows what a trouble they make if the potatoes are "caught".'

'Then,' thought Paul to himself, 'you shouldn't let them make a trouble.'

After a while Edgar came in. He wore leggings and his boots were covered with earth. He was rather small, rather formal, for a farmer. He glanced at Paul, nodded to him distantly, and said:

'Dinner ready?'

'Nearly, Edgar,' replied the mother apologetically.

'I'm ready for mine,' said the young man, taking up the newspaper and reading. Presently the rest of the family trooped in. Dinner was served. The meal went rather brutally. The over-gentleness and apologetic tone of the mother brought out all the brutality of manners in the sons. Edgar tasted the potatoes, moved his mouth quickly like a rabbit, looked indignantly at his mother, and said:

'These potatoes are burnt, mother.'

'Yes, Edgar. I forgot them for a minute. Perhaps you'll have bread if you can't eat them.'

Edgar looked in anger across at Miriam.

'What was Miriam doing that she couldn't attend to them?' he said.

Miriam looked up. Her mouth opened, her dark eyes blazed and winced, but she said nothing. She swallowed her anger and her shame, bowing her dark head.

'I'm sure she was trying hard,' said the mother.

'She hasn't got sense even to boil the potatoes,' said Edgar. 'What is she kept at home for?'

'On'y for eating everything that's left in th' pantry,' said Maurice.

'They don't forget that potato-pie against our Miriam,' laughed the father.

She was utterly humiliated. The mother sat in silence, suffering, like some saint out of place at the brutal board.

It puzzled Paul. He wondered vaguely why all this intense feeling went running because of a few burnt potatoes.

The mother exalted everything – even a bit of housework – to the plane of a religious trust. The sons resented this; they felt themselves cut away underneath, and they answered with brutality and also with a sneering superciliousness.

Paul was just opening out from childhood into manhood. This atmosphere, where everything took a religious value, came with a subtle fascination to him. There was something in the air. His own mother was logical. Here there was something different, something he loved, something that at times he hated.

Miriam quarrelled with her brothers fiercely. Later in the afternoon, when they had gone away again, her mother said:

'You disappointed me at dinner-time, Miriam.'

The girl dropped her head.

'They are such *brutes!*' she suddenly cried, looking up with flashing eyes.

'But hadn't you promised not to answer them?' said the mother. 'And I believed in you. I *can't* stand it when you wrangle.'

'But they're so hateful!' cried Miriam, 'and – and low.'

'Yes, dear. But how often have I asked you not to answer Edgar back? Can't you let him saw what he likes?'

'But why should he say what he likes?'

'Aren't you strong enough to bear it, Miriam, if even for my sake? Are you so weak that you must wrangle with them?'

Mrs Leivers stuck unflinchingly to this doctrine of 'the other cheek.' She could not instil it at all into the boys. With the girls she succeeded better, and Miriam was the child of her heart. The boys loathed the other cheek when it was presented to them. Miriam was often sufficiently lofty to turn it. Then they spat on her and hated her. But she walked in her proud humility, living within herself.

There was always this feeling of jangle and discord in the Leivers family. Although the boys resented so bitterly this eternal appeal to their deeper feelings of resignation and proud humility, yet it had its effect on them. They could not establish between themselves and an outsider just the ordinary human feeling and unexaggerated friendship; they were always restless for the something deeper. Ordinary folk seemed shallow to them, trivial and inconsiderable. And so they were unaccustomed, painfully uncouth in the simplest social intercourse, suffering, and yet insolent in their superiority. Then beneath was the yearning for the soul-intimacy to which they could not attain because they were too dumb, and every approach to close connection was blocked by their clumsy contempt of other people. They wanted genuine intimacy, but they could not get even normally near to anyone, because they scorned to take the first steps, they scorned the triviality which forms common human intercourse.

Paul fell under Mrs Leivers' spell. Everything had a religious and intensified meaning when he was with her. His soul, hurt, highly developed, sought her as if for nourishment. Together they seemed to sift the vital fact from an experience.

Miriam was her mother's daughter. In the sunshine of the afternoon mother and daughter went down the fields with him. They looked for nests. There was a jenny wren's in the hedge by the orchard.

'I *do* want you to see this,' said Mrs Leivers.

He crouched down and carefully put his finger through the thorns into the round door of the nest.

'It's almost as if you were feeling inside the live body of the bird,' he said, 'it's so warm. They saw a bird makes its nest round like a cup with pressing its breast on it. Then how did it make the ceiling round, I wonder?'

The nest seemed to start into life for the two women. After that, Miriam came to see it every day. It seemed so close to her. Again, going down the hedge-side with the girl, he noticed the celandines, scalloped splashes of gold, on the side of the ditch.

'I like them,' he said, 'when their petals go flat back with the sunshine. They seem to be pressing themselves at the sun.'

And then the celandines ever after drew her with a little spell. Anthropomorphic as she was, she stimulated him into appreciating things thus, and then they lived for her. She seemed to need things kindling in her imagination or in her soul before she felt she had them. And she was cut off from ordinary life by her religious intensity which made the world for her either a nunnery garden or a paradise where sin and knowledge were not, or else an ugly, cruel thing.

So it was in this atmosphere of subtle intimacy, this meeting in their common feeling for something in Nature, that their love started.

Personally, he was a long time before he realised her. For ten months he had to stay at home after his illness. For a while he went to Skegness with his mother, and was perfectly happy. But even from the seaside he wrote long letters to Mrs Leivers about the shore and the sea. And he brought back his beloved sketches of the flat Lincoln coast, anxious for them to see. Almost they would interest the Leivers more than they interested his mother. It was not his art Mrs Morel cared about; it was himself and his achievement. But Mrs Leivers and her children were almost his disciples. They kindled him and made him glow to his work, whereas his mother's influence was to make him quietly determined, patient, dogged, unwearied.

He soon was friends with the boys, whose rudeness was only superficial. They had all, when they could trust themselves, a strange gentleness and lovableness.

'Will you come with me on to the fallow?' asked Edgar, rather hesitatingly.

Paul went joyfully, and spent the afternoon helping to hoe or to single turnips with his friend. He used to lie with the three brothers in the hay piled up in the barn and tell them about Nottingham and about Jordan's. In return they taught him to milk, and let him do little jobs chopping hay or pulping turnips – just as much as he liked. At midsummer he worked all through hay-harvest with them, and then he loved them. The family was so cut off from the world actually. They seemed, somehow, like 'les derniers fils d'une race epuisée*.' Though the lads were strong and healthy, yet they had all that over-sensitiveness and hanging-back which made them so lonely, yet also such close, delicate friends once their intimacy was won. Paul loved them dearly, and they him.

* (Fr.) the last of a vanishing tribe.

Miriam came later. But he had come into her life before she made any mark on his. One dull afternoon, when the men were on the land and the rest at school, only Miriam and her mother at home, the girl said to him, after having hesitated for some time:

'Have you seen the swing?'

'No,' he answered. 'Where?'

'In the cowshed,' she replied.

She always hesitated to offer or to show him anything. Men have such different standards of worth from women, and her-dear things – the valuable things to her – her brothers had so often mocked or flouted.

'Come on, then,' he replied, jumping up.

There were two cowsheds, one on either side of the barn. In the lower, darker shed there was standing for four cows. Hens flew scolding over the manger-wall as the youth and girl went forward for the great thick rope which hung from the beam in the darkness overhead, and was pushed back over a peg in the wall.

'It's something like a rope!' he exclaimed appreciatively; and he sat down on it, anxious to try it. Then immediately he rose.

'Come on, then, and have first go,' he said to the girl.

'See,' she answered, going into the barn, 'we put some bags on the seat'; and she made the swing comfortable for him. That gave her pleasure. He held the rope.

'Come on, then,' he said to her.

'No, I won't go first,' she answered.

She stood aside in her still, aloof fashion.

'Why?'

'You go,' she pleaded.

Almost for the first time in her life she had the pleasure of giving up to a man, of spoiling him. Paul looked at her.

'All right,' he said, sitting down. 'Mind out?'

He set off with a spring, and in a moment was flying through the air, almost out of the door of the shed, the upper half of which was open, showing outside the drizzling rain, the filthy yard, the cattle standing disconsolate against the black cart-shed, and at the back of all the grey-green wall of the wood. She stood below in her crimson tam-o'-shanter and watched. He looked down at her, and she saw his blue eyes sparkling.

'It's a treat of a swing,' he said.

'Yes.'

He was swinging through the air, every bit of him swinging, like a bird that swoops for joy of movement. And he looked down at her. Her crimson cap hung over her dark curls, her beautiful warm face, so still in a kind of brooding, was lifted towards him. It was dark and rather cold in the shed. Suddenly a swallow came down from the high roof and darted out of the door.

'I didn't know a bird was watching,' he called.

He swung negligently. She could feel him falling and lifting through the air, as if he were lying on some force.

'Now I'll die,' he said, in a detached, dreamy voice, as though he were the dying motion of the swing. She watched him, fascinated. Suddenly he put on the brake and jumped out.

'I've had a long turn,' he said. 'But it's a treat of a swing – it's a real treat of a swing!'

Miriam was amused that he took a swing so seriously and felt so warmly over it.

'No; you go on,' she said.

'Why, don't you want one?' he asked, astonished.

'Well, not much. I'll have just a little.'

She sat down, whilst he kept the bags in place for her.

'It's so ripping!' he said, setting her in motion. 'Keep your heels up, or they'll bang the manger-wall.'

She felt the accuracy with which he caught her, exactly at the right moment, and the exactly proportionate strength of his thrust, and she was afraid. Down to her bowels went the hot wave of fear. She was in his hands. Again, firm and inevitable came the thrust at the right moment. She gripped the rope, almost swooning.

'Ha!' she laughed in fear. 'No higher!'

'But you're not a *bit* high,' he remonstrated.

'But no higher.'

He heard the fear in her voice, and desisted. Her heart melted in hot pain when the moment came for him to thrust her forward again. But he left her alone. She began to breathe.

'Won't you really go any farther?' he asked. 'Should I keep you there?'

'No; let me go by myself,' she answered.

He moved aside and watched her.

'Why, you're scarcely moving,' he said.

She laughed slightly with shame, and in a moment got down.

'They say if you can swing you won't be sea-sick,' he said, as he mounted again. 'I don't believe I should ever be sea-sick.'

Away he went. There was something fascinating to her in him. For the moment he was nothing but a piece of swinging stuff; not a particle of him that did not swing. She could never lose herself so, nor could her brothers. It roused a warmth in her. It were almost as if he were a flame that had lit a warmth in her whilst he swung in the middle air.

And gradually the intimacy with the family concentrated for Paul on three persons – the mother, Edgar, and Miriam. To the mother he went for that sympathy and that appeal which seemed to draw him out. Edgar was his very close friend. And to Miriam he more or less condescended, because she seemed so humble.

But the girl gradually sought him out. If he brought up his sketchbook, it was she who pondered longest over the last picture. Then she would look up at him. Suddenly, her dark eyes alight like water that shakes with a stream of gold in the dark, she would ask:

'Why do I like this so?'

Always something in his breast shrank from these close, intimate, dazzled looks of hers.

'Why *do* you?' he asked.

'I don't know. It seems so true.'

'It's because – it's because there is scarcely any shadow in it; it's more shimmery, as if I'd painted the shimmering protoplasm in the leaves and everywhere, and not the stiffness of the shape. That seems dead to me. Only this shimmeriness is the real living. The shape is a dead crust. The shimmer is inside really.'

And she, with her little finger in her mouth, would ponder these sayings. They gave her a feeling of life again, and vivified things which had meant nothing to her. She managed to find some meaning in his struggling, abstract speeches. And they were the medium through which she came distinctly at her beloved objects.

Another day she sat at sunset whilst he was painting some pine trees which caught the red glare from the west. He had been quiet.

'There you are!' he said suddenly. 'I wanted that. Now, look at them and tell me, are they pine-trunks or are they red coals, up-up pieces of fire in that darkness. There's God's burning bush for you, that burned not away.'

Miriam looked, and was frightened. But the pine-trunks were wonderful to her, and distinct. He packed his box and rose. Suddenly he looked at her.

'Why are you always sad?' he asked her.

'Sad!' she exclaimed, looking up at him with startled, wonderful brown eyes.

'Yes,' he replied. 'You are always, always sad.'

'I am not – oh, not a bit!' she cried.

'But even your joy is like a flame coming off of sadness,' he persisted. 'You're never jolly, or even just all right.'

'No,' she pondered. 'I wonder – why.'

'Because you're not; because you're different inside, like a pine-tree, and then you flare up; but you're not just like an ordinary tree, with fidgety leaves and jolly – '

He got tangled up in his own speech; but she brooded on it, and he had a strange, roused sensation, as if his feelings were new. She got so near him. It was a strange stimulant.

Then sometimes he hated her. Her youngest brother was only five. He was a frail lad, with immense brown eyes in his quaint fragile face one of Reynolds's 'Choir of Angels,' with a touch of elf. Often Miriam kneeled to the child and drew him to her.

'Eh, my Hubert!' she sang, in a voice heavy and surcharged with love. 'Eh, my Hubert!'

And, folding him in her arms, she swayed slightly from side to side with love, her face half lifted, her eyes half closed, her voice drenched with love.

'Don't!' said the child, uneasy – 'don't, Miriam!'

'Yes; you love me, don't you!' she murmured deep in her throat, almost as if she were in a trance, and swaying also as if she were swooned in an ecstasy of love.

'Don't!' repeated the child, a frown on his clear brow.

'You love me, don't you?' she murmured.

'What do you make such a *fuss* for?' cried Paul, all in suffering because of her extreme emotion. 'Why can't you be ordinary with him?'

She let the child go and rose, and said nothing. Her intensity, which would leave no emotion on a normal plane, irritated the youth into a frenzy. And this fearful, naked contact of her on small occasions shocked him. He was used to his mother's reserve. And on such occasions he was thankful in his heart and soul that he had his mother, so sane and wholesome.

All the life of Miriam's body was in her eyes, which were usually dark as a dark church, but could flame with light like a conflagration. Her face scarcely ever altered from its look of brooding. She might have been one of the women who went with Mary when Jesus was dead. Her body was not flexible and living. She walked with a swing, rather heavily, her head bowed forward, pondering. She was not clumsy, and yet none of her movements seemed quite *the* movement. Often, when wiping the dishes, she would stand in bewilderment and chagrin because she had pulled in two halves a cup or a tumbler. It was as if, in her fear and self-mistrust, she put too much strength into the effort. There was no looseness or abandon about her. Everything was gripped stiff with intensity, and her effort, overcharged, closed in on itself.

She rarely varied from her swinging, forward, intense walk. Occasionally she ran with Paul down the fields. Then her eyes blazed naked in a kind of ecstasy that frightened him. But she was physically afraid. If she were getting over a stile, she gripped his hands in a little hard anguish, and began to lose her presence of mind. And he could not persuade her to jump from even a small height. Her eyes dilated, became exposed and palpitating.

'No!' she cried, half laughing in terror – 'no!'

'You shall!' he cried once, and, jerking her forward, he brought her falling from the fence. But her wild 'Ah!' of pain, as if she were losing consciousness, cut him. She landed on her feet safely, and afterwards had courage in this respect.

She was very much dissatisfied with her lot.

'Don't you like being at home?' Paul asked her, surprised.

'Who would?' she answered, low and intense. 'What is it? I'm all day cleaning what the boys make just as bad in five minutes. I don't *want* to be at home.'

'What do you want, then?'

'I want to do something. I want a chance like anybody else. Why should I, because I'm a girl, be kept at home and not allowed to be anything? What chance *have* I?'

'Chance of what?'

'Of knowing anything – of learning, of doing anything. It's not fair, because I'm a woman.'

She seemed very bitter. Paul wondered. In his own home Annie was almost glad to be a girl. She had not so much responsibility; things were lighter for her. She never wanted to be other than a girl. But Miriam almost fiercely wished she were a man. And yet she hated men at the same time.

'But it's as well to be a woman as a man,' he said, frowning.

'Ha! Is it? Men have everything.'

'I should think women ought to be as glad to be women as men are to be men,' he answered.

'No!' she shook her head – 'no! Everything the men have.'

'But what do you want?' he asked.

'I want to learn. Why *should* it be that I know nothing?'

'What! such as mathematics and French?'

'Why *shouldn't* I know mathematics? Yes!' she cried, her eye expanding in a kind of defiance.

Well, you can learn as much as I know,' he said. 'I'll teach you, if you like.'

Her eyes dilated. She mistrusted him as teacher.

Would you?' he asked.

Her head had dropped, and she was sucking her finger broodingly. 'Yes,' she said hesitatingly.

He used to tell his mother all these things.

'I'm going to teach Miriam algebra,' he said.

Well,' replied Mrs Morel, 'I hope she'll get fat on it.'

When he went up to the farm on the Monday evening, it was drawing twilight. Miriam was just sweeping up the kitchen, and was kneeling at the hearth when he entered. Everyone was out but her. She looked round at him, flushed, her dark eyes shining, her fine hair falling about her face.

'Hello!' she said, soft and musical. 'I knew it was you.'

'How?'

'I knew your step. Nobody treads so quick and firm.'

He sat down, sighing.

'Ready to do some algebra?' he asked, drawing a little book from his pocket.

'But – '

He could feel her backing away.

'You said you wanted,' he insisted.

'Tonight, though?' she faltered.

'But I came on purpose. And if you want to learn it, you must begin.' She took up her ashes in the dustpan and looked at him, half tremulously, laughing.

'Yes, but tonight! You see, I haven't thought of it.'

Well, my goodness! Take the ashes and come.'

He went and sat on the stone bench in the back-yard where the big milk-cans were standing, tipped up, to air. The men were in the cowsheds. He could hear the little sing-song of the milk spurting into the pails. Presently she came, bringing some big greenish apples.

'You know you like them,' she said.

He took a bite.

'Sit down,' he said, with his mouth full.

She was short-sighted, and peered over his shoulder. It irritated him. He gave her the book quickly.

'Here,' he said. 'It's only letters for figures. You put down "a" instead of "2" or "6." '

They worked, he talking, she with her head down on the book. He was quick and hasty. She never answered. Occasionally, when he demanded of her, 'Do you see?' she looked up at him, her eyes wide with the half-laugh that comes of fear. 'Don't you?' he cried.

He had been too fast. But she said nothing. He questioned her more, then got hot. It made his blood rouse to see her there, as it were, at his mercy, her mouth open, her eyes dilated with laughter that was afraid, apologetic ashamed. Then Edgar came along with two buckets of milk. 'Hello!' he said. 'What are you doing?'

'Algebra,' replied Paul.

'Algebra!' repeated Edgar curiously. Then he passed on with a laugh. Paul took a bite at his forgotten apple looked at the miserable cabbages in the garden, pecked into lace by the fowls, and he wanted to pull them up. Then he glanced at Miriam. She was poring over the book, seemed absorbed in it, yet trembling lest she could not get at it. It made him cross. She was ruddy and beautiful. Yet her soul seemed to be intensely supplicating. The algebra-book she closed, shrinking, knowing he was angered; and at the same instant he grew gentle, seeing her hurt because she did not understand.

But things came slowly to her. And when she held herself in a grip, seemed so utterly humble before the lesson, it made his blood rouse. He stormed at her, got ashamed, continued the lesson, and grew furious again, abusing her. She listened in silence. Occasionally, very rarely, she defended herself. Her liquid dark eyes blazed at him.

'You don't give me time to learn it,' she said.

'All right,' he answered, throwing the book on the table and lighting a cigarette. Then, after awhile, he went back to her repentant. So the lessons went. He was always either in a rage or very gentle.

'What do you tremble your *soul* before it for?' he cried. 'You don't learn algebra with your blessed soul. Can't you look at it with your clear simple wits?'

Often, when he went again into the kitchen, Mrs Leivers would look at him reproachfully, saying:

'Paul, don't be so hard on Miriam She may not be quick, but I'm sure she tries.'

'I can't help it,' he said rather pitiably: 'I go off like it.'

'You don't mind me, Miriam, do you?' he asked of the girl later.

'No,' she reassured him in her beautiful deep tones – 'no, I don't mind.'

'Don't mind me; it's my fault.'

But, in spite of himself, his blood began to boil with her. It was strange that no one else made him in such fury. He flared against her. Once he threw the pencil in her face. There was a silence. She turned her face slightly aside.

'I didn't – ' he began, but got no farther, feeling weak in all his bones. She never reproached him or was angry with him. He was often cruelly ashamed. But still again his anger burst like a bubble surcharged; and still, when he saw her eager, silent, as it were, blind face, he felt he wanted to throw the pencil in it; and still, when he saw her hand trembling and her mouth parted with suffering, his heart was scalded with pain for her. And because of the intensity to which she roused him, he sought her.

Then he often avoided her and went with Edgar. Miriam and her brother were naturally antagonistic. Edgar was a rationalist, who was curious, and had a sort of scientific interest in life. It was a great bitterness to Miriam to see herself deserted by Paul for Edgar, who seemed so much lower. But the youth was very happy with her elder brother. The two men spent afternoons together on the land or in the loft doing carpentry, when it rained. And they talked together, or Paul taught Edgar the songs he himself had learned from Annie at the piano. And often all the men, Mr Leivers as well, had bitter debates on the nationalising of the land and similar problems. Paul had already heard his mother's views, and as these were as yet his own, he argued for her. Miriam attended and took part, but was all the time waiting until it should be over and a personal communication might begin.

'After all,' she said within herself, 'if the land were nationalised, Edgar and Paul and I would be just the same.' So she waited for the youth to come back to her.

He was studying for his painting. He loved to sit at home, alone with his mother, at night, working and working. She sewed or read. Then, looking up from his task, he would rest his eyes for a moment on her face, that was bright with living warmth, and he returned gladly to his work.

'I can do my best things when you sit there in your rocking-chair, mother,' he said.

'I'm sure!' she exclaimed, sniffing with mock scepticism. But she felt it was so, and her heart quivered with brightness. For many hours she sat still, slightly conscious of him labouring away, whilst she worked or read her book. And he, with all his soul's intensity directing his pencil, could feel her warmth inside him like strength. They were both very happy so, and both unconscious of it. These times, that meant so much, and which were real living, they almost ignored.

He was conscious only when stimulated. A sketch finished, he always wanted to take it to Miriam. Then he was stimulated into knowledge of the work he had produced unconsciously. In contact with Miriam he gained insight; his vision went deeper. From his mother he drew the life-warmth, the strength to produce; Miriam urged this warmth into intensity like a white light.

When he returned to the factory the conditions of work were better. He had Wednesday afternoon off to go to the Art School – Miss Jordan's provision – returning in the evening. Then the factory closed at six instead of at eight on Thursday and Friday evenings.

One evening in the summer Miriam and he went over the fields by Herod's Farm on their way from the library home. So it was only three miles to Willey Farm. There was a yellow glow over the mowing-grass, and the sorrel-heads burned crimson. Gradually, as they walked along the high land, the gold in the west sank down to red, the red to crimson, and then the chill blue crept up against the glow.

They came out upon the high road to Alfreton which ran white between the darkening fields. There Paul hesitated. It was two miles home for him, one mile forward for Miriam. They both looked up the road that ran in shadow right under the glow of the north-west sky. On the crest of the hill, Selby, with its stork houses and the up-pricked headstocks of the pit, stood in black silhouette small against the sky.

He looked at his watch.

'Nine o'clock!' he said.

The pair stood, loth to part, hugging their books.

'The wood is so lovely now,' she said. 'I wanted you to see it.'

He followed her slowly across the road to the white gate.

'They grumble so if I'm late,' he said.

'But you're not doing anything wrong,' she answered impatiently.

He followed her across the nibbled pasture in the dusk. There was a coolness in the wood, a scent of leaves, of honeysuckle, and a twilight. The two walked in silence. Night came wonderfully there, among the throng of dark tree-trunks. He looked round, expectant.

She wanted to show him a certain wild-rose bush she had discovered. She knew it was wonderful. And yet, till he had seen it, she felt it had not come into her soul. Only he could make it her own, immortal. She was dissatisfied.

Dew was already on the paths. In the old oak-wood a mist was rising, and he hesitated, wondering whether one whiteness were a strand of fog or only campion-flowers pallid in a cloud.

By the time they came to the pine-trees Miriam was getting very eager and very tense. Her bush might be gone. She might not be able to find it; and she wanted it so much. Almost passionately she wanted to be with him when he stood before the flowers. They were going to have a communion together – something that thrilled her, something holy. He was walking beside her in silence. They were very near to each other. She trembled, and he listened, vaguely anxious.

Coming to the edge of the wood, they saw the sky in front, like mother-of-pearl, and the earth growing dark. Somewhere on the outermost branches of the pine-wood the honeysuckle was streaming scent.

'Where?' he asked.

'Down the middle path,' she murmured, quivering.

When they turned the corner of the path she stood still. In the wide walk between the pines, gazing rather frightened, she could distinguish nothing for some moments; the greying light robbed things of their colour. Then she saw her bush.

'Ah!' she cried, hastening forward.

It was very still. The tree was tall and straggling. It had thrown its briers over a hawthorn-bush, and its long streamers trailed thick, right down to the grass, splashing the darkness everywhere with great spilt stars, pure white. In bosses of ivory and in large splashed stars the roses gleamed on the darkness of foliage and stems and grass. Paul and Miriam stood close together, silent, and watched. Point after point the steady roses shone out to them, seeming to kindle something in their souls. The dusk came like smoke around, and still did not put out the roses.

Paul looked into Miriam's eyes. She was pale and expectant with wonder, her lips were parted, and her dark eyes lay open to him. His look seemed to travel down into her. Her soul quivered. It was the communion she wanted. He turned aside, as if pained. He turned to the bush.

'They seem as if they walk like butterflies, and shake themselves,' he said.

She looked at her roses. They were white, some incurved and holy, others expanded in an ecstasy. The tree was dark as a shadow. She lifted her hand impulsively to the flowers; she went forward and touched them in worship.

'Let us go,' he said.

There was a cool scent of ivory roses – a white, virgin scent. Something made him feel anxious and imprisoned. The two walked in silence.

'Till Sunday,' he said quietly, and left her; and she walked home slowly, feeling her soul satisfied with the holiness of the night. He stumbled down the path. And as soon as he was out of the wood, in the free open meadow, where he could breathe, he started to run as fast as he could. It was like a delicious delirium in his veins.

Always when he went with Miriam, and it grew rather late, he knew his mother was fretting and getting angry about him – why, he could not understand. As he went into the house, flinging down his cap, his mother looked up at the clock. She had been sitting thinking, because a chill to her eyes prevented her reading. She could feel Paul being drawn away by this girl. And she did not care for Miriam. 'She is one of those who will want to suck a man's soul out till he has none of his own left,' she said to herself; 'and he is just such a gaby as to let himself be absorbed. She will never let him become a man; she never will.' So, while he was away with Miriam, Mrs Morel grew more and more worked up.

She glanced at the clock and said, coldly and rather tired:

'You have been far enough tonight.'

His soul, warm and exposed from contact with the girl, shrank.

'You must have been right home with her,' his mother continued.

He would not answer. Mrs Morel, looking at him quickly, saw his hair was damp on his forehead with haste, saw him frowning in his heavy fashion, resentfully.

'She must be wonderfully fascinating, that you can't get away from her, but must go trailing eight miles at this time of night.'

He was hurt between the past glamour with Miriam and the knowledge that his mother fretted. He had meant not to saw anything, to refuse to answer. But he could not harden his heart to ignore his mother.

'I *do* like to talk to her,' he answered irritably.

'Is there nobody else to talk to?'

'You wouldn't say anything if I went with Edgar.'

'You know I should. You know, whoever you went with, I should say it was too far for you to go trailing, late at night, when you've been to Nottingham. Besides' – her voice suddenly flashed into anger and contempt – 'it is disgusting – bits of lads and girls courting.'

'It is *not* courting,' he cried.

'I don't know what else you call it.'

'It's not! Do you think we *spoon* and do? We only talk.'

'Till goodness knows what time and distance,' was the sarcastic rejoinder.

Paul snapped at the laces of his boots angrily.

'What are you so mad about?' he asked. 'Because you don't like her.'

'I don't saw I don't like her. But I don't hold with children keeping company, and never did.'

'But you don't mind our Annie going out with Jim Inger.'

'They've more sense than you two.'

Why?'

'Our Annie's not one of the deep sort.'

He failed to see the meaning of this remark. But his mother looked tired. She was never so strong after William's death; and her eyes hurt her.

'Well,' he said, 'it's so pretty in the country. Mr Sleath asked about you. He said he'd missed you. Are you a bit better?'

'I ought to have been in bed a long time ago,' she replied.

'Why, mother, you know you wouldn't have gone before quarter-past ten.'

'Oh yes, I should!'

'Oh, little woman, you'd say anything now you're disagreeable with me, wouldn't you?'

He kissed her forehead that he knew so well: the deep marks between the brows, the rising of the fine hair, greying now, and the proud setting of the temples. His hand lingered on her shoulder after his kiss. Then he went slowly to bed. He had forgotten Miriam; he only saw how his mother's hair was lifted back from her warm, broad brow. And somehow, she was hurt.

Then the next time he saw Miriam he said to her:

'Don't let me be late tonight – not later than ten o'clock. My mother gets so upset.'

Miriam dropped her head, brooding.

Why does she get upset?' she asked.

'Because she says I oughtn't to be out late when I have to get up early.'

'Very well!' said Miriam, rather quietly, with just a touch of a sneer.

He resented that. And he was usually late again.

That there was any love growing between him and Miriam neither of them would have acknowledged. He thought he was too sane for such sentimentality, and she thought herself too lofty. They both were late in coming to maturity, and psychical ripeness was much behind even the physical. Miriam was exceedingly sensitive, as her mother had always been. The slightest grossness made her recoil almost in anguish. Her brothers were brutal, but never coarse in speech. The men did all the discussing of farm matters outside. But, perhaps, because of the continual business of birth and of begetting which goes on upon every farm, Miriam was the more hypersensitive to the matter, and her blood was chastened almost to disgust of the faintest suggestion of such intercourse. Paul took his pitch from her, and their intimacy went on in an utterly blanched and chaste fashion. It could never be mentioned that the mare was in foal.

When he was nineteen, he was earning only twenty shillings a week, but he was happy. His painting went well, and life went well enough. On the Good Friday he organised a walk to the Hemlock Stone. There were three lads of his own age, then Annie and Arthur, Miriam and Geoffrey. Arthur, apprenticed as an electrician in Nottingham, was home for the holiday. Morel, as usual, was up early, whistling and sawing in the yard. At seven o'clock the family heard him buy threepennyworth of hot-cross buns; he talked with gusto to the little girl who brought them, calling her 'my darling.' He turned away several boys who came with more buns, telling them they had been 'kested'* by a little lass. Then Mrs Morel got up, and the family straggled down. It was an immense luxury to everybody, this lying in bed just beyond the ordinary time on a weekday. And Paul and Arthur read before breakfast, and had the meal unwashed, sitting in their shirt-sleeves. This was another holiday luxury. The room was warm. Everything felt free of care and anxiety. There was a sense of plenty in the house.

* beaten.

While the boys were reading, Mrs Morel went into the garden. They were now in another house, an old one, near the Scargill Street home, which had been left soon after William had died. Directly came an excited cry from the garden:

'Paul, Paul! come and look!'

It was his mother's voice. He threw down his book and went out. There was a long garden that ran to a field. It was a grey, cold day, with a sharp wind blowing out of Derbyshire. Two fields away Bestwood began, with a jumble of roofs and red house-ends, out of which rose the church tower and the spire of the Congregational Chapel. And beyond went woods and hills, right away to the pale grey heights of the Pennine Chain.

Paul looked down the garden for his mother. Her head appeared among the young currant-bushes.

'Come here!' she cried.

What for?' he answered.

'Come and see.'

She had been looking at the buds on the currant-trees. Paul went up.

'To think,' she said, 'that here I might never have seen them!'

Her son went to her side. Under the fence, in a little bed, was a ravel of poor grassy leaves, such as come from very immature bulbs, and three scyllas in bloom. Mrs Morel pointed to the deep blue flowers.

'Now, just see those!' she exclaimed. 'I was looking at the currant bushes, when, thinks I to myself, "There's something very blue; is it a bit of sugar-bag" and there, behold you! Sugar-bag! Three glories of the snow, and *such* beauties! But where on earth did they come from!'

'I don't know,' said Paul.

Well, that's a marvel, now! I *thought* I knew every weed and blade in this garden. But *haven't* they done well? You see, that gooseberry-bush just shelters them. Not nipped, not touched!'

He crouched down and turned up the bells of the little blue flowers.

'They're a glorious colour!' he said.

'Aren't they!' she cried. 'I guess they come from Switzerland, where they saw they have such lovely things. Fancy them against the snow! But where have they come from? They can't have *blown* here, can they?'

Then he remembered having set here a lot of little trash of bulbs to mature.

'And you never told me,' she said.

'No; I thought I'd leave it till they might flower.'

'And now, you see! I might have missed them. And I've never had a glory of the snow in my garden in my life.'

She was full of excitement and elation. The garden was an endless joy to her. Paul was thankful for her sake at last to be in a house with a long garden that went down to a field. Every morning after breakfast she went out and was happy pottering about in it. And it was true, she knew every weed and blade.

Everybody turned up for the walk. Food was packed, and they set off, a merry, delighted party. They hung over the wall of the mill-race, dropped paper in the water on one side the tunnel and watched it shoot out on the other. They stood on the footbridge over Boathouse Station and looked at the metals gleaming coldly.

'You should see the Flying Scotchman come through at half-past six!' said Leonard, whose father was a signalman. 'Lad, but she doesn't half buzz!' and the little party looked up the lines one way, to London, and the other way, to Scotland, and they felt the touch of these two magical places.

In Ilkeston the colliers were waiting in gongs for the public-houses to open. It was a town of idleness and lounging. At Stanton Gate the iron foundry blazed. Over everything there were great discussions. At Trowell they crossed again from Derbyshire into Nottinghamshire. They came to the Hemlock Stone at dinner-time. Its field was crowded with folk from Nottingham and Ilkeston.

They had expected a venerable and dignified monument. They found a little, gnarled, twisted stump of rock, something like a decayed mushroom, standing out pathetically on the side of a field. Leonard and Dick immediately proceeded to carve their initials, 'L. W.' and 'R. P.,' in the old red sandstone; but Paul desisted, because he had read in the newspaper satirical remarks about initial-carvers, who could find no other road to immortality. Then all the lads climbed to the top of the rock to look round.

Everywhere in the field below, factory girls and lads were eating lunch or sporting about. Beyond was the garden of an old manor. It had yewhedges and thick clumps and borders of yellow crocuses round the lawn.

'See,' said Paul to Miriam, 'what a quiet garden!'

She saw the dark yews and the golden crocuses, then she looked at him gratefully. He had not seemed to belong to her among all these others; he was different then – not her Paul, who understood the slightest quiver of her innermost soul; but something else, speaking another language than hers. How it hurt her, and deadened her very perceptions. Only when he came right back to her, leaving his other, his lesser self, as she thought, would she feel alive again. And now he asked her to look at this garden, wanting the contact with her again. Impatient of the set in the field, she turned to the quiet lawn, surrounded by sheaves of shut-up crocuses. A feeling of stillness, almost of ecstasy, came over her. It felt almost as if she were alone with him in this garden.

Then he left her again and joined the others. Soon they started home. Miriam loitered behind, alone. She did not fit in with the others; she could very rarely get into human relation with anyone: so her friend, her companion, her lover, was Nature. She saw the sun declining wanly. In the dusky, cold hedgerows were some red leaves. She lingered to gather them, tenderly, passionately. The love in her finger-tips caressed the leaves; the passion in her heart came to a glow upon the leaves.

Suddenly she realised she was alone in a strange road, and she hurried forward. Turning a corner in the lane, she came upon Paul, who stood bent over something, his mind fixed on it, working away steadily, patiently, a little hopelessly, She hesitated in her approach, to watch.

He remained concentrated in the middle of the road. Beyond, one rift of rich gold in that colourless grey evening seemed to make him stand out in dark relief. She saw him, slender and firm, as if the setting sun had given him to her. A deep pain took hold of her, and she knew she must love him. And she had discovered him, discovered in him a rare potentiality, discovered his loneliness. Quivering as at some 'annunciation,' she went slowly forward.

At last he looked up.

Why,' he exclaimed gratefully, 'have you waited for me!'

She saw a deep shadow in his eyes.

What is it?' she asked.

'The spring broken here'; and he showed her where his umbrella was injured.

Instantly, with some shame, she knew he had not done the damage himself, but that Geoffrey was responsible.

'It is only an old umbrella, isn't it?' she asked.

She wondered why he, who did not usually trouble over trifles, made such a mountain of this molehill.

'But it was William's, an' my mother can't help but know,' he said quietly, still patiently working at the umbrella.

The words went through Miriam like a blade. This, then, was the confirmation of her vision of him. She looked at him; But there was about him a certain reserve, and she dared not comfort him, not even speak softly to him.

'Come on,' he said. 'I can't do it'; and they went in silence along the road.

That same evening they were walking along under the trees by Nether Green. He was talking to her fretfully, seemed to be struggling to convince himself.

'You know,' he said, with an effort, 'if one person loves, the other does.'

'Ah!' she answered. 'Like mother said to me when I was little, "Love begets love." '

'Yes, something like that, I think it *must* be.'

'I hope so, because, if it were not, love might be a very terrible thing,' she said.

'Yes, but it is – at least with most people,' he answered.

And Miriam, thinking he had assured himself, felt strong in herself. She always regarded that sudden coming upon him in the lane as a revelation. And this conversation remained graven in her mind as one of the letters of the law.

Now she stood with him and for him. When, about this time, he outraged the family feeling at Willey Farm by some overbearing insult, she stuck to him, and believed he was right. 'And at this time she dreamed dreams of him, vivid, unforgettable. These dreams came again later on, developed to a more subtle psychological stage.

On the Easter Monday the same party took an excursion to Wingfield Manor. It was great excitement to Miriam to catch a train at Sethley Bridge, amid all the bustle of the Bank Holiday crowd. They left the train at Alfreton. Paul was interested in the street and in the colliers with their dogs. Here was a new race of miners. Miriam did not live till they came to the church. They were all rather timid of entering, with their bags of food, for fear of being turned out. Leonard, a comic, thin fellow, went first; Paul, who would have died rather than be sent back, went last. The place was decorated for Easter. In the font hundreds of white narcissi seemed to be growing. The air was dim and coloured from the windows, and thrilled with a subtle scent of lilies and narcissi. In that atmosphere Miriam's soul came into a glow. Paul was afraid of the things he mustn't do; and he was sensitive to the feel of the place. Miriam turned to him. He answered. They were together. He would not go beyond the Communion-rail. She loved him for that. Her soul expanded into prayer beside him. He felt the strange fascination of shadowy religious places. All his latent mysticism quivered into life. She was drawn to him. He was a prayer along with her.

Miriam very rarely talked to the other lads. They at once became awkward in conversation with her. So usually she was silent.

It was past midday when they climbed the steep path to the manor. All things shone softly in the sun, which was wonderfully warm and enlivening. Celandines and violets were out. Everybody was tip-top full with happiness. The glitter of the ivy, the soft, atmospheric grey of the castle walls, the gentleness of everything near the ruin, was perfect.

The manor is of hard, pale grey stone, and the outer walls are blank and calm. The young folk were in raptures. They went in trepidation, almost afraid that the delight of exploring this ruin might be denied them. In the first courtyard, within the high broken walls, were farm-carts, with their shafts lying idle on the ground, the tyres of the wheels brilliant with gold-red rust. It was very still.

All eagerly paid their sixpences, and went timidly through the fine clean arch of the inner courtyard. They were shy. Here on the pavement, where the hall had been, an old thorn-tree was budding. All kinds of strange openings and broken rooms were in the shadow around them.

After lunch they set off once more to explore the ruin.

This time the girls went with the boys, who could act as guides and expositors. There was one tall tower in a corner, rather tottering, where they saw Mary Queen of Scots was imprisoned.

'Think of the Queen going up here!' said Miriam in a low voice, as she climbed the hollow stairs.

'If she could get up,' said Paul, 'for she had rheumatism like anything. I reckon they treated her rottenly.'

'You don't think she deserved it?' asked Miriam.

'No, I don't. She was only lively.'

They continued to mount the winding staircase. A high wind, blowing through the loopholes, went rushing up the shaft, and filled the girl's skirts like a balloon, so that she was ashamed, until he took the hem of her dress and held it down for her. He did it perfectly simply, as he would have picked up her glove. She remembered this always.

Round the broken top of the tower the ivy bushed out, old and handsome. Also, there were a few chill gillivers, in pale cold bud. Miriam wanted to lean over for some ivy, but he would not let her. Instead, she had to wait behind him, and take from him each spray as he gathered it and held it to her, each one separately, in the purest manner of chivalry. The tower seemed to rock in the wind. They looked over miles and miles of wooded country, and country with gleams of pasture.

The crypt underneath the manor was beautiful, and in perfect preservation. Paul made a drawing: Miriam stayed with him. She was thinking of Mary Queen of Scots looking with her strained, hopeless eyes, that could not understand misery, over the hills whence no help came, or sitting in this crypt, being told of a God as cold as the place she sat in.

They set off again gaily, looking round on their beloved manor that stood so clean and big on its hill.

'Supposing you could have *that* farm,' said Paul to Miriam.

'Yes!'

'Wouldn't it be lovely to come and see you!'

They were now in the bare country of stone walls, which he loved, and which, though only ten miles from home, seemed so foreign to Miriam. The party was straggling. As they were crossing a large meadow that sloped away from the sun, along a path embedded with innumerable tiny glittering points, Paul, walking alongside, laced his fingers in the strings of the bag Miriam was carrying, and instantly she felt Annie behind, watchful and jealous. But the meadow was bathed in a glory of sunshine, and the path was jewelled, and it was seldom that he gave her any sign. She held her fingers very still among the strings of the bag, his fingers touching; and the place was golden as a vision.

At last they came into the straggling grey village of Crich, that lies high. Beyond the village was the famous Crich Stand that

Paul could see from the garden at home. The party pushed on. Great expanses of country spread around and below. The lads were eager to get to the top of the hill. It was capped by a round knoll, half of which was by now cut away, and on the top of which stood on ancient monument, sturdy and squat, for signalling in old days far down into the level lands of Nottinghamshire and Leicestershire.

It was blowing so hard, high up there in the exposed place, that the only way to be safe was to stand nailed by the wind to the wall of the tower. At their feet fell the precipice where the limestone was quarried away. Below was a jumble of hills and tiny villages – Matlock, Ambergate, Stoney Middleton. The lads were eager to spy out the church of Bestwood, far away among the rather crowded country on the left. They were disgusted that it seemed to stand on a plain. They saw the hills of Derbyshire fall into the monotony of the Midlands that swept away South.

Miriam was somewhat scored by the wind, but the lads enjoyed it. They went on, miles and miles, to Whatstandwell. All the food was eaten, everybody was hungry, and there was very little money to get home with. But they managed to procure a loaf and a currant-loaf, which they hacked into pieces with shut-knives, and ate sitting on the wall near the bridge, watching the bright Derwent rushing by, and the brakes from Matlock pulling up at the inn.

Paul was now pale with weariness. He had been responsible for the party all day, and now he was done. Miriam understood, and kept close to him, and he left himself in her hands.

They had an hour to wait at Ambergate Station. Trains came, crowded with excursionists returning to Manchester, Birmingham, and London.

'We might be going there – folk easily might think we're going that far,' said Paul.

They got back rather late. Miriam, walking home with Geoffrey, watched the moon rise big and red and misty. She felt something was fulfilled in her.

She had an elder sister, Agatha, who was a school-teacher. Between the two girls was a feud. Miriam considered Agatha worldly. And she wanted herself to be a school-teacher.

One Saturday afternoon Agatha and Miriam were upstairs dressing. Their bedroom was over the stable. It was a low room, not very large, and bare. Miriam had nailed on the wall a reproduction of Veronese's 'St Catherine.' She loved the woman who sat in the window, dreaming. Her own windows were too small to sit in. But the front one was dripped over with honeysuckle and virginia creeper, and looked upon the tree tops of the oak-wood across the yard, while the little back window, no bigger than a handkerchief, was a loophole to the east, to the down beating up against the beloved round hills.

The two sisters did not talk much to each other. Agatha, who was fair and small and determined, had rebelled against the home atmosphere, again the doctrine of 'the other cheek.' She was out in the world now, in a fair way to be independent. And she insisted on worldly values, on appearance, on manners, on position, which Miriam would fain have ignored.

Both girls liked to be upstairs, out of the way, when Paul came. They preferred to come running down, open the stair-foot door, and see him watching, expectant of them. Miriam stood painfully pulling over her head a rosary he had given her. It caught in the fine mesh of her hair. But at last she had it on, and the red-brown wooden beads looked well against her cool brown neck. She was a well-developed girl, and very handsome. But in the little looking-glass nailed against the whitewashed wall she could only see a fragment of herself at a time. Agatha had bought a little mirror of her own, which she propped up to suit herself. Miriam was near the window. Suddenly she heard the well-known click of the chain, and she saw Paul fling open the gate, push his bicycle into the yard. She saw him look at the house, and she shrank away. He walked in a nonchalant fashion, and his bicycle went with him as if it were a live thing.

'Paul's come!' she exclaimed.

'Aren't you glad?' said Agatha cuttingly.

Miriam stood still in amazement and bewilderment.

'Well, aren't you?' she asked.

'Yes, but I'm not going to let him see it, and think I wanted him.'

Miriam was startled. She heard him putting his bicycle in the stable underneath, and talking to Jimmy, who had been a pit-horse and who was seedy.

'Well, Jimmy my lad, how are ter? Nobbut sick an' sadly, like? Why, then, it's a shame, my owd lad.'

She heard the rope run through the hole as the horse lifted its head from the lad's caress. How she loved to listen when he thought only the horse could hear. But there was a serpent in her Eden. She searched earnestly in herself to see if she wanted Paul Morel. She felt there would be some disgrace in it. Full of twisted feeling, she was afraid she did want him. She stood self-convicted. Then came on agony of new shame. She shrank within herself in a coil of torture. Did she want Paul Morel, and did he know she wanted him? What a subtle infamy upon her! She felt as if her whole soul coiled into knots of shame.

Agatha was dressed first, and ran downstairs. Miriam heard her greet the lad gaily, knew exactly how brilliant her grey eyes became with that tone. She herself would have felt it bold to have greeted him in such wise. Yet there she stood under the self-accusation of wanting him, tied to that stoke of torture. In bitter perplexity she kneeled down and prayed:

'O Lord, let me not love Paul Morel. Keep me from loving him, if I ought not to love him.'

Something anomalous in the prayer arrested her. She lifted her head and pondered. How could it be wrong to love him? Love was God's gift. And yet it caused her shame. That was because of him, Paul Morel. But, then, it was not his affair, it was her own, between herself and God. She was to be a sacrifice. But it was God's sacrifice, not Paul Morel's or her own. After a few minutes she hid her face in the pillow again, and said:

'But, Lord, if it is Thy will that I should love him, make me love him – as Christ would, who died for the souls of men. Make me love him splendidly, because he is Thy son.'

She remained kneeling for some time, quite still, and deeply moved, her black hair against the red squares and the lavender-sprigged squares of the patchwork-quilt. Prayer was almost essential to her. Then she fell into that rapture of self-sacrifice, identifying herself with a God who was sacrificed, which gives to so many human souls their deepest bliss.

When she went downstairs Paul was lying back in an armchair, holding forth with much vehemence to Agatha, who was scorning a little painting he had brought to show her. Miriam glanced at the two, and avoided their levity. She went into the parlour to be alone.

It was teatime before she was able to speak to Paul, and then her manner was so distant he thought he had offended her.

Miriam discontinued her practice of going each Thursday evening to the library in Bestwood. After calling for Paul regularly during the whole spring, a number of trifling incidents and tiny insults from his family awakened her to their attitude towards her, and she decided to go no more. So she announced to Paul one evening she would not call at his house again for him on Thursday nights.

'Why?' he asked, very short.

'Nothing. Only I'd rather not.'

'Very well.'

'But,' she faltered, 'if you'd care to meet me, we could still go together.'

'Meet you where?'

'Somewhere – where you like.'

'I shan't meet you anywhere. I don't see why you shouldn't keep calling for me. But if you won't, I don't want to meet you.'

So the Thursday evenings which had been so precious to her, and to him, were dropped. He worked instead. Mrs Morel sniffed with satisfaction at this arrangement.

He would not have it that they were lovers. The intimacy between them had been kept so abstract, such a matter of the soul, all thought and weary struggle into consciousness, that he saw it only as a platonic friendship. He stoutly denied there was anything else between them. Miriam was silent, or else she very quietly agreed. He was a fool who did not know what was happening to himself. By tacit agreement they ignored the remarks and insinuations of their acquaintances.

'We aren't lovers, we are friends,' he said to her. 'We know it. Let them talk. What does it matter what they say.'

Sometimes, as they were walking together, she slipped her arm timidly into his. But he always resented it, and she knew it. It caused a violent conflict in him. With Miriam he was always on the high plane of abstraction, when his natural fire of love was transmitted into the fine steam of thought. She would have it so. If he were jolly and, as she put it, flippant, she waited till he came back to her, till the change had taken place in him again, and he was wrestling with his own soul, frowning, passionate in' his desire for understanding. And in this passion for understanding her soul lay close to his; she had him all to herself. But he must be made abstract first.

Then, if she put her arm in his, it caused him almost torture. His consciousness seemed to split. The place where she was touching him ran hot with friction. He was one internecine battle, and he became cruel to her because of it.

One evening in midsummer Miriam called at the house, warm from climbing. Paul was alone in the kitchen; his mother could be heard moving about upstairs.

'Come and look at the sweet-peas,' he said to the girl.

They went into the garden. The sky behind the townlet and the church was orange-red; the flower-garden was flooded with a strange warm light that lifted every leaf into significance. Paul passed along a fine row of sweet-peas, gathering a blossom here and there, all cream and pale blue. Miriam followed, breathing the fragrance. To her, flowers appealed with such strength she felt she must make them part of herself. When she bent and breathed a flower, it was as if she and the flower were loving each other. Paul hated her for it. There seemed a sort of exposure about the action, something too intimate.

When he had got a fair bunch, they returned to the house. He listened for a moment to his mother's quiet movement upstairs, then he said:

'Come here, and let me pin them in for you.' He arranged them two or three at a time in the bosom of her dress, stepping back now and then to see the effect. 'You know,' he said, taking the pin out of his mouth, 'a woman ought always to arrange her flowers before her glass.'

Miriam laughed. She thought flowers ought to be pinned in one's dress without any care. That Paul should take pains to fix her flowers for her was his whim.

He was rather offended at her laughter.

'Some women do – those who look decent,' he said.

Miriam laughed again, but mirthlessly, to hear him thus mix her up with women in a general way. From most men she would have ignored it. But from him it hurt her.

He had nearly finished arranging the flowers when he heard his mother's footstep on the stairs. Hurriedly he pushed in the last pin and turned away.

'Don't let mater know,' he said.

Miriam picked up her books and stood in the doorway looking with chagrin at the beautiful sunset. She would call for Paul no more, she said.

'Good-evening, Mrs Morel,' she said, in a deferential way. She sounded as if she felt she had no right to be there.

'Oh, is it you, Miriam?' replied Mrs Morel coolly.

But Paul insisted on everybody's accepting his friendship with the girl, and Mrs Morel was too wise to have any open rupture.

It was not till he was twenty years old that the family could ever afford to go away for a holiday. Mrs Morel had never been away for a holiday, except to see her sister, since she had been married. Now at last Paul had saved enough money, and they were all going. There was to be a party: some of Annie's friends, one friend of Paul's, a young man in the same office where William had previously been, and Miriam.

It was great excitement writing for rooms. Paul and his mother debated it endlessly between them. They wanted a furnished cottage for two weeks. She thought one week would be enough, but he insisted on two.

At last they got on answer from Mablethorpe, a cottage such as they wished for thirty shillings a week. There was immense jubilation. Paul was wild with joy for his mother's sake. She would have a real holiday now. He and she sat at evening picturing what it would be like. Annie came in, and Leonard, and Alice, and Kitty. There was wild rejoicing and anticipation. Paul told Miriam. She seemed to brood with joy over it. But the Morel's house rang with excitement.

They were to go on Saturday morning by the seven train.

Paul suggested that Miriam should sleep at his house, because it was so far for her to walk. She came down for supper. Everybody was so excited that even Miriam was accepted with warmth. But almost as soon as she entered the feeling in the family became close and tight. He had discovered a poem by Jean Ingelow which mentioned Mablethorpe, and so he must read it to Miriam. He would never have got so far in the direction of sentimentality as to read poetry to his own family. But now they condescended to listen. Miriam sat on the sofa absorbed in him. She always seemed absorbed in him, and by him, when he was present. Mrs Morel sat jealously in her own chair. She was going to hear also. And even Annie and the father attended, Morel with his head cocked on one side, like somebody listening to a sermon and feeling conscious of the fact. Paul ducked his head over the book. He had got now all the audience he cared for. And Mrs Morel and Annie almost contested with Miriam who should listen best and win his favour. He was in very high feather.

'But,' interrupted Mrs Morel, 'what if the "Bride of Enderby" that the bells are supposed to ring?'

'It's an old tune they used to play on the bells for a warning against water. I suppose the Bride of Enderby was drowned in a flood,' he replied. He had not the faintest knowledge what it really was, but he would never have sunk so low as to confess that to his womenfolk. They listened and believed him. He believed himself.

'And the people knew what that tune meant?' said his mother.

'Yes – just like the Scotch when they heard "The Flowers o' the Forest" – and when they used to ring the bells backward for alarm.'

'How?' said Annie. 'A bell sounds the same whether it's rung backwards or forwards.'

'But,' he said, 'if you start with the deep bell and ring up to the high one – der – der – der – der – der – der – der – der!'

He ran up the scale. Everybody thought it clever. He thought so too. Then, waiting a minute, he continued the poem.

'Hm!' said Mrs Morel curiously, when he finished. 'But I wish everything that's written weren't so sad.'

'I canna see what they want drownin' theirselves for,' said Morel. There was a pause. Annie got up to clear the table.

Miriam rose to help with the pots.

'Let *me* help to wash up,' she said.

'Certainly not,' cried Annie. 'You sit down again. There aren't many.' And Miriam, who could not be familiar and insist, sat down again to look at the book with Paul.

He was master of the party; his father was no good. And great tortures he suffered lest the tin box should be put out at Firsby instead of at Mablethorpe. And he wasn't equal to getting a carriage. His bold little mother did that.

'Here!' she cried to a man. 'Here!'

Paul and Annie got behind the rest, convulsed with shamed laughter. 'How much will it be to drive to Brook Cottage?' said Mrs Morel. Two shillings.'

'Why, how far is it?'

'A good way.'

'I don't believe it,' she said.

But she scrambled in. There were eight crowded in one old seaside carriage.

'You see,' said Mrs Morel, 'it's only threepence each, and if it were a tram-car – '

They drove along. Each cottage they came to, Mrs Morel cried:

'Is it this? Now, this is it!'

Everybody sat breathless. They drove past. There was a universal sigh. 'I'm thankful it wasn't that brute,' said Mrs Morel. 'I *was* frightened.' They drove on and on.

At last they descended at a house that stood alone over the dyke by the highroad. There was wild excitement because they had to cross a little bridge to get into the front garden. But they loved the house that lay so solitary, with a sea-meadow on one side, and immense expanse of land patched in white barley, yellow oats, red wheat, and green root-crops, flat and stretching level to the sky.

Paul kept accounts. He and his mother ran the show. The total expenses – lodging, food, everything – was sixteen shillings a week per person. He and Leonard went bathing in the morning. Morel was wandering abroad quite early.

'You, Paul,' his mother called from the bedroom, 'eat a piece of bread and-butter.'

'All right,' he answered.

And when he got back he saw his mother presiding in state at the breakfast-table. The woman of the house was young. Her husband was blind, and she did laundry work. So Mrs Morel always washed the pots in the kitchen and made the beds.

'But you said you'd have a real holiday,' said Paul, 'and now you work.

'Work!' she exclaimed. 'What are you talking about!'

He loved to go with her across the fields to the village and the sea. She was afraid of the plank bridges, and he abused her for being a baby. On the whole he stuck to her as if he were her man.

Miriam did not get much of him, except, perhaps, when all the others went to the 'Coons.'[*] Coons were insufferably stupid to Miriam, so he thought they were to himself also, and he preached priggishly to Annie about the fatuity of listening to them. Yet he, too, knew all their songs, and sang them along the roads roisterously. And if he found himself listening, the stupidity pleased him very much. Yet to Annie he said:

'Such rot! there isn't a grain of intelligence in it. Nobody with more gumption than a grasshopper could go and sit and listen.' And to Miriam he said, with much scorn of Annie and the others: 'I suppose they're at the "Coons." '

It was queer to see Miriam singing coon songs. She had a straight chin that went in a perpendicular line from the lower lip to the turn. She always reminded Paul of some sad Botticelli angel when she sang, even when it was:

> 'Come down lover's lane
> For a walk with me, talk with me.'

Only when he sketched, or at evening when the others were at the 'Coons,' she had him to herself. He talked to her endlessly about his love of horizontals: how they, the great levels of sky and land in Lincolnshire, meant to him the eternality of the will, just as the bowed Norman arches of the church, repeating themselves, meant the dogged leaping forward of the persistent human soul, on and on, nobody knows where; in contradiction to the perpendicular lines and to the Gothic arch, which, he said, leapt up at heaven and touched the ecstasy and lost itself in the divine. Himself, he said, was Norman, Miriam was Gothic. She bowed in consent even to that.

* (U.S.) A song-and-dance show.

One evening he and she went up the great sweeping shore of sand towards Theddlethorpe. The long breakers plunged and ran in a hiss of foam along the coast. It was a warm evening. There was not a figure but themselves on the far reaches of sand, no noise but the sound of the sea. Paul loved to see it clanging at the land. He loved to feel himself between the noise of it and the silence of the sandy shore. Miriam was with him. Everything grew very intense. It was quite dark when they turned again. The way home was through a gap in the sandhills, and then along a raised grass road between two dykes. The country was black and still. From behind the sandhills came the whisper of the sea. Paul and Miriam walked in silence. Suddenly he started. The whole of his blood seemed to burst into flame, and he could scarcely breathe. An enormous orange moon was staring at them from the rim of the sandhills. He stood still, looking at it.

'Ah!' cried Miriam, when she saw it.

He remained perfectly still, staring at the immense and ruddy moon, the only thing in the far-reaching darkness of the level. His heart beat heavily, the muscles of his arms contracted.

'What is it?' murmured Miriam, waiting for him.

He turned and looked at her. She stood beside him, for ever in shadow. Her face, covered with the darkness of her hat, was watching him unseen. But she was brooding. She was slightly afraid – deeply moved and religious. That was her best state. He was impotent against it. His blood was concentrated like a flame in his chest. But he could not get across to her. There were flashes in his blood. But somehow she ignored them. She was expecting some religious state in him. Still yearning, she was half aware of his passion, and gazed at him, troubled. 'What is it?' she murmured again.

'It's the moon,' he answered, frowning.

'Yes,' she assented. 'Isn't it wonderful?' she was curious about him. The crisis was past.

He did not know himself what was the matter. He was naturally so young, and their intimacy was so abstract, he did not know he wanted to crush her on to his breast to ease the ache there. He was afraid of her. The fact that he might want her as a man wants a woman had in him been suppressed into a shame. When she shrank in her convulsed, coiled torture from the thought of such a thing he had winced to the depths of his soul. And now this 'purity' prevented even their first love-kiss. It was as if she could scarcely stand the shock of physical love, even a passionate kiss, and then he was too shrinking and sensitive to give it.

As they walked along the dark fen-meadow he watched the moon and did not speak. She plodded beside him. He hated her, for she seemed in some way to make him despise himself. Looking ahead – he saw the one light in the darkness, the window of their lamp-lit cottage.

He loved to think of his mother, and the other jolly people.

'Well, everybody else has been in long ago!' said his mother as they entered.

'What does that matter!' he cried irritably. 'I can go a walk if I like, can't I?'

'And I should have thought you could get in to supper with the rest,' said Mrs Morel.

'I shall please myself,' he retorted. 'It's not *late*. I shall do as I like.'

'Very well,' said his mother cuttingly, 'then *do* as you like.' And she took no further notice of him that evening. Which he pretended neither to notice nor to care about, but sat reading. Miriam read also, obliterating herself. Mrs Morel hated her for making her son like this. She watched Paul growing irritable, priggish, and melancholic. For this she put the blame on Miriam. Annie and all her friends joined against the girl. Miriam had no friend of her own, only Paul. But she did not suffer so much, because she despised the triviality of these other people.

And Paul hated her because, somehow, she spoilt his ease and naturalness. And he writhed himself with a feeling of humiliation.

CHAPTER 8

Strife in Love

ARTHUR FINISHED his apprenticeship, and got a job on the electrical plant at Minton Pit. He earned very little, but had a good chance of getting on. But he was wild and restless. He did not drink nor gamble. Yet he somehow contrived to get into endless scrapes, always through some hot-headed thoughtlessness. Either he went rabbiting in the woods, like a poacher, or he stayed in Nottingham all night instead of coming home, or he miscalculated his dive into the canal at Bestwood, and scored his chest into one mass of wounds on the raw stones and tins at the bottom.

He had not been at his work many months when again he did not come home one night.

'Do you know where Arthur is?' asked Paul at breakfast.

'I do not,' replied his mother.

'He is a fool,' said Paul. 'And if he *did* anything I shouldn't mind. But no, he simply can't come away from a game of whist, or else he must see a girl home from the skating-rink – quite proprietously – and so can't get home. He's a fool.'

'I don't know that it would make it any better if he did something to make us all ashamed,' said Mrs Morel.

Well, *I* should respect him more,' said Paul.

'I very much doubt it,' said his mother coldly.

They went on with breakfast.

'Are you fearfully fond of him?' Paul asked his mother.

What do you ask that for?'

'Because they say a woman always likes the youngest best.'

'She may do – but I don't. No, he wearies me.'

'And you'd actually rather he was good?'

'I'd rather he showed some of a man's common sense.'

Paul was raw and irritable. He also wearied his mother very often. She saw the sunshine going out of him, and she resented it.

As they were finishing breakfast came the postman with a letter from Derby. Mrs Morel screwed up her eyes to look at the address.

'Give it here, blind eye!' exclaimed her son, snitching it away from her.

She started, and almost boxed his ears.

'It's from your son, Arthur,' he said.

What now!' cried Mrs Morel.

' "My dearest Mother," ' Paul read, ' "I don't know what made me such a fool. I want you to come and fetch me back from here. I came with Jack Bredon yesterday, instead of going to work, and enlisted. He said he was sick of wearing the seat of a stool out, and, like the idiot you know I am, I came away with him." '

' "I have taken the King's shilling, but perhaps if you came for me they would let me go back with you. I was a fool when I did it. I don't want to be in the army. My dear mother, I am nothing but a trouble to you. But if you get me out of this, I promise I will have more sense and consideration. ..." '

Mrs Morel sat down in her rocking-chair.

Well, *now,*' she cried, 'let him stop!'

'Yes,' said Paul, 'let him stop.'

There was silence. The mother sat with her hands folded in her apron, her face set, thinking.

'If I'm not *sick!*' she cried suddenly. 'Sick!'

'Now,' said Paul, beginning to frown, 'you're not going to worry your soul out about this, do you hear.'

'I suppose I'm to take it as a blessing,' she flashed, turning on her son.

'You're not going to mount it up to a tragedy, so there,' he retorted.

'The *fool!* – the young fool!' she cried.

'He'll look well in uniform,' said Paul irritatingly.

His mother turned on him like a fury.

'Oh, will he!' she cried. 'Not in my eyes!'

'He should get in a cavalry regiment; he'll have the time of his life, and will look on awful swell.'

'Swell! – *swell!* – a mighty swell indeed! – a common soldier!'

Well,' said Paul, 'what am I but a common clerk?'

'A good deal, my boy!' cried his mother, stung.

What?'

'At any rate, a *man,* and not a thing in a red coat.'

'I shouldn't mind being in a red coat – or dark blue, that would suit me better – if they didn't boss me about too much.'

But his mother had ceased to listen.

'Just as he was getting on, or might have been getting on, at his job – a young nuisance – here he goes and ruins himself for life. What good will he be, do you think, after *this?*'

'It may lick him into shape beautifully,' said Paul.

'Lick him into shape! – lick what marrow there *was* out of his bones. A *soldier!* – a common *soldier!* – nothing but a body that makes movements when it hears a shout! It's a fine thing!'

'I can't understand why it upsets you,' said Paul. 'No, perhaps you can't. But *I* understand'; and she sat back in her chair, her chin in one hand, holding her elbow with the other, brimmed up with wrath and chagrin.

'And shall you go to Derby?' asked Paul.

'Yes.'

'It's no good.'

'I'll see for myself.'

'And why on earth don't you let him stop. It's just what he wants.'

'Of course,' cried the mother, '*you* know what he wants!'

She got ready and went by the first train to Derby, where she saw her son and the sergeant. It was, however, no good.

When Morel was having his dinner in the evening, she said suddenly:

'I've had to go to Derby today.'

The miner turned up his eyes, showing the whites in his black face.

'Has ter, lass. What took thee there?'

'That Arthur!'

'Oh – an' what's agate now?'*

'He's only enlisted.'

Morel put down his knife and leaned back in his chair.

'Nay,' he said, 'that he niver 'as!'

'And is going down to Aldershot tomorrow.'

'Well!' exclaimed the miner. 'That's a winder.' He considered it a moment, said 'H'm!' and proceeded with his dinner. Suddenly his face contracted with wrath. 'I hope he may never set foot i' my house again,' he said.

'The idea!' cried Mrs Morel. 'Saying such a thing!'

'I do,' repeated Morel. 'A fool as runs away for a soldier, let 'im look after 'issen; I s'll do no more for 'im.'

'A fat sight you have done as it is,' she said.

And Morel was almost ashamed to go to his public-house that evening.

'Well, did you go?' said Paul to his mother when he came home.

'I did.'

'And could you see him?'

'Yes.'

'And what did he say?'

'He blubbered when I came away.'

'H'm!'

'And so did I, so you needn't "h'm!" '

Mrs Morel fretted after her son. She knew he would not like the army. He did not. The discipline was intolerable to him.

'But the doctor,' she said with some pride to Paul, 'said he was perfectly proportioned – almost exactly – all his measurements were correct. He's good-looking, you know.'

* "What's happening!"

'He's awfully nice-looking. But he doesn't fetch the girls like William, does he?'

'No; it's a different character. He's a good deal like his father, irresponsible.'

To console his mother, Paul did not go much to Willey Farm at this time. And in the autumn exhibition of student's work in the Castle he had two studies, a landscape in watercolour and a still life in oil, both of which had first-prize awards. He was highly excited.

'What do you think I've got for my pictures, mother?' he asked coming home one evening. She saw by his eyes he was glad. Her face flushed.

'Now, how should I know, my boy!'

'A first prize for those glass jars – '

'H'm!'

'And a first prize for that sketch up at Willey Farm.'

'Both first?'

'Yes.'

'H'm!'

There was a rosy, bright look about her, though she said nothing.

'It's nice,' he said, 'isn't it?'

'It is.'

'Why don't you praise me up to the skies?'

She laughed.

'I should have the trouble of dragging you down again,' she said.

But she was full of joy, nevertheless. William had brought her his sporting trophies. She kept them still, and she did not forgive his death. Arthur was handsome – at least, a good specimen – and warm and generous, and probably would do well in the end. But Paul was going to distinguish himself. She had a great belief in him, the more because he was unaware of his own powers. There was so much to come out of him. Life for her was rich with promise. She was to see herself fulfilled. Not for nothing had been her struggle.

Several times during the exhibition Mrs Morel went to the Castle unknown to Paul. She wandered down the long room looking at the other exhibits. Yes, they were good. But they had not in them a certain something which she demanded for her satisfaction. Some made her jealous, they were so good. She looked at them a long time trying to find fault with them. Then suddenly she had a shock that made her heart beat. There hung Paul's picture! She knew it as if it were printed on her heart.

'Name – Paul Morel – First Prize.'

It looked so strange, there in public, on the walls of the Castle gallery, where in her lifetime she had seen so many pictures. And she glanced round to see if anyone had noticed her again in front of the same sketch.

But she felt a proud woman. When she met well-dressed ladies going home to the Park, she thought to herself:

'Yes, you look very well – but I wonder if *your* son has two first prizes in the Castle.'

And she walked on, as proud a little woman as any in Nottingham. And Paul felt he had done something for her, if only a trifle. All his work was hers.

One day, as he was going up Castle Gate, he met Miriam. He had seen her on the Sunday, and had not expected to meet her in town. She was walking with a rather striking woman, blonde, with a sullen expression, and a defiant carriage. It was strange how Miriam, in her bowed, meditative bearing, looked dwarfed beside this woman with the handsome shoulders. Miriam watched Paul searchingly. His gaze was on the stranger, who ignored him. The girl saw his masculine spirit rear its head.

'Hello!' he said, 'you didn't tell me you were coming to town.'

'No,' replied Miriam, half apologetically. 'I drove in to Cattle Market with father.'

He looked at her companion.

'I've told you about Mrs Dawes,' said Miriam huskily; she was nervous. 'Clara, do you know Paul?'

'I think I've seen him before,' replied Mrs Dawes indifferently, as she shook hands with him. She had scornful grey eyes, a skin like white honey, and a full mouth, with a slightly lifted upper lip that did not know whether it was raised in scorn of all men or out of eagerness to be kissed but which believed the former. She carried her head back, as if she had drawn away in contempt, perhaps from men also. She wore a large, dowdy hat of black beaver, and a sort of slightly affected simple dress that made her look rather sacklike. She was evidently poor, and had not much taste. Miriam usually looked nice.

Where have you seen me?' Paul asked of the woman.

She looked at him as if she would not trouble to answer. Then: 'Walking with Louie Travers,' she said.

Louie was one of the 'spiral' girls.

Why, do you know her?' he asked.

She did not answer. He turned to Miriam.

Where are you going?' he asked.

'To the Castle.'

What train are you going home by?'

'I am driving with father. I wish you could come too. What time are you free?'

'You know not till eight tonight, damn it!'

And directly the two women moved on.

Paul remembered that Clara Dawes was the daughter of an old friend of Mrs Leivers. Miriam had sought her out because she had once been spiral overseer at Jordan's, and because her husband, Baxter Dawes, was smith for the factory, making the irons for cripple instruments, and so on. Through her Miriam felt she got into direct contact with Jordan's, and could estimate better Paul's position. But Mrs Dawes was separated from her husband, and had taken up Women's Rights. She was supposed to be clever. It interested Paul.

Baxter Dawes he knew and disliked. The smith was a man of thirty-one or thirty-two. He came occasionally through Paul's corner – a big, well-set man, also striking to look at, and handsome. There was a peculiar similarity between himself and his wife. He had the same white skin, with a clear golden tinge. His hair was of soft brown, his moustache was golden. And he had a similar defiance in his bearing and manner. But then came the difference. His eyes, dark brown and quick-shifting, were dissolute. They protruded very slightly, and his eyelids hung over them in a way that was half hate. His mouth, too, was sensual. His whole manner was of cowed defiance, as if he were ready to knock anybody down who disapproved of him – perhaps because he really disapproved of himself.

From the first day he had hated Paul. Finding the lad's impersonal, deliberate gaze of on artist on his face, he got into a fury.

What are yer lookin' at?' he sneered, bullying.

The boy glanced away. But the smith used to stand behind the counter and talk to Mr Pappleworth. His speech was dirty, with a kind of rottenness. Again he found the youth with his cool, critical gaze fixed on his face. The smith started round as if he had been stung.

What'r yer lookin' at, three hap'orth o' pap?' he snarled.

The boy shrugged his shoulders slightly.

Why yer – !' shouted Dawes.

'Leave him alone,' said Mr Pappleworth, in that insinuating voice which means, 'he's only one of your good little sops who can't help it.'

Since that time the boy used to look at the man every time he came through with the same curious criticism, glancing away before he met the smith's eye. It made Dawes furious. They hated each other in silence.

Clara Dawes had no children. When she had left her husband the home had been broken up, and she had gone to live with her mother. Dawes lodged with his sister. In the same house was a sister-in-law, and somehow Paul knew that this girl, Louie Travers, was now Dawes' woman. She was a handsome, insolent hussy, who mocked at the youth, and yet flushed if he walked along to the station with her as she went home.

The next time he went to see Miriam it was Saturday evening. She had a fire in the parlour, and was waiting for him. The others, except her father and mother and the young children, had gone out, so the two had the parlour together. It was a long, low, warm room. There were three of Paul's small sketches on the wall, and his photo was on the mantelpiece. On the table and on the high old rosewood piano were bowls of coloured leaves. He sat in the armchair, she crouched on the hearthrug near his feet. The glow was warm on her handsome, pensive face as she kneeled there like a devotee.

What did you think of Mrs Dawes?' she asked quietly.

'She doesn't look very amiable,' he replied.

'No, but don't you think she's a fine woman?' she said, in a deep tone.

'Yes – in stature. But without a grain of taste. I like her for some things. *Is* she disagreeable?'

'I don't think so. I think she's dissatisfied.'

What with?'

'Well – how would *you* like to be tied for life to a man like that?'

Why did she marry him, then, if she was to have revulsions so soon?'

'Ay, why did she!' repeated Miriam bitterly.

'And I should have thought she had enough fight in her to match him,' he said.

Miriam bowed her head.

'Ay?' she queried satirically. 'What makes you think so?'

'Look at her mouth – made for passion – and the very setback of her throat – ' he threw his head back in Clara's defiant manner.

Miriam bowed a little lower.

'Yes,' she said.

There was a silence for some moments, while he thought of Clara. 'And what were the things you liked about her?' she asked.

'I don't know – her skin and the texture of her – and her – I don't know – there's a sort of fierceness somewhere in her. I appreciate her as an artist, that's all.'

'Yes.'

He wondered why Miriam crouched there brooding in that strange way. It irritated him.

'You don't really like her, do you?' he asked the girl.

She looked at him with her great, dazzled dark eyes.

'I do,' she said.

'You don't – you can't – not really.'

'Then what?' she asked slowly.

'Eh, I don't know – perhaps you like her because she's got a grudge against men.'

That was more probably one of his own reasons for liking Mrs Dawes, but this did not occur to him. They were silent. There had come into his forehead a knitting of the brows which was becoming habitual with him, particularly when he was with Miriam. She longed to smooth it away, and she was afraid of it. It seemed the stamp of a man who was not her man in Paul Morel.

There were some crimson berries among the leaves in the bowl. He reached over and pulled out a bunch.

'If you put red berries in your hair,' he said, 'why would you look like some witch or priestess, and never like a reveller?'

She laughed with a naked, painful sound. 'I don't know,' she said.

His vigorous warm hands were playing excitedly with the berries.

'Why can't you laugh?' he said. 'You never laugh laughter. You only laugh when something is odd or incongruous, and then it almost seems to hurt you.'

She bowed her head as if he were scolding her.

'I wish you could laugh at me just for one minute – just for one minute. I feel as if it would set something free.'

'But' – and she looked up at him with eyes frightened and struggling – 'I do laugh at you – I *do*.'

'Never! There's always a kind of intensity. When you laugh I could always cry; it seems as if it shows up your suffering. Oh, you make me knit the brows of my very soul and cogitate.'

Slowly she shook her head despairingly.

'I'm sure I don't want to,' she said.

'I'm so damned spiritual with *you* always!' he cried.

She remained silent, thinking, 'Then why don't you be otherwise.' But he saw her crouching, brooding figure, and it seemed to tear him in two.

'But, there, it's autumn,' he said, 'and everybody feels like a disembodied spirit then.'

There was still another silence. This peculiar sadness between them thrilled her soul. He seemed so beautiful with his eyes gone dark, and looking as if they were deep as the deepest well.

'You make me so spiritual!' he lamented. 'And I don't want to be spiritual.'

She took her finger from her mouth with a little pop, and looked up at him almost challenging. But still her soul was naked in her great dark eyes, and there was the same yearning appeal upon her. If he could have kissed her in abstract purity he would have done so. But he could not kiss her thus – and she seemed to leave no other way. And she yearned to him.

He gave a brief laugh.

Well,' he said, 'get that French and we'll do some – some Verlaine.'

'Yes,' she said in a deep tone, almost of resignation. And she rose and got the books. And her rather red, nervous hands looked so pitiful, he was mad to comfort her and kiss her. But then he dared not – or could not. There was something prevented him. His kisses were wrong for her. They continued the reading till ten o'clock, when they went into the kitchen, and Paul was natural and jolly again with the father and mother. His eyes were dark and shining; there was a kind of fascination about him.

When he went into the barn for his bicycle he found the front wheel punctured.

'Fetch me a drop of water in a bowl,' he said to her. 'I shall be late, and then I s'll catch it.'

He lighted the hurricane lamp, took off his coat, turned up the bicycle, and set speedily to work. Miriam came with the bowl of water and stood close to him, watching. She loved to see his hands doing things. He was slim and vigorous, with a kind of easiness even in his most hasty movements. And busy at his work he seemed to forget her. She loved him absorbedly. She wanted to run her hands down his sides. She always wanted to embrace him, so long as he did not want her.

'There!' he said, rising suddenly. 'Now, could you have done it quicker?'

'No!' she laughed.

He straightened himself. His back was towards her. She put her two hands on his sides, and ran them quickly down.

'You are so *fine!*' she said.

He laughed, hating her voice, but his blood roused to a wave of flame by her hands. She did not seem to realise him in all this. He might have been an object. She never realised the male he was.

He lighted his bicycle-lamp, bounced the machine on the barn floor to see that the tyres were sound, and buttoned his coat.

'That's all right!' he said.

She was trying the brakes, that she knew were broken.

'Did you have them mended?' she asked.

'No!'

'But why didn't you?'

'The back one goes on a bit.'

'But it's not safe.'

'I can use my toe.'

'I wish you'd had them mended,' she murmured.

'Don't worry – come to tea tomorrow, with Edgar.'

'Shall we?'

'Do – about four. I'll come to meet you.'

'Very well.'

She was pleased. They went across the dark yard to the gate. Looking across, he saw through the uncurtained window of the kitchen the heads of Mr and Mrs Leivers in the warm glow. It looked very cosy. The road, with pine-trees, was quite black in front.

'Till tomorrow,' he said, jumping on his bicycle.

'You'll take care, won't you?' she pleaded.

'Yes.'

His voice already came out of the darkness. She stood a moment watching the light from his lamp race into obscurity along the ground. She turned very slowly indoors. Orion was wheeling up over the wood, his dog twinkling after him, half smothered. For the rest the world was full of darkness, and silent, save for the breathing of cattle in their stalls. She prayed earnestly for his safety that night. When he left her, she often lay in anxiety, wondering if he had got home safely.

He dropped down the hills on his bicycle. The roads were greasy, so he had to let it go. He felt a pleasure as the machine plunged over the second, steeper drop in the hill. 'Here goes!' he said. It was risky, because of the curve in the darkness at the bottom, and because of the brewers' waggons with drunken waggoners asleep. His bicycle seemed to fall beneath him, and he loved it. Recklessness is almost a man's revenge on his woman. He feels he is not valued, so he will risk destroying himself to deprive her altogether.

The stars on the lake seemed to leap like grasshoppers, silver upon the blackness, as he spun past. Then there was the long climb home.

'See, mother!' he said, as he threw her the berries and leaves on to the table.

'H'm!' she said, glancing at them, then away again. She sat reading, alone, as she always did.

'Aren't they pretty?'

'Yes.'

He knew she was cross with him. After a few minutes he said:

'Edgar and Miriam are coming to tea tomorrow.'

She did not answer.

'You don't mind?'

Still she did not answer.

'Do you?' he asked.

'You know whether I mind or not.'

'I don't see why you should. I have plenty of meals there.'

'You do.'

'Then why do you begrudge them tea?'

'I begrudge whom tea?'

'What are you so horrid for?'

'Oh, say no more! You've asked her to tea, it's quite sufficient. She'll come.'

He was very angry with his mother. He knew it was merely Miriam she objected to. He flung off his boots and went to bed.

Paul went to meet his friends the next afternoon. He was glad to see them coming. They arrived home at about four o'clock. Everywhere was clean and still for Sunday afternoon. Mrs Morel sat in her black dress and black apron. She rose to meet the visitors. With Edgar she was cordial, but with Miriam cold and rather grudging. Yet Paul thought the girl looked so nice in her brown cashmere frock.

He helped his mother to get the tea ready. Miriam would have gladly proffered, but was afraid. He was rather proud of his home. There was about it now, he thought, a certain distinction. The chairs were only wooden, and the sofa was old. But the hearthrug and cushions were cosy; the pictures were prints in good taste; there was a simplicity in everything, and plenty of books. He was never ashamed in the least of his home, nor was Miriam of hers, because both were what they should be, and warm. And then he was proud of the table; the china was pretty, the cloth was fine. It did not matter that the spoons were not silver nor the knives ivory-handled; everything looked nice. Mrs Morel had managed wonderfully while her children were growing up, so that nothing was out of place.

Miriam talked books a little. That was her unfailing topic. But Mrs Morel was not cordial, and turned soon to Edgar.

At first Edgar and Miriam used to go into Mrs Morel's pew. Morel never went to chapel, preferring the public-house. Mrs Morel, like a little champion, sat at the head of her pew, Paul at the other end; and at first Miriam sat next to him. Then the chapel was like home. It was a pretty place, with dark pews and slim, elegant pillars, and flowers. And the same people had sat in the same places ever since he was a boy. It was wonderfully sweet and soothing to sit there for an hour and a half, next to Miriam, and near to his mother, uniting his two loves under the spell of the place of worship. Then he felt warm and happy and religious at once. And after chapel he walked home with Miriam, whilst Mrs Morel spent the rest of the evening with her old friend, Mrs Burns. He was keenly alive on his walks on Sunday nights with Edgar and Miriam. He never went past the pits at night, by the lighted lamp-house, the tall black head-stocks and lines of trucks, past the fans spinning slowly like shadows, without the feeling of Miriam returning to him, keen and almost unbearable.

She did not very long occupy the Morels' pew. Her father took one for themselves once more. It was under the little gallery, opposite the Morels'. When Paul and his mother came in the chapel the Leivers' pew was always empty. He was anxious for fear she would not come: it was so far, and there were so many rainy Sundays. Then, often very late indeed, she came in, with her long stride, her head bowed, her face hidden under her hat of dark green velvet. Her face, as she sat opposite, was always in shadow. But it gave him a very keen feeling, as if all his soul stirred within him, to see her there. It was not the same glow, happiness, and pride, that he felt in having his mother in charge: something more wonderful, less human, and tinged to intensity by a pain, as if there were something he could not get to.

At this time he was beginning to question the orthodox creed. He was twenty-one, and she was twenty. She was beginning to dread the spring: he became so wild, and hurt her so much. All the way he went cruelly smashing her beliefs. Edgar enjoyed it. He was by nature critical and rather dispassionate. But Miriam suffered exquisite pain, as, with an intellect like a knife, the man she loved examined her religion in which she lived and moved and had her being. But he did not spare her. He was cruel. And when they went alone he was even more fierce, as if he would kill her soul. He bled her beliefs till she almost lost consciousness.

'She exults – she exults as she carries him off from me,' Mrs Morel cried in her heart when Paul had gone. 'She's not like an ordinary woman, who can leave me my share in him. She wants to absorb him. She wants to draw him out and absorb him till there is nothing left of him, even for himself. He will never be a man on his own feet – she will suck him up.' So the mother sat, and battled and brooded bitterly.

And he, coming home from his walks with Miriam, was wild with torture. He walked biting his lips and with clenched fists, going at a great rate. Then, brought up against a stile, he stood for some minutes, and did not move. There was a great hollow of darkness fronting him, and on the black up-slopes patches of tiny lights, and in the lowest trough of the night, a flare of the pit. It was all weird and dreadful. Why was he torn so, almost bewildered, and unable to move? Why did his mother sit at home and suffer? He knew she suffered badly. But why should she? And why did he hate Miriam, and feel so cruel towards her, at the thought of his mother. If Miriam caused his mother suffering, then he hated her – and he easily hated her. Why did she make him feel as if he were uncertain of himself, insecure, an indefinite thing, as if he had not sufficient sheathing to prevent the night and the space breaking into him? How he hated her! And then, what a rush of tenderness and humility!

Suddenly he plunged on again, running home. His mother saw on him the marks of some agony, and she said nothing. But he had to make her talk to him. Then she was angry with him for going so far with Miriam.

'Why don't you like her, mother?' he cried in despair.

'I don't know, my boy,' she replied piteously. 'I'm sure I've tried to like her. I've tried and tried, but I can't – I can't!'

And he felt dreary and hopeless between the two.

Spring was the worst time. He was changeable, and intense and cruel. So he decided to stay away from her. Then came the hours when he knew Miriam was expecting him. His mother watched him growing restless. He could not go on with his work. He could do nothing. It was as if something were drawing his soul out towards Willey Farm. Then he put on his hat and went, saying nothing. And his mother knew he was gone. And as soon as he was on the way he sighed with relief. And when he was with her he was cruel again.

One day in March he lay on the bank of Nethermere, with Miriam sitting beside him. It was a glistening, white-and-blue day. Big clouds, so brilliant, went by overhead, while shadows stole along on the water. The clear spaces in the sky were of clean, cold blue. Paul lay on his back in the old grass, looking up. He could not bear to look at Miriam. She seemed to want him, and he resisted. He resisted all the time. He wanted now to give her passion and tenderness, and he could not. He felt that she wanted the soul out of his body, – and not him. All his strength and energy she drew into herself through some channel which united them. She did not want to meet him, so that there were two of them, man and woman together. She wanted to draw all of him into her. It urged him to an intensity like madness, which fascinated him, as drug-taking might.

He was discussing Michaelangelo. It felt to her as if she were fingering the very quivering tissue, the very protoplasm of life, as she heard him. It gave her her deepest satisfaction. And in the end it frightened her. There he lay in the white intensity of his search, and his voice gradually filled her with fear, so level it was, almost inhuman, as if in a trance.

'Don't talk any more,' she pleaded softly, laying her hand on his forehead.

He lay quite still, almost unable to move. His body was somewhere discarded.

'Why not? Are you tired?'

'Yes, and it wears you out.'

He laughed shortly, realising.

'Yet you always make me like it,' he said.

'I don't wish to,' she said, very low.

'Not when you've gone too far, and you feel you can't bear it. But your unconscious self always asks it of me. And I suppose I want it.'

He went on, in his dead fashion:

'If only you could want *me,* and not want what I can reel off for you!'

'I!' she cried bitterly – 'I! Why, when would you let me take you?'

'Then it's my fault,' he said, and, gathering himself together, he got up and began to talk trivialities. He felt insubstantial. In a vague way he hated her for it. And he knew he was as much to blame himself. This, however, did not prevent his hating her.

One evening about this time he had walked along the home road with her. They stood by the pasture leading down to the wood, unable to part. As the stars came out the clouds closed. They had glimpses of their own constellation, Orion, towards the west. His jewels glimmered for a moment, his dog ran low, struggling with difficulty through the spume of cloud.

Orion was for them chief in significance among the constellations. They had gazed at him in their strange, surcharged hours of feeling, until they seemed themselves to live in every one of his stars. This evening Paul had been moody and perverse. Orion had seemed just an ordinary constellation to him. He had fought against his glamour and fascination. Miriam was watching her lover's mood carefully. But he said nothing that gave him away, till the moment came to part, when he stood frowning gloomily at the gathered clouds, behind which the great constellation must be striding still.

There was to be a little party at his house the next day, at which she was to attend.

'I shan't come and meet you,' he said.

'Oh, very well; it's not very nice out,' she replied slowly.

'It's not that – only they don't like me to. They say I care more for you than for them. And you understand, don't you? You know it's only friendship.'

Miriam was astonished and hurt for him. It had cost him an effort. She left him, wanting to spare him any further humiliation. A fine rain blew in her face as she walked along the road. She was hurt deep down; and she despised him for being blown about by any wind of authority. And in her heart of hearts, unconsciously, she felt that he was trying to get away from her. This she would never have acknowledged. She pitied him.

At this time Paul became an important factor in Jordan's warehouse. Mr Pappleworth left to set up a business of his own, and Paul remained with Mr Jordan as spiral overseer. His wages were to be raised to thirty shillings at the year-end, if things went well.

Still on Friday night Miriam often came down for her French lesson. Paul did not go so frequently to Willey Farm, and she grieved at the thought of her education's coming to an end; moreover, they both loved to be together, in spite of discords. So they read Balzac, and did compositions, and felt highly cultured.

Friday night was reckoning night for the miners. Morel 'reckoned' – shared up the money of the stall – either in the New Inn at Bretty or in his own house, according as his fellow-butties wished. Barker had turned a non-drinker, so now the men reckoned at Morel's house.

Annie, who had been teaching away, was at home again. She was still a tomboy; and she was engaged to be married. Paul was studying design.

Morel was always in good spirits on Friday evening, unless the week's earnings were small. He bustled immediately after his dinner, prepared to get washed. It was decorum for the women to absent themselves while the men reckoned. Women were not supposed to spy into such a masculine privacy as the butties' reckoning, nor were they to know the exact amount of the week's earnings. So, whilst her father was spluttering in the scullery, Annie went out to spend an hour with a neighbour. Mrs Morel attended to her baking.

'Shut that doo-er!' bowled Morel furiously.

Annie banged it behind her, and was gone.

'If tha oppens it again while I'm weshin' me, I'll ma'e thy jaw rattle,' he threatened from the midst of his soapsuds. Paul and the mother frowned to hear him.

Presently he came running out of the scullery with the soapy water dripping from him, dithering with cold.

'Oh, my sirs!' he said. 'Wheer's my towel?'

It was hung on a chair to warm before the fire, otherwise he would have bullied and blustered. He squatted on his heels before the hot baking-fire to dry himself.

'F-ff-f!' he went, pretending to shudder with cold.

'Goodness, man, don't be such a kid!' said Mrs Morel 'It's *not* cold.'

'Thee strip thysen stark nak'd to wesh thy flesh i' that scullery,' said the miner, as he rubbed his hair; 'nowt b'r a ice-'ouse!'

'And I shouldn't make that fuss,' replied his wife.

'No, tha'd drop down stiff, as dead as a door-knob, wi' thy nesh sides.'

'Why is a door-knob deader than anything else?' asked Paul, curious. 'Eh, I dunno; that's what they say,' replied his father. 'But there's that much draught i' yon scullery, as it blows through your ribs like through a five-barred gate.'

'It would have some difficulty in blowing through yours,' said Mrs Morel.

Morel looked down ruefully at his sides.

'Me!' he exclaimed. 'I'm nowt b't a skinned rabbit. My bones fair juts out on me.'

'I should like to know where,' retorted his wife.

'Iv'ry-wheer! I'm nobbut a sock o' faggots.'

Mrs Morel laughed. He had still a wonderfully young body, muscular, without any fat. His skin was smooth and clear; It might have been the body of a man of twenty-eight, except that there were, perhaps, too many blue scars, like tattoo-marks, where the coal-dust remained under the skin, and that his chest was too hairy. But he put his hand on his sides ruefully. It was his fixed belief that, because he did not get fat, he was as thin as a starved rat.

Paul looked at his father's thick, brownish hands all scarred, with broken nails, rubbing the fine smoothness of his sides, and the incongruity struck him. It seemed strange they were the same flesh.

'I suppose,' he said to his father, 'you had a good figure once.'

'Eh!' exclaimed the miner, glancing round, startled and timid, like a child.

'He had,' exclaimed Mrs Morel, 'if he didn't hurtle himself up as if he was trying to get in the smallest space he could.'

'Me!' exclaimed Morel – 'me a good figure! I wor niver much more n'r a skeleton.'

'Man!' cried his wife, 'don't be such a pulamiter*!'

'Strewth!' he said. 'Tha's niver knowed me but what I looked as if I wor goin' off in a rapid decline.'

She sat and laughed.

---

* grumbler.

'You've had a constitution like iron,' she said; 'and never a man had a better start, if it was body that counted. You should have seen him as a young man,' she cried suddenly to Paul, drawing herself up to imitate her husband's once handsome bearing.

Morel watched her shyly. He saw again the passion she had had for him. It blazed upon her for a moment. He was shy, rather scored, and humble. Yet again he felt his old glow. And then immediately he felt the ruin he had made during these years. He wanted to bustle about, to run away from it.

'Gi'e my back a bit of a wesh,' he asked her.

His wife brought a well-soaped flannel and clapped it on his shoulders. He gave a jump.

'Eh, tha mucky little 'ussy!' he cried. 'Cowd as death!'

'You ought to have been a salamander,' she laughed, washing his back. It was very rarely she would do anything so personal for him. The children did those things.

'The next world won't be half hot enough for you,' she added.

'No,' he said; 'tha'lt see as it's draughty for me.'

But she had finished. She wiped him in a desultory fashion, and went upstairs, returning immediately with his shifting-trousers. When he was dried he struggled into his shirt. Then, ruddy and shiny, with hair on end, and his flannelette shirt hanging over his pit-trousers, he stood warming the garments he was going to put on. He turned them, he pulled them inside out, he scorched them.

'Goodness, man!' cried Mrs Morel; 'get dressed!'

'Should thee like to clap thysen into britches as cowd as a tub o' water?' he said.

At last he took off his pit-trousers and donned decent black. He did all this on the hearthrug, as he would have done if Annie and her familiar friends had been present.

Mrs Morel turned the bread in the oven. Then from the red earthenware panchion* of dough that stood in a corner she took another handful of paste, worked it to the proper shape, and dropped it into a tin. As she was doing so Barker knocked and

* a large clay bowl.

entered. He was a quiet, compact little man who looked as if he would go through a stone wall. His black hair was cropped short, his head was bony. Like most miners, he was pale, but healthy and taut.

'Evenin', missis,' he nodded to Mrs Morel, and he seated himself with a sigh.

'Good-evening,' she replied cordially.

'Tha's made thy heels crack,' said Morel.

'I dunno as I have,' said Barker.

He sat, as the men always did in Mrs Morel's kitchen, effacing himself rather.

'How's missis?' she asked of him.

Be had told her some time back:

'We're expectin' us third just now, you see.'

Well,' he answered, rubbing his head, 'she keeps pretty middlin', I think.'

'Let's see – when?' asked Mrs Morel.

Well, I shouldn't be surprised any time now.'

'Ah! And she's kept fairly?'

'Yes, tidy.'

'That's a blessing, for she's none too strong.'

'No. An' I've done another silly trick.'

What's that?'

Mrs Morel knew Barker wouldn't do anything very silly. 'I'm come be-out th' market-bag.'

'You can have mine.'

'Nay, you'll be wantin' that yourself.'

'I shan't. I take a string bag always.'

She saw the determined little collier buying in the week's groceries and meat on the Friday nights, and she admired him.

'Barker's little, but he's ten times the man you are,' she said to her husband.

Just then Wesson entered. He was thin, rather frail-looking, with a boyish ingenuousness and a slightly foolish smile, despite his seven children. But his wife was a passionate woman.

'I see you've kested me,' he said, smiling rather vapidly. 'Yes,' replied Barker.

The newcomer took off his cap and his big woollen muffler. His nose was pointed and red.

'I'm afraid you're cold, Mr Wesson,' said Mrs Morel.

'It's a bit nippy,' he replied.

'Then come to the fire.'

'Nay, I s'll do where I am.'

Both colliers sat away back. They could not be induced to come on to the hearth. The hearth is sacred to the family.

'Go thy ways i' th' armchair,' cried Morel cheerily.

'Nay, thank yer; I'm very nicely here.'

'Yes, come, of course,' insisted Mrs Morel.

He rose and went awkwardly. He sat in Morel's armchair awkwardly. It was too great a familiarity. But the fire made him blissfully happy.

'And how's that chest of yours?' demanded Mrs Morel. He smiled again, with his blue eyes rather sunny.

'Oh, it's very middlin',' he said.

'Wi' a rattle in it like a kettle-drum,' said Barker shortly. 'T-t-t-t!' went Mrs Morel rapidly with her tongue. 'Did you have that flannel singlet made?'

'Not yet,' he smiled.

'Then, why didn't you?' she cried.

'It'll come,' he smiled.

'Ah, an' Doomsday!' exclaimed Barker.

Barker and Morel were both impatient of Wesson. But, then, they were both as hard as nails, physically.

When Morel was nearly ready he pushed the bag of money to Paul.

'Count it, boy,' he asked humbly.

Paul impatiently turned from his books and pencil, tipped the bag upside down on the table. There was a five-pound bag of silver, sovereigns and loose money. He counted quickly, referred to the checks – the written papers giving amount of coal – put the money in order. Then Barker glanced at the checks.

Mrs Morel went upstairs, and the three men came to table. Morel, as master of the house, sat in his armchair, with his back to the hot fire. The two butties had cooler seats. None of them counted the money.

What did we say Simpson's was?' asked Morel; and the butties cavilled for a minute over the dayman's earnings. Then the amount was put aside.

'An' Bill Naylor's?'

This money also was taken from the pack.

Then, because Wesson lived in one of the company's houses, and his rent had been deducted, Morel and Barker took four-and-six each. And because Morel's coals had come, and the leading was stopped, Barker and Wesson took four shillings each. Then it was plain soiling. Morel gave each of them a sovereign till there were no more sovereigns; each half a crown till there were no more half-crowns; each a shilling till there were no more shillings. If there was anything at the end that wouldn't split, Morel took it and stood drinks.

Then the three men rose and went. Morel scuttled out of the house before his wife came down. She heard the door close, and descended. She looked hastily at the bread in the oven. Then, glancing on the table, she saw her money lying. Paul had been working all the time. But now he felt his mother counting the week's money, and her wrath rising.

'T-t-t-t-t!' went her tongue.

He frowned. He could not work when she was cross. She counted again.

'A measly twenty-five shillings!' she exclaimed. 'How much was the cheque?'

'Ten pounds eleven,' said Paul irritably. He dreaded what was coming.

'And he gives me a scrattlin' twenty-five, an' his club this week! But I know him. He thinks because *you're* earning he needn't keep the house any longer. No, all he has to do with his money is to guttle it.[*] But I'll show him!'

'Oh, mother; don't!' cried Paul.

'Don't what, I should like to know?' she exclaimed.

'Don't carry on again. I can't work.'

She went very quiet.

'Yes, it's all very well,' she said; 'but how do you think I'm going to manage?'

'Well, it won't make it any better to whittle about it.'

'I should like to know what you'd do if you had it to put up with.'

'It won't be long. You can have my money. Let him go to hell.'

He went back to his work, and she tied her bonnet-strings grimly. When she was fretted he could not bear it. But now he began to insist on her recognising him.

'The two loaves at the top,' she said, 'will be done in twenty minutes. Don't forget them.'

'All right,' he answered; and she went to market.

He remained alone working. But his usual intense concentration became unsettled. He listened for the yard-gate. At a quarter-past seven came a low knock, and Miriam entered.

'All alone?' she said.

'Yes.'

As if at home, she took off her tam-o'-shanter and her long coat, hanging them up. It gave him a thrill. This might be their own house, his and hers. Then she came back and peered over his work.

'What is it?' she asked.

'Still design, for decorating stuffs, and for embroidery.'

---

[*] to bust it.

She bent short-sightedly over the drawings.

It irritated him that she peered so into everything that was his, searching him out. He went into the parlour and returned with a bundle of brownish linen. Carefully unfolding it, he spread it on the floor. It proved to be a curtain or *portière,* beautifully stencilled with a design on roses.

'Ah, how beautiful!' she cried.

The spread cloth, with its wonderful reddish roses and dark green stems, all so simple, and somehow so wicked-looking, lay at her feet. She went on her knees before it, her dark curls dropping. He saw her crouched voluptuously before his work, and his heart beat quickly. Suddenly she looked up at him.

'Why does it seem cruel?' she asked.

'What?'

'There seems a feeling of cruelty about it,' she said.

'It's jolly good, whether or not,' he replied, folding up his work with a lover's hands.

She rose slowly, pondering.

'And what will you do with it?' she asked.

'Send it to Liberty's. I did it for my mother, but I think she'd rather have the money.'

'Yes,' said Miriam. He had spoken with a touch of bitterness, and Miriam sympathised. Money would have been nothing to her.

He took the cloth back into the parlour. When he returned, he threw to Miriam a smaller piece. It was a cushion cover with the same design.

'I did that for you,' he said.

She fingered the work with trembling hands, and did not speak. He became embarrassed.

'By Jove, the bread!' he cried.

He took the top loaves out, topped them vigorously. They were done.

He put them on the hearth to cool. Then he went to the scullery, wetted his hands, scooped the last white dough out of the punchion, and dropped it in a baking-tin. Miriam was still bent over her painted cloth. He stood rubbing the bits of dough from his hands.

'You do like it?' he asked.

She looked up at him, with her dark eyes one flame of love. He laughed uncomfortably. Then he began to talk about the design. There was for him the most intense pleasure in talking about his work to Miriam. All his passion, all his wild blood, went into this intercourse with her, when he talked and conceived his work. She brought forth to him his imaginations. She did not understand, any more than a woman understands when she conceives a child in her womb. But this was life for her and for him.

While they were talking, a young woman of about twenty-two, small and pale, hollow-eyed, yet with a relentless look about her, entered the room. She was a friend at the Morels'.

'Take your things off,' said Paul.

'No, I'm not stopping.'

She sat down in the armchair opposite Paul and Miriam, who were on the sofa. Miriam moved a little farther from him. The room was hot, with a scent of new bread. Brown, crisp loaves stood on the hearth.

'I shouldn't have expected to see you here tonight, Miriam Leivers,' said Beatrice wickedly.

Why not?' murmured Miriam huskily.

Why, let's look at your shoes.'

Miriam remained uncomfortably still.

'If tha doesna tha durs'na,' laughed Beatrice.

Miriam put her feet from under her dress. Her boots had that queer, irresolute, rather pathetic look about them, which showed how selfconscious and self-mistrustful she was. And they were covered with mud.

'Glory! You're a positive muck-heap,' exclaimed Beatrice. 'Who cleans your boots?'

'I clean them myself.'

'Then you wanted a job,' said Beatrice. 'It would ha' taken a lot of men to ha' brought me down here tonight. But love laughs at sludge, doesn't it, 'Postle my duck?'

'Inter alia,' he said.

'Oh, Lord! are you going to spout foreign languages? What does it mean, Miriam?'

There was a fine sarcasm in the last question, but Miriam did not see it.

' "Among other things," I believe,' she said humbly.

Beatrice put her tongue between her teeth and laughed wickedly.

' "Among other things," 'Postle?' she repeated. 'Do you mean love laughs at mothers, and fathers, and sisters, and. brothers, and men friends, and lady friends, and even at the b'loved himself?'

She affected a great innocence.

'In fact, it's one big smile,' he replied.

'Up its sleeve, 'Postle Morel – you believe me,' she said; and she went off into another burst of wicked, silent laughter.

Miriam sat silent, withdrawn into herself. Everyone of Paul's friends delighted in taking sides against her, and he left her in the lurch seemed almost to have a sort of revenge upon her then.

'Are you still at school?' asked Miriam of Beatrice.

'Yes.'

'You've not had your notice, then?'

'I expect it at Easter.'

'Isn't it on awful shame, to turn you off merely because you didn't pass the exam?'

'I don't know,' said Beatrice coldly.

'Agatha says you're as good as any teacher anywhere. It seems to me ridiculous. I wonder why you didn't pass.'

'Short of brains, eh 'Postle?' said Beatrice briefly.

'Only brains to bite with,' replied Paul, laughing.

'Nuisance!' she cried; and, springing from her seat, she rushed and boxed his ears. She had beautiful small hands. He held her wrists while she wrestled with him. At last she broke free, and seized two handfuls of his thick, dark brown hair, which she shook.

'Beat!' he said, as he pulled his hair straight with his fingers. 'I hate you!'

She laughed with glee.

'Mind!' she said. 'I want to sit next to you.'

'I'd as lief be neighbours with a vixen,' he said, nevertheless making place for her between him and Miriam.

'Did it ruffle his pretty hair, then!' she cried; and, with her hair-comb, she combed him straight. 'And his nice lime moustache!' she exclaimed. She tilted his head back and combed his young moustache. 'It's a wicked moustache, 'Postle,' she said. 'It's a red for danger. Have you got any of those cigarettes?'

He pulled his cigarette-case from his pocket. Beatrice looked inside it.

'And fancy me having Connie's last cig,' said Beatrice, putting the thing between her teeth. He held a lit match to her, and she puffed daintily.

'Thanks so much, darling,' she said mockingly.

It gave her a wicked delight.

'Don't you think he does it nicely, Miriam?' she asked.

'Oh, very!' said Miriam.

He took a cigarette for himself

'Light, old boy?' said Beatrice, tilting her cigarette at him.

He bent forward to her to light his cigarette at hers. She was winking at him as he did so. Miriam saw his eyes trembling with mischief, and his full, almost sensual, mouth quivering. He was not himself, and she could not bear it. As he was now, she had no connection with him; she might as well not have existed. She saw the cigarette dancing on his full red lips. She hated his thick hair for being tumbled loose on his forehead.

'Sweet boy!' said Beatrice, tipping up his chin and giving him a lime kiss on the cheek.

'I s'll kiss thee back, Beat,' he said.

'Tha wunna!' she giggled, jumping up and going away. 'Isn't he shameless, Miriam? '

'Quite,' said Miriam. 'By the way, aren't you forgetting the bread?'

'By Jove!' he cried, flinging open the oven-door.

Out puffed the bluish smoke and a smell of burned bread.

'Oh, golly!' cried Beatrice, coming to his side. He crouched before the oven, she peered over his shoulder. 'This is what comes of the oblivion of love, my boy.'

Paul was ruefully removing the loaves. One was burnt black on the hot side; another was hard as a brick.

'Poor mater!' said Paul.

'You want to grate it,' said Beatrice. 'Fetch me the nutmeg-grater.'

She arranged the bread in the oven. He brought the grater, and she grated the bread on to a newspaper on the table. He set the doors open to blow away the smell of burned bread. Beatrice grated away, puffing her cigarette, knocking the charcoal off the poor loaf.

My word, Miriam! you're in for it this time,' said Beatrice.

'I!' exclaimed Miriam in amazement.

'You'd better be gone when his mother comes in. I know why King Alfred burned the cakes. Now I see it! 'Postle would fix up a tale about his work making him forget, if he thought it would wash. If that old woman had come in a bit sooner, she'd have boxed the brazen thing's ears who made the oblivion, instead of poor Alfred's.'

She giggled as she scraped the loaf. Even Miriam laughed in spite of herself. Paul mended the fire ruefully.

The garden-gate was heard to bang.

'Quick!' cried Beatrice, giving Paul the scraped loaf. 'Wrap it up in a damp towel.'

Paul disappeared into the scullery. Beatrice hastily blew her scrapings into the fire, and sat down innocently. Annie came bursting in. She was on abrupt, quite smart young woman. She blinked in the strong light.

'Smell of burning!' she exclaimed.

'It's the cigarettes,' replied Beatrice demurely.

'Where's Paul?'

Leonard had followed Annie. He had a long comic face and blue eyes, very sad.

'I suppose he's left you to settle it between you,' he said. He nodded sympathetically to Miriam, and became gently sarcastic to Beatrice.

'No,' said Beatrice, 'he's gone off with number nine.'

'I just met number five inquiring for him,' said Leonard.

'Yes – we're going to share him up like Solomon's baby, said Beatrice. Annie laughed.

'Oh, ay,' said Leonard. 'And which bit should you have?'

'I don't know,' said Beatrice. 'I'll let all the others pick first.'

'An' you'd have the leavings, like?' said Leonard, twisting up a comic face. '

Annie was looking in the oven. Miriam sat ignored. Paul entered.

'This bread's a fine sight, our Paul,' said Annie.

'Then you should stop an' look after it,' said Paul.

'You mean *you* should do what you're reckoning to do,' replied Annie.

'He should, shouldn't he!' cried Beatrice.

'I s'd think he'd got plenty on hand,' said Leonard.

'You had a nasty walk, didn't you, Miriam?' said Annie.

'Yes – but I'd been in all week – '

'And you wanted a bit of a change, like,' insinuated Leonard kindly.

'Well, you can't be stuck in the house for ever,' Annie agreed. She was quite amiable. Beatrice pulled on her coat, and went out with Leonard and Annie. She would meet her own boy.

'Don't forget that bread, our Paul,' cried Annie. 'Good-night, Miriam. I don't think it will rain.'

When they had all gone, Paul fetched the swathed loaf, unwrapped it, and surveyed it sadly.

'It's a mess!' he said.

'But,' answered Miriam impatiently, 'what is it, after all – twopence ha'penny.'

'Yes, but – it's the mater's precious baking, and she'll take it to heart. However, it's no good bothering.'

He took the loaf back into the scullery. There was a little distance between him and Miriam. He stood balanced opposite her for some moments considering, thinking of his behaviour with Beatrice. He felt guilty inside himself, and yet glad. For some inscrutable reason it served Miriam right. He was not going to repent. She wondered what he was thinking of as he stood suspended. His thick hair was tumbled over his forehead. Why might she not push it back for him, and remove the marks of Beatrice's comb? Why might she not press his body with her two hands. It looked so firm, and every whit living. And he would let other girls, why not her?

Suddenly he started into life. It made her quiver almost with terror as he quickly pushed the hair off his forehead and came towards her.

'Half-past eight!' he said. 'We'd better buck up. Where's your French?'

Miriam shyly and rather bitterly produced her exercise-book. Every week she wrote for him a sort of diary of her inner life, in her own French. He had found this was the only way to get her to do compositions. And her diary was mostly a love-letter. He would read it now; she felt as if her soul's history were going to be desecrated by him in his present mood. He sat beside her. She watched his hand firm and warm, rigorously scoring her work. He was reading only the French, ignoring her soul that was there. But gradually his hand forgot its work. He read in silence, motionless. She quivered.

' "Ce matin les oiseaux m'ont éveille," ' he read. ' "Il faisait encore un crépuscule. Mais la petite fenêtre de ma chambre était blême, et puis, jaûne, et tous les oiseaux du bois éclaterent dans un chanson vif et résonnant. Toute l'aûbe tressaillit. J'avais revé de vous. Est-ce que vous voyez aussi l'aûbe? Les oiseaux m'éveillent presque tous les matins, et toujours il y a quelque chose de terreur dans le cri des grives. Il est si clair – " '

Miriam sat tremulous, half ashamed. He remained quite still, trying to understand. He only knew she loved him.

He was afraid of her love for him. It was too good for him, and he was inadequate. His own love was, at fault, not hers. Ashamed, he corrected her work, humbly writing above her words.

'Look,' he said quietly, 'the past participle conjugated with *avoir* agrees with the direct object when it precedes.'

She bent forward, trying to see and to understand. Her free, fine curls tickled his face. He started as if they had been red hot, shuddering. He saw her peering forward at the page, her red lips parted piteously, the black hair springing in fine strands across her tawny, ruddy cheek. She was coloured like a pomegranate for richness. His breath came short as he watched her. Suddenly she looked up at him. Her dark eyes were naked with their love, afraid, and yearning. His eyes, too, were dark, and they hurt her. They seemed to master her. She lost all her self-control, was exposed in fear. And he knew, before he could kiss her, he must drive something out of himself. And a touch of hate for her crept back again into his heart. He returned to her exercise.

Suddenly he flung down the pencil, and was at the oven in a leap, turning the bread. For Miriam he was too quick. She started violently, and it hurt her with real pain. Even the way he crouched before the oven hurt her. There seemed to be something cruel in it, something cruel in the swift way he pitched the bread out of the tins, caught it up again. If only he had been gentle in his movements she would have felt so rich and warm. As it was, she was hurt.

He returned and finished the exercise.

'You've done well this week,' he said.

She saw he was flattered by her diary. It did not repay her entirely.

'You really do blossom out sometimes,' he said. 'You ought to write poetry.'

She lifted her head with joy, then she shook it mistrustfully.

'I don't trust myself,' she said.

'You should try!'

Again she shook her head.

'Shall we read, or is it too late?' he asked.

'It is late – but we can read just a little,' she pleaded.

She was really getting now the food for her life during the next week. He made her copy Baudelaire's 'Le Balcon.'

Then he read it for her. His voice was soft and caressing, but growing almost brutal. He had a way of lifting his lips and showing his teeth, passionately and bitterly, when he was much moved. This he did now. It made Miriam feel as if he were trampling on her. She dared not look at him, but sat with her head bowed. She could not understand why he got into such a tumult and fury. It made her wretched. She did not like Baudelaire, on the whole – nor Verlaine.

'Behold her singing in the field
Yon solitary highland lass.'

That nourished her heart. So did 'Fair Ines.' And –

'It was a beauteous evening, calm and pure,
And breathing holy quiet like a nun.'

These were like herself. And there was he, saying in his throat bitterly:

'Tu te rappeleras la beaûté des carresses.'*

The poem was finished; he took the bread out of the oven, arranging the burnt loaves at the bottom of the panchion, the good ones at the top. The desiccated loaf remained swathed up in the scullery.

'Mater needn't know till morning,' he said. 'It won't upset her so much then as at night.'

Miriam looked in the bookcase, saw what postcards and letters he had received, saw what books were there. She took one that had interested him. Then he turned down the gas and they set off. He did not trouble to lock the door.

He was not home again until a quarter to eleven. His mother was seated in the rocking-chair. Annie, with a rope of hair hanging down her back, remained sitting on a low stool before the fire, her elbows on her knees, gloomily. On the table stood the offending loaf unswathed. Paul entered rather breathless. No one spoke. His mother was reading the little local newspaper. He took off his coat, and went to sit down on the sofa. His mother moved curtly aside to let him pass. No one spoke. He was very uncomfortable. For some minutes he sat pretending to read a piece of paper he found on the table. Then –

'I forgot that bread, mother,' he said.

There was no answer from either woman.

Well,' he said, 'it's only twopence ha'penny. I can pay you for that.'

Being angry he put three pennies on the table, and slid them towards his mother. She turned away her head. Her mouth was shut tightly.

'Yes,' said Annie, 'you don't know how badly my mother is!'

The girl sat staring glumly into the fire.

* (Fr.) You will remember the beauty of our embraces.

Why is she badly?' asked Paul, in his overbearing way.

Well!' said Annie. 'She could scarcely get home.'

He looked closely at his mother. She looked ill.

'*Why* could you scarcely get home?' he asked her, still sharply. She would not answer.

'I found her as white as a sheet sitting here,' said Annie, with a suggestion of tears in her voice.

'Well, *why?*' insisted Paul. His brows were knitting, his eyes dilating passionately.

'It was enough to upset anybody,' said Mrs Morel, 'hugging those parcels – meat, and green-groceries, and a pair of curtains – '

'Well, why *did* you hug them; you needn't have done.'

'Then who would?'

'Let Annie fetch the meat.'

'Yes, and I *would* fetch the meat, but how was I to know. You were off with Miriam, instead of being in when my mother came.'

'And what was the matter with you?' asked Paul of his mother.

'I suppose it's my heart,' she replied. Certainly she looked bluish round the mouth.

'And have you felt it before?'

'Yes – often enough.'

'Then why haven't you told me? – and why haven't you seen a doctor?'

Mrs Morel shifted in her chair, angry with him for his hectoring.

'You'd never notice anything,' said Annie. 'You're too eager to be off with Miriam.'

'Oh, am I – and any worse than you with Leonard?'

'I was in at a quarter to ten.'

There was silence in the room for a time.

'I should have thought,' said Mrs Morel bitterly, 'that she wouldn't have occupied you so entirely as to burn a whole ovenful of bread.'

'Beatrice was here as well as she.'

'Very likely. But we know why the bread is spoilt.'

Why?' he flashed.

'Because you were engrossed with Miriam,' replied Mrs Morel hotly.

'Oh, very well – then it was *not!*' he replied angrily.

He was distressed and wretched. Seizing a paper, he began to read. Annie, her blouse unfastened, her long ropes of hair twisted into a plait, went up to bed, bidding him a very curt good-night.

Paul sat pretending to read. He knew his mother wanted to upbraid him. He also wanted to know what had made her ill, for he was troubled. So, instead of running away to bed, as he would have liked to do, he sat and waited. There was a tense silence. The clock ticked loudly.

'You'd better go to bed before your father comes in,' said the mother harshly. 'And if you're going to have anything to eat, you'd better get it.'

'I don't want anything.'

It was his mother's custom to bring him some trifle for supper on Friday night, the night of luxury for the colliers. He was too angry to go and find it in the pantry this night. This insulted her.

'If I *wanted* you to go to Selby on Friday night, I can imagine the scene,' said Mrs Morel. 'But you're never too tired to go if *she* will come for you. Nay, you neither want to eat nor drink then.'

'I can't let her go alone.'

'Can't you? And why does she come?'

'Not because I ask her.'

'She doesn't come without you want her – '

'Well, what if I *do* want her – ' he replied.

'Why, nothing, if it was sensible or reasonable. But to go trapesing up there miles and miles in the mud, coming home at midnight, and got to go to Nottingham in the morning – '

'If I hadn't, you'd be just the same.'

'Yes, I should, because there's no sense in it. Is she so fascinating that you must follow her all that way?' Mrs Morel was bitterly sarcastic. She sat still, with averted face, stroking with a rhythmic, jerked movement, the black sateen of her apron. It was a movement that hurt Paul to see.

'I do like her,' he said, 'but – '

'*Like* her!' said Mrs Morel, in the same biting tones. 'It seems to me you like nothing and nobody else. There's neither Annie, nor me, nor anyone now for you.'

'What nonsense, mother – you know I don't love her – I – I tell you I *don't* love her – she doesn't even walk with my arm, because I don't want, her to.'

'Then why do you fly to her so often!'

'I do like to talk to her – I never said I didn't. But! *don't* love her.'

'Is there nobody else to talk to?'

'Not about the things we talk of. There's lots of things that you're not interested in, that – '

What things?'

Mrs Morel was so intense that Paul began to pant.

'Why – painting – and books. *You* don't care about Herbert Spencer.'

'No,' was the sad reply. 'And you won't at my age.'

Well, but I do now – and Miriam does – '

'And how do you know,' Mrs Morel flashed defiantly, 'that *I* shouldn't? Do you ever try me!'

'But you don't, mother, you know you don't care whether a picture's decorative or not; you don't care what *manner* it is in.'

'How do you know I don't care? Do you ever try me? Do you ever talk to me about these things, to try?'

'But it's not that that matters to you, mother, you know it's not'

'What is it, then – what is it, then, that matters to me?' she flashed. He knitted his brows with pain.

'You're old, mother, and we're young.'

He only meant that the interests of *her* age were not the interests of his. But he realised the moment he had spoken that he had said the wrong thing.

'Yes, I know it well – I am old. And therefore I may stand aside; I have nothing more to do with you. You only want me to wait on you – the rest is for Miriam.'

He could not bear it. Instinctively he realised that he was life to her. And, after all, she was the chief thing to him, the only supreme thing.

'You know it isn't, mother, you mow it isn't!'

She was moved to pity by his cry.

'It looks a great deal like it,' she said, half putting aside her despair. 'No, mother – I really *don't* love her. I talk to her, but I want to come home to you.'

He had taken off his collar and tie, and rose, bare-throated, to go to bed. As he stooped to kiss his mother, she threw her arms round his neck, hid her face on his shoulder, and cried, in a whimpering voice, so unlike her own that he writhed in agony:

'I can't bear it. I could let another woman – but not her. She'd leave me no room, not a bit of room – '

And immediately he hated Miriam bitterly.

'And I've never – you know, Paul – I've never had a husband – not really – '

He stroked his mother's hair, and his mouth was on her throat.

'And she exults so in taking you from me – she's not like ordinary girls.'

'Well, I don't love her, mother,' he murmured, bowing his head and hiding his eyes on her shoulder in misery. His mother kissed him a long, fervent kiss.

'My boy!' she said, in a voice trembling with passionate love.

Without knowing, he gently stroked her face.

'There,' said his mother, 'now go to bed. You'll be so tired in the morning.' As she was speaking she heard her husband coming.

'There's your father – now go.' Suddenly she looked at him almost as if in fear. 'Perhaps I'm selfish. If you want her, take her, my boy.'

His mother looked so strange, Paul kissed her, trembling.

'Ha – mother!' he said softly.

Morel came in, walking unevenly. His hat was over one corner of his eye. He balanced in the doorway.

'At your mischief again?' he said venomously.

Mrs Morel's emotion turned into sudden hate of the drunkard who had come in thus upon her.

'At any rate, it is sober,' she said.

'H'm – h'm! h'm – h'm!' he sneered. He went into the passage, hung up his hat and coat. Then they heard him go down three steps to the pantry. He returned with a piece of pork-pie in his fist. It was what Mrs Morel had bought for her son.

'Nor was that bought for you. If you can give me no more than twenty-five shillings, I'm sure I'm not going to buy you pork-pie to stuff, after you've swilled a bellyful of beer.'

'Wha-at – wha-at!' snarled Morel, toppling in his balance. 'Wha-at not for me?' he looked at the piece of meat and crust, and suddenly, in a vicious spurt of temper, flung it into the fire.

Paul started to his feet.

'Waste your own stuff!' he cried.

'What – what!' suddenly shouted Morel, jumping up and clenching his fist. 'I'll show yer, yer young jockey!'

'All right!' said Paul viciously, putting his head on one side. 'Show me!'

He would at that moment dearly have loved to have a smack at something. Morel was half crouching, fists up, ready to spring. The young man stood, smiling with his lips.

'Ussha!' hissed the father, swiping round with a great stroke just past his son's face. He dared not, even though so close, really touch the young man, but swerved an inch away.

'Right!' said Paul, his eyes upon the side of his father's mouth, where in another instant his fist would have hit. He ached for that stroke. But he heard a faint moan from behind. His mother was deadly pale, and dark at the mouth. Morel was dancing up to deliver another blow.

'Father!' said Paul, so that the word rang.

Morel started, and stood at attention.

'Mother!' moaned the boy. 'Mother!'

She began to struggle with herself. Her open eyes watched him, although she could not move. Gradually she was coming to herself. He laid her down on the sofa, and ran upstairs for a little whisky, which at last she could sip. The tears were hopping down his face. As he kneeled in front of her he did not cry, but the tears ran down his face quickly. Morel on the opposite side of the room, sat with his elbows on his knees glaring across.

What's a-matter with 'er?' he asked.

'Faint!' replied Paul.

'H'm!'

The elderly man began to unlace his boots. He stumbled off to bed. His last fight was fought in that home.

Paul kneeled there, stroking his mother's hand.

'Don't be poorly, mother – don't be poorly!' he said time after time. 'It's nothing, my boy,' she murmured.

At last he rose, fetched in a large piece of coal, and raked the fire. Then he cleared the room, put everything straight, laid the things for breakfast, and brought his mother's candle.

'Can you go to bed, mother?'

'Yes, I'll come.'

'Sleep with Annie, mother, not with him.'

'No. I'll sleep in my own bed.'

'Don't sleep with him, mother.'

'I'll sleep in my own bed.'

She rose, and he turned out the gas, then followed her closely upstairs, carrying her candle. On the landing he kissed her close.

'Good-night, mother.'

'Good-night!' she said.

He pressed his face upon the pillow in a fury of misery. And yet, somewhere in his soul, he was at peace because he still loved his mother best. It was the bitter peace of resignation.

The efforts of his father to conciliate him next day were a great humiliation to him.

Everybody tried to forget the scene.

CHAPTER 9

Defeat of Miriam

PAUL WAS dissatisfied with himself and with everything. The deepest of his love belonged to his mother. When he felt he had hurt her, or wounded his love for her he could not bear it. Now it was spring, and there was battle between him and Miriam. This year he had a good deal against her. She was vaguely aware of it. The old feeling that she was to be a sacrifice to this love, which she had had when she prayed, was mingled in all her emotions. She did not at the bottom believe she ever would have him. She did not believe in herself primarily: doubted whether she could ever be what he would demand of her. Certainly she never saw herself living happily through a lifetime with him. She saw tragedy, sorrow, and sacrifice ahead. And in sacrifice she was proud, in renunciation she was strong, for she did not trust herself to support everyday life. She was prepared for the big things and the deep things, like tragedy. It was the sufficiency of the small day-life she could not trust.

The Easter holidays began happily. Paul was his own frank self. Yet she felt it would go wrong. On the Sunday afternoon she stood at her bedroom window, looking across at the oak-trees of the wood, in whose branches a twilight was tangled, below the bright sky of the afternoon. Grey-green rosettes of honeysuckle leaves hung before the window, some already, she fancied, showing bud. It was spring, which she loved and dreaded.

Hearing the clack of the gate she stood in suspense. It was a bright grey day. Paul came into the yard with his bicycle, which glittered as he walked. Usually he rang his bell and laughed towards the house. Today he walked with shut lips and cold, cruel bearing, that had something of a slouch and a sneer in it. She knew him well by now, and could tell from that keen-looking, aloof young body of his what was happening inside him. There was a cold correctness in the way he put his bicycle in its place, that made her heart sink.

She came downstairs nervously. She was wearing a new net blouse that she thought became her. It had a high collar with a tiny ruff, reminding her of Mary, Queen of Scots, and making her, she thought, look wonderfully a woman, and dignified. At twenty she was full-breasted and luxuriously formed. Her face was still like a soft rich mask, unchangeable. But her eyes, once lifted, were wonderful. She was afraid of him. He would notice her new blouse.

He, being in a hard, ironical mood, was entertaining the family to a description of a service given in the Primitive Methodist Chapel, conducted by one of the well-known preachers of the sect. He sat at the head of the table, his mobile face, with the eyes that could be so beautiful, shining with tenderness or dancing with laughter, now taking on one expression and then another, in imitation of various people he was mocking. His mockery always hurt her; it was too near the reality. He was too clever and cruel. She felt that when his eyes were like this, hard with mocking hate, he would spare neither himself nor anybody else. But Mrs Leivers was wiping her eyes with laughter, and Mr Leivers, just awake from his Sunday nap, was rubbing his head in amusement. The three brothers sat with ruffled, sleepy appearance in their shirt-sleeves, giving a guffaw from time to time. The whole family loved a 'take-off more than anything.

He took no notice of Miriam. Later, she saw him remark her new blouse, saw that the artist approved, but it won from him not a spark of warmth. She was nervous, could hardly reach the teacups from the shelves.

When the men went out to milk, she ventured to address him personally.

'You were late,' she said.

'Was I?' he answered.

There was silence for a while.

'Was it rough riding?' she asked.

'I didn't notice it.'

She continued quickly to lay the table. When she had finished –

'Tea won't be for a few minutes. Will you come and look at the daffodils?' she said.

He rose without answering. They went out into the back garden under the budding damson-trees. The hills and the sky were clean and cold. Everything looked washed, rather hard. Miriam glanced at Paul. He was pale and impassive. It seemed cruel to her that his eyes and brows, which she loved, could look so hurting.

'Has the wind made you tired?' she asked. She detected an underneath feeling of weariness about him.

'No, I think not,' he answered.

'It must be rough on the road – the wood moans so.'

'You can see by the clouds it's a south-west wind; that helps me here.'

'You see, I don't cycle, so I don't understand,' she murmured.

'Is there need to cycle to know that!' he said.

She thought his sarcasms were unnecessary. They went forward in silence. Round the wild, tussocky lawn at the back of the house was a thorn hedge, under which daffodils were craning forward from among their sheaves of grey-green blades. The cheeks of the flowers were greenish with cold. But still some had burst, and their gold ruined and glowed. Miriam went on her knees before one cluster, took a wild looking daffodil between her hands, turned up its face of gold to her, and bowed down, caressing it with her mouth and cheeks and brow. He stood aside, with his hands in his pockets, watching her. One after another she turned up to him the faces of the yellow, bursten flowers appealingly, fondling them lavishly all the while.

'Aren't they magnificent?' she murmured.

'Magnificent! it's a bit thick – they're pretty!'

She bowed again to her flowers at his censure of her praise. He watched her crouching, sipping the flowers with fervid kisses.

'Why must you always be fondling things!' he said irritably.

'But I love to touch them,' she replied, hurt.

'Can you never like things without clutching them as if you wanted to pull the heart out of them? Why don't you have a bit more restraint, or reserve, or something?'

She looked up at him full of pain, then continued slowly to stroke her lips against a ruffled flower. Their scent, as she smelled it, was so much kinder than he; it almost made her cry.

'You wheedle the soul out of things,' he said. 'I would never wheedle – at any rate, I'd go straight.'

He scarcely knew what he was saying. These things came from him mechanically. She looked at him. His body seemed one weapon, firm and hard against her.

'You're always begging things to love you,' he said, 'as if you were a beggar for love. Even the flowers, you have to fawn on them – '

Rhythmically, Miriam was swaying and stroking the flower

with her mouth, inhaling the scent which ever after made her shudder as it came to her nostrils.

'You don't want to love – your eternal and abnormal craving is to be loved. You aren't positive, you're negative. You absorb, absorb, as if you must fill yourself up with love, and because you've got a shortage somewhere.'

She was stunned by his cruelty, and did not hear. He had not the faintest notion of what he was saying. It was as if his fretted, tortured soul, run hot by thwarted passion, jetted off these sayings like sparks from electricity. She did not grasp anything he said. She only sat crouched beneath his cruelty and his hatred of her. She never realised in a flash. Over everything she brooded and brooded.

After tea he stayed with Edgar and the brothers, taking no notice of Miriam. She, extremely unhappy on this looked-for holiday, waited for him. And at last he yielded and came to her. She was determined to track this mood of his to its origin. She counted it not much more than a mood.

'Shall we go through the wood a little way?' she asked him, knowing he never refused a direct request.

They went down to the warren. On the middle path they passed a trap, a narrow horseshoe hedge of small fir-boughs, baited with the guts of a rabbit. Paul glanced at it frowning. She caught his eye.

'Isn't it dreadful?' she asked.

'I don't know! Is it worse than a weasel with its teeth in a rabbit's throat? One weasel or many rabbits? One or the other must go!'

He was taking the bitterness of life badly. She was rather sorry for him.

'We will go back to the house,' he said. 'I don't want to walk out.'

They went past the lilac-tree, whose bronze leaf-buds were coming unfastened. Just a fragment remained of the haystack, a monument squared and brown, like a pillar of stone. There was a little bed of hay from the last cutting.

'Let us sit here a minute,' said Miriam.

He sat down against his will, resting his back against the hard wall of hay. They faced the amphitheatre of round hills that glowed with sunset, tiny white farms standing out, the meadows golden, the woods dark and yet luminous, tree-tops folded over tree-tops, distinct in the distance. The evening had cleared, and the east was tender with a magenta flush under which the land lay still and rich.

'Isn't it beautiful?' she pleaded.

But he only scowled. He would rather have had it ugly just then.

At that moment a big bull-terrier came rushing up, open-mouthed, pranced his two paws on the youth's shoulders, licking his face. Paul drew back, laughing. Bill was a great relief to him. He pushed the dog aside, but it came leaping back.

'Get out,' said the lad, 'or I'll dot thee one.'

But the dog was not to be pushed away. So Paul had a little battle with the creature, pitching poor Bill away from him, who, however, only floundered tumultuously back again, wild with joy. The two fought together, the man laughing grudgingly, the dog grinning all over. Miriam watched them. There was something pathetic about the man. He wanted so badly to love, to be tender. The rough way he bowled the dog over was really loving. Bill got up, panting with happiness, his brown eyes rolling in his white face, and lumbered back again. He adored Paul. The lad frowned.

'Bill, I've had enough o' thee,' he said.

But the dog only stood with two heavy paws, that quivered with love, upon his thigh, and flickered a red tongue at him. He drew back.

'No,' he said – 'no – I've had enough.'

And in a minute the dog trotted off happily, to vary the fun.

He remained staring miserably across at the hills, whose still beauty be begrudged. He wanted to go and cycle with Edgar. Yet he had not the courage to leave Miriam.

'Why are you sad?' she asked humbly.

'I'm not sad; why should I be?' he answered. 'I'm only normal.'

She wondered why he always claimed to be normal when he was disagreeable.

'But what is the matter?' she pleaded, coaxing him soothingly.

'Nothing!'

'Nay!' she murmured.

He picked up a stick and began to stab the earth with it.

'You'd far better not talk,' he said.

'But I wish to know – ' she replied.

He laughed resentfully.

'You always do,' he said.

'It's not fair to me,' she murmured.

He thrust, thrust, thrust at the ground with the pointed stick, digging up little clods of earth as if he were in a fever of irritation. She gently and firmly laid her hand on his wrist.

'Don't!' she said. 'Put it away.'

He flung the stick into the currant-bushes, and leaned back. Now he was bottled up.

'What is it?' she pleaded softly.

He lay perfectly still, only his eyes alive, and they full of torment.

'You know,' he said at length, rather wearily – 'you know – we'd better break off.'

It was what she dreaded. Swiftly everything seemed to darken before her eyes.

'Why!' she murmured. 'What has happened?'

'Nothing has happened. We only realise where we are. It's no good – '

She waited in silence, sadly, patiently. It was no good being impatient with him. At any rate, he would tell her now what ailed him.

'We agreed on friendship,' he went on in a dull, monotonous voice. 'How often *have* we agreed for friendship! And yet – it neither stops there, nor gets anywhere else.'

He was silent again. She brooded. What did he mean? He was so wearying. There was something he would not yield. Yet she must be patient with him.

'I can only give friendship – it's all I'm capable of – it's a flaw in my make-up. The thing overbalances to one side – I hate a toppling balance. Let us have done.'

There was warmth of fury in his last phrases. He meant she loved him more than he her. Perhaps he could not love her. Perhaps she had not in herself that which he wanted. It was the deepest motive of her soul, this self-mistrust. It was so deep she dared neither realise nor acknowledge it. Perhaps she was deficient. Like an infinitely subtle shame, it kept her always back. If it were so, she would do without him. She would never let herself want him. She would merely see.

'But what has happened?' she said.

'Nothing – it's all in myself – it only comes out just now. We're always like this towards Easter-time.'

He grovelled so helplessly, she pitied him. At least she never floundered in such a pitiable way. After all, it was he who was chiefly humiliated.

'What do you want?' she asked him.

'Why – I mustn't come often – that's all. Why should I monopolise you when I'm not – You see, I'm deficient in something with regard to you – '

He was telling her he did not love her, and so ought to leave her a chance with another man. How foolish and blind and shamefully clumsy he was! What were other men to her! What were men to her at all! But he, ah! she loved his soul. Was he deficient in something? Perhaps he was.

'But I don't understand,' she said huskily. 'Yesterday – '

The night was turning jangled and hateful to him as the twilight faded. And she bowed under her suffering.

'I know,' he cried, 'you never will! You'll never believe that I can't can't physically, any more than I can fly up like a skylark – '

'What?' she murmured. Now she dreaded.

'Love you.'

He hated her bitterly at that moment because he made her suffer.

Love her! She knew he loved her. He really belonged to her. This about not loving her, physically, bodily, was a mere perversity on his part, because he knew she loved him. He was stupid like a child. He belonged to her. His soul wanted her. She guessed somebody had been influencing him. She felt upon him the hardness, the foreignness of another influence.

'What have they been saying at home?' she asked.

'It's not that,' he answered.

And then she knew it was. She despised them for their commonness, his people. They did not know what things were really worth.

He and she talked very little more that night. After all he left her to cycle with Edgar.

He had come back to his mother. Hers was the strongest tie in his life. When he thought round, Miriam shrank away. There was a vague, unreal feel about her. And nobody else mattered. There was one place in the world that stood solid and did not melt into unreality: the place where his mother was. Everybody else could grow shadowy, almost nonexistent to him, but she could not. It was as if the pivot and pole of his life, from which he could not escape, was his mother.

And in the same way she waited for him. In him was established her life now. After all, the life beyond offered very little to Mrs Morel. She saw that our chance for doing is here, and doing counted with her. Paul was going to prove that she had been right; he was going to make a man whom nothing should shift off his feet; he was going to alter the face of the earth in some way which mattered. Wherever he went she felt her soul went with him. Whatever he did she felt her soul stood by him, ready, as it were, to hand him his tools. She could not bear it when he was with Miriam. William was dead. She would fight to keep Paul.

And he came back to her. And in his soul was a feeling of the satisfaction of self-sacrifice because he was faithful to her. She loved him first; he loved her first. And yet it was not enough. His new young life, so strong and imperious, was urged towards something else. It made him mad with restlessness. She saw this, and wished bitterly that Miriam had been a woman who could take this new life of his, and leave her the roots. He fought against his mother almost as he fought against Miriam.

It was a week before he went again to Willey Farm. Miriam had suffered a great deal, and was afraid to see him again. Was she now to endure the ignominy of his abandoning her? That would only be superficial and temporary. He would come back. She held the keys to his soul. But meanwhile, how he would torture her with his battle against her. She shrank from it.

However, the Sunday after Easter he came to tea. Mrs Leivers was glad to see him. She gathered something was fretting him, that he found things hard. He seemed to drift to her for comfort. And she was good to him. She did him that great kindness of treating him almost with reverence.

He met her with the young children in the front garden.

'I'm glad you've come,' said the mother, looking at him with her great appealing brown eyes. 'It is such a sunny day. I was just going down the fields for the first time this year.'

He felt she would like him to come. That soothed him. They went, talking simply, he gentle and humble. He could have wept with gratitude that she was deferential to him. He was feeling humiliated.

At the bottom of the Mow Close they found a thrush's nest.

'Shall I show you the eggs?' he said.

'Do!' replied Mrs Leivers: 'They seem *such* a sign of spring, and so hopeful.'

He put aside the thorns, and took out the eggs, holding them in the palm of his hand.

'They are quite hot – I think we frightened her off them,'

'Ay, poor thing!' said Mrs Leivers.

Miriam could not help touching the eggs, and his hand which, it seemed to her, cradled them so well.

'Isn't it a strange warmth!' she murmured, to get near him.

'Blood heat,' he answered.

She watched him putting them back, his body pressed against the hedge, his arm reaching slowly through the thorns, his hand folded carefully over the eggs. He was concentrated on the act. Seeing him so, she loved him; he seemed so simple and sufficient to himself. And she could not get to him.

After tea she stood hesitating at the bookshelf. He took 'Tartarin de Tarascon.' Again they sat on the bank of hay at the foot of the stock. He read a couple of pages, but without any heart for it. Again the dog came racing up to repeat the fun of the other day. He shoved his muzzle in the man's chest. Paul fingered his ear for a moment. Then he pushed him away.

'Go away, Bill,' he said. 'I don't want you.'

Bill slunk off, and Miriam wondered and dreaded what was coming. There was a silence about the youth that made her still with apprehension. It was not his furies, but his quiet resolutions that she feared.

Turning his face a little to one side, so that she could not see him, he began, speaking slowly and painfully:

Do you think – if I didn't come up so much – you might get to like somebody else – another man?'

So this was what he was still harping on.

'But I don't know any other men. Why do you ask?' she replied, in a low tone that should have been a reproach to him.

'Why,' he blurted, 'because they say I've no right to come up like this – without we mean to marry – '

Miriam was indignant at anybody's forcing the issues between them. She had been furious with her own father for suggesting to Paul, laughingly, that he knew why he came so much.

Who says?' she asked, wondering if her people had anything to do with it. They had not.

'Mother – and the others. They say at this rate everybody will consider me engaged, and I ought to consider myself so, because it's not fair to you. And I've tried to find out – and I don't think I love you as a man ought to love his wife. What do *you* think about it?'

Miriam bowed her head moodily. She was angry at having this struggle. People should leave him and her alone.

'I don't know,' she murmured.

'Do you think we love each other enough to marry?' he asked definitely. It made her tremble.

'No,' she answered truthfully. 'I don't think so – we're too young.'

'I thought perhaps,' he went on miserably, 'that you, with your intensity in things, might have given me more – than I could ever make up to you. And even now – if you think it better – we'll be engaged.'

Now Miriam wanted to cry. And she was angry, too. He was always such a child for people to do as they liked with.

'No, I don't think so,' she said firmly.

He pondered a minute.

'You see,' he said, 'with me – I don't think one person would ever monopolise me – be everything to me – I think never.'

This she did not consider.

'No,' she murmured. Then, after a pause, she looked at him, and her dark eyes flashed.

'This is your mother,' she said. 'I know she never liked me.'

'No, no, it isn't,' he said hastily. 'It was for your sake she spoke this time. She only said, if I was going on, I ought to consider myself engaged.' There was a silence. 'And if I ask you to come down any time, you won't stop away, will you?'

She did not answer. By this time she was very angry.

Well, what shall we do?' she said shortly. 'I suppose I'd better drop French. I was just beginning to get on with it. But I suppose I can go on alone.'

'I don't see that we need,' he said. 'I can give you a French lesson, surely.'

'Well – and there are Sunday nights. I shan't stop coming to chapel, because I enjoy it, and it's all the social life I get. But you've no need to come home with me. I can go alone.'

'All right,' he answered, rather taken aback. 'But if I ask Edgar, he'll always come with us, and then they can say nothing.'

There was silence. After all, then, she would not lose much. For all their talk down at his home there would not be much difference. She wished they would mind their own business.

'And you won't think about it, and let it trouble you, will you?' he asked.

'Oh no,' replied Miriam, without looking at him.

He was silent. She thought him unstable. He had no fixity of purpose, no anchor of righteousness that held him.

'Because,' he continued, 'a man gets across his bicycle – and goes to work – and does all sorts of things. But a woman broods.'

'No, I shan't bother,' said Miriam. And she meant it.

It had gone rather chilly. They went indoors.

'How white Paul looks!' Mrs Leivers exclaimed. 'Miriam, you shouldn't have let him sit out of doors. Do you think you've taken cold, Paul?'

'Oh, no!' he laughed.

But he felt done up. It wore him out, the conflict in himself. Miriam pitied him now. But quite early, before nine o'clock, he rose to go.

'You're not going home, are you?' asked Mrs Leivers anxiously.

'Yes,' he replied. 'I said I'd be early.' He was very awkward.

'But this is early,' said Mr Leivers.

Miriam sat in the rocking-chair, and did not speak. He hesitated, expecting her to rise and go with him to the barn as usual for his bicycle. She remained as she was. He was at a loss.

Well – good-night all!' he faltered.

She spoke her good-night along with all the others. But as he went past the window he looked in. She saw him pale, his brows knit slightly in a way that had become constant with him, his eyes dark with pain.

She rose and went to the doorway to wave goodbye to him as he passed through the gate. He rode slowly under the pine-trees, feeling a cur and a miserable wretch. His bicycle went tilting down the hills at random. He thought it would be a relief to break one's neck.

Two days later he sent her up a book and a little note, urging her to read and be busy.

At this time he gave all his friendship to Edgar. He loved the family so much, he loved the farm so much; it was the dearest place on earth to him. His home was not so lovable. It was his mother. But then he would have been just as happy with his mother anywhere. Whereas Willey Farm he loved passionately. He loved the little pokey kitchen, where men's boots tramped, and the dog slept with one eye open for fear of being trodden on; where the lamp hung over the table at night, and everything was so silent. He loved Miriam's long, low parlour, with its atmosphere of romance, its flowers, its books, its high rosewood piano. He loved the gardens and the buildings that stood with their scarlet roofs on the naked edges of the fields, crept towards the wood as if for cosiness, the wild country scooping down a valley and up the uncultured hills of the other side. Only to be there was an exhilaration and a joy to him. He loved Mrs Leivers, with her unworldliness and her quaint cynicism; he loved Mr Leivers so warm and young and lovable; he loved Edgar, who lit up when he came, and the boys and the children and Bill – even the sow Circe and the Indian game-cock called Tippoo. All this besides Miriam. He could not give it up.

So he went as often, but he was usually with Edgar. Only all the family, including the father, joined in charades and games at evening. And later, Miriam drew them together, and they read

'Macbeth' out of penny books, taking parts. It was great
excitement. Miriam was glad, and Mrs Leivers was glad, and
Mr Leivers enjoyed it. Then they all learned songs together from
tonic sol-fa, singing in a circle round the fire. But now Paul was
very rarely alone with Miriam. She waited. When she and Edgar
and he walked home together from chapel or from the literary
society in Bestwood, she knew his talk, so passionate and so
unorthodox nowadays, was for her. She did envy Edgar,
however, his cycling with Paul, his Friday nights, his days
working in the fields. For her Friday nights and her French
lessons were gone. She was nearly always alone, walking,
pondering in the wood, reading, studying, dreaming, waiting. And
he wrote to her frequently.

One Sunday evening they attained to their old rare harmony.
Edgar had stayed to Communion – he wondered what it was like
– with Mrs Morel. So Paul came on alone with Miriam to his
home. He was more or less under her spell again. As usual, they
were discussing the sermon. He was setting now full soil towards
Agnosticism, but such a religious Agnosticism that Miriam did
not suffer so badly. They were at the Renan 'Vie de Jesus' stage.
Miriam was the threshing-floor on which he threshed out all his
beliefs. While he trampled his ideas upon her soul, the truth came
out for him. She alone was his threshing-floor. She alone helped
him towards realisation. Almost impassive, she submitted to his
argument and expounding. And somehow, because of her, he
gradually realised where he was wrong. And what he realised,
she realised. She felt he could not do without her.

They came to the silent house. He took the key out of the
scullery window, and they entered. All the time he went on with
his discussion. He lit the gas, mended the fire, and brought her
some cakes from the pantry. She sat on the sofa, quietly, with a
plate on her knee. She wore a large white hat with some pinkish
flowers. It was a cheap hat, but he liked it. Her face beneath was
still and pensive, golden-brown and ruddy. Always her ears were
hid in her short curls. She watched him.

She liked him on Sundays. Then he wore a dark suit that showed the lithe movement of his body. There was a clean, clear-cut look about him. He went on with his thinking to her. Suddenly he reached for a Bible. Miriam liked the way he reached up – so sharp, straight to the mark. He turned the pages quickly, and read her a chapter of St John. As he sat in the armchair reading, intent, his voice only thinking, she felt as if he were using her unconsciously as a man uses his tools at some work he is bent on. She loved it. And the wistfulness of his voice was like a reaching to something, and it was as if she were what he reached with. She sat back on the sofa away from him, and yet feeling herself the very instrument his hand grasped. It gave her great pleasure.

Then he began to falter and to get self-conscious. And when he came to the verse, 'A woman, when she is in travail hath sorrow because her hour is come,' he missed it out. Miriam had felt him growing uncomfortable. She shrank when the well-known words did not follow. He went on reading, but she did not hear. A grief and shame made her bend her head. Six months ago he would have read it simply. Now there was a scotch in his running with her. Now she felt there was really something hostile between them, something of which they were ashamed.

She ate her cake mechanically. He tried to go on with his argument, but could not get back the right note. Soon Edgar came in. Mrs Morel had gone to her friends'. The three set off to Willey Farm.

Miriam brooded over his split with her. There was something else he wanted. He could not be satisfied; he could give her no peace. There was between them now always a ground for strife. She wanted to prove him. She believed that his chief need in life was herself. If she could prove it, both to herself and to him, the rest might go, she could simply trust to the future.

So in May she asked him to come to Willey Farm and meet Mrs Dawes. There was something he hankered after. She saw him, whenever they spoke of Clara Dawes, rouse and get slightly angry. He said he did not like her. Yet he was keen to know about her. Well, he should put himself to the test. She believed that there were in him desires for higher things, and desires for lower, and that the desire for the higher would conquer. At any rate, he should try. She forgot that her 'higher' and lower were arbitrary.

He was rather excited at the idea of meeting Clara at Willey Farm. Mrs Dawes came for the day. Her heavy, dun-coloured hair was coiled on top of her head. She wore a white blouse and navy skirt, and somehow, wherever she was, seemed to make things look paltry and insignificant. When she was in the room, the kitchen seemed too small and mean altogether. Miriam's beautiful twilighty parlour looked stiff and stupid.

All the Leivers were eclipsed like candles. They found her rather hard to put up with. Yet she was perfectly amiable, but indifferent, and rather hard.

Paul did not come till afternoon. He was early. As he swung off his bicycle, Miriam saw him look round at the house eagerly. He would be disappointed if the visitor had not come. Miriam went out to meet him, bowing her head because of the sunshine. Nasturtiums were coming out crimson under the cool green shadow of their leaves. The girl stood, dark-haired, glad to see him.

'Hasn't Clara come?' he asked.

'Yes,' replied Miriam in her musical tone. 'She's reading.'

He wheeled his bicycle into the barn. He had put on a handsome tie, of which he was rather proud, and socks to match.

'She came this morning?' he asked.

'Yes,' replied Miriam, as she walked at his side. 'You said you'd bring me that letter from the man at Liberty's. Have you remembered?'

'Oh dash, no!' he said. 'But nag at me till you get it.'

'I don't like to nag at you.'

'Do it whether or not. And is she any more agreeable?' he continued.

'You know I always think she is quite agreeable.'

He was silent. Evidently his eagerness to be early today had been the newcomer. Miriam already began to suffer. They went together towards the house. He took the clips off his trousers, but was too lazy to brush the dust from his shoes, in spite of the socks and tie.

Clara sat in the cool parlour reading. He saw the nape of her white neck, and the fine hair lifted from it. She rose, looking at him indifferently. To shake hands she lifted her arm straight, in a manner that seemed at once to keep him at a distance, and yet to fling something to him. He noticed how her breasts swelled inside her blouse, and how her shoulder curved handsomely under the thin muslin at the top of her arm.

'You have chosen a fine day,' he said.

'It happens so,' she said.

'Yes,' he said; 'I am glad.'

She sat down, not thanking him for his politeness.

What have you been doing all morning?' asked Paul of Miriam.

Well you see,' said Miriam, coughing huskily, 'Clara only came with father – and so – she's not been here very long.'

Clara sat leaning on the table, holding aloof. He noticed her hands were large, but well kept. And the skin on them seemed almost coarse, opaque, and white, with fine golden hairs. She did not mind if he observed her hands. She intended to scorn him. Her heavy arm lay negligently on the table. Her mouth was closed as if she were offended, and she kept her face slightly averted.

'You were at Margaret Bonford's meeting the other evening,' he said to her.

Miriam did not know this courteous Paul. Clara glanced at him.

'Yes,' she said.

'Why,' asked Miriam, 'how do you know?'

'I went in for a few minutes before the train came,' he answered.

Clara turned away again rather disdainfully.

'I think she's a lovable little woman,' said Paul.

'Margaret Bonford!' exclaimed Clara. 'She's a great deal cleverer than most men.'

'Well, I didn't say she wasn't,' he said, deprecating. 'She's lovable for all that.'

'And, of course, that is all that matters,' said Clara witheringly.

He rubbed his head, rather perplexed, rather annoyed.

'I suppose it matters more than her cleverness,' he said; 'which, after all, would never get her to heaven.'

'It's not heaven she wants to get – it's her fair share on earth,' retorted Clara. She spoke as if he were responsible for some deprivation which Miss Bonford suffered.

'Well,' he said, 'I thought she was warm, and awfully nice – only too frail. I wished she was sitting comfortably in peace – '

' "Darning her husband's stockings," ' said Clara scathingly.

'I'm sure she wouldn't mind darning even my stockings,' he said. 'And I'm sure she'd do them well. Just as I wouldn't mind blacking her boots if she wanted me to.'

But Clara refused to answer this sally of his. He talked to Miriam for a little while. The other woman held aloof.

Well,' he said, 'I think I'll go and see Edgar. Is he on the land?'

'I believe,' said Miriam, 'he's gone for a load of coal. He should be back directly.'

'Then,' he said, 'I'll go and meet him.'

Miriam dared not propose anything for the three of them. He rose and left them.

On the top road, where the gorse was out, he saw Edgar walking lazily beside the mare, who nodded her white-starred forehead as she dragged the clanking load of coal. The young farmer's face lighted up as he saw his friend. Edgar was good-looking, with dark, warm eyes. His clothes were old and rather disreputable, and he walked with considerable pride.

'Hello!' he said, seeing Paul bareheaded. 'Where are you going?'

'Came to meet you. Can't stand "Nevermore." '

Edgar's teeth flashed in a laugh of amusement.

'Who is "Nevermore"?' he asked.

'The lady – Mrs Dawes – it ought to be Mrs The Raven that quothed "Nevermore." '

Edgar laughed with glee.

'Don't you like her?' he asked.

'Not a fat kit,' said Paul. 'Why, do you?'

'No!' The answer came with a deep ring of conviction. 'No!' Edgar pursed up his lips. 'I can't say she's much in my line.' He mused a little. Then: 'But why do you call her "Nevermore"?' he asked.

'Well,' said Paul, 'if she looks at a man she says haughtily "Nevermore," and if she looks at herself in the looking-glass she says disdainfully "Nevermore," and if she thinks back she says it in disgust, and if she looks forward she says it cynically.'

Edgar considered this speech, failed to make much out of it, and said, laughing:

'You think she's a man-hater?'

'*She* thinks she is,' replied Paul.

'But you don't think so?'

'No,' replied Paul.

Wasn't she nice with you, then?'

'Could you imagine her *nice* with anybody?' asked the young man. Edgar laughed. Together they unloaded the coal in the yard. Paul was rather self-conscious, because he knew Clara could see if she looked out of the window. She didn't look.

On Saturday afternoons the horses were brushed down and groomed. Paul and Edgar worked together, sneezing with the dust that came from the pelts of Jimmy and Flower.

'Do you know a new song to teach me?' said Edgar.

He continued to work all the time. The back of his neck was sun-red when he bent down, and his fingers that held the brush were thick. Paul watched him sometimes.

' "Mary Morrison"?' suggested the younger.

Edgar agreed. He had a good tenor voice, and he loved to learn all the songs his friend could teach him, so that he could sing whilst he was carting. Paul had a very indifferent baritone voice, but a good ear. However, he sang softly, for fear of Clara. Edgar repeated the line in a clear tenor. At times they both broke off to sneeze, and first one, then the other, abused his horse.

Miriam was impatient of men. It took so little to amuse them – even Paul. She thought it anomalous in him that he could be so thoroughly absorbed in a triviality.

It was teatime when they had finished.

'What song was that?' asked Miriam.

Edgar told her. The conversation turned to singing.

We have such jolly times,' Miriam said to Clara.

Mrs Dawes ate her meal in a slow, dignified way. Whenever the men were present she grew distant.

'Do you like singing?' Miriam asked her.

'If it is good,' she said.

Paul, of course, coloured.

'You mean if it is high-class and trained?' he said.

'I think a voice needs training before the singing is anything,' she said. 'You might as well insist on having people's voices trained before you allowed them to talk,' he replied. 'Really, people sing for their own pleasure, as a rule.'

'And it may be for other people's discomfort.'

'Then the other people should have flaps to their ears,' he replied. The boys laughed. There was a silence. He flushed deeply, and ate in silence.

After tea, when all the men had gone but Paul, Mrs Leivers said to Clara:

'And you find life happier now?'

'Infinitely.'

'And you are satisfied?'

'So long as I can be free and independent.'

'And you don't *miss* anything in your life?' asked Mrs Leivers gently. 'I've put all that behind me.'

Paul had been feeling uncomfortable during this discourse. He got up. 'You'll find you're always tumbling over the things you've put behind you,' he said. Then he took his departure to the cowsheds. He felt he had been witty, and his manly pride was high. He whistled as he went down the brick track.

Miriam came for him a little later to know if he would go with Clara and her for a walk. They set off down to Strelley Mill Farm. As they were going beside the brook, on the Willey Water side, looking through the brake at the edge of the wood, where pink campions glowed under a few sunbeams, they saw, beyond the tree-trunks and the thin hazel bushes, a man leading a great bay horse through the gullies. The big red beast seemed to dance romantically through that dimness of green hazel drift away there where the air was shadowy, as if it were in the past, among the fading bluebells that might have bloomed for Deidre or Iseult.

The three stood charmed.

'What a treat to be a knight,' he said, 'and to have a pavilion here.'

'And to have us shut up safely?' replied Clara.

'Yes,' he answered, 'singing with your maids at your broidery. I would carry your banner of white and green and heliotrope. I would have "W.S.P.U." emblazoned on my shield, beneath a woman rampant.'

'I have no doubt,' said Clara, 'that you would much rather fight for a woman than let her fight for herself.'

'I would. When she fights for herself she seems like a dog before a looking-glass, gone into a mad fury with its own shadow.'

'And *you* are the looking-glass?' she asked, with a curl of the lip.

'Or the shadow,' he replied.

'I am afraid,' she said, 'that you are too clever.'

Well, I leave it to you to be *good,*' he retorted, laughing. 'Be good, sweet maid, and just let *me* be clever.'

But Clara wearied of his flippancy. Suddenly, looking at her, he saw that the upward lifting of her face was misery and not scorn. His heart grew tender for everybody. He turned and was gentle with Miriam, whom he had neglected till then.

At the wood's edge they met Limb, a thin, swarthy man of forty, tenant of Strelley Mill, which he ran as a cattle-raising farm. He held the halter of the powerful stallion indifferently, as if he were tired. The three stood to let him pass over the stepping-stones of the first brook. Paul admired that so large on animal should walk on such springy toes, with an endless excess of vigour. Limb pulled up before them.

Tell your father, Miss Leivers,' he said, in a peculiar piping voice, 'that his young beas'es 'as broke that bottom fence three days an' runnin'.'

'Which?' asked Miriam, tremulous.

The great horse breathed heavily, shifting round its red flanks, and looking suspiciously with its wonderful big eyes upwards from under its lowered head and falling mane.

'Come along a bit,' replied Limb, 'an' I'll show you.'

The man and the stallion went forward. It danced sideways, shaking its white fetlocks and looking frightened, as it felt itself in the brook.

'No hanky-pankyin',' said the man affectionately to the beast.

It went up the bank in little leaps, then splashed finely through the second brook. Clara, walking with a kind of sulky abandon, watched it half-fascinated, half-contemptuous. Limb stopped and pointed to the fence under some willows.

There, you see where they got through,' he said. 'My man's druv 'em back three times.'

'Yes,' answered Miriam, colouring as if she were at fault.

'Are you comin' in?' asked the man.

'No, thanks; but we should like to go by the pond.'

'Well, just as you've a mind,' he said.

The horse gave little whinneys of pleasure at being so near home.

'He is glad to be back,' said Clara, who was interested in the creature.

'Yes – 'e's been a tidy step today.'

They went through the gate, and saw approaching them from the big farmhouse a smallish, dark, excitable-looking woman of about thirty-five. Her hair was touched with grey, her dark eyes looked wild. She walked with her hands behind her back. Her brother went forward. As it saw her, the big bay stallion whinneyed again. She came up excitedly.

'Are you home again, my boy!' she said tenderly to the horse, not to the man. The great beast shifted round to her, ducking his head. She smuggled into his mouth the wrinkled yellow apple she had been hiding behind her back, then she kissed him near the eyes. He gave a big sigh of pleasure. She held his head in her arms against her breast.

'Isn't he splendid!' said Miriam to her.

Miss Limb looked up. Her dark eyes glanced straight at Paul.

'Oh, good-evening, Miss Leivers,' she said. 'It's ages since you've been down.'

Miriam introduced her friends.

'Your horse *is* a fine fellow!' said Clara.

'Isn't he!' Again she kissed him. 'As loving as any man!'

'More loving than most men, I should think,' replied Clara.

'He's a nice boy!' cried the woman, again embracing the horse.

Clara fascinated by the big beast, went up to stroke his neck.

'He's quite gentle,' said Miss Limb. 'Don't you think big fellows are?'

'He's a beauty!' replied Clara

She wanted to look in his eyes. She wanted him to look at her.

'It's a pity he can't talk,' she said.

'Oh, but he can – all but,' replied the other woman.

Then her brother moved on with the horse.

'Are you coming in? *Do* come in, Mr – I didn't catch it.'

'Morel,' said Miriam. 'No, we won't come in, but we should like to go by the mill-pond.'

'Yes – yes, do. Do you fish, Mr Morel?'

'No,' said Paul.

'Because if you do you might come and fish any time,' said Miss Limb. 'We scarcely see a soul from week's end to week's end. I should be thankful.'

'What fish are there in the pond?' he asked.

They went through the front garden, over the sluice, and up the steep bank to the pond, which lay in shadow, with its two wooded islets. Paul walked with Miss Limb.

'I shouldn't mind swimming here,' he said.

'Do,' she replied. 'Come when you like. My brother will be awfully pleased to talk with you. He is so quiet because there is no one to talk to. Do come and swim.'

Clara came up.

'It's a fine depth,' she said, 'and so clear.'

'Yes,' said Miss Limb.

'Do you swim?' said Paul. 'Miss Limb was just saying we could come when we liked.'

'Of course there's the farm-hands,' said Miss Limb.

They talked a few moments, then went on up the wild hill, leaving the lonely, haggard-eyed woman on the bank.

The hillside was all ripe with sunshine. It was wild and tussocky, given over to rabbits. The three walked in silence. Then:

'She makes me feel uncomfortable,' said Paul.

'You mean Miss Limb?' asked Miriam. 'Yes'

'What's a matter with her? Is she going dotty with being too lonely?'

'Yes,' said Miriam. 'It's not the right sort of life for her. I think it's cruel to bury her there. I really ought to go and see her more. But – she upsets me.'

'She makes me feel sorry for her – yes, and she bothers me,' he said. 'I suppose,' blurted Clara suddenly, 'she wants a man.'

The other two were silent for a few moments.

'But it's the loneliness sends her cracked,' said Paul.

Clara did not answer, but strode on uphill. She was walking with her head hanging, her legs swinging as she kicked through the dead thistles and the tussocky grass, her arms hanging loose. Rather than walking, her handsome body seemed to be blundering up the hill. A hot wave went over Paul. He was curious about her. Perhaps life had been cruel to her. He forgot Miriam, who was walking beside him talking to him. She glanced at him, finding he did not answer her. His eyes were fixed ahead on Clara.

'Do you still think she is disagreeable?' she asked.

He did not notice that the question was sudden. It ran with his thoughts.

'Something's the matter with her,' he said.

'Yes,' answered Miriam.

They found at the top of the hill a hidden wild field, two sides of which were backed by the wood, the other sides by high loose hedges of hawthorn and elder-bushes. Between these overgrown bushes were gaps that the cattle might have walked through had there been any cattle now. There the turf was smooth as velveteen, padded and holed by the rabbits. The field itself was coarse, and crowded with tall, big cowslips that had never been cut. Clusters of strong flowers rose everywhere above the coarse tussocks of bent. It was like a roadstead crowded with tall, fairy shipping.

'Ah!' cried Miriam, and she looked at Paul, her dark eyes dilating. He smiled. Together they enjoyed the field of flowers. Clara, a little way off, was looking at the cowslips disconsolately. Paul and Miriam stayed close together, talking in subdued tones. He kneeled on one knee, quickly gathering the best blossoms, moving from tuft to tuft restlessly, talking softly all the time. Miriam plucked the flowers lovingly, lingering over them. He always seemed to her too quick and almost scientific. Yet his bunches had a natural beauty more than hers. He loved them, but as if they were his and he had a right to them. She had more reverence for them: they held something she had not.

The flowers were very fresh and sweet. He wanted to drink them. As he gathered them, he ate the little yellow trumpets. Clara was still wandering about disconsolately. Going towards her, he said:

'Why don't you get some?'

'I don't believe in it. They look better growing.'

'But you'd like some?'

'They want to be left.'

'I don't believe they do.'

'I don't want the corpses of flowers about me,' she said.

'That's a stiff, artificial notion,' he said. 'They don't die any quicker in water than on their roots. And besides they *look* nice in a bowl – they look jolly. And you only call a thing a corpse because it looks corpselike.'

Whether it is one or not?' she argued.

'It isn't one to me. A dead flower isn't a corpse of a flower.'

Clara now ignored him.

'And even so – what right have you to pull them?' she asked.

'Because I like them, and want them – and there's plenty of them.'

'And that is sufficient?'

'Yes. Why not? I'm sure they'd smell nice in your room in Nottingham.'

'And I should have the pleasure of watching them die.'

'But then – it does not matter if they do die.'

Whereupon he left her, and went stooping over the clumps of tangled flowers which thickly sprinkled the field like pale luminous foam-clots. Miriam had come close. Clara was kneeling, breathing some scent from the cowslips.

'I think,' said Miriam, 'if you treat them with reverence you don't do them any harm. It is the spirit you pluck them in that matters.'

Yes, he said. But no, you get 'em because you want 'em, and that's all.' He held out his bunch.

Miriam was silent. He picked some more.

'Look at these!' he continued; 'sturdy and lusty like little trees and like boys with fat legs.'

Clara's hat lay on the grass not far off. She was kneeling, bending forward still to smell the flowers. Her neck gave him a sharp pang, such a beautiful thing, yet not proud of itself just now. Her breasts swung slightly in her blouse. The arching curve of her back was beautiful and strong; she wore no stays. Suddenly, without knowing, he was scattering a handful of cowslips over her hair and neck, saying:

> 'Ashes to ashes and dust to dust,
>   If the Lord won't have you the devil must.'

The chill flowers fell on her neck. She looked up at him, with almost pitiful, scared grey eyes, wondering what he was doing. Flowers fell on her face, and she shut her eyes.

Suddenly, standing there above her, he felt awkward. 'I thought you wanted a funeral,' he said, ill at ease.

Clara laughed strangely, and rose, picking the cowslips from her hair. She took up her hat and pinned it on. One flower had remained tangled in her hair. He saw, but would not tell her. He gathered up the flowers he had sprinkled over her.

At the edge of the wood the bluebells had flowed over into the field and stood there like flood-water. But they were fading now. Clara strayed up to them. He wandered after her. The bluebells pleased him.

'Look how they've come out of the wood!' he said.

Then she turned with a flash of warmth and of gratitude.

'Yes,' she smiled.

His blood beat up.

'It makes me think of the wild men of the woods, how terrified they would be when they got breast to breast with the open space.'

'Do you think they were?' she asked.

'I wonder which was more frightened among old tribes – those bursting out of their darkness of woods upon all the space of light, or those from the open tip toeing into the forests.'

'I should think the second,' she answered.

'Yes, you *do* feel like one of the open space sort, trying to force yourself into the dark, don't you?'

'How should I know?' she answered queerly.

The conversation ended there.

The evening was deepening over the earth. Already the valley was full of shadow. One tiny square of light stood opposite at Crossleigh Bank Farm. Brightness was swimming on the tops of the hills. Miriam came up slowly, her face in her big, loose bunch of flowers, walking ankle deep through the scattered froth of the cowslips. Beyond her the trees were coming into shape, all shadow.

'Shall we go?' she asked.

And the three turned away. They were all silent. Going down the path they could see the light of home right across, and on the ridge of the hill a thin dark outline with little lights, where the colliery village touched the sky.

'It has been nice, hasn't it?' he asked.

Miriam murmured assent. Clara was silent.

'Don't you think so?' he persisted.

But she walked with her head up, and still did not answer. He could tell by the way she moved, as if she didn't care, that she suffered.

At this time Paul took his mother to Lincoln. She was bright and enthusiastic as ever, but as he sat opposite her in the railway carriage, she seemed to look frail. He had a momentary sensation as if she were slipping away from him. Then he wanted to get hold of her, to fasten her, almost to chain her. He felt he must keep hold of her with his hand. They drew near to the city. Both were at the window looking for the cathedral.

'There she is, mother!' he cried.

They saw the great cathedral lying couchant above the plain.

'Ah!' she exclaimed. 'So she is!'

He looked at his mother. Her blue eyes were watching the cathedral quietly. She seemed again to be beyond him. Something in the eternal repose of the uplifted cathedral, blue and noble against the sky, was reflected in her, something of the fatality. What was, *was*. With all his young will he could not alter it. He saw her face, the skin still fresh and pink and downy, but crow's-feet near her eyes, her eyelids steady, Sinking a little, her mouth always closed with disillusion; and there was on her the same eternal look, as if she knew fate at last. He beat against it with all the strength of his soul.

'Look, mother, how big she is above the town! Think, there are streets and streets below her! She looks bigger than the city altogether.'

So she does!' exclaimed his mother, breaking bright into life again. But he had seen her sitting, looking steady out of the window at the cathedral, her face and eyes fixed, reflecting the relentlessness of life. And the crow's-feet near her eyes, and her mouth shut so hard, made him feel he would go mad.

They ate a meal that she considered wildly extravagant.

'Don't imagine I like it,' she said, as she ate her cutlet. 'I *don't* like it, I really don't! Just *think* of your money wasted!'

'You never mind my money,' he said. 'You forget I'm a fellow taking his girl for an outing.'

And he bought her some blue violets.

'Stop it at once, sir!' she commanded. 'How can I do it?'

'*You've* got nothing to do. Stand still!'

And in the middle of High Street he stuck the flowers in her coat.

'An old thing like me!' she said, sniffing.

'You see,' he said, 'I want people to think we're awful swells. So look ikey.'

'I'll jowl your head,' she laughed.

'Strut!' he commanded. 'Be a fantail pigeon.'

It took him an hour to get her through the street. She stood above Glory Hole, she stood before Stone Bow, she stood everywhere, and exclaimed.

A man came up, took off his hat, and bowed to her.

'Can I show you the town, madam?'

'No, thank you,' she answered. 'I've got my son.'

Then Paul was cross with her for not answering with more dignity.

'You go away with you!' she exclaimed. 'Ha! that's the Jew's House. Now, do you remember that lecture, Paul –?'

But she could scarcely climb the cathedral hill. He did not notice. Then suddenly he found her unable to speak. He took her into a little public-house, where she rested.

'It's nothing,' she said. 'My heart is only a bit old; one must expect it.'

He did not answer, but looked at her. Again his heart was crushed in a hot grip. He wanted to cry, he wanted to smash things in fury.

They set off again, pace by pace, so slowly. And every step seemed like a weight on his chest. He felt as if his heart would burst. At last they came to the top. She stood enchanted, looking at the castle gate, looking at the cathedral front. She had quite forgotten herself.

'Now *this* is better than I thought it could be!' she cried.

But he hated it. Everywhere he followed her, brooding. They sat together in the cathedral. They attended a little service in the choir. She was timid.

'I suppose it is open to anybody?' she asked him.

'Yes,' he replied. 'Do you think they'd have the damned cheek to send us away?'

'Well, I'm sure,' she exclaimed, 'they would if they heard your language.'

Her face seemed to shine again with joy and peace during the service. And all the time he was wanting to rage and smash things and cry.

Afterwards, when they were leaning over the wall, looking at the town below, he blurted suddenly:

'Why can't a man have a *young* mother? What is she old for?'

'Well,' his mother laughed, 'she can scarcely help it.'

'And why wasn't I the oldest son? Look – they say the young ones have the advantage – but look, *they* had the young mother. You should have had me for your eldest son.'

'I didn't arrange it,' she remonstrated. 'Come to consider, you're as much to blame as me.'

He turned on her, white, his eyes furious.

'What are you old for!' he said, mad with his impotence. '*Why* can't you walk? *Why* can't you come with me to places?'

'At one time,' she replied, 'I could have run up that hill a good deal better than you.'

'What's the good of that to me?' he cried, hitting his fist on the wall. Then he became plaintive. 'It's too bad of you to be ill, Little, it is – '

'Ill!' she cried. 'I'm a bit old, and you'll have to put up with it, that's all.'

They were quiet. But it was as much as they could bear. They got jolly again over tea. As they sat by Brayford watching the boats, he told her about Clara. His mother asked him innumerable questions.

'Then who does she live with!'

With her mother, on Bluebell Hill.'

'And have they enough to keep them?'

'I don't think so. I think they do lace work.'

'And wherein lies her charm, my boy?'

'I don't know that she's charming, mother. But she's nice. And she seems straight, you know – not a bit deep, not a bit.'

'But she's a good deal older than you.'

'She's thirty, I'm going on twenty-three.'

'You haven't told me what you like her for.'

'Because I don't know – a sort of defiant way she's got – a sort of angry way.'

Mrs Morel considered. She would have been glad now for her son to fall in love with some woman who would – she did not know what. But he fretted so, got so furious suddenly, and again was melancholic. She wished he knew some nice woman. She did not know what she wished, but left it vague. At any rate she was not hostile to the idea of Clara.

Annie, too, was getting married. Leonard had gone away to work in Birmingham. One week-end when he was home she had said to him:

'You don't look very well, my lad.'

'I dunno,' he said. 'I feel anyhow or nohow, ma.'

He called her 'ma' already in his boyish fashion.

Are you sure they're good lodgings?' she asked.

'Yes – yes. Only – it's a winder when you have to pour your own tea out – an' nobody to grouse if you team it in your saucer and sup it up. It somehow takes a' the taste out of it.'

Mrs Morel laughed. 'And so it knocks you up!' she said.

'I dunno. I want to get married,' he blurted, twisting his fingers and looking down at his boots. There was a silence.

'But,' she exclaimed, 'I thought you said you'd wait another year.'

'Yes, I did say so,' he replied stubbornly.

Again she considered.

'And you know,' she said, 'Annie's a bit of a spendthrift. She's saved no more than eleven pounds. And I know, lad, you haven't had much chance.'

He coloured up to the ears.

'I've got thirty-three quid,' he said.

'It doesn't go far,' she answered.

He said nothing, but twisted his fingers.

'And you know,' she said, 'I've nothing – '

'I didn't want, ma!' he cried, very red, suffering and remonstrating.

'No, my lad, I know. I was only wishing I had. And take away five pounds for the wedding and things – it leaves twenty-nine pounds. You won't do much on that.'

He twisted still, impotent, stubborn, not looking up.

'But do you really want to get married?' she asked. 'Do you feel as if you ought?'

He gave her one straight look from his blue eyes.

'Yes,' he said.

'Then,' she replied, 'we must all do the best we can for it, lad.'

The next time he looked up there were tears in his eyes.

'I don't want Annie to feel handicapped,' he said, struggling.

'My lad,' she said, 'you're steady – you've got a decent place. If a man had *needed* me I'd have married him on his last week's wages. She may find it a bit hard to start humbly. Young girls *are* like that. They look forward to the fine home they think they'll have. But I had expensive furniture. It's not everything.'

So the wedding took place almost immediately. Arthur came home, and was splendid in uniform. Annie looked nice in a dove-grey dress that she could take for Sundays. Morel called her a fool for getting married, and was cool with his son-in-law. Mrs Morel had white tips in her bonnet, and some white on her blouse, and was teased by both her sons for fancying herself so grand. Leonard was jolly and cordial, and felt a fearful fool. Paul could not quite see what Annie wanted to get married for. He was fond of her, and she of him. Still, he hoped rather lugubriously that it would turn out all right. Arthur was astonishingly handsome in his scarlet and yellow, and he knew it well, but was secretly ashamed of the uniform. Annie cried her eyes up in the kitchen, on leaving her mother. Mrs Morel cried a little, then patted her on the back and said:

'But don't cry, child, he'll be good to you.'

Morel stamped and said she was a fool to go and tie herself up. Leonard looked white and overwrought. Mrs Morel said to him:

'I s'll trust her to you, my lad, and hold you responsible for her.'

'You can,' he said, nearly dead with the ordeal. And it was all over.

When Morel and Arthur were in bed, Paul sat talking, as he often did, with his mother.

'You're not sorry she's married, mother, are you?' he asked.

'I'm not sorry she's married – but – it seems strange that she should go from me. It even seems to me hard that she can prefer to go with her Leonard. That's how mothers are – I know it's silly.'

'And shall you be miserable about her?'

When I think of my own wedding day,' his mother answered, 'I can only hope her life will be different.'

'But you can trust him to be good to her?'

'Yes, yes. They say he's not good enough for her. But I say if a man is *genuine,* as he is, and a girl is fond of him – then – it should be all right. He's as good as she.'

'So you don't mind?'

'I would *never* have let a daughter of mine marry a man I didn't *feel* to be genuine through and through. And yet, there's a gap now she's gone.'

They were both miserable, and wanted her back again. It seemed to Paul his mother looked lonely, in her new black silk blouse with its bit of white trimming.

'At any rate, mother, I s'll never marry,' he said.

'Ay, they all say that, my lad. You've not met the one yet. Only wait a year or two.'

'But I shan't marry, mother. I shall live with you, and we'll have a servant.'

'Ay, my lad, it's easy to talk. We'll see when the time comes.'

What time? I'm nearly twenty-three.'

'Yes, you are not the one that would marry young. But in three years' time – '

'I shall be with you just the same.'

We'll see, my boy, we'll see.'

'But you don't want me to marry?'

'I shouldn't like to think of you going through your life without anybody to care for you and do – no.'

And you think I ought to marry?'

'Sooner or later every man ought.'

'But you'd rather it were later.'

'It would be hard – and very hard. It's as they say:

'A son's my son till he takes him a wife,
 But my daughter's my daughter the whole of her life.'

'And you think I'd let a wife take me from you?'

'Well, you wouldn't ask her to marry your mother as well as you,' Mrs Morel smiled.

'She could do what she liked; she wouldn't have to interfere.'

'She wouldn't – till she'd got you – and then you'd see.'

'I never will see. I'll never marry while I've got you – I won't.'

'But I shouldn't like to leave you with nobody, my boy,' she cried.

'You're not going to leave me. What are you? Fifty-three! I'll give you till seventy-five. There you are, I'm fat and forty-four. Then I'll marry a staid body. See!'

His mother sat and laughed.

'Go to bed,' she said – 'go to bed.'

'And we'll have a pretty house, you and me, and a servant, and it'll be just all right. I s'll perhaps be rich with my painting.'

'Will you go to bed!'

'And then you s'll have a pony-carriage. See yourself – a little Queen Victoria trotting round.'

'I tell you to go to bed,' she laughed.

He kissed her and went. His plans for the future were always the same.

Mrs Morel sat brooding – about her daughter, about Paul, about Arthur. She fretted at losing Annie. The family was very closely bound. And she felt she must live now, to be with her children. Life was so rich for her. Paul wanted her, and so did Arthur. Arthur never knew how deeply he loved her. He was a creature of the moment. Never yet had he been forced to realise himself. The army had disciplined his body, but not his soul. He was in perfect health and very handsome. His dark, vigorous hair sat close to his smallish head. There was something childish about his nose, something almost girlish about his dark blue eyes. But he had the full red mouth of a man under his brown moustache, and his jaw was strong. It was his father's mouth; it was the nose and eyes of her own mother's people – good-looking, weak principled folk. Mrs Morel was anxious about him. Once he had really run the rig he was safe. But how far would he go?

The army had not really done him any good. He resented bitterly the authority of the petty officers. He hated having to obey as if he were an animal. But he had too much sense to kick. So he turned his attention to getting the best out of it. He could sing, he was a boon-companion. Often he got into scrapes, but they were the manly scrapes that are easily condoned. So he made a good time out of it, whilst his self-respect was in suppression. He trusted to his good looks and handsome figure, his refinement, his decent education to get him most of what he wanted, and he was not disappointed. Yet he was restless. Something seemed to gnaw him inside. He was never still, he was never alone. With his mother he was rather humble. Paul he admired and loved and despised slightly. And Paul admired and loved and despised him slightly.

Mrs Morel had had a few pounds left to her by her father, and she decided to buy her son out of the army. He was wild with joy. Now he was like a lad taking a holiday.

He had always been fond of Beatrice Wyld, and during his furlough he picked up with her again. She was stronger and better in health. The two often went long walks together, Arthur taking her arm in soldier's fashion, rather stiffly. And she came to play the piano whilst he sang. Then Arthur would unhook his tunic collar. He grew flushed, his eyes were bright, he sang in a manly tenor. Afterwards they sat together on the sofa. He seemed to flaunt his body: she was aware of him so – the strong chest, the sides, the thighs in their close-fitting trousers.

He liked to lapse into the dialect when he talked to her. She would sometimes smoke with him. Occasionally she would only take a few whiffs at his cigarette.

'Nay,' he said to her one evening, when she reached for his cigarette. 'Nay, tha doesna. I'll gi'e thee a smoke kiss if ter's a mind.'

'I wanted a whiff, no kiss at all,' she answered.

Well, an' tha s'lt ha' e a whiff,' he said, 'along wi' t' kiss.'

'I want a draw at thy fag,' she cried, snatching for the cigarette between his lips.

He was sitting with his shoulder touching her. She was small and quick as lightning. He just escaped.

'I'll gi'e thee a smoke kiss,' he said.

Tha'rt a knivey* nuisance, Arty Morel,' she said, sitting back.

'Ha'e a smoke kiss?'

The soldier leaned forward to her, smiling. His face was near hers.

Shonna!' she replied, turning away her head.

He took a draw at his cigarette, and pursed up his mouth, and put his lips close to her. His dark-brown cropped moustache

* trickey and mean.

stood out like a brush. She looked at the puckered crimson lips, then suddenly snatched cigarette from his fingers and darted away. He, leaping after her, seized the comb from her back hair. She turned, threw the cigarette at him. He picked it up, put it in his mouth, and sat down.

'Nuisance!' she cried. 'Give me my comb!'

She was afraid that her hair, specially done for him, would come down. She stood with her hands to her head. He hid the comb between his knees.

'I've non got it,' he said.

The cigarette trembled between his lips with laughter as he spoke.

'Liar!' she said.

" 'S true as I'm here!' he laughed, showing his hands.

'You brazen imp!' she exclaimed, rushing and scuffling for the comb, which he had under his knees. As she wrestled with him, pulling at his smooth, tight-covered knees, he laughed till he lay back on the sofa shaking with laughter. The cigarette fell from his mouth, almost singeing his throat. Under his delicate tan the blood flushed up, and he laughed till his blue eyes were blinded, his throat swollen almost to choking. Then he sat up. Beatrice was putting in her comb.

'Tha tickled me, Beat,' he said thickly.

Like a flash her small white hand went out and smacked his face. He started up, glaring at her. They stared at each other. Slowly the flush mounted her cheek, she dropped her eyes, then her head. He sat down sulkily. She went into the scullery to adjust her hair. In private there she shed a few tears, she did not know what for.

When she returned she was pursed up close. But it was only a film over her fire. He, with ruffled hair, was sulking upon the sofa. She sat down opposite, in the armchair, and neither spoke. The clock ticked in the silence like blows.

'You are a little cat, Beat,' he said at length, half apologetically.

'Well, you shouldn't be brazen,' she replied.

There was again a long silence. He whistled to himself, like a man much agitated but defiant. Suddenly she went across to him and kissed him.

'Did it, pore fing!' she mocked.

He lifted his face, smiling curiously.

'Kiss?' he invited her.

'Daren't I?' she asked.

'Go on!' he challenged, his mouth lifted to her.

Deliberately, and with a peculiar quivering smile that seemed to overspread her whole body, she put her mouth on his. Immediately his arms folded round her. As soon as the long kiss was finished she drew back her head from him, put her delicate fingers on his neck, through the open collar. Then she closed her eyes, giving herself up again in a kiss.

She acted of her own free will. What she would do she did, and made nobody responsible.

Paul felt life changing around him. The conditions of youth were gone. Now it was a home of grown-up people. Annie was a married woman, Arthur was following his own pleasure in a way unknown to his folk. For so long they had all lived at home, and gone out to pass their time. But now, for Annie and Arthur, life lay outside their mother's house. They came home for holiday and for rest. So there was that strange, half-empty feeling about the house, as if the birds had flown. Paul became more and more unsettled. Annie and Arthur had gone. He was restless to follow. Yet home was for him beside his mother. And still there was something else, something outside, something he wanted.

He grew more and more restless. Miriam did not satisfy him. His old mad desire to be with her grew weaker. Sometimes he met Clara in Nottingham, sometimes he went to meetings with her, sometimes he saw her at Willey Farm. But on these last occasions the situation became strained. There was a triangle of antagonism between Paul and Clara and Miriam. With Clara he took on a smart, worldly, mocking tone very antagonistic to

Miriam. It did not matter what went before. She might be intimate and sad with him. Then as soon as Clara appeared, it all vanished, and he played to the newcomer.

Miriam had one beautiful evening with him in the hay. He had been on the horse-rake, and, having finished, came to help her to put the hay in cocks. Then he talked to her of his hopes and despairs, and his whole soul seemed to lie bare before her. She felt as if she watched the very quivering stuff of life in him. The moon came out: they walked home together: he seemed to have come to her because he needed her so badly, and she listened to him, gave him all her love and her faith. It seemed to her he brought her the best of himself to keep, and that she would guard it all her life. Nay, the sky did not cherish the stars more surely and eternally than she would guard the good in the soul of Paul Morel. She went on home alone, feeling exalted, glad in her faith.

And then, the next day, Clara came. They were to have tea in the hayfield. Miriam watched the evening drawing to gold and shadow. And all the time Paul was sporting with Clara. He made higher and higher heaps of hay that they were jumping over. Miriam did not care for the game, and stood aside. Edgar and Geoffrey and Maurice and Clara and Paul jumped. Paul won, because he was light. Clara's blood was roused. She could run like on Amazon. Paul loved the determined way she rushed at the haycock and leaped, landed on the other side, her breasts shaken, her thick hair coming undone.

'You touched!' he cried. 'You touched?'

'No!' she flashed, turning to Edgar. 'I didn't touch, did I? Wasn't I clear?'

'I couldn't say,' laughed Edgar.

None of them could say.

'But you touched,' said Paul. 'You're beaten.'

'I did *not* touch!' she cried.

'As plain as anything,' said Paul.

'Box his ears for me!' she cried to Edgar.

'Nay,' Edgar laughed. 'I daren't. You must do it yourself'

'And nothing can alter the fact that you touched,' laughed Paul.

She was furious with him. Her little triumph before these lads and men was gone. She had forgotten herself in the game. Now he was to humble her.

'I think you are despicable!' she said.'

And again he laughed, in a way that tortured Miriam.

'And I *knew* you couldn't jump that heap,' he teased.

She turned her back on him. Yet everybody could see that the only person she listened to, or was conscious of, was he, and he of her. It pleased the men to see this battle between them. But Miriam was tortured.

Paul could choose the lesser in place of the higher, she saw. He could be unfaithful to himself, unfaithful to the real, deep Paul Morel. There was a danger of his becoming frivolous, of his running after his satisfactions like any Arthur, or like his father. It made Miriam bitter to think that he should throw away his soul for this flippant traffic of triviality with Clara. She walked in bitterness and silence, while the other two rallied each other, and Paul sported.

And afterwards, he would not own it, but he was rather ashamed of himself, and prostrated himself before Miriam. Then again he rebelled.

'It's not religious to be religious,' he said. 'I reckon a crow is religious when it sails across the sky. But it only does it because it feels itself carried to where it's going, not because it thinks it is being eternal.'

But Miriam knew that one should be religious in everything, have God, whatever God might be, present in everything.

'I don't believe God knows such a lot about Himself,' he cried. 'God doesn't *know* things, He *is* things. And I'm sure He's not soulful.'

And then it seemed to her that Paul was arguing God on to his own side, because he wanted his own way and his own pleasure. There was a long battle between him and her. He was utterly unfaithful to her even in her own presence; then he was ashamed, then repentant; then he hated her, and went off again. Those were the ever-recurring conditions.

She fretted him to the bottom of his soul. There she remained – sad, pensive, a worshipper. And he caused her sorrow. Half the time he grieved for her, half the time he hated her. She was his conscience; and he felt, somehow, he had got a conscience that was too much for him. He could not leave her, because in one way she did hold the best of him. He could not stay with her because she did not take the rest of him, which was three-quarters. So he chafed himself into rawness over her.

When she was twenty-one he wrote her a letter which could only have been written to her.

'May I speak of our old, worn love, this last time. It, too, is changing, is it not? Say, has not the body of that love died, and left you its invulnerable soul? You see, I can give you a spirit love, I have given it you this long, long time; but not embodied passion. See, you are a nun. I have given you what I would give a holy nun – as a mystic monk to a mystic nun. Surely you esteem it best. Yet you regret – no, have regretted – the other. In all our relations no body enters. I do not talk to you through the senses – rather through the spirit. That is why we cannot love in the common sense. Ours is not an everyday affection. As yet we are mortal, and to live side by side with one another would be dreadful, for somehow with you I cannot long be trivial, and, you know, to be always beyond this mortal state would be to lose it. If people marry, they must live together as affectionate humans, who may be commonplace with each other without feeling awkward – not as two souls. So I feel it.

'Ought I to send this letter – I doubt it. But there – it is best to understand. Au revoir.'

Miriam read this letter twice, after which she sealed it up. A year later she broke the seal to show her mother the letter.

'You are a nun – you are a nun.' The words went into her heart again and again. Nothing he ever had said had gone into her so deeply, fixedly, like a mortal wound.

She answered him two days after the party.

' "Our intimacy would have been all-beautiful but for one little mistake." ' she quoted. 'Was the mistake mine?'

Almost immediately he replied to her from Nottingham, sending her at the same time a little 'Omar Khayyam.'

'I am glad you answered; you are so calm and natural you put me to shame. What a ranter I am! We are often out of sympathy. But in fundamentals we may always be together I think.

'I must thank you for your sympathy with my painting and drawing. Many a sketch is dedicated to you. I do look forward to your criticisms, which, to my shame and glory, are always grand appreciations. It is a lovely joke, that. Au revoir.'

This was the end of the first phase of Paul's love-affair. He was now about twenty-three years old, and, though still virgin, the sex instinct that Miriam had over-refined for so long now grew particularly strong. Often, as he talked to Clara Dawes, came that thickening and quickening of his blood, that peculiar concentration in the breast, as if something were alive there, a new self or a new centre of consciousness, warning him that sooner or later he would have to ask one woman or another. But he belonged to Miriam. Of that she was so fixedly sure that he allowed her right.

CHAPTER 10

Clara

WHEN HE was twenty-three years old Paul sent in a landscape to the winter exhibition at Nottingham Castle. Miss Jordan had taken a good deal of interest in him, had invited him to her house, where he met other artists. He was beginning to grow ambitious.

One morning the postman came just as he was washing in the scullery. Suddenly he heard a wild noise from his mother. Rushing into the kitchen, he found her standing on the hearthrug wildly waving a letter and crying 'Hurrah!' as if she had gone mad. He was shocked and frightened.

'Why, mother!' he exclaimed.

She flew to him, flung her arms round him for a moment, then waved the letter, crying:

'Hurrah, my boy! I knew we should do it!'

He was afraid of her – the small, severe woman with greying hair suddenly bursting out in such frenzy. The postman came running back, afraid something had happened. They saw his tipped cap over the short curtain. Mrs Morel rushed to the door.

'His picture's got first prize, Fred,' she cried, 'and is sold for twenty guineas. '

'My word, that's something like!' said the young postman, whom they had known all his life.

'And Major Moreton has bought it!' she cried.

'It looks like meanin' something, that does, Mrs Morel,' said the postman, his blue eyes bright. He was glad to have brought such a lucky letter. Mrs Morel went indoors and sat down, trembling. Paul was afraid lest she might have misread the letter, and might be disappointed after all. He scrutinised it once, twice. Yes, he became convinced it was true. Then he sat down, his heart beating with joy.

'Mother!' he exclaimed.

'Didn't I *say* we should do it!' she said, pretending she was not crying.

He took the kettle off the fire and mashed the tea.

'You didn't think, mother – ' he began tentatively.

'No, my son – not so much – but I expected a good deal.'

'But not so much,' he said.

'No – no – but I knew we should do it'

And then she recovered her composure, apparently at least. He sat with his shirt turned back, showing his young throat almost like a girl's, and the towel in his hand, his hair sticking up wet.

'Twenty guineas, mother! That's just what you wanted to buy Arthur out. Now you needn't borrow any. It'll just do.'

'Indeed, I shan't take it all,' she said

'But why?'

'Because I shan't.'

'Well – you have twelve pounds, I'll have nine.'

They cavilled about sharing the twenty guineas. She wanted to take only the five pounds she needed. He would not hear of it. So they got over the stress of emotion by quarrelling.

Morel came home at night from the pit, saying:

'They tell me Paul's got first prize for his picture, and sold it to Lord Henry Bentley for fifty pound.'

'Oh, what stories people do tell!' she cried.

'Ha!' he answered. 'I said I war sure it war a lie. But they said tha'd told Fred Hodgkisson.'

'As if I would tell him such stuff!'

'Ha!' assented the miner.

But he was disappointed nevertheless.

'It's true he has got the first prize,' said Mrs Morel.

The miner sat heavily in his chair.

'Has he, beguy!' he exclaimed.

He stored across the room fixedly.

'But as for fifty pounds such nonsense!' she was silent awhile. 'Major Moreton bought it for twenty guineas, that's true.'

'Twenty guineas! Tha niver says!' exclaimed Morel.

'Yes, and it was worth it.'

'Ay!' he said. 'I don't misdoubt it. But twenty guineas for a bit of a paintin' as he knocked off in an hour or two!'

He was silent with conceit of his son. Mrs Morel sniffed, as if it were nothing.

'And when does he handle th' money?' asked the collier:

'That I couldn't tell you. When the picture is sent home, I suppose.'

There was silence. Morel stared at the sugar-basin instead of eating his dinner. His black arm, with the hand all gnarled with work lay on the table. His wife pretended not to see him rub the back of his hand across his eyes, nor the smear in the coal-dust on his black face.

'Yes, an' that other lad 'ud 'a done as much if they hadna ha' killed 'im,' he said quietly.

The thought of William went through Mrs Morel like a cold blade. It left her feeling she was tired, and wanted rest.

Paul was invited to dinner at Mr Jordan's. Afterwards he said:

'Mother, I want an evening suit.'

'Yes, I was afraid you would,' she said. She was glad. There was a moment or two of silence. 'There's that one of William's,' she continued, 'that I know cost four pounds ten and which he'd only worn three times.'

'Should you like me to wear it, mother?' he asked.

'Yes. I think it would fit you – at least the coat. The trousers would want shortening.'

He went upstairs and put on the coat and vest. Coming down, he looked strange in a flannel collar and a flannel shirt-front, with an evening coat and vest. It was rather large.

'The tailor can make it right,' she said, smoothing her hand over his shoulder. 'It's beautiful stuff. I never could find in my heart to let your father wear the trousers, and very glad I am now.'

And as she smoothed her hand over the silk collar she thought of her eldest son. But this son was living enough inside the clothes. She passed her hand down his back to feel him. He was alive and hers. The other was dead.

He went out to dinner several times in his evening suit that had been William's. Each time his mother's heart was firm with pride and joy. He was started now. The studs she and the children had bought for William were in his shirt-front; he wore one of William's dress shirts. But he had an elegant figure. His face was rough, but warm-looking and rather pleasing. He did not look particularly a gentleman, but she thought he looked quite a man.

He told her everything that took place, everything that was said. It was as if she had been there. And he was dying to introduce her to these new friends who had dinner at seven-thirty in the evening.

'Go along with you!' she said. 'What do they want to know me for?'

'They do!' he cried indignantly. 'If they want to know me – and they say they do – then they want to know you, because you are quite as clever as I am.'

'Go along with you, child!' she laughed.

But she began to spare her hands. They, too, were work-gnarled now. The skin was shiny with so much hot water, the knuckles rather swollen. But she began to be careful to keep them out of soda. She regretted what they had been – so small and exquisite. And when Annie insisted on her having more stylish blouses to suit her age, she submitted. She even went so far as to allow a black velvet bow to be placed on her hair. Then she sniffed in her sarcastic manner, and was sure she looked a sight. But she looked a lady, Paul declared, as much as Mrs Major Moreton, and far, far nicer. The family was coming on. Only Morel remained unchanged, or rather, lapsed slowly.

Paul and his mother now had long discussions about life. Religion was fading into the background. He had shovelled away all the beliefs that would hamper him, had cleared the ground, and come more or less to the bedrock of belief that one should feel inside oneself for right and wrong, and should have the patience to gradually realise one's God. Now life interested him more.

'You know,' he said to his mother, 'I don't want to belong to the well-to-do middle class. I like my common people best. I belong to the common people.'

'But if anyone else said so, my son, wouldn't you be in a tear. *You* know you consider yourself equal to any gentleman.'

'In myself,' he answered, 'not in my class or my education or my manners. But in myself I am.'

'Very well, then. They why talk about the common people?'

'Because – the difference between people isn't in their class, but in themselves. Only from the middle classes one gets ideas, and from the common people – life itself, warmth. You feel their hates and loves.'

'It's all very well, my boy. But, then, why don't you go and talk to your father's pals?'

'But they're rather different.'

'Not at all. They're the common people. After all, whom do you mix with now   among the common people? Those that exchange ideas, like the middle classes. The rest don't interest you.'

'But – there's the life – '

'I don't believe there's a jot more life from Miriam than you could get from any educated girl – say Miss Moreton. It is *you* who are snobbish about class.'

She frankly *wanted* him to climb into the middle classes, a thing not very difficult, she knew. And she wanted him in the end to marry a lady.

Now she began to combat him in his restless fretting. He still kept up his connection with Miriam, could neither break free nor go the whole length of engagement. And this indecision seemed to bleed him of his energy. Moreover, his mother suspected him of an unrecognised leaning towards Clara, and, since the latter was a married woman, she wished he would fall in love with one of the girls in a better station of life. But he was stupid, and would refuse to love or even to admire a girl much, just because she was his social superior.

My boy,' said his mother to him, 'all your cleverness, your breaking away from old things, and taking life in your own hands, doesn't seem to bring you much happiness.'

'What is happiness!' he cried. 'It's nothing to me! How *am* I to be happy?'

The plump question disturbed her.

'That's for you to judge, my lad. But if you could meet some *good* woman who would *make* you happy – and you began to think of settling your life – when you have the means – so that you could work without all this fretting – it would be much better for you.'

He frowned. His mother caught him on the raw of his wound of Miriam. He pushed the tumbled hair off his forehead, his eyes full of pain and fire.

'You mean easy, mother,' he cried. 'That's a woman's whole doctrine for life – ease of soul and physical comfort. And I do despise it.'

'Oh, do you!' replied his mother. 'And do you call yours a divine discontent?'

'Yes. I don't care about its divinity. But damn your happiness! So long as life's full, it doesn't matter whether it's happy or not. I'm afraid your happiness would bore me.'

'You never give it a chance,' she said. Then suddenly all her passion of grief over him broke out. 'But it does matter!' she cried. 'And you *ought* to be happy, you ought to try to be happy, to live to be happy. How could I bear to think your life wouldn't be a happy one!'

'Your own's been bad enough, mater, but it hasn't left you so much worse off than the folk who've been happier. I reckon you've done well. And I am the same. Aren't I well enough off?'

'You're not, my son. Battle – battle – and suffer. It's about all you do, as far as I can see.'

'But why not, my dear? I tell you it's the best – '

'It isn't. And one *ought* to be happy, one *ought.* '

By this time Mrs Morel was trembling violently. Struggles of this kind often took place between her and her son, when she seemed to fight for his very life against his own will to die. He took her in his arms. She was ill and pitiful.

'Never mind, Little,' he murmured. 'So long as you don't feel life's paltry and a miserable business, the rest doesn't matter, happiness or unhappiness.'

She pressed him to her.

'But I want you to be happy,' she said pathetically.

'Eh, my dear – say rather you want me to live.'

Mrs Morel felt as if her heart would break for him. At this rate she knew he would not live. He had that poignant carelessness about himself his own suffering, his own life, which is a form of slow suicide. It almost broke her heart. With all the passion of her strong nature she hated Miriam for having in this subtle way undermined his joy. It did not matter to her that Miriam could not help it. Miriam did it, and she hated her.

She wished so much he would fall in love with a girl equal to be his mate – educated and strong. But he would not look at anybody above him in station. He seemed to like Mrs Dawes. At any rate that feeling was wholesome. His mother prayed and prayed for him, that he might not be wasted. That was all her prayer – not for his soul or his righteousness, but that he might not be wasted. And while he slept, for hours and hours she thought and prayed for him.

He drifted away from Miriam imperceptibly, without knowing he was going. Arthur only left the army to be married. The baby was born six months after his wedding. Mrs Morel got him a job under the firm again, at twenty-one shillings a week. She furnished for him, with the help of Beatrice's mother, a little cottage of two rooms. He was caught now. It did not matter how he kicked and struggled, he was fast. For a time he chafed, was irritable with his young wife, who loved him; he went almost distracted when the baby, which was delicate, cried or gave trouble. He grumbled for hours to his mother. She only said, 'Well, my lad, you did it yourself, now you must make the best of it.' And then the grit came out in him. He buckled to work, undertook his responsibilities, acknowledged that he belonged to his wife and child, and did make a good best of it. He had never been very closely inbound into the family. Now he was gone altogether.

The months went slowly along. Paul had more or less got into connection with the Socialist, Suffragette, Unitarian* people in Nottingham, owing to his acquaintance with Clara. One day a friend of his and of Clara's, in Bestwood, asked him to take a message to Mrs Dawes. He went in the evening across Sneinton Market to Bluebell Hill. He found the house in a mean little street paved with granite cobbles and having causeways of dark blue, grooved bricks. The front door went up a step from off this rough pavement, where the feet of the passers-by rasped and clattered. The brown paint on the door was so old that the naked wood showed between the rents. He stood on the street below and knocked. There came a heavy footstep; a large, stout woman of about sixty towered above him. He looked up at her from the pavement. She had a rather severe face.

She admitted him into the parlour, which opened on to the street. It was a small, stuffy, defunct room, of mahogany, and deathly enlargements photographs of departed people done in carbon. Mrs Radford left him. She was stately, almost martial. In a moment Clara appeared. She flushed deeply, and he was covered with confusion. It seemed as if she did not like being discovered in her home circumstances.

'I thought it couldn't be your voice,' she said.

* Christian sect who held that God was one, and did not believe in the doctrine of the Trinity (of Israel, Jesus, and the Holy Spirit).

But she might as well be hung for a sheep as for a lamb.

She invited him out of the mausoleum of a parlour into the kitchen.

That was a little, darkish room too, but it was smothered in white lace. The mother had seated herself again by the cupboard, and was drawing thread from a vast web of lace. A clump of fluff and ravelled cotton was at her right hand, a heap of three-quarter-inch lace lay on her left, whilst in front of her was the mountain of the lace web, piling the hearthrug. Threads of curly cotton, pulled out from between the lengths of lace, strewed over the fender and the fireplace. Paul dared not go forward, for fear of treading on piles of white stuff.

On the table was a jenny for carding the lace. There was a pack of brown cardboard squares, a pack of cards of lace, a little box of pins, and on the sofa lay a heap of drawn lace.

The room was all lace, and it was so dark and warm that the white, snowy stuff seemed the more distinct.

'If you're coming in you won't have to mind the work,' said Mrs Radford. 'I know we're about blocked up. But sit you down.'

Clara, much embarrassed, gave him a chair against the wall opposite the white heaps. Then she herself took her place on the sofa, shamedly.

Will you drink a bottle of stout?' Mrs Radford asked. 'Clara, get him a bottle of stout.'

He protested, but Mrs Radford insisted.

'You look as if you could do with it,' she said. 'Haven't you never any more colour than that?'

'It's only a thick skin I've got that doesn't show the blood through,' he answered.

Clara, ashamed and chagrined, brought him a bottle of stout and a glass. He poured out some of the black stuff.

Well,' he said, lifting the glass, 'here's health!'

'And thank you,' said Mrs Radford.

He took a drink of stout.

'And light yourself a cigarette, so long as you don't set the house on fire,' said Mrs Radford.

'Thank you,' he replied.

'Nay, you needn't thank me,' she answered. 'I s'll be glad to smell a bit of smoke in th' 'ouse again. A house o' women is as dead as a house wi' no fire, to my thinkin'. I'm not a spider as likes a corner to myself. I like a man about, if he's only something to snap at.'

Clara began to work. Her jenny spun with a subdued buzz; the white lace hopped from between her fingers on to the card. It was filled; she snipped off the length, and pinned the end down to the banded lace.

Then she put a new card in her jenny. Paul watched her. She sat square and magnificent. Her throat and arms were bare. The blood still mantled below her ears; she bent her head in shame of her humility. Her face was set on her work. Her arms were creamy and full of life beside the white lace; her large, well-kept hands worked with a balanced movement, as if nothing would hurry them. He, not knowing, watched her all the time. He saw the arch of her neck from the shoulder, as she bent her head; he saw the coil of dun hair; he watched her moving, gleaming arms.

'I've heard a bit about you from Clara,' continued the mother. 'You're in Jordan's, aren't you?' she drew her lace unceasing.

'Yes.'

'Ay, well, and I can remember when Thomas Jordan used to ask *me* for one of my toffies.'

'Did he?' laughed Paul. 'And did he get it?'

'Sometimes he did, sometimes he didn't – which was latterly. For he's the sort that takes all and gives naught, he is or used to be.'

'I think he's very decent,' said Paul.

'Yes; well, I'm glad to hear it.'

Mrs Radford looked across at him steadily. There was something determined about her that he liked. Her face was falling loose, but her eyes were calm, and there was something strong in her that made it seem she was not old; merely her wrinkles and loose cheeks were on anachronism. She had the strength and sang-froid of a woman in the prime of life. She continued drawing the lace with slow, dignified movements. The big web came up inevitably over her apron; the length of lace fell away at her side. Her arms were finely shapen, but glossy and yellow as old ivory. They had not the peculiar dull gleam that made Clara's so fascinating to him.

'And you've been going with Miriam Leivers?' the mother asked him.

'Well – ' he answered.

'Yes, she's a nice girl,' she continued. 'She's very nice, but she's a bit too much above this world to suit my fancy.'

'She is a bit like that,' he agreed.

'She'll never be satisfied till she's got wings and can fly over everybody's head, she won't,' she said.

Clara broke in, and he told her his message. She spoke humbly to him. He had surprised her in her drudgery. To have her humble made him feel as if he were lifting his head in expectation.

'Do you like jennying?' he asked.

'What can a woman do!' she replied bitterly.

'Is It sweated?'

'More or less. Isn't *all* woman's work? That's another trick the men have played, since we force ourselves into the labour market.'

'Now then, you shut up about the men,' said her mother. 'If the women wasn't fools, the men wouldn't be bad 'uns, that's what I say. No man was ever that bad wi' me but what he got it back again. Not but what they're a lousy lot, there's no denying it.'

'But they're all right really, aren't they?' he asked.

Well, they're a bit different from women,' she answered.

Would you care to be back at Jordan's?' he asked Clara.

'I don't think so,' she replied.

'Yes, she would!' cried her mother; 'thank her stars if she could get back. Don't you listen to her. She's for ever on that 'igh horse of hers, an' it's back's that thin an' starved it'll cut her i' two one of these days.'

Clara suffered badly from her mother. Paul felt as if his eyes were coming very wide open. Wasn't he to take Clara's fulminations so seriously, after all? She spun steadily at her work. He experienced a thrill of joy, thinking she might need his help. She seemed denied and deprived of so much. And her arm moved mechanically, that should never have been subdued to a mechanism, and her head was bowed to the lace, that never should have been bowed. She seemed to be stranded there among the refuse that life has thrown away doing her jennying. It was a bitter thing to her to be put aside by life, as if it had no use for her. No wonder she protested.

She came with him to the door. He stood below in the mean street, looking up at her. So fine she was in her stature and her bearing, she reminded him of Juno dethroned. As she stood in the doorway, she winced from the street, from her surroundings.

'And you will go with Mrs Hodgkisson to Hucknall?'

He was talking quite meaninglessly, only watching her. Her grey eyes at last met his. They looked dumb with humiliation, pleading with a kind of captive misery. He was shaken and at a loss. He had thought her high and mighty.

When he left her, he wanted to run. He went to the station in a sort of dream, and was at home without realising he had moved out of her street.

He had an idea that Susan, the overseer of the spiral girls, was about to be married. He asked her the next day.

'I say, Susan, I heard a whisper of your getting married. What about it?'

Susan flushed red.

'Who's been talking to you?' she replied.

'Nobody. I merely heard a whisper that you *were* thinking –'

Well, I am, though you needn't tell anybody. What's more, I wish I wasn't!'

'Nay, Susan, you won't make me believe that.'

'Shan't I? You *can* believe it, though. I'd rather stop here a thousand times.'

Paul was perturbed.

'Why, Susan?'

The girl's colour was high, and her eyes flashed.

That's why!'

'And must you?'

For answer, she looked at him. There was about him a candour and gentleness which made the women trust him. He understood.

'Ah, I'm sorry,' he said.

Tears came to her eyes.

'But you'll see it'll turn out all right. You'll make the best of it,' he continued rather wistfully.

There's nothing else for it.'

'Yea, there's making the worst of it. Try and make it all right.'

He soon made occasion to call again on Clara.

Would you,' he said, 'care, to come back to Jordan's?'

She put down her work, laid her beautiful arms on the table, and looked at him for some moments without answering. Gradually the flush mounted her cheek.

'Why?' she asked.

Paul felt rather awkward.

'Well, because Susan is thinking of leaving,' he said.

Clara went on with her jennying. The white lace leaped in lime jumps and bounds on to the card. He waited for her. Without raising her head, she said at last, in a peculiar low voice:

'Have you said anything about it?'

'Except to you, not a word.'

There was again a long silence.

'I will apply when the advertisement is out,' she said

'You will apply before that. I will let you know exactly when.'

She went on spinning her lime machine, and did not contradict him.

Clara came to Jordan's. Some of the older hands, Fanny among them, remembered her earlier rule, and cordially disliked the memory. Clara had always been 'ikey,' reserved, and superior. She had never mixed with the girls as one of themselves. If she had occasion to find fault, she did it coolly and with perfect politeness, which the defaulter felt to be a bigger insult than crossness. Towards Fanny, the poor, overstrung hunchback, Clara was unfailingly compassionate and gentle, as a result of which Fanny shed more bitter tears than ever the rough tongues of the other overseers had caused her.

There was something in Clara that Paul disliked, and much that piqued him. If she were about, he always watched her strong throat or her neck, upon which the blonde hair grew low and fluffy. There was a fine down, almost invisible, upon the skin of her face and arms, and when once he had perceived it, he saw it always.

When he was at his work, painting in the afternoon, she would come and stand near to him, perfectly motionless. Then he felt her, though she neither spoke nor touched him. Although she stood a yard away he felt as if he were in contact with her. Then he could paint no more. He flung down the brushes, and turned to talk to her.

Sometimes she praised his work; sometimes she was critical and cold.

'You are affected in that piece,' she would say; and, as there was an element of truth in her condemnation, his blood boiled with anger.

Again: 'What of this?' he would ask enthusiastically.

'H'm!' She made a small doubtful sound. 'It doesn't interest me much.'

'Because you don't understand it,' he retorted.

'Then why ask me about it?'

'Because I thought you would understand.'

She would shrug her shoulders in scorn of his work. She maddened him. He was furious. Then he abused her, and went into passionate exposition of his stuff. This amused and stimulated her. But she never owned that she had been wrong.

During the ten years that she had belonged to the women's movement she had acquired a fair amount of education, and having had some of Miriam's passion to be instructed, had taught herself French, and could read in that language with a struggle. She considered herself as a woman apart, and particularly apart, from her class. The girls in the spiral department were all of good homes. It was a small, special industry, and had a certain distinction. There was on air of refinement in both rooms. But Clara was aloof also from her fellow-workers.

None of these things, however, did she reveal to Paul. She was not the one to give herself away. There was a sense of mystery about her. She was so reserved, he felt she had much to reserve. Her history was open on the surface, but its inner meaning was hidden from everybody. It was exciting. And then sometimes he caught her looking at him from under her brows with on almost furtive, sullen scrutiny which made him move quickly. Often she met his eyes. But then her own were, as it were, covered over, revealing nothing. She gave him a little, lenient smile. She was to him extraordinarily provocative, because of the knowledge she seemed to possess, and gathered fruit of experience he could not attain.

One day he picked up a copy of 'Lettres de mon Moulin' from her work-bench.

'You read French, do you?' he cried.

Clara glanced round negligently. She was making an elastic stocking of heliotrope silk, turning the spiral machine with slow, balanced regularity, occasionally bending down to see her work or to adjust the needles; then her magnificent neck, with its down and fine pencils of hair, shone white against the lavender, lustrous silk. She turned a few more rounds, and stopped.

What did you say?' she asked, smiling sweetly.

Paul's eyes glittered at her insolent indifference to him.

'I did not know you read French,' he said, very polite.

'Did you not?' she replied, with a faint, sarcastic smile.

'Rotten swank!' he said, but scarcely loud enough to be heard.

He shut his mouth angrily as he watched her. She seemed to scorn the work she mechanically produced; yet the hose she made were as nearly perfect as possible.'

'You don't like spiral work,' he said.

'Oh, well, all work is work,' she answered, as if she knew all about it. He marvelled at her coldness. He had to do everything hotly. She must be something special.

What would you prefer to do?' he asked.

She laughed at him indulgently, as she said:

'There is so little likelihood of my ever being given a choice, that I haven't wasted time considering.'

'Pah!' he said, contemptuous on his side now. 'You only say that, because you're too proud to own up what you want and can't get.'

'You know me very well,' she replied coldly.

'I know you think you're terrific great shakes, and that you live under the eternal insult of working in a factory.'

He was very angry and very rude. She merely turned away from him in disdain. He walked whistling down the room, flirted and laughed with Hilda.'

Later on he said to himself:

'What was I so impudent to Clara for?' he was rather annoyed with himself, at the same time glad. 'Serve her right; she stinks with silent pride,' he said to himself angrily.

In the afternoon he came down. There was a certain weight on his heart which he wanted to remove. He thought to do it by offering her chocolates.

'Have one?' he said. 'I bought a handful to sweeten me up.'

To his great relief, she accepted. He sat on the work-bench beside her machine, twisting a piece of silk round his finger. She loved him for his quick, unexpected movements, like a young animal. His feet swung as he pondered. The sweets lay strewn on the bench. She bent over her machine, grinding rhythmically, then stooping to see the stocking that ling beneath, pulled down by the weight. He watched the handsome crouching of her back, and the apron-strings curling on the floor.

'There is always about you,' he said, 'a sort of waiting. Whatever I see you doing you're not really there: you are waiting – like Penelope* when she did her weaving.' He could not help a spurt of wickedness. 'I'll call you Penelope,' he said.

Would it make any difference?' she said, carefully removing one of her needles.

'That doesn't matter, so long as it pleases me. Here, I say you seem to forget I'm your boss. It just occurs to me.'

'And what does that mean?' she asked coolly.

'It means I've got a right to boss you.'

'Is there anything you want to complain about?'

'Oh, I say, you needn't be nasty,' he said angrily.

'I don't know what you want,' she said, continuing her task.

'I want you to treat me nicely and respectfully.'

'Call you "sir," perhaps?' she asked quietly.

'Yes, call me "sir." I should love it.'

'Then I wish you would go upstairs, sir.'

His mouth closed, and a frown came on his face. He jumped suddenly down.

'You're too blessed superior for anything,' he said.

And he went away to the other girls. He felt he was being angrier than he had any need to be. In fact, he doubted slightly that he was showing off. But if he were, then he would. Clara heard him laughing, in a way she hated, with the girls down the next room.

---

* In Homer's *Odyssey*, the wife of Odysseus awaits her husband's return for two decades, knitting and undoing the work.

When at evening he went through the department after the girls had gone, he saw his chocolates lying untouched in front of Clara's machine. He left them. In the morning they were still there, and Clara was at work. Later on Minnie, a little brunette they called Pussy, called to him:

'Hey, haven't you got a chocolate for anybody?'

'Sorry, Pussy,' he replied. 'I meant to have offered them; then I went and forgot 'em.'

'I think you did,' she answered.

'I'll bring you some this afternoon. You don't want them after they've been lying about, do you?'

'Oh, I'm not particular,' smiled Pussy.

'Oh no,' he said. 'They'll be dusty.'

He went up to Clara's bench.

'Sorry I left these things littering about,' he said.

She flushed scarlet. He gathered them together in his fist.

'They'll be dirty now,' he said. 'You should have taken them. I wonder why you didn't. I meant to have told you I wanted you to.'

He flung them out of the window into the yard below. He just glanced at her. She winced from his eyes.

In the afternoon he brought another packet.

'Will you take some?' he said, offering them first to Clara. 'These are fresh.'

She accepted one, and put it on to the bench.

'Oh, take several – for luck,' he said.

She took a couple more, and put them on the bench also. Then she turned in confusion to her work. He went on up the room.

'Here you are, Pussy,' he said. 'Don't be greedy!'

'Are they all for her?' cried the others, rushing up.

'Of course they're not,' he said.

The girls clamoured round. Pussy drew back from her mates.

'Come out!' she cried. 'I can have first pick, can't I, Paul?'

'Be nice with 'em,' he said, and went away.

'You are a dear,' the girls cried.

'Ten pence,' he answered.

He went past Clara without speaking. She felt the three chocolate creams would burn her if she touched them. It needed all her courage to slip them into the pocket of her apron.

The girls loved him and were afraid of him. He was so nice while he was nice, but if he were offended, so distant, treating them as if they scarcely existed, or not more than the bobbins of thread. And then, if they were impudent, he said quietly: 'Do you mind going on with your work,' and stood and watched.

When he celebrated his twenty-third birthday, the house was in trouble. Arthur was just going to be married. His mother was not well. His father, getting an old man, and lame from his accidents, was given a paltry, poor job. Miriam was an eternal reproach. He felt he owed himself to her, yet could not give himself. The house, moreover, needed his support. He was pulled in all directions. He was not glad it was his birthday. It made him bitter.

He got to work at eight o'clock. Most of the clerks had not turned up. The girls were not due till 8.30. As he was changing his coat, he heard a voice behind him say:

'Paul, Paul, I want you.'

It was Fanny, the hunchback, standing at the top of her stairs, her face radiant with a secret. Paul looked at her in astonishment.

'I want you,' she said.

He stood, at a loss.

'Come on,' she coaxed. 'Come before you begin of the letters.'

He went down the half-dozen steps into her dry, narrow, 'finishing-off' room. Fanny walked before him: her black bodice was short – the waist was under her armpits – and her green-black cashmere skirt seemed very long, as she strode with big strides before the young man, himself so graceful. She went to her seat at the narrow end of the room, where the window opened on to chimney-pots. Paul watched her thin hands and her flat red wrists as she excitedly twitched her white apron, which was spread on the bench in front of her. She hesitated.

'You didn't think we'd forgot you?' she asked, reproachful.

Why?' he asked. He had forgotten his birthday himself.

'Why," he says! "Why!" Why, look here!' she pointed to the calendar, and he saw, surrounding the big black number '21,' hundreds of little crosses in blacklead.

'Oh, kisses for my birthday,' he laughed. 'How did you know?'

'Yes, you want to know, don't you?' Fanny mocked, hugely delighted.

'There's one from everybody – except Lady Clara – and two from some. But I shan't tell you how many *I* put.'

'Oh, I know, you're spooney,' he said.

'There you *are* mistaken!' she cried indignant. 'I could never be so soft.' Her voice was strong and contralto.

'You always pretend to be such a hard-hearted hussy,' he laughed. 'And you know you're as sentimental – '

'I'd rather be called sentimental than frozen meat,' Fanny blurted. Paul knew she referred to Clara, and he smiled.

'Do you say such nasty things about me?' he laughed.

'No, my duck,' the hunchback woman answered, lavishly tender. She was thirty-nine. 'No, my duck, because you don't think yourself a fine figure in marble and us nothing but dirt. I'm as good as you, aren't I, Paul?' and the question delighted her.

Why, we're not better than one another, are we?' he replied.

'But I'm as good as you, aren't I, Paul?' she persisted daringly.

'Of course you are. If it comes to goodness, you're better.'

She was rather afraid of the situation. She might get hysterical.

'I thought I'd get here before the others – won't they say I'm deep! Now shut your eyes – ' she said.

'And open your mouth, and see what God sends you,' he continued, suiting action to words, and expecting a piece of chocolate. He heard the rustle of the apron, and a faint clink of metal. 'I'm going to look,' he said

He opened his eyes. Fanny, her long cheeks flushed, her blue eyes shining, was gazing at him. There was a little bundle of paint-tubes on the bench before him. He turned pale.

'No, Fanny,' he said quickly.

'From us all,' she answered hastily.

'No, but – '

'Are they the right sort?' she asked, rocking herself with delight.

'Jove! they're the best in the catalogue.'

'But they're the right sorts?' she cried.

'They're off the little list I'd made to get when my ship came in.' He bit his lip.

Fanny was overcome with emotion. She must turn the conversation.

'They was all on thorns to do it; they all paid their shares, all except the Queen of Sheba.'

The Queen of Sheba was Clara.

'And wouldn't she join?' Paul asked.

'She didn't get the chance; we never told her; we wasn't going to have *her* bossing *this* show. We didn't *want* her to join.'

Paul laughed at the woman. He was much moved. At last he must go. She was very close to him. Suddenly she flung her arms round his neck and kissed him vehemently.

'I can give you a kiss today,' she said apologetically. 'You've looked so white, it's made my heart ache.'

Paul kissed her, and left her. Her arms were so pitifully thin that his heart ached also.

That day he met Clara as he ran downstairs to wash his hands at dinner-time.

'You have stayed to dinner!' he exclaimed. It was unusual for her.

'Yes; and I seem to have dined on old surgical-appliance stock. I *must* go out now, or I shall feel stole india-rubber right through.'

She lingered. He instantly caught at her wish.

'You are going anywhere?' he asked.

They went together up to the Castle. Outdoors she dressed very plainly, down to ugliness; indoors she always looked nice. She walked with hesitating steps alongside Paul, bowing and turning away from him. Dowdy in dress, and drooping, she showed to great disadvantage. He could scarcely recognise her strong form, that seemed to slumber with power. She appeared almost insignificant, drowning her stature in her stoop, as she shrank from the public gaze.

The Castle grounds were very green and fresh. Climbing the precipitous ascent, he laughed and chattered, but she was silent, seeming to brood over something. There was scarcely time to go inside the squat, square building that crowns the bluff of rock. They leaned upon the wall there the cliff runs sheer down to the Park. Below them, in their holes on the sandstone, pigeons preened themselves and cooed softly. Away down upon the boulevard at the foot of the rock, tiny trees stood in their own pools of shadow, and tiny people went scurrying about in almost ludicrous importance.

'You feel as if you could scoop up the folk like tadpoles, and have a handful of them,' he said.

She laughed, answering:

'Yes it is not necessary to get far off in order to see us proportionately. The trees are much more significant.'

'Bulk only,' he said.

She laughed cynically.

Away beyond the boulevard the thin stripes of the metals showed upon the railway track, whose margin was crowded with little stocks of timber, beside which smoking toy engines fussed. Then the silver string of the canal lay at random among the black heaps. Beyond, the dwellings, very dense on the river flat, looked like black, poisonous herbage, in thick rows and crowded beds, stretching right away, broken now and then by taller plants, right to where the river glistened in a hieroglyph across the country. The steep scarp cliffs across the river looked puny. Great stretches of country darkened with trees and faintly brightened with corn-land spread towards the haze, where the hills rose blue beyond grey.

'It is comforting,' said Mrs Dawes, 'to think the town goes no farther. It is only a *little* sore upon the country yet.'

'A little scab,' Paul said.

She shivered. She loathed the town. Looking drearily across at the country which was forbidden her, her impassive face, pale and hostile, she reminded Paul of one of the bitter, remorseful angels.

'But the town's all right,' he said, 'it's only temporary. This is the crude, clumsy make-shift we've practised on, till we find out what the idea is. The town will come all right.'

The pigeons in the pockets of rock, among the perched bushes, cooed comfortably. To the left the large church of St Mary rose into space, to keep close company with the castle, above the heaped rubble of the town. Mrs Dawes smiled brightly as she looked across the country.

'I feel better,' she said.

'Thank you,' he replied. 'Great compliment!'

'Oh, my brother!' she laughed.

'H'm! that's snatching back with the left hand what you gave with the right, and no mistake,' he said.

She laughed in amusement at him.

'But what was the matter with you?' he asked. 'I know you were brooding something special. I can see the stamp of it on your face yet.'

'I think I will not tell you,' she said.

'All right, hug it,' he answered.

She flushed and bit her lip.

'No,' she said, 'it was the girls.'

'What about 'em?' Paul asked.

'They have been plotting something for a week now, and today they seem particularly full of it. All alike they insult me with their secrecy.'

'Do they?' he asked in concern.

'I should not mind,' she went on, in the metallic, angry tone, 'if they did not thrust it into my face – the fact that they have a secret.'

Just like women,' said he.

'It is hateful, their mean gloating,' she said intensely.

Paul was silent. He knew what the girls gloated over. He was sorry to be the cause of this new dissension.

'They can have all the secrets in the world,' she went on, brooding bitterly; 'but they might refrain from glorying in them, and making me feel more out of it than ever. It is – it is almost unbearable.'

Paul thought for a few minutes. He was much perturbed.

'I will tell you what it's all about,' he said, pale and nervous. 'It's my birthday, and they've bought me a fine lot of paints, all the girls. They're jealous of you' – he felt her stiffen coldly at the word "jealous" – merely because I sometimes bring you a book,' he added slowly. 'But, you see, it's only a trifle. Don't bother about it, will you – because' – he laughed quickly – 'well, what would they say if they saw us here now, in spite of their victory?'

She was angry with him for his clumsy reference to their present intimacy. It was almost insolent of him. Yet he was so quiet, she forgave him, although it cost her an effort.

Their two hands lay on the rough stone parapet of the Castle wall. He had inherited from his mother a fineness of mould, so that his hands were small and vigorous. Hers were large, to match her large limbs, but white and powerful looking. As Paul looked at them he knew her. 'She is wanting somebody to take her hands – for all she is so contemptuous of us,' he said to himself. And she saw nothing but his two hands, so warm and alive, which seemed to live for her. He was brooding now, staring out over the country from under sullen brows. The little, interesting diversity of shapes had vanished from the scene; all that remained was a vast, dark matrix of sorrow and tragedy, the same in all the houses and the river-flats and the people and the birds, they were only shapen differently. And now that the farms seemed to have melted away, there remained the mass from which all the landscape was composed, a dark mass of struggle and pain. The factory, the girls, his mother, the large, uplifted church, the thicket of the town, merged into one atmosphere – dark, brooding, and sorrowful, every bit.

'Is that two o'clock striking?' Mrs Dawes said in surprise.

Paul started, and everything sprang into form, regained its individuality, its forgetfulness, and its cheerfulness.

They hurried back to work.

When he was in the rush of preparing for the night's post, examining the work up from Fanny's room, which smelt of ironing, the evening postman came in.

' "Mr Paul Morel," ' he said smiling, handing Paul a package. 'A lady's handwriting! Don't let the girls see it.'

The postman, himself a favourite, was pleased to make fun of the girls' affection for Paul.

It was a volume of verse with a brief note: 'You will allow me to send you this, and so spare me my isolation. I also sympathise and wish you well. – C. D.' Paul flushed hot.

'Good Lord! Mrs Dawes. She can't afford it. Good Lord, who ever'd have thought it!'

He was suddenly intensely moved. He was filled with the warmth of her. In the glow he could almost feel her as if she were present – her arms, her shoulders, her bosom, see them, feel them, almost contain them.

This move on the part of Clara brought them into closer intimacy. The other girls noticed that when Paul met Mrs Dawes his eyes lifted and gave that peculiar bright greeting which they could interpret. Knowing he was unaware, Clara made no sign,

save that occasionally she turned aside her face from him when
he came upon her.

They walked out together very often at dinner-time; it was
quite open, quite frank. Everybody seemed to feel that he was
quite unaware of the state of his own feeling, and that nothing
was wrong. He talked to her now with some of the old fervour
with which he had talked to Miriam, but he cared less about the
talk; he did not bother about his conclusions.

One day in October they went out to Lambley for tea. Suddenly
they came to a halt on top of the hill. He climbed and sat on a gate,
she sat on the stile. The afternoon was perfectly still, with a dim
haze, and yellow sheaves glowing through. They were quiet.

'How old were you when you married?' he asked quietly.
'Twenty-two.'

Her voice was subdued, almost submissive. She would tell
him now. 'It is eight years ago?'

'Yes.'

'And when did you leave him?'

'Three years ago.'

'Five years! Did you love him when you married him?'

She was silent for some time; then she said slowly:

'I thought I did – more or less. I didn't think much about it.
And he wanted me. I was very prudish then.'

'And you sort of walked into it without thinking?'

'Yes. I seemed to have been asleep nearly all my life.'

'Somnambule? But – when did you wake up?'

'I don't know that I ever did, or ever have – since I was a child.'

'You went to sleep as you grew to be a woman? How queer!
And he didn't wake you?'

'No; he never got there,' she replied, in a monotone.

The brown birds dashed over the hedges where the rosehips
stood naked and scarlet.

'Got where?' he asked.

'At me. He never really mattered to me.'

The afternoon was so gently warm and dim. Red roofs of the cottages burned among the blue haze. He loved the day. He could feel, but he could not understand, what Clara was saying.

'But why did you leave him? Was he horrid to you? '

She shuddered lightly.

'He – he sort of degraded me. He wanted to bully me because he hadn't got me. And then I felt as if I wanted to run, as if I was fastened and bound up. And he seemed dirty.'

'I see.'

He did not at all see.

'And was he always dirty?' he asked.

'A bit,' she replied slowly. 'And then he seemed as if he couldn't get *at* me, really. And then he got brutal – he *was* brutal!'

'And why did you leave him finally?'

'Because – because he was unfaithful to me – '

They were both silent for some time. Her hand lay on the gate-post as she balanced. He put his own over it. His heart beat quickly.

'But did you – were you ever – did you ever give him a chance?'

'Chance? How?'

'To come near to you.'

'I married him – and I was willing – '

They both strove to keep their voices steady.

'I believe he loves you,' he said.

'It looks like it,' she replied.

He wanted to take his hand away, and could not. She saved him by removing her own. After a silence, he began again:

'Did you leave him out of count all along?'

'He left me,' she said.

'And I suppose he couldn't *make* himself mean everything to you?'

'He tried to bully me into it.'

But the conversation had got them both out of their depth. Suddenly Paul Jumped down.

'Come on,' he said. 'Let's go and get some tea.'

They found a cottage, where they sat in the cold parlour. She poured out his tea. She was very quiet. He felt she had withdrawn again from him. After tea, she stared broodingly into her teacup, twisting her wedding ring all the time. In her abstraction she took the ring off her finger, stood it up, and spun it upon the table. The gold became a diaphanous, glittering globe. It fell, and the ring was quivering upon the table. She spun it again and again. Paul watched, fascinated.

But she was a married woman, and he believed in simple friendship. And he considered that he was perfectly honourable with regard to her. It was only a friendship between man and woman, such as any civilised persons might have.

He was like so many young men of his own age. Sex had become so complicated in him that he would have denied that he ever could want Clara or Miriam or any woman whom he *knew*. Sex desire was a sort of detached thing, that did not belong to a woman. He loved Miriam with his soul. He grew warm at the thought of Clara, he battled with her. He knew the curves of her breast and shoulders as if they had been moulded inside him; and yet he did not positively desire her. He would have denied it for ever. He believed himself really bound to Miriam. If ever he should marry, sometime in the far future, it would be his duty to marry Miriam. That he gave Clara to understand, and she said nothing, but left him to his courses. He came to her, Mrs Dawes, whenever he could. Then he wrote frequently to Miriam, and visited the girl occasionally. So he went on through the winter; but he seemed not so fretted. His mother was easier about him. She thought he was getting away from Miriam.

Miriam knew now how strong was the attraction of Clara for him; but still she was certain that the best in him would triumph. His feeling for Mrs Dawes – who, moreover, was a married woman – was shallow and temporal, compared with his love for herself.

He would come back to her, she was sure with some of his young freshness gone, perhaps, but cured of his desire for the lesser things which other women than herself could give him. She could bear all if he were inwardly true to her and must come back.

He saw none of the anomaly of his position. Miriam was his old friend, lover, and she belonged to Bestwood and home and his youth. Clara was a newer friend, and she belonged to Nottingham, to life, to the world. It seemed to him quite plain.

Mrs Dawes and he had many periods of coolness, when they saw little of each other; but they always came together again.

'Were you horrid with Baxter Dawes?' he asked her. It was a thing that seemed to trouble him.

'In what way?'

'Oh, I don't know. But weren't you horrid with him? Didn't you do something that knocked him to pieces?'

'What, pray?'

'Making him feel as if he were nothing – *I* know,' Paul declared.

'You are so clever, my friend,' she said coolly.

The conversation broke off there. But it made her cool with him for some time.

She very rarely saw Miriam now. The friendship between the two women was not broken off, but considerably weakened.

Will you come into the concert on Sunday afternoon?' Clara asked him just after Christmas.

'I promised to go up to Willey Farm,' he replied.

'Oh, very well.'

'You don't mind, do you?' he asked.

Why should I?' she answered.

Which almost annoyed him.

'You know,' he said, 'Miriam and I have been a lot to each other ever since I was sixteen – that's seven years now.'

'It's a long time,' Clara replied.

'Yes; but somehow she – it doesn't go right – '

'How?' asked Clara.

'She seems to draw me and draw me, and she wouldn't leave a single hair of me free to fall out and blow away – she'd keep it.'

'But you like to be kept.'

'No,' he said, 'I don't. I wish it could be normal, give and take – like me and you. I want a woman to keep me, but not in her pocket.'

'But if you love her, it couldn't be normal, like me and you.'

'Yes; I should love her better then. She sort of wants me so much that I can't give myself.'

Wants you how?'

'Wants the soul out of my body. I can't help shrinking back from her.'

'And yet you love her!'

'No, I don't love her. I never even kiss her.'

Why not?' Clara asked.

'I don't know.'

'I suppose you're afraid,' she said.

'I'm not. Something in me shrinks from her like hell – she's so good, when I'm not good.'

'How do you know what she is?'

'I do! I know she wants a sort of soul union.'

'But how do you know what she wants?'

'I've been with her for seven years.'

'And you haven't found out the very first thing about her.'

'What's that?'

'That she doesn't want any of your soul communion. That's your own imagination. She wants you.'

He pondered over this. Perhaps he was wrong.

'But she seems – ' he began.

'You've never tried,' she answered.

———◆━━━◆———

CHAPTER 11

The Test on Miriam

WITH THE spring came again the old madness and battle. Now he knew he would have to go to Miriam. But what was his reluctance? He told himself it was only a sort of overstrong virginity in her and him which neither could break through. He might have married her; but his circumstances at home made it difficult, and, moreover, he did not want to marry. Marriage was for life, and because they had become close companions, he and she, he did not see that it should inevitably follow they should be man and wife. He did not feel that he wanted marriage with Miriam. He wished he did. He would have given his head to have felt a joyous desire to marry her and to have her. Then why couldn't he bring it off? There was some obstacle; and what was the obstacle? It lay in the physical bondage. He shrank from the physical contact. But why? With her he felt bound up inside himself. He could not go out to her. Something struggled in him, but he could not get to her. Why? She loved him. Clara said she even wanted him; then why couldn't he go to her, make love to her, kiss her? Why, when she put her arm in his, timidly, as they walked, did he feel he would burst forth in brutality and recoil? He owed himself to her; he wanted to belong to her? Perhaps the recoil and the shrinking from her was love in its first fierce modesty. He had no aversion for her. No, it was the opposite; it was a strong desire battling with a still stronger shyness and virginity. It seemed as if virginity were a positive force, which fought and won in both of them. And with her he felt it so hard to overcome; yet he was nearest to her, and with her alone could he deliberately break through. And he owed himself to her. Then, if they could get things right, they could marry; but he would not marry unless he could feel strong in the joy of it – never. He could not have faced his mother. It seemed to him that to sacrifice himself in a marriage he did not want would be degrading, and would undo all his life, make it a nullity. He would try what he *could* do.

And he had a great tenderness for Miriam. Always, she was sad, dreaming her religion; and he was nearly a religion to her. He could not bear to fail her. It would all come right if they tried.

He looked round. A good many of the nicest men he knew were like himself, bound in by their own virginity, which they could not break out of. They were so sensitive to their women that they would go without them for ever rather than do them a hurt, an injustice. Being the sons of mothers whose husbands had blundered rather brutally through their feminine sanctities, they were themselves too diffident and shy. They could easier deny themselves than incur any reproach from a woman; for a woman was like their mother, and they were full of the sense of their mother. They preferred themselves to suffer the misery of celibacy, rather than risk the other person.

He went back to her. Something in her, when he looked at her, brought the tears almost to his eyes. One day he stood behind her as she sang. Annie was playing a song on the piano. As Miriam sang her mouth seemed hopeless. She sang like a nun singing to heaven. It reminded him so much of the mouth and eyes of one who sings beside a Botticelli Madonna, so spiritual. Again, hot as steel, came up the pain in him. Why must he ask her for the other thing? Why was there his blood battling with her? If only he could have been always gentle, tender with her, breathing with her the atmosphere of reverie and religious dreams, he would give his right hand. It was not fair to hurt her. There seemed an eternal maidenhood about her; and when he thought of her mother, he saw the great brown eyes of a maiden who was nearly scored and shocked out of her virgin maidenhood, but not quite, in spite of her seven children. They had been born almost leaving her out of count, not of her, but upon her. So she could never let them go, because she never had possessed them.

Mrs Morel saw him going again frequently to Miriam, and was astonished. He said nothing to his mother. He did not explain nor excuse himself. If he came home late, and she reproached him, he frowned and turned on her in an overbearing way:

'I shall come home when I like,' he said; 'I am old enough.'

'Must she keep you till this time?'

'It is I who stay,' he answered.

'And she lets you? But very well,' she said.

And she went to bed, leaving the door unlocked for him; but she lay listening until he came, often long after. It was a great bitterness to her at he had gone back to Miriam. She recognised, however, the uselessness of any further interference. He went to Willey Farm as a man now, as a youth. She had no right over him. There was a coldness between him and her. He hardly told her anything. Discarded, she waited on him, cooked for him, and loved to slave for him; but her face closed again like a mask. There was nothing for her to do now but the housework; for all the rest he had gone to Miriam. She could not forgive him. Miriam killed the joy and the warmth in him. He had been such a jolly lad, and full of the warmest affection; now he grew colder, more and more irritable and gloomy. It reminded her of William; but Paul was worse. He did things with more intensity, and more realisation of what he was about. His mother knew how he was suffering for want of a woman, and she saw him going to Miriam. If he had made up his mind, nothing on earth would alter him. Mrs Morel was tired. She began to give up at last; she had finished. She was in the way.

He went on determinedly. He realised more or less what his mother felt. It only hardened his soul. He made himself callow towards her; but it was like being callous to his own health. It undermined him quickly; yet he persisted.

He lay back in the rocking-chair at Willey Farm one evening. He had been talking to Miriam for some weeks, but had not come to the point Now he said suddenly:

'I am twenty-four, almost.'

She had been brooding. She looked up at him suddenly in surprise.

'Yes. What makes you say it?'

There was something in the charged atmosphere that she dreaded.

'Sir Thomas More says one can marry at twenty-four.'

She laughed quaintly, saying:

'Does it need Sir Thomas More's sanction?'

'No; but one ought to marry about then.'

'Ay,' she answered broodingly; and she waited.

'I can't marry you,' he continued slowly, 'not now, because we've no money, and they depend on me at home.'

She sat half-guessing what was coming.

'But I want to marry now – '

'You want to marry?' she repeated.

'A woman – you know what I mean.'

She was silent.

'Now, at last, I must,' he said.

'Ay,' she answered.

'And you love me?'

She laughed bitterly.

'Why are you ashamed of it,' he answered. 'You wouldn't be ashamed before your God, why are you before people?'

'Nay,' she answered deeply, 'I am not ashamed.'

'You are,' he replied bitterly; 'and it's my fault. But you know I can't help being – as I am – don't you?'

'I know you can't help it,' she replied.

'I love you an awful lot – then there is something short.'

'Where?' she answered, looking at him.

'Oh, in me! It is I who ought to be ashamed – like a spiritual cripple. And I am ashamed. It is misery. Why is it?'

'I don't know,' replied Miriam.

'And I don't know,' he repeated. 'Don't you think we have been too fierce in our what they call purity? Don't you think that to be so much afraid and averse is a sort of dirtiness?

She looked at him with startled dark eyes.

'You recoiled away from anything of the sort, and I took the motion from you, and recoiled also, perhaps worse.'

There was silence in the room for some time.

'Yes,' she said, 'it is so.'

'There is between us,' he said, 'all these years of intimacy. I feel naked enough before you. Do you understand?'

'I think so,' she answered.

'And you love me?'

She laughed.

'Don't be bitter,' he pleaded.

She looked at him and was sorry for him; his eyes were dark with torture. She was sorry for him; it was worse for him to have this deflected love than for herself, who could never be properly mated. He was restless, for ever urging forward and trying to find a way out. He might do as he liked, and have what he liked of her.

'Nay,' she said softly, 'I am not bitter.'

She felt she could bear anything for him; she would suffer for him. She put her hand on his knee as he leaned forward in his chair. He took it and kissed it; but it hurt to do so. He felt he was putting himself aside. He sat there sacrificed to her purity, which felt more like nullity. How could he kiss her hand passionately, when it would drive her away, and leave nothing but pain? Yet slowly he drew her to him and kissed her.

They knew each other too well to pretend anything. As she kissed him, she watched his eyes; they were staring across the room, with a peculiar dark blaze in them that fascinated her. He was perfectly still. She could feel his heart throbbing heavily in his breast.

'What are you thinking about?' she asked.

The blaze in his eyes shuddered, became uncertain.

'I was thinking, all the while, I love you. I have been obstinate.'

She sank her head on his breast.

'Yes,' she answered.

'That's all,' he said, and his voice seemed sure, and his mouth was kissing her throat.

Then she raised her head and looked into his eyes with her full gaze of love. The blaze struggled, seemed to try to get away from her, and then was quenched. He turned his head quickly aside. It was a moment of anguish.

'Kiss me,' she whispered.

He shut his eyes, and kissed her, and his arms folded her closer and closer.

When she walked home with him over the fields, he said:

'I am glad I came back to you. I feel so simple with you – as if there was nothing to hide. We will be happy?'

'Yes,' she murmured, and the tears came to her eyes.

'Some sort of perversity in our souls,' he said, 'makes us not want, get away from, the very thing, we want. We have to fight against that.'

'Yes,' she said, and she felt stunned.

As she stood under the drooping thorn-tree, in the dark by the roadside, he kissed her, and his fingers wandered over her face. In the darkness, where he could not see her but only feel her, his passion flooded him. He clasped her very close.

'Sometime you will have me?' he murmured, hiding his face on her shoulder. It was so difficult.

'Not now,' she said.

His hopes and his heart sunk. A dreariness came over him.

'No,' he said.

His clasp of her slackened.

'I love to feel your arm. *there!*' she said, pressing his arm against her back, where it went round her waist. 'It rests me so.'

He tightened the pressure of his arm upon the small of her back to rest her.

'We belong to each other,' he said.

'Yes.'

'Then why shouldn't we belong to each other altogether?'

'But – ' she faltered.

'I know it's a lot to ask,' he said; 'but there's not much risk for you really – not in the Gretchen way. You can trust me there?'

'Oh, I can trust you.' The answer came quick and strong. 'It's not that – it's not that at all – but – '

What?'

She hid her face in his neck with a little cry of misery.

'I don't know!' she cried.

She seemed slightly hysterical, but with a sort of horror. His heart died in him.

'You don't think it ugly?' he asked.

'No, not now. You have *taught* me it isn't.'

'You are afraid?'

She calmed herself hastily.

'Yes, I am only afraid,' she said.

He kissed her tenderly.

'Never mind,' he said. 'You shall please yourself.'

Suddenly she gripped his arms round her, and clenched her body stiff. 'You *shall* have me,' she said, through her shut teeth.

His heart beat up again like fire. He folded her close, and his mouth was on her throat. She could not bear it. She drew away. He disengaged her.

'Won't you be late?' she asked gently.

He sighed, scarcely hearing what she said. She waited, wishing he would go. At last he kissed her quickly and climbed the fence. Looking round he saw the pale blotch of her face down in the darkness under the hanging tree. There was no more of her but this pale blotch.

'Goodbye!' she called softly. She had no body, only a voice and a dim face. He turned away and ran down the road, his fists clenched; and when he came to the wall over the lake he leaned there, almost stunned, looking up the black water.

Miriam plunged home over the meadows. She was not afraid of people, what they might say; but she dreaded the issue with him. Yes, she would let him have her if he insisted; and then, when she thought of it afterwards, her heart went down. He would be disappointed, he would find no satisfaction, and then he would go away. Yet he was so insistent; and over this, which did not seem so all-important to her, was their love to break down. After all, he was only like other men, seeking his satisfaction. Oh, but there was something more in him, something deeper! She could trust to it, in spite of all desires. He said that possession was a great moment in life. All strong emotions concentrated there. Perhaps it was so. There was something divine in it; then she would submit, religiously, to the sacrifice. He should have her. And at the thought her whole body clenched itself involuntarily, hard, as if against something; but Life forced her through this gate of suffering, too, and she would submit. At any rate, it would give him what he wanted, which was her deepest wish. She brooded and brooded and brooded herself towards accepting him.

He courted her now like a lover. Often, when he grew hot, she put his face from her, held it between her hands, and looked in his eyes. He could not meet her gaze. Her dark eyes, full of love, earnest and searching, made him turn away. Not for an instant would she let him forget. Back again he had to torture himself into a sense of his responsibility and hers. Never any relaxing, never any leaving himself to the great hunger and impersonality of passion; he must be brought back to a deliberate, reflective creature. As if from a swoon of passion she called him back to the littleness, the personal relationship. He could not bear it.

'Leave me alone – leave me alone!' he wanted to cry; but she wanted him to look at her with eyes full of love. His eyes, full of the dark, impersonal fire of desire, did not belong to her.

There was a great crop of cherries at the farm. The trees at the back of the house, very large and tall, hung thick with scarlet and crimson drops, under the dark leaves. Paul and Edgar were gathering the fruit one evening. It had been a hot day, and now the clouds were rolling in the sky, dark and warm. Paul climbed high in the tree, above the scarlet roofs of the buildings. The wind, moaning steadily, made the whole tree rock with a subtle, thrilling motion that stirred the blood. The young man, perched insecurely in the slender branches, rocked till he felt slightly drunk, reached down the boughs, where the scarlet beady cherries hung thick underneath, and tore off handful after handful of the sleek, cool-fleshed fruit. Cherries touched his ears and his neck as he stretched forward, their chill fingertips sending a flash down his blood. All shades of red, from a golden vermilion to a rich crimson, glowed and met his eyes under a darkness of leaves.

The sun, going down, suddenly caught the broken clouds. Immense piles of gold flared out in the south-east, headed in soft, glowing yellow right up the sky. The world, till now dusk and grey, reflected the gold glow, astonished. Everywhere the trees, and the grass, and the far-off water, seemed roused from the twilight and shining.

Miriam came out wondering.

'Oh!' Paul heard her mellow voice call, 'isn't it wonderful?'

He looked down. There was a faint gold glimmer on her face, that looked very soft, turned up to him.

'How high you are!' she said.

Beside her, on the rhubarb leaves, were four dead birds, thieves that had been shot. Paul saw some cherry-stones hanging quite bleached, like skeletons, picked clear of flesh. He looked down again to Miriam.

'Clouds are on fire,' he said.

'Beautiful!' she cried.

She seemed so small, so soft, so tender, down there. He threw a handful of cherries at her. She was startled and frightened. He laughed with a low, chuckling sound, and pelted her. She ran for shelter, picking up some cherries. Two fine red pairs she hung over her ears; then she looked up again.

'Haven't you got enough?' she asked.

'Nearly. It is like being on a ship up here.'

'And how long will you stay?'

'While the sunset lasts.'

She went to the fence and sat there, watching the gold clouds fall to pieces, and go in immense, rose-coloured ruin towards the darkness. Gold flamed to scarlet, like pain in its intense brightness. Then the scarlet sank to rose, and rose to crimson, and quickly the passion went out of the sky. All the world was dark grey. Paul scrambled quickly down with his basket, tearing his shirt-sleeve as he did so.

'They are lovely,' said Miriam, fingering the cherries.

'I've torn my sleeve,' he answered.

She took the three-cornered rip, saying:

'I shall have to mend it.' It was near the shoulder. She put her fingers through the tear. 'How warm!' she said.

He laughed. There was a new, strange note in his voice, one that made her pant.

'Shall we stay out?' he said.

'Won't it rain?' she asked.

'No let us walk a little way.'

They went down the fields and into the thick plantation of fir-trees and pines.

'Shall we go in among the trees?' he asked.

'Do you want to?'

'Yes.'

It was very dark among the firs, and the sharp spines pricked her face. She was afraid. Paul was silent and strange.

'I like the darkness,' he said. 'I wish it were thicker – good, thick darkness.'

He seemed to be almost unaware of her as a person: she was only to him then a woman. She was afraid.

He stood against a pine-tree trunk and took her in his arms. She relinquished herself to him, but it was a sacrifice in which she felt something of horror. This thick-voiced, oblivious man was a stranger to her.

Later it began to rain. The pine-trees smelled very strong.

Paul lay with his head on the ground, on the dead pine-needles, listening to the sharp hiss of the rain – a steady, keen noise. His heart was down, very heavy. Now he realised that she had not been with him all the time, that her soul had stood apart, in a sort of horror. He was physically at rest, but no more. Very dreary at heart, very sad, and very tender, his fingers wandered over her face pitifully. Now again she loved in deeply. He was tender and beautiful.

'The rain!' he said.

'Yes'– Is it coming on you?'

She put her hands over him, on his hair, on his shoulders, to feel if the rain drops fell on him. She loved him dearly. He, as he lay with his face dead pile-leaves, felt extraordinarily quiet. He did not mind if the rain drops came on him: he would have lain and got wet through: he felt as if nothing mattered, as if his living were smeared away into the beyond, near and quite lovable. This strange, gentle reaching-out to death was new to him

'We must go,' said Miriam.

'Yes,' he answered, but did not move.

To him now, life seemed a shadow, day a white shadow; night, and death, and stillness, and inaction, this seemed like *being*. To be alive, to be urgent and insistent – that was *not-to-be*. The highest of all was to melt out into the darkness and sway there, identified with the great Being.

'The rain is coming in on us,' said Miriam.

He rose, and assisted her.

'It is a pity,' he said.

What?'

'To have to go. I feel so still.'

'Still!' she repeated.

'Stiller than I have ever been in my life.'

He was walking with his hand in hers. She pressed his fingers, feeling a slight fear. Now he seemed beyond her; she had a fear lest she should lose him.

'The fir-trees are like presences on the darkness: each one only a presence.'

She was afraid, and said nothing.

'A sort of hush: the whole night wondering and asleep: *I* suppose that's what we do in death – sleep in wonder.'

She had been afraid before of the brute in him: now of the mystic. She trod beside him in silence. The rain fell with a heavy 'Hush!' on the trees. At last they gained the cart-shed.

'Let us stay here awhile,' he said.

There was a sound of rain everywhere, smothering everything.

'I feel so strange and still,' he said, 'along with everything.'

'Ay,' she answered patiently.

He seemed again unaware of her, though he held her hand close.

'To be rid of our individuality, which is our will, which is our effort to live effortless, a kind of conscious sleep – that is very beautiful, I think; that is our after-life – our immortality.'

'Yes?'

'Yes – and very beautiful to have.'

'You don't usually say that.'

'No.'

In a while they went indoors. Everybody looked at them curiously. He still kept the quiet, heavy look in his eyes, the stillness in his voice. Instinctively, they all left him alone.

About this time Miriam's grandmother, who lived in a tiny cottage Woodlinton, fell ill, and the girl was sent to keep house. It was a beautiful little place. The cottage had a big garden in front, with red brick walls, against which the plum-trees were nailed. At the back another garden was separated from the fields by a tall old hedge. It was very pretty. Miriam had not much to do, so she found time for her beloved reading, and for writing little introspective pieces which interested her.

At the holiday-time her grandmother, being better, was driven to Derby to stay with her daughter for a day or two. She was a crotchety old lady, and might return the second day or the third; so Miriam stayed alone in the cottage, which also pleased her.

Paul used often to cycle over, and they had as a rule peaceful and happy times. He did not embarrass her much; but then on the Monday of the holiday he was to spend a whole day with her.

It was perfect weather. He left his mother, telling her where he was going. She would be alone all the day. It cast a shadow over him; but he had three days that were all his own, when he was going to do as he liked. It was sweet to rush through the morning lanes on his bicycle.

He got to the cottage at about eleven o'clock. Miriam was busy preparing dinner. She looked so perfectly in keeping with the little kitchen, ruddy and busy. He kissed her and sat down to watch. The room was small and cosy. The sofa was covered all over with a sort of linen in squares of red and pale blue, old, much washed, but pretty. There was a stuffed owl in a case over a corner cupboard. The sunlight came through the leaves of the scented geraniums in the window. She was cooking a chicken in his honour. It was their cottage for the day, and they were man and wife. He beat the eggs for her and peeled the potatoes. He thought she gave a feeling of home almost like his mother; and no one could look more beautiful, with her tumbled curls, when she was flushed from the fire.

The dinner was a great success. Like a young husband, he carved. They talked all the time with unflagging zest. Then he wiped the dishes she had washed, and they went out down the fields. There was a bright little brook that ran into a bog at the foot of a very steep bank. Here they wandered, picking still a few marsh-marigolds and many big blue forget-me-nots. Then she

sat on the bank with her hands full of flowers, mostly golden
water-blobs. As she put her face down into the marigolds, it was
all overcast with a yellow shine.

Your face is bright,' he said, 'like a transfiguration.'

She looked at him, questioning. He laughed pleadingly to her,
laying his hand on hers. Then he kissed her fingers, then her face.

The world was all steeped in sunshine, and quite still, yet not
asleep, but quivering with a kind of expectancy.

'I have never seen anything more beautiful than this,' he said.
He held her hand fast all the time.

'And the water singing to itself as it runs – do you love it?' She
looked at him full of love. His eyes were very dark, very bright.

'Don't you think it's a great day?' he asked.

She murmured her assent. She was happy, and he saw it.

'And our day – just between us,' he said.

They lingered a little while. Then they stood up upon the
Sweet thyme, and he looked down at her simply.

'Will you come?' he asked.

They went back to the house, hand-in-hand, in silence. The
chickens came scampering down the path to her. He locked the
door, and they had the little house to themselves.

He never forgot seeing her as she lay on the bed, when he
was unfastening his collar. First he saw only her beauty, and was
blind with it. She had the most beautiful body he had ever imagined.
He stood unable to move or speak, looking at her, his face half
smiling with wonder. And then he wanted her, but as he went
forward to her, her hands lifted in a little pleading movement, and
he looked at her face, and stopped. Her big brown eyes were
watching him, still and resigned and loving; she lay as if she had
given herself up to sacrifice: there was her body for him; but the
look at the back of her eyes, like a creature awaiting immolation,
arrested him, and all his blood fell back.

'You are sure you want me?' he asked, as if a cold shadow
had come over him.

'Yes, quite sure.'

She was very quiet, very calm. She only realised that she was doing something for him. He could hardly bear it. She lay to be sacrificed for him because she loved him so much. And he had to sacrifice her. For a second, he wished he were sexless or dead. Then he shut his eyes again to her, and his blood beat back again.

And afterwards he loved her – loved her to the last fibre of his being. He loved her. But he wanted, somehow, to cry. There was something he could not bear for her sake. He stayed with her till quite late at night. As he rode home he felt that he was finally initiated. He was a youth no longer. But why had he the dull pain in his soul? Why did the thought of death, the after-life, seem so sweet and consoling?

He spent the week with Miriam, and wore her out with his passion before it was gone. He had always, almost willfully, to put her out of count, and act from the brute strength of his own feelings. And he could not do it often, and there remained afterwards always the sense of failure and of death. If he were really with her, he had to put aside himself and his desire. If he would have her, he had to put her aside.

'When I come to you,' he asked her, his eyes dark with pain and shame, 'you don't really want me, do you?'

'Ah, yes!' she replied quickly.

He looked at her.

'Nay,' he said.

She began to tremble.

'You see,' she said, taking his face and shutting it out against her shoulder – 'you see – as we are – how can I get used to you? It would come all right if we were married.'

He lifted her head and looked at her.

'You mean, now, it is always too much shock?'

'Yes – and – '

'You are always clenched against me.'

She was trembling with agitation.

'You see,' she said, 'I'm not used to the thought – '

'You are lately,' he said.

'But all my life. Mother said to me, "There is one thing in marriage that is always dreadful, but you have to bear it." And I believed it.'

'And still believe,' he said.

'No!' she cried hastily. 'I believe, as you do, that loving, even in *that* way, is the high-water mark of living.'

'That doesn't alter the fact that you never *want* it.'

'No,' she said, taking his head in her arms and rocking in despair.

'Don't say so! You don't understand.' She rocked with pain. 'Don't I want your children?'

'But not me.'

'How can you say so? But we must be married to have children –'

'Shall we be married, then? I want you to have my children.'

He kissed her hand reverently. She pondered sadly, watching him.

We are too young,' she said at length.

'Twenty-four and twenty-three – '

'Not yet,' she pleaded, as she rocked herself in distress.

'When you will,' he said.

She bowed her head gravely. The tone of hopelessness in which he said these things grieved her deeply. It had always been a failure between them. Tacitly, she acquiesced in what he felt.

And after a week of love he said to his mother suddenly one Sunday night, just as they were going to bed:

'I shan't go so much to Miriam's, mother.'

She was surprised, but she would not ask him anything.

'You please yourself,' she said.

So he went to bed. But there was a new quietness about him which she had wondered at. She almost guessed. She would leave him alone, however. Precipitation might spoil things. She watched him in his loneliness, wondering where he would end.

He was sick, and much too quiet for him. There was a perpetual little knitting of his brows, such as she had seen when he was a small baby, and which had been gone for many years. Now it was the same again. And she could do nothing for him. He had to go on alone, make his own way.

He continued faithful to Miriam. For one day he had loved her utterly. But it never came again. The sense of failure grew stronger. At first it was only a sadness. Then he began to feel he could not go on. He wanted to run, to go abroad, anything. Gradually he ceased to ask her to have him. Instead of drawing them together, it put them apart. And then he realised, consciously, that it was no good. It was useless trying: it would never be a success between them.

For some months he had seen very little of Clara. They had occasionally walked out for half an hour at dinner-time. But he always reserved himself for Miriam. With Clara, however, his brow cleared, and he was gay again. She treated him indulgently, as if he were a child. He thought he did not mind. But deep below the surface it piqued him.

Sometimes Miriam said:

'What about Clara? I hear nothing of her lately.'

'I walked with her about twenty minutes yesterday,' he replied.

'And what did she talk about?'

'I don't know. I suppose I did all the jawing – I usually do. I think I was telling her about the strike, and how the women took it.'

'Yes.'

So he gave the account of himself.

But insidiously, without his knowing it, the warmth he felt for Clara drew him away from Miriam, for whom he felt responsible, and to whom he felt he belonged. He thought he was being quite faithful to her. It was not easy to estimate exactly the strength and warmth of one's feelings for a woman till they have run away with one.

He began to give more time to his men friends. There was Jessop, at the Art School; Swain, who was chemistry demonstrator at the University; Newton, who was a teacher; besides Edgar and Miriam's younger brothers. Pleading work, he sketched and studied with Jessop. He called in the University for Swain, and the two went 'down town' together. Having come home in the train with Newton, he called and had a game of billiards with him in the Moon and Stars. If he gave to Miriam the excuse of his men friends, he felt quite justified. His mother began to be relieved. He always told her where he had been.

During the summer Clara wore sometimes a dress of soft cotton stuff with loose sleeves. When she lifted her hands, her sleeves fell back, and her beautiful strong arms shone out.

'Half a minute,' he cried. 'Hold your arm still.'

He made sketches of her hand and arm, and the drawings contained some of the fascination the real thing had for him. Miriam, who always went scrupulously through his books and papers, saw the drawings.

'I think Clara has such beautiful arms,' he said.

'Yes! When did you draw them?'

'On Tuesday, in the work-room. You know, I've got a corner where I can work. Often I can do every single thing they need in the department, before dinner. Then I work for myself in the afternoon, and just see to things at night.'

'Yes,' she said, turning the leaves of his sketch-book.

Frequently he hated Miriam. He hated her as she bent forward and pored over his things. He hated her way of patiently casting him up, as if he were an endless psychological account. When he was with her, he hated her for having got him, and yet not got him, and he tortured her. She took all and gave nothing, he said. At least, she gave no living warmth. She was never alive, and giving off life. Looking for her was like looking for something which did not exist. She was only his conscience, not his mate. He hated her violently, and was more cruel to her. They dragged on till the next summer. He saw more and more of Clara.

At last he spoke. He had been sitting working at home one evening. There was between him and his mother a peculiar condition of people frankly finding fault with each other. Mrs Morel was strong on her feet again. He was not going to stick to Miriam. Very well; then she would stand aloof till he said something. It had been coming a long time, this bursting of the storm in him, when he would come back to her. This evening there was between them a peculiar condition of suspense. He worked feverishly and mechanically, so that he could escape from himself. It grew late. Through the open door, stealthily, came the scent of madonna lilies, almost as if it were prowling abroad. Suddenly he got up and went out of doors.

The beauty of the night made him want to shout. A half-moon, dusky gold, was sinking behind the black sycamore at the end of the garden, making the sky dull purple with its glow. Nearer, a dim white fence of lillies went across the garden, and the air all round seemed to stir with scent, as if it were alive. He went across the bed of pinks, whose keen perfume came sharply across the rocking, heavy scent of the lilies, and stood alongside the white barrier of flowers. They flagged all loose, as if they were panting. The scent made him drunk. He went down to the to watch the moon sink under.

A corncrake in the hay-close called insistently. The moon slid quite quickly downwards, growing more flushed. Behind him the great flowers leaned as if they were calling. And then, like a shock, he caught another perfume, something raw and coarse. Hunting round, he found the purple iris, touched their fleshy throats and their dark, grasping hands. At any rate, he had found something. They stood stiff in the darkness. Their scent was brutal. The moon was melting down upon the crest of the hill. It was gone; all was dark. The corncrake called still.

Breaking off a pink, he suddenly went indoors.

'Come, my boy,' said his mother. 'I'm sure it's time you went to bed.'

He stood with the pink against his lips.

'I shall break off with Miriam, mother,' he answered calmly.

She looked up at him over her spectacles. He was staring back at her, unswerving. She met his eyes for a moment then took off her glasses, He was white. The male was up in him, dominant. She did not want to see him too clearly.

'But I thought – ' she began.

'Well,' he answered, 'I don't love her. I don't want to marry her – so I shall have done.'

'But,' exclaimed his mother, amazed, 'I thought lately you had made up your mind to have her, and so I said nothing.'

'I had – I wanted to – but now I don't want. It's no good. I shall break off on Sunday. I ought to, oughtn't I?'

'You know best. You know I said so long ago.'

'I can't help that now. I shall break off on Sunday.'

'Well,' said his mother, 'I think it will be best. But lately I decided you had made up your mind to have her, so I said nothing, and should have said nothing. But I say as I have always said, I *don't* think she is suited to you.'

'On Sunday I break off,' he said, smelling the pink. He put the flower in his mouth. Unthinking, he bared his teeth, closed them on the blossom slowly, and had a mouthful of petals. These he spat into the fire, kissed his mother, and went to bed.

On Sunday he went up to the farm in the early afternoon. He had written Miriam that they would walk over the fields to Hucknall. His mother was very tender with him. He said nothing. But she saw the effort it was costing. The peculiar set look on his face stilled her.

'Never mind, my son,' she said. 'You will be so much better when it is all over.'

Paul glanced swiftly at his mother in surprise and resentment. He did not want sympathy.

Miriam met him at the lane-end. She was wearing a new dress of figured muslin that had short sleeves. Those short sleeves, and Miriam's brown-skinned arms beneath them – such pitiful, resigned arms – gave him so much pain that they helped to make him cruel. She had made herself look so beautiful and fresh for him. She seemed to blossom for him alone. Every time he looked at her – a mature young woman now, and beautiful in her new dress – it hurt so much that his heart seemed almost to be bursting with the restraint he put on it. But he had decided, and it was irrevocable.

On the hills they sat down, and he lay with his head in her lap, whilst she fingered his hair. She knew that 'he was not there,' as she put it. Often, when she had him with her, she looked for him, and could not find him. But this afternoon she was not prepared.

It was nearly five o'clock when he told her. They were sitting on the bank of a stream, where the lip of turf hung over a hollow bank of yellow earth, and he was hacking away with a stick, as he did when he was perturbed and cruel.

'I have been thinking,' he said, 'we ought to break off.'

'Why?' she cried in surprise.

'Because it's no good going on.'

'Why is it no good?'

'It isn't. I don't want to marry. I don't want ever to marry. And if we're not going to marry, it's no good going on.'

'But why do you say this now?'

'Because I've made up my mind.'

'And what about these last months, and the things you told me then?'

'I can't help it; I don't want to go on.'

'You don't want any more of me?'

'I want us to break off – you be free of me, I free of you.'

'And what about these last months?'

'I don't know. I've not told you anything but what I thought was true.'

'Then why are you different now?'

'I'm not – I'm the same – only I know it's no good going on.'

'You haven't told me why it's no good.'

'Because I don't want to go on – and I don't want to marry.'

'How many times have you offered to marry me, and I wouldn't?'

'I know; but I want us to break off.'

There was silence for a moment or two, while he dug viciously at the earth. She bent her head, pondering. He was an unreasonable child. He was like an infant which, when it has drunk its fill throws away and smashes the cup. She looked at him, feeling she could get hold of him and *wring* some consistency out of him. But she was helpless. Then she cried:

'I have said you were only fourteen – you are only *four!"*

He still dug at the earth viciously. He heard.

'You are a child of four,' she repeated in her anger.

He did not answer, but said in his heart: 'All right; if I'm a child of four, what do you want me for? *I* don't want another mother.' But he said nothing to her, and there was silence.

'And have you told your people?' she asked.

'I have told my mother.'

There was another long interval of silence.

Then what do you *want?*' she asked.

'Why, I want us to separate. We have lived on each other all these years; now let us stop. I will go my own way without you, and you will go your way without me. You will have an independent life of your own then.'

There was in it some truth that, in spite of her bitterness, she could not help registering. She knew she felt in a sort of bondage to him, which she hated because she could not control it. She had hated her love for him from the moment it grew too strong for her. And, deep down, she had hated him because she loved him and he dominated her. She had resisted his domination. She had fought to keep herself free of him in the last issue. And she *was* free of him, even more than he of her.

'And,' he continued, 'we shall always be more or less each other's work. You have done a lot for me, I for you. Now let us start and live by ourselves.'

'What do you want to do?' she asked.

'Nothing – only be free,' he answered.

She, however, knew in her heart that Clara's influence was over him to liberate him. But she said nothing.

'And what have I to tell my mother?' she asked.

'I told my mother,' he answered, 'that I was breaking off – clean and altogether.'

'I shall not tell them at home,' she said.

Frowning, 'You please yourself,' he said.

He knew he had landed her in a nasty hole, and was leaving her in the lurch. It angered him.

'Tell them you wouldn't and won't marry me, and have broken off,' he said. 'It's true enough.'

She bit her finger moodily. She thought over their whole affair. She had known it would come to this; she had seen it all along. It chimed with her bitter expectation.

'Always – it has always been so!' she cried. 'It has been one long battle between us – you fighting away from me.'

It came from her unawares, like a flash of lightning. The man's heart stood still. Was this how she saw it?

'But we've had *some* perfect hours, *some* perfect times, when we were together!' he pleaded.

'Never!' she cried; 'never! It has always been you fighting me off.'

'Not always – not at first!' he pleaded.

'Always, from the very beginning – always the same!'

She had finished, but she had done enough. He sat aghast. He had wanted to say, 'It has been good, but it is at an end.' And she – she whose love he had believed in when he had despised himself – denied that their love had ever been love. 'He had always fought away from her?' Then it had been monstrous. There had never been anything really between them, all the time he had been imagining something where there was nothing! And she had known. She had known so much, and had told him so little. She had known all the time. All the time this was at the bottom of her!

He sat silent in bitterness. At last the whole affair appeared in a cynical aspect to him. She had really played with him, not he with her. She had hidden all her condemnation from him, had flattered him, and despised him. She despised him now. He grew intellectual and cruel.

'You ought to marry a man who worships you,' he said; 'then you could do as you liked with him. Plenty of men will worship you, if you get on the private side of their natures. You ought to marry one such. They would never fight you off.'

'Thank you!' she said. 'But don't advise me *to* marry someone else any more. You've done it before.'

'Very well,' he said; 'I will say no more.'

He sat still, feeling as if he had had a blow, instead of giving one. Their eight years of friendship and love, *the* eight years of his life, were nullified.

When did you think of this?' she asked.

'I thought definitely on Thursday night.'

'I knew it was coming,' she said.

That pleased him bitterly. 'Oh, very well! If she knew then it doesn't come as a surprise to her,' he thought.

'And have you said anything to Clara?' she asked.

'No; but I shall tell her now.'

There was a silence.

'Do you remember the things you said this time last year, in my grandmother's house – nay last month even?'

'Yes,' he said; 'I do! And I meant them! I can't help that it's failed.'

'It has failed because you want something else.'

'It would have failed whether or not. You never believed in me.'

She laughed strangely.

He sat in silence. He was full of a feeling that she had deceived him. She had despised him when he thought she worshipped him. She had let him say wrong things, and had not contradicted him. She had let him fight alone. But it stuck in his throat that she had despised him whilst he thought she worshipped him. She should have told him when she found fault with him. She had not played fair. He hated her. All these years she had treated him as if he were a hero, and thought of him secretly as an infant, a foolish child. Then why had she left the foolish child to his folly? His heart was hard against her.

She sat full of bitterness. She had known – oh, well she had known! All the time he was away from her she had summed him up, seen his littleness, his meanness, and his folly. Even she had guarded her soul against him. She was not overthrown, nor prostrated, not even much hurt. She had known. Only why, as he sat there, had he still this strange dominance over her? His very movements fascinated her as if she were hypnotised by him. Yet he was despicable, false, inconsistent, and mean. Why this bondage for her? Why was it the movement of his arm stirred her as nothing else in the world could? Why was she fastened to him? Why, even now, if he looked at her and commanded her, would she have to obey? She would obey him in his trifling commands. But once he was obeyed, then she had him in her power, she knew, to lead him where she would. She was sure of herself. Only, this new influence! Ah, he was not a man! He was a baby that cries for the newest toy. And all the attachment of his soul would not keep him. Very well, he would have to go. But he would come back when he had tired of his new sensation.

He hacked at the earth till she was fretted to death. She rose. He sat flinging lumps of earth in the stream.

We will go and have tea here?' he asked.

'Yes,' she answered.

They chattered over irrelevant subjects during tea. He held forth on the love of ornament – the cottage parlour moved him thereto – and its connection with aesthetics.

She was cold and quiet. As they walked home, she asked:

'And we shall not see each other?'

'No – or rarely,' he answered.

'Nor write?' she asked, almost sarcastically.

'As you will,' he answered. 'We're not strangers – never should be, whatever happened. I will write to you now and again. You please yourself.'

'I see!' she answered cuttingly.

But he was at that stage at which nothing else hurts. He had made a great cleavage in his life. He had had a great shock when she had told him their love had been always a conflict. Nothing more mattered. If it never had been much, there was no need to make a fuss that it was ended.

He left her at the lane-end. As she went home, solitary, in her new frock, having her people to face at the other end, he stood still with shame and pain in the highroad, thinking of the suffering he caused her.

In the reaction towards restoring his self-esteem, he went into the Willow Tree for a drink. There were four girls who had been out for the day, drinking a modest glass of port. They had some chocolates on the table. Paul sat near with his whisky. He noticed the girls whispering and nudging. presently one, a bonny dark hussy, leaned to him and said:

'Have a chocolate?'

The others laughed loudly at her impudence.

'All right,' said Paul. 'Give me a hard one – nut. I don't like creams.'

'Here you are, then,' said the girl; 'here's an almond for you.'

She held the sweet between her fingers. He opened his mouth. She popped it in, and blushed.

'You *are* nice!' he said.

'Well,' she answered, 'we thought you looked overcast, and they dared me offer you a chocolate.'

'I don't mind if I have another – another sort,' he said.

And presently they were all laughing together.

It was nine o'clock when he got home, falling dark. He entered the house in silence. His mother, who had been waiting, rose anxiously.

'I told her,' he said.

'I'm glad,' replied the mother, with great relief.

He hung up his cap wearily.

'I said we'd have done altogether,' he said.

'That's right, my son,' said the mother. 'It's hard for her now, but best in the long run. I know. You weren't suited for her.'

He laughed shakily as he sat down.

'I've had such a lark with some girls in a pub,' he said. His mother looked at him. He had forgotten Miriam now. He told her about the girls in the Willow Tree. Mrs Morel looked at him. It seemed unreal, his gaiety. At the back of it was too much horror and misery.

'Now have some supper,' she said very gently.

Afterwards he said wistfully:

'She never thought she'd have me, mother, not from the first, and so she's not disappointed.'

'I'm afraid,' said his mother, 'she doesn't give up hopes of you yet.'

'No,' he said, 'perhaps not.'

'You'll find it's better to have done,' she said.

'I don't know,' he said desperately.

'Well, leave her alone,' replied his mother.

So he left her, and she was alone. Very few people cared for her, and she for very few people. She remained alone with herself, waiting.

CHAPTER 12

Passion

HE WAS gradually making it possible to earn a livelihood by his art. Liberty's had taken several of his painted designs on various stuffs, and he could sell designs for embroideries for altar-cloths, and similar things, in one or two places It was not very much he made at present, but he might extend it. He had also made friends with the designer for a pottery firm, and was gaining some knowledge of his new acquaintance's art. The applied arts interested him very much. At the same time he laboured slowly at his pictures. He loved to paint large figures, full of light, but not merely made up of lights and cast shadows, like the impressionists; rather definite figures that had a certain luminous quality, like some of Michaelangelo's people. And these he fitted into a landscape, in what he thought true proportion. He worked a great deal from memory, using everybody he knew. He believed firmly in his work, that it was good and valuable. In spite of fits of depression, shrinking, everything, he believed in his work.

He was twenty-four when he said his first confident thing to his mother.

'Mother,' he said, 'I s'll make a painter that they'll attend to.'

She sniffed in her quaint fashion. It was like a half-pleased shrug of the shoulders.

'Very well, my boy, we'll see,' she said.

'You shall see, my pigeon! You see if you're not swanky one of these days!'

'I'm quite content, my boy,' she smiled.

'But you'll have to alter. Look at you with Minnie!'

Minnie was the small servant, a girl of fourteen.

'And what about Minnie?' asked Mrs Morel, with dignity. 'I

heard her this morning: "Eh, Mrs Morel! I was going to do that, when you went out in the rain for some coal," he said. 'That looks a lot like your being able to manage servants!'

'Well, it was only the child's niceness,' said Mrs Morel.

'And you apologising to her: "You can't do two things at once, can you?"'

'She *was* busy washing up,' replied Mrs Morel.

'And what did she say? "It could easy have waited a bit. Now look how your feet paddle!"'

'Yes – brazen young baggage!' said Mrs Morel, smiling.

He looked at his mother, laughing. She was quite warm and rosy again with love of him. It seemed as if all the sunshine were on her for a moment. He continued his work gladly. She seemed so well when she was happy that he forgot her grey hair.

And that year she went with him to the Isle of Wight for a holiday. It was too exciting for them both, and too beautiful. Mrs Morel was full of joy and wonder. But he would have her walk with him more than she was able. She had a bad fainting bout. So grey her face was, so blue her mouth! It was agony to him. He felt as if someone were pushing a knife in his chest. Then she was better again, and he forgot. But the anxiety remained inside him, like a wound that did not close.

After leaving Miriam he went almost straight to Clara. On the Monday following the day of the rupture he went down to the work room. She looked up at him and smiled. They had grown very intimate unawares. She saw a new brightness about him.

'Well, Queen of Sheba!' he said, laughing.

'But why?' she asked.

'I think it suits you. You've got a new frock on.'

She flushed, asking: 'and what of it?'

'Suits you – awfully! *I* could design you a dress.'

'How would it be?'

He stood in front of her, his eyes glittering as he expounded. He kept her eyes fixed with his. Then suddenly he took hold of her. She half started back. He drew the stuff of her blouse tighter, smoothed it over her breast.

'More *so!'* he explained.

But they were both of them flaming with blushes, and immediately he ran away. He had touched her. His whole body was quivering with the sensation.

There was already a sort of secret understanding between them. The next evening he went into the cinematograph with her for a few minutes before train-time. As they sat, he saw her hand lying near him. For some moments he dared not touch it. The pictures danced and dithered. Then he took her hand in his. It was large and firm; it filled his grasp. He held it fast. She neither moved nor made any sign. When they came out his train was due. He hesitated.

'Good-night,' she said. He darted away across the road.

The next day he came again, talking to her. She was rather superior with him.

'Shall we go a walk on Monday?' he asked.

She turned her face aside.

'Shall you tell Miriam?' she replied sarcastically.

'I have broken off with her,' he said.

'When?'

'Last Sunday.'

'You quarrelled?'

'No! I had made up my mind. I told her quite definitely I should consider myself free.'

Clara did not answer, and he returned to his work. She was so quiet and so superb!

On the Saturday evening he asked her to come and drink coffee with him in a restaurant, meeting him after work was over. She came, looking very reserved and very distant. He had three-quarters of an hour to train-time.

'We will walk a little while,' he said.

She agreed, and they went past the Castle into the Park. He was afraid of her. She walked moodily at his side, with a kind of resentful, reluctant, angry walk. He was afraid to take her hand.

'Which way shall we go?' he asked as they walked in darkness.

'I don't mind.'

'Then we'll go up the steps.'

He suddenly turned round. They had passed the Park steps. She stood still in resentment at his suddenly abandoning her. He looked for her. She stood aloof. He caught her suddenly in his arms, held her strained for a moment, kissed her. Then he let her go.

'Come along' he said, penitent.

She followed him. He took her hand and kissed her fingertips. They went in silence. When they came to the light, he let go her hand. Neither spoke till they reached the station. Then they looked each other in the eyes.

'Good-night,' she said.

And he went for his train. His body acted mechanically. People talked to him. He heard faint echoes answering them. He was in a delirium. He felt that he would go mad if Monday did not come at once. On Monday he would see her again. All himself was pitched there, ahead. Sunday intervened. He could not bear it. He could not see her till Monday. And Sunday intervened – hour after hour of tension. He wanted to beat his head against the door of the carriage. But he sat still. He drank some whisky on the way home, but it only made it worse. His mother must not be upset, that was all. He dissembled, and got quickly to bed. There he sat, dressed, with his chin on his knees, staring out of the window at the far hill, with its few lights. He neither thought nor slept, but sat perfectly still, staring. And when at last he was so cold that he came to himself, he found his watch had stopped at half-past two. It was after three o'clock. He was exhausted, but still there was the torment of knowing it was only Sunday morning. He went to bed and slept. Then he cycled all day long, till he was fagged out. And he scarcely knew where he had been. But the day after was Monday. He slept till four o' clock. Then he lay and thought. He was coming nearer to himself – he could see himself, real, somewhere in front. She would go a walk with him in the afternoon. Afternoon! It seemed years ahead.

Slowly the hours crawled. His father got up; he heard him pottering about. Then the miner set off to the pit, his heavy boots scraping the yard. Cocks were still crowing. A cart went down the road. His mother got up. She knocked the fire. Presently she called him softly. He answered as if he were asleep. This shell of himself did well.

He was walking to the station – another mile! The train was near Nottingham. Would it stop before the tunnels? But it did not matter; it would get there before dinner-time. He was at Jordan's. She would come in half an hour. At any rate, she would be near. He had done the letters. She would be there. Perhaps she had not come. He ran downstairs. Ah! he saw her through the glass door. Her shoulders stooping a little to her work made him feel he could not go forward; he could not stand. He went in. He was pale, nervous, awkward, and quite cold. Would she misunderstand him? He could not write his real self with this shell.

'And this afternoon,' he struggled to say. 'You will come?'

'I think so,' she replied, murmuring.

He stood before her, unable to say a word. She hid her face from him. Again came over him the feeling that he would lose consciousness. He set his teeth and went upstairs. He had done everything correctly yet, and he would do so. All the morning things seemed a long way off, as they do to a man under chloroform. He himself seemed under a tight band of constraint. Then there was his other self, in the distance, doing things, entering stuff in a ledger, and he watched that far-off him carefully to see he made no mistake.

But the ache and strain of it could not go on much longer. He worked incessantly. Still it was only twelve o'clock. As if he had nailed his clothing against the desk, he stood there and worked, forcing every stroke out of himself. It was a quarter to one; he could clear away. Then he ran downstairs.

'You will meet me at the Fountain at two o'clock,' he said.

'I can't be there till half-past.'

'Yes!' he said.

She saw his dark, mad eyes.

'I will try at a quarter past.'

And he had to be content. He went and got some dinner. All the time he was still under chloroform, and every minute was stretched out indefinitely. He walked miles of street. Then he thought he would be late at the meeting-place. He was at the Fountain at five past two. The torture of the next quarter of an hour was refined beyond expression. It was the anguish of combining the living self with the shell. Then he saw her. She came! And he was there.

'You are late,' he said.

'Only five minutes,' she answered.

'I'd never have done it to you,' he laughed.

She was in a dark blue costume. He looked at her beautiful figure.

'You want some flowers,' he said, going to the nearest florists.

She followed him in silence. He bought her a bunch of scarlet, brick-red carnations. She put them in her coat, flushing.

'That's a fine colour!' he said.

'I'd rather have had something softer,' she said.

He laughed.

'Do you feel like a blot of vermilion walking down the street?' he said.

She hung her head, afraid of the people they met. He looked sideways at her as they walked. There was a wonderful close down on her face near the ear that he wanted to touch. And a certain heaviness, the heaviness of a very full ear of corn that dips slightly in the wind, that there was about her, made his brain spin. He seemed to be spinning down the street, everything going round.

As they sat in the tramcar, she leaned her heavy shoulder against him, and he took her hand. He felt himself coming round from the anaesthetic, beginning to breathe. Her ear, half hidden among her blonde hair, was near to him. The temptation to kiss it was almost too great. But there were other people on top of the car. It still remained to him to kiss it. After all, he was not himself, he was some attribute of hers, like the sunshine that fell on her.

He looked quickly away. It had been raining. The big bluff of the Castle rock was streaked with rain, as it reared above the flat of the town. They crossed the wide, black space of the Midland Railway, and passed the cattle enclosure that stood out white. Then they ran down sordid Wilford Road.

She rocked slightly to the tram's motion, and as she leaned against him, rocked upon him. He was a vigorous, slender man, with exhaustless energy. His face was rough, with rough-hewn features, like the common people's; but his eyes under the deep brows were so full of life that they fascinated her. They seemed to dance, and yet they were still, trembling on the finest balance of laughter. His mouth the same was just going to spring into a laugh of triumph, yet did not. There was a sharp suspense about him. She bit her lip moodily. His hand was hard clenched over hers.

They paid their two halfpennies at the turnstile and crossed the bridge. The Trent was very full. It swept silent and insidious under the bridge, travelling in a soft body. There had been a great deal of rain. On the river levels were flat gleams of flood water. The sky was grey, with glisten of silver here and there. In Wilford Churchyard the dahlias were sodden with rain – wet black-crimson balls. No one was on the path that went along the green river meadow, along the elm-tree colonnade.

There was the faintest haze over the silvery-dark water and the green meadow-banks, and the elm-trees that were spangled with gold. The river slid by in a body, utterly silent and swift, intertwining among itself like some subtle, complex creature. Clara walked moodily beside him.

Why,' she asked at length, in rather a jarring tone, 'did you leave Miriam?'

He frowned.

'Because I *wanted* to leave her,' he said.

'Why?'

'Because I didn't want to go on with her. And I didn't want to marry.' She was silent for a moment. They picked their way down the muddy path. Drops of water fell from the elm-trees.

'You didn't want to marry Miriam, or you didn't want to marry at all?' she asked.

'Both,' he answered – 'both!'

They had to manoeuvre to get to the stile, because of the pools of water.

'And what did she say?' Clara asked.

'Miriam? She said I was a baby of four, and that I always *had* battled her off.'

Clara pondered over this for a time.

'But you have really been going with her for some time?' she asked.

'Yes.'

'And now you don't want any more of her?'

'No. I know it's no good.'

She pondered again.

'Don't you think you've treated her rather badly?' she asked.

'Yes; I ought to have dropped it years back. But it would have been no good going on. Two wrongs don't make a right.'

'How old *are* you?' Clara asked.

'Twenty-five.'

'And I am thirty,' she said.

'I know you are.'

'I shall be thirty-one – or *am* I thirty-one?'

'I neither know nor care. What does it matter!'

They were at the entrance to the Grove. The wet, red track, already sticky with fallen leaves, went up the steep bank between the grass. On either side stood the elm-trees like pillars along a great aisle, arching over and making high up a roof from which the dead leaves fell. All was empty and silent and wet. She stood on top of the stile, and he held both her hands. Laughing, she looked down into his eyes. Then she leaped. Her breast came against his; he held her, and covered her face with kisses.

They went on up the slippery, steep red path. Presently she released his hand and put it round her waist.

'You press the vein in my arm, holding it so tightly,' she said.

They walked along. His finger-tips felt the rocking of her breast. All was silent and deserted. On the left the red wet plough-land showed through the doorways between the elm-boles and their branches. On the right, looking down, they could see the tree-tops of elms growing far beneath them, hear occasionally the gurgle of the river. Sometimes there below they caught glimpses of the full, soft-sliding Trent, and of water-meadows dotted with small cattle.

'It has scarcely altered since little Kirke White used to come,' he said. But he was watching her throat below the ear, where the flush was fusing into the honey-white, and her mouth that pouted disconsolate. She stirred against him as she walked, and his body was like a taut string.

Half-way up the big colonnade of elms, where the Grove rose highest above the river, their forward movement faltered to an end. He led her across to the grass, under the trees at the edge of the path. The cliff of red earth sloped swiftly down, through trees and bushes, to the river that glimmered and was dark between the foliage. The far-below water-meadows were very green. He and she stood leaning against one another, silent, afraid, their bodies touching all along. There came a quick gurgle from the river below.

'Why,' he asked at length, 'did you hate Baxter Dawes?' She turned to him with a splendid movement. Her mouth was offered him, and her throat; her eyes were half shut; her breast was tilted as if it asked for him. He flashed with a small laugh, shut his eyes, and met her in a long, whole kiss. Her mouth fused with his; their bodies were sealed and annealed. It was some minutes before they withdrew. They were standing beside the public path.

'Will you go down to the river?' he asked.

She looked at him, leaving herself in his hands. He went over the brim of the declivity and began to climb down.

'It is slippery,' he said.

'Never mind,' she replied.

The red clay went down almost sheer. He slid, went from one tuft of grass to the next, hanging on to the bushes, making for a little platform at the foot of a tree. There he waited for her, laughing with excitement. Her shoes were clogged with red earth. It was hard for her. He frowned. At last he caught her hand, and she stood beside him. The cliff rose above them and fell away below. Her colour was up, her eyes flashed. He looked at the big drop below them.

'It's risky,' he said; 'or messy, at any rate. Shall we go back?'

'Not for my sake,' she said quickly.

'All right. You see, I can't help you; I should only hinder. Give me that little parcel and your gloves. Your poor shoes!'

They stood perched on the face of the declivity, under the trees.

'Well, I'll go again,' he said.

Away he went, slipping, staggering, sliding to the next tree, into which he fell with a slam that nearly shook the breath out of him. She came after cautiously, hanging on to the twigs and grasses. So they descended, stage by stage, to the river's brink. There, to his disgust, the flood had eaten away the path, and the red decline ran straight into the water. He dug in his heels and brought himself up violently. The string of the parcel broke with a snap; the brown parcel bounded down, leaped into the water, and soiled smoothly away. He hung on to his tree.

'Well, I'll be damned!' he cried crossly. Then he laughed. She was coming perilously down.

'Mind!' he warned her. He stood with his back to the tree, waiting. 'Come now,' he called, opening his arms.

She let herself run. He caught her, and together they stood watching the dark water scoop at the raw edge of the bank. The parcel had soiled out of sight.

'It doesn't matter,' she said.

He held her close and kissed her. There was only room for their four feet.

'It's a swindle!' he said. 'But there's a rut where a man has been, so if we go on I guess we shall find the path again.'

The river slid and twined its great volume. On the other bank cattle were feeding on the desolate flats. The cliff rose high above Paul and Clara on their right hand. They stood against the tree in the watery silence.

'Let us try going forward,' he said; and they struggled in the red clay along the groove a man's nailed boots had made. They were hot and flushed. Their barkled shoes hung heavy on their steps. At last they found the broken path. It was littered with rubble from the water, but at any rate it was easier. They cleaned their boots with twigs. His heart was beating thick and fast.

Suddenly, coming on to the lime level, he saw two figures of men standing silent at the water's edge. His heart leaped. They were fishing.

He turned and put his hand up warningly to Clara. She hesitated, buttoned her coat. The two went on together.

The fishermen turned curiously to watch the two intruders on their privacy and solitude. They had had a fire, but it was nearly out. All kept perfectly still. The men turned again to their fishing, stood over the grey glinting river like statues. Clara went with bowed head, flushing; he was laughing to himself. Directly they passed out of sight behind the willows.

'Now they ought to be drowned,' said Paul softly.

Clara did not answer. They toiled forward along a tiny path on the river's lip. Suddenly it vanished. The bank was sheer red solid clay in front of them, sloping straight into the river. He stood and cursed beneath his breath, setting his teeth.

'It is impossible!' said Clara.

He stood erect, looking round. Just ahead were two islets in the stream, covered with osiers. But they were unattainable. The cliff came down like a sloping wall from far above their heads. Behind, not far back, were the fishermen. Across the river the distant cattle fed silently in the desolate afternoon. He cursed again deeply under his breath. He gazed up the great steep bank. Was there no hope but to scale back to the public path?

'Stop a minute,' he said, and, digging his heels sideways into the steep bank of red clay, he began nimbly to mount. He looked across at every tree foot. At last he found what he wanted. Two beech-trees side by side on the hill held a little level on the upper face between their roots. It was littered with damp leaves, but it would do. The fishermen were perhaps sufficiently out of sight. He threw down his rainproof and waved to her to come.

She toiled to his side. Arriving there, she looked at him heavily, dumbly, and laid her head on his shoulder. He held her fast as he looked round. They were safe enough from all but the small, lonely cows over the river. He sunk his mouth on her throat, where he felt her heavy pulse beat under his lips. Everything was perfectly still. There was nothing in the afternoon but themselves.

When she arose, he, looking on the ground all the time, saw suddenly sprinkled on the black wet beech-roots many scarlet carnation petals, like splashed drops of blood; and red, small splashes fell from her bosom, streaming down her dress to her feet.

'Your flowers are smashed,' he said.

She looked at him heavily as she put back her hair. Suddenly he put his finger-tips on her cheek.

'Why dost look so heavy?' he reproached her.

She smiled sadly, as if she felt alone in herself. He caressed her cheek with his fingers, and kissed her.

'Nay!' he said. 'Never thee bother!'

She gripped his fingers tight, and laughed shakily. Then she dropped her hand. He put the hair back from her brows, stroking her temples, kissing them lightly.

'But tha shouldna worrit!' he said softly, pleading.

'No, I don't worry!' she laughed tenderly and resigned.

'Yea, tha does! Dunna thee worrit,' he implored, caressing.

'No!' she consoled him, kissing him.

They had a stiff climb to get to the top again. It took them a quarter of an hour. When he got on to the level grass, he threw off his cap, wiped the sweat from his forehead, and sighed.

'Now we're back at the ordinary level,' he said.

She sat down, panting, on the tussocky grass. Her cheeks were flushed pink. He kissed her, and she gave way to joy.

'And now I'll clean thy boots and make thee fit for respectable folk,' he said.

He kneeled at her feet, worked away with a stick and tufts of grass. She put her fingers in his hair, drew his head to her, and kissed it.

'What am I supposed to be doing,' he said, looking at her laughing; 'cleaning shoes or dibbling with love? Answer me that!'

Just whichever I please,' she replied.

'I'm your boot-boy for the time being, and nothing else!' But they remained looking into each other's eyes and laughing. Then they kissed with little nibbling kisses.

'T-t-t-t!' he went with his tongue, like his mother. 'I tell you, nothing gets done when there's a woman about.'

And he returned to his boot-cleaning, singing softly. She touched his thick hair, and he kissed her fingers. He worked away at her shoes. At last they were quite presentable.

'There you are, you see!' he said. 'Aren't I a great hand at restoring you to respectability? Stand up! There, you look as irreproachable as Britannia herself!'

He cleaned his own boots a little, washed his hands in a puddle, and sang. They went on into Clifton village. He was madly in love with her every movement she made, every crease in her garments, sent a hot flash rough him and seemed adorable.

The old lady at whose house they had tea was roused into gaiety by them.

'I could wish you'd had something of a better day,' she said, hovering round.

'Nay!' he laughed. 'We've been saying how nice it is.'

The old lady looked at him curiously. There was a peculiar glow and charm about him. His eyes were dark and laughing. He rubbed his moustache with a glad movement.

'Have you been saying *so!*' she exclaimed, a light rousing in her old eyes.

'Truly!' he laughed.

'Then I'm sure the day's good enough,' said the old lady.

She fussed about, and did not want to leave them.

'I don't know whether you'd like some radishes as well,' she said to Clara; 'but I've got some in the garden and a cucumber.'

Clara flushed. She looked very handsome.

'I should like some radishes,' she answered.

And the old lady pottered off gleefully.

'If she knew!' said Clara quietly to him.

'Well, she doesn't know; and it shows we're nice in ourselves, at any rate. You look quite enough to satisfy on archangel, and I'm sure I feel harmless – so – if it makes you look nice, and makes folk happy when they have us, and makes us happy – why, we're not cheating them out of much!'

They went on with the meal. When they were going away, the old lady came timidly with three tiny dahlias in full blow, neat as bees, and speckled scarlet and white. She stood before Clara, pleased with herself, saying:

'I don't know whether – ' and holding the flowers forward in her old hand.

'Oh, how pretty!' cried Clara, accepting the flowers.

'Shall she have them am' asked Paul reproachfully of the old woman.

'Yes, she shall have them all,' she replied, beaming with joy. 'You have got enough for your share.'

'Ah, but I shall ask her to give me one!' he teased.

'Then she does as she pleases,' said the old lady, smiling. And she bobbed a little curtsey of delight.

Clara was rather quiet and uncomfortable. As they walked along, he said:

'You don't feel criminal, do you?'

She looked at him with startled grey eyes.

'Criminal!' she said. 'No.'

'But you seem to feel you have done a wrong?'

'No,' she said. 'I only think, "If they knew!"'

'If they knew, they'd cease to understand. As it is, they do understand, and they like it. What do they matter? Here, with only the trees and me, you don't feel not the least bit wrong, do you?'

He took her by the arm, held her facing him, holding her eyes with his. Something fretted him.

'Not sinners, are we?' he said, with an uneasy little frown.

'No' she replied.

He kissed her, laughing.

'You like your little bit of guiltiness, I believe,' he said. 'I believe Eve enjoyed it, when she went cowering out of Paradise.'

But there was a certain glow and quietness about her that made him glad. When he was alone in the railway-carriage, he found himself tumultuously happy, and the people exceedingly nice, and the night lovely, and everything good.

Mrs Morel was sitting reading when he got home. Her health was not good now, and there had come that ivory pallor into her face which he never noticed, and which afterwards he never forgot. She did not mention her own ill-health to him. After all, she thought, it was not much.

'You are late!' she said, looking at him.

His eyes were shining; his face seemed to glow. He smiled to her.

'Yes; I've been down Clifton Grove with Clara.'

His mother looked at him again.

'But won't people talk?' she said.

'Why? They know she's a suffragette, and so on. And what if they do talk!'

'Of course, there may be nothing wrong in it,' said his mother. 'But you know what folk are, and if once she gets talked about – '

Well, I can't help it. Their jaw isn't so almighty important, after all.'

'I think you ought to consider *her.*'

'So I *do!* What can people say? – that we take a walk together. I believe you're jealous.'

'You know I should be *glad* if she weren't a married woman.'

'Well, my dear, she lives separate from her husband, and talks on platforms; so she's already singled out from the sheep, and, as far as I can see, hasn't much to lose. No; her life's nothing to her, so what's the worth of nothing? She goes with me – it becomes something. Then she must pay – we both must pay! Folk are so frightened of paying; they'd rather starve and die.'

'Very well, my son. We'll see how it will end.'

'Very well my mother. I'll abide by the end.'

'We'll see!'

And she's – she's *awfully* nice, mother; she is really! You don't know!'

'That's not the same as marrying her.'

'It's perhaps better.'

There was silence for a while. He wanted to ask his mother something, but was afraid.

'Should you like to know her?' he hesitated.

'Yes,' said Mrs Morel coolly. 'I should like to know what she's like.'

'But she's nice, mother, she is! And not a bit common!'

'I never suggested she was.'

'But you seem to think she's – not as good as – She's better than ninety-nine folk out of a hundred, I tell you! She's *better,* she is! She's fair, she's honest, she's straight! There isn't anything underhand or superior about her. Don't be mean about her!'

Mrs Morel flushed.

'I am sure I am not mean about her. She may be quite as you say, but – '

'You don't approve,' he finished.

'And do you expect me to?' she answered coldly.

'Yes! – yes! – if you'd anything about you, you'd be glad! Do you *want* to see her?'

'I said I did.'

Then I'll bring her – shall I bring her here?'

'You please yourself.'

'Then I *will* bring her here – one Sunday – to tea. If you think a horrid thing about her, I shan't forgive you.'

His mother laughed.

'As if it would make any difference!' she said. He knew he had won.

'Oh, but it feels so fine, mother, when she's there! She's such a queen in her way.'

Occasionally he still walked a little way from chapel with Miriam and Edgar. He did not go up to the farm. She, however, was very much the same with him, and he did not feel embarrassed in her presence. One evening she was alone when he accompanied her. They began by talking books: it was their unfailing topic. Mrs Morel had said that his and Miriam's affair was like a fire fed on books – if there were no more volumes it would die out. Miriam, for her part, boasted that she could read him like a book, could place her finger any minute on the chapter and the line. He, easily taken in, believed that Miriam knew more about him than anyone else. So it pleased him to talk to her about himself, like the simplest egoist. Very soon the conversation drifted to his own doings. It flattered him immensely that he was of such supreme interest.

'And what have you been doing lately?'

'I – oh, not much! I made a sketch of Bestwood from the garden, that is nearly right at last. It's the hundredth try.'

So they went on. Then she said:

'You've not been out, then, lately?'

'Yes I went up Clifton Grove on Monday afternoon with Clara.'

'It was not very nice weather,' said Miriam, 'was it?'

'But I wanted to go out, and it was all right. The Trent is full.'

'And did you go to Barton?' she asked.

'No; we had tea in Clifton.'

'*Did* you! That would be nice.'

'It was! The jolliest old woman! She gave us several pom-pom dahlias, as pretty as you like.'

Miriam bowed her head and brooded. He was quite unconscious of concealing anything from her.

'What made her give them you?' she asked.

He laughed.

'Because she liked us – because we were jolly, I should think.' Miriam put her finger in her mouth.

'Were you late home?' she asked.

At last he resented her tone.

'I caught the seven-thirty.'

'Ha!'

They walked on in silence, and he was angry.

'And how *is* Clara?' asked Miriam.

'Quite all right, I think.'

'That's good!' she said, with a tinge of irony. 'By the way, what of her husband? One never hears anything of him.'

'He's got some other woman, 'and is also quite all right,' he replied. 'At least, so I think.'

'I see – you don't know for certain. Don't you think a position like that is hard on a woman?'

'Rottenly hard!'

'It's so unjust!' said Miriam. 'The man does as he likes – '

'Then let the woman also,' he said.

'How can she? And if she does, look at her position!'

'What of it?'

'Why, it's impossible! You don't understand what a woman forfeits – '

'No, I don't. But if a woman's got nothing but her fair fame to feed on, why, it's thin tack, and a donkey would die of it!'

So she understood his moral attitude, at least, and she knew he would act accordingly.

She never asked him anything direct, but she got to know enough.

Another day, when he saw Miriam, the conversation turned to marriage, then to Clara's marriage with Dawes.

'You see,' he said; 'she never knew the fearful importance of marriage. She thought it was all in the day's march – it would have to come – and Dawes – well, a good many women would have given their souls to get him; so why not him? Then she developed into the *femme incomprise,* and treated him badly I'll bet my boots.'

'And she left him because he didn't understand her?'

'I suppose so. I suppose she had to. It isn't altogether a question of understanding; it's a question of living. With him, she was only half alive; the rest was dormant, deadened. And the dormant woman was the *femme incomprise* and she *had* to be awakened.'

'And what about him?'

'I don't know. I rather think he loves her as much as he can, but he's a fool.'

'It was something like your mother and father,' said Miriam.

'Yes; but my mother, I believe, got *real* joy and satisfaction out of my father at first. I believe she had a passion for him; that's why she stayed with him. After all, they were bound to each other.'

'Yes,' said Miriam.

'That's what one I must *have,* I think,' he continued – 'the real, real flame of feeling through another person – once, only once, if it only lasts three months. See, my mother looks as if she'd *had* everything that was necessary for her living and developing. There's not a tiny bit of a feeling of sterility about her.'

'No,' said Miriam.

'And with my father, at first, I'm sure she had the real thing. She knows; she has been there. You can feel it about her, and about him, and about hundreds of people you meet every day; and, once it has happened to you, you can go on with anything and ripen.'

What has happened, exactly?' asked Miriam.

'It's so hard to say, but the samething big and intense that changes you when you really come together with somebody else. It almost seems to fertilise your soul and make it that you can go on and mature.'

'And you think your mother had it with your father?'

'Yes; and at the bottom she feels grateful to him for giving it her, even now, though they are miles apart.'

'And you think Clara never had it?'

'I'm sure.'

Miriam pondered this. She saw what he was seeking – a sort of baptism of fire in passion, it seemed to her. She realised that he would never be satisfied till he had it. Perhaps it was essential to him, as to same men, tosaw wild oats; and afterwards, when he was satisfied, he would not rage with restlessness any more, but could settle down and give her his life into her hands. Well, then, if he must go, let him go and have his fill – something big and intense, he called it. At any rate, when he had got it, he would not want it – that he said himself he would want the other thing that she could give him. He would want to be owned, so that he could work. It seemed to her a bitter thing that he must go, but she could let him go into an inn for a glass of whisky, so she could let him go to Clara, so long as it was something that would satisfy a need in him and leave him free for herself to possess.

'Have you told your mother about Clara?' she asked.

She knew this would be a test of the seriousness of his feeling for the other woman; she knew he was going to Clara for something vital, not as man goes for pleasure to a prostitute, if he told his mother.

'Yes,' he said, 'and she is coming to tea on Sunday.

'To your house?'

'Yes; I want mater to see her.'

'Ah!'

There was a silence. Things had gone quicker than she thought. She felt a sudden bitterness that he could leave her so soon and so entirely. And was Clara to be accepted by his people, who had been so hostile to herself?

'I may call in as I go to chapel,' she said. 'It is a long time since I saw Clara.'

'Very well,' he said, astonished, and unconsciously angry.

On the Sunday afternoon he went to Keston to meet Clara at the station. As he stood on the platform he was trying to examine in himself if he had a premonition.

'Do I *feel* as if she'd come?' he said to himself, and he tried to find out. His heart felt queer and contracted. That seemed like foreboding. Then he had a foreboding she would not come! Then she would not come, and instead of taking her over the fields home, as he had imagined, he would have to go alone. The train was late; the afternoon would be wasted, and the evening. He hated her for not coming. Why had she promised, then, if she could not keep her promise? Perhaps she had missed her train – he himself was always missing trains, but that was no reason why she should miss this particular one. He was angry with her; he was furious.

Suddenly he saw the train crawling, sneaking round the corner. Here, then, was the train, but of course she had not come. The green engine hissed along the platform, the row of brown carriages drew up, several doors opened. No; she had not come! No! Yes; ah, there she was! She had a big black hat on! He was at her side in a moment.

'I thought you weren't coming,' he said.

She was laughing rather breathlessly as she put out her hand to him; their eyes met. He took her quickly along the platform, talking at a great rate to hide his feeling. She looked beautiful. In her hat were large silk roses, coloured like tarnished gold. Her costume of dark cloth fitted so beautifully over her breast and shoulders. His pride went up as he walked with her. He felt the station people, who knew him, eyed her with awe and admiration.

'I was sure you weren't coming,' he laughed shakily.

She laughed in answer, almost with a little cry.

'And I wondered, when I was in the train, whatever I should do if you weren't there!' she said.

He caught her hand impulsively, and they went along the narrow twitchel.* They took the road into Nuttall and over the Reckoning House Farm. It was a blue, mild day. Everywhere the brown leaves lay scattered; many scarlet hips stood upon the hedge beside the wood. He gathered a few for her to wear.

'Though, really,' he said, as he fitted them into the breast of her coat, 'you ought to object to my getting them, because of the birds. But they don't care much for rose-hips in this part, where they can get plenty of stuff. You often find the berries going rotten in the springtime.'

So he chattered, scarcely aware of what he said, only knowing he was putting berries in the bosom of her coat, while she stood patiently for him. And she watched his quick hands, so full of life, and it seemed to her she had never *seen* anything before. Till now, everything had been indistinct.'

They came near to the colliery. It stood quite still and black among the corn-fields, its immense heap of slag seen rising almost from the oats.

'What a pity there is a coal-pit here where it is so pretty!' said Clara.

'Do you think so?' he answered. 'You see, I am so used to it I should miss it. No; and I like the pits here and there. I like the rows of trucks and the headstocks, and the steam in the daytime,

* alley.

and the lights at night When I was a boy, I always thought a pillar
of cloud by day and a pillar of fire by night was a pit, with its
steam, and its lights, and the burning bank, – and I thought the
Lord was always at the pit-top.'

As they drew near home she walked in silence, and seemed
to hang back. He pressed her fingers in his own. She flushed, but
gave no response.

'Don't you want to come home?' he asked.

'Yes, I want to come,' she replied.

It did not occur to him that her position in his home would be
rather a peculiar and difficult one. To him it seemed just as if one
of his men friends were going to be introduced to his mother,
only nicer.

The Morels lived in a house in an ugly street that ran down a
steep hill. The street itself was hideous. The house was rather
superior to most. It was old, grimy, with a big bay window, and it
was semi-detached; but it looked gloomy. Then Paul opened the
door to the garden, and all was different. The sunny afternoon was
there, like another land. By the path grew tansy and little trees. In
front of the window was a plot of sunny grass, with old lilacs
round it. And away went the garden, with heaps of dishevelled
chrysanthemums in the sunshine, down to the sycamore-tree, and
the field, and beyond one looked over a few red-roofed cottages
to the hills with all the glow of the autumn afternoon.

Mrs Morel sat in her rocking-chair, wearing her black silk
blouse. Her grey-brown hair was taken smooth back from her
brow and her high temples; her face was rather pale. Clara,
suffering, followed Paul into the kitchen. Mrs Morel rose. Clara
thought her a lady, even rather stiff. The young woman was very
nervous. She had almost a wistful look, almost resigned.

'Mother – Clara,' said Paul.

Mrs Morel held out her hand and smiled.

'He has told me a good deal about you,' she said.

The blood flamed in Clara's cheek.

'I hope you don't mind my coming,' she faltered.

'I was pleased when he said he would bring you,' replied Mrs Morel.

Paul, watching, felt his heart contract with pain. His mother looked so small, and sallow, and done-for beside the luxuriant Clara.

'It's such a pretty day, mother!' he said. 'And we saw a jay.'

His mother looked at him; he had turned to her. She thought what a man he seemed, in his dark, well-made clothes. He was pale and detached-looking; it would be hard for any woman to keep him. Her heart glowed; then she was sorry for Clara.

'Perhaps you'll leave your things in the parlour,' said Mrs Morel nicely to the young woman.

'Oh, thank you,' she replied.

'Come on,' said Paul, and he led the way into the little front-room, with its old piano, its mahogany furniture, its yellowing marble mantelpiece. A fire was burning; the place was littered with books and drawing boards. 'I leave my things lying about,' he said. 'It's so much easier.'

She loved his artist's paraphernalia, and the books, and the photos of people. Soon he was telling her: this was William, this was William's young lady in the evening dress, this was Annie and her husband, this was Arthur and his wife and the baby. She felt as if she were being taken in into the family. He showed her photos, books, sketches, and they talked a little while. Then they returned to the kitchen. Mrs Morel put aside her book. Clara wore a blouse of fine silk chiffon, with narrow black-and-white stripes; her hair was done simply, coiled on top of her head. She looked rather stately and reserved.

'You have gone to live down Sneinton Boulevard?' said Mrs Morel. 'When I was a girl – girl, I say! – when I was a young woman *we* lived in Minerva Terrace.'

'Oh, did you!' said Clara. 'I have a friend in Number 6.'

And the conversation had started. They talked Nottingham and Nottingham people; it interested them both. Clara was still rather nervous; Mrs Morel was still somewhat on her dignity. She clipped her language very clear and precise. But they were going to get on well together, Paul saw.

Mrs Morel measured herself against the younger woman, and found herself easily stronger. Clara was deferential. She knew Paul's surprising regard for his mother, and she had dreaded the meeting, expecting someone rather hard and cold. She was surprised to find this little interested woman chatting with such readiness; and then she felt, as she felt with Paul, that she would not care to stand in Mrs Morel's way. There was something so hard and certain in his mother, as if she never had a misgiving in her life.

Presently Morel came down, ruffled and yawning, from his afternoon sleep. He scratched his grizzled head, he podded in his stocking feet, his waistcoat hung open over his shirt. He seemed incongruous.

'This is Mrs Dawes, father,' said Paul.

Then Morel pulled himself together. Clara saw Paul's manner of bowing and shaking hands.

'Oh, indeed!' exclaimed Morel. 'I am very glad to see you – I am, I assure you. But don't disturb yourself. No, no; make yourself quite comfortable, and be very welcome.'

Clara was astonished at this flood of hospitality from the old collier. He was so courteous, so gallant! She thought him most delightful. 'And may you have come far?' he asked.

'Only from Nottingham,' she said.

'From Nottingham! Then you have had a beautiful day for your journey.'

Then he strayed into the scullery to wash his hands and face, and from force of habit came on to the hearth with the towel to dry himself.

At tea Clara felt the refinement and sang-froid of the household. Mrs Morel was perfectly at her ease. The pouring out the tea and attending to the people went on unconsciously, without interrupting her in her talk. There was a lot of room at the oval table; the china of dark blue willow pattern looked pretty on the glossy cloth. There was a little bowl of small, yellow chrysanthemums. Clara felt she completed the circle, and it was a pleasure to her. But she was rather afraid of the self-possession of the Morels, father and all. She took their tone; there was a feeling of balance. It was a cool, clear atmosphere, where everyone was himself, and in harmony. Clara enjoyed it, but there was a fear deep at the bottom of her.

Paul cleared the table whilst his mother and Clara talked. Clara was conscious of his quick, vigorous body as it came and went, seeming blown quickly by a wind at its work. It was almost like the hither and thither of a leaf that comes unexpected. Most of herself went with him. By the way she leaned forward, as if listening, Mrs Morel could see she was possessed elsewhere as she talked, and again the elder woman was sorry for her.

Having finished, he strolled down the garden, leaving the two women talk. It was a hazy, sunny afternoon, mild and soft. Clara glanced through the window after him as he loitered among the chrysanthemums. She felt as if something almost tangible fastened her to him; yet he seemed so easy in his graceful, indolent movement, so detached as he tied up the too-heavy flower-branches to their stokes, that she wanted to shriek in her helplessness.

Mrs Morel rose.

'You will let me help you wash up,' said Clara.

'Eh, there are so few, it will only take me a minute,' said the other.

Clara, however, dried the tea-things, and was glad to be on such good terms with his mother, but it was torture not to be able to follow him down the garden. At last she allowed herself to go; she felt as if a rope were taken off her ankle.

The afternoon was golden over the hills of Derbyshire. He stood across in the other garden, beside a bush of pale Michaelmas daisies, watching the last bees crawl into the hive. Hearing her coming, he turned to her with an easy motion, saying:

'It's the end of the run with these chaps.'

Clara stood near him. Over the low red wall in front was the country and the far-off hills, all golden dim.

At that moment Miriam was entering through the garden door. She saw Clara go up to him, saw him turn, and saw them come to rest together. Something in their perfect isolation together made her know that it was accomplished between them, that they were, as she put it, married. She walked very slowly down the cinder-track of the long garden.

Clara had pulled a button from a hollyhock spire, and was breaking it to get seeds. Above her bowed head the pink flowers stored, as if defending her. The last bees were falling down to the hive.

'Count your money,' laughed Paul, as she broke the flat seeds one by one, from the roll of coin. She looked at him.

'I'm well off,' she said, smiling.

'How much? Pf!' he snapped his fingers. 'Can I turn them into gold?'

'I'm afraid not,' she laughed.

They looked into each other's eyes, laughing. At that moment they became aware of Miriam. There was a click, and everything had altered.

'Hello, Miriam!' he exclaimed. 'You said you'd come!'

'Yes. Had you forgotten?'

She shook hands with Clara, saying:

'It seems strange to see you here.'

'Yes,' replied the other; 'it seems strange to be here.'

There was a hesitation.

'It is pretty, isn't it?' said Miriam.

'I like it very much,' replied Clara.

Then Miriam realised that Clara was accepted as she had never been.

'Have you come down alone?' asked Paul.

'Yes; I went to Agatha's to tea. We are going to chapel. I only called in for a moment to see Clara.'

'You should have come in here to tea,' he said.

Miriam laughed shortly, and Clara turned impatiently aside.

'Do you like the chrysanthemums?' he asked.

'Yes; they are very fine,' replied Miriam.

'Which sort do you like best?' he asked

'I don't know. The bronze, I think.'

'I don't think you've seen all the sorts. Come and look. Come and see which are your favourites, Clara.'

He led the two women back to his own garden, where the towzled bushes of flowers of all colours stood raggedly along the path down to the field. The situation did not embarrass him, to his knowledge.

'Look, Miriam; these are the white ones that came from your garden. They aren't so fine here, are they?'

No,' said Miriam.

'But they're hardier. You're so sheltered; things grow big and tender, and then die. These little yellow ones I like. Will you have some?'

While they were out there the bells began to ring in the church, sounding loud across the town and the field. Miriam looked at the tower, proud among the clustering roofs, and remembered the sketches he had brought her. It had been different then, but he had not left her even yet. She asked him for a book to read. He ran indoors.

'What! is that Miriam?' asked his mother coldly.

'Yes; she said she'd call and see Clara.'

'You told her, then?' came the sarcastic answer.

'Yes; why shouldn't I?'

There's certainly no reason why you shouldn't,' said Mrs Morel, and she returned to her book. He winced from his mother's irony, frowned irritably, thinking: 'Why can't I do as I like?'

'You've not seen Mrs Morel before?' Miriam was saying to Clara.

'No; but she's *so* nice!'

'Yes,' said Miriam, dropping her head; 'in some ways she's very fine.

'I should think so.'

'Had Paul told you much about her?'

'He had talked a good deal'

'Ha!'

There was silence until he returned with the book.

'When will you want it back?' Miriam asked.

'When you like,' he answered.

Clara turned to go indoors, whilst he accompanied Miriam to the gate.

'When will you come up to Willey Farm?' the latter asked.

'I couldn't say,' replied Clara.

'Mother asked me to say she'd be pleased to see you any time, if you cared to come.'

'Thank you; I should like to, but I can't say when.'

'Oh, very well!' exclaimed Miriam rather bitterly, turning away. She went down the path with her mouth to the flowers he had given her.

'You're sure you won't come in?' he said.

'No, thanks.'

'We are going to chapel.'

'Ha, I shall see you, then!' Miriam was very bitter.

'Yes.'

They parted. He felt guiltily towards her. She was bitter, and she scorned him. He still belonged to herself, she believed; yet he could have Clara, take her home, sit with her next his mother in chapel, give her the same hymn-book he had given herself years before. She heard him running quickly indoors.

But he did not go straight in. Halting on the plot of grass, he heard his mother's voice, then Clara's answer:

'What I hate is the bloodhound quality in Miriam.'

'Yes,' said his mother quickly, 'yes; *doesn't* it make you hate her, now?'

His heart went hot, and he was angry with them for talking about the girl. What right had they to say that? Something in the speech itself stung him into a flame of hate against Miriam. Then his own heart rebelled furiously at Clara's taking the liberty of speaking so about Miriam. After all, the girl was the better woman of the two, he thought, if it came to goodness. He went indoors. His mother looked excited. She was beating with her hand rhythmically on the sofa-arm, as women do who are wearing out. He could never bear to see the movement. There was silence; then he began to talk.

In chapel Miriam saw him find the place in the hymn-book for Clara, in exactly the same way as he used for herself. And during the sermon he could see the girl across the chapel, her hat throwing a dark shadow over her face. What did she think, seeing Clara with him? He did not stop to consider. He felt himself cruel towards Miriam.

After chapel he went over Pentrich with Clara. It was a dark autumn night. They had said goodbye to Miriam, and his heart had smitten him as he left the girl alone. 'But it serves her right,' he said inside himself, and it almost gave him pleasure to go off under her eyes with this other handsome woman.

There was a scent of damp leaves in the darkness. Clara's hand lay warm and inert in his own as they walked. He was full of conflict. The battle that raged inside him made him feel desperate.

Up Pentrich Hill Clara leaned against him as he went. He slid his arm round her waist. Feeling the strong motion of her body under his arm as she walked, the tightness in his chest because of Miriam relaxed, and the hot blood bathed him. He held her closer and closer.

Then: 'You still keep on with Miriam,' she said quietly.

'Only talk. There never *was* a great deal more than talk between us,' he said bitterly.

'Your mother doesn't care for her,' said Clara.

'No, or I might have married her. But it's all up, really!'

Suddenly his voice went passionate with hate.

'If I was with her now, we should be jawing about the "Christian Mystery," or some such tack Thank God, I'm not!'

They walked on in silence for some time.

'But you can't really give her up,' said Clara.

'I don't give her up, because there's nothing to give,' he said.

'There is for her.'

'I don't know why she and I shouldn't be friends as long as we live,' he said. 'But it'll only be friends.'

Clara drew away from him, leaning away from contact with him.

'What are you drawing away for?' he asked.

She did not answer, but drew farther from him.

Why do you want to walk alone?' he asked.

Still there was no answer. She walked resentfully, hanging her head.

'Because I said I would be friends with Miriam!' he exclaimed.

She would not answer him anything.

'I tell you it's only words that go between us,' he persisted, trying to take her again.

She resisted. Suddenly he strode across in front of her, barring her way.

'Damn it!' he said. 'What do you want now?'

'You'd better run after Miriam,' mocked Clara.

The blood flamed up in him. He stood showing his teeth. She drooped sulkily. The lane was dark, quite lonely. He suddenly caught her in his arms, stretched forward, and put his mouth on her face in a kiss of rage. She turned frantically to avoid him. He held her fast. Hard and relentless his mouth came for her. Her breasts hurt against the wall of his chest. Helpless, she went loose in his arms, and he kissed her, and kissed her.

He heard people coming down the hill.

'Stand up! stand up!' he said thickly, gripping her arm till it hurt. If he had let go, she would have sunk to the ground.

She sighed and walked dizzily beside him. They went on in silence.

'We will go over the fields,' he said; and then she woke up.

But she let herself be helped over the stile, and she walked in silence with him over the first dark field. It was the way to Nottingham and to the station, she knew. He seemed to be looking about. They came out on a bare hilltop where stood the dark figure of the ruined windmill. There he halted. They stood together high up in the darkness, looking at the lights scattered on the night before them, handfuls of glittering points, villages lying high and low on the dark, here and there.

'Like treading among the stars,' he said, with a quaky laugh.

Then he took her in his arms, and held her fast. She moved aside her mouth to ask, dogged and low:

What time is it?'

'It doesn't matter,' he pleaded thickly.

'Yes it does – yes! I must go!'

'It's early yet,' he said.

What time is it?' she insisted.

All round lay the black night, speckled and spangled with lights.

'I don't know.'

She put her hand on his chest, feeling for his watch. He felt the joints fuse into fire. She groped in his waistcoat pocket, while he stood panting. In the darkness she could see the round, pale face of the watch, but not the figures. She stooped over it. He was panting till he could take her in his arms again.

'I can't see,' she said.

'Then don't bother.'

'Yes; I'm going!' she said, turning away.

'Wait! I'll look!' But he could not see. 'I'll strike a match.'

He secretly hoped it was too late to catch the train. She saw the glowing lantern of his hands as he cradled the light; then his face lit up, his eyes fixed on the watch. Instantly all was dark again. All was black before her eyes; only a glowing match was red near her feet. Where was he?

'What is it?' she asked, afraid.

'You can't do it,' his voice answered out of the darkness.

There was a pause. She felt in his power. She had heard the ring in his voice. It frightened her.

'What time is it?' she asked, quiet, definite, hopeless.

'Two minutes to nine,' he replied, telling the truth with a struggle.

'And can I get from here to the station in fourteen minutes?'

'No. At any rate – '

She could distinguish his dark form again a yard or so away. She wanted to escape.

'But can't I do it?' she pleaded.

'If you hurry,' he said brusquely. 'But you could easily walk it, Clara; it's only seven miles to the tram. I'll come with you.'

'No; I want to catch the train.'

'But why?'

'I do – I want to catch the train.'

Suddenly his voice altered.

'Very well,' he said, dry and hard. 'Come along, then.'

And he plunged ahead into the darkness. She ran after him, wanting to cry. Now he was hard and cruel to her. She ran over the rough, dark fields behind him, out of breath, ready to drop. But the double row of lights at the station drew nearer. Suddenly:

'There she is!' he cried, breaking into a run.

There was a faint rattling noise. Away to the right the train, like a luminous caterpillar, was threading across the night. The rattling ceased.

'She's over the viaduct. You'll just do it.'

Clara ran, quite out of breath, and fell at last into the train. The whistle blew. He was gone. Gone! – and she was in a carriage full of people. She felt the cruelty of it.

He turned round and plunged home. Before he knew where he was he was in the kitchen at home. He was very pale. His eyes were dark and dangerous-looking, as if he were drunk. His mother looked at him.

Well, I must say your boots are in a nice state!' she said.

He looked at his feet. Then he took off his overcoat. His mother wondered if he were drunk.

'She caught the train, then?' she said.

'Yes.'

'I hope *her* feet weren't so filthy. Where on earth you dragged her I don't know!'

He was silent and motionless for some time.

'Did you like her?' he asked grudgingly at last.

'Yes, I liked her. But you'll tire of her, my son; you know you will.'

He did not answer. She noticed how he laboured in his breathing.

'Have you been running?' she asked.

'We had to run for the train.'

'You'll go and knock yourself up. You'd better drink hot milk.'

It was as good a stimulant as he could have, but he refused and went to bed. There he lay face down on the counterpane, and shed tears of rage pain. There was a physical pain that made him bite his lips till they bled and the chaos inside him left him unable to think, almost to feel.

'This is how she serves me, is it?' he said in his heart over and over, pressing his face in the quilt. And he hated her. Again he went over the scene, and again he hated her.

The next day there was a new aloofness about him. Clara was very gentle, almost loving. But he treated her distantly, with a touch of contempt. She sighed, continuing to be gentle. He came round.

One evening of that week Sarah Bernhardt was at the Theatre Royal in Nottingham, giving 'La Dome aux Camélias.' Paul wanted to see this old and famous actress, and he asked Clara to accompany him. He told his mother to leave the key in the window for him.

'Shall I book seats?' he asked of Clara.

'Yes. And put on an evening suit, will you? I've never seen you in it.'

'But, good Lord, Clara! Think of me in evening suit at the theatre!' he remonstrated.

Would you rather not?' she asked.

'I will if you *want* me to; but I s'll feel a fool.'

She laughed at him.

'Then feel a fool for my sake, once, won't you?'

The request made his blood flush up.

'I suppose I s'll have to.'

What are you taking a suit-case for?' his mother asked.

He blushed furiously.

'Clara asked me,' he said.

'And what seats are you going in?'

'Circle – three-and-six each!'

Well, I'm sure!' exclaimed his mother sarcastically.

'It's only once in the bluest of blue moons,' he said.

He dressed at Jordan's, put on an overcoat and a cap, and met Clara in a cafe. She was with one of her suffragette friends. She wore an old long coat, which did not suit her, and had a little wrap over her head, which he hated. The three went to the theatre together.

Clara took off her coat on the stairs, and he discovered she was in a sort of semi-evening dress, that left her arms and neck and part of her breast bare. Her hair was done fashionably. The dress, a simple thing of green crape, suited her.

She looked quite grand, he thought. He could see her figure inside the frock, as if that were wrapped closely round her. The firmness and the softness of her upright body could almost be felt as he looked at her. He clenched his fists.

And he was to sit all the evening beside her beautiful naked arm, watching the strong throat rise from the strong chest, watching the breasts under the green stuff, the curve of her limbs in the tight dress. Something in him hated her again for submitting him to this torture of nearness. And he loved her as she balanced her head and stared straight in front of her, pouting, wistful, immobile, as if she yielded herself to her fate because it was too strong for her. She could not help herself; she was in the grip of something bigger than herself. A kind of eternal look about her, as if she were a wistful sphinx, made it necessary for him to kiss her. He dropped his programme, and crouched down on the floor to get it, so that he could kiss her hand and wrist. Her beauty was a torture to him. She sat immobile. Only, when the lights went down, she sank a little against him, and he caressed her hand and arm with his fingers. He could smell her faint perfume. All the time his blood kept sweeping up in great white-hot waves that killed his consciousness momentarily.

The drama continued. He saw it all in the distance, going on somewhere; he did not know where, but it seemed far away inside him. He was Clara's white heavy arms, her throat, her moving bosom. That seemed to be himself. Then away somewhere the play went on, and he was identified with that also. There was no himself. The grey and black eyes of Clara, her bosom coming down on him, her arm that he held gripped between his hands, were all that existed. Then he felt himself small and helpless, her towering in her force above him.

Only the intervals, when the lights came up, hurt him expressibly. He wanted to run anywhere, so long as it would be dark again. In a maze, he wandered out for a drink. Then the lights were out, and the strange, insane reality of Clara and the drama took hold of him again.

The play went on. But he was obsessed by the desire to kiss the tiny blue vein that nestled in the bend of her arm. He could feel it. His whole life seemed suspended till he had put his lips there. It must be done. And the other people!

At last he bent quickly forward and touched it with his lips. His moustache brushed the sensitive flesh. Clara shivered, drew away her arm.

When all was over, the lights up, the people clapping, he came to himself and looked at his watch. His train was gone.

'I s'll have to walk home!' he said.

Clara looked at him.

'Is it too late?' she asked.

He nodded. Then he helped her on with her coat.

'I love you! You look beautiful in that dress,' he murmured over her shoulder, among the throng of bustling people.

She remained quiet. Together they went out of the theatre. He saw the cabs waiting, the people passing. It seemed he met a pair of brown eyes which hated him. But he did not know. He and Clara turned away, mechanically taking the direction to the station.

The train had gone. He would have to walk the ten miles home.

'It doesn't matter,' he said. 'I shall enjoy it.'

'Won't you,' she said, flushing, 'come home for the night? I can sleep with mother.'

He looked at her. Their eyes met.

'What will your mother say?' he asked.

'She won't mind.'

'You're sure?'

'Quite!'

'*Shall* I come?'

'If you will.'

'Very well.'

And they turned away. At the first stopping-place they took the car. The wind blew fresh in their faces. The town was dark; the tram tipped in its haste. He sat with her hand fast in his.

Will your mother be gone to bed?' he asked.

'She may be. I hope not.'

They hurried along the silent, dark little street, the only people out of doors. Clara quickly entered the house. He hesitated.

'Come in,' she said.

He leaped up the step and was in the room. Her mother appeared in the inner doorway, large and hostile.

'Who have you got there?' she asked.

'It's Mr Morel; he has missed his train. I thought we might put him up for the night, and save him a ten-mile walk.'

'H'm!' exclaimed Mrs Radford. 'That's *your* lookout! If you've invited him, he's very welcome as far as I'm concerned. *You* keep the house!'

'If you don't like me, I'll go away again,' he said.

'Nay, nay, you needn't! Come along in! I dunno what you'll think of the supper I'd got her.'

It was a little dish of chip potatoes and a piece of bacon. The table was roughly laid for one.

'You can have some more bacon,' continued Mrs Radford. 'More chips you can't have.'

'It's a shame to bother you,' he said:

'Oh don't you be apologetic! It doesn't *do* wi' me! You treated her to the theatre, didn't you?' There was a sarcasm in the last question.

'Well?' laughed Paul uncomfortably.

'Well?' and what's an inch of bacon! Take your coat off.'

The big, straight-standing woman was trying to estimate the situation. She moved about the cupboard. Clara took his coat. The room was very warm and cosy in the lamplight.

'My sirs!' exclaimed Mrs Radford; 'but you two's a pair of bright beauties, I must say! What's all that get-up for?'

'I believe we don't know,' he said, feeling a victim.

'There isn't room in *this* house for two such bobby-dazzlers, if you fly your kites *that* high!' she rallied them. It was a nasty thrust.

He in his dinner jacket, and Clara in her green dress and bare arms, were confused. They felt they must shelter each other in that little kitchen.

'And look at *that* blossom!' continued Mrs Radford, pointing to Clara. 'What does she reckon she did it for?'

Paul looked at Clara. She was rosy; her neck was warm with blushes. There was a moment of silence.

'You like to see it, don't you?' he asked.

The mother had them in her power. All the time his heart was beating hard, and he was tight with anxiety. But he would fight her.

'Me like to see it!' exclaimed the old woman. 'What should I like to see her make a fool of herself for?'

'I've seen people look bigger fools,' he said. Clara was under his protection now.

'Oh, ay! and when was that?' came the sarcastic rejoinder.

'When they made frights of themselves,' he answered.

Mrs Radford, large and threatening, stood suspended on the hearthrug, holding her fork.

'They're fools either road,' she answered at length, turning to the Dutch oven.

'No,' he said, fighting stoutly. 'Folk ought to look as well as they can.'

'And do you call *that* looking nice!' cried the mother, pointing a scornful fork at Clara. 'That – that looks as if it wasn't properly dressed!'

'I believe you're jealous that you can't swank as well,' he said laughing.

'Me! I could have worn evening dress with anybody, if I'd wanted to!' came the scornful answer.

'And why didn't you want to?' he asked pertinently. 'Or *did* you wear it?'

There was a long pause. Mrs Radford readjusted the bacon in the Dutch oven. His heart beat fast, for fear he had offended her.

'Me!' she exclaimed at last. 'No, I didn't! And when I was in service, I knew as soon as one of the maids came out in bare shoulders what sort *she* was, going to her sixpenny hop!'

'Were you too good to go to a sixpenny hop?' he said.

Clara sat with bowed head. His eyes were dark and glittering. Radford took the Dutch oven from the fire, and stood near him, putting bits of bacon on his plate.

There's a nice crozzly* bit!' she said.

'Don't give me the best!' he said.

* crispy.

'*She's* got what *she* wants,' was the answer.

There was a sort of scornful forbearance in the woman's tone that made Paul know she was mollified.

'But *do* have some!' he said to Clara.

She looked up at him with her grey eyes, humiliated and lonely.

'No thanks!' she said.

'Why won't you?' he answered caressively,

The blood was beating up like fire in his veins. Mrs Radford sat down again, large and impressive and aloof. He left Clara altogether to attend to the mother.

'They say Sarah Bernhardt's fifty,' he said.

'Fifty! She's turned sixty!' came the scornful answer.

'Well,' he said, 'you'd never think it! She made me want to howl even now.'

'I should like to see myself howling at *that* bad old baggage!' said Mrs Radford. 'It's time she began to think herself a grandmother, not a shrieking catamaran – '

He laughed.

'A catamaran is a boat the Malays use,' he said.

'And it's a word as *I* use,' she retorted.

'My mother does sometimes, and it's no good my telling her,' he said.

'I s'd think she boxes your ears,' said Mrs Radford, good-humouredly.

'She'd like to, and she says she will, so I give her a little stool to stand on.'

'That's the worst of my mother,' said Clara. 'She never wants a stool for anything.'

'But she often can't touch *that* lady with a long prop,' retorted Mrs Radford to Paul.

'I s'd think she doesn't want touching with a prop,' he laughed. '*I* shouldn't.'

'It might do the pair of you good to give you a crack on the head with one,' said the mother, laughing suddenly.

'Why are you so vindictive towards me?' he said. 'I've not stolen anything from you.'

'No; I'll watch that,' laughed the older woman.

Soon supper was finished. Mrs Radford sat guard in her chair. Paul lit a cigarette. Clara went upstairs, returning with a sleeping-suit, which she spread on the fender to air.

Why, I'd forgot all about *them!*' said Mrs Radford. 'Where have they sprung from?'

'Out of my drawer.'

'H'm! You bought 'em for Baxter, an' he wouldn't wear 'em, would he?' – laughing. 'Said he reckoned to do wi'out trousers i' bed.' She turned confidentially to Paul, saying: 'He couldn't *bear* 'em, them pyjama things.'

The young man sat making rings of smoke.

'Well, it's everyone to his taste,' he laughed.

Then followed a little discussion of the merits of pyjamas.

'My mother loves me in them,' he said. 'She says I'm a pierrot.'

'I can imagine they'd suit you,' said Mrs Radford.

After a while he glanced at the little clock that was ticking on the mantelpiece. It was half-past twelve.

'It is funny,' he said, 'but it takes hours to settle down to sleep after the theatre.'

'It's about time you did,' said Mrs Radford, clearing the table.

'Are you tired?' he asked of Clara.

'Not the least bit,' she answered, avoiding his eyes.

'Shall we have a game at cribbage?' he said.

'I've forgotten it.'

'Well, I'll teach you again. May we play crib, Mrs Radford?' he asked.

'You'll please yourselves,' she said; 'but it's pretty late.'

'A game or so will make us sleepy,' he answered.

Clara brought the cards, and sat spinning her wedding-ring whilst he shuffled them. Mrs Radford was washing up in the scullery. As it grew later Paul felt the situation getting more and more tense.

'Fifteen two, fifteen four, fifteen six, and two's eight!'

The clock struck one. Still the game continued. Mrs Radford had done all the little jobs preparatory to going to bed, had locked the door and filled the kettle. Still Paul went on dealing and counting. He was obsessed by Clara's arms and throat. He believed he could see where the division was just beginning for her breasts. He could not leave her. She watched his hands, and felt her joints melt as they moved quickly. She was so near, it was almost as if he touched her, and yet not quite. His mettle was roused. He hated Mrs Radford. She sat on, nearly dropping asleep, but determined and obstinate in her chair. Paul glanced at her, then at Clara. She met his eyes, that were angry, mocking, and hard as steel. Her own answered him in shame. He knew she, at any rate, was of his mind. He played on.

At last Mrs Radford roused herself stiffly, and said:

'Isn't it nigh on time you two was thinking o' bed?'

Paul played on without answering. He hated her sufficiently to murder her.

'Half a minute,' he said.

The elder woman rose and soiled stubbornly into the scullery, returning with his candle, which she put on the mantelpiece. Then she sat down again. The hatred of her went so hot down his veins, he dropped his cards.

'We'll stop, then,' he said, but his voice was still a challenge.

Clara saw his mouth shut hard. Again he glanced at her. It seemed like an agreement. She bent over the cards, coughing, to clear her throat.

'Well, I'm glad you've finished,' said Mrs Radford. 'Here, take your things' – she thrust the warm suit in his hand – 'and this is your candle. Your room's over this; there's only two, so you can't go far wrong. Well, good-night. I hope you'll rest well.'

'I'm sure I shall; I always do,' he said.

'Yes; and so you ought at your age,' she replied.

He bade good-night to Clara, and went. The twisting stairs of white, scrubbed wood creaked and clanged at every step. He went doggedly. The two doors faced each other. He went in his room, pushed the door to, without fastening the latch.

It was a small room with a large bed. Some of Clara's hairpins were on the dressing-table – her hair-brush. Her clothes and some skirts hung under a cloth in a corner. There was actually a pair of stockings over a chair. He explored the room. Two books of his own were there on the shelf. He undressed, folded his suit, and sat on the bed listening. Then he blew out the candle, lay down, and in two minutes was almost asleep. Then click! – he was wide awake and writhing in torment. It was as if, when he had nearly got to sleep, something had bitten him suddenly and sent him mad. He sat up and looked at the room in the darkness, his feet doubled under him, perfectly motionless, listening. He heard a cat somewhere away outside; then the heavy, poised tread of the mother; then Clara's distinct voice:

'Will you unfasten my dress?'

There was silence for some time. At last the mother said:

'Now then! aren't you coming up?'

'No, not yet,' replied the daughter calmly.

'Oh, very well then! If it's not late enough, stop a bit longer. Only you needn't come waking me up when I've got to sleep.'

'I shan't be long,' said Clara.

Immediately afterwards Paul heard the mother slowly mounting the stairs. The candle-light flashed through the cracks in his door. Her dress brushed the door, and his heart jumped. Then it was dark, and he heard the latter of her latch. She was very leisurely indeed in her preparations for sleep. After a long time it was quite still. He sat strung up on the bed, shivering slightly. His door was an inch open. As Clara came upstairs, he would intercept her. He waited. All was dead silence. The clock struck two. Then heard a slight scrape of the fender downstairs. Now he could not help himself. His shivering was uncontrollable. He felt he must go or die.

He stepped off the bed, and stood a moment, shuddering. Then he went straight to the door. He tried to step lightly. The first stair cracked like a shot. He listened. The old woman stirred in her bed. The staircase was dark. There was a slit of light under the stair-foot door, which opened into the kitchen. He stood a moment. Then he went on, mechanically. Every step creaked, and his back was creeping, lest the old woman's door should open behind him up above. He fumbled with the door at the bottom. The latch opened with a loud clack. He went through into the kitchen, and shut the door noisily behind him. The old woman daren't come now.

Then he stood, arrested. Clara was kneeling on a pile of white underclothing on the hearthrug, her back towards him, warming herself. She did not look round, but sat crouching on her heels, and her rounded, beautiful back was towards him, and her face was hidden. She was warming her body at the fire for consolation. The glow was rosy on one side, the shadow was dark and warm on the other. Her arms hung slack.

He shuddered violently, clenching his teeth and fists hard to keep control. Then he went forward to her. He put one hand on her shoulder, the finger of the other hand under her chin to raise her face. A convulsed shiver ran through her, once, twice, at his touch. She kept her head bent.

'Sorry!' he murmured, realizing that his hands were very cold.

Then she looked up at him, frightened, like a thing that is afraid of death.

'My hands are so cold,' he murmured.

'I like it,' she whispered, closing her eyes.

The breath of her words was on his mouth. Her arms clasped his knees. The cord of his sleeping-suit dangled against her and made her shiver. As the warmth went into him, his shuddering became less.

At length, unable to stand so any more, he raised her, and she buried her head on his shoulder. His hand went over slowly with an infinite tenderness of caress. She clung close to him, trying to hide herself against him. He clasped her very fast. Then at last she looked at him, mute, imploring, looking to see if she must be ashamed.

His eyes were dark, very deep, and very quiet. It was as if her beauty and his talking it hurt him, made him sorrowful. He looked at her with a little pain, and was afraid. He was so humble before her. She kissed him fervently on the eyes, first one, then the other, and she folded herself to him. She gave herself. He held her fast. It was a moment intense almost to agony.

She stood letting him adore her and tremble with joy of her. It healed her hurt pride. It healed her; It made her glad. It made her feel erect and proud again. Her pride had been wounded inside her. She had been cheapened. Now she radiated with joy and pride again. It was her restoration and her recognition.

Then he looked at her, his face radiant. They laughed to each other, and he strained her to his chest. The seconds ticked off, the minutes passed; and still the two stood clasped rigid together, mouth to mouth, like a statue in one block.

But again his fingers went seeking over her, restless, wandering, dissatisfied. The hot blood came up wave upon wave. She laid her head on his shoulder.

'Come you to my room,' he murmured.

She looked at him and shook her head, her mouth pouring disconsolately, her eyes heavy with passion. He watched her fixedly.

'Yes!' he said.

Again she shook her head.

'Why not?' he asked.

She looked at him still heavily, sorrowfully, and again she shook her head. His eyes hardened, and he gave way.

When, later on, he was back in bed, he wondered why she had refused to come to him openly, so that her mother would know. At any rate, then things would have been definite. And she could have stayed with him the night, without having to go, as she was, to her mother's bed. It was strange, and he could not understand it. And then almost immediately he fell asleep.

He awoke in the morning with someone speaking to him. Opening his eyes, he saw Mrs Radford, big and stately, looking down on him. She held a cup of tea in her hand.

'Do you think you're going to sleep till Doomsday?' she said.

He laughed at once.

'It ought only to be about five o'clock,' he said.

'Well,' she answered, 'it's half-past seven, whether or not. Here, I've brought you a cup of tea.'

He rubbed his face, pushed the tumbled hair off his forehead, and roused himself

'What's it so' late for!' he grumbled.

He resented being wakened. It amused her. She saw his neck in the flannel sleeping-jacket, as white and round as a girl's. He rubbed his hair crossly.

'It's no good your scratching your head,' she said. 'It won't make it no earlier. Here, an' how long d'you think I'm going to stand waiting wi' this here cup?'

'Oh, dash the cup!' he said.

'You should go to bed earlier,' said the woman.

He looked up at her, laughing with impudence.

'I went to bed before *you* did,' he said.

'Yes, my Guyney,* you did!' she exclaimed.

'Fancy,' he said, stirring his tea, 'having tea brought to bed to me! My mother'll think I'm ruined for life.'

'Don't she never do it?' asked Mrs Radford.

'She'd as leave think of flying.'

'Ah, I always spoilt my lot! That's why they've turned out such bad 'uns,' said the elderly woman.

---

* "my God."

'You'd only Clara,' he said. 'And Mr Radford's in heaven. So I suppose there's only you left to be the bad un.'

'I'm not bad; I'm only soft,' she said, as she went out of the bedroom. 'I'm only a fool, I am!'

Clara was very quiet at breakfast, but she had a sort of air of proprietorship over him that pleased him infinitely. Mrs Radford was evidently fond of him. He began to talk of his painting.

'What's the good,' exclaimed the mother, 'of your whittling and worrying and twistin' and too-in' at that painting of yours? What *good* does it do you, I should like to know? You'd better be enjoyin' yourself.'

'Oh, but,' exclaimed Paul, 'I made over thirty guineas last year.'

'Did you! Well, that's a consideration, but it's nothing to the time you put in.'

'And I've got four pounds owing. A man said he'd give me five pounds if I'd paint him and his missis and the dog and the cottage. And I went and put the fowls in instead of the dog, and he was waxy[*], so I had to knock a quid off. I was sick of it, and I didn't like the dog. I made a picture of it. What shall I do when he pays me the four pounds?'

'Nay! you know your own uses for your money,' said Mrs Radford.

'But I'm going to bust this four pounds. Should we go to the seaside for a day or two?'

'Who?'

'You and Clara and me.'

'What, on your money!' she exclaimed, half wrathful.

'Why not?'

'*You* wouldn't be long in breaking your neck at a hurdle race!' she said.

'So long as I get a good run for my money! Will you?'

'Nay; you may settle that atween you.'

'And you're willing?' he asked, amazed and rejoicing.

'You'll do as you like,' said Mrs Radford, 'whether I'm willing or not.'

---

* irritable.

CHAPTER 13

Baxter Dawes

SOON AFTER Paul had been to the theatre with Clara, he was drinking in the Punch Bowl with some friends of his when Dawes came in. Clara's husband was growing stout; his eyelids were getting slack over his brown eyes; he was losing his healthy firmness of flesh. He was very evidently on the downward track. Having quarrelled with his sister, he had gone into cheap lodgings. His mistress had left him for a man who would marry her. He had been in prison one night for fighting when he was drunk, and there was a shady betting episode in which he was concerned.

Paul and he were confirmed enemies, and yet there was between them that peculiar feeling of intimacy, as if they were secretly near to each other, which sometimes exists between two people, although they never speak to one another. Paul often thought of Baxter Dawes, often wanted to get at him and be friends with him. He knew that Dawes often thought about him, and that the man was drawn to him by some bond or other. And yet the two never looked at each other save in hostility.

Since he was a superior employee at Jordan's, it was the thing for Paul to offer Dawes a drink.

'What'll you have?' he asked of him.

'Nowt wi' a bleeder like you!' replied the man.

Paul turned away with a slight disdainful movement of the shoulders, very irritating.

'The aristocracy,' he continued, 'is really a military institution. Take Germany, now. She's got thousands of aristocrats whose only means of existence is the army. They're deadly poor, and life's deadly slow. So they hope for a war. They look for war as a chance of getting on. Till there's a war they are idle good-for-nothings. When there's a war, they are leaders and commanders. There you are, then – they *want* war!'

He was not a favourite debater in the public-house, being too quick and overbearing. He irritated the older men by his assertive manner, and his cocksureness. They listened in silence, and were not sorry when he finished.

Dawes interrupted the young man's flow of eloquence by asking, in a loud sneer:

'Did you learn all that at th' theatre th' other night?'

Paul looked at him their eyes met. Then he knew Dawes had seen him coming out of the theatre with Clara.

'Why, what about th' theatre?' asked one of Paul's associates, glad to get a dig at the young fellow, and sniffing something tasty.

'Oh, him in a bob-tailed evening suit, on the lardy-da!' sneered Dawes, jerking his head contemptuously at Paul.

'That's comin' it strong,' said the mutual friend. 'Tart an' all?'

'Tart, begod!' said Dawes.

'Go on; let's have it!' cried the mutual friend.

'You've got it,' said Dawes, 'an' I reckon Morelly had it an' all.'

'Well, I'll be jiggered!' said the mutual friend. 'An' was it a proper tart?'

'Tart, God blimey – yes!'

'How do you know?'

'Oh,' said Dawes, 'I reckon he spent th' night – '

There was a good deal of laughter at Paul's expense.

'But who *was* she? D'you know her?' asked the mutual friend.

'I should *shay sho*,' said Dawes.

This brought another burst of laughter.

'Then spit it out,' said the mutual friend.

Dawes shook his head, and took a gulp of beer.

'It's a wonder he hasn't let on himself,' he said. 'He'll be braggin' of it in a bit.'

'Come on, Paul,' said the friend; 'it's no good. You might just as well own up.'

'Own up what? That I happened to take a friend to the theatre?'

'Oh well, if it was all right, tell us who she was, lad,' said the friend.

'She *was* all right,' said Dawes.

Paul was furious. Dawes wiped his golden moustache with his fingers, sneering.

'Strike me –! One o' that sort?' said the mutual friend. 'Paul, boy, I'm surprised at you. And do you know her, Baxter?'

'Just a bit, like!'

He winked at the other men.

'Oh well,' said Paul, 'I'll be going!'

The mutual friend laid a detaining hand on his shoulder.

'Nay,' he said, 'you don't get off as easy as that, my lad. We've got to have a full account of this business.'

'Then get it from Dawes!' he said.

'You shouldn't funk your own deeds, man,' remonstrated the friend.

Then Dawes made a remark which caused Paul to throw half a glass of beer in his face.

'Oh, Mr Morel!' cried the barmaid, and she rang the bell for the 'chucker-out.'

Dawes spat and rushed for the young man. At that minute a brawny fellow with his shirt-sleeves rolled up and his trousers tight over his haunches intervened.

'Now, then!' he said, pushing his chest in front of Dawes.

'Come out!' cried Dawes.

Paul was leaning, white and quivering, against the brass rail of the bar. He hated Dawes, wished something could exterminate him at that minute; and at the same time, seeing the wet hair on the man's forehead, he thought he looked pathetic. He did not move.

'Come out, you,' said Dawes.

'That's enough, Dawes,' cried the barmaid.

'Come on,' said the 'chucker-out,' with kindly insistence, 'you'd better be getting on.'

And, by making Dawes edge away from his own close proximity, he worked him to the door.

'*That's* the little sod as started it!' cried Dawes, half cowed, pointing to Paul Morel.

'Why, what a story, Mr Dawes!' said the barmaid 'You know it was you all the time.'

Still the 'chucker-out' kept thrusting his chest forward at him, still he kept edging back, until he was in the doorway and on the steps outside; then he turned round.

'All right,' he said, nodding straight at his rival.

Paul had a curious sensation of pity, almost of affection mingled with violent hate, for the man. The coloured door swung to; there was silence in the bar.

'Serve him jolly well right!' said the barmaid.

'But it's a nasty thing to get a glass of beer in your eyes,' said the mutual friend.

'I tell you *I* was glad he did,' said the barmaid. 'Will you have another, Mr Morel?'

She held up Paul's glass questioningly. He nodded.

'He's a man as doesn't care for anything, is Baxter Dawes,' said one.

'Pooh! is he?' said the barmaid. 'He's a loud-mouthed one, he is, and they're never much good. Give me a pleasant spoken chap, if you want a devil!'

'Well, Paul, my lad,' said the friend, 'you'll have to take care of yourself now for a while.'

'You won't have to give him a chance over you, that's all,' said the barmaid.

'Can you box?' asked a friend.

'Not a bit,' he answered, still very white.

'I might give you a turn or two,' said the friend.

'Thanks, I haven't time.'

And presently he took his departure.

'Go along with him, Mr Jenkinson,' whispered the barmaid, tipping Mr Jenkinson the wink.

The man nodded, took his hat, said 'Good-night all!' very heartily, and followed Paul, calling:

'Half a minute, old man. You an' me's going the same road, I believe.'

'Mr Morel doesn't like it,' said the barmaid. 'You'll see, we shan't have him in much more. I'm sorry; he's good company. And Baxter Dawes wants locking up, that's what he wants.'

Paul would have died rather than his mother should get to know of this affair. He suffered tortures of humiliation and self-consciousness. There was now a good deal of his life of which necessarily he could not speak to his mother. He had a life apart from her – his sexual life. The rest she still kept. But he felt he had to conceal something from her, and it irked him. There was a certain silence between them, and he felt he had, in that silence, to defend himself against her; he felt condemned by her. Then sometimes he hated her, and pulled at her bondage. His life wanted to free itself of her. It was like a circle where life turned back on itself, and got no farther. She bore him, loved him, kept him, and his love turned back into her, so that he could not be free to go forward with his own life, really love another woman. At this period, unknowingly, he resisted his mother's influence. He did not tell her things; there was a distance between them.

Clara was happy, almost sure of him. She felt she had at last got him for herself; and then again came the uncertainty. He told her jestingly of the affair with her husband. Her colour came up, her grey eyes flashed.

'That's him to a "T," she cried – 'like a navvy! He's not fit for mixing with decent folk.'

'Yet you married him,' he said.

It made her furious that he reminded her.

'I did!' she cried. 'But how was I to know!'

'I think he might have been rather nice,' he said.

'You think *I* made him what he is!' she exclaimed.

'Oh no! he made himself. But there's something about him – '

Clara looked at her lover closely. There was something in him she hated, a sort of detached criticism of herself, a coldness which made her woman's soul harden against him.

'And what are you going to do?' she asked.

'How?'

'About Baxter.'

'There's nothing to do, is there?' he replied.

'You can fight him if you have to, I suppose?' she said.

'No; I haven't the least sense of the "fist." It's funny. With most men there's the instinct to clench the fist and hit. It's not so with me. I should want a knife or a pistol or something to fight with.'

'Then you'd better carry something,' she said.

'Nay,' he laughed; 'I'm not daggeroso*.'

'But he'll do something to you. You don't know him.'

'All right,' he said, 'we'll see.'

'And you'll let him?'

'Perhaps, if I can't help it.'

'And if he kills you?' she said.

'I should be sorry, for his sake and mine.'

Clara was silent for a moment.

'You *do* make me angry!' she exclaimed.

'That's nothing afresh,' he laughed.

'But why are you so silly? You don't know him.'

'And don't want.'

'Yes, but you're not going to let a man do as he likes with you?'

'What must I do?' he replied, laughing.

'*I* should carry a revolver,' she said. 'I'm sure he's dangerous.'

'I might blow my fingers off,' he said.

'No; but won't you?' she pleaded

'No.'

---

* (It.) hiding a dagger.

'Not anything?'

'No.'

'And you'll leave, him to –?'

'Yes.'

'You are a fool!'

'Fact!'

She set her teeth with anger. 'I could *shake* you!' she cried, trembling with passion.

'Let a man like *him* do as he likes with you.'

'You can go back to him if he triumphs,' he said.

'Do you want me to hate you?' she asked.

'Well, I only tell you,' he said.

'And *you* say you *love* me!' she exclaimed, low and indignant.

'Ought I to slay him to please you?' he said. 'But if I did, see what a hold he'd have over me.'

'Do you think I'm a fool!' she exclaimed.

'Not at all. But you don't understand me, my dear.'

There was a pause between them.

'But you ought *not* to expose yourself,' she pleaded. He shrugged his shoulders.

> 'The man in righteousness arrayed
> The pure and blameless liver
> Needs not the keen Toledo blade
> Nor venom-freighted quiver,'

he quoted.

She looked at him searchingly.

'I wish I could understand you,' she said.

'There's simply nothing to understand,' he laughed.

She bowed her head, brooding. He did not see Dawes for several days; then one morning as he ran upstairs from the spiral room he almost collided with the burly metal-worker.

'What the –!' cried the smith.

'Sorry!' said Paul, and passed on.

'*Sorry*' sneered Dawes.

Paul whistled lightly, 'Put Me among the Girls.'

'I'll stop your whistle, my jockey!' he said.

The other took no notice.

'You're goin' to answer for that job of the other night.'

Paul went to his desk in his corner, and turned over the leaves of the ledger.

'Go and tell Fanny I want order 097, quick!' he said to his boy.

Dawes stood in the doorway, tall and threatening, looking at the top of the young man's head.

'Six and five's eleven and seven's one-and-six,' Paul added aloud.

'An' you hear, do you!' said Dawes.

'*Five and ninepence!*' He wrote a figure. 'What's that?' he said.

'I'm going to show you what it is,' said the smith.

The other went on adding the figures aloud.

'Yer crawlin' little – , yer daresn't face me proper!'

Paul quickly snatched the heavy ruler. Dawes started. The young man ruled some lines in his ledger. The elder man was infuriated.

'But wait till I light on you, no matter where it is, I'll settle your hash for a bit, yer little swine!'

'All right,' said Paul.

At that the smith started heavily from the doorway. Just then a whistle piped shrilly. Paul went to the speaking tube.

'Yes!' he said, and he listened. 'Er – yes!' He listened, then he laughed. 'I'll come down directly. I've got a visitor just now.'

Dawes knew from his tone that he had been speaking to Clara. He stepped forward.

'Yer little devil!' he said. 'I'll visitor you, inside of two minutes! Think I'm goin' ter have *you* whipperty-snappin' round?'

The other clerks in the warehouse looked up. Paul's office-boy appeared, holding some white article.

'Fanny says you could have had it last night if you'd let her know,' he said.

'All right,' answered Paul, looking at the stocking. 'Get it off.'

Dawes stood frustrated, helpless with rage. Morel turned round.

'Excuse me a minute,' he said to Dawes, and he would have run downstairs.

'By God, I'll stop your gallop!' shouted the smith, seizing him by the arm. He turned quickly.

'Hey! hey!' cried the office-boy, alarmed.

Thomas Jordan started out of his little glass office, and came running down the room.

'What's a-matter, what's a-matter?' he said, in his old man's sharp voice.

'I'm just goin' ter settle this little – , that's all,' said Dawes desperately. 'What do you mean?' snapped Thomas Jordan.

'What I say,' said Dawes, but he hung fire.

Morel was leaning against the counter, ashamed, half grinning.

'What's it all about?' snapped Thomas Jordan.

'Couldn't say,' said Paul, shaking his head and shrugging his shoulders.

'Couldn't yer, couldn't yer!' cried Dawes, thrusting forward his handsome, furious face, and squaring his fist.

'Have you finished?' cried the old man, strutting. 'Get off about your business, and don't come here tipsy in the morning.'

Dawes turned his big frame slowly upon him.

'Tipsy!' he said. 'Who's tipsy? I'm no more tipsy than *you* are!'

'We've heard that song before,' snapped the old man. 'Now you get off, and don't be long about it. Comin' *here* with your rowdying.'

The smith looked down contemptuously on his employer. His hands, large, and grimy, and yet well shaped for his labour, worked restlessly. Paul remembered they were the hands of Clara's husband, and a flash of hate went through him.

'Get out before you're turned out!' snapped Thomas Jordan.

'Why, who'll turn me out?' said Dawes, beginning to sneer.

Mr Jordan started, marched up to the smith, waving him off, thrusting his stout little figure at the man, saying:

'Get off my premises – get off!'

He seized and twitched Dawes' arm.

'Come off!' said the smith, and with a jerk of the elbow he sent the little manufacturer staggering backwards.

Before anyone could help him, Thomas Jordan had collided with the flimsy spring-door. It had given way, and let him crash down the half-dozen steps into Fanny's room. There was a second of amazement; then men and girls were running. Dawes stood a moment looking bitterly on the scene, then he took his departure.

Thomas Jordan was shaken and bruised, not otherwise hurt. He was, however, beside himself with rage. He dismissed Dawes from his employment, and summoned him for assault.

At the trial Paul Morel had to give evidence. Asked how the trouble began, he said:

'Dawes took occasion to insult Mrs Dawes and me because I accompanied her to the theatre one evening; then I threw some beer at him, and he wanted his revenge.'

'Cherchez la femme!'[*] smiled the magistrate.

The case was dismissed after the magistrate had told Dawes he thought him a skunk.

'You gave the case away,' snapped Mr Jordan to Paul.

'I don't think I did,' replied the latter. 'Besides, you didn't really want a conviction, did you?'

'What do you think I took the case up for?'

'Well,' said Paul, 'I'm sorry if I said the wrong thing.' Clara was also very angry.

'Why need *my* name have been dragged in?' she said.

'Better speak it openly than leave it to be whispered.'

---

* (Fr.) Look for a woman (behind a dispute in men).

'There was no need for anything at all,' she declared.

'We are none the poorer,' he said indifferently.

'*You* may not be,' she said.

'And you?' he asked.

'I need never have been mentioned.'

'I'm sorry,' he said; but he did not sound sorry.

He told himself easily: 'She will come round.' And she did.

He told his mother about the fall of Mr Jordan and the trial of Dawes. Mrs Morel watched him closely.

'And what do you think of it all?' she asked him.

'I think he's a fool,' he said.

But he was very uncomfortable, nevertheless.

'Have you ever considered where it will end?' his mother said.

'No,' he answered; 'things work out of themselves.'

'They do, in a way one doesn't like, as a rule,' said his mother.

'And then one has to put up with them,' he said.

'You'll find you're not as good at "putting up" as you imagine,' she said.

He went on working rapidly at his design.

'Do you ever ask *her* opinion?' she said at length.

'What of?'

'Of you, and the whole thing.'

'I don't care what her opinion of me is. She's fearfully in love with me, but it's nc ery deep.'

'But quite as deep as your feeling for her.'

He looked up at his mother curiously.

'Yes,' he said. 'You know, mother, I think there must be something the matter with me, that I *can't* love. When she's there, as a rule, I *do* love her. Sometimes, when I see her just as *the woman,* I love her, mother, but then, when she talks and criticises, I often don't listen to her.'

'Yet she's as much sense as Miriam.'

'Perhaps; and I love her better than Miriam. But *why* don't they hold me?'

The last question was almost a lamentation. His mother turned away her face, sat looking across the room, very quiet, grave, with something of renunciation.

'But you wouldn't want to marry Clara?' she said.

'No; at first perhaps I would. But why – why don't I want to marry her or anybody? I feel sometimes as if I wronged my women, mother.'

'How wronged them, my son?'

'I don't know.'

He went on painting rather despairingly; he had touched the quick of the trouble.

'And as for wanting to marry,' said his mother, 'there's plenty of time yet.'

'But no, mother. I even love Clara, and I did Miriam; but to *give* myself to them in marriage I couldn't. I couldn't belong to them. They seem to want *me,* and I can't ever give; it them.'

'You haven't met the right woman.'

'And I never shall meet the right woman while you live,' he said.

She was very quiet. Now she began to feel again tired, as if she were done.

'We'll see, my son,' she answered.

The feeling that things were going in a circle made him mad.

Clara was, indeed, passionately in love with him, and he with her, as far as passion went. In the daytime he forgot her a good deal. She was working in the same building, but he was not aware of it. He was busy, and her existence was of no matter to him. But all the time she was in her spiral room she had a sense that he was upstairs, a physical sense of his person in the same building. Every second she expected him to come through the door, and when he came it was a shock to her. But he was often short and off-hand with her. He gave her his directions in an official manner, keeping her at bay. With what wits she had left she listened to him. She dared not misunderstand or fail to remember, but it was a cruelty to her. She wanted to touch his chest. She knew exactly how his breast was shapen under the waistcoat, and she wanted to touch it. It maddened her to hear his mechanical voice giving orders about the work. She wanted to break through the sham of it, smash the trivial coating of business which covered him with hardness, get at the man again, but she was afraid, and before she could feel one touch of his warmth he was gone, and she ached again.

He knew that she was dreary every evening she did not see him, so he gave her a good deal of his time. The days were often a misery to her, but the evenings and the nights were usually a bliss to them both. Then they were silent. For hours they sat together, or walked together in the dark, and talked only a few, almost meaningless words. But he had her hand in his, and her bosom left its warmth in his chest making him feel whole.

One evening they were walking down by the canal, and something was troubling him. She knew she had not got him. All the time he whistled softly and persistently to himself. She listened, feeling she could learn more from his whistling than from his speech. It was a sad dissatisfied tune – a tune that made her feel he would not stay with her. She walked on in silence. When they came to the swing bridge he sat down on the great pole, looking at the stars in the water. He was a long way from her. She had been thinking.

'Will you always stay at Jordan's?' she asked.

'No,' he answered without reflecting. 'No; I s'll leave Nottingham and go abroad – soon.'

'Go abroad! What for?'

'I dunno! I feel restless.'

'But what shall you do?'

'I shall have to get some steady designing work, and some sort of sale for my pictures first,' he said. 'I am gradually making my way. I know I am.'

'And when do you think you'll go?'

'I don't know. I shall hardly go far long, while there's my mother.'

'You couldn't leave her?'

'Not for long.'

She looked at the stars in the black water. They lay very white and staring. It was an agony to know he would leave her, but it was almost an agony to have him near her.

'And if you made a nice lot of money, what would you do?' she asked.

'Go somewhere in a pretty house near London with my mother.'

'I see.'

There was a long pause.

'I could still come and see you,' he said. 'I don't know. Don't ask me what I should do; I don't know.'

There was a silence. The stars shuddered and broke upon the water. There came a breath of wind. He went suddenly to her, and put his hand on her shoulder.

'Don't ask me anything about the future,' he said miserably. 'I don't know anything. Be with me now, will you, no matter what it is?'

And she took him in her arms. After all, she was a married woman, and she had no right even to what he gave her. He needed her badly. She had him in her arms, and he was miserable. With her warmth she folded-him over, consoled him, loved him. She would let the moment stand for itself.

After a moment he lifted his head as if he wanted to speak.

'Clara,' he said, struggling.

She caught him passionately to her, pressed his head down on her breast with her hand. She could not bear the suffering in his voice. She was afraid in her soul. He might have anything of her – anything; but she did not want to *know*. She felt she could not bear it. She wanted him to be soothed upon her – soothed.

She stood clasping him and caressing him, and he was something unknown to her – something almost uncanny. She wanted to soothe him into forgetfulness.

And soon the struggle went down in his soul, and he forgot. But then Clara was not there for him, only a woman, warm, something he loved and almost worshipped, there in the dark. But it was not Clara, and she submitted to him. The naked hunger and inevitability of his loving her, something strong and blind and ruthless in its primitiveness, made the hour almost terrible to her. She knew how stark and alone he was, and she felt it was great that he came to her; and she took him simply because his need was bigger either than her or him, and her soul was still within her. She did this for him in his need, even if he left her, for she loved him.

All the while the peewits were screaming in the field. When he came to, he wondered what was near his eyes, curving and strong with life in the dark, and what voice it was speaking. Then he realised it was the grass, and the peewit was calling. The warmth was Clara's breathing heaving. He lifted his head, and looked into her eyes. They were dark and shining and strange, life wild at the source staring into his life, stranger to him, yet meeting him; and he put his face down on her throat, afraid. What was she? A strong, strange, wild life, that breathed with his in the darkness through this hour. It was all so much bigger than themselves that he was hushed. They had met, and included in their meeting the thrust of the manifold grass-stems, the cry of the peewit, the wheel of the stars.

When they stood up they saw other lovers stealing down the opposite hedge. It seemed natural they were there; the night contained them.

And after such an evening they both were very still, having known the immensity of passion. They felt small, half afraid, childish, and wondering, like Adam and Eve when they lost their innocence and realised the magnificence of the power which drove them out of Paradise and across the great night and the great day of humanity. It was for each of them an initiation and a satisfaction. To know their own nothingness, to know the tremendous living flood which carried them always, gave them rest within themselves. If so great a magnificent power could overwhelm them, identify them altogether with itself, so that they knew they were only grains in the tremendous heave that lifted every grass-blade its little height, and every tree, and living thing, then why fret about themselves? They could let themselves be carried by life, and they felt a sort of peace each in the other. There was a verification which they had had together. Nothing could nullify it, nothing could take it away; it was almost their belief in life.

But Clara was not satisfied. Something great was there, she knew; something great enveloped her. But it did not keep her. In the morning it was not the same. They had *known,* but she could not keep the moment. She wanted it again; she wanted something permanent. She had not realised fully. She thought it was he whom she wanted. He was not safe to her. This that had been between them might never be again; he might leave her. She had not got him; she was not satisfied. She had been there, but she had not gripped the – the something – she knew not what – which she was mad to have.

In the morning he had considerable peace, and was happy in himself. It seemed almost as if he had known the baptism of fire in passion, and it left him at rest. But it was not Clara. It was something that happened because of her, but it was not her. They were scarcely any nearer each other. It was as if they had been blind agents of a great force.

When she saw him that day at the factory her heart melted like a drop of fire. It was his body, his brows. The drop of fire grew more intense in her breast; she must hold him. But he, very quiet, very subdued this morning, went on giving his instructions. She followed him into the dark, ugly basement, and lifted her arms to him. He kissed her, and the intensity of passion began to burn him again. Somebody was at the door. He ran upstairs; she returned to her room, moving as if in a trance.

After that the fire slowly went down. He felt more and more that his experience had been impersonal, and not Clara. He loved her. There was a big tenderness, as after a strong emotion they had known together; but it was not she who could keep his soul steady. He had wanted her to be something she could not be.

And she was mad with desire of him. She could not see him without touching him. In the factory, as he talked to her about spiral hose, she ran her hand secretly along his side. She followed him out into the basement for a quick kiss; her eyes, always mute and yearning, full of unrestrained passion, she kept fixed on his. He was afraid of her, lest she should too flagrantly give herself away before the other girls. She invariably waited for him at dinner-time for him to embrace her before she went. He felt as if she were helpless, almost a burden to him, and it irritated him.

'But what do you always want to be kissing and embracing for?' he said. 'Surely there's a time for everything?'

She looked up at him, and the hate came into her eyes.

'*Do* I always want to be kissing you?' she said.

'Always, even if I come to ask you about the work. I don't want anything to do with love when I'm at work. Work's work –'

'And what is love?' she asked. 'Has it to have special hours?'

'Yes; out-of-work hours.'

'And you'll regulate it according to Mr Jordan's closing time?'

'Yes; and according to the freedom from business of any sort.'

'It is only to exist in spare time?'

'That's all, and not always then – not the kissing sort of love.'

'And that's all you think of it?'

'It's quite enough.'

'I'm glad you think so.'

And she was cold to him for some time – she hated him; and while she was cold and contemptuous, he was uneasy till she had forgiven him again. But when they started afresh they were not any nearer. He kept her because he never satisfied her.

In the spring they went together to the seaside. They had rooms at a little cottage near Theddlethorpe, and lived as man and wife. Mrs Radford sometimes went with them.

It was known in Nottingham that Paul Morel and Mrs Dawes were going together, but as nothing was very obvious, and Clara was always a solitary person, and he seemed so simple and innocent, it did not make much difference.

He loved the Lincolnshire coast, and she loved the sea. In the early morning they often went out together to bathe. The grey of the dawn, the far, desolate reaches of the fenland smitten with winter, the seameadows rank with herbage, were stark enough to rejoice his soul. As they stepped on to the highroad from their plank bridge, and looked round at the endless monotony of levels, the land a little darker than the sky, the sea sounding small beyond the sand hills, his heart filled strong with the sweeping relentlessness of life. She loved him then. He was solitary and strong, and his eyes had a beautiful light.

They shuddered with cold; then he raced her down the road to the green turf bridge. She could run well. Her colour soon came, her throat was bare, her eyes shone. He loved her for being so luxuriously heavy, and yet so quick. Himself was light; she went with a beautiful rush. They grew warm, and walked hand in hand.

A flush came into the sky, the wan moon, half-way down the west, sank into insignificance. On the shadowy land things began to take life, plants with great leaves became distinct. They came through a pass in the big, cold sandhills on to the beach. The long waste of foreshore lay moaning under the dawn and the sea; the ocean was a flat dark strip with a white edge. Over the gloomy sea the sky grew red. Quickly the fire spread among the clouds and scattered them. Crimson burned to orange, orange to dull gold, and in a golden glitter the sun came up, dribbling fierily over the waves in little splashes, as if someone had gone along and the light had spilled from her pail as she walked.

The breakers ran down the shore in long, hoarse strokes. Tiny seagulls, like specks of spray, wheeled above the line of surf. Their crying seemed larger than they. Far away the coast reached out, and melted into the morning, the tussocky sandhills seeming to sink to a level with the beach. Mablethorpe was tiny on their right. They had alone the space of all this level shore, the sea, and the upcoming sun, the faint noise of the waters, the sharp crying of the gulls.

They had a warm hollow in the sandhills where the wind did not come. He stood looking out to sea.

'It's very fine,' he said.

'Now don't get sentimental,' she said.

It irritated her to see him standing gazing at the sea, like a solitary and poetic person. He laughed. She quickly undressed.

'There are some fine waves this morning,' she said triumphantly.

She was a better swimmer than he; he stood idly watching her.

'Aren't you coming?' she said.

'In a minute,' he answered.

She was white and velvet skinned, with heavy shoulders. A little wind, coming from the sea, blew across her body and ruffled her hair.

The morning was of a lovely limpid gold colour. Veils of shadow seemed to be drifting away on the north and the south. Clara stood shrinking slightly from the touch of the wind, twisting her hair. The sea-grass rose behind the white stripped woman. She glanced at the sea, then looked at him. He was watching her with dark eyes which she loved and could not understand. She hugged her breasts between her arms, cringing, laughing:

'Oo, it will be so cold!' she said.

He bent forward and kissed her, held her suddenly close, and kissed her again. She stood waiting. He looked into her eyes, then away at the pale sands.

'Go, then!' he said quietly.

She flung her arms round his neck, drew him against her, kissed him passionately, and went, saying:

'But you'll come in?'

'In a minute.'

She went plodding heavily over the sand that was soft as velvet. He, on the sandhills, watched the great pale coast envelop her. She grew smaller, lost proportion, seemed only like a large white bird toiling forward.

'Not much more than a big white pebble on the beach, not much more than a clot of foam being blown and rolled over the sand,' he said to himself.

She seemed to move very slowly across the vast sounding shore. As he watched, he lost her. She was dazzled out of sight by the sunshine. Again he saw her, the merest white speck moving against the white, muttering sea-edge.

'Look how little she is!' he said to himself. 'She's lost like a grain of sand in the beach – just a concentrated speck blown along, a tiny white foam-bubble, almost nothing among the morning. Why does she absorb me?'

The morning was altogether uninterrupted: she was gone in the water. Far and wide the beach, the sandhills with their blue marram[*], the shining water, glowed together in immense, unbroken solitude.

'What is she, after all?' he said to himself. 'Here's the sea-coast morning, big and permanent and beautiful; there is she, fretting, always unsatisfied, and temporary as a bubble of foam. What does she mean to me, after all? She represents something, like a bubble of foam represents the sea. But what is *she*? It's not her I care for.'

Then, startled by his own unconscious thoughts, that seemed to speak so distinctly that all the morning could hear, he undressed and ran quickly down the sands. She was watching for him. Her arm flashed up to him, she heaved on a wave, subsided, her shoulders in a pool of liquid silver. He jumped through the breakers, and in a moment her hand was on his shoulder.

He was a poor swimmer, and could not stay long in the water. She played round him in triumph, sporting with her superiority, which he begrudged her. The sunshine stood deep and fine on

* a type of hardy grass.

the water. They laughed in the sea for a minute or two, then raced each other back to the sandhills.

When they were drying themselves, panting heavily, he watched her laughing, breathless face, her bright shoulders, her breasts that swayed and made him frightened as she rubbed them, and he thought again:

'But she is magnificent, and even bigger than the morning and the sea.

Is she —? is she —?'

She, seeing his dark eyes fixed on her, broke off from her drying with a laugh.

'What are you looking at?' she said

'You,' he answered, laughing.

Her eyes met his, and in a moment he was kissing her white 'goose fleshed' shoulder, and thinking:

'What is she? What is she?'

She loved him in the morning. There was something detached, hard, and elemental about his kisses then, as if he were only conscious of his own will, not in the least of her and her wanting him.

Later in the day he went out sketching.

'You,' he said to her, 'go with your mother to Sutton. I am so dull.'

She stood and looked at him. He knew she wanted to come with him, but he preferred to be alone. She made him feel imprisoned when she was there, as if he could not get a free deep breath, as if there were something on top of him. She felt his desire to be free of her.

In the evening he came back to her. They walked down the shore in the darkness, then sat for a while in the shelter of the sandhills.

'It seems,' she said, as they stared over the darkness of the sea, where no light was to be seen – 'it seemed as if you only loved me at night – as if you didn't love me in the daytime.'

He ran the cold sand through his fingers, feeling guilty under the accusation.

'The night is free to you,' he replied. 'In the daytime I want to be by myself.'

'But why?' she said. 'Why, even now, when we are on this short holiday? '

'I don't know. Love-making stifles me in the daytime.'

'But it needn't be always love-making,' she said.

'It always is,' he answered, 'when you and I are together.'

She sat feeling very bitter.

'Do you ever want to marry me?' he asked curiously.

'Do you me?' she replied.

'Yes, yes; I should like us to have children,' he answered slowly.

She sat with her head bent, fingering the sand.

'But you don't really want a divorce from Baxter, do you?' he said.

It was some minutes before she replied.

'No,' she said, very deliberately; 'I don't think I do.'

'Why?'

'I don't know.'

'Do you feel as if you belonged to him?'

'No; I don't think so.'

'What, then?'

'I think he belongs to me,' she replied.

He was silent for some minutes, listening to the wind blowing over the hoarse, dark sea.

'And you never really intended to belong to *me*?' he said.

'Yes, I do belong to you,' she answered.

'No,' he said; 'because you don't want to be divorced.'

It was a knot they could not untie, so they left it, took what they could get; and what they could not attain they ignored.

'I consider you treated Baxter rottenly,' he said another time.

He half expected Clara to answer him, as his mother would: 'You consider your own affairs, and don't know so much about other people's.' But she took him seriously, almost to his own surprise.

'Why?' she said.

'I suppose you thought he was a lily of the valley, and so you put him in an appropriate pot, and tended him according. You made up your mind he was a lily of the valley, and it was no good his being a cow-parsnip. You wouldn't have it.'

'I certainly never imagined him a lily of the valley.'

'You imagined him something he wasn't. That's just what a woman is. She thinks she knows what's good for a man, and she's going to see he gets it; and no matter if he's starving, he may sit and whistle for what he needs, while she's got him, and is giving him what's good for him.'

'And what are you doing?' she asked.

'I'm thinking what tune I shall whistle,' he laughed.

And instead of boxing his ears, she considered him in earnest.

'You think I want to give you what's good for you?' she asked.

'I hope so; but love should give a sense of freedom, not of prison. Miriam made me feel tied up like a donkey to a stake. I must feed on her patch, and nowhere else. It's sickening!'

'And would *you* let a *woman* do as she likes?'

'Yes; I'll see that she likes to love me. If she doesn't – well, I don't hold her.'

'If you were as wonderful as you say – ' replied Clara.

'I should be the marvel I am,' he laughed.

There was a silence in which they hated each other, though they laughed.

'Love's a dog in the manger,' he said.

'And which of us is the dog?' she asked.

'Oh well, you, of course.'

So there went on a battle between them. She knew she never fully had him. Some part, big and vital in him, she had no hold over, nor did she ever try to get it, or even to realise what it was. And he knew in some way that she held herself still as Mrs Dawes. She did not love Dawes, never had loved him; but she believed he loved her, at least depended on her. She felt a certain surety about him that she never felt with Paul Morel. Her passion *for* the young man had filled her soul, given her a certain satisfaction, eased her of her self-mistrust, her doubt. Whatever else she was, she was inwardly assured. It was almost as if she had gained *herself,* and stood now distinct and complete. She had received her confirmation; but she never believed that her life belonged to Paul Morel, nor his to her. They would separate in the end, and the rest of her life would be an ache after him. But at any rate, she *knew* now, she was sure of herself. And the same could almost be said of him. Together they had received the baptism of life, each through the other; but now their missions were separate. Where he wanted to go she could not come with him. They would have to part sooner or later. Even if they married, and were faithful to each other, still he would have to leave her, go on alone, and she would only have to attend to him when he came home. But it was not possible. Each wanted a mate to go side by side with.

Clara had gone to live with her mother upon Mapperley Plains. One evening, as Paul and she were walking along Woodborough Road, they met Dawes. Morel knew something about the bearing of the man approaching, but he was absorbed in his thinking at the moment, so that only his artist's eye watched the form of the stranger. Then he suddenly turned to Clara with a laugh, and put his hand on her shoulder, saying, laughing:

'But we walk side by side, and yet I'm in London arguing with an imaginary Orpen; and where are you? '

At that instant Dawes passed, almost touching Morel. The young man glanced, saw the dark brown eyes burning, full of hate and yet tired.

'Who was that?' he asked of Clara.

'It was Baxter,' she replied.

Paul took his hand from her shoulder and glanced round; then he saw again distinctly the man's form as it approached him. Dawes still walked erect, with his fine shoulders flung back, and his face lifted; but there was a furtive look in his eyes that gave one the impression he was trying to get unnoticed past every person he met, glancing suspiciously to see what they thought of him. And his hands seemed to be wanting to hide. He wore old clothes, the trousers were torn at the knee, and the handkerchief tied round his throat was dirty; but his cap was still defiantly over one eye. As she saw him Clara felt guilty. There was a tiredness and despair on his face that made her hate him, because it hurt her.

'He looks shady,' said Paul.

But the note of pity in his voice reproached her, and made her feel hard.

'His true commonness comes out,' she answered.

'Do you hate him?' he asked.

'You talk,' she said, 'about the cruelty of women; I wish you knew the cruelty of men in their brute force. They simply don't know that the woman exists.'

'Don't *I*?' he said.

'No,' she answered.

'Don't I know you exist?'

'About *me* you know nothing,' she said bitterly – 'about *me*!'

'Not more than Baxter knew?' he asked.

'Perhaps not as much.'

He felt puzzled, and helpless, and angry. There she walked unknown to him, though they had been through such experience together.

'But you know *me* pretty well,' he said.

She did not answer.

'Did you know Baxter as well as you know me?' he asked.

'He wouldn't let me,' she said.

'And I have let you know me?'

'It's what men *won't* let you do. They won't let you get really near to them,' she said.

'And haven't I let you?'

'Yes,' she answered slowly; 'but you've never come near to me. You can't come out of yourself, you can't. Baxter could do that better than you.'

He walked on pondering. He was angry with her for preferring Baxter to him.

'You begin to value Baxter now you've not got him,' he said.

'No; I can only see where he was different from you.'

But he felt she had a grudge against him.

One evening, as they were coming home over the fields, she startled him by asking:

'Do you think it's worth it – the – the sex part?'

'The act of loving, itself?'

'Yes; is it worth anything to you?'

'But how can you separate it?' he said. 'It's the culmination of everything. All our intimacy culminates then.'

'Not for me,' she said.

He was silent. A flash of hate for her came up. After all she was dissatisfied with him, even there, where he thought they fulfilled each other. But he believed her too implicitly.

'I feel,' she continued slowly, 'as if I hadn't got you, as if all of you weren't there, and as if it weren't *me* you were taking – '

'Who, then?'

'Something just for yourself. It has been fine, so that I daren't think of it. But is it *me* you want, or is it *It*?'

He again felt guilty. Did he leave Clara out of count, and take simply woman? But he thought that was splitting a hair.

'When I had Baxter, actually had him, then I *did* feel as if I had all of him,' she said.

'And it was better?' he asked.

'Yes, yes; it was more whole. I don't say you haven't given me more than he ever gave me.'

'Or could give you.'

'Yes, perhaps; but you've never given me yourself.'

He knitted his brows angrily.

'If I start to make love to you,' he said, 'I just go like a leaf down the wind.'

'And leave me out of count,' she said.

'And then is it nothing to you?' he asked, almost rigid with chagrin.

'It's something; and sometimes you have carried me away – right away – I know – and – I reverence you for it – but – '

'Don't "but" me,' he said, kissing her quickly, as a fire ran through him.

She submitted, and was silent.

It was true as he said. As a rule, when he started love-making, the emotion was strong enough to carry with it everything – reason, soul, blood – in a great sweep, like the Trent carries bodily its back-swirls and intertwinings, noiselessly. Gradually the little criticisms, the little sensations, were lost, thought also went, everything borne along in one flood. He became, not a man with a mind, but a great instinct. His hands were like creatures, living; his limbs, his body, were all life and consciousness, subject to no will of his, but living in themselves. Just as he was, so it seemed the vigorous, wintry stars were strong also with life. He and they struck with the same pulse of fire, and the same joy of strength which held the bracken-frond stiff near his eyes held his own body firm. It was as if he and the stars, and the dark herbage, and Clara were licked up in an immense tongue of flame, which tore onwards and upwards. Everything rushed along in living beside him; everything was still, perfect in itself, along with him. This wonderful stillness in each thing in itself, while it was being borne along in a very ecstasy of living, seemed the highest point of bliss.

And Clara knew this held him to her, so she trusted altogether to the passion. It, however, failed her very often. They did not often reach again the height of that once when the peewits had called. Gradually, some mechanical effort spoilt their loving, or, where they had splendid moments, they had them separately, and not so satisfactorily. So often he seemed merely to be running on alone; often they realised it had been a failure, not what they had wanted. He left her, knowing that evening had only made a little split between them. Their loving grew more mechanical, without the marvellous glamour. Gradually they began to introduce novelties, to get back some of the feeling of satisfaction. They would be very near, almost dangerously near to the river, so that the black water ran not far from his face, and it gave a little thrill; or they loved sometimes in a little hollow below the fence of the path where people were passing occasionally, on the edge of the town, and they heard footsteps coming, almost felt the vibration of the tread, and they heard what the passers-by said – strange little things that were never intended to be heard. And afterwards each of them was rather ashamed, and these things caused a distance between the two of them. He began to despise her a little, as if she had merited it!

One night he left her to go to Daybrook Station over the fields. It was very dark, with an attempt at snow, although the spring was so far advanced. Morel had not much time; he plunged forward. The town ceases almost abruptly on the edge of a steep hollow; there the houses with their yellow lights stand up against the darkness. He went over the stile, and dropped quickly into the hollow of the fields. Under the orchard one warm window shone in Swineshead Farm. Paul glanced round. Behind, the houses stood on the brim of the dip, bleak against the sky, like wild beasts glaring curiously with yellow eyes down into the darkness. It was the town that seemed savage and uncouth, glaring on the clouds at the back of him. Some creature stirred under the willows of the farm pond. It was too dark to distinguish anything:

He was close up to the next stile before he saw a dark shape leaning against it. The man moved aside.

'Good-evening!' he said.

'Good-evening!' Morel answered, not noticing.

'Paul Morel?' said the man.

Then he knew it was Dawes. The man stopped his way.

'I've got yer, have I?' he said awkwardly.

'I shall miss my train,' said Paul.

He could see nothing of Dawes' face. The man's teeth seemed to chatter as he talked.

'You're going to get it from me now,' said Dawes.

Morel attempted to move forward; the other man stepped in front of him.

'Are yer goin' to take that top-coat off,' he said, 'or are you goin' to lie down to it?'

Paul was afraid the man was mad.

'But,' he said, 'I don't know how to fight.'

'All right, then,' answered Dawes, and before the younger man knew where he was he was staggering backwards from a blow across the face.

The whole night went black. He tore off his overcoat and coat, dodging a blow, and flung the garments over Dawes. The latter swore savagely. Morel, in his shirt-sleeves, was now alert and furious. He felt his whole body unsheath itself like a claw. He could not fight, so he would use his wits. The other man became more distinct to him; he could see particularly the shirt-breast. Dawes stumbled over Paul's coats, then came rushing forward. The young man's mouth was bleeding. It was the other man's mouth he was dying to get at, and the desire was anguish in its strength. He stepped quickly through the stile, and as Dawes was coming through after him, like a flash he got a blow in over the other's mouth. He shivered with pleasure. Dawes advanced slowly, spitting. Paul was afraid; he moved round to get to the stile again. Suddenly, from out of nowhere, came a great blow against his ear, that sent him falling helpless backwards. He heard

Dawes' heavy panting, like a wild beast's; then came a kick on the knee, giving him such agony that he got up and, quite blind, leapt clean under his enemy's guard. He felt blows and kicks, but they did not hurt. He hung on to the bigger man like a wild cat, till at last Dawes fell with a crash, losing his presence of mind. Paul went down with him. Pure instinct brought his hands to the man's neck, and before Dawes, in frenzy and agony, could wrench him free, he had got his fists twisted in the scarf and, his knuckles dug in the throat of the other man. He was a pure instinct, without reason or feeling. His body, hard and wonderful in itself, cleaved against the struggling body of the other man; not a muscle in him relaxed. He was quite unconscious, only his body had taken upon itself to kill this other man. For himself, he had neither feeling nor reason. He lay pressed hard against his adversary, his body adjusting itself to its one pure purpose of choking the other man, resisting exactly at the right moment, with exactly the right amount of strength, the struggles of the other, silent, intent, unchanging, gradually pressing its knuckles deeper, feeling the struggles of the other body become wilder and more frenzied. Tighter and tighter grew his body, like a screw that is gradually increasing in pressure, till something breaks.

Then suddenly he relaxed, full of wonder and misgiving.

Dawes had been yielding. Morel felt his body flame with pain, as he realised what he was doing; he was all bewildered. Dawes' struggles suddenly renewed themselves in a furious spasm. Paul's hands were wrenched, torn out of the scarf in which they were knotted, and he was flung away, helpless. He heard the horrid sound of the other's gasping, but he lay stunned; then, still dazed, he felt the blows of the other's feet, and lost consciousness.

Dawes, grunting with pain like a beast, was kicking the prostrate body of his rival. Suddenly the whistle of the train shrieked two fields away. He turned round and glared suspiciously. What was coming? He saw the lights of the train draw across his vision. It seemed to him people were approaching. He made off across the field into Nottingham, and dimly in his consciousness as he went, he felt on his foot the place where his boot had knocked against one of the lad's bones. The knock seemed to re-echo inside him; he hurried to get away from it.

Morel gradually came to himself. He knew where he was and what had happened, but he did not want to move. He lay still, with tiny bits of snow tickling his face. It was pleasant to lie quite, quite still. The time passed. It was the bits of snow that kept rousing him when he did not want to be roused. At last his will clicked into action.

'I mustn't lie here,' he said: 'it's silly.'

But still he did not move.

'I said I was going to get up,' he repeated. 'Why don't I?'

And still it was some time before he had sufficiently pulled himself together to stir; then gradually he got up. Pain made him sick and dazed, but his brain was clear. Reeling, he groped for his coats and got them on, buttoning his overcoat up to his ears. It was some time before he found his cap. He did not know whether his face was still bleeding. Walking blindly, every step making him sick with pain, he went back to the pond and washed his face and hands. The icy water hurt, but helped to bring him back to himself. He crawled back up the hill to the tram. He wanted to get to his mother – he must get to his mother – that was his blind intention. He covered his face as much as he could, and struggled sickly along. Continually the ground seemed to fall away from him as he walked, and he felt himself dropping with a sickening feeling into space; so, like a nightmare, he got through with the journey home.

Everybody was in bed. He looked at himself. His face was discoloured and smeared with blood, almost like a dead man's face. He washed it, and went to bed. The night went by in delirium. In the morning he found his mother looking at him. Her blue eyes – they were all he wanted to see. She was there; he was in her hands.

'It's not much, mother,' he said. 'It was Baxter Dawes.'

'Tell me where it hurts you,' she said quietly.

'I don't know – my shoulder. Say it was a bicycle accident, mother.'

He could not move his arm. Presently Minnie, the little servant, came upstairs with some tea. 'Your mother's nearly frightened me out of my wits – fainted away,' she said.

He felt he could not bear it. His mother nursed him; he told her about it.

'And now I should have done with them all,' she said quietly.

'I will, mother.'

She covered him up.

'And don't think about it,' she said – 'only try to go to sleep. The doctor won't be here till eleven.'

He had a dislocated shoulder, and the second day acute bronchitis set in. His mother was pale as death now, and very thin. She would sit and look at him, then away into space. There was something between them that neither dared mention. Clara came to see him. Afterwards he said to his mother:

'She makes me tired, mother.'

'Yes; I wish she wouldn't come,' Mrs Morel replied.

Another day Miriam came, but she seemed almost like a stranger to him.

'You know, I don't care about them, mother,' he said.

'I'm afraid you don't, my son,' she replied sadly.

It was given out everywhere that it was a bicycle accident. Soon he was able to go to work again, but now there was a constant sickness and gnawing at his heart. He went to Clara, but there seemed, as it were, nobody there. He could not work. He and his mother seemed almost to avoid each other. There was some secret between them which they could not bear. He was not aware of it. He only knew that his life seemed unbalanced, as if it were going to smash into pieces.

Clara did not know what was the matter with him. She realised that he seemed unaware of her. Even when he came to her he seemed unaware of her; always he was somewhere else. She felt she was clutching for him, and he was somewhere else. It tortured her, and so she tortured him. For a month at a time she kept him at arm's length. He almost hated her, and was driven to her in spite of himself. He went mostly into the company of men, was always at the George or the White Horse. His mother was ill, distant quiet, shadowy. He was terrified of something; he dared not look at her. Her eyes seemed to grow darker, her face more waxen; still she dragged about at her work.

At Whitsuntide he said he would go to Blackpool for four days with his friend Newton. The latter was a big, jolly fellow, with a touch of the bounder about him. Paul said his mother must go to Sheffield to stay a week with Annie, who lived there. Perhaps the change would do her good. Mrs Morel was attending a woman's doctor in Nottingham. He said her heart and her digestion were wrong. She consented to go to Sheffield, though she did not want to; but now she would do everything her son wished of her. Paul said he would come for her on the fifth day, and stay also in Sheffield till the holiday was up. It was agreed.

The two young men set off gaily for Blackpool. Mrs Morel was quite lively as Paul kissed her and left her. Once at the station, he forgot everything. Four days were clear – not an anxiety, not a thought. The two young men simply enjoyed themselves. Paul was like another man. None of himself remained – no Clara, no Miriam, no mother that fretted him. He wrote to them all, and long letters to his mother; but they were jolly letters that made her laugh. He was having a good time, as young fellows will in a place like Blackpool. And underneath it all was a shadow for her.

Paul was very gay, excited at the thought of staying with his mother in Sheffield. Newton was to spend the day with them. Their train was late. Joking, laughing, with their pipes between their teeth, the young men swung their bags on to the tram-car. Paul had bought his mother a little collar of real lace that he wanted to see her wear, so that he could tease her about it.

Annie lived in a nice house, and had a little maid. Paul ran gaily up the steps. He expected his mother laughing in the hall, but it was Annie who opened to him. She seemed distant to him. He stood a second in display. Annie let him kiss her cheek.

'Is my mother ill?' he said.

'Yes; she's not very well. Don't upset her.'

'Is she in bed?'

'Yes.'

And then the queer feeling went over him, as if all the sunshine had gone out of him, and it was all shadow. He dropped the bag and ran upstairs. Hesitating, he opened the door. His mother sat up in bed, wearing a dressing-gown of old rose colour. She looked at him almost as if she were ashamed of herself, pleading to him, humble. He saw the ashy look about her.

'Mother!' he said.

'I thought you were never coming,' she answered gaily. But he only fell on his knees at the bedside, and buried his face in the bedclothes, crying in agony, and saying:

'Mother – mother – mother!'

She stroked his hair slowly with her thin hand.

'Don't cry,' she said. 'Don't cry – it's nothing.'

But he felt as if his blood was melting into tears, and he cried in terror and pain.

'Don't – don't cry,' his mother faltered.

Slowly she stroked his hair. Shocked out of himself, he cried, and the tears hurt in every fibre of his body. Suddenly he stopped, but he dared not lift his face out of the bedclothes.

'You *are* late. Where have you been?' his mother asked.

'The train was late,' he replied, muffled in the sheet.

'Yes that miserable Central! Is Newton come?'

'Yes.'

'I'm sure you must be hungry, and they've kept dinner waiting.'

With a wrench he looked up at her.

'What is it, mother?' he asked brutally.

She averted her eyes as she answered:

'Only a bit of a tumour, my boy. You needn't trouble. It's been there the lump has – a long time.'

Up came the tears again. His mind was clear and hard, but his body was crying

'Where?' he said.

She put her hand on her side.

'Here. But you know they can sweal a tumour away.'

He stood feeling dazed and helpless, like a child. He thought perhaps it was as she said. Yes he reassured himself it was so. But all the while his blood and his body knew definitely what it was. He sat down on the bed, and took her hand. She had never had but the one ring – her wedding ring.

'When were you poorly?' he asked.

'It was yesterday it began,' she answered submissively.

'Pains!'

'Yes but not more than I've often had at home. I believe Dr Ansell is an alarmist.'

'You ought not to have travelled alone,' he said, to himself more than to her.

'As if that had anything to do with it!' she answered quickly.

They were silent for a while.

'Now go and have your dinner,' she said. 'You *must* be hungry.'

'Have you had yours?'

'Yes a beautiful sole I had. Annie *is* good to me.'

They talked a little while, then he went downstairs. He was very white and strained. Newton sat in miserable sympathy.

After dinner he went into the scullery to help Annie to wash up. The little maid had gone on an errand.

'Is it really a tumour?' he asked.

Annie began to cry again.

'The pain she had yesterday – I never saw anybody suffer like it!' she cried. 'Leonard ran like a madman for Dr Ansell, and when she'd got to bed she said to me: "Annie, look at this lump on my side. I wonder what it is?" And there I looked, and I thought I should have dropped. Paul, as true as I'm here, it's a lump as big as my double fist. I said: "Good gracious, mother, whenever did that come?"

"Why, child," she said, "it's been there a long time." I thought I should have died, our Paul, I did. She's been having these pains for months at home, and nobody looking after her.'

The tears came to his eyes, then dried suddenly.

'But she's been attending the doctor in Nottingham – and she never told me,' he said.

'If I'd have been at home,' said Annie, 'I should have seen for myself.'

He felt like a man walking in unrealities. In the afternoon he went to see the doctor. The latter was a shrewd, lovable man.

'But what is it?' he said.

The doctor looked at the young man, then knitted his fingers.

'It may be a large tumour which has formed in the membrane,' he said slowly, 'and which we *may* be able to make go away.'

'Can't you operate?' asked Paul.

'Not there,' replied the doctor.

'Are you sure?'

'*Quite!*'

Paul meditated a while.

'Are you sure it's a tumour?' he asked. 'Why did Dr Jameson in Nottingham never find out anything about it? She's been going to him for weeks, and he's treated her for heart and indigestion.'

'Mrs Morel never told Dr Jameson about the lump,' said the doctor.

'And do you *know* it's a tumour?'

'No, I am not sure.'

'What else *might* it be? You asked my sister if there was cancer in the family. Might it be cancer?'

'I don't know.'

'And what shall you do?'

'I should like an examination, with Dr Jameson.'

'Then have one.'

'You must arrange about that. His fee wouldn't be less than ten guineas to come here from Nottingham.'

'When would you like him to come?'

'I will call in this evening, and we will talk it over.'

Paul went away, biting his lip.

His mother could come downstairs for tea, the doctor said. Her son went upstairs to help her. She wore the old-rose dressing-gown that Leonard had given Annie, and, with a little colour in her face, was quite young again.

'But you look quite pretty in that,' he said.

'Yes they make me so fine, I hardly know myself,' she answered.

But when she stood up to walk, the colour went. Paul helped her, half carrying her. At the top of the stairs she was gone. He lifted her up and carried her quickly downstairs laid her on the couch. She was light and frail. Her face looked as if she were dead, with the blue lips shut tight. Her eyes opencd – her blue, unfailing eyes – and she looked at him pleadingly, almost wanting him to forgive her. He held brandy to her lips, but her mouth would not open. All the time she watched him lovingly. She was only sorry for him. The tears ran down his face without ceasing, but not a muscle moved. He was intent on getting a little brandy between her lips. Soon she was able to swallow a teaspoonful. She lay back, so tired. The tears continued to run down his face.

'But,' she panted, 'it'll go off. Don't cry!'

'I'm not doing,' he said.

After a while she was better again. He was kneeling beside the couch.

They looked into each other's eyes.

'I don't want you to make a trouble of it,' she said.

'No, mother. You'll have to be quite still, and then you'll get better soon.'

But he was white to the lips, and their eyes as they looked at each other understood. Her eyes were so blue – such a wonderful forget-me-not blue! He felt if only they had been of a different colour he could have borne it better. His heart seemed to be ripping slowly in his breast. He kneeled there, holding her hand, and neither said anything. Then Annie came in.

'Are you all right?' she murmured timidly to her mother.

'Of course,' said Mrs Morel.

Paul sat down and told her about Blackpool. She was curious.

A day or two after, he went to see Dr Jameson in Nottingham, to arrange for a consultation. Paul had practically no money in the world. But he could borrow.

His mother had been used to go to the public consultation on Saturday morning, when she could see the doctor for only a nominal sum. Her son went on the same day. The waiting-room was full of poor women, who sat patiently on a bench around the wall. Paul thought of his mother, in her little black costume, sitting waiting likewise. The doctor was late. The women all looked rather frightened. Paul asked the nurse in attendance if he could see the doctor immediately he came. It was arranged so. The women sitting patiently round the walls of the room eyed the young man curiously.

At last the doctor came. He was about forty, good looking, brownskinned. His wife had died, and he, who had loved her, had specialised on women's ailments. Paul told his name and his mother's. The doctor did not remember.

'Number forty-six M.,' said the nurse; and the doctor looked up the case in his book.

'There is a big lump that may be a tumour,' said Paul. 'But Dr Ansell is going to write you a letter.'

'Ah, yes!' replied the doctor, drawing the letter from his pocket. He was very friendly, affable, busy, kind. He would come to Sheffield the next day.

'What is your father?' he asked.

'He is a coal-miner' replied Paul.

'Not very well off, I suppose?'

'No, I see after this.' said Paul.

'And you?' smiled the doctor.

'I am a clerk in Jordan's Appliance Factory.'

The doctor smiled at him.

'Er – to go to Sheffield!' he said, putting the tips of his fingers together, and smiling with his eyes. 'Eight guineas?'

'Thank you!' said Paul, flushing and rising. 'And you'll come tomorrow?'

'Tomorrow – Sunday? Yes! Can you tell me about what time there is a train in the afternoon?'

'There is a Central gets in at four-fifteen.'

'And will there be any way of getting up to the house? Shall I have to walk?' The doctor smiled.

'There is the tram,' said Paul; 'the Western Park Tram.'

The doctor made a note of it.

'Thank you!' he said and shook hands.

Then Paul went on home to see his father, who was left in the charge of Minnie. Walter Morel was getting very grey now. Paul found him digging in the garden. He had written him a letter. He shook hands with his father.

'Hello, son! Tha has landed then?' said the father.

'Yes,' replied the son. 'But I'm going back tonight.'

'Are ter, beguy!' exclaimed the collier. 'An' has ter eaten owt?'

'No.'

'That's just like thee,' said Morel. 'Come thy ways in.'

The father was afraid of the mention of his wife. The two went indoors. Paul ate in silence; his father, with earthy hands, and sleeves rolled up, sat in the armchair opposite and looked at him.

'Well, and how is she?' asked the miner at length, in a little voice. 'She can sit up; she can be carried down to tea.' said Paul.

'That's a blessin'!' exclaimed Morel. 'I hope we s'll soon be having her whoam, then. An' what's that Nottingham doctor say?'

'He's going tomorrow to have an examination of her.'

'Is he, beguy! That's a tidy penny, I'm thinkin'!'

'Eight guineas.'

'Eight guineas!' The miner spoke breathlessly. 'Well we mun find it from somewhere.'

'I can pay that,' said Paul.

There was a silence between them for some time.

'She says she hopes you're getting on all right with Minnie,' Paul said.

'Yes, I'm all right, an' I wish she was,' answered Morel. 'But Minnie's a good little wench, bless 'er heart!' He sat looking dismal.

'I s'll have to be going at half-past three,' said Paul.

'It' a trapse for thee lad! Eight guineas! An' when dost think she'll be able to get as far as this?'

'We must see what the doctors say tomorrow,' Paul said.

Morel sighed deeply. The house seemed strangely empty, and Paul thought his father looked lost, forlorn and old.

'You'll have to go and see her next week, father,' he said.

'I hope she'll be a-whoam by that time,' said Morel.

'If she's not,' said Paul, 'then you must come.'

'I dunno wheer I s'll find th' money,' said Morel.

'And I'll write to you what the doctor says,' said Paul.

'But tha writes i' such a fashion, I canna ma'e it out,' said Morel.

'Well, I'll write plain.'

It was no good asking Morel to answer, for he could scarcely do more than write his own name.

The doctor came. Leonard felt it his duty to meet him with a cab. The examination did not take long. Annie, Arthur, Paul, and Leonard were waiting in the parlour anxiously. The doctors came down. Paul glanced at them. He had never had any hope, except when he had deceived himself.

'It *may* be a tumour; we must wait and see,' said Dr Jameson.

'And if it is,' said Annie, 'can you sweal it away?'

'Probably,' said the doctor.

Paul put eight sovereigns and half a sovereign on the table. The doctor counted them, took a florin out of his purse, and put that down.

'Thank you!' he said. 'I'm sorry Mrs Morel is so ill. But we must see what we can do.'

'There can't be an operation?' said Paul.

The doctor shook his head.

'No,' he said; 'and even if there could, her heart wouldn't stand it.'

'Is her heart risky?' asked Paul.

'Yes; you must be careful with her.'

'Very risky?'

'No – er – no, no! Just take care.'

And the doctor was gone.

Then Paul carried his mother downstairs. She lay simply, like a child. But when he was on the stairs, she put her arms round his neck, clinging. 'I'm so frightened of these beastly stairs,' she said.

And he was frightened, too. He would let Leonard do it another time. He felt he could not carry her.

'He thinks it's only a tumour!' cried Annie to her mother. 'And he can sweal it away.'

'I *knew* he could,' protested Mrs Morel scornfully.

She pretended not to notice that Paul had gone out of the room. He sat in the kitchen, smoking. Then he tried to brush some grey ash off his coat. He looked again. It was one of his mother's grey hairs. It was so long! He held it up, and it drifted into the chimney. He let go. The long grey hair floated and was gone in the blackness of the chimney.

The next day he kissed her before going back to work. It was very early in the morning, and they were alone.

'You won't fret, my boy!' she said.

'No, mother.'

'No; it would be silly. And take care of yourself.'

'Yes,' he answered. Then, after a while: 'And I shall come next Saturday, and shall bring my father?'

'I suppose he wants to come,' she replied. 'At any rate, if he does you'll have to let him.'

He kissed her again, and stroked the hair from her temples, gently, tenderly, as if she were a lover.

'Shan't you be late?' she murmured.

'I'm going,' he said, very low.

Still he sat a few minutes, stroking the brown and grey hair from her temples.

'And you won't be any worse, mother?'

'No, my son.'

'You promise me?'

'Yes; I won't be any worse.'

He kissed her, held her in his arms for a moment, and was gone. In the early sunny morning he ran to the station, crying all the way, he did not know what for. And her blue eyes were wide and staring as she thought of him.

In the afternoon he went a walk with Clara. They sat in the little wood where bluebells were standing. He took her hand.

'You'll see,' he said to Clara, 'she'll never be better.'

'Oh, you don't know!' replied the other.

'I do,' he said.

She caught him impulsively to her breast.

'Try and forget it, dear,' she said; 'try and forget it.'

'I will,' he answered.

Her breast was there, warm for him; her hands were in his hair. It was comforting, and he held his anus round her. But he did not forget. He only talked to Clara of something else. And it was always so. When she felt it coming, the agony, she cried to him:

'Don't think of it, Paul! Don't think of it, my darling!'

And she pressed him to her breast, rocked him, soothed him like a child. So he put the trouble aside for her sake, to take it up again immediately he was alone. All the time, as he went about, he cried mechanically. His mind and hands were busy. He cried, he did not know why. It was his blood weeping. He was just as much alone whether he was with Clara or with the men in the White Horse. Just himself and this pressure inside him, that was all that existed. He read sometimes. He had to keep his mind occupied. And Clara was a way of occupying his mind.

On the Saturday Walter Morel went to Sheffield. He was a forlorn figure, looking rather as if nobody owned him. Paul ran upstairs.

'My father's come,' he said, kissing his mother.

'Has he?' she answered weariedly.

The old collier came rather frightened into the bedroom.

'How dun I find thee, lass?' he said, going forward and kissing her in a hasty, timid fashion.

'Well, I'm middlin',' she replied.

'I see tha art,' he said. He stood looking down on her. Then he wiped his eyes with his handkerchief. Helpless, and as if nobody owned him, he looked.

'Have you gone on all right?' asked the wife, rather wearily, as if it were an effort to talk to him.

'Yis,' he answered. 'Er's a bit behint-hand now and again, as yer might expect.'

'Does she have your dinner ready?' asked Mrs Morel.

'Well, I've 'ad to shout at 'er once or twice,' he said.

'And you *must* shout at her if she's not ready. She *will* leave things to the last minute.'

She gave him a few instructions. He sat looking at her as if she were almost a stranger to him, before whom he was awkward and humble, and also as if he had lost his presence of mind, and wanted to run. This feeling that he wanted to run away, that he was on thorns to be gone from so trying a situation, and yet must linger because it looked better, made his presence so trying. He put up his eyebrows for misery and clenched his fists on his knees, feeling so awkward in presence of a big trouble.

Mrs Morel did not change much. She stayed in Sheffield for two months. If anything, at the end she was rather worse. But she wanted to go home. Annie had her children. Mrs Morel wanted to go home. So they got a motor-car from Nottingham – for she was too ill to go by train – and she was driven through the sunshine. It was just August, everything was bright and warm. Under the blue sky they could all see she was dying. Yet she was jollier than she had been for weeks. They all laughed and talked.

'Annie,' she exclaimed, 'I saw a lizard dart on that rock!'

Her eyes were so quick; she was still so full of life.

Morel knew she was coming. He had the front-door open. Everybody was on tiptoe. Half the street turned out. They heard the sound of the great motor-car. Mrs Morel, smiling, drove home down the street.

'And just look at them all come out to see me!' she said. 'But there, I suppose I should have done the same. How do you do, Mrs Matthews? How are you, Mrs Harrison?'

They none of them could hear, but they saw her smile and nod. And they all saw death on her face, they said. It was a great event in the street.

Morel wanted to carry her indoors, but he was too old. Arthur took her as if she were a child. They had set her a big, deep chair by the hearth where her rocking-chair used to stand. When she was unwrapped and seated, and had drunk a little brandy, she looked round the room.

'Don't think I didn't like your house, Annie,' she said; 'but it's nice to be in my own home again.'

And Morel answered huskily:

'It is, lass, it is.'

And Minnie, the little quaint maid, said:

'An' we glad t' 'ave yer.'

There was a lovely yellow ravel of sunflowers in the garden. He looked out of the window.

'There are my sunflowers!' she said.

CHAPTER 14

The Release

'BY THE WAY,' said Dr Ansell one evening when Morel was in Sheffield, 'we've got a man in the fever hospital here who comes from Nottingham – Dawes. He doesn't seem to have many belongings in this world.'

'Baxter Dawes!' Paul exclaimed.

'That's the man – has been a fine fellow, physically, I should think. Been in a bit of a mess lately. You know him?'

'He used to work at the place where I am.'

'Did he? Do you know anything about him? He's just sulking, or he'd be a lot better than he is by now.'

'I don't know anything of his home circumstances, except that he's separated from his wife and has been a bit down, I believe. But tell him about me, will you? Tell him I'll come and see him.'

The next time Morel saw the doctor he said:

'And what about Dawes?'

'I said to him,' answered the other, " 'Do you know a man from Nottingham named Morel?" and he looked at me as if he'd jump at my throat. So I said, "I see you know the name; it's Paul Morel." Then I told him about your saying you would go and see him. "What does he want?" he said, as if you were a policeman.'

'And did he say he would see me?' asked Paul.

'He wouldn't say anything – good, bad, or indifferent,' replied the doctor.

'Why not?'

'That's what I want to know. There he lies and sulks, day in, day out. Can't get a word of information out of him.'

'Do you think I might go?' asked Paul.

'You might.'

There was a feeling of connection between the rival men more than ever since they had fought. In a way Morel felt guilty towards the other, and more or less responsible. And being in such a state of soul himself, he felt an almost painful nearness to Dawes, who was suffering and despairing too. Besides, they had met in a naked extremity of hate and it was a bond. At any rate, the elemental man in each had met.

He went down to the isolation hospital, with Dr Ansell's card. The sister, a healthy young Irishwoman, led him down the ward.

'A visitor to see you, Jim Crow,' she said.

Dawes turned over suddenly with a startled grunt.

'Eh?'

'Caw!' she mocked. 'He can only say "Caw!" I have brought you a gentleman to see you. Now say "Thank you," and show some manners.'

Dawes looked swiftly with his dark, startled eyes beyond the sister at Paul. His look was full of fear, mistrust, hate, and misery. Morel met the swift, dark eyes, and hesitated. The two men were afraid of the naked selves they had been.

'Dr Ansell told me you were here,' said Morel, holding out his hand.

Dawes mechanically shook hands.

'So I thought I'd come in,' continued Paul.

There was no answer. Dawes lay staring at the opposite wall.

'Say "Caw!" ' mocked the nurse. 'Say "Caw!" Jim Crow.'

'He is getting on all right?' said Paul to her.

'Oh yes! He lies and imagines he's going to die,' said the nurse, 'and it frightens every word out of his mouth.'

'And you must have somebody to talk to,' laughed Morel.

'That's it!' laughed the nurse. 'Only two old men and a boy who always cries. It is hard lines! Here am I dying to hear Jim Crow's voice, and nothing but an odd "Caw!" will he give!'

'So rough on you!' said Morel.

'Isn't it?' said the nurse.

'I suppose I am a godsend,' he laughed.

'Oh, dropped straight from heaven!' laughed the nurse.

Presently she left the two men alone. Dawes was thinner, and handsome again, but life seemed low in him. As the doctor said, he was lying sulking, and would not move forward towards convalescence. He seemed to grudge every beat of his heart.

'Have you had a bad time?' asked Paul.

Suddenly again Dawes looked at him.

'What are you doing in Sheffield?' he asked

'My mother was taken ill at my sister's in Thurston Street. What are you doing here?'

There was no answer.

'How long have you been in?' Morel asked.

'I couldn't say for sure,' Dawes answered grudgingly.

He lay staring across at the wall opposite, as if trying to believe Morel was not there. Paul felt his heart go hard and angry,

'Dr Ansell told me you were here,' he said coldly.

The other man did not answer.

'Typhoid's pretty bad, I know,' Morel persisted.

Suddenly Dawes said:

'What did you come for?'

'Because Dr Ansell said you didn't know anybody here. Do you?'

'I know nobody nowhere,' said Dawes.

'Well,' said Paul, 'it's because you don't choose to, then.'

There was another silence.

'We s'll be taking my mother home as soon as we can,' said Paul.

'What's a-matter with her?' asked Dawes, with a sick man's interest in illness.

'She's got a cancer.'

There was another silence.

'But we want to get her home,' said Paul. 'We s'll have to get a motor-car.'

Dawes lay thinking.

'Why don't you ask Thomas Jordan to lend you his?' said Dawes.

'It's not big enough,' Morel answered.

Dawes blinked his dark eyes as he lay thinking.

'Then ask Jack Pilkington; he'd lend it you. You know him.'

'I think I s'll hire one,' said Paul.

'You're a fool if you do,' said Dawes.

The sick man was gaunt and handsome again. Paul was sorry for him because his eyes looked so tired.

'Did you get a job here?' he asked.

'I was only here a day or two before I was taken bad,' Dawes replied.

'You want to get in a convalescent home,' said Paul.

The other's face clouded again.

'I'm goin' in no convalescent home,' he said.

'My father's been in the one at Seathorpe, an' he liked it. Dr Ansell would get you a recommend.'

Dawes lay thinking. It was evident he dared not face the world again. 'The seaside would be all right just now,' Morel said. 'Sun on those sandhills, and the waves not far out.'

The other did not answer.

'By Gad!' Paul concluded, too miserable to bother much; 'it's all right when you know you're going to walk again, and swim!'

Dawes glanced at him quickly. The man's dark eyes were afraid to meet any other eyes in the world. But the real misery and helplessness in Paul's tone gave him a feeling of relief.

'Is she far gone?' he asked.

'She's going like wax,' Paul answered; 'but cheerful-lively!'

He bit his lip. After a minute he rose.

'Well, I'll be going,' he said. 'I'll leave you this half-crown.'

'I don't want it,' Dawes muttered.

Morel did not answer, but left the coin on the table.

'Well,' he said, 'I'll try and run in when I'm back in Sheffield. Happen you might like to see my brother-in-law. He works in Pyecrofts.'

'I don't know him,' said Dawes.

'He's all right. Should I tell him to come? He might bring you some papers to look at.'

The other man did not answer. Paul went. The strong emotion that Dawes aroused in him, repressed, made him shiver.

He did not tell his mother, but next day he spoke to Clara about this interview. It was in the dinner-hour. The two did not often go out together now, but this day he asked her to go with him to the Castle grounds. There they sat while the scarlet geraniums and the yellow calceolarias blazed in the sunlight. She was now always rather protective, and rather resentful towards him.

'Did you know Baxter was in Sheffield Hospital with typhoid?' he asked.

She looked at him with startled grey eyes, and her face went pale.

'No,' she said, frightened.

'He's getting better. I went to see him yesterday – the doctor told me.'

Clara seemed stricken by the news.

'Is he very bad?' she asked guiltily.

'He has been. He's mending now.'

'What did he say to you?'

'Oh, nothing! He seems to be sulking.'

There was a distance between the two of them. He gave her more information.

She went about shut up and silent. The next time they took a walk together, she disengaged herself from his arm, and walked at a distance from him. He was wanting her comfort badly.

'Won't you be nice with me?' he asked.

She did not answer.

'What's the matter?' he said, putting his arm across her shoulder.

'Don't!' she said, disengaging herself.

He left her alone, and returned to his own brooding.

'Is it Baxter that upsets you?' he asked at length.

'I *have* been *vile* to him!' she said.

'I've said many a time you haven't treated him well,' he replied.

And there was a hostility between them. Each pursued his own train of thought.

'I've treated him – no, I've treated him badly,' she said. 'And now you treat *me* badly. It serves me right.'

'How do I treat you badly?' he said.

'It serves me right,' she repeated. 'I never considered him worth having, and now you don't consider *me*. But it serves me right. He loved me a thousand times better than you ever did.'

'He didn't!' protested Paul.

'He did! At any rate, he did respect me, and that's what you don't do.'

'It looked as if he respected you!' he said.

'He did! And I *made* him horrid – I know I did! You've taught me that. And he loved me a thousand times better than ever you do.'

'All right,' said Paul.

He only wanted to be left alone now. He had his own trouble, which was almost too much to bear. Clara only tormented him and made him tired. He was not sorry when he left her.

She went on the first opportunity to Sheffield to see her husband. The meeting was not a success. But she left him roses and fruit and money. She wanted to make restitution. It was not that she loved him. As she looked at him lying there her heart did not warm with love. Only she wanted to humble herself to him, to kneel before him. She wanted now to be self-sacrificial. After all, she had failed to make Morel really love her. She was morally frightened. She wanted to do penance. So she kneeled to Dawes, and it gave him a subtle pleasure. But the distance between them was still very great – too great. It frightened the man. It almost pleased the woman. She liked to feel she was serving him across an insuperable distance. She was proud now.

Morel went to see Dawes once or twice. There was a sort of friendship between the two men, who were all the while deadly rivals. But they never mentioned the woman who was between them.

Mrs Morel got gradually worse. At first they used to carry her downstairs, sometimes even into the garden. She sat propped in her chair, smiling, and so pretty. The gold wedding-ring shone on her white hand; her hair was carefully brushed. And she watched the tangled sunflowers dying, the chrysanthemums coming out, and the dahlias.

Paul and she were afraid of each other. He knew, and she knew, that she was dying. But they kept up a pretence of cheerfulness. Every morning, when he got up, he went into her room in his pyjamas.

'Did you sleep, my dear?' he asked.

'Yes,' she answered.

'Not very well?'

'Well, yes!'

Then he knew she had lain awake. He saw her hand under the bedclothes, pressing the place on her side where the pain was.

'Has it been bad?' he asked.

'No. It hurt a bit, but nothing to mention.'

And she sniffed in her old scornful way. As she lay she looked like a girl. And all the while her blue eyes watched him. But there were the dark pain-circles beneath that made him ache again.

'It's a sunny day,' he said.

'It's a beautiful day.'

'Do you think you'll be carried down?'

'I shall see.'

Then he went away to get her breakfast. All day long he was conscious of nothing but her. It was a long ache that made him feverish. Then, when he got home in the early evening, he glanced through the kitchen window. She was not there; she had not got up.

He ran straight upstairs and kissed her. He was almost afraid to ask:

'Didn't you get up, Pigeon?'

'No,' she said. 'It was that morphia; it made me tired.'

'I think he gives you too much,' he said.

'I think he does,' she answered.

He sat down by the bed, miserably. She had a way of curling and lying on her side, like a child. The grey and brown hair was loose over her ear.

'Doesn't it tickle you?' he said, gently putting it back.

'It does,' she replied.

His face was near hers. Her blue eyes smiled straight into his, like a girl's – warm, laughing with tender love. It made him pant with terror, agony, and love.

'You want your hair doing in a plait,' he said. 'Lie still.'

And going behind her, he carefully loosened her hair, brushed it out. It was like fine long silk of brown and grey. Her head was snuggled between her shoulders. As he lightly brushed and plaited her hair, he bit his lip and felt dazed. It all seemed unreal, he could not understand it.

At night he often worked in her room, looking up from time to time. And so often he found her blue eyes fixed on him. And when their eyes met, she smiled. He worked away again mechanically, producing good stuff without knowing what he was doing.

Sometimes he came in, very pale and still, with watchful, sudden eyes, like a man who is drunk almost to death. They were both afraid of the veils that were ripping between them.

Then she pretended to be better, chattered to him gaily; made a great fuss over some scraps of news. For they had both come to the condition when they had to make much of the trifles, lest they should give in to the big thing, and their human independence would go smash. They were afraid, so they made light of things and were gay.

Sometimes as she lay he knew she was thinking of the past. Her mouth gradually shut hard in a line. She was holding herself rigid, so that she might die without ever uttering the great cry that was tearing from her. He never forgot that hard, utterly lonely and stubborn clenching of her mouth, which persisted for weeks. Sometimes, when it was lighter, she talked about her husband. Now she hated him. She did not forgive him. She could not bear him to be in the room. And a few things, the things that had been most bitter to her, came up again so strongly that they broke from her, and she told her son.

He felt as if his life were being destroyed, piece-by-piece, within him. Often the tears came suddenly. He ran to the station, the tear-drops falling on the pavement. Often he could not go on with his work. The pen stopped writing. He sat staring, quite unconscious. And when he came round again he felt sick, and trembled in his limbs. He never questioned what it was. His mind did not try to analyse or understand. He merely submitted, and kept his eyes shut; let the thing go over him.

His mother did the same. She thought of the pain, of the morphia, of the next day; hardly ever of the death. That was coming, she knew. She had to submit to it. But she would never entreat it or make friends with it. Blind, with her face shut hard and blind, she was pushed towards the door. The days passed, the weeks, the months.

Sometimes, in the sunny afternoons, she seemed almost happy.

'I try to think of the nice times – when we went to Mablethorpe, and Robin Hood's Bay, and Shanklin,' she said. 'After all, not everybody has seen those beautiful places. And wasn't it beautiful! I try to think of that, not of the other things.'

Then, again, for a whole evening she spoke not a word; neither did he. They were together, rigid, stubborn, silent. He went into his room at last to go to bed, and leaned against the doorway as if paralysed, unable to go any farther. His consciousness went. A furious storm, he knew not what, seemed to ravage inside him. He stood leaning there, submitting, never questioning.

In the morning they were both normal again, though her face was grey with the morphia, and her body felt like ash. But they were bright again, nevertheless. Often, especially if Annie or Arthur were at home, he neglected her. He did not see much of Clara. Usually he was with men. He was quick and active and lively; but when his friends saw him go white to the gills, his eyes dark and glittering, they had a certain mistrust of him. Sometimes he went to Clara, but she was almost cold to him.

'Take me!' he said simply.

Occasionally she would. But she was afraid. When he had her then, there was something in it that made her shrink away from him something unnatural. She grew to dread him. He was so quiet, yet so strange. She was afraid of the man who was not there with her, whom she could feel behind this make-belief lover; somebody sinister, that filled her with horror. She began to have a kind of horror of him. It was almost as if he were a criminal. He wanted her – he had her – and it made her feel as if death itself had her in its grip. She lay in horror. There was no man there loving her. She almost hated him. Then came little bouts of tenderness. But she dared not pity him.

Dawes had come to Colonel Seely's Home near Nottingham. There Paul visited him sometimes, Clara very occasionally. Between the two men the friendship had developed peculiarly. Dawes, who mended very slowly and seemed very feeble, seemed to leave himself in the hands of Morel.

In the beginning of November Clara reminded Paul that it was her birthday.

'I'd nearly forgotten,' he said.

'I thought quite,' she replied.

'No. Shall we go to the seaside for the week-end?'

They went. It was cold and rather dismal. She waited for him to be warm and tender with her, instead of which he seemed hardly aware of her. He sat in, the railway-carriage, looking out, and was startled when she spoke to him. He was not definitely thinking. Things seemed as if they did not exist. She went across to him.

'What is it, dear?' she asked.

'Nothing!' he said. 'Don't those windmill sails look monotonous?'

He sat holding her hand. He could not talk nor think. It was a comfort, however, to sit holding her hand. She was dissatisfied and miserable. He was not with her; she was nothing.

And in the evening they sat among the sandhills, looking at the black, heavy sea.

'She will never give in,' he said quietly.

Clara's heart sank.

'No,' she replied.

'There are different ways of dying. My father's people are frightened, and have to be hauled out of life into death like cattle into a slaughter house, pulled by the neck; but my mother's people are pushed from behind, inch by inch. They are stubborn people, and won't die.'

'Yes,' said Clara.

'And she won't die. She can't. Mr Renshaw, the parson was in the other day. "Think!" he said to her; "you will have your mother and father, and your sisters, and your son, in the Other Land." And she said: "I have done without them for a long time, and *can* do without them now. It is the living I want, not the dead." She wants to live even now.'

'Oh, how horrible!' said Clara, too frightened to speak.

'And she looks at me, and she wants to stay with me,' he went on monotonously. 'She's got such a will, it seems as if she would never go-never!'

'Don't think of it!' cried Clara.

'And she was religious – she is religious now – but it is no good. She simply won't give in. And do you know, I said to her on Thursday, "Mother, if I had to die, I'd die. I'd *will* to die." And she said to me, sharp: "Do you think I haven't? Do you think you can die when you like?"'

His voice ceased. He did not cry, only went on speaking monotonously. Clara wanted to run. She looked round. There was the black, re-echoing shore, the dark sky down on her. She got up terrified. She wanted to be where there was light, where there were other people. She wanted to be away from him. He sat with his head dropped, not moving a muscle.

'And I don't want her to eat,' he said, 'and she knows it. When I ask her, "Shall you have anything?" she's almost afraid to say "Yes." "I'll have a cup of Benger's." she says. "It'll only keep your strength up," I said to her. "Yes" – and she almost cried – "but there's such a gnawing when I eat nothing, I can't bear it." So I went and made her the food. It's the cancer that gnaws like that at her. I wish she'd die!'

'Come!' said Clara roughly. 'I'm going.'

He followed her down the darkness of the sands. He did not come to her. He seemed scarcely aware of her existence. And she was afraid of him, and disliked him.

In the same acute daze they went back to Nottingham. He was always busy, always doing something, always going from one to the other of his friends.

On the Monday he went to see Baxter Dawes. Listless and pale, the mall rose to greet the other, clinging to his chair as he held out his hand.

'You shouldn't get up' said Paul.

Dawes sat down heavily, eyeing Morel with a sort of suspicion.

'Don't you waste your time on me,' he said, 'if you've owt better to do.'

'I wanted to come,' said Paul. 'Here! I brought you some sweets.'

The invalid put them aside.

'It's not been much of a weekend,' said Morel.

'How's your mother?' asked the other.

'Hardly any different.'

'I thought she was perhaps worse, being as you didn't come on Sunday.'

'I was at Skegness,' said Paul. 'I wanted a change.'

The other looked at him with dark eyes. He seemed to be waiting, not quite daring to ask, trusting to be told.

'I went with Clara,' said Paul.

'I knew as much,' said Dawes quietly.

'It was an old promise,' said Paul.

'You have it your own way,' said Dawes.

This was the first time Clara had been definitely mentioned between them.

'Nay,' said Morel slowly; 'she's tired of me.'

Again Dawes looked at him.

'Since August she's been getting tired of me,' Morel repeated.

The two men were very quiet together. Paul suggested a game of draughts. They played in silence.

'I s'll go abroad when my mother's dead,' said Paul.

'Abroad!' repeated Dawes.

'Yes; I don't care what I do.'

They continued the game. Dawes was winning.

'I s'll have to begin a new start of some sort,' said Paul; 'and you as well, suppose.'

He took one of Dawes' pieces.

'I dunno where,' said the other.

'Things have to happen,' Morel said. 'It's no good doing anything – at least – no, I don't know. Give me some toffee.'

The two men ate sweets, and began another game of draughts.

'What made that scar on your mouth?' asked Dawes.

Paul put his hand hastily to his lips, and looked over the garden.

'I had a bicycle accident,' he said.

Dawes' hand trembled as he moved the piece.

'You shouldn't ha' laughed at me,' he said very low.

'When?'

'That night on Wood borough Road, when you and her passed me you with your hand on her shoulder.'

'I never laughed at you,' said Paul.

Dawes kept his fingers on the draught-piece.

'I never knew you were there till the very second when you passed,' said Morel.

'It was that as did me,' he said, very low.

Paul took another sweet.

'I never laughed,' he said, 'except as I'm always laughing.'

They finished the game.

That night Morel walked home from Nottingham, in order to have something to do. The furnaces flared in a red blotch over Bulwell; the black clouds were like a low ceiling. As he went along the ten miles of highroad, he felt as if he were walking out of life, between the black levels of the sky and the earth. But at the end was only the sick-room. If he walked and walked for ever, there was only that place to come to.

He was not tired when he got near home, or he did not know it. Across the field he could see the red firelight leaping in her bedroom window.

'When she's dead,' he said to himself, 'that fire will go out.'

He took off his boots quietly and crept upstairs. His mother's door was wide open, because she slept alone still. The red firelight dashed its glow on the landing. Soft as a shadow, he peeped in her doorway.

'Paul!' she murmured.

His heart seemed to break again. He went in and sat by the bed.

'How late you are!' she murmured.

'Not very,' he said.

'Why, what time is it?' The murmur came plaintive and helpless.

'It's only just gone eleven.'

That was not true; it was nearly one o'clock.

'Oh!' she said; 'I thought it was later.'

And he knew the unutterable misery of her nights that would not go.

'Can't you sleep, my pigeon?' he said.

'No, I can't,' she wailed.

'Never mind, Little!' he said, crooning. 'Never mind my love. I'll stop with you half an hour, my pigeon; then perhaps it will be better.'

And he sat by the bedside, slowly, rhythmically stroking her brows with his finger-tips, stroking her eyes shut, soothing her, holding her fingers in his free hand. They could hear the sleepers' breathing in the other rooms.

'Now go to bed,' she murmured, lying quite still under his fingers and his love.

'Will you sleep?' he asked.

'Yes, I think so.'

'You feel better, my Little, don't you?'

'Yes,' she said, like a fretful, half-soothed child.

Still the days and the weeks went by. He hardly ever went to see Clara now. But he wandered restlessly from one person to another for some help, and there was none anywhere. Miriam had written to him tenderly. He went to see her. Her heart was very sore when she saw him, white, gaunt, with his eyes dark and bewildered. Her pity came up, hurting her till she could not bear it.

'How is she?' she asked.

'The same – the same!' he said. 'The doctor says she can't last, but I know she will. She'll be here at Christmas.'

Miriam shuddered. She drew him to her; she pressed him to her bosom; she kissed him and kissed him. He submitted, but it was torture. She could not kiss his agony. That remained alone and apart. She kissed his face, and roused his blood, while his soul was apart writhing with the agony of death. And she kissed him and fingered his body, till at last, feeling he would go mad, he got away from her. It was not that he wanted just then – not that. And she thought she had soothed him and done him good.

December came, and some snow. He stayed at home all the while now. They could not afford a nurse. Annie came to look after her mother; the parish nurse, whom they loved, came in morning and evening. Paul shared the nursing with Annie. Often, in the evenings, when friends were in the kitchen with them, they all laughed together and shook with laughter. It was reaction. Paul was so comical, Annie was so quaint. The whole party laughed till they cried, trying to subdue the sound. And Mrs Morel, lying alone in the darkness heard them, and among her bitterness was a feeling of relief.

Then Paul would go upstairs gingerly, guiltily, to see if she had heard.

'Shall I give you some milk?' he asked.

'A little,' she replied plaintively.

And he would put some water with it, so that it should not nourish her. Yet he loved her more than his own life.

She had morphia every night, and her heart got fitful. Annie slept beside her. Paul would go in in the early morning, when his sister got up. His mother was wasted and almost ashen in the morning with the morphia. Darker and darker grew her eyes, all pupil, with the torture. In the mornings the weariness and ache was too much to bear. Yet she could not – would not – weep, or even complain much.

'You slept a bit later this morning, little one,' he would say to her.

'Did I?' she answered, with fretful weariness.

'Yes; it's nearly eight o'clock.'

He stood looking out of the window. The whole country was bleak and pallid under the snow. Then he felt her pulse. There was a strong stroke and a weak one, like a sound and its echo.

That was supposed to betaken the end. She let him feel her wrist, knowing what he wanted.

Sometimes they looked in each other's eyes. Then they almost seemed to make an agreement. It was almost as if he were agreeing to die also. But she did not consent to die; she would not. Her body was wasted to a fragment of ash. Her eyes were dark and full of torture.

'Can't you give her something to put an end to it?' he asked the doctor at last.

But the doctor shook his head.

'She can't last many days now, Mr Morel,' he said.

Paul went indoors.

'I can't bear it much longer; we shall all go mad,' said Annie.

The two sat down to breakfast.

'Go and sit with her while we have breakfast, Minnie,' said Annie. But the girl was frightened.

Paul went through the country, through the woods, over the snow. He saw the marks of rabbits and birds in the white snow. He wandered miles and miles. A smoky red sunset came on slowly, painfully, lingering. He thought she would die that day. There was a donkey that came up to him over the snow by the wood's edge, and put its head against him and walked with him alongside. He put his arms round the donkey's neck, and stroked his cheeks against his ears.

His mother, silent, was still alive, with her hard mouth gripped grimly, her eyes of dark torture only living.

It was nearing Christmas; there was more snow. Annie and he felt as if they could go on no more. Still her dark eyes were alive. Morel, silent and frightened, obliterated himself. Sometimes he would go into the sick-room and look at her. Then he backed out, bewildered.

She kept her hold on life still. The miners had been out on strike, and returned a fortnight or so before Christmas. Minnie went upstairs with the feeding-cup. It was two days after the men had been in.

'Have the men been saying their hands are sore, Minnie?' she asked, in the faint, querulous voice that would not give in. Minnie stood surprised.

'Not as I know of, Mrs Morel,' she answered.

'But I'll bet they are sore,' said the dying woman, as she moved her head with a sigh of weariness. 'But, at any rate there'll be something to buy in with this week.'

Not a thing did she let slip.

'Your father's pit things will want well airing, Annie,' she said, when the men were going back to work.

'Don't you bother about that, my dear,' said Annie.

One night Annie and Paul were alone. Nurse was upstairs.

'She'll live over Christmas,' said Annie. They were both full of horror.

'She won't,' he replied grimly. 'I s'll give her morphia.'

'Which?' said Annie.

'All that came from Sheffield,' said Paul.

'Ay – do!' said Annie.

The next day he was painting in the bedroom. She seemed to be asleep. He stepped softly backwards and forwards at his painting. Suddenly her small voice wailed:

'Don't walk about, Paul.'

He looked round. Her eyes, like dark bubbles in her face were looking at him.

'No, my dear,' he said gently. Another fibre seemed to snap in his heart.

That evening he got all the morphia pills there were, and took them downstairs. Carefully he crushed them to powder.

'What are you doing?' said Annie.

'I s'll put 'em in her night milk.'

Then they both laughed together like two conspiring children. On top of all their horror flickered this little sanity.

Nurse did not come that night to settle Mrs Morel down. Paul went up with the hot milk in a feeding-cup. It was nine o'clock.

She was reared up in bed, and he put the feeding-cup between her lips that he would have died to save from any hurt. She took a sip, then put the spout of the cup away and looked at him with her dark, wondering eyes. He looked at her.

'Oh, it *is* bitter, Paul!' she said, making a little grimace.

'It's a new sleeping draught the doctor gave me for you,' he said. 'He thought it wouldn't leave you in such a state in the morning.'

'And I hope it won't,' she said, like a child.

She drank some more of the milk.

'But it *is* horrid?' she said.

He saw her frail fingers over the cup, her lips making a little move.

'I know – I tasted it,' he said. 'But I'll give you some clean milk afterwards.'

'I think so,' she said, and she went on with the draught. She was obedient to him like a child. He wondered if she knew. He saw her poor wasted throat moving as she drank with difficulty. Then he ran downstairs for more milk. There were no grains in the bottom of the cup.

'Has she had it?' whispered Annie.

'Yes – and she said it was bitter.'

'Oh!' laughed Annie, putting her under lip between her teeth. 'And I told her it was a new draught. Where's that milk?'

They both went upstairs.

'I wonder why nurse didn't come to settle me down?' complained the mother, like a child, wistfully.

'She said she was going to a concert, my love,' replied Annie.

'Did she?'

They were silent a minute. Mrs Morel gulped the little clean milk.

'Annie, that draught was horrid!' she said plaintively.

'Was it, my love? Well, never mind.'

The mother sighed again with weariness. Her pulse was very irregular.

'Let *us* settle you down,' said Annie. 'Perhaps nurse will be so late.'

'Ay,' said the mother – 'try.'

They turned the clothes back. Paul saw his mother like a girl curled up in her flannel nightdress. Quickly they made one half the bed, moved her, made the other, straightened her nightgown over her small feet, and covered her up.

'There,' said Paul, stroking her softly. 'There! – now you'll sleep.'

'Yes,' she said. 'I didn't think you could do the bed so nicely,' she added, almost gaily. Then she curled up, with her cheek on her hand, her head snugged between her shoulder. Paul put the long thin plait of grey hair over her shoulder and kissed her.

'You'll sleep, my love,' he said.

'Yes,' she answered trustfully. 'Good-night.'

They put out the light, and it was still.

Morel was in bed. Nurse did not come. Annie and Paul came to look at her at about eleven. She seemed to be sleeping as usual after her draught. Her mouth had come a bit open.

'Shall we sit up?' said Paul.

'I s'll lie with her as I always do,' said Annie. 'She might wake up.'

'All right. And call me if you see any difference.'

'Yes.'

They lingered before the bedroom fire, feeling the night big and black and snowy outside, their two selves alone in the world. At last he went into the next room and went to bed.

He slept almost immediately, but kept waking every now and again. Then he went sound asleep. He started awake at Annie's whispered, 'Paul, Paul!' He saw his sister in her white nightdress, with her long plait of hair down her back, standing in the darkness.

'Yes?' he whispered, sitting up. 'Come and look at her.'

He slipped out of bed. A bud of gas was burning in the sick chamber. His mother lay with her cheek on her hand curled up as she had gone to sleep. But her mouth had fallen open, and she breathed with great, hoarse breaths, like snoring, and there were long intervals between.

'She's going!' he whispered.

'Yes,' said Annie.

'How long has she been like it?'

'I only just woke up.'

Annie huddled into the dressing-gown, Paul wrapped himself in a brown blanket. It was three o'clock. He mended the fire. Then the two sat waiting. The great, snoring breath was taken – held awhile – then given back. There was a space – a long space. Then they started. The great, snoring breath was taken again. He bent close down and looked at her.

'Isn't it awful!' whispered Annie.

He nodded. They sat down again helplessly. Again came the great, snoring breath. Again they hung suspended. Again it was given back, long and harsh. The sound, so irregular, at such wide intervals, sounded through the house. Morel, in his room, slept on. Paul and Annie sat crouched, huddled, motionless. The great, snoring sound began again there was a painful pause while the breath was held – back came the rasping breath. Minute after minute passed. Paul looked at her again, bending low over her.

'She may last like this,' he said.

They were both silent. He looked out of the window, and could faintly discern the snow on the garden.

'You go to my bed,' he said to Annie. 'I'll sit up.'

'No,' she said, 'I'll stop with you.'

'I'd rather you didn't,' he said.

At last Annie crept out of the room, and he was alone. He hugged himself in his brown blanket, crouched in front of his mother, watching. She looked dreadful, with the bottom jaw fallen back. He watched. Sometimes he thought the great breath would never begin again. He could not bear it – the waiting. Then suddenly, startling him, came the great harsh sound. He mended the fire again, noiselessly. She must not be disturbed. The minutes went by. The night was going, breath by breath. Each time the sound came he felt it wring him, till at last he could not feel so much.

His father got up. Paul heard the miner drawing his stocking on, yawning. Then Morel, in shirt and stockings, entered.

'Hush!' said Paul.

Morel stood watching. Then he looked at his son, helplessly, and in horror.

'Had I better stop a-whoam?' he whispered.

'No. Go to work. She'll last through tomorrow.'

'I don't think so.'

'Yes. Go to work.'

The miner looked at her again, in fear, and went obediently out of the room. Paul saw the tape of his garters swinging against his legs.

After another half-hour Paul went downstairs and drank a cup of tea, then returned. Morel, dressed for the pit, came upstairs again.

'Am I to go?' he said.

'Yes.'

And in a few minutes Paul heard his father's heavy steps go thudding over the deadening snow. Miners called in the street as they tramped in gangs to work. The terrible, long drawn breaths continued – heave – heave – heave; then a long pause – then ah – ah-h-h-h-h! as it came back. Far away over the snow sounded the hooters of the ironworks. One after another they crowed and boomed, some small and far away, some near, the blowers of the collieries and the other works. Then there was silence. He mended the fire. The great breaths broke the silence – she looked just the same. He put back the blind and peered out. Still it was dark. Perhaps there was a lighter tinge. Perhaps the snow was bluer. He drew up the blind and got dressed. Then, shuddering, he drank brandy from the bottle on the washstand. The snow *was* growing blue. He heard a cart clanking down the street. Yes, it was seven o'clock, and it was coming a little bit light. He heard some people calling. The world was waking. A grey, deathly dawn crept over the snow. Yes, he could see the houses. He put out the gas. It seemed very dark. The breathing came still, but he was almost used to it. He could see her. She was just the same. He wondered if he piled heavy clothes on top of her it would make it heavier and the horrible breathing would stop. He looked at her. That was not her – not her a bit. If he piled the blanket and heavy coats on her

Suddenly the door opened, and Annie entered. She looked at him questioningly.

'Just the same,' he said calmly.

They whispered together a minute, then went downstairs to get breakfast. It was twenty to eight. Soon Annie came down.

'Isn't it awful! Doesn't she look awful!' she whispered dazed with horror.

He nodded.

'If she looks like that!' said Annie.

'Drink some tea,' he said.

They went upstairs again. Soon the neighbours came with their frightened question:

'How is she?'

It went on just the same. She lay with her cheek in her hand, her mouth fallen open, and the great, ghastly snores came and went.

At ten o'clock nurse came. She looked strange and woe-begone.

'Nurse,' cried Paul, 'she'll last like this for days?'

'She can't, Mr Morel,' said nurse, 'she can't.'

There was a silence.

'Isn't it dreadful!' wailed the nurse. 'Who would have thought she could stand it? Go down now, Mr Morel, go down.'

At last, at about eleven o'clock, he went downstairs and sat in the neighbour's house. Annie was downstairs also. Nurse and Arthur were upstairs. Paul sat with his head in his hands. Suddenly Annie came flying across the yard crying, half mad:

'Paul – Paul – she's gone!'

In a second he was back in his own house and upstairs. She lay curled up and still, with her face on her hand, and nurse was wiping her mouth. They all stood back. He kneeled down, and put his face to hers and his arms round her:

'My love – my love – oh, my love!' he whispered again and again. 'My love – oh, my love!'

Then he heard the nurse behind him, crying, saying:

'She's better, Mr Morel, she's better.'

When he took his face up from his warm, dead mother he went straight downstairs and began blacking his boots.

There was a good deal to do, letters to write, and so on. The doctor came and glanced at her, and sighed.

'Ay – poor thing!' he said, then turned away. 'Well, call at the surgery about six for the certificate.'

The father came home from work at about four o'clock. He dragged silently into the house and sat down. Minnie bustled to give him his dinner. Tired, he laid his black arms on the table. There were swede turnips for his dinner, which he liked. Paul wondered if he knew. It was some time, and nobody had spoken. At last the son said:

'You noticed the blinds were down?'

Morel looked up.

'No,' he said. 'Why – has she gone?'

'Yes.'

'When wor that?'

'About twelve this morning.'

'H'm!'

The miner sat still for a moment, then began his dinner. It was as if nothing had happened. He ate his turnips in silence. Afterwards he washed and went upstairs to dress. The door of her room was shut.

'Have you seen her?' Annie asked of him when he came down.

'No' he said.

In a little while he went out. Annie went away, and Paul called on the undertaker, the clergyman, the doctor, the registrar. It was a long business. He got back at nearly eight o'clock. The undertaker was coming soon to measure for the coffin. The house was empty except for her. He took a candle and went upstairs.

The room was cold that had been warm for so long. Flowers, bottles, plates, all sick-room litter was taken away; everything was harsh and austere. She lay raised on the bed, the sweep of the sheet from the raised feet was like a clean curve of snow, so silent. She lay like a maiden asleep. With his candle in his hand, he bent over her. She lay like a girl asleep and dreaming of her love. The mouth was a little open, as if wondering from the suffering, but her face was young, her brow clear and white as if life had never touched it. He looked again at the eyebrows, at the small, winsome nose a bit on one side. She was young again. Only the hair as it arched so beautifully from her temples was mixed with silver, and the two simple plaits that lay on her shoulders were filigree of silver and brown. She would wake up. She would lift her eyelids. She was with him still. He bent and kissed her passionately. But there was coldness against his mouth. He bit his lip with horror. Looking at her, he felt he could never, never let her go. No! He stroked the hair from her temples. That, too, was cold. He saw the mouth so dumb and wondering at the hurt.

Then he crouched on the floor, whispering to her:

'Mother, mother!'

He was still with her when the undertakers came, young men who had been to school with him. They touched her reverently, and in a quiet, businesslike fashion. They did not look at her. He watched jealously. He and Annie guarded her fiercely. They would not let anybody come to see her, and the neighbours were offended.

After a while Paul went out of the house, and played cards at a friend's. It was midnight when he got back. His father rose from the couch as he entered, saying in a plaintive way:

'I thought tha wor niver comin' lad.'

'I didn't think you'd sit up,' said Paul.

His father looked so forlorn. Morel had been a man without fear simply nothing frightened him. Paul realised with a start that he had been afraid to go to bed, alone in the house with his dead. He was sorry.

'I forgot you'd be alone, father,' he said.

'Dost want owt to eat?' asked Morel.

'No.'

'Sithee – I made thee a drop o' hot milk. Get it down thee; it's cold enough for owt.'

Paul drank it.

'I must go to Nottingham tomorrow,' he said.

After a while Morel went to bed. He hurried past the closed door, and left his own door open. Soon the son came upstairs also. He went in to kiss her good-night, as usual. It was cold and dark. He wished they had kept her fire burning. Still she dreamed her young dream. But she would be cold.

'My dear!' he whispered. 'My dear!'

And he did not kiss her, for fear she should be cold and strange to him.

It eased him she slept so beautifully. He shut her door softly, not to wake her, and went to bed.

In the morning Morel summoned his courage, hearing Annie downstairs and Paul coughing in the room across the landing. He opened her door, and went into the darkened room. He saw the white uplifted form in the twilight, but her he dared not see. Bewildered, too frightened to possess any of his faculties, he got out of the room again and left her. He never looked at her again. He had not seen her for months, because he had not dared to look. And she looked like his young wife again.

'Have you seen her?' Annie asked of him sharply after breakfast. 'Yes,' he said.

'And don't you think she looks nice?'

'Yes.'

He went out of the house soon after. And all the time he seemed to be creeping aside to avoid it.

Paul went about from place to place, doing the business of the death. He met Clara in Nottingham, and they had tea together in a cafe, when they were quite jolly again. She was infinitely relieved to find he did not take it tragically.

Later, when the relatives began to come for the funeral, the affair became public, and the children became social beings. They put themselves aside. They buried her in a furious storm of rain and wind. The wet clay glistened, all the white flowers were soaked. Annie gripped his arm and leaned forward. Down below she saw a dark corner of William's coffin. The oak box sank steadily. She was gone. The rain poured in the grave. The procession of black, with its umbrellas glistening, turned away. The cemetery was deserted under the drenching cold rain.

Paul went home and busied himself supplying the guests with drinks. His father sat in the kitchen with Mrs Morel's relatives, 'superior' people, and wept, and said what a good lass she'd been, and how he'd tried to do everything he could for her – everything. He had striven all his life to do what he could for her, and he'd nothing to reproach himself with. She was gone, but he'd done his best for her. He wiped his eyes with his white handkerchief. He'd nothing to reproach himself for, he repeated. All his life he'd done his best for her.

And that was how he tried to dismiss her. He never thought of her personally. Everything deep in him he denied. Paul hated his father for sitting sentimentalising over her. He knew he would do it in the publichouses. For the real tragedy went on in Morel in spite of himself. Sometimes, later, he came down from his afternoon sleep, white and cowering.

'I *have* been dreaming of thy mother,' he said in a small voice.

'Have you, father? When I dream of her it's always just as she was when she was well. I dream of her often, but it seems quite nice and natural, as if nothing had altered.'

But Morel crouched in front of the fire in terror.

The weeks passed half real, not much pain, not much of anything, perhaps a little relief, mostly a *nuit blanche*. Paul went restlessly from place to place. For some months, since his mother had been worse, he had not made love to Clara. She was, as it were, dumb to him, rather distant. Dawes saw her very occasionally, but the two could not get an inch across the great distance between them. The three of them were drifting forward.

Dawes mended very slowly. He was in the convalescent home at Skegness at Christmas, nearly well again. Paul went to the seaside for a few days. His father was with Annie in Sheffield. Dawes came to Paul's lodgings. His time in the home was up. The two men, between whom was such a big reserve, seemed faithful to each other. Dawes depended on Morel now. He knew Paul and Clara had practically separated.

Two days after Christmas Paul was to go back to Nottingham. The evening before he sat with Dawes smoking before the fire.

'You know Clara's coming down for the day tomorrow?' he said.

The other man glanced at him.

'Yes, you told me,' he replied.

Paul drank the remainder of his glass of whisky.

'I told the landlady your wife was coming,' he said.

'Did you?' said Dawes, shrinking, but almost leaving himself in the other's hands. He got up rather stiffly, and reached for Morel's glass.

'Let me fill you up,' he said.

Paul jumped up.

'You sit still,' he said.

But Dawes, with rather shaky hand, continued to mix the drink.

'Say when,' he said.

'Thanks!' replied the other. 'But you've no business to get up.'

'It does me good, lad,' replied Dawes. 'I begin to think I'm right again, then.'

'You are about right, you know.'

'I am, certainly I am,' said Dawes, nodding to him.

'And Len says he can get you on in Sheffield.'

Dawes glanced at him again, with dark eyes that agreed with everything the other would say, perhaps a trifle dominated by him.

'It's funny,' said Paul, 'starting again. I feel in a lot bigger mess than you.'

'In what way, lad?'

'I don't know. I don't know. It's as if I was in a tangled sort of hole, rather dark and dreary, and no road anywhere.'

'I know – I understand it,' Dawes said, nodding. 'But you'll find it'll come all right.'

He spoke caressingly.

'I suppose so,' said Paul.

Dawes knocked his pipe in a hopeless fashion.

'You've not done for yourself like I have,' he said.

Morel saw the wrist and the white hand of the other man gripping the stem of the pipe and knocking out the ash, as if he had given up.

'How old are you?' Paul asked.

'Thirty-nine,' replied Dawes, glancing at him.

Those brown eyes, full of the consciousness of failure, almost pleading for reassurance, for someone to re-establish the man in himself, to warm him, to set him up firm again, troubled Paul.

'You'll just be in your prime,' said Morel. 'You don't look as if much life had gone out of you.'

The brown eyes of the other flashed suddenly.

'It hasn't,' he said. 'The go is there.'

Paul looked up and laughed.

'We've both got plenty of life in us yet to make things fly,' he said.

The eyes of the two men met. They exchanged one look. Having recognised the stress of passion each in the other, they both drank their whisky.

'Yes, begod!' said Dawes, breathless.

There was a pause.

'And I don't see,' said Paul, 'why you shouldn't go on where you left off.'

'What – ' said Dawes, suggestively.

'Yes – fit your old home together again.'

Dawes hid his face and shook his head.

'Couldn't be done,' he said, and he looked up with an ironic smile.

'Why? Because you don't want?'

'Perhaps.'

They smoked in silence. Dawes showed his teeth as he bit his pipe stem.

'You mean you don't want her?' asked Paul.

Dawes stared up at the picture with a caustic expression on his face.

'I hardly know,' he said.

The smoke floated softly up.

'I believe she wants you,' said Paul

'Do you?' replied the other, soft, satirical, abstract.

'Yes. She never really hitched on to me – you were always there in the background. That's why she wouldn't get a divorce.'

Dawes continued to stare in a satirical fashion at the picture over the mantelpiece.

'That's how women are with me,' said Paul. 'They want me like mad, but they don't want to belong to me. And she *belonged* to you all the time. I knew.'

The triumphant male came up in Dawes. He showed his teeth more distinctly.

'Perhaps I was a fool,' he said.

'You were a big fool,' said Morel.

'But perhaps even *then* you were a bigger fool,' said Dawes.

There was a touch of triumph and malice in it.

'Do you think so?' said Paul.

They were silent for a time.

'At any rate, I'm clearing out tomorrow,' said Morel.

'I see,' answered Dawes.

Then they did not talk any more. The instinct to murder each other had returned. They almost avoided each other.

They shared the same bedroom. When they retired Dawes seemed abstract, thinking of something. He sat on the side of the bed in his shirt, looking at his legs.

'Aren't you getting cold?' asked Morel.

'I was lookin' at these legs,' replied the other.

'What' up with 'em? They look all right,' replied Paul from his bed.

'They look all right. But there' some water in 'em yct,'

'And what about it?'

'Come and look'

Paul reluctantly got out of bed and went to look at the rather handsome legs of the other man that were covered with glistening, dark gold hair.

'Look here,' said Dawes, pointing to his shin. 'Look at the water under here.'

'Where?' said Paul.

The man pressed his finger-tips. They left little dents that filled up slowly.

'It's nothing,' said Paul.

'You feel,' said Dawes.

Paul tried with his fingers. It made little dents.

'H'm!' he said.

'Rotten, isn't it?' said Dawes.

'Why? It's nothing much.'

'You're not much of a man with water in your legs.'

'I can't see as it makes any difference,' said Morel. 'I've got a weak chest.'

He returned to his own bed.

'I suppose the rest of me's all right,' said Dawes, and he put out the light.

In the morning it was raining. Morel packed his bag. The sea was grey and shaggy and dismal. He seemed to be cutting himself off from life more and more. It gave him a wicked pleasure to do it.

The two men were at the station. Clara stepped out of the train, and came along the platform, very erect and coldly composed. She wore a long coat and tweed hat. Paul shook hands with her at the barrier. Dawes was leaning against the bookstall, watching. His black overcoat was buttoned up to the chin because of the rain. He was pale, with almost a touch of nobility in his quietness. He came forward, limping slightly.

'You ought to look better than this,' she said.

'Oh, I'm all right now.'

The three stood at a loss. She kept the two men hesitating near her.

'Shall we go to the lodging straight off,' said Paul, 'or somewhere else?'

'We may as well go home,' said Dawes.

Paul walked on the outside of the pavement, then Dawes, then Clara. They made polite conversation. The sitting-room faced the sea, whose tide, grey and shaggy, hissed not far off.

Morel swung up the big armchair.

'Sit down, Jack,' he said.

'I don't want that chair,' said Dawes.

'Sit down!' Morel repeated.

Clara took off her things and laid them on the couch. She had a slight air of resentment. Lifting her hair with her fingers, she sat down, rather aloof and composed. Paul ran downstairs to speak to the landlady.

'I should think you're cold,' said Dawes to his wife. 'Come nearer to the fire.'

'Thank you, I'm quite warm,' she answered.

She looked out of the window at the rain and at the sea. 'When are you going back?' she asked.

'Well, the rooms are taken until tomorrow, so he wants me to stop.

He's going back tonight.'

'And then you're thinking of going to Sheffield?'

'Yes.'

'Are you fit to start work?

'I'm going to start.'

'You've really got a place?'

'Yes – begin on Monday.'

'You don't look fit.'

'Why don't I?'

She looked again out of the window instead of answering. 'And have you got lodgings in Sheffield?'

'Yes.'

Again she looked away out of the window. The panes were blurred with streaming rain.

'And can you manage all right?' she asked.

'I s'd think so. I s'll have to!'

They were silent when Morel returned.

'I shall go by the four-twenty,' he said as he entered.

Nobody answered.

'I wish you'd take your boots off,' he said to Clara.

'There's a pair of slippers of mine'.

'Thank you,' she said. 'They aren't wet.'

He put the slippers near her feet. She felt them there.

Morel sat down. Both the men seemed helpless, and each of them had a rather hunted look. But Dawes now carried himself quietly, seemed to yield himself, while Paul seemed to screw himself up. Clara thought she had never seen him look so small and mean. He was as if trying to get himself into the smallest possible compass. And as he went about arranging, and as he sat talking, there seemed something false about him and out of tune. Watching him unknown, she said to herself there was no stability about him. He was fine in his way, passionate, and able to give her drinks of pure life when he was in one mood. And now he looked paltry and insignificant. There was nothing stable about him. Her husband had more manly dignity. At any rate *he* did not waft about with any wind. There was something evanescent about Morel, she thought, something shifting and false. He would never make sure ground for any woman to stand on.

She despised him rather for his shrinking together, getting smaller. Her husband at least was manly, and when he was beaten gave in. But this other would never own to being beaten. He would shift round and round, prowl, get smaller. She despised him. And yet she watched him rather than Dawes, and it seemed as if their three fates lay in his hands. She hated him for it.

She seemed to understand better now about men, and what they could or would do. She was less afraid of them, more sure of herself. That they were not the small egoists she had imagined them made her more comfortable. She had learned a good deal – almost as much as she wanted to learn. Her cup had been full. It was still as full as she could carry. On the whole, she would not be sorry when he was gone.

They had dinner, and sat eating nuts and drinking by the fire. Not a serious word had been spoken. Yet Clara realised that Morel was withdrawing from the circle, leaving her the option to stay with her husband. It angered her. He was a mean fellow, after all, to take what he wanted and then give her back. She did not remember that she herself had had what she wanted, and really, at the bottom of her heart, wished to be given back.

Paul felt crumpled up and lonely. His mother had really supported his life. He had loved her; they two had, in fact, faced the world together. Now she was gone, and for ever behind him was the gap in life, the tear in the veil, through which his life seemed to drift slowly, as if he were drawn towards death. He wanted someone of their own free initiative to help him. The lesser things he began to let go from him, for fear of this big thing, the lapse towards death, following in the wake of his beloved. Clara could not stand for him to hold on to. She wanted him, but not to understand him. He felt she wanted the man on top, not the real him that was in trouble. That would be too much trouble to her; he dared not give it her. She could not cope with him. It made him ashamed. So, secretly ashamed because he was in such a mess, because his own hold on life was so unsure, because nobody held him, feeling unsubstantial, shadowy, as if he did not count for much in this concrete world, he drew himself together smaller and smaller. He did not want to die; he would not give in. But he was not afraid of death. If nobody would help, he would go on alone.

Dawes had been driven to the extremity of life, until he was afraid. He could go to the brink of death, he could lie on the edge and look in. Then, cowed, afraid, he had to crawl back, and like a beggar take what offered. There was a certain nobility in it. As Clara saw, he owned himself beaten, and he wanted to be taken back whether or not. That she could do for him.

It was three o'clock.

'I am going by the four-twenty,' said Paul again to Clara.

'Are you coming then or later?'

'I don't know,' she said.

'I'm meeting my father in Nottingham at seven-fifteen,' he said.

'Then,' she answered, 'I'll come later.'

Dawes jerked suddenly, as if he had been held on a strain. He looked out over the sea, but he saw nothing.

'There are one or two books in the corner,' said Morel. 'I've done with 'em.'

At about four o'clock he went.

'I shall see you both later,' he said, as he shook hands.

'I suppose so,' said Dawes. 'An' perhaps – one day – I s'll be able to pay you back the money as – '

'I shall come for it, you'll see,' laughed Paul. 'I s'll be on the rocks before I'm very much older.'

'Ay – well – ' said Dawes.

'Goodbye,' he said to Clara.

'Goodbye,' she said, giving him her hand. Then she glanced at him for the last time, dumb and humble.

He was gone. Dawes and his wife sat down again.

'It's a nasty day for travelling,' said the man.

'Yes,' she answered.

They talked in a desultory fashion until it grew dark. The landlady brought in the tea. Dawes drew up his chair to the table without being invited, like a husband. Then he sat humbly waiting for his cup. She served him as she would, like a wife, not consulting his wish.

After tea, as it drew near to six o'clock, he went to the window. All was dark outside. The sea was roaring.

'It's raining yet,' he said.

'Is it?' she answered.

'You won't go tonight, shall you?' he said, hesitating.

She did not answer. He waited.

'I shouldn't go in this rain,' he said.

'Do you *want* me to stay?' she asked.

His hand as he held the dark curtain trembled.

'Yes,' he said.

He remained with his back to her. She rose and went slowly to him. He let go the curtain, turned, hesitating, towards her. She stood with her hands behind her back, looking up at him in a heavy, inscrutable fashion.

'Do you want me, Baxter?' she asked.

His voice was hoarse as he answered:

'Do you want to come back to me?'

She made a moaning noise, lifted her arms, and put them round his neck, drawing him to her. He hid his face on her shoulder, holding her clasped.

'Take me back!' she whispered, ecstatic. 'Take me back, take me back!' And she put her fingers through his fine, thin dark hair, as if she were only semi-conscious. He tightened his grasp on her.

'Do you want me again?' he murmured, broken.

CHAPTER 15

Derelict

CLARA WENT with her husband to Sheffield, and Paul scarcely saw her again. Walter Morel seemed to have let all the trouble go over him, and there he was, crawling about on the mud of it, just the same. There was scarcely any bond between father and son, save that each felt he must not let the other go in any actual want. As there was no one to keep on the home, and as they could neither of them bear the emptiness of the house, Paul took lodgings in Nottingham, and Morel went to live with a friendly family in Bestwood.

Everything seemed to have gone smash for the young man. He could not paint. The picture he finished on the day of his mother's death – one that satisfied him – was the last thing he did. At work there was no Clara. When he came home he could not take up his brushes again. There was nothing left.

So he was always in the town at one place or another, drinking, knocking about with the men he knew. It really wearied him. He talked to barmaids, to almost any woman, but there was that dark, strained look in his eyes, as if he were hunting something.

Everything seemed so different, so unreal. There seemed no reason why people should go along the street, and houses pile up in the daylight. There seemed no reason why these things should occupy the space, instead of leaving it empty. His friends talked to him: he heard the sounds, and he answered. But why there should be the noise of speech he could not understand.

He was most himself when he was alone, or working hard and mechanically at the factory. In the latter case there was pure forgetfulness; when he lapsed from consciousness. But it had to come to an end. It hurt him so, that things had lost their reality. The first snowdrops came. He saw the tiny drop-pearls among the grey. They would have given him the liveliest emotion at one time. Now they were there, but they did not seem to mean anything. In a few moments they would cease to occupy that place and just the space would be, where they had been. Tall, brilliant tram-cars ran along the street at night. It seemed almost a wonder they should trouble to rustle backwards and forwards. 'Why trouble to go tilting down to Trent Bridges?' he asked of the big trams. It seemed they just as well might *not* be as be.

The realest thing was the thick darkness at night. That seemed to him whole and comprehensible and restful. He could leave himself to it. Suddenly a piece of paper started near his feet and blew along down the pavement. He stood still, rigid, with clenched fists, a flame of agony going over him. And he saw again the sick-room, his mother, her eyes. Unconsciously he had been with her, in her company. The swift hop of the paper reminded him she was gone. But he had been with her. He wanted everything to stand still, so that he could be with her again.

The days passed, the weeks. But everything seemed to have fused, gone into a conglomerated mass. He could not tell one day from another, one week from another, hardly one place from another. Nothing was distinct or distinguishable. Often he lost himself for an hour at a time, could not remember what he had done.

One evening he came home late to his lodging. The fire was burning low; everybody was in bed. He threw on some more coal, glanced at the table, and decided he wanted no supper. Then he sat down in the armchair. It was perfectly still. He did not know anything, yet he saw the dim smoke wavering up the chimney. Presently two mice came out, cautiously, nibbling the fallen crumbs. He watched them as it were from a long way off. The church clock struck two. Far away he could hear the sharp clinking of the trucks on the railway. No, it was not they that were far away. They were there in their places. But where was he himself?

The time passed. The two mice, careering wildly, scampered cheekily over his slippers. He had not moved a muscle. He did not want to move. He was not thinking of anything. It was easier so. There was no wrench of knowing anything. Then, from time to time, some other consciousness, working mechanically, flashed into sharp phrases.

'What am I doing?'

And out of the semi-intoxicated trance came the answer:

'Destroying myself.'

Then a dull, live feeling, gone in an instant, told him that it was wrong. After a while, suddenly came the question:

'Why wrong?'

Again there was no answer, but a stroke of hot stubbornness inside his chest resisted his own annihilation.

There was a sound of a heavy cart clanking down the road. Suddenly the electric light went out; there was a bruising thud in the penny-in the-slot meter. He did not stir, but sat gazing in front of him. Only the mice had scuttled, and the fire glowed red in the dark room.

Then, quite mechanically and more distinctly, the conversation began again inside him.

'She's dead. What was it all for – her struggle?'

That was his despair wanting to go after her.

'You're alive.'

'She's not.'

'She is – in you.'

Suddenly he felt tired with the burden of it.

'You've got to keep alive for her sake,' said his will in him. Something felt sulky, as if it would not rouse.

'You've got to carry forward her living, and what she had done, go on with it.'

But he did not want to. He wanted to give up.

'But you can go on with your painting,' said the will in him. 'Or else you can beget children. They both carry on her effort.'

'Painting is not living.'

'Then live.'

'Marry whom?' came the sulky question.

'As best you can.'

'Miriam?'

But he did not trust that.

He rose suddenly, went straight to bed. When he got inside his bedroom and closed the door, he stood with clenched fists.

'Mater, my dear – ' he began, with the whole force of his soul. Then he stopped. He would not say it. He would not admit that he wanted to die, to have done. He would not own that life had beaten him, or that death had beaten him.

Going straight to bed, he slept at once, abandoning himself to the sleep.

So the weeks went on. Always alone, his soul oscillated, first on the side of death, then on the side of life, doggedly. The real agony was that he had nowhere to go, nothing to do, nothing to say, and *was* nothing himself. Sometimes he ran down the streets as if he were mad: sometimes he was mad; things weren't there, things were there. It made him pant. Sometimes he stood before the bar of the public-house where he had called for a drink. Everything suddenly stood back away from him. He saw the face of the barmaid, the gabbling drinkers, his own glass on the slopped, mahogany board, in the distance. There was something between him and them. He could not get into touch. He did not want them; he did not want his drink. Turning abruptly, he went out. On the threshold he stood and looked at the lighted street. But he was not of it or in it. Something separated him. Everything went on there below those lamps, shut away from him. He could not get at them. He felt he couldn't touch the lamp-posts, not if he reached. Where could he go? There was nowhere to go, neither back into the inn, or forward anywhere. He felt stifled. There was nowhere for him. The stress grew inside him; he felt he should smash.

'I mustn't,' he said; and, turning blindly, he went in and drank. Sometimes the drink did him good – sometimes it made him worse. He ran down the road. For ever restless, he went here, there, everywhere. He determined to work. But when he had made six strokes, he loathed the pencil violently, got up, and went away, hurried off to a club where he could play cards or billiards, to a place where he could flirt with a barmaid who was no more to him than the brass pump-handle she drew.

He was very thin and lantern-jawed. He dared not meet his own eyes in the mirror; he never looked at himself. He wanted to get away from himself, but there was nothing to get hold of. In despair he thought of Miriam. Perhaps – perhaps –?

Then, happening to go into the Unitarian Church one Sunday evening, when they stood up to sing the second hymn he saw her before him. The light glistened on her lower lip as she sang. She looked as if she had got something, at any rate: some hope in heaven, if not in earth. Her comfort and her life seemed in the after-world. A warm, strong feeling for her came up. She seemed to yearn, as she sang, for the mystery and comfort. He put his hope in her. He longed for the sermon to be over, to speak to her.

The throng carried her out just before him. He could nearly touch her. She did not know he was there. He saw the brown humble nape of her neck under its black curls. He would leave himself to her. She was better and bigger than he. He would depend on her.

She went wandering, in her blind way, through the little throngs of people outside the church. She always looked so lost and out of place among people. He went forward and put his hand on her arm. She started violently. Her great brown eyes dilated in fear, then went questioning at the sight of him. He shrank slightly from her.

'I didn't know – ' she faltered.

'Nor I,' he said.

He looked away. His sudden, flaring hope sank again.

'What are you doing in town?' he asked.

'I'm staying at Cousin Anne's.'

'Ha! For long?'

'No; only till tomorrow.'

'Must you go straight home?'

She looked at him, then hid her face under her hat-brim.

'No,' she said – 'no; it's not necessary.'

He turned away; and she went with him. They threaded through the throng of church-people. The organ was still sounding in St Mary's. Dark figures came through the lighted doors; people were coming down the steps. The large coloured windows glowed up in the night. The church was like a great lantern suspended. They went down Hollow Stone, and he took the car for the Bridges.

'You will just have supper with me,' he said; 'then I'll bring you back.'

'Very well,' she replied, low and husky.

They scarcely spoke while they were on the car. The Trent ran dark and full under the bridge. Away towards Colwich all was black night. He lived down Holme Road, on the naked edge of the town, facing across the river meadows towards Sneinton Hermitage and the steep scarp of Colwick Wood. The floods were out. The silent water and the darkness spread away on their left. Almost afraid, they hurried along by the houses.

Supper was laid. He swung the curtain over the window. There was a bowl of freesias and scarlet anemones on the table.

She bent to them. Still touching them with her finger-tips, she looked up at him, saying:

'Aren't they beautiful?'

'Yes,' he said. 'What will you drink – coffee?'

'I should like it,' she said.

'Then excuse me a moment.'

He went out to the kitchen.

Miriam took off her things and looked round. It was a bare, severe room. Her photo, Clara's, Annie's, were on the wall. She looked on the drawing-board to see what, he was doing. There were only a few meaningless lines. She looked to see what books he was reading. Evidently just an ordinary novel. The letters in the rack she saw were from Annie, Arthur, and from some man or other she did not know. Everything he had touched, everything that was in the least personal to him, she examined with lingering absorption. He had been gone from her for so long, she wanted to rediscover him, his position, what he was now. But there was not much in the room to help her. It only made her feel rather sad, it was so hard and comfortless.

She was curiously examining a sketch-book when he returned with the coffee.

'There's nothing new in it,' he said, 'and nothing very interesting.'

He put down the tray, and went to look over her shoulder. She turned the pages slowly, intent on examining everything.

'H'm!' he said, as she paused at a sketch. 'I'd forgotten that. It's not bad, is it?'

'No,' she said. 'I don't quite understand it.'

He took the book from her and went through it. Again he made a curious sound of surprise and pleasure.

'There's some not bad stuff in there,' he said.

'Not at all bad,' she answered gravely.

He felt again her interest in his work. Or was it for himself? Why was she always most interested in him as he appeared in his work?

They sat down to supper.

'By the way,' he said, 'didn't I hear something about your earning your own living?'

'Yes,' she replied, bowing her dark head over her cup.

'And what of it?'

'I'm merely going to the farming college at Broughton for three months, and I shall probably be kept on as a teacher there.'

'I say – that sounds all right for you! You always wanted to, be independent.'

'Yes.'

'Why didn't you tell me?'

'I only knew last week.'

'But I heard a month ago,' he said.

'Yes; but nothing was settled then.'

'I should have thought,' he said, 'you'd have told me you were trying.'

She ate her food in the deliberate, constrained way, almost as if she recoiled a little from doing anything so publicly, that he knew so well.

'I suppose you're glad,' he said.

'Very glad.'

'Yes – it will be something.'

He was rather disappointed.

'I think it will be a great deal,' she said, almost haughtily, resentfully.

He laughed shortly.

'Why do you think it won't?' she asked.

'Oh, I don't think it won't be a great deal. Only you'll find earning your own living isn't everything.'

'No,' she said, swallowing with difficulty; 'I don't suppose it is.'

'I suppose work *can* be nearly everything to a man,' he said, 'though it isn't to me. But a woman only works with a part of herself. The real and vital part is covered up.'

'But a man can give *all* himself to a work?' she asked.

'Yes, practically.'

'And a woman only the unimportant part of herself?'

'That's it.'

She looked up at him, and her eyes dilated with anger.

'Then,' she said, 'if it's true, it's a great shame.'

'It is. But I don't know everything,' he answered.

After supper they drew up to the fire. He swung her a chair facing him, and they sat down. She was wearing a dress of dark claret colour, that suited her dark complexion and her large features. Still, the curls were fine and free, but her face was much older, the brown throat much thinner. She seemed old to him, older than Clara. Her bloom of youth had quickly gone. A sort of stiffness, almost of woodenness, had come upon her. She meditated a little while, then looked at him.

'And how are things with you?' she asked.

'About all right,' he answered.

She looked at him, waiting.

'Nay,' she said, very low.

Her brown, nervous hands were clasped over her knee. They had still the lack of confidence or repose, the almost hysterical look. He winced as he saw them. Then he laughed mirthlessly. She put her fingers between her lips. His slim, black, tortured body lay quite still in the chair. She suddenly took her finger from her mouth and looked at him.

'And you have broken off with Clara?'

'Yes.'

His body lay like an abandoned thing, strewn in the chair.

'You know,' she said, 'I think we ought to be married.'

He opened his eyes for the first time since many months and attended to her with respect.

'Why?' he said.

'See,' she said, 'how you waste yourself! You might be ill, you might die, and I never know – be no more then than if I had never known you.'

'And if we married?' he asked.

'At any rate, I could prevent you wasting yourself and being a prey to other women – like – like Clara.'

'A prey?' he repeated, smiling.

She bowed her head in silence. He lay feeling his despair come up again.

'I'm not sure,' he said slowly, 'that marriage would be much good.'

'I only think of you,' she replied.

'I know you do. But – you love me so much, you want to put me in your pocket. And I should die there smothered.'

She bent her head, put her finger between her lips, while the bitterness surged up in her heart.

'And what will you do otherwise?' she asked.

'I don't know – go on, I suppose. Perhaps I shall soon go abroad.'

The despairing doggedness in his tone made her go on her knees on the rug before the fire, very near to him. There she crouched as if she were crushed by something, and could not raise her head. His hands lay quite inert on the arms of his chair. She was aware of them. She felt that now he lay at her mercy. If she could rise, take him, put her aims round him, and say, 'You are mine,' then he would leave himself to her. But dare she? She could easily sacrifice herself. But dare she assert herself? She was aware of his dark-clothed, slender body, that seemed one stroke of life, sprawled in the chair close to her. But no; she dared not put her arms round it, take it up, and say, 'It is mine, this body. Leave it to me.' And she wanted to. It called to all her woman's instinct. But she crouched, and dared not. She was afraid he would not let her. She was afraid it was too much. It lay there, his body, abandoned. She knew she ought to take it up and claim it, and claim every right to it. But – could she do it? Her impotence before him, before the strong demand of some unknown thing in him, was her extremity. Her hands fluttered; she half lifted her head. Her eyes, shuddering, appealing, gone almost distracted, pleaded to him suddenly. His heart caught with pity. He took her hands, drew her to him, and comforted her.

'Will you have me, to marry me?' he said very low.

Oh, why did not he take her? Her very soul belonged to him. Why would he not take what was his? She had borne so long the cruelty of belonging to him and not being claimed by him. Now he was straining her again. It was too much for her. She drew back her head, held his face between her hands, and looked him in the eyes. No, he was hard. He wanted something else. She pleaded to him with all her love not to make it *her* choice. She could not cope with it, with him, she knew not with what. But it strained her till she felt she would break.

'Do you want it?' she asked, very gravely.

'Not much,' he replied, with pain.

She turned her face aside; then, raising herself with dignity, she took his head to her bosom, and rocked him softly. She was not to have him, then! So she could comfort him. She put her fingers through his hair. For her, the anguished sweetness of self-sacrifice. For him, the hate and misery of another failure. He could not bear it – that breast which was warm and which cradled him without taking the burden of him. So much he wanted to rest on her that the feint of rest only tortured him. He drew away.

'And without marriage we can do nothing?' he asked.

His mouth was lifted from his teeth with pain. She put her little finger between her lips.

'No,' she said, low and like the toll of a bell. 'No, I think not.'

It was the end then between them. She could not take him and relieve him of the responsibility of himself. She could only sacrifice herself to him – sacrifice herself every day, gladly. And that he did not want. He wanted her to hold him and say, with joy and authority: 'Stop all this restlessness and beating against death.

You are mine for a mate.' She had not the strength. Or was it a mate she wanted? or did she want a Christ in him?

He felt, in leaving her, he was defrauding her of life. But he knew that, in staying, stifling the inner, desperate man, he was denying his own life. And he did not hope to give life to her by denying his own.

She sat very quiet. He lit a cigarette. The smoke went up from it, wavering. He was thinking of his mother, and had forgotten Miriam. She suddenly looked at him. Her bitterness came surging up. Her sacrifice, then, was useless. He lay there aloof, careless about her. Suddenly she saw again his lack of religion, his restless instability. He would destroy himself like a perverse child. Well, then, he would!

'I think I must go,' she said softly.

By her tone he knew she was despising him. He rose quietly.

'I'll come along with you,' he answered.

She stood before the mirror pinning on her hat. How bitter, how unutterably bitter, it made her that he rejected her sacrifice! Life ahead looked dead, as if the glow were gone out. She bowed her face over the flowers – the freesias so sweet and spring-like, the scarlet anemones flaunting over the table. It was like him to have those flowers.

He moved about the room with a certain sureness of touch, swift and relentless and quiet. She knew she could not cope with him. He would escape like a weasel out of her hands. Yet without him her life would trail on lifeless. Brooding, she touched the flowers.

'Have them!' he said; and he took them out of the jar, dripping as they were, and went quickly into the kitchen. She waited for him, took the flowers, and they went out together, he talking, she feeling dead.

She was going from him now. In her misery she leaned against him as they sat on the car. He was unresponsive. Where would he go? What would be the end of him? She could not bear it, the vacant feeling where he should be. He was so foolish, so wasteful, never at peace with himself. And now where would he go? And what did he care that he wasted her? He had no religion; it was all for the moment's attraction that he cared, nothing else, nothing deeper. Well, she would wait and see how it turned out with him. When he had had enough he would give in and come to her.

He shook hands and left her at the door of her cousin's house. When he turned away he felt the last hold for him had gone. The town, as he sat upon the car, stretched away over the bay of railway, a level fume of lights. Beyond the town the country, little smouldering spots for more towns – the sea – the night – on and on! And he had no place in it! Whatever spot he stood on, there he stood alone. From his breast, from his mouth, sprang the endless space, and it was there behind him, everywhere. The people hurrying along the streets offered no obstruction to the void in which he found himself. They were small shadows whose footsteps and voices could be heard, but in each of them the same night, the same silence. He got off the car. In the country all was dead still. Little stars shone high up; little stars spread far away in the floodwaters, a firmament below. Everywhere the vastness and terror of the immense night which is roused and stirred for a brief while by the day but which returns, and will remain at last eternal, holding everything in its silence and its living gloom. There was no Time, only Space. Who could say his mother had lived and did not live? She had been in one place, and was in another; that was all. And his soul could not leave her, wherever she was. Now she was gone abroad into the night, and he was with her still. They were together. But yet there was his body, his chest, that leaned against the stile, his hands on the wooden bar. They seemed something. Where was he? – one tiny upright speck of flesh, less than an ear of wheat lost in the field. He could not bear it. On every side the immense dark silence seemed pressing him, so tiny a spark, into extinction, and yet, almost nothing, he could not be extinct. Night, in which everything was lost, went reaching out, beyond stars and sun. Stars and sun, a few bright grains, went spinning round for terror, and holding each other in embrace, there in a darkness that outpassed them all, and left them tiny and daunted. So much, and himself, infinitesimal, at the core a nothingness, and yet not nothing.

'Mother!' he whimpered – 'mother!'

She was the only thing that held him up, himself, amid all this. And she was gone, intermingled herself. He wanted her to touch him, have him alongside with her.

But no, he would not give in. Turning sharply, he walked towards the city's gold phosphorescence. His fists were shut, his mouth set fast. He would not take that direction, to the darkness, to follow her. He walked towards the faintly humming, glowing town, quickly.

THE END

WOMEN IN LOVE

CONTENTS

CONTENTS

CHAPTER 1

Sisters

URSULA AND GUDRUN Brangwen sat one morning in the window-bay of their father's house in Beldover, working and talking. Ursula was stitching a piece of brightly-coloured embroidery, and Gudrun was drawing upon a board which she held on her knee. They were mostly silent, talking as their thoughts strayed through their minds.

'Ursula,' said Gudrun, 'don't you *really want* to get married?' Ursula laid her embroidery in her lap and looked up. Her face was calm and considerate.

'I don't know,' she replied. 'It depends how you mean.'

Gudrun was slightly taken aback. She watched her sister for some moments.

'Well,' she said, ironically, 'it usually means one thing! But don't you think anyhow, you'd be – 'she darkened slightly – 'in a better position than you are in now.'

A shadow came over Ursula's face.

'I might,' she said. 'But I'm not sure.'

Again Gudrun paused, slightly irritated. She wanted to be quite definite.

'You don't think one needs the *experience* of having been married?' she asked.

'Do you think it need *be* an experience?' replied Ursula.

'Bound to be, in some way or other,' said Gudrun, coolly. 'Possibly undesirable, but bound to be an experience of some sort.'

'Not really,' said Ursula. 'More likely to be the end of experience.'

Gudrun sat very still, to attend to this.

'Of course,' she said, 'there's *that* to consider.' This brought the conversation to a close. Gudrun, almost angrily, took up her rubber and began to rub out part of her drawing. Ursula stitched absorbedly.

'You wouldn't consider a good offer?' asked Gudrun.

'I think I've rejected several,' said Ursula.

'*Really!*' Gudrun flushed dark – 'But anything really worth while?

Have you *really?*'

'A thousand a year, and an awfully nice man. I liked him awfully,' said Ursula.

'Really! But weren't you fearfully tempted?'

'In the abstract but not in the concrete,' said Ursula. 'When it comes to the point, one isn't even tempted – oh, if I were tempted, I'd marry like a shot. I'm only tempted *not* to.' The faces of both sisters suddenly lit up with amusement.

'Isn't it an amazing thing,' cried Gudrun, 'how strong the temptation is, not to!' They both laughed, looking at each other. In their hearts they were frightened.

There was a long pause, whilst Ursula stitched and Gudrun went on with her sketch. The sisters were women, Ursula twenty-six, and Gudrun twenty-five. But both had the remote, virgin look of modem girls, sisters of Artemis rather than of Hebe.* Gudrun was very beautiful, passive, soft-skinned, soft-limbed. She wore a dress of dark-blue silky stuff, with ruches of blue and green linen lace in the neck and sleeves; and she had emerald-green stockings. Her look of confidence and diffidence contrasted with Ursula's sensitive expectancy. The provincial people, intimidated by Gudrun's perfect sang-froid and exclusive bareness of manner, said of her: 'She is a smart woman.' She had just come back from London, where she had spent several years, working at an art-school, as a student, and living a studio life.

'I was hoping now for a man to come along,' Gudrun said, suddenly catching her underlip between her teeth, and making a strange grimace, half sly smiling, half anguish. Ursula was afraid.

'So you have come home, expecting him here?' she laughed.

* Virtuous daughters of Greek god Zeus.

'Oh my dear,' cried Gudrun, strident, 'I wouldn't go out of my way to look for him. But if there did happen to come along a highly attractive individual of sufficient means – well – ' she tailed off ironically. Then she looked searchingly at Ursula, as if to probe her. 'Don't you find yourself getting bored?' she asked of her sister. 'Don't you find, that things fail to materialise? *Nothing materialises!* Everything withers in the bud.'

'What withers in the bud?' asked Ursula.

'Oh, everything – oneself – things in general.' There was a pause, whilst each sister vaguely considered her fate.

'It does frighten one,' said Ursula, and again there was a pause. 'But do you hope to get anywhere by just marrying?'

'It seems to be the inevitable next step,' said Gudrun. Ursula pondered this, with a little bitterness. She was a class mistress herself, in Willey Green Grammar School, as she had been for some years.

'I know,' she said, 'it seems like that when one thinks in the abstract. But really imagine it: imagine any man one knows, imagine him coming home to one every evening, and saying "Hello" and giving one a kiss – '

There was a blank pause.

'Yes,' said Gudrun, in a narrowed voice. 'It's just impossible. The man makes it impossible.'

'Of course there's children – ' said Ursula doubtfully.

Gudrun's face hardened.

'Do you *really* want children, Ursula?' she asked coldly. A dazzled, baffled look came on Ursula's face.

'One feels it is still beyond one,' she said.

'*Do* you feel like that?' asked Gudrun. 'I get no feeling whatever from the thought of bearing children.'

Gudrun looked at Ursula with a masklike, expressionless face. Ursula knitted her brows.

'Perhaps it isn't genuine,' she faltered. 'Perhaps one doesn't really want them, in one's soul – only superficially.' A hardness came over Gudrun's face. She did not want to be too definite.

'When one thinks of other people's children – ' said Ursula.

Again Gudrun looked at her sister, almost hostile.

'Exactly,' she said, to close the conversation.

The two sisters worked on in silence, Ursula having always that strange brightness of an essential flame that is caught, meshed, contravened. She lived a good deal by herself, to herself, working, passing on from day to day, and always thinking, trying to lay hold on life, to grasp it in her own understanding. Her active living was suspended, but underneath, in the darkness, something was coming to pass. If only she could break through the last integuments! She seemed to try and put her hands out, like an infant in the womb, and she could not, not yet. Still she had a strange prescience, an intimation of something yet to come.

She laid down her work and looked at her sister. She thought Gudrun so *charming,* so infinitely charming, in her softness and her fine, exquisite richness of texture and delicacy of line. There was a certain playfulness about her too, such a piquancy or ironic suggestion, such an untouched reserve. Ursula admired her with all her soul.

'Why did you come home, Prune?' she asked.

Gudrun knew she was being admired. She sat back from her drawing and looked at Ursula, from under her finely-curved lashes.

'Why did I come back, Ursula?' she repeated. 'I have asked myself a thousand times.'

'And don't you know?'

'Yes, I think I do. I think my coming back home was just *reculer pour mieux sauter.'**

And she looked with a long, slow look of knowledge at Ursula.

'I know!' cried Ursula, looking slightly dazzled and falsified, and as if she did *not* know. 'But where can one jump to?'

---

* To jump back after a retreat.

'Oh, it doesn't matter,' said Gudrun, somewhat superbly. 'If one jumps over the edge, one is bound to land somewhere.'

'But isn't it very risky?' asked Ursula.

A slow mocking smile dawned on Gudrun's face.

'Ah!' she said laughing. 'What is it all but words!' And so again she closed the conversation. But Ursula was still brooding.

'And how do you find home, now you have come back to it?' she asked.

Gudrun paused for some moments, coldly, before answering. Then, in a cold truthful voice, she said:

'I find myself completely out of it.'

'And father?'

Gudrun looked at Ursula, almost with resentment, as if brought to bay.

'I haven't thought about him: I've refrained,' she said coldly.

'Yes,' wavered Ursula; and the conversation was really at an end. The sisters found themselves confronted by a void, a terrifying chasm, as if they had looked over the edge.

They worked on in silence for some time, Gudrun's cheek was flushed with repressed emotion. She resented its having been called into being.

'Shall we go out and look at that wedding?' she asked at length, in a voice that was too casual.

'Yes!' cried Ursula, too eagerly, throwing aside her sewing and leaping up, as if to escape something, thus betraying the tension of the situation and causing a friction of dislike to go over Gudrun's nerves.

As she went upstairs, Ursula was aware of the house, of her home round about her. And she loathed it, the sordid, too-familiar place! She was afraid at the depth of her feeling against the home, the milieu, the whole atmosphere and condition of this obsolete life. Her feeling frightened her.

The two girls were soon walking swiftly down the main road of Beldover, a wide street, part shops, part dwelling-houses, utterly formless and sordid, without poverty. Gudrun, new from her life in Chelsea and Sussex, shrank cruelly from this amorphous ugliness of a small colliery town in the Midlands. Yet forward she went, through the whole sordid gamut of pettiness, the long amorphous, gritty street. She was exposed to every stare, she passed on through a stretch of torment. It was strange that she should have chosen to come back and test the full effect of this shapeless, barren ugliness upon herself. Why had she wanted to submit herself to it, did she still want to submit herself to it, the insufferable torture of these ugly, meaningless people, this defaced countryside? She felt like a beetle toiling in the dust. She was filled with repulsion.

They turned off the main road, past a black patch of common-garden, where sooty cabbage stumps stood shameless. No one thought to be ashamed. No one was ashamed of it all.

'It is like a country in an underworld,' said Gudrun. 'The colliers bring it above-ground with them, shovel it up. Ursula, it's marvellous, it's really marvellous – it's really wonderful, another world. The people are all ghouls, and everything is ghostly. Everything is a ghoulish replica of the real world, a replica, a ghoul, all soiled, everything sordid. It's like being mad, Ursula.'

The sisters were crossing a black path through a dark, soiled field. On the left was a large landscape, a valley with collieries, and opposite hills with cornfields and woods, all blackened with distance, as if seen through a veil of crape. White and black smoke rose up in steady columns, magic within the dark air. Near at hand came the long rows of dwellings, approaching curved up the hill-slope, in straight lines along the brow of the hill. They were of darkened red brick, brittle, with dark slate roofs. The path on which the sisters walked was black, trodden-in by the feet of the recurrent colliers, and bounded from the field by iron fences; the stile that led again into the road was rubbed shiny by the moleskins of the passing miners. Now the two girls were going between some rows of dwellings, of the poorer sort. Women, their arms folded over their coarse aprons, standing gossiping at the end of their block, stared after the Brangwen sisters with that long, unwearying stare of aborigines; children called out names.

Gudrun went on her way half dazed. If this were human life, if these were human beings, living in a complete world, then what was her own world, outside? She was aware of her grass-green stockings, her large grass-green velour hat, her full soft coat, of a strong blue colour. And she felt as if she were treading in the air, quite unstable, her heart was contracted, as if at any minute she might be precipitated to the ground. She was afraid.

She clung to Ursula, who, through long usage was inured to this violation of a dark, uncreated, hostile world. But all the time her heart was crying, as if in the midst of some ordeal: 'I want to go back, I want to go away, I want not to know it, not to know that this exists.' Yet she must go forward.

Ursula could feel her suffering.

'You hate this, don't you?' she asked.

'It bewilders me,' stammered Gudrun.

'You won't stay long,' replied Ursula.

And Gudrun went along, grasping at release.

They drew away from the colliery region, over the curve of the hill, into the purer country of the other side, towards Willey Green. Still the faint glamour of blackness persisted over the fields and the wooded hills, and seemed darkly to gleam in the air. It was a spring day, chill, with snatches of sunshine. Yellow celandines showed out from the hedge-bottoms, and in the cottage gardens of Willey Green, currant-bushes were breaking into leaf, and little flowers were coming white on the grey alyssum that hung over the stone walls.

Turning, they passed down the high-road, that went between high banks towards the church. There, in the lowest bend of the road, low under the trees, stood a little group of expectant people, waiting to see the wedding. The daughter of the chief mine-owner of the district, Thomas Crich, was getting married to a naval officer.

'Let us go back,' said Gudrun, swerving away. 'There are all those people.'

And she hung wavering in the road.

'Never mind them,' said Ursula, 'they're all right. They all know me, they don't matter.'

'But must we go through them?' asked Gudrun.

'They're quite all right, really,' said Ursula, going forward. And together the two sisters approached the group of uneasy, watchful common people. They were chiefly women, colliers' wives of the more shiftless sort. They had watchful, underworld faces.

The two sisters held themselves tense, and went straight towards the gate. The women made way for them, but barely sufficient, as if grudging to yield ground. The sisters passed in silence through the stone gateway and up the steps, on the red carpet, a policeman estimating their progress.

'What price the stockings!' said a voice at the back of Gudrun. A sudden fierce anger swept over the girl, violent and murderous. She would have liked them all annihilated, cleared away, so that the world was left clear for her. How she hated walking up the churchyard path, along the red carpet, continuing in motion, in their sight.

'I won't go into the church,' she said suddenly, with such final decision that Ursula immediately halted, turned round, and branched off up a small side path which led to the little private gate of the Grammar School, whose grounds adjoined those of the church.

Just inside the gate of the school shrubbery, outside the churchyard, Ursula sat down for a moment on the low stone wall under the laurel bushes, to rest. Behind her, the large red building of the school rose up peacefully, the windows all open for the holiday. Over the shrubs, before her, were the pale roofs and tower of the old church. The sisters were hidden by the foliage.

Gudrun sat down in silence. Her mouth was shut close, her face averted. She was regretting bitterly that she had ever come back. Ursula looked at her, and thought how amazingly beautiful she was, flushed with discomfiture. But she caused a constraint over Ursula's nature, a certain weariness. Ursula wished to be alone, freed from the tightness, the enclosure of Gudrun's presence.

'Are we going to stay here?' asked Gudrun.

'I was only resting a minute,' said Ursula, getting up as if rebuked. 'We will stand in the corner by the fives-court, we shall see everything from there.'

For the moment, the sunshine fell brightly into the churchyard, there was a vague scent of sap and of spring, perhaps of violets from off the graves. Some white daisies were out, bright as angels. In the air, the unfolding leaves of a copper-beech were blood-red.

Punctually at eleven o'clock, the carriages began to arrive. There was a stir in the crowd at the gate, a concentration as a carriage drove up, wedding guests were mounting up the steps and passing along the red carpet to the church. They were all gay and excited because the sun was shining.

Gudrun watched them closely, with objective curiosity. She saw each one as a complete figure, like a character in a book, or a subject in a picture, or a marionette in a theatre, a finished creation. She loved to recognise their various characteristics, to place them in their true light, give them their own surroundings, settle them for ever as they passed before her along the path to the church. She knew them, they were finished, sealed and stamped and finished with, for her. There was none that had anything unknown, unresolved, until the Criches themselves began to appear. Then her interest was piqued. Here was something not quite so preconcluded.

There came the mother, Mrs Crich, with her eldest son Gerald. She was a queer unkempt figure, in spite of the attempts that had obviously been made to bring her into line for the day. Her face was pale, yellowish, with a clear, transparent skin, she leaned forward rather, her features were strongly marked, handsome, with a tense, unseeing, predative look. Her colourless hair was untidy, wisps floating down on to her sac coat of dark blue silk, from under her blue silk hat. She looked like a woman with a monomania, furtive almost, but heavily proud.

Her son was of a fair, sun-tanned type, rather above middle height, well-made, and almost exaggeratedly well-dressed. But about him also was the strange, guarded look, the unconscious glisten, as if he did not belong to the same creation as the people about him. Gudrun lighted on him at once. There was something northern about him that magnetised her. In his clear northern flesh and his fair hair was a glisten like sunshine refracted through crystals of ice. And he looked so new, unbroached, pure as an arctic thing. Perhaps he was thirty years old, perhaps more. His gleaming beauty, maleness, like a young, good-humoured, smiling wolf, did not blind her to the significant, sinister stillness in his bearing, the lurking danger of his unsubdued temper. 'His totem is the wolf,' she repeated to herself. 'His mother is an old, unbroken wolf.' And then she experienced a keen paroxysm, a transport, as if she had made some incredible discovery, known to nobody else on earth. A strange transport took possession of her, all her veins were in a paroxysm of violent sensation. 'Good God!' she exclaimed to herself, 'what is this?' And then, a moment after, she was saying assuredly, 'I shall know more of that man.' She was tortured with desire to see him again, a nostalgia, a necessity to see him again, to make sure it was not all a mistake, that she was not deluding herself, that she really felt this strange and overwhelming sensation on his account, this knowledge of him in her essence, this powerful apprehension of him. 'Am I *really* singled out for him in some way, is there really some pale gold, arctic light that envelopes only us two?' she asked herself. And she could not believe it, she remained in a muse, scarcely conscious of what was going on around.

The bridesmaids were here, and yet the bridegroom had not come. Ursula wondered if something was amiss, and if the wedding would yet all go wrong. She felt troubled, as if it rested upon her. The chief bridesmaids had arrived. Ursula watched them come up the steps. One of them she knew, a tall, slow, reluctant woman with a weight of fair hair and a pale, long face. This was Hermione Roddice, a friend of the Criches. Now she came along, with her head held up, balancing an enormous flat hat of pale yellow velvet, on which were streaks of ostrich feathers, natural and grey. She drifted forward as if scarcely conscious, her long blanched face lifted up, not to see the world. She was rich. She wore a dress of silky, frail velvet, of pale yellow colour, and she carried a lot of small rose-coloured cyclamens. Her shoes and stockings were of brownish grey, like the feathers on her hat, her hair was heavy, she drifted along with a peculiar fixity of the hips, a strange unwilling motion. She was impressive, in her lovely pale-yellow and brownish-rose, yet macabre, something repulsive. People were silent when she passed, impressed, roused, wanting to jeer, yet for some reason silenced. Her long, pale face, that she carried lifted up, somewhat in the Rossetti* fashion, seemed almost drugged, as if a strange mass of thoughts coiled in the darkness within her; and she was never allowed to escape.

Ursula watched her with fascination. She knew her a little. She was the most remarkable woman in the Midlands. Her father was a Derbyshire Baronet of the old school, she was a woman of – the new school, full of intellectuality, and heavy, nerve-worn with consciousness. She was passionately interested in reform, her soul was given up to the public cause. But she was a man's woman, it was the manly world that held her.

She had various intimacies of mind and soul with various men of capacity. Ursula knew, among these men, only Rupert Birkin, who was one of the school inspectors of the county. But Gudrun had met others, in London. Moving with her artist friends in different kinds of society, Gudrun had already come to know a good many people of repute and standing. She had met Hermione twice, but they did not take to each other. It would be queer to meet again down here in the Midlands, where their social standing was so diverse, after they had known each other on terms of equality in the houses of sundry acquaintances in town. For Gudrun had been a social success, and had her friends among the slack aristocracy that keeps touch with the arts.

*British painter and poet (1828-82).

Hermione knew herself to be well-dressed; she knew herself to be the social equal, if not far the superior, of anyone she was likely to meet in Willey Green. She knew she was accepted in the world of culture and of intellect. She was a *Kulturträger,* a medium for the culture of ideas. With all that was highest, whether in society or in thought or in public action, or even in art, she was at one, she moved among the foremost, at home with them. No one could put her down, no one could make mock of her, because she stood among the first, and those that were against her were below her, either in rank, or in wealth, or in high association of thought and progress and Understanding. So, she was invulnerable. All her life, she had sought to make herself invulnerable, unassailable, beyond reach of the world's judgment.

And yet her soul was tortured, exposed. Even walking up the path to the church, confident as she was that in every respect she stood beyond all vulgar judgment, knowing perfectly that her appearance was complete and perfect, according to the first standards, yet she suffered a torture, under her confidence and her pride, feeling herself exposed to wounds and to mockery and to despite. She always felt vulnerable, vulnerable, there was always a secret chink in her armour. She did not know herself what it was. It was a lack of robust self, she had no natural sufficiency, there was a terrible void, a lack, a deficiency of being within her.

And she wanted someone to close up this deficiency, to close it up for ever. She craved for Rupert Birkin. When he was there, she felt complete, she was sufficient, whole. For the rest of time she was established on the sand, built over a chasm, and, in spite of all her vanity and securities, any common maid-servant of positive, robust temper could fling her down this bottomless pit of insufficiency, by the slightest movement of jeering or contempt. And all the while the pensive, tortured woman piled up her own defences of aesthetic knowledge, and culture, and world-visions, and disinterestedness. Yet she could never stop up the terrible gap of insufficiency.

If only Birkin would form a close and abiding connection with her, she would be safe during this fretful voyage of life. He could make her sound and triumphant, triumphant over the very angels of heaven. If only he would do it! But she was tortured with fear, with misgiving. She made herself beautiful, she strove so hard to come to that degree of beauty and advantage, when he should be convinced. But always there was a deficiency.

He was perverse too. He fought her off, he always fought her off. The more she strove to bring him to her, the more he battled her back. And they had been lovers now, for years. Oh, it was so wearying, so aching; she was so tired. But still she believed in herself. She knew he was trying to leave her. She knew he was trying to break away from her finally, to be free. But still she believed in her strength to keep him, she believed in her own higher knowledge. His own knowledge was high, she was the central touchstone of truth. She only needed his conjunction with her.

And this, this conjunction with her, which was his highest fulfilment also, with the perverseness of a wilful child he wanted to deny. With the wilfulness of an obstinate child, he wanted to break the holy connection that was between them.

He would be at this wedding; he was to be groom's man. He would be in the church, waiting. He would know when she came. She shuddered with nervous apprehension and desire as she went through the church-door. He would be there, surely he would see how beautiful her dress was, surely he would see how she had made herself beautiful for him. He would understand, he would be able to see how she was made for him, the first, how she was, for him, the highest. Surely at last he would be able to accept his highest fate, he would not deny her.

In a little convulsion of too-tired yearning, she entered the church and looked slowly along her cheeks for him, her slender body convulsed with agitation. As best man, he would be standing beside the altar. She looked slowly, deferring in her certainty.

And then, he was not there. A terrible storm came over her, as if she were drowning. She was possessed by a devastating hopelessness. And she approached mechanically to the altar. Never had she known such a pang of utter and final hopelessness. It was beyond death, so utterly null, desert.

The bridegroom and the groom's man had not yet come. There was a growing consternation outside. Ursula felt almost responsible. She could not bear it that the bride should arrive, and no groom. The wedding must not be a fiasco, it must not.

But here was the bride's carriage, adorned with ribbons and cockades. Gaily the grey horses curvetted to their destination at the church-gate, a laughter in the whole movement. Here was the quick of all laughter and pleasure. The door of the carriage was thrown open, to let out the very blossom of the day. The people on the roadway murmured faintly with the discontented murmuring of a crowd.

The father stepped out first into the air of the morning, like a shadow. He was a tall, thin, careworn man, with a thin black beard that was touched with grey. He waited at the door of the carriage patiently, self-obliterated.

In the opening of the doorway was a shower of fine foliage and flowers, a whiteness of satin and lace, and a sound of a gay voice saying:

'How do I get out?'

A ripple of satisfaction ran through the expectant people. They pressed near to receive her, looking with zest at the stooping blond head with its flower buds, and at the delicate, white, tentative foot that was reaching down to the step of the carriage. There was a sudden foaming rush, and the bride like a sudden surf-rush, floating all white beside her father in the morning shadow of trees, her veil flowing with laughter.

'That's done it!' she said.

She put her hand on the arm of her care-worn, sallow father, and frothing her light draperies, proceeded over the eternal red carpet. Her father, mute and yellowish, his black beard making him look more careworn, mounted the steps stiffly, as if his spirit were absent; but the laughing mist of the bride went along with him undiminished.

And no bridegroom had arrived! It was intolerable for her. Ursula, her heart strained with anxiety, was watching the hill beyond; the white, descending road, that should give sight of him. There was a carriage. It was running. It had just come into sight. Yes, it was he. Ursula turned towards the bride and the people, and, from her place of vantage, gave an inarticulate cry. She wanted to warn them that he was coming: But her cry was inarticulate and inaudible, and she flushed deeply, between her desire and her wincing confusion.

The carriage rattled down the hill, and drew near. There was a shout from the people. The bride, who had just reached the top of the steps, turned round gaily to see what was the commotion. She saw a confusion among the people, a cab pulling up, and her lover dropping out of the carriage, and dodging among the horses and into the crowd.

'Tibs! Tibs!' she cried in her sudden, mocking excitement, standing high on the path in the sunlight and waving her bouquet. He, dodging with his hat in his hand, had not heard.

'Tibs!' she cried again, looking down to him.

He glanced up, unaware, and saw the bride and her father standing on the path above him. A queer, startled look went over his face. He hesitated for a moment. Then he gathered himself together for a leap, to overtake her.

'Ah-h-h!' came her strange, intaken cry, as, on the reflex, she started, turned and fled, scudding with an unthinkable swift beating of her white feet and fraying of her white garments, towards the church. Like a hound the young man was after her, leaping the steps and swinging past her father, his supple haunches working like those of a hound that bears down on the quarry.

'Ay, after her!' cried the vulgar women below, carried suddenly into the sport.

She, her flowers shaken from her like froth, was steadying herself to turn the angle of the church. She glanced behind, and with a wild cry of laughter and challenge, veered, poised, and was gone beyond the grey stone buttress. In another instant the bridegroom, bent forward as he ran, had caught the angle of the silent stone with his hand, and had swung himself out of sight, his supple, strong loins vanishing in pursuit.

Instantly cries and exclamations of excitement burst from the crowd at the gate. And then Ursula noticed again the dark, rather stooping figure of Mr Crich, waiting suspended on the path, watching with expressionless face the flight to the church. It was over, and he turned round to look behind him, at the figure of Rupert Birkin, who at once came forward and joined him.

'We'll bring up the rear,' said Birkin, a faint smile on his face.

'Ay!' replied the father laconically. And the two men turned together up the path.

Birkin was as thin as Mr Crich, pale and ill-looking. His figure was narrow but nicely made. He went with a slight trail of one foot, which came only from self-consciousness. Although he was dressed correctly for his part, yet there was an innate incongruity which caused a slight ridiculousness in his appearance. His nature was clever and separate, he did not fit at all in the conventional occasion. Yet he subordinated himself to the common idea, travestied himself.

He affected to be quite ordinary, perfectly and marvellously commonplace. And he did it so well, taking the tone of his surroundings, adjusting himself quickly to his interlocutor and his circumstance, that he achieved a verisimilitude of ordinary commonplaceness that usually propitiated his onlookers for the moment, disarmed them from attacking his singleness.

Now he spoke quite easily and pleasantly to Mr Crich, as they walked along the path; he played with situations like a man on a tightrope: but always on a tight-rope, pretending nothing but ease.

'I'm sorry we are so late,' he was saying. 'We couldn't find a buttonhook, so it took us a long time to button our boots. But you were to the moment.'

'We are usually to time,' said Mr Crich.

'And I'm always late,' said Birkin. 'But today I was *really* punctual, only accidentally not so. I'm sorry.'

The two men were gone, there was nothing more to see, for the time. Ursula was left thinking about Birkin. He piqued her, attracted her, and annoyed her.

She wanted to know him more. She had spoken with him once or twice, but only in his official capacity as inspector. She thought he seemed to acknowledge some kinship between her and him, a natural, tacit understanding, a using of the same language. But there had been no time for the understanding to develop. And something kept her from him, as well as attracted her to him. There was a certain hostility, a hidden ultimate reserve in him, cold and inaccessible.

Yet she wanted to know him.

'What do you think of Rupert Birkin?' she asked, a little reluctantly, of Gudrun. She did not want to discuss him.

'What do I think of Rupert Birkin?' repeated Gudrun. 'I think he's attractive – decidedly attractive. What I can't stand about him is his way with other people – his way of treating any little fool as if she were his greatest consideration. One feels so awfully sold, oneself.'

'Why does he do it?' said Ursula.

'Because he has no real critical faculty – of people, at all events,' said

Gudrun. 'I tell you, he treats any little fool as he treats me or you – and it's such an insult.'

'Oh, it is,' said Ursula. 'One must discriminate.'

'One *must* discriminate,' repeated Gudrun. 'But he's a wonderful chap, in other respects – a marvellous personality. But you can't trust him.'

'Yes, said Ursula vaguely. She was always forced to assent to Gudrun's pronouncements, even when she was not in accord altogether.

The sisters sat silent, waiting for the wedding party to come out. Gudrun was impatient of talk. She wanted to think about Gerald Crich. She wanted to see if the strong feeling she had got from him was real. She wanted to have herself ready.

Inside the church, the wedding was going on. Hermione Roddice was thinking only of Birkin. He stood near her. She seemed to gravitate physically towards him. She wanted to stand touching him. She could hardly be sure he was near her, if she did not touch him. Yet she stood subjected through the wedding service.

She had suffered so bitterly when he did not come, that still she was dazed. Still she was gnawed as by a neuralgia, tormented by his potential absence from her. She had awaited him in a faint delirium of nervous torture. As she stood bearing herself pensively, the rapt look on her face, that seemed spiritual, like the angels, but which came from torture, gave her a certain poignancy that tore his heart with pity. He saw her bowed head, her rapt face, the face of an almost demoniacal ecstatic. Feeling him looking, she lifted her face and sought his eyes, her own beautiful grey eyes flaring him a great signal. But he avoided her look, she sank her head in torment and shame, the gnawing at her heart going on. And he too was tortured with shame, and ultimate dislike, and with acute pity for her, because he did not want to meet her eyes, he did not want to receive her flare of recognition.

The bride and bridegroom were married, the party went into the vestry. Hermione crowded involuntarily up against Birkin, to touch him. And he endured it.

Outside, Gudrun and Ursula listened for their father's playing on the organ. He would enjoy playing a wedding march. Now the married pair were coming! The bells were ringing, making the air shake. Ursula wondered if the trees and the flowers could feel the vibration, and what they thought of it, this strange motion in the air. The bride was quite demure on the – arm of the bridegroom, who stared up into the sky before him, shutting and opening his eyes unconsciously, as if he were neither here nor there. He looked rather comical, blinking and trying to be in the scene, when emotionally he was violated by his exposure to a crowd. He looked a typical naval officer, manly, and up to his duty.

Birkin came with Hermione. She had a rapt, triumphant look, like the fallen angels restored, yet still subtly demoniacal, now she held Birkin by the arm. And he was expressionless, neutralised, possessed by her as if it were his fate, without question.

Gerald Crich came, fair, good-looking, healthy, with a great reserve of energy. He was erect and complete, there was a strange stealth glistening through his amiable, almost happy appearance. Gudrun rose sharply and went away. She could not bear it. She wanted to be alone, to know this strange, sharp inoculation that had changed the whole temper of her blood.

◆━■━◆━━━━━━━━◆━■━◆

CHAPTER 2

Shortlands

THE BRANGWENS went home to Beldover, the wedding-party gathered at Shortlands, the Criches' home. It was a long, low old house, a sort of manor farm, that spread along the top of a slope just beyond the narrow little lake of Willey Water. Shortlands looked across a sloping meadow that might be a park, because of the large, solitary trees that stood here and there, across the water of the narrow lake, at the wooded hill that successfully hid the colliery valley beyond, but did not quite hide the rising smoke. Nevertheless, the scene was rural and picturesque, very peaceful, and the house had a charm of its own.

It was crowded now with the family and the wedding guests. The father, who was not well, withdrew to rest. Gerald was host. He stood in the homely entrance hall, friendly and easy, attending to the men. He seemed to take pleasure in his social functions, he smiled, and was abundant in hospitality.

The women wandered about in a little confusion, chased hither and thither by the three married daughters of the house. All the while there could be heard the characteristic, imperious voice of one Crich woman or another calling 'Helen, come here a minute,' 'Marjory, I want you here.' 'Oh, I say, Mrs Witham – ' There was a great rustling of skirts, swift glimpses of smartly-dressed women, a child danced through the hall and back again, a maidservant came and went hurriedly.

Meanwhile the men stood in calm little groups, chatting, smoking, pretending to pay no heed to the rustling animation of the women's world. But they could not really talk, because of the glassy ravel of women's excited, cold laughter and running voices. They waited, uneasy, suspended, rather bored. But Gerald remained as if genial and happy, unaware that he was waiting or unoccupied, knowing himself the very pivot of the occasion.

Suddenly Mrs Crich came noiselessly into the room, peering about with her strong, clear face. She was still wearing her hat, and her sac coat of blue silk.

'What is it, mother?' said Gerald.

'Nothing, nothing!' she answered vaguely. And she went straight towards Birkin, who was talking to a Crich brother-in-law.

'How do you do, Mr Birkin,' she said, in her low voice, that seemed to take no count of her guests. She held out her hand to him.

'Oh Mrs Crich,' replied Birkin, in his readily-changing voice, 'I couldn't come to you before.'

'I don't know half the people here,' she said, in her low voice. Her son-in-law moved uneasily away.

'And you don't like strangers?' laughed Birkin. 'I myself can never see why one should take account of people, just because they happen to be in the room with one: why *should* I know they are there?'

'Why indeed, why indeed!' said Mrs Crich, in her low, tense voice. 'Except that they *are* there. *I* don't know people whom I find in the house. The children introduce them to me – "Mother, this is Mr So-and-so." I am no further. What has Mr So-and-so to do with his own name? – and what have I to do with either him or his name?'

She looked up at Birkin. She startled him. He was flattered too that she came to talk to him, for she took hardly any notice of anybody. He looked down at her tense clear face, with its heavy features, but he was afraid to look into her heavy-seeing blue eyes. He noticed instead how her hair looped in slack, slovenly strands over her rather beautiful ears, which were not quite clean. Neither was her neck perfectly clean. Even in that he seemed to belong to her, rather than to the rest of the company; though, he thought to himself, he was always well washed, at any rate at the neck and ears.

He smiled faintly, thinking these things. Yet he was tense, feeling that he and the elderly, estranged woman were conferring together like traitors, like enemies within the camp of the other people. He resembled a deer, that throws one ear back upon the trail behind, and one ear forward, to know what is ahead.

'People don't really matter,' he said, rather unwilling to continue.

The mother looked up at him with sudden, dark interrogation, as if doubting his sincerity.

'How do you mean, *matter?*' she asked sharply.

'Not many people are anything at all,' he answered, forced to go deeper than he wanted to. 'They jingle and giggle. It would be much better if they were just wiped out. Essentially, they don't exist, they aren't there.'

She watched him steadily while he spoke.

'But we didn't imagine them,' she said sharply.

'There's nothing to imagine, that's why they don't exist.'

'Well,' she said, 'I would hardly go as far as that. There they are, whether they exist or no. It doesn't rest with me to decide on their existence. I only know that I can't be expected to take count of them all. You can't expect me to know them, just because they happen to be there. As far as *I* go they might as well not be there.'

'Exactly,' he replied.

'Mightn't they?' she asked again.

'Just as well,' he repeated. And there was a little pause.

'Except that they *are* there, and that's a nuisance,' she said. 'There are my sons-in-law,' she went on, in a sort of monologue. 'Now Laura's got married, there's another. And I really don't know John from James yet. They come up to me and call me mother. I know what they will say – "how are you, mother?" I ought to say, "I am not your mother, in any sense." But what is the use? There they are. I have had children of my own. I suppose I know them from another woman's children.'

'One would suppose so,' he said.

She looked at him, somewhat surprised, forgetting perhaps that she was talking to him. And she lost her thread.

She looked round the room, vaguely. Birkin could not guess what she was looking for, nor what she was thinking. Evidently she noticed her sons.

'Are my children all there?' she asked him abruptly.

He laughed, startled, afraid perhaps.

'I scarcely know them, except Gerald,' he replied.

'Gerald!' she exclaimed. 'He's the most wanting of them all. You'd never think it, to look at him now, would you?'

'No,' said Birkin.

The mother looked across at her eldest son, stared at him heavily for some time.

'Ay,' she said, in an incomprehensible monosyllable, that sounded profoundly cynical. Birkin felt afraid, as if he dared not realise. And Mrs Crich moved away, forgetting him. But she returned on her traces.

'I should like him to have a friend,' she said. 'He has never had a friend.'

Birkin looked down into her eyes, which were blue, and watching heavily. He could not understand them. 'Am I my brother's keeper?' he said to himself, almost flippantly.

Then he remembered, with a slight shock, that that was Cain's cry. And Gerald was Cain,* if anybody. Not that he was Cain, either, although he had slain his brother. There was such a thing as pure accident, and the consequences did not attach to one, even though one had killed one's brother in such wise. Gerald as a boy had accidentally killed his brother. What then? Why seek to draw a brand and a curse across the life that had caused the accident? A man can live by accident, and die by accident. Or can he not? Is every man's life subject to pure accident, is it only the race, the genus, the species, that has a universal reference? Or is this not true, is there no such thing as pure accident? Has *everything* that happens a universal significance? Has it? Birkin, pondering as he stood there, had forgotten Mrs Crich, as she had forgotten him.

He did not believe that there was any such thing as accident. It all hung together, in the deepest sense.

Just as he had decided this, one of the Crich daughters came up, saying:

'Won't you come and take your hat off, mother dear? We shall be sitting down to eat in a minute, and it's a formal occasion, darling, isn't it?' She drew her arm through her mother's, and they went away. Birkin immediately went to talk to the nearest man.

The gong sounded for the luncheon. The men looked up, but no move was made to the dining-room. The women of the house seemed not to feel that the sound had meaning for them. Five minutes passed by. The elderly manservant, Crowther, appeared in the doorway exasperatedly. He looked with appeal at Gerald. The latter took up a large, curved conch shell, that lay on a shelf, and without reference to anybody, blew a shattering blast. It was a strange rousing noise, that made the heart beat. The summons was almost magical. Everybody came running, as if at a signal. And then the crowd in one impulse moved to the dining-room.

* The first child of Adam and Eve who killed his sibling Able. (Genesis: 4.)

Gerald waited a moment, for his sister to play hostess. He knew his mother would pay no attention to her duties. But his sister merely crowded to her seat. Therefore the young man, slightly too dictatorial, directed the guests to their places.

There was a moment's lull, as everybody looked at the *hors d'oeuvres* that were being handed round. And out of this lull, a girl of thirteen or fourteen, with her long hair down her back, said in a calm, self-possessed voice:

'Gerald, you forget father, when you make that unearthly noise.'

'Do I?' he answered. And then, to the company, 'Father is lying down, he is not quite well.'

'How is he, really?' called one of the married daughters, peeping round the immense wedding cake that towered up in the middle of the table shedding its artificial flowers.

'He has no pain, but he feels tired,' replied Winifred, the girl with the hair down her back.

The wine was filled, and everybody was talking boisterously. At the far end of the table sat the mother, with her loosely-looped hair. She had Birkin for a neighbour. Sometimes she glanced fiercely down the rows of faces, bending forwards and staring unceremoniously. And she would say in a low voice to Birkin:

'Who is that young man?'

'I don't know,' Birkin answered discreetly.

'Have I seen him before?' she asked.

'I don't think so. *I* haven't,' he replied. And she was satisfied. Her eyes closed wearily, a peace came over her face, she looked like a queen in repose. Then she started, a little social smile came on her face, for a moment she looked the pleasant hostess. For a moment she bent graciously, as if everyone were welcome and delightful. And then immediately the shadow came back, a sullen, eagle look was on her face, she glanced from under her brows like a sinister creature at bay, hating them all.

'Mother,' called Diana, a handsome girl a little older than Winifred, 'I may have wine, mayn't I?'

'Yes, you may have wine,' replied the mother automatically, for she was perfectly indifferent to the question.

And Diana beckoned to the footman to fill her glass.

'Gerald shouldn't forbid me,' she said calmly, to the company at large.

'All right, Di,' said her brother amiably. And she glanced challenge at him as she drank from her glass.

There was a strange freedom, that almost amounted to anarchy, in the house. It was rather a resistance to authority, than liberty. Gerald had some command, by mere force of personality, not because of any granted position. There was a quality in his voice, amiable but dominant, that cowed the others, who were all younger than he.

Hermione was having a discussion with the bridegroom about nationality.

'No,' she said, 'I think that the appeal to patriotism is a mistake. It is like one house of business rivalling another house of business.'

'Well you can hardly say that, can you?' exclaimed Gerald, who had a real *passion* for discussion. 'You couldn't call a race a business concern, could you? – and nationality roughly corresponds to race, I think. I think it is *meant* to.'

There was a moment's pause. Gerald and Hermione were always strangely but politely and evenly inimical.

'*Do* you think race corresponds with nationality?' she asked musingly, with expressionless indecision.

Birkin knew she was waiting for him to participate. And dutifully he spoke up.

'I think Gerald is right – race is the essential element in nationality, in Europe at least,' he said.

Again Hermione paused, as if to allow this statement to cool. Then she said with strange assumption of authority:

'Yes, but even so, is the patriotic appeal an appeal to the racial instinct? Is it not rather an appeal to the proprietory instinct, the *commercial* instinct? And isn't this what we mean by nationality?'

'Probably,' said Birkin, who felt that such a discussion was out of place and out of time.

But Gerald was now on the scent of argument.

'A race may have its commercial aspect,' he said. 'In fact it must. It is like a family. You *must* make provision. And to make provision you have got to strive against other families, other nations. I don't see why you shouldn't.'

Again Hermione made a pause, domineering and cold, before she replied: 'Yes, I think it is always wrong to provoke a spirit of rivalry. It makes bad blood. And bad blood accumulates.'

'But you can't do away with the spirit of emulation altogether?' said Gerald. 'It is one of the necessary incentives to production and improvement.'

'Yes,' came Hermione's sauntering response. 'I think you can do away with it.'

'I must say,' said Birkin, 'I detest the spirit of emulation.' Hermione was biting a piece of bread, pulling it from between her teeth with her fingers, in a slow, slightly derisive movement. She turned to Birkin.

'You do hate it, yes,' she said, intimate and gratified.

'Detest it,' he repeated.

'Yes,' she murmured, assured and satisfied.

'But,' Gerald insisted, 'you don't allow one man to take away his neighbour's living, so why should you allow one nation to take away the living from another nation?'

There was a long slow murmur from Hermione before she broke into speech, saying with a laconic indifference:

'It is not always a question of possessions, is it? It is not all a question of goods?'

Gerald was nettled by this implication of vulgar materialism.

'Yes, more or less,' he retorted. 'If I go and take a man's hat from off his head, that hat becomes a symbol of that man's liberty. When he fights me for his hat, he is fighting me for his liberty.'

Hermione was nonplussed.

'Yes,' she said, irritated. 'But that way of arguing by imaginary instances is not supposed to be genuine, is it? A man does *not* come and take my hat from off my head, does he?'

'Only because the law prevents him,' said Gerald.

'Not only,' said Birkin. 'Ninety-nine men out of a hundred don't want my hat.'

'That's a matter of opinion,' said Gerald.

'Or the hat,' laughed the bridegroom.

'And if he does want my hat, such as it is,' said Birkin, 'why, surely it is open to me to decide, which is a greater loss to me, my hat, or my liberty as a free and indifferent man. If I am compelled to offer fight, I lose the latter. It is a question which is worth more to me, my pleasant liberty of conduct, or my hat.'

'Yes,' said Hermione, watching Birkin strangely. 'Yes.'

'But would you let somebody come and snatch your hat off your head?' the bride asked of Hermione.

The face of the tall straight woman turned slowly and as if drugged to this new speaker.

'No,' she replied, in a low inhuman tone, that seemed to contain a chuckle. 'No, I shouldn't let anybody take my hat off my head.'

'How would you prevent it?' asked Gerald.

'I don't know,' replied Hermione slowly. 'Probably I should kill him.'

There was a strange chuckle in her tone, a dangerous and convincing humour in her bearing.

'Of course,' said Gerald, 'I can see Rupert's point. It is a question to him whether his hat or his peace of mind is more important.'

'Peace of body,' said Birkin.

'Well, as you like there,' replied Gerald. 'But how are you going to decide this for a nation?'

'Heaven preserve me,' laughed Birkin.

'Yes, but suppose you have to?' Gerald persisted.

'Then it is the same. If the national crown-piece is an old hat, then the thieving gent may have it.'

'But *can* the national or racial hat be an old hat?' insisted Gerald.

'Pretty well bound to be, I believe,' said Birkin.

'I'm not so sure,' said Gerald.

'I don't agree, Rupert,' said Hermione.

'All right,' said Birkin.

'I'm all for the old national hat,' laughed Gerald.

'And a fool you look in it,' cried Diana, his pert sister who was just in her teens.

'Oh, we're quite out of our depths with these old hats,' cried Laura Crich. 'Dry up now, Gerald. We're going to drink toasts. Let us drink toasts. Toasts – glasses, glasses – now then, toasts! Speech! Speech!'

Birkin, thinking about race or national death, watched his glass being filled with champagne. The bubbles broke at the rim, the man withdrew, and feeling a sudden thirst at the sight of the fresh wine, Birkin drank up his glass. A queer little tension in the room roused him. He felt a sharp constraint.

'Did I do it by accident, or on purpose?' he asked himself. And he decided that, according to the vulgar phrase, he had done it 'accidentally on purpose.' He looked round at the hired footman. And the hired footman came, with a silent step of cold servant-like disapprobation. Birkin decided that he detested toasts, and footmen, and assemblies, and mankind altogether, in most of its aspects. Then he rose to make a speech. But he was somehow disgusted.

At length it was over, the meal. Several men strolled out into the garden. There was a lawn, and flower-beds, and at the boundary an iron fence shutting off the little field or park. The view was pleasant; a highroad curving round the edge of a low lake, under the trees. In the spring air, the water gleamed and the opposite woods were purplish with new life. Charming Jersey cattle came to the fence, breathing hoarsely from their velvet muzzles at the human beings, expecting perhaps a crust.

Birkin leaned on the fence. A cow was breathing wet hotness on his hand.

'Pretty cattle, very pretty,' said Marshall, one of the brothers-in-law. 'They give the best milk you can have.'

'Yes,' said Birkin.

'Eh, my little beauty, eh, my beauty!' said Marshall, in a queer high falsetto voice, that caused the other man to have convulsions of laughter in his stomach.

'Who won the race, Lupton?' he called to the bridegroom, to hide the fact that he was laughing.

The bridegroom took his cigar from his mouth.

'The race?' he exclaimed. Then a rather thin smile came over his face. He did not want to say anything about the flight to the church door. 'We got there together. At least she touched first, but I had my hand on her shoulder.'

'What's this?' asked Gerald.

Birkin told him about the race of the bride and the bridegroom.

'H'm!' said Gerald, in disapproval. 'What made you late then?'

'Lupton would talk about the immortality of the soul,' said Birkin, 'and then he hadn't got a button-hook.'

'Oh God!' cried Marshall. 'The immortality of the soul on your wedding day! Hadn't you got anything better to occupy your mind?'

'What's wrong with it?' asked the bridegroom, a clean-shaven naval man, flushing sensitively.

'Sounds as if you were going to be executed instead of married. *The immortality of the soul!*' repeated the brother-in-law, with most killing emphasis.

But he fell quite flat.

'And what did you decide?' asked Gerald, at once pricking up his ears at the thought of a metaphysical discussion.

'You don't want a soul today, my boy,' said Marshall. 'It'd be in your road.'

'Christ! Marshall, go and talk to somebody else,' cried Gerald, with sudden impatience.

'By God, I'm willing,' said Marshall, in a temper. 'Too much bloody soul and talk altogether – '

He withdrew in a dudgeon, Gerald staring after him with angry eyes, that grew gradually calm and amiable as the stoutly-built form of the other man passed into the distance.

'There's one thing, Lupton,' said Gerald, turning suddenly to the bridegroom. 'Laura won't have brought such a fool into the family as Lottie did.'

'Comfort yourself with that,' laughed Birkin.

'I take no notice of them,' laughed the bridegroom.

'What about this race then – who began it?' Gerald asked.

'We were late. Laura was at the top of the churchyard steps when our cab came up. She saw Lupton bolting towards her. And she fled. But why do you look so cross? Does it hurt your sense of the family dignity?'

'It does, rather,' said Gerald. 'If you're doing a thing, do it properly, and if you're not going to do it properly, leave it alone.'

'Very nice aphorism,' said Birkin.

'Don't you agree?' asked Gerald.

'Quite,' said Birkin. 'Only it bores me rather, when you become aphoristic.'

'Damn you, Rupert, you want all the aphorisms your own way,' said Gerald.

'No. I want them out of the way, and you're always shoving them in it.'

Gerald smiled grimly at this humorism. Then he made a little gesture of dismissal, with his eyebrows.

'You don't believe in having any standard of behaviour at all, do you?' he challenged Birkin, censoriously.

'Standard – no. I hate standards. But they're necessary for the common ruck. Anybody who is anything can just be himself and do as he likes.'

'But what do you mean by being himself?' said Gerald. 'Is that an aphorism or a cliché?'

'I mean just doing what you want to do. I think it was perfect good form in Laura to bolt from Lupton to the church door. It was almost a masterpiece in good form. It's the hardest thing in the world to act spontaneously on one's impulses – and it's the only really gentlemanly thing to do – provided you're fit to do it.'

'You don't expect me to take you seriously, do you?' asked Gerald.

'Yes, Gerald, you're one of the very few people I do expect that of.'

'Then I'm afraid I can't come up to your expectations here, at any rate. You think people should just do as they like.'

'I think they always do. But I should like them to like the purely individual thing in themselves, which makes them act in singleness. And they only like to do the collective thing.'

'And I,' said Gerald grimly, 'Shouldn't like to be in a world of people who acted individually and spontaneously, as you call it. We should have everybody cutting everybody else's throat in five minutes.'

'That means *you* would like to be cutting everybody's throat,' said Birkin.

'How does that follow?' asked Gerald crossly.

'No man,' said Birkin, 'cuts another man's throat unless he wants to cut it, and unless the other man wants it cutting. This is a complete truth. It takes two people to make a murder: a murderer and a murderee. And a murderee is a man who is murderable. And a man who is murderable is a man who in a profound if hidden lust desires to be murdered.'

'Sometimes you talk pure nonsense,' said Gerald to Birkin. 'As a matter of fact, none of us wants our throat cut, and most other people would like to cut it for us – some time or other – '

'It's a nasty view of things, Gerald,' said Birkin, 'and no wonder you are afraid of yourself and your own unhappiness.'

'How am I afraid of myself?' said Gerald; 'and I don't think I am unhappy.'

'You seem to have a lurking desire to have your gizzard slit, and imagine every man has his knife up his sleeve for you,' Birkin said.

'How do you make that out?' said Gerald.

'From you,' said Birkin.

There was a pause of strange enmity between the two men, that was very near to love. It was always the same between them; always their talk brought them into a deadly nearness of contact, a strange, perilous intimacy which was either hate or love, or both. They parted with apparent unconcern, as if their going apart were a trivial occurrence. And they really kept it to the level of trivial occurrence. Yet the heart of each burned from the other. They burned with each other, inwardly. This they would never admit. They intended to keep their relationship a casual free-and-easy friendship, they were not going to be so unmanly and unnatural as to allow any heart-burning between them. They had not the faintest belief in deep relationship between men and men, and their disbelief prevented any development of their powerful but suppressed friendliness.

CHAPTER 3

Classroom

A SCHOOL-DAY was drawing to a close. In the classroom the last lesson was in progress, peaceful and still. It was elementary botany. The desks were littered with catkins, hazel and willow, which the children had been sketching. But the sky had come overdark, as the end of the afternoon approached: there was scarcely light to draw any more. Ursula stood in front of the class, leading the children by questions to understand the structure and the meaning of the catkins.

A heavy, copper-coloured beam of light came in at the west window, gilding the outlines of the children's heads with red gold, and falling on the wall opposite in a rich, ruddy illumination. Ursula, however, was scarcely conscious of it. She was busy, the end of the day was here, the work went on as a peaceful tide that is at flood, hushed to retire.

This day had gone by like so many more, in an activity that was like a trance. At the end there was a little haste, to finish what was in hand. She was pressing the children with questions, so that they should know all they were to know, by the time the gong went. She stood in shadow in front of the class, with catkins in her hand, and she leaned towards the children, absorbed in the passion of instruction.

She heard, but did not notice the click of the door. Suddenly she started. She saw, in the shaft of ruddy, copper-coloured light near her, the face of a man. It was gleaming like fire, watching her, waiting for her to be aware. It startled her terribly. She thought she was going to faint. All her suppressed, subconscious fear sprang into being, with anguish.

'Did I startle you?' said Birkin, shaking hands with her. 'I thought you had heard me come in.'

'No,' she faltered, scarcely able to speak. He laughed, saying he was sorry. She wondered why it amused him.

'It is so dark,' he said. 'Shall we have the light?'

And moving aside, he switched on the strong electric lights. The classroom was distinct and hard, a strange place after the soft dim magic that filled it before he came. Birkin turned curiously to look at Ursula. Her eyes were round and wondering, bewildered, her mouth quivered slightly. She looked like one who is suddenly wakened. There was a living, tender beauty, like a tender light of dawn shining from her face. He looked at her with a new pleasure, feeling gay in his heart, irresponsible.

'You are doing catkins?' he asked, picking up a piece of hazel from a scholar's desk in front of him. 'Are they as far out as this? I hadn't noticed them this year.'

He looked absorbedly at the tassel of hazel in his hand.

'The red ones too!' he said, looking at the flickers of crimson that came from the female bud.

Then he went in among the desks, to see the scholars' books. Ursula watched his intent progress. There was a stillness in his motion that hushed the activities of her heart. She seemed to be standing aside in arrested silence, watching him move in another, concentrated world. His presence was so quiet, almost like a vacancy in the corporate air.

Suddenly he lifted his face to her, and her heart quickened at the flicker of his voice.

'Give them some crayons, won't you?' he said, 'So that they can make the gynaecious flowers red, and the androgynous yellow. I'd chalk them in plain, chalk in nothing else, merely the red and the yellow. Outline scarcely matters in this case. There is just the one fact to emphasise.'

'I haven't any crayons,' said Ursula.

'There will be some somewhere – red and yellow, that's all you want.'

Ursula sent out a boy on a quest.

'It will make the books untidy,' she said to Birkin, flushing deeply.

'Not very,' he said. 'You must mark in these things obviously. It's the fact you want to emphasise, not the subjective impression to record. What's the fact? – red little spiky stigmas of the female flower, dangling yellow male catkin, yellow pollen flying from one to the other. Make a pictorial record of the fact, as a child does when drawing a face – two eyes, one nose, mouth with teeth – so – 'And he drew a figure on the blackboard.

At that moment another vision was seen through the glass panels of the door. It was Hermione Roddice. Birkin went and opened to her.

'I saw your car,' she said to him. 'Do you mind my coming to find you? I wanted to see you when you were on duty.'

She looked at him for a long time, intimate and playful, then she gave a short little laugh. And then only she turned to Ursula, who, with all the class, had been watching the little scene between the lovers.

'How do you do, Miss Brangwen,' sang Hermione, in her low, odd, singing fashion, that sounded almost as if she were poking fun. 'Do you mind my coming in?'

Her grey, almost sardonic eyes rested all the while on Ursula, as if summing her up.

'Oh no,' said Ursula.

'Are you *sure?*' repeated Hermione, with complete sang froid, and an odd, half-bullying effrontery.

'Oh no, I like it awfully,' laughed Ursula, a little bit excited and bewildered, because Hermione seemed to be compelling her, coming very close to her, as if intimate with her; and yet, how could she be intimate?

This was the answer Hermione wanted. She turned satisfied to Birkin.

'What are you doing?' she sang, in her casual, inquisitive fashion.

'Catkins,' he replied.

'Really!' she said. 'And what do you learn about them?' She spoke all the while in a mocking, half teasing fashion, as if making game of the whole business. She picked up a twig of the catkin, piqued by Birkin's attention to it.

She was a strange figure in the classroom, wearing a large, old cloak of greenish cloth, on which was a raised pattern of dull gold. The high collar, and the inside of the cloak, was lined with dark fur. Beneath she had a dress of fine lavender-coloured cloth, trimmed with fur, and her hat was close-fitting, made of fur and of the dull, green-and-gold figured stuff. She was tall and strange, she looked as if she had come out of some new, bizarre picture.

'Do you know the little red ovary flowers, that produce the nuts? Have you ever noticed them?' he asked her. And he came close and pointed them out to her, on the sprig she held.

'No,' she replied. 'What are they?'

'Those are the 'little seed-producing flowers, and the long catkins, they only produce pollen, to fertilise them.'

'Do they, do they!' repeated Hermione, looking closely.

'From those little red bits, the nuts come; if they receive pollen from the long danglers.'

'Little red flames, little red flames,' murmured Hermione to herself. And she remained for some moments looking only at the small buds out of which the red flickers of the stigma issued.

'Aren't they beautiful? I think they're so beautiful,' she said, moving close to Birkin, and pointing to the red filaments with her long, white finger.

'Had you never noticed them before?' he asked.

'No, never before,' she replied.

'And now you will always see them,' he said.

'Now I shall always see them,' she repeated. 'Thank you so much for showing me. I think they're so beautiful – little red flames – '

Her absorption was strange, almost rhapsodic. Both Birkin and Ursula were suspended. The little red pistillate flowers had some strange, almost mystic-passionate attraction for her.

The lesson was finished, the books were put away, at last the class was dismissed. And still Hermione sat at the table, with her chin in her hand, her elbow on the table, her long white face pushed up, not attending to anything. Birkin had gone to the window, and was looking from the brilliantly-lighted room on to the grey, colourless outside, where rain was noiselessly falling. Ursula put away her things in the cupboard.

At length Hermione rose and came near to her.

'Your sister has come home?' she said.

'Yes,' said Ursula.

'And does she like being back in Beldover?'

'No,' said Ursula.

'No, I wonder she can bear it. It takes all my strength, to bear the ugliness of this district, when I stay here. Won't you come and see me? Won't you come with your sister to stay at Breadalby for a few days? – do – '

'Thank you very much,' said Ursula.

'Then I will write to you,' said Hermione. 'You think your sister will come? I should be so glad. I think she is wonderful. I think some of her work is really wonderful. I have two water-wagtails, carved in wood, and painted – perhaps you have seen it?'

'No,' said Ursula.

'I think it is perfectly wonderful – like a flash of instinct.'

'Her little carvings *are* strange,' said Ursula.

'Perfectly beautiful – full of primitive passion – '

'Isn't it queer that she always likes little things? – she must always work small things, that one can put between one's hands, birds and tiny animals. She likes to look through the wrong end of the opera glasses, and see the world that way – why is it, do you think?'

Hermione looked down at Ursula with that long, detached scrutinising gaze that excited the younger woman.

'Yes,' said Hermione at length. 'It is curious. The little things seem to be more subtle to her – '

'But they aren't, are they? A mouse isn't any more subtle than a lion, is it?'

Again Hermione looked down at Ursula with that long scrutiny, as if she were following some train of thought of her own, and barely attending to the other's speech.

'I don't know,' she replied.

'Rupert, Rupert,' she sang mildly, calling him to her. He approached in silence.

'Are little things more subtle than big things?' she asked, with the odd grunt of laughter in her voice, as if she were making game of him in the question.

'Dunno,' he said.

'I hate subtleties,' said Ursula.

Hermione looked at her slowly.

'Do you?' she said.

'I always think they are a sign of weakness,' said Ursula, up in arms, as if her prestige were threatened.

Hermione took no notice. Suddenly her face puckered, her brow was knit with thought, she seemed twisted in troublesome effort for utterance.

'Do you really think, Rupert,' she asked, as if Ursula were not present, 'do you really think it is worthwhile? Do you really think the children are better for being roused to consciousness?'

A dark flash went over his face, a silent fury. He was hollow-cheeked and pale, almost unearthly. And the woman, with her serious, conscience-harrowing question tortured him on the quick.

'They are not roused to consciousness,' he said. 'Consciousness comes to them, willy-nilly.'

'But do you think they are better for having it quickened, stimulated? Isn't it better that they should remain unconscious of the hazel, isn't it better that they should see as a whole, without all this pulling to pieces, all this knowledge?'

'Would you rather, for yourself, know or not know, that the little red flowers are there, putting out for the pollen?' he asked harshly. His voice was brutal, scornful, cruel.

Hermione remained with her face lifted up, abstracted. He hung silent in irritation.

'I don't know,' she replied, balancing mildly. 'I don't know.'

'But knowing is everything to you, it is all your life,' he broke out. She slowly looked at him.

'Is it?' she said.

'To know, that is your all, that is your life – you have only this, this knowledge,' he cried. 'There is only one tree, there is only one fruit, in your mouth.'

Again she was some time silent.

'Is there?' she said at last, with the same untouched calm. And then in a tone of whimsical inquisitiveness: 'What fruit, Rupert?'

'The eternal apple,'* he replied in exasperation, hating his own metaphors.

'Yes,' she said. There was a look of exhaustion about her. For some moments there was silence. Then, pulling herself together with a convulsed movement, Hermione resumed, in a sing-song, casual voice:

'But leaving me apart, Rupert; do you think the children are better, richer, happier, for all this knowledge; do you really think they are? Or is it better to leave them untouched, spontaneous. Hadn't they better be animals, simple animals, crude, violent, *anything,* rather than this self-consciousness, this incapacity to be spontaneous.'

They thought she had finished. But with a queer rumbling in her throat she resumed, 'Hadn't they better be anything than

*Eve's fruit that tempted Adam.

grow up crippled; crippled in their souls, crippled in their feelings
– so thrown back – so turned back on themselves – incapable –
'Hermione clenched her fist like one in a trance – 'of any
spontaneous action, always deliberate, always burdened with
choice, never carried away.'

Again they thought she had finished. But just as he was going
to reply, she resumed her queer rhapsody – 'never carried away,
out of themselves, always conscious, always self-conscious,
always aware of themselves. Isn't *anything* better than this? Better
be animals, mere animals with no mind at all, than this, this
nothingness – '

'But do you think it is knowledge that makes us unliving and
self-conscious?' he asked irritably.

She opened her eyes and looked at him slowly.

'Yes,' she said. She paused, watching him all the while, her
eyes vague. Then she wiped her fingers across her brow, with a
vague weariness. It irritated him bitterly. 'It is the mind,' she
said, 'and that is death.' She raised her eyes slowly to him: 'Isn't
the mind – ' she said, with the convulsed movement of her body,
'isn't it our death? Doesn't it destroy all our spontaneity, all our
instincts? Are not the young people growing up today, really dead
before they have a chance to live?'

'Not because they have too much mind, but too little,' he
said brutally.

'Are you *sure?*' she cried. 'It seems to me the reverse. They
are over conscious, burdened to death with consciousness.'

'Imprisoned within a limited, false set of concepts,' he cried.

But she took no notice of this, only went on with her own
rhapsodic interrogation.

'When we have knowledge, don't we lose everything but
knowledge?' she asked pathetically. 'If I know about the flower,
don't I lose the flower and have only the knowledge? Aren't we
exchanging the substance for the shadow, aren't we forfeiting
life for this dead quality of knowledge? And what does it mean to

me, after all? What does all this knowing mean to me? It means nothing.'

'You are merely making words,' he said; 'knowledge means everything to you. Even your animalism, you want it in your head. You don't want to *be* an animal, you want to observe your own animal functions, to get a mental thrill out of them. It is all purely secondary – and more decadent than the most hide-bound intellectualism. What is it but the worst and last form of intellectualism, this love of yours for passion and the animal instincts? Passion and the instincts – you want them hard enough, but through your head, in your consciousness. It all takes place in your head, under that skull of yours. Only you won't be conscious of what *actually* is: you want the lie that will match the rest of your furniture.'

Hermione set hard and poisonous against this attack. Ursula stood covered with wonder and shame. It frightened her, to see how they hated each other.

'It's all that Lady of Shalott* business,' he said, in his strong abstract voice. He seemed to be charging her before the unseeing air. 'You've got that mirror, your own fixed will, your immortal understanding, your own tight conscious world, and there is nothing beyond it. There, in the mirror, you must have everything. But now you have come to all your conclusions, you want to go back and be like a savage, without knowledge. You want a life of pure sensation and "passion." '

He quoted the last word satirically against her. She sat convulsed with fury and violation, speechless, like a stricken pythoness of the Greek oracle.

'But your passion is a lie,' he went on violently. 'It isn't passion at all, it is your *will*. It's your bullying will. You want to clutch things and have them in your power. You want to have things in your power. And why? Because you haven't got any real body, any dark sensual body of life. You have no sensuality. You have only your will and your conceit of consciousness, and your lust for power, to *know*.'

*Refers to Lord Tennyson's poem.

He looked at her in mingled hate and contempt, also in pain because she suffered, and in shame because he knew he tortured her. He had an impulse to kneel and plead for forgiveness. But a bitterer red anger burned up to fury in him. He became unconscious of her, he was only a passionate voice speaking.

'Spontaneous!' he cried. 'You and spontaneity! You, the most deliberate thing that ever walked or crawled! You'd be verily deliberately spontaneous – that's you. Because you want to have everything in your own volition, your deliberate voluntary consciousness. You want it all in that loathsome little skull of yours, that ought to be cracked like a nut. For you'll be the same till it is cracked, like an insect in its skin. If one cracked your skull perhaps one might get a spontaneous, passionate woman out of you, with real sensuality. As it is, what you want is pornography – looking at yourself in mirrors, watching your naked animal actions in mirrors, so that you can have it all in your consciousness, make it all mental.'

There was a sense of violation in the air, as if too much was said, the unforgivable. Yet Ursula was concerned now only with solving her own problems, in the light of his words. She was pale and abstracted.

'But do you really *want* sensuality?' she asked, puzzled.

Birkin looked at her, and became intent in his explanation.

'Yes,' he said, 'that and nothing else, at this point. It is a fulfilment the great dark knowledge you can't have in your head – the dark involuntary being. It is death to one's self – but it is the coming into being of another.'

'But how? How can you have knowledge not in your head?' she asked, quite unable to interpret his phrases.

'In the blood,' he answered; 'when the mind and the known world is drowned in darkness everything must go – there must be the deluge. Then you find yourself a palpable body of darkness, a demon – '

'But why should I be a demon –?' she asked.

' "*Woman wailing for her demon lover*" – he quoted – 'why, I don't know.'

Hermione roused herself as from a death – annihilation.

'He is such a *dreadful* satanist, isn't he?' she drawled to Ursula, in a queer resonant voice, that ended on a shrill little laugh of pure ridicule. The two women were jeering at him, jeering him into nothingness. The laugh of the shrill, triumphant female sounded from Hermione, jeering him as if he were a neuter.

'No,' he said. 'You are the real devil who won't let life exist.'

She looked at him with a long, slow look, malevolent, supercilious.

'You know all about it, don't you?' she said, with slow, cold, cunning mockery.

'Enough,' he replied, his face fixing fine and clear like steel. A horrible despair, and at the same time a sense of release, liberation, came over Hermione. She turned with a pleasant intimacy to Ursula.

'You are sure you will come to Breadalby?' she said, urging.

'Yes, I should like to very much,' replied Ursula.

Hermione looked down at her, gratified, reflecting, and strangely absent, as if possessed, as if not quite there.

'I'm so glad,' she said, pulling herself together. 'Some time in about a fortnight. Yes? I will write to you here, at the school, shall I? Yes. And you'll be sure to come? Yes. I shall be so glad. Good-bye! Good-bye!'

Hermione held out her hand and looked into the eyes of the other woman. She knew Ursula as an immediate rival, and the knowledge strangely exhilarated her. Also she was taking leave. It always gave her a sense of strength, advantage, to be departing and leaving the other behind. Moreover she was taking the man with her, if only in hate.

Birkin stood aside, fixed and unreal. But now, when it was his turn to bid good-bye, he began to speak again.

'There's the whole difference in the world,' he said, 'between the actual sensual being, and the vicious mental-deliberate profligacy our lot goes in for. In our night-time, there's always the electricity switched on, we watch ourselves, we get it all in the head, really. You've got to lapse out before you can know

what sensual reality is, lapse into unknowingness, and give up
your volition. You've got to do it. You've got to learn not-to-be,
before you can come into being.

'But we have got such a conceit of ourselves – that's where
it is. We are so conceited, and so unproud. We've got no pride,
we're all conceit, so conceited in our own papier-mâché realised
selves. We'd rather die than give up our little self-righteous self-
opinionated self-will.'

There was silence in the room. Both women were hostile and
resentful. He sounded as if he were addressing a meeting.
Hermione merely paid no attention, stood with her shoulders tight
in a shrug of dislike.

Ursula was watching him as if furtively, not really aware of
what she was seeing. There was a great physical attractiveness
in him – a curious hidden richness, that came through his thinness
and his pallor like another voice, conveying another knowledge
of him. It was in the curves of his brows and his chin, rich, fine,
exquisite curves, the powerful beauty of life itself. She could not
say what it was. But there was a sense of richness and of liberty.

'But we are sensual enough, without making ourselves so,
aren't we?' she asked, turning to him with a certain golden
laughter flickering' under her greenish eyes, like a challenge. And
immediately the queer, careless, terribly attractive smile came
over his eyes and brows, though his mouth did not relax.

'No,' he said, 'we aren't. We're too full of ourselves.'

'Surely it isn't a matter of conceit,' she cried.

'That and nothing else.'

She was frankly puzzled.

'Don't you think that people are most conceited of all about
their sensual powers?' she asked.

'That's why they aren't sensual – only sensuous – which is
another matter. They're *always* aware of themselves – and they're
so conceited, that rather than release themselves, and live in another
world, from another centre, they'd – '

'You want your tea, don't you,' said Hermione, turning to
Ursula with a gracious kindliness. 'You've worked all day – '

Birkin stopped short. A spasm of anger and chagrin went over Ursula. His face set. And he bade good-bye, as if he had ceased to notice her.

They were gone. Ursula stood looking at the door for some moments. Then she put out the lights. And having done so, she sat down again in her chair, absorbed and lost. And then she began to cry, bitterly, bitterly weeping: but whether for misery or joy, she never knew.

CHAPTER 4

Diver

THE WEEK passed away. On the Saturday it rained, a soft drizzling rain that held off at times. In one of the intervals Gudrun and Ursula set out for a walk, going towards Willey Water. The atmosphere was grey and translucent, the birds sang sharply on the young twigs, the earth would be quickening and hastening in growth. The two girls walked swiftly, gladly, because of the soft, subtle rush of morning that filled the wet haze. By the road the black-thorn was in blossom, white and wet, its tiny amber grains burning faintly in the white smoke of blossom. Purple twigs were darkly luminous in the grey air, high hedges glowed like living shadows, hovering nearer, coming into creation. The morning was full of a new creation.

When the sisters came to Willey Water, the lake lay all grey and visionary, stretching into the moist, translucent vista of trees and meadow. Fine electric activity in sound came from the dumbles below the road, the birds piping one against the other, and water mysteriously plashing, issuing from the lake.

The two girls drifted swiftly along. In front of them, at the corner of the lake, near the road, was a mossy boat-house under a walnut tree, and a little landing-stage where a boat was moored, wavering like a shadow on the still grey water, below the green, decayed poles. All was shadowy with coming summer.

Suddenly, from the boat-house, a white figure ran out, frightening in its swift sharp transit, across the old landing-stage. It launched in a white arc through the air, there was a bursting of the water, and among the smooth ripples a swimmer was making out to space, in a centre of faintly heaving motion. The whole otherworld, wet and remote, he had to himself. He could move into the pure translucency of the grey, uncreated water.

Gudrun stood by the stone wall, watching.

'How I envy him,' she said, in low, desirous tones.

'Ugh!' shivered Ursula. 'So cold!'

'Yes, but how good, how really fine, to swim out there!' The sisters stood watching the swimmer move further into the grey, moist, full space of the water, pulsing with his own small, invading motion, and arched over with mist and dim woods.

'Don't you wish it were you?' asked Gudrun, looking at Ursula.

'I do,' said Ursula. 'But I'm not sure – it's so wet.'

'No,' said Gudrun, reluctantly. She stood watching the motion on the bosom of the water, as if fascinated. He, having swum a certain distance, turned round and was swimming on his back, looking along the water at the two girls by the wall. In the faint wash of motion, they could see his ruddy face, and could feel him watching them.

'It is Gerald Crich,' said Ursula.

'I know,' replied Gudrun.

And she stood motionless gazing over the water at the face which washed up and down on the flood, as he swam steadily. From his separate element he saw them and he exulted to himself because of his own advantage, his possession of a world to himself. He was immune and perfect. He loved his own vigorous, thrusting motion, and the violent impulse of the very cold water against his limbs, buoying him up. He could see the girls watching him a way off, outside, and that pleased him. He lifted his arm from the water, in a sign to them.

'He is waving,' said Ursula.

'Yes,' replied Gudrun. They watched him. He waved again, with a strange movement of recognition across the difference.

'Like a Nibelung,' laughed Ursula. Gudrun said nothing, only stood still looking over the water.

Gerald suddenly turned, and was swimming away swiftly, with a side stroke. He was alone now, alone and immune in the middle of the waters, which he had all to himself. He exulted in his isolation in the new element, unquestioned and unconditioned. He was happy, thrusting with his legs and all his body, without bond or connection anywhere, just himself in the watery world.

Gudrun envied him almost painfully. Even this momentary possession of pure isolation and fluidity seemed to her so terribly desirable that she felt herself as if damned, out there on the high-road.

'God, what it is to be a man!' she cried.

'What?' exclaimed Ursula in surprise.

'The freedom, the liberty, the mobility!' cried Gudrun, strangely flushed and brilliant. 'You're a man, you want to do a thing, you do it. You haven't the *thousand* obstacles a woman has in front of her.'

Ursula wondered what was in Gudrun's mind, to occasion this outburst. She could not understand.

'What do you want to do?' she asked.

'Nothing,' cried Gudrun, in swift refutation. 'But supposing I did. Supposing I want to swim up that water. It is impossible, it is one of the impossibilities of life, for me to take my clothes off now and jump in. But isn't it *ridiculous,* doesn't it simply prevent our living!'

She was so hot, so flushed, so furious, that Ursula was puzzled.

The two sisters went on, up the road. They were passing between the trees just below Shortlands. They looked up at the long, low house, dim and glamorous in the wet morning, its cedar trees slanting before the windows. Gudrun seemed to be studying it closely.

'Don't you think it's attractive, Ursula?' asked Gudrun.

'Very,' said Ursula. 'Very peaceful and charming.'

'It has form, too – it has a period.'

'What period?'

'Oh, eighteenth century, for certain; Dorothy Wordsworth and Jane Austen, don't you think?'

Ursula laughed.

'Don't you think so?' repeated Gudrun.

'Perhaps. But I don't think the Criches fit the period. I know Gerald is putting in a private electric plant, for lighting the house; and is making all kinds of latest improvements.'

Gudrun shrugged her shoulders swiftly.

'Of course,' she said, 'that's quite inevitable.'

'Quite,' laughed Ursula. 'He is several generations of youngness at one go. They hate him for it. He takes them all by the scruff of the neck, and fairly flings them along. He'll have to die soon, when he's made every possible improvement, and there will be nothing more to improve. He's got *go,* anyhow.'

'Certainly, he's got go,' said Gudrun. 'In fact I've never seen a man that showed signs of so much. The unfortunate thing is, where does his *go* go to, what becomes of it?'

'Oh I know,' said Ursula. 'It goes in applying the latest appliances!'

'Exactly,' said Gudrun.

'You know he shot his brother?' said Ursula.

'Shot his brother?' cried Gudrun, frowning as if in disapprobation.

'Didn't you know? Oh yes! – I thought you knew. He and his brother were playing together with a gun. He told his brother to look down the gun, and it was loaded, and blew the top of his head off. Isn't it a horrible story?'

'How fearful!' cried Gudrun. 'But it is long ago?'

'Oh yes, they were quite boys,' said Ursula. 'I think it is one of the most horrible stories I know.'

'And he of course did not know that the gun was loaded?'

'Yes. You see it was an old thing that had been lying in the stable for years. Nobody dreamed it would ever go off, and of course, no one imagined it was loaded. But isn't it dreadful, that it should happen?'

'Frightful!' cried Gudrun. 'And isn't it horrible too to think of such a thing happening to one, when one was a child, and having to carry the responsibility of it all through one's life. Imagine it, two boys playing together – then this comes upon them, for no reason whatever – out of the air. Ursula, it's very frightening! Oh, it's one of the things I can't bear. Murder, that is thinkable, because there's a will behind it. But a thing like that to *happen* to one – '

'Perhaps there *was* an unconscious will behind it,' said Ursula. 'This playing at killing has some primitive *desire* for killing in it, don't you think?'

'Desire!' said Gudrun, coldly, stiffening a little. 'I can't see that they were even playing at killing. I suppose one boy said to the other, "You look down the barrel while I pull the trigger, and see what happens." It seems to me the purest form of accident.'

'No,' said Ursula. 'I couldn't pull the trigger of the emptiest gun in the world, not if someone were looking down the barrel. One instinctively doesn't do it – one can't.'

Gudrun was silent for some moments, in sharp disagreement.

'Of course,' she said coldly. 'If one is a woman, and grown up, one's instinct prevents one. But I cannot see how that applies to a couple of boys playing together.'

Her voice was cold and angry.

'Yes,' persisted Ursula. At that moment they heard a woman's voice a few yards off say loudly:

'Oh damn the thing!' They went forward and saw Laura Crich and Hermione Roddice in the field on the other side of the hedge, and Laura Crich struggling with the gate, to get out. Ursula at once hurried up and helped to lift the gate.

'Thanks so much,' said Laura, looking up flushed and amazon-like, yet rather confused. 'It isn't right on the hinges.'

'No,' said Ursula. 'And they're so heavy.'

'Surprising!' cried Laura.

'How do you do,' sang Hermione, from out of the field, the moment she could make her voice heard. 'It's nice now. Are you going for a walk? Yes. Isn't the young green beautiful? So beautiful – quite burning. Good morning – good morning – you'll come and see me? thank you so much – next week – yes – good-bye, g-o-o-d b-y-e.'

Gudrun and Ursula stood and watched her slowly waving her head up and down, and waving her hand slowly in dismissal, smiling a strange affected smile, making a tall queer, frightening figure, with her heavy fair hair slipping to her eyes. Then they moved off, as if they had been dismissed like inferiors. The four women parted.

As soon as they had gone far enough, Ursula said, her cheeks burning,

'I do think she's impudent.'

'Who, Hermione Roddice?' asked Gudrun. 'Why?'

'The way she treats one – impudence!'

'Why, Ursula, what did you notice that was so impudent?' asked Gudrun rather coldly.

'Her whole manner. Oh, it's impossible, the way she tries to bully one. Pure bullying. She's an impudent woman. "You'll come and see me," as if we should be falling over ourselves for the privilege.'

'I can't understand, Ursula, what you are so much put out about,' said Gudrun, in some exasperation. 'One knows those women are impudent – these free women who have emancipated themselves from the aristocracy.'

'But it is so *unnecessary* – so vulgar,' cried Ursula.

'No, I don't see it. And if I did – pour moi, elle n'existe pas.* I don't grant her the power to be impudent to me.'

'Do you think she likes you?' asked Ursula.

'Well, no, I shouldn't think she did.'

'Then why does she ask you to go to Breadalby and stay with her?'

---

* For me she ceases to exist.

Gudrun lifted her shoulders in a low shrug.

'After all, she's got the sense to know we're not just the ordinary run,' said Gudrun. 'Whatever she is, she's not a fool. And I'd rather have somebody I detested, than the ordinary woman who keeps to her own set. Hermione Roddice does risk herself in some respects.'

Ursula pondered this for a time.

'I doubt it,' she replied. 'Really she risks nothing. I suppose we ought to admire her for knowing she *can* invite us school teachers – and risk nothing.'

'Precisely!' said Gudrun. 'Think of the myriads of women that daren't do it. She makes the most of her privileges – that's something. I suppose, really, we should do the same, in her place.'

'No,' said Ursula. 'No. It would bore me: I couldn't spend my time playing her games. It's infra dig.'

The two sisters were like a pair of scissors, snipping off everything that came athwart them; or like a knife and a whetstone, the one sharpened against the other.

'Of course,' cried Ursula suddenly, 'She ought to thank her stars if we will go and see her. You are perfectly beautiful, a thousand times more beautiful than ever she is or was, and to my thinking, a thousand times more beautifully dressed, for she never looks fresh and natural, like a flower, always old, thought-out; and we *are* more intelligent than most people.'

'Undoubtedly!' said Gudrun.

'And it ought to be admitted, simply,' said Ursula.

'Certainly it ought,' said Gudrun. 'But you'll find that the really chic thing is to be so absolutely ordinary, so perfectly commonplace and like the person in the street, that you really are a masterpiece of humanity, not the person in the street actually, but the artistic creation of her – '

'How awful!' cried Ursula.

'Yes, Ursula, it if awful, in most respects. You daren't be anything that isn't amazingly *à terre,** so* much *à terre* that it is the artistic creation of ordinariness.'

'It's very dull to create oneself into nothing better,' laughed Ursula.

* Down to earth.

'Very dull!' retorted Gudrun. 'Really Ursula, it is dull, that's just the word. One longs to be high-flown, and make speeches like Corneille, after it.'

Gudrun was becoming flushed and excited over her own cleverness.

'Strut,' said Ursula. 'One wants to strut, to be a swan among geese.'

'Exactly,' cried Gudrun, 'a swan among geese.'

'They are all so busy playing the ugly duckling,' cried Ursula, with mocking laughter. 'And I don't feel a bit like a humble and pathetic ugly duckling. I do feel like a swan among geese – I can't help it. They make one feel so. And I don't care what *they* think of me. *Je m'en fiche.'* *

Gudrun looked up at Ursula with a queer, uncertain envy and dislike.

'Of course, the only thing to do is to despise them all – just all,' she said.

The sisters went home again, to read and talk and work, and wait for Monday, for school. Ursula often wondered what else she waited for, besides the beginning and end of the school week, and the beginning and end of the holidays. This was a whole life! Sometimes she had periods of tight horror, when it seemed to her that her life would pass away, and be gone, without having been more than this. But she never really accepted it. Her spirit was active, her life like a shoot that is growing steadily, but which has not yet come above ground.

CHAPTER 5

In the Train

ONE DAY at this time Birkin was called to London. He was not very fixed in his abode. He had rooms in Nottingham, because his work lay chiefly in that town. But often he was in London, or in Oxford. He moved about a great deal, his life seemed uncertain, without any definite rhythm, any organic meaning.

* I don't care a damn.

On the platform of the railway station he saw Gerald Crich, reading a newspaper, and evidently waiting for the train. Birkin stood some distance off, among the people. It was against his instinct to approach anybody.

From time to time, in a manner characteristic of him, Gerald lifted his head and looked round. Even though he was reading the newspaper closely, he must keep a watchful eye on his external surroundings. There seemed to be a dual consciousness running in him. He was thinking vigorously of something he read in the newspaper, and at the same time his eye ran over the surfaces of the life round him, and he missed nothing. Birkin, who was watching him, was irritated by his duality. He noticed too, that Gerald seemed always to be at bay against everybody, in spite of his queer, genial, social manner when roused.

Now Birkin started violently at seeing this genial look flash on to Gerald's face, at seeing Gerald approaching with hand outstretched.

'Hallo, Rupert, where are you going?'

'London. So are you, I suppose.'

'Yes – '

Gerald's eyes went over Birkin's face in curiosity.

'We'll travel together if you like,' he said.

'Don't you usually go first?' asked Birkin.

'I can't stand the crowd,' replied Gerald. 'But third'll be all right. There's a restaurant car, we can have some tea.'

The two men looked at the station clock, having nothing further to say.

'What were you reading in the paper?' Birkin asked.

Gerald looked at him quickly.

'Isn't it funny, what they *do* put in the newspapers,' he said. 'Here are two leaders – ' he held out his *Daily Telegraph,* 'full of the ordinary newspaper cant – ' he scanned the columns down – 'and then there's this little – I dunno what you'd call it, essay, almost – appearing with the leaders, and saying there must arise a man who will give new values to things, give us new truths, a new attitude to life, or else we shall be a crumbling nothingness in a few years, a country in ruin – '

'I suppose that's a bit of newspaper cant, as well,' said Birkin.

'It sounds as if the man meant it, and quite genuinely,' said Gerald.

'Give it to me,' said Birkin, holding out his hand for the paper.

The train came, and they went on board, sitting on either side a little table, by the window, in the restaurant car. Birkin glanced over his paper, then looked up at Gerald, who was waiting for him.

'I believe the man means it,' he said, 'as far as he means anything.'

'And do you think it's true? Do you think we really want a new gospel?' asked Gerald.

Birkin shrugged his shoulders.

'I think the people who say they want a new religion are the last to accept anything new. They want novelty right enough. But to stare straight at this life that we've brought upon ourselves, and reject it, absolutely smash up the old idols of ourselves, that we sh'll never do. You've got very badly to want to get rid of the old, before anything new will appear – even in the self.'

Gerald watched him closely.

'You think we ought to break up this life, just start and let fly?' he asked.

'This life. Yes I do. We've got to bust it completely, or shrivel inside it, as in a tight skin. For it won't expand any more.'

There was a queer little smile in Gerald's eyes, a look of amusement, calm and curious.

'And how do you propose to begin? I suppose you mean, reform the whole order of society?' he asked.

Birkin had a slight, tense frown between the brows. He too was impatient of the conversation.

'I don't propose at all,' he replied. 'When we really want to go for something better, we shall smash the old. Until then, any sort of proposal, or making proposals, is no more than a tiresome game for self-important people.'

The little smile began to die out of Gerald's eyes, and he said, looking with a cool stare at Birkin:

'So you really think things are very bad?'

'Completely bad.'

The smile appeared again.

'In what way?'

'Every way,' said Birkin. 'We are such dreary liars. Our one idea is to lie to ourselves. We have an ideal of a perfect world, clean and straight and sufficient. So we cover the earth with foulness; life is a blotch of labour, like insects scurrying in filth, so that your collier can have a pianoforte in his parlour, and you can have a butler and a motor-car in your up-to-date house, and as a nation we can sport the Ritz, or the Empire, Gaby Deslys and the Sunday newspapers. It is very dreary.'

Gerald took a little time to re-adjust himself after this tirade.

'Would you have us live without houses – return to nature?' he asked.

'I would have nothing at all. People only do what they want to do and what they are capable of doing. If they were capable of anything else, there would be something else.'

Again Gerald pondered. He was not going to take offence at Birkin.

'Don't you think the collier's *pianoforte,* as you call it, is a symbol for something very real, a real desire for something higher, in the collier's life?'

'Higher!' cried Birkin. 'Yes. Amazing heights of upright grandeur. It makes him so much higher in his neighbouring collier's eyes. He sees himself reflected in the neighbouring opinion, like in a Brocken mist, several feet taller on the strength of the pianoforte, and he is satisfied. He lives for the sake of that Brocken spectre, the reflection of himself in the human opinion. You do the same. If you are of high importance to humanity you are of high importance to yourself. That is why you work so hard at the mines. If you can produce coal to cook five thousand dinners a day, you are five thousand times more important than if you cooked only your own dinner.'

'I suppose I am,' laughed Gerald.

'Can't you see,' said Birkin, 'that to help my neighbour to eat is no more than eating myself. "I eat, thou eatest, he eats, we eat, you eat, they eat" – and what then? Why should every man decline the whole verb. First person singular is enough for me.'

'You've got to start with material things,' said Gerald. Which statement Birkin ignored.

'And we've got to live for *something,* we're not just cattle that can graze and have done with it,' said Gerald.

'Tell me,' said Birkin. 'What do you live for?'

Gerald's face went baffled.

'What do I live for?' he repeated. 'I suppose I live to work, to produce something, in so far as I am a purposive being. Apart from that, I live because I am living.'

'And what's your work? Getting so many more thousands of tons of coal out of the earth every day. And when we've got all the coal we want, and all the plush furniture, and pianofortes, and the rabbits are all stewed and eaten, and we're all warm and our bellies are filled and we're listening to the young lady performing on the pianoforte – what then? What then, when you've made a real fair start with your material things?'

Gerald sat laughing at the words and the mocking humour of the other man. But he was cogitating too.

'We haven't got there yet,' he replied. 'A good many people are still waiting for the rabbit and the fire to cook it.'

'So while you get the coal I must chase the rabbit?' said Birkin, mocking at Gerald.

'Something like that,' said Gerald.

Birkin watched him narrowly. He saw the perfect good-humoured callousness, even strange, glistening malice, in Gerald, glistening through the plausible ethics of productivity.

'Gerald,' he said, 'I rather hate you.'

'I know you do,' said Gerald. 'Why do you?'

Birkin mused inscrutably for some minutes.

'I should like to know if you are conscious of hating me,' he said at last. 'Do you ever consciously detest me – hate me with mystic hate? There are odd moments when I hate you starrily.'

Gerald was rather taken aback, even a little disconcerted. He did not quite know what to say.

'I may, of course, hate you sometimes,' he said. 'But I'm not aware of it – never acutely aware of it, that is.'

'So much the worse,' said Birkin.

Gerald watched him with curious eyes. He could not quite make him out.

'So much the worse, is it?' he repeated.

There was a silence between the two men for some time, as the train ran on. In Birkin's face was a little irritable tension, a sharp knitting of the brows, keen and difficult. Gerald watched him warily, carefully, rather calculatingly, for he could not decide what he was after.

Suddenly Birkin's eyes looked straight and overpowering into those of the other man.

'What do you think is the aim and object of your life, Gerald?' he asked.

Again Gerald was taken aback. He could not think what his friend was getting at. Was he poking fun, or not?

'At this moment, I couldn't say off-hand,' he replied, with faintly ironic humour.

'Do you think love is the be-all and the end-all of life?' Birkin asked, with direct, attentive seriousness.

'Of my own life?' said Gerald.

'Yes.'

There was a really puzzled pause.

'I can't say,' said Gerald. 'It hasn't been, so far.'

'What has your life been, so far?'

'Oh – finding out things for myself – and getting experiences – and making things *go*.'

Birkin knitted his brows like sharply moulded steel.

'I find,' he said, 'that one needs some one *really* pure single activity – I should call love a single pure activity. But I *don't* really love anybody – not now.'

'Have you ever really loved anybody?' asked Gerald.

'Yes and no,' replied Birkin.

'Not finally?' said Gerald.

'Finally – finally – no,' said Birkin.

'Nor I,' said Gerald.

'And do you want to?' said Birkin.

Gerald looked with a long, twinkling, almost sardonic look into the eyes of the other man.

'I don't know,' he said.

'I do – I want to love,' said Birkin.

'You do?'

'Yes. I want the finality of love.'

'The finality of love,' repeated Gerald. And he waited for a moment.

'Just one woman?' he added. The evening light, flooding yellow along the fields, lit up Birkin's face with a tense, abstract steadfastness. Gerald still could not make it out.

'Yes, one woman,' said Birkin.

But to Gerald it sounded as if he were insistent rather than confident. 'I don't believe a woman, and nothing but a woman, will ever make my life,' said Gerald.

'Not the centre and core of it – the love between you and a woman?' asked Birkin.

Gerald's eyes narrowed with a queer dangerous smile as he watched the other man.

'I never quite feel it that way,' he said.

'You don't? Then wherein does life centre, for you?'

'I don't know – that's what I want somebody to tell me. As far as I can make out, it doesn't centre at all. It is artificially held *together* by the social mechanism.'

Birkin pondered as if he would crack something.

'I know,' he said, 'it just doesn't centre. The old ideals are dead as nails – nothing there. It seems to me there remains only this perfect union with a woman – sort of ultimate marriage – and there isn't anything else.'

'And you mean if there isn't the woman, there's nothing?' said Gerald.

'Pretty well that – seeing there's no God.'

'Then we're hard put to it,' said Gerald. And he turned to look out of the window at the flying, golden landscape.

Birkin could not help seeing how beautiful and soldierly his face was, with a certain courage to be indifferent.

'You think its heavy odds against us?' said Birkin.

'If we've got to make our life up out of a woman, one woman, woman only, yes, I do,' said Gerald. 'I don't believe I shall ever make up *my* life, at that rate.'

Birkin watched him almost angrily.

'You are a born Unbeliever,' he said.

'I only feel what I feel,' said Gerald. And he looked again at Birkin almost sardonically, with his blue, manly, sharp-lighted eyes. Birkin's eyes were at the moment full of anger. But swiftly they became troubled, doubtful, then full of a warm, rich affectionateness and laughter.

'It troubles me very much, Gerald,' he said, wrinkling his brows.

'I can see it does,' said Gerald, uncovering his mouth in a manly, quick, soldierly laugh.

Gerald was held unconsciously by the other man. He wanted to be near him, he wanted to be within his sphere of influence. There was something very congenial to him in Birkin. But yet, beyond this, he did not take much notice. He felt that he, himself, Gerald, had harder and more durable truths than any the other man knew. He felt himself older, more knowing. It was the quick-changing warmth and venality and brilliant warm utterance he loved in his friend. It was the rich play of words and quick interchange of feelings he enjoyed. The real content of the words he never really considered: he himself knew better.

Birkin knew this. He knew that Gerald wanted to be *fond* of him without taking him seriously. And this made him go hard and cold. As the train ran on, he sat looking at the land, and Gerald fell away, became as nothing to him.

Birkin looked at the land, at the evening, and was thinking: 'Well, if mankind is destroyed, if our race is destroyed like Sodom,* and there is this beautiful evening with the luminous land and trees, I am satisfied. That which informs it all is there, and can never be lost. After all, what is mankind but just one expression of the incomprehensible. And if mankind passes away, it will only mean that this particular expression is completed and done. That which is expressed, and that which is to be expressed, cannot be diminished. There it is, in the shining evening. Let mankind pass away – time it did. The creative utterances will not cease, they will only be there. Humanity doesn't embody the utterance of the incomprehensible any more. Humanity is a dead letter. There will be a new embodiment, in a new way. Let humanity disappear as quick as possible.'

Gerald interrupted him by asking:

'Where are you staying in London?'

Birkin looked up.

'With a man in Soho. I pay part of the rent of a flat, and stop there when I like.'

'Good idea – have a place more or less your own,' said Gerald.

'Yes. But I don't care for it much. I'm tired of the people I am bound to find there.'

'What kind of people?'

'Art – music – London Bohemia – the most pettifogging calculating Bohemia that ever reckoned its pennies. But there are a few decent people, decent in some respects. They are really very thorough rejecters of the world – perhaps they live only in the gesture of rejection and negation – but negatively something, at any rate.'

'What are they? – painters, musicians?'

'Painters, musicians, writers – hangers-on, models, advanced young people, anybody who is openly at outs with the conventions,

---

* The evil cities of Sodom and Gomorrah were destroyed by God for their immorality. (Gen. 19:24-5).

and belongs to nowhere particularly. They are often young fellows down from the University, and girls who are living their own lives, as they say.'

'All loose?' said Gerald.

Birkin could see his curiosity roused.

'In one way. Most bound, in another. For all their shockingness, all on one note.'

He looked at Gerald, and saw how his blue eyes were lit up with a little flame of curious desire. He saw too how good-looking he was. Gerald was attractive, his blood seemed fluid and electric. His blue eyes burned with a keen, yet cold light, there was a certain beauty, a beautiful passivity in all his body, his moulding.

'We might see something of each other – I am in London for two or three days,' said Gerald.

'Yes,' said Birkin, 'I don't want to go to the theatre, or the music hall – you'd better come round to the flat, and see what you can make of Halliday and his crowd.'

'Thanks – I should like to,' laughed Gerald. 'What are you doing tonight?'

'I promised to meet Halliday at the Pompadour. It's a bad place, but there is nowhere else.'

'Where is it?' asked Gerald.

'Piccadilly Circus.'

'Oh yes – well, shall I come round there?'

'By all means, it might amuse you.'

The evening was falling. They had passed Bedford. Birkin watched the country, and was filled with a sort of hopelessness. He always felt this, on approaching London.

His dislike of mankind, of the mass of mankind, amounted almost to an illness.

' "Where the quiet coloured end of evening smiles
      Miles and miles – " '

he was murmuring to himself, like a man condemned to death. Gerald, who was very subtly alert, wary in all his senses, leaned forward and asked smilingly:

'What were you saying?' Birkin glanced at him, laughed, and repeated:

> ' "Where the quiet coloured end of evening smiles,
>   Miles and miles,
>   Over pastures where the something something sheep
>   Half asleep – " '

Gerald also looked now at the country. And Birkin, who, for some reason was now tired and dispirited, said to him:

'I always feel doomed when the train is running into London. I feel such a despair, so hopeless, as if it were the end of the world.'

'Really!' said Gerald. 'And does the end of the world frighten you?'

Birkin lifted his shoulders in a slow shrug.

'I don't know,' he said. 'It does while it hangs imminent and doesn't fall. But people give me a bad feeling – very bad.'

There was a roused glad smile in Gerald's eyes.

'Do they?' he said. And he watched the other man critically.

In a few minutes the train was running through the disgrace of outspread London. Everybody in the carriage was on the alert, waiting to escape. At last they were under the huge arch of the station, in the tremendous shadow of the town. Birkin shut himself together – he was in now.

The two men went together in a taxi-cab.

'Don't you feel like one of the damned?' asked Birkin, as they sat in a little, swiftly-running enclosure, and watched the hideous great street.

'No,' laughed Gerald.

'It is real death,' said Birkin.

CHAPTER 6

Crême de Menthe

THEY MET again in the café several hours later. Gerald went through the push doors into the large, lofty room where the faces and heads of the drinkers showed dimly through the haze of smoke, reflected more dimly, and repeated ad infinitum in the great mirrors on the walls, so that one seemed to enter a vague, dim world of shadowy drinkers humming within an atmosphere of blue tobacco smoke. There was, however, the red plush of the seats to give substance within the bubble of pleasure.

Gerald moved in his slow, observant, glistening-attentive motion down between the tables and the people whose shadowy faces looked up as he passed. He seemed to be entering in some strange element, passing into an illuminated new region, among a host of licentious souls. He was pleased, and entertained. He looked over all the dim, evanescent, strangely illuminated faces that bent across the tables. Then he saw Birkin rise and signal to him.

At Birkin's table was a girl with dark, soft, fluffy hair cut short in the artist fashion, hanging level and full almost like the Egyptian princess's. She was small and delicately made, with warm colouring and large, dark hostile eyes. There was a delicacy, almost a beauty in all her form, and at the same time a certain attractive grossness of spirit, that made a little spark leap instantly alight in Gerald's eyes.

Birkin, who looked muted, unreal, his presence left out, introduced her as Miss Darrington. She gave her hand with a sudden, unwilling movement, looking all the while at Gerald with a dark, exposed stare. A glow came over him as he sat down.

The waiter appeared. Gerald glanced at the glasses of the other two. Birkin was drinking something green, Miss Darrington had a small liqueur glass that was empty save for a tiny drop.

'Won't you have some more –?'

'Brandy,' she said, sipping her last drop and putting down the glass. The waiter disappeared.

'No,' she said to Birkin. 'He doesn't know I'm back. He'll be terrified when he sees me here.'

She spoke her r's like w's, lisping with a slightly babyish pronunciation which was at once affected and true to her character. Her voice was dull and toneless.

'Where is he then?' asked Birkin.

'He's doing a private show at Lady Snellgrove's,' said the girl. 'Warens is there too.'

There was a pause.

'Well, then,' said Birkin, in a dispassionate protective manner, 'what do you intend to do?'

The girl paused sullenly. She hated the question.

'I don't intend to do anything,' she replied. 'I shall look for some sittings tomorrow.'

'Who shall you go to?' asked Birkin.

'I shall go to Bentley's first. But I believe he's angwy with me for running away.'

'That is from the Madonna?'

'Yes. And then if he doesn't want me, I know I can get work with Carmarthen.'

'Carmarthen?'

'Lord Carmarthen – he does photographs.'

'Chiffon and shoulders' –

'Yes. But he's awfully decent.' There was a pause.

'And what are you going to do about Julius?' he asked.

'Nothing,' she said. 'I shall just ignore him.'

'You've done with him altogether?' But she turned aside her face sullenly, and did not answer the question.

Another young man came hurrying up to the table.

'Hallo Birkin! Hallo *Pussum,* when did you come back?' he said eagerly.

'Today.'

'Does Halliday know?'

'I don't know. I don't care either.'

'Ha-ha! The wind still sits in that quarter, does it? Do you mind if come over to this table?'

'I'm talking to Wupert, do you mind?' she replied, coolly and yet appealingly, like a child.

'Open confession – good for the soul, eh?' said the young man.

'Well, so long.'

And giving a sharp look at Birkin and at Gerald, the young man moved off, with a swing of his coat skirts.

All this time Gerald had been completely ignored. And yet he felt that the girl was physically aware of his proximity. He waited, listened, and tried to piece together the conversation.

'Are you staying at the flat?' the girl asked, of Birkin.

'For three days,' replied Birkin. 'And you?'

'I don't know yet. I can always go to Bertha's.' There was a silence.

Suddenly the girl turned to Gerald, and said, in a rather formal, polite voice, with the distant manner of a woman who accepts her position as a social inferior, yet assumes intimate *camaraderie* with the male she addresses:

'Do you know London well?'

'I can hardly say,' he laughed. 'I've been up a good many times, but I was never in this place before.'

'You're not an artist, then?' she said, in a tone that placed him an outsider.

'No,' he replied.

'He's a soldier, and an explorer, and a Napoleon of industry,' said Birkin, giving Gerald his credentials for Bohemia.

'Are you a soldier?' asked the girl, with a cold yet lively curiosity.

'No, I resigned my commission,' said Gerald, 'Some years ago.'

'He was in the last war,' said Birkin.

'Were you really?' said the girl.

'And then he explored the Amazon,' said Birkin, 'and now he is ruling over coal-mines.'

The girl looked at Gerald with steady, calm curiosity. He laughed, hearing himself described. He felt proud too, full of male strength. His blue, keen eyes were lit up with laughter, his ruddy face, with its sharp fair hair, was full of satisfaction, and glowing with life. He piqued her.

'How long are you staying?' she asked him.

'A day or two,' he replied. 'But there is no particular hurry.'

Still she stared into his face with that slow, full gaze which was so curious and so exciting to him. He was acutely and delightfully conscious of himself, of his own attractiveness. He felt full of strength, able to give off a sort of electric power. And he was aware of her dark, hot-looking eyes upon him. She had beautiful eyes, dark, fully-opened, hot, naked in their looking at him. And on them there seemed to float a film of disintegration, a sort of misery and sullenness, like oil on water. She wore no hat in the heated café, her loose, simple jumper was strung on a string round her neck. But it was made of rich peach-coloured *crêpe-de-chine*, that hung heavily and softly from her young throat and her slender wrists. Her appearance was simple and complete, really beautiful, because of her regularity and form, her soft dark hair falling full and level on either side of her head, her straight, small, softened features, Egyptian in the slight fulness of their curves, her slender neck and the simple, rich-coloured smock hanging on her slender shoulders. She was very still, almost null, in her manner, apart and watchful.

She appealed to Gerald strongly. He felt an awful, enjoyable power over her, an instinctive cherishing very near to cruelty. For she was a victim. He felt that she was in his power, and he was generous. The electricity was turgid and voluptuously rich, in his limbs. He would be able to destroy her utterly in the strength of his discharge. But she was waiting in her separation, given.

They talked banalities for some time. Suddenly Birkin said:

'There's Julius!' and he half rose to his feet, motioning to the newcomer. The girl, with a curious, almost evil motion, looked round over her shoulder without moving her body. Gerald watched her dark, soft hair swing over her ears. He felt her watching intensely the man who was approaching, so he looked too. He saw a pale, full-built young man with rather long, solid fair hair hanging from under his black hat, moving cumbrously down the room, his face lit up with a smile at once naive and warm, and vapid. He approached towards Birkin, with a haste of welcome.

It was not till he was quite close that he perceived the girl. He recoiled, went pale, and said, in a high squealing voice:

'Pussum, what are *you* doing here?'

The café looked up like animals when they hear a cry. Halliday hung motionless, an almost imbecile smile flickering palely on ills face. The girl only stared at him with a black look in which flared an unfathomable hell of knowledge, and a certain impotence. She was limited by him.

'Why have you come back?' repeated Halliday, in the same high, hysterical voice. 'I told you not to come back.'

The girl did not answer, only stared in the same viscous, heavy fashion, straight at him, as he stood recoiled, as if for safety, against the next table.

'You know you wanted her to come back – come and sit down,' said Birkin to him.

'No I didn't want her to come back, and I told her not to come back. What have you come for, Pussum?'

'For nothing from *you*,' she said in a heavy voice of resentment.

'Then why have you come back at *all?*' cried Halliday, his voice rising to a kind of squeal.

'She comes as she likes,' said Birkin. 'Are you going to sit down, or are you not?'

'No, I won't sit down with Pussum,' cried Halliday.

'I won't hurt you, you needn't be afraid,' she said to him, very curtly, and yet with a sort of protectiveness towards him, in her voice.

Halliday came and sat at the table, putting his hand on his heart, and crying:

'Oh, it's given me such a turn! Pussum, I wish you wouldn't do these things. Why did you come back?'

'Not for anything from you,' she repeated.

'You've said that before,' he cried in a high voice.

She turned completely away from him, to Gerald Crich, whose eyes were shining with a subtle amusement.

'Were you ever vewy much afraid of the savages?' she asked in her calm, dull childish voice.

'No – never very much afraid. On the whole they're harmless they're not born yet, you can't feel really afraid of them. You know you can manage them.'

'Do you weally? Aren't they very fierce?'

'Not very. There aren't many fierce things, as a matter of fact. There aren't many things, neither people nor animals, that have it in them to be really dangerous.'

'Except in herds,' interrupted Birkin.

'Aren't there really?' she said. 'Oh, I thought savages were all so dangerous, they'd have your life before you could look round.'

'Did you?' he laughed. 'They are over-rated, savages. They're too much like other people, not exciting, after the first acquaintance.'

'Oh, it's not so very wonderfully brave then, to be an explorer?'

'No. It's more a question of hardships than of terrors.'

'Oh! And weren't you ever afraid?'

'In my life? I don't know. Yes, I'm afraid of some things – of being shut up, locked up anywhere – or being fastened. I'm afraid of being bound hand and foot.'

She looked at him steadily with her dark eyes, that rested on him and roused him so deeply, that it left his upper self quite calm. It was rather delicious, to feel her drawing his self-revelations from him, as from the very innermost dark marrow of his body. She wanted to know. And her dark eyes seemed to be looking through into his naked organism. He felt, she was compelled to him, she was fated to come into contact with him, must have the seeing him and knowing him. And this roused a curious exultance.

Also he felt, she must relinquish herself into his hands, and be subject to him. She was so profane, slave-like, watching him, absorbed by him. It was not that she was interested in what he said; she was absorbed by his self-revelation, by *him,* she wanted the secret of him, the experience of his male being.

Gerald's face was lit up with an uncanny smile, full of light and rousedness, yet unconscious. He sat with his arms on the table, his sun-browned, rather sinister hands, that were animal and yet very shapely and attractive, pushed forward towards her. And they fascinated her. And she knew, she watched her own fascination.

Other men had come to the table, to talk with Birkin and Halliday. Gerald said in a low voice, apart, to Pussum:

'Where have you come back from?'

'From the country,' replied Pussum, in a very low, yet fully resonant voice. Her face closed hard. Continually she glanced at Halliday, and then a black flare came over her eyes. The heavy, fair young man ignored her completely; he was really afraid of her. For some moments she would be unaware of Gerald. He had not conquered her yet.

'And what has Halliday to do with it?' he asked, his voice still muted.

She would not answer for some seconds. Then she said, unwillingly:

'He made me go and live with him, and now he wants to throw me over. And yet he won't let me go to anybody else. He wants me to live hidden in the country. And then he says I persecute him, that he can't get rid of me.'

'Doesn't know his own mind,' said Gerald.

'He hasn't any mind, so he can't know it,' she said. 'He waits for what somebody tells him to do. He never does anything he wants to do himself – because he doesn't know what he wants. He's a perfect baby.'

Gerald looked at Halliday for some moments, watching the soft, rather degenerate face of the young man. Its very softness

was an attraction; it was a soft, warm, corrupt nature, into which
one might plunge with gratification.

'But he has no hold over you, has he?' Gerald asked.

'You see he *made* me go and live with him, when I didn't
want to,' she replied. 'He came and cried to me, tears, you never
saw so many, saying *he couldn't* bear it unless I went back to
him. And he wouldn't go away, he would have stayed for ever.
He made me go back. Then every time he behaves in this fashion.
And now I'm going to have a baby, he wants to give me a hundred
pounds and send me into the country, so that he would never see
me nor hear of me again. But I'm not going to do it, after – '

A queer look came over Gerald's face.

'Are you going to have a child?' he asked incredulous. It
seemed, to look at her, impossible, she was so young and so far
in spirit from any child-bearing.

She looked full into his face, and her dark, inchoate eyes had
now a furtive look, and a look of a knowledge of evil, dark and
indomitable. A flame ran secretly to his heart.

'Yes,' she said. 'Isn't it beastly?'

'Don't you want it?' he asked.

'I don't,' she replied emphatically.

'But – ' he said, 'how long have you known?'

'Ten weeks,' she said.

All the time she kept her dark, inchoate eyes full upon him.
He remained silent, thinking. Then, switching off and becoming
cold, he asked, in a voice full of considerate kindness:

'Is there anything we can eat here? Is there anything you
would like?'

'Yes,' she said, 'I should adore some oysters.'

'All right,' he said. 'We'll have oysters.' And he beckoned to
the waiter.

Halliday took no notice, until the little plate was set before
her. Then suddenly he cried:

'Pussum, you can't eat oysters when you're drinking brandy.'

'What has it go to do with you?' she asked.

'Nothing, nothing,' he cried. 'But you can't eat oysters when you're drinking brandy.'

'I'm not drinking brandy,' she replied, and she sprinkled the last drops of her liqueur over his face. He gave an odd squeal. She sat looking at him, as if indifferent.

'Pussum, why do you do that?' he cried in panic. He gave Gerald the impression that he was terrified of her, and that he loved his terror. He seemed to relish his own horror and hatred of her, turn it over and extract every flavour from it, in real panic. Gerald thought him a strange fool, and yet piquant.

'But Pussum,' said another man, in a very small, quick Eton voice, 'you promised not to hurt him.'

'I haven't hurt him,' she answered.

'What will you drink?' the young man asked. He was dark, and smooth-skinned, and full of a stealthy vigour.

'I don't like porter, Maxim,' she replied.

'You must ask for champagne,' came the whispering, gentlemanly voice of the other.

Gerald suddenly realised that this was a hint to him.

'Shall we have champagne?' he asked, laughing.

'Yes please, dwy,' she lisped childishly.

Gerald watched her eating the oysters. She was delicate and finicking in her eating, her fingers were fine and seemed very sensitive in the tips, so she put her food apart with fine, small motions, she ate carefully, delicately. It pleased him very much to see her, and it irritated Birkin. They were all drinking champagne. Maxim, the prim young Russian with the smooth, warm-coloured face and black, oiled hair was the only one who seemed to be perfectly calm and sober. Birkin was white and abstract, unnatural, Gerald was smiling with a constant bright, amused, cold light in his eyes, leaning a little protectively towards the Pussum, who was very handsome, and soft, unfolded like some red lotus in dreadful flowering nakedness, vainglorious now, flushed with wine and with the excitement of men. Halliday looked foolish.

One glass of wine was enough to make him drunk and giggling. Yet there was always a pleasant, warm naiveté about him, that made him attractive.

'I'm not afwaid of anything except black-beetles,' said the Pussum, looking up suddenly and staring with her black eyes, on which there seemed an unseeing film of flame, fully upon Gerald. He laughed dangerously, from the blood. Her childish speech caressed his nerves, and her burning, filmed eyes, turned now full upon him, oblivious of all her antecedents, gave him a sort of licence.

'I'm not,' she protested. 'I'm not afraid of other things. But blackbeetles – ugh!' she shuddered convulsively, as if the very thought were too much to bear.

'Do you mean,' said Gerald, with the punctiliousness of a man who has been drinking, 'that you are afraid of the sight of a black-beetle, or you are afraid of a black-beetle biting you, or doing you some harm?'

'Do they bite?' cried the girl.

'How perfectly loathsome!' exclaimed Halliday.

'I don't know,' replied Gerald, looking round the table. 'Do black-beetles bite? But that isn't the point. Are you afraid of their biting, or is it a metaphysical antipathy?'

The girl was looking full upon him all the time with inchoate eyes.

'Oh, I think they're beastly, they're horrid,' she cried. 'If I see one, it gives me the creeps all over. If one were to crawl on me, I'm *sure* I should die – I'm sure I should.'

'I hope not,' whispered the young Russian.

'I'm sure I should, Maxim,' she asseverated.

'Then one won't crawl on you,' said Gerald, smiling and knowing. In some strange way he understood her.

'It's metaphysical, as Gerald says,' Birkin stated.

There was a little pause of uneasiness.

'And are you afraid of nothing else, Pussum?' asked the young Russian, in his quick, hushed, elegant manner.

'Not weally,' she said. 'I am afwaid of some things, but not weally the same. I'm not afwaid of *blood.*'

'Not afwaid of blood!' exclaimed a young man with a thick, pale, jeering face, who had just come to the table and was drinking whisky.

The Pussum turned on him a sulky look of dislike, low and ugly.

'Aren't you really afraid of blud?' the other persisted, a sneer all over his face.

'No, I'm not,' she retorted.

'Why, have you ever seen blood, except in a dentist's spittoon?' jeered the young man.

'I wasn't speaking to you,' she replied rather superbly.

'You can answer me, can't you?' he said.

For reply, she suddenly jabbed a knife across his thick, pale hand. He started up with a vulgar curse.

'Show's what you are,' said the Pussum in contempt.

'Curse you,' said the young man, standing by the table and looking down at her with acrid malevolence.

'Stop that,' said Gerald, in quick, instinctive command.

The young man stood looking down at her with sardonic contempt, a cowed, self-conscious look on his thick, pale face. The blood began to flow from his hand.

'Oh, how horrible, take it away!' squealed Halliday, turning green and averting his face.

'D'you feel ill?' asked the sardonic young man, in some concern. 'Do you feel ill, Julius? Garn, it's nothing, man, don't give her the pleasure of letting her think she's performed a feat – don't give her the satisfaction, man – it's just what she wants.'

'Oh!' squealed Halliday.

'He's going to cat,* Maxim,' said the Pussum warningly. The suave young Russian rose and took Halliday by the arm, leading him away. Birkin, white and diminished, looked on as if he were displeased. The wounded, sardonic young man moved away, ignoring his bleeding hand in the most conspicuous fashion.

* vomit.

'He's an awful coward, really,' said the Pussum to Gerald. 'He's got such an influence over Julius.'

'Who is he?' asked Gerald.

'He's a Jew, really. I can't bear him.'

'Well, he's quite unimportant. But what's wrong with Halliday?'

'Julius's the most awful coward you've ever seen,' she cried. 'He always faints if I lift a knife – he's tewwified of me.'

'H'm!' said Gerald.

'They're all afwaid of me,' she said. 'Only the Jew thinks he's going to show his courage. But he's the biggest coward of them all, really, because he's afwaid what people will think about him – and Julius doesn't care about that.'

'They've a lot of valour between them,' said Gerald good-humouredly.

The Pussum looked at him with a slow, slow smile. She was very handsome, flushed, and confident in dreadful knowledge. Two little points of light glinted on Gerald's eyes.

'Why do they call you Pussum, because you're like a cat?' he asked her.

'I expect so,' she said.

The smile grew more intense on his face.

'You are, rather; or a young, female panther.'

'Oh God, Gerald!' said Birkin, in some disgust.

They both looked uneasily at Birkin.

'You're silent tonight, Wupert,' she said to him, with a slight insolence, being safe with the other man.

Halliday was coming back, looking forlorn and sick.

'Pussum,' he said, 'I wish you wouldn't do these things – Oh!' He sank in his chair with a groan.

'You'd better go home,' she said to him.

'I *will* go home,' he said. 'But won't you all come along. Won't you come round to the flat?' he said to Gerald. 'I should be so glad if you would. Do – that'll be splendid. I say?' He looked round for a waiter. 'Get me a taxi.' Then he groaned again. 'Oh I do feel – perfectly ghastly! Pussum, you see what you do to me.'

'Then why are you such an idiot?' she said with sullen calm.

'But I'm not an idiot! Oh, how awful! Do come, everybody, it will be so splendid. Pussum, you are coming. What? Oh but you *must* come, yes, you must. What? Oh, my dear girl, don't make a fuss now, I feel perfectly – Oh, it's so ghastly – Ho! – er! oh!'

'You know you can't drink,' she said to him, coldly.

'I tell you it isn't drink – it's your disgusting behaviour, Pussum, it's nothing else. Oh, how awful! Libidnikov, do let us go.'

'He's only drunk one glass – only one glass,' came the rapid, hushed voice of the young Russian.

They all moved off to the door. The girl kept near to Gerald, and seemed to be at one in her motion with him. He was aware of this, and filled with demon-satisfaction that his motion held good for two. He held her in the hollow of his will, and she was soft, secret, invisible in her stirring there.

They crowded five of them into the taxi-cab. Halliday lurched in first, and dropped into his seat against the other window. Then the Pussum took her place, and Gerald sat next to her. They heard the young Russian giving orders to the driver, then they were all seated in the dark, crowded close together, Halliday groaning and leaning out of the window. They felt the swift, muffled motion of the car.

The Pussum sat near to Gerald, and she seemed to become soft, subtly to infuse herself into his bones, as if she were passing into him in a black, electric flow. Her being suffused into his veins like a magnetic darkness, and concentrated at the base of his spine like a fearful source of power. Meanwhile her voice sounded out reedy and nonchalant, as she talked indifferently with Birkin and with Maxim. Between her and Gerald was this silence and this black, electric comprehension in the darkness. Then she found his hand, and grasped it in her own firm, small clasp. It was so utterly dark, and yet such a naked statement, that rapid vibrations ran through his blood and over his brain, he was no longer responsible. Still her voice rang on like a bell, tinged with a tone of mockery. And as she swung her head, her fine mane of hair just swept his face, and all his nerves were on fire, as with a subtle friction of electricity. But the great centre of his force held steady, a magnificent pride to him, at the base of his spine.

They arrived at a large block of buildings, went up in a lift, and presently a door was being opened for them by a Hindu. Gerald looked in surprise, wondering if he were a gentleman, one of the Hindus down from Oxford, perhaps. But no, he was the man-servant.

'Make tea, Hasan,' said Halliday.

'There is a room for me?' said Birkin.

To both of which questions the man grinned, and murmured.

He made Gerald uncertain, because, being tall and slender and reticent, he looked like a gentleman.

'Who is your servant?' he asked of Halliday. 'He looks a swell.'

'Oh yes – that's because he's dressed in another man's clothes. He's anything but a swell, really. We found him in the road, starving. So I took him here, and another man gave him clothes. He's anything but what he seems to be – his only advantage is that he can't speak English and can't understand it, so he's perfectly safe.'

'He's very dirty,' said the young Russian swiftly and silently.

Directly, the man appeared in the doorway.

'What is it?' said Halliday.

The Hindu grinned, and murmured shyly:

'Want to speak to master.'

Gerald watched curiously. The fellow in the doorway was good-looking and clean-limbed, his bearing was calm, he looked elegant, aristocratic. Yet he was half a savage, grinning foolishly. Halliday went out into the corridor to speak with him.

'What?' they heard his voice. 'What? What do you say? Tell me again. What? Want money? Want *more* money? But what do

you want money for?' There was the confused sound of the
Hindu's talking, then Halliday appeared in the room, smiling also
foolishly, and saying:

'He says he wants money to buy underclothing. Can anybody
lend me a shilling? Oh thanks, a shilling will do to buy all the
underclothes he wants.' He took the money from Gerald and
went out into the passage again, where they heard him saying,
'You can't want more money, you had three and six yesterday.
You mustn't ask for any more. Bring the tea in quickly.'

Gerald looked round the room. It was an ordinary London
sitting-room in a flat, evidently taken furnished, rather common
and ugly. But there were several negro statues, wood-carvings
from West Africa? strange and disturbing, the carved negroes
looked almost like the fœtus of a human being. One was a woman
sitting naked in a strange posture, and looking tortured, her
abdomen stuck out. The young Russian explained that she was
sitting in child-birth, clutching the ends of the band that hung
from her neck, one in each hand, so that she could bear down,
and help labour. The strange, transfixed, rudimentary face of the
Woman again reminded Gerald of a fœtus, it was also rather
wonderful, conveying the suggestion of the extreme of physical
sensation, beyond the limits of mental consciousness.

'Aren't they rather obscene?' he asked, disapproving.

'I don't know,' murmured the other rapidly. 'I have never
defined the obscene. I think they are very good.'

Gerald turned away. There were one or two new pictures in
the room, in the Futurist manner; there was a large piano. And
these, with some ordinary London lodging-house furniture of the
better sort, completed the whole.

The Pussum had taken off her hat and coat, and was seated
on the sofa. She was evidently quite at home in the house, but
uncertain, suspended. She did not quite know her position. Her
alliance for the time being was with Gerald, and she did not know
how far this was admitted by any of the men. She was considering
how she should carry off the situation. She was determined to
have her experience. Now, at this eleventh hour, she was not to

be baulked. Her face was flushed as with battle, her eye was brooding but inevitable.

The man came in with tea and a bottle of Kümmel. He set the tray on a little table before the couch.

'Pussum,' said Halliday, 'pour out the tea.'

She did not move.

'Won't you do it?' Halliday repeated, in a state of nervous apprehension. 'I've not come back here as it was before,' she said. 'I only came because the others wanted me to, not for your sake.'

'My dear Pussum, you know you are your own mistress. I don't want you to do anything but use the flat for your own convenience – you know it, I've told you so many times.'

She did not reply, but silently, reservedly reached for the teapot. They all sat round and drank tea. Gerald could feel the electric connection between him and her so strongly, as she sat there quiet and withheld, that another set of conditions altogether had come to pass. Her silence and her immutability' perplexed him. *How* was he going to come to her? And yet he felt it quite inevitable. He trusted completely to the current that held them. His perplexity was only superficial, new conditions reigned, the old were surpassed; here one did as one was possessed to do, no matter what it was.

Birkin rose. It was nearly one o'clock.

'I'm going to bed,' he said. 'Gerald, I'll ring you up in the morning at your place or you ring me up here.'

'Right,' said Gerald, and Birkin went out.

When he was well gone, Halliday said in a stimulated voice, to Gerald:

'I say, won't you stay here – oh do!'

'You can't put everybody up,' said Gerald.

'Oh but I can, perfectly – there are three more beds besides mine – do stay, won't you. Everything is quite ready – there is always somebody here – I always put people up – I love having the house crowded.'

'But there are only two rooms,' said the Pussum, in a cold, hostile voice, 'now Rupert's here.'

'I know there are only two rooms,' said Halliday, in his odd, high way of speaking. 'But what does that matter?'

He was smiling rather foolishly, and he spoke eagerly, with an insinuating determination.

'Julius and I will share one room,' said the Russian in his discreet, precise voice. Halliday and he were friends since Eton.

'It's very simple,' said Gerald, rising and pressing back his arms, stretching himself. Then he went again to look at one of the pictures. Every one of his limbs was turgid with electric force, and his back was tense like a tiger's, with slumbering fire. He was very proud.

The Pussum rose. She gave a black look at Halliday, black and deadly, which brought the rather foolishly pleased smile to that young man's face: Then she went out of the room, with a cold good-night to them all generally.

There was a brief interval, they heard a door close, then Maxim said, in his refined voice:

'That's all right.'

He looked significantly at Gerald, and said again, with a silent nod. 'That's all right – you're all right.'

Gerald looked at the smooth, ruddy, comely face, and at the strange, significant eyes, and it seemed as if the voice of the young Russian, so small and perfect, sounded in the blood rather than in the air.

'*I'm* all right then,' said Gerald.

'Yes! Yes! You're all right,' said the Russian.

Halliday continued to smile, and to say nothing.

Suddenly the Pussum appeared again in the door, her small, childish face looking sullen and vindictive.

'I know you want to catch me out,' came her cold, rather resonant voice. 'But I don't care, I don't care how much you catch me out.'

She turned and was gone again. She had been wearing a loose dressing-gown of purple silk, tied round her waist. She looked so small and childish and vulnerable, almost pitiful. And yet the black looks of her eyes made Gerald feel drowned in some potent darkness that almost frightened him.

The men lit another cigarette and talked casually.

CHAPTER 7

Fetish

IN THE morning Gerald woke late. He had slept heavily. Pussum was still asleep, sleeping childishly and pathetically. There was something small and curled up and defenceless about her, that roused an unsatisfied flame of passion in the young man's blood, a devouring avid pity. He looked at her again. But it would be too cruel to wake her. He subdued himself, and went away.

Hearing voices coming from the sitting-room, Halliday talking to Libidnikov, he went to the door and glanced in. He had on a silk wrap of a beautiful bluish colour, with an amethyst hem.

To his surprise he saw the two young men by the fire, stark naked. Halliday looked up, rather pleased.

'Good-morning,' he said. 'Oh – did you want towels?' And stark naked he went out into the hall, striding a strange, white figure between the unliving furniture. He came back with the towels, and took his former position, crouching seated before the fire on the fender.

'Don't you love to feel the fire on your skin?' he said.

'It *is* rather pleasant,' said Gerald.

'How perfectly splendid it must be to be in a climate where one could do without clothing altogether,' said Halliday.

'Yes,' said Gerald, 'if there weren't so many things that sting and bite.'

''That's a disadvantage,' murmured Maxim.

Gerald looked at him, and with a slight revulsion saw the human animal, golden skinned and bare, somehow humiliating. Halliday was different. He had a rather heavy, slack, broken beauty, white and firm. He was like a Christ in a Pietà.* The animal was not there at all, only the heavy, broken beauty. And Gerald realised how Halliday's eyes were beautiful too, so blue and warm and confused, broken also in their expression. The fireglow fell on his heavy, rather bowed shoulders, he sat slackly crouched on the fender, his face was uplifted, weak, perhaps slightly disintegrate, and yet with a moving beauty of its own.

'Of course,' said Maxim, 'you've been in hot countries where the people go about naked.'

'Oh really!' exclaimed Halliday. 'Where?'

'South America – Amazon,' said Gerald.

'Oh but how perfectly splendid! It's one of the things I want most to do – to live from day to day without *ever* putting on any sort of clothing whatever. If I could do that, I should feel I had lived.'

'But why?' said Gerald. 'I can't see that it makes so much difference.'

'Oh, I think it would be perfectly splendid. I'm sure life would be entirely another thing – entirely different, and perfectly wonderful.'

'But why?' asked Gerald. 'Why should it?'

'Oh – one would *feel* things instead of merely looking at them. I should feel the air move against me, and feel the things I touched, instead of having only to look at them. I'm sure life is all wrong because it has become much too visual – we can neither hear nor feel nor understand, we can only see. I'm sure that is entirely wrong.'

'Yes, that is true, that is true,' said the Russian.

Gerald glanced at him, and saw him, his suave, golden coloured body with the black hair growing fine and freely, like tendrils, and his limbs like smooth plant-stems. He was so healthy

---

* Like Virgin Mary holding the dead Christ.

and well-made, why did he make one ashamed, why did one feel repelled? Why should Gerald even dislike it, why did it seem to him to detract from his own dignity. Was that all a human being amounted to? So uninspired! Thought Gerald.

Birkin suddenly appeared in the doorway, in white pyjamas and wet hair, and a towel over his arm. He was aloof and white, and somehow evanescent.

'There's the bath-room now, if you want it,' he said generally, and was going away again, when Gerald called:

'I say, Rupert!'

'What?' The single white figure appeared again, a presence in the room.

'What do you think of that figure there? I want to know,' Gerald asked.

Birkin, white and strangely ghostly, went over to the carved figure of the negro woman in labour. Her nude, protuberant body crouched in a strange, clutching posture, her hands gripping the ends of the band, above her breast.

'It is art,' said Birkin.

'Very beautiful, it's very beautiful,' said the Russian.

They all drew near to look. Gerald looked at the group of men, the Russian golden and like a water-plant, Halliday tall and heavily, brokenly beautiful, Birkin very white and indefinite, not to be assigned, as he looked closely at the carven woman. Strangely elated, Gerald also lifted his eyes to the face of the wooden figure. And his heart contracted.

He saw vividly with his spirit the grey, forward-stretching face of the negro woman, African and tense, abstracted in utter physical stress. It was a terrible face, void, peaked, abstracted almost into meaninglessness by the weight of sensation beneath. He saw the Pussum in it. As in a dream, he knew her.

'Why is it art?' Gerald asked, shocked, resentful.

'It conveys a complete truth,' said Birkin. 'It contains the whole truth of that state, whatever you feel about it'

'But you can't call it *high* art,' said Gerald.

'High! There are centuries and hundreds of centuries of development in a straight line, behind that carving; it is an awful pitch of culture, of a definite sort.'

'What culture?' Gerald asked, in opposition. He hated the sheer African thing.

'Pure culture in sensation, culture in the physical consciousness, really ultimate *physical* consciousness, mindless, utterly sensual. It is so sensual as to be final, supreme.'

But Gerald resented it. He wanted to keep certain illusions, certain ideas like clothing.

'You like the wrong things, Rupert,' he said, 'things against yourself.'

'Oh, I know, this isn't everything,' Birkin replied, moving away.

When Gerald went back to his room from the bath, he also carried his clothes. He was so conventional at home, that when he was really away, and on the loose, as now, he enjoyed nothing so much as full outrageousness. So he strode with his blue silk wrap over his arm and felt defiant.

The Pussum lay in her bed, motionless, her round, dark eyes like black, unhappy pools. He could only see the black, bottomless pools of her eyes. Perhaps she suffered. The sensation of her inchoate suffering roused the old sharp flame in him, a mordant pity, a passion almost of cruelty.

'You are awake now,' he said to her. 'What time is it?' came her muted voice.

She seemed to flow back, almost like liquid, from his approach, to sink helplessly away from him. Her inchoate look of a violated slave, whose fulfilment lies in her further and further violation, made his nerves quiver with acutely desirable sensation. After all, his was the only will, she was the passive substance of his will. He tingled with the subtle, biting sensation. And then he knew, he must go away from her, there must be pure separation between them.

It was a quiet and ordinary breakfast, the four men all looking very clean and bathed. Gerald and the Russian were both correct and *comme il faut** in appearance and manner, Birkin was gaunt and sick, and looked a failure in his attempt to be a properly dressed man, like Gerald and Maxim. Halliday wore tweeds and a green flannel shirt, and a rag of a tie, which was just right for him. The Hindu brought in a great deal of soft toast, and looked exactly the same as he had looked the night before, statically the same.

At the end of the breakfast the Pussum appeared, in a purple silk wrap with a shimmering sash. She had recovered herself somewhat, but was mute and lifeless still. It was a torment to her when anybody spoke to her. Her face was like a small, fine mask, sinister too, masked with unwilling suffering. It was almost midday. Gerald rose and went away to his business, glad to get out. But he bad not finished. He was coming back again at evening, they were all dining together, and he had booked seats for the party, excepting Birkin, at a music-hall.

At night they came back to the flat very late again, again flushed with drink. Again the man-servant – who invariably disappeared between the hours of ten and twelve at night – came in silently and inscrutably with tea, bending in a slow, strange, leopard-like fashion to put the tray softly on the table. His face was immutable, aristocratic-looking, tinged slightly with grey under the skin; he was young and good-looking. But Birkin felt a slight sickness, looking at him, and feeling the slight greyness as an ash or a corruption, in the aristocratic inscrutability of expression a nauseating, bestial stupidity.

Again they talked cordially and rousedly together. But already a certain friability was coming over the party, Birkin was mad with irritation, Halliday was turning in an insane hatred against Gerald, the Pussum was becoming hard and cold, like a flint knife, and Halliday was laying himself out to her. And her intention, ultimately, was to capture Halliday, to have complete power over him.

* correctly stylish.

In the morning they all stalked and lounged about again. But Gerald could feel a strange hostility to himself in the air. It roused his obstinacy, and he stood up against it. He hung on for two more days. The result was a nasty and insane scene with Halliday on the fourth evening. Halliday turned with absurd animosity upon Gerald, in the café. There was a row. Gerald was on the point of knocking-in Halliday's face; when he was filled with sudden disgust and indifference, and he went away, leaving Halliday in a foolish state of gloating triumph, the Pussum hard and established, and Maxim standing clear. Birkin was absent, he had gone out of town again.

Gerald was piqued because he had left without giving the Pussum money. It was true, she did not care whether he gave her money or not, and he knew it. But she would have been glad of ten pounds, and he would have been *very* glad to give them to her. Now he felt in a false position. He went away chewing his lips to get at the ends of his short clipped moustache. He knew the Pussum was merely glad to be rid of him. She had got her Halliday whom she wanted. She wanted him completely in her power. Then she would marry him. She wanted to marry him. She had set her will on marrying Halliday. She never wanted to hear of Gerald again; unless, perhaps, she were in difficulty; because after all, Gerald was what she called a man, and these others, Halliday, Libidnikov, Birkin, the whole Bohemian set, they were only half men. But it was half men she could deal with. She felt sure of herself with them. The real men, like Gerald, put her in her place too much.

Still, she respected Gerald, she really respected him. She had managed to get his address, so that she could appeal to him in time of distress. She knew he wanted to give her money. She would perhaps write to him on that inevitable rainy day.

CHAPTER 8

Breadalby

BREADALBY WAS a Georgian house with Corinthian pillars, standing among the softer, greener hills of Derbyshire, not far from Cromford. In front, it looked over a lawn, over a few trees, down to a string of fish ponds in the hollow of the silent park. At the back were trees, among which were to be found the stables, and the big kitchen garden, behind which was a wood.

It was a very quiet place, some miles from the high-road, back from the Derwent Valley, outside the show scenery. Silent and forsaken, the golden stucco showed between the trees, the house-front looked down the park, unchanged and unchanging.

Of late, however, Hermione had lived a good deal at the house. She had turned away from London, away from Oxford, towards the silence of the country. Her father was mostly absent, abroad, she was either alone in the house, with her visitors, of whom there were always several, or she had with her, her brother, a bachelor, and a Liberal Member of Parliament. He always came down when the House was not sitting, seemed always to be present in Breadalby, although he was most conscientious in his attendance to duty.

The summer was just coming in when Ursula and Gudrun went to stay the second time with Hermione. Coming along in the car, after they had entered the park, they looked across the dip, where the fish ponds lay in silence, at the pillared front of the house, sunny and small like an English drawing of the old school, on the brow of the green hill, against the trees. There were small figures on the green lawn, women in lavender and yellow moving to the shade of the enormous, beautifully balanced cedar tree.

'Isn't it complete!' said Gudrun. 'It is as final as an old aquatint.' She spoke with some resentment in her voice, as if she were captivated unwillingly, as if she must admire against her will.

'Do you love it?' asked Ursula.

'I don't *love* it, but in its way, I think it is quite complete.'

The motor-car ran down the hill and up again in one breath, and they were curving to the side door. A parlour-maid appeared, and then Hermione, coming forward with her pale face lifted, and her hands outstretched, advancing straight to the new-comers, her voice singing:

'Here you are – I'm so glad to see you – ' she kissed Gudrun – 'So glad to see you – ' she kissed Ursula and remained with her arm round her. 'Are you very tired?'

'Not at all tired,' said Ursula.

'Are you tired, Gudrun?'

'Not at all, thanks,' said Gudrun.

'No – ' drawled Hermione. And she stood and looked at them. The two girls were embarrassed because she would not move into the house, but must have her little scene of welcome there on the path. The servants waited.

'Come in,' said Hermione at last, having fully taken in the pair of them. Gudrun was the more beautiful and attractive, she had decided again, Ursula was more physical, more womanly. She admired Gudrun's dress more. It was of green poplin, with a loose coat above it, of broad, dark-green and dark-brown stripes. The hat was of a pale, greenish straw, the colour of new hay, and it had a plaited ribbon of black and orange, the stockings were dark green, the shoes black. It was a good get-up, at once fashionable and individual. Ursula, in dark blue, was more ordinary, though she also looked well.

Hermione herself wore a dress of prune-coloured silk, with coral beads and coral coloured stockings. But her dress was both shabby and soiled, even rather dirty.

'You would like to see your rooms now, wouldn't you! Yes. We will go up now, shall we?'

Ursula was glad when she could be left alone in her room. Hermione lingered so long, made such a stress on one. She stood so near to one, pressing herself near upon one, in a way that was most embarrassing and oppressive. She seemed to hinder one's workings.

Lunch was served on the lawn, under the great tree, whose thick, blackish boughs came down close to the grass. There were present a young Italian woman, slight and fashionable, a young, athletic-looking Miss Bradley, a learned, dry Baronet of fifty, who was always making witticisms and laughing at them heartily in a harsh, horse-laugh, there was Rupert Birkin, and then a woman secretary, a Fräulein März, young and slim and pretty.

The food was very good, that was one thing. Gudrun, critical of everything, gave it her full approval. Ursula loved the situation, the white table by the cedar tree, the scent of new sunshine, the little vision of the leafy park, with far-off deer feeding peacefully. There seemed a magic circle drawn about the place, shutting out the present, enclosing the delightful, precious past, trees and deer and silence, like a dream.

But in spirit she was unhappy. The talk went on like a rattle of small artillery, always slightly sententious, with a sententiousness that was only emphasised by the continual crackling of a witticism, the continual spatter of verbal jest, designed to give a tone of flippancy to a stream of conversation that was all critical and general, a canal of conversation rather than a stream.

The attitude was mental and very wearying. Only the elderly sociologist, whose mental fibre was so tough as to be insentient, seemed to be thoroughly happy. Birkin was down in the mouth. Hermione appeared, with amazing persistence, to wish to ridicule him and make him look ignominious in the eyes of everybody. And it was surprising how she seemed to succeed, how helpless he seemed against her. He looked completely insignificant. Ursula and Gudrun, both very unused, were mostly silent, listening to the slow, rhapsodic sing-song of Hermione, or the verbal sallies of Sir Joshua, or the prattle of Fräulein, or the responses of the other two women.

Luncheon was over, coffee was brought out on the grass, the party left the table and sat about in lounge chairs, in the shade or in the sunshine as they wished. Fräulein departed into the house, Hermione took up her embroidery, the little Contessa took a book, Miss Bradley was weaving a basket out of fine grass, and there they all were on the lawn in the early summer afternoon, working leisurely and spattering with half-intellectual, deliberate talk.

Suddenly there was the sound of the brakes and the shutting off of a motor-car.

'There's Salsie!' sang Hermione, in her slow, amusing sing-song. And laying down her work, she rose slowly, and slowly passed over the lawn, round the bushes, out of sight

'Who is it?' asked Gudrun.

'Mr Roddice – Miss Roddice's brother – at least, I suppose it's he,' said Sir Joshua.

'Salsie, yes, it is her brother,' said the little Contessa, lifting her head for a moment from her book, and speaking as if to give information, in her slightly deepened, guttural English.

They all waited. And then round the bushes came the tall form of Alexander Roddice, striding romantically like a Meredith hero who remembers Disraeli. He was cordial with everybody, he was at once a host, with an easy, offhand hospitality that he had learned for Hermione's friends. He had just come down from London, from the House. At once the atmosphere of the House of Commons made itself felt over the lawn: the Home Secretary had said such and such a thing, and he, Roddice, on the other hand, thought such and such a thing, and had said so-and-so to the PM.

Now Hermione came round the bushes with Gerald Crich. He had come along with Alexander. Gerald was presented to everybody, was kept by Hermione for a few moments in full view, then he was led away, still by Hermione. He was evidently her guest of the moment.

There had been a split in the Cabinet; the minister for Education had resigned owing to adverse criticism. This started a conversation on education.

'Of course,' said Hermione, lifting her face like a rhapsodist, 'there *can* be no reason, no *excuse* for education, except the joy and beauty of knowledge in itself.' She seemed to rumble and ruminate with subterranean thoughts for a minute, then she proceeded: 'Vocational education *isn't* education, it is the close of education.'

Gerald, on the brink of discussion, sniffed the air with delight and prepared for action.

'Not necessarily,' he said. 'But isn't education really like gymnastics, isn't the end of education the production of a well-trained, vigorous, energetic mind?'

Just as athletics produce a healthy body, ready for anything,' cried Miss Bradley, in hearty accord.

Gudrun looked at her in silent loathing.

'Well – ' rumbled Hermione, 'I don't know. To me the pleasure of knowing is so great, so *wonderful* – nothing has meant so much to me in all life, as certain knowledge – no, I am sure – nothing.'

'What knowledge, for example, Hermione?' asked Alexander.

Hermione lifted her face and rumbled –

'M-m-m – I don't know. . . But one thing was the stars, when I really understood something about the stars. One feels so *uplifted,* so *unbounded.* . .'

Birkin looked at her in a white fury.

'What do you want to feel unbounded for?' he said sarcastically. 'You don't want to *be* unbounded.'

Hermione recoiled in offence.

'Yes, but one does have that limitless feeling,' said Gerald. 'It's like getting on top of the mountain and seeing the Pacific.'

'Silent, upon a peak in Dariayn,'* murmured the Italian, lifting her face for a moment from her book.

'Not necessarily in Darien,' said Gerald, while Ursula began to laugh.

Hermione waited for the dust to settle, and then she said, untouched:

'Yes, it is the greatest thing in life – to *know.* It is really to be happy, to be *free.* '

'Knowledge is, of course, liberty,' said Mattheson.

'In compressed tabloids,' said Birkin, looking at the dry, stiff little body of the Baronet. Immediately Gudrun saw the famous

* From Keat's poem: 'On First Looking into Chapman's Homer'.

sociologist as a flat bottle, containing tabloids of compressed liberty. That pleased her. Sir Joshua was labelled and placed forever in her mind.

'What does that mean, Rupert?' sang Hermione, in a calm snub.

'You can only have knowledge, strictly,' he replied, 'of things concluded, in the past. It's like bottling the liberty of last summer in the bottled gooseberries.'

'*Can* one have knowledge only of the past?' asked the Baronet, pointedly. 'Could we call our knowledge of the laws of gravitation for instance, knowledge of the past?'

'Yes,' said Birkin.

'There is a most beautiful thing in my book,' suddenly piped the little Italian woman. 'It says the man came to the door and threw his eyes down the street.'

There was a general laugh in the company. Miss Bradley went and looked over the shoulder of the Contessa.

'See!' said the Contessa.

'Bazarov came to the door and threw his eyes hurriedly down the street,' she read.

Again there was a loud laugh, the most startling of which was the Baronet's, which rattled out like a clatter of falling stones.

'What is the book?' asked Alexander, promptly.

'Fathers and Sons, by Turgenev,' said the little foreigner, pronouncing every syllable distinctly. She looked at the cover, to verify herself.

'An old American edition,' said Birkin.

'Ha! – of course – translated from the French,' said Alexander, with a fine declamatory voice. 'Bazarov ouvra la porte et jeta les yeux dans la rue.'

He looked brightly round the company.

'I wonder what the "hurriedly" was,' said Ursula.

They all began to guess.

And then, to the amazement of everybody, the maid came hurrying with a large tea-tray. The afternoon had passed so swiftly.

After tea, they were all gathered for a walk.

'Would you like to come for a walk?' said Hermione to each of them, one by one. And they all said yes, feeling somehow like prisoners marshalled for exercise. Birkin only refused.

'Will you come for a walk, Rupert?'

'No, Hermione.'

'But are you *sure?*'

'Quite sure.' There was a second's hesitation.

'And why not?' sang Hermione's question. It made her blood run sharp, to 'be thwarted in even so trifling a matter. She intended them all to walk with her in the park.

'Because I don't like trooping off in a gang,' he said.

Her voice rumbled in her throat for a moment. Then she said, with a curious stray calm:

'Then we'll leave a little boy behind, if he's sulky.'

And she looked really gay, while she insulted him. But it merely made him stiff.

She trailed off to the rest of the company, only turning to wave her handkerchief to him, and to chuckle with laughter, singing out:

'Good-bye, good-bye, little boy.'

'Good-bye, impudent hag,' he said to himself

They all went through the park. Hermione wanted to show them the wild daffodils on a little slope. 'This way, this way,' sang her leisurely voice at intervals. And they had all to come this way. The daffodils were pretty, but who could see them? Ursula was stiff all over with resentment by this time, resentment of the whole atmosphere. Gudrun, mocking and objective, watched and registered everything.

They looked at the shy deer, and Hermione talked to the stag, as if he too were a boy she wanted to wheedle and fondle. He was male, so she must exert some kind of power over him. They trailed home by the fish-ponds, and Hermione told them about the quarrel of two male swans, who had striven for the love of the one lady. She chuckled and laughed as she told how the ousted lover had sat with his head buried under his wing, on the gravel.

When they arrived back at the house, Hermione stood on the lawn and sang out, in a strange, small, high voice that carried very far:

'Rupert! Rupert!' The first syllable was high and slow, the second dropped down. 'Roo-o-opert.'

But there was no answer. A maid appeared.

'Where is Mr Birkin, Alice?' asked the mild straying voice of Hermione. But under the straying voice, what a persistent, almost insane *will!*

'I think he's in his room, madam.'

'Is he?'

Hermione went slowly up the stairs, along the corridor, singing out in her high, small call:

'Ru-oo-pert! Ru-oo pert!'

She came to his door, and tapped, still crying: 'Roo-pert.'

'Yes,' sounded his voice at last.

'What are you doing?'

The question was mild and curious.

There was no answer. Then he opened the door.

'We've come back,' said Hermione. 'The daffodils are *so* beautiful.'

'Yes,' he said, 'I've seen them.'

She looked at him with her long, slow, impassive look, along her cheeks.

'Have you?' she echoed. And she remained looking at him. She was stimulated above all things by this conflict with him, when he was like a sulky boy, helpless, and she had him safe at Breadalby. But underneath she knew the split was coming, and her hatred of him was subconscious and intense.

'What were you doing?' she reiterated, in her mild, indifferent tone. He did not answer, and she made her way, almost unconsciously into his room. He had taken a Chinese drawing of geese from the boudoir, and was copying it, with much skill and vividness.

'You are copying the drawing,' she said, standing near the table, and looking down at his work. 'Yes. How beautifully you do it! You like it very much, don't you?'

'It's a marvellous drawing,' he said.

'Is it? I'm so glad you like it, because I've always been fond of it. The Chinese Ambassador gave it me.'

'I know,' he said.

'But why do you copy it?' she asked, casual and sing-song. 'Why not do something original?'

'I want to know it,' he replied. 'One gets more of China, copying this picture, than reading all the books.'

'And what do you get?'

She was at once roused, she laid as it were violent hands on him, to extract his secrets from him. She *must* know. It was a dreadful tyranny, an obsession in her, to know all he knew. For some time he was silent, hating to answer her. Then, compelled, he began:

'I know what centres they live from – what they perceive and feel – the hot, stinging centrality of a goose in the flux of cold water and mud – the curious bitter stinging heat of a goose's blood, entering their own blood like an inoculation of corruptive fire – fire of the cold-burning mud – the lotus mystery.'

Hermione looked at him along her narrow, pallid cheeks. Her eyes were strange and drugged, heavy under their heavy, drooping lids. Her thin bosom shrugged convulsively. He stared back at her, devilish and unchanging. With another strange, sick convulsion, she turned away, as if she were sick, could feel dissolution setting-in in her body. For with her mind she was unable to attend to his words, he caught her, as it were, beneath all her defences, and destroyed her with some insidious occult potency.

'Yes,' she said, as if she did not know what she were saying. 'Yes,' and she swallowed, and tried to regain her mind. But she could not, she was witless, decentralised. Use all her will as she might, she could not recover. She suffered the ghastliness of dissolution, broken and gone in a horrible corruption. And he stood and looked at her unmoved. She strayed out, pallid and preyed-upon like a ghost, like one attacked by the tomb-influences which dog us. And she was gone like a corpse, that has no presence, no connection. He remained hard and vindictive.

Hermione came down to dinner strange and sepulchral, her eyes heavy and full of sepulchral darkness, strength. She had put on a dress of stiff old greenish brocade, that fitted tight and made her look tall and rather terrible, ghastly. In the gay light of the drawing-room she was uncanny and oppressive. But seated in the half-light of the dining room, sitting stiffly before the shaded candles on the table, she seemed a power, a presence. She listened and attended with a drugged attention.

The party was gay and extravagant in appearance, everybody had put on evening dress except Birkin and Joshua Mattheson. The little Italian Contessa wore a dress of tissue, of orange and gold and black velvet in soft wide stripes, Gudrun was emerald green with strange net-work, Ursula was in yellow with dull silver veiling, Miss Bradley was of grey, crimson and jet, Fräulein März wore pale blue. It gave Hermione a sudden convulsive sensation of pleasure, to see these rich colours under the candle-light. She was aware of the talk going on, ceaselessly, Joshua's voice dominating; of the ceaseless pitter-patter of women's light laughter and responses; of the brilliant colours and the white table and the shadow above and below; and she seemed in a swoon of gratification, convulsed with pleasure and yet sick, like a *revenant*.* She took very little part in the conversation, yet she heard it all, it was all hers.

They all went together into the drawing-room, as if they were one family, easily, without any attention to ceremony. Fräulein handed the coffee, everybody smoked cigarettes, or else long warden pipes of white clay, of which a sheaf was provided.

'Will you smoke? – cigarettes or pipe?' asked Fräulein prettily. There was a circle of people, Sir Joshua with his eighteenth-century appearance, Gerald the amused, handsome young Englishman, Alexander tall and the handsome politician, democratic and lucid, Hermione strange like a long Cassandra, and the women

* Like a ghost.

lurid with colour, all dutifully smoking their long white pipes, and sitting in a half-moon in the comfortable, soft-lighted drawing-room, round the logs that flickered on the marble hearth.

The talk was very often political or sociological, and interesting, curiously anarchistic. There was an accumulation of powerful force in the room, powerful and destructive. Everything seemed to be thrown into the melting pot, and it seemed to Ursula they were all witches, helping the pot to bubble. There was an elation and a satisfaction in it all, but it was cruelly exhausting for the new-comers, this ruthless mental pressure, this powerful, consuming, destructive mentality that emanated from Joshua and Hermione and Birkin and dominated the rest.

But a sickness, a fearful nausea gathered possession of Hermione. There was a lull in the talk, as it was arrested by her unconscious but all-powerful will.

'Salsie, won't you play something?' said Hermione, breaking off completely. 'Won't somebody dance? Gudrun, you will dance, won't you? I wish you would. Anche tu, Palestra, ballerai? – si, per piacere.[1] You too, Ursula.'

Hermione rose and slowly pulled the gold-embroidered band that hung by the mantel, clinging to it for a moment, then releasing it suddenly. Like a priestess she looked, unconscious, sunk in a heavy half-trance.

A servant came, and soon reappeared with armfuls of silk robes and shawls and scarves, mostly oriental, things that Hermione, with her love for beautiful extravagant dress, had collected gradually.

'The three women will dance together,' she said.

'What shall it be?' asked Alexander, rising briskly.

'Vergini Delle Rocchette,'[2] said the Contessa at once.

'They are so languid,' said Ursula.

'The three witches from Macbeth,' suggested Fräulein usefully. It was finally decided to do Naomi and Ruth and Orpah.[3]

---

1 Italian: "Will you dance Palestra? Please – Yes?
2 Italian: The Virgins of the little rocks, as appearing in the play of Italian writer Gabriele D'Annunzio.
3 In the Old Testament widowed Naomi has two widowed daughters-in-law, Ruth and Oprah.

Ursula was Naomi, Gudrun was Ruth, the Contessa was Orpah. The idea was to make a little ballet, in the style of the Russian Ballet of Pavlova and Nijinsky.

The Contessa was ready first, Alexander went to the piano, a space was cleared. Orpah, in beautiful oriental clothes, began slowly to dance the death of her husband. Then Ruth came, and they wept together, and lamented, then Naomi came to comfort them. It was all done in dumb show, the women danced their emotion in gesture and motion. The little drama went on for a quarter of an hour.

Ursula was beautiful as Naomi. All her men were dead, it remained to her only to stand alone in indomitable assertion, demanding nothing. Ruth, woman-loving, loved her. Orpah, a vivid, sensational, subtle widow, would go back to the former life, a repetition. The interplay between the women was real and rather frightening. It was strange to see how Gudrun clung with heavy, desperate passion to Ursula, yet smiled with subtle malevolence against her, how Ursula accepted silently, unable to provide any more either for herself or for the other, but dangerous and indomitable, refuting her grief.

Hermione loved to watch. She could see the Contessa's rapid, stoat-like sensationalism, Gudrun's ultimate but treacherous cleaving to the woman in her sister, Ursula's dangerous helplessness, as if she were helplessly weighted, and unreleased.

'That was very beautiful,' everybody cried with one accord. But Hermione writhed in her soul, knowing what she could not know. She cried out for more dancing, and it was her will that set the Contessa and Birkin moving mockingly in Malbrouk.

Gerald was excited by the desperate cleaving of Gudrun to Naomi. The essence of that female, subterranean recklessness and mockery penetrated his blood. He could not forget Gudrun's lifted, offered, cleaving, reckless, yet withal mocking weight. And Birkin, watching like a hermit crab from its hole, had seen the brilliant frustration and helplessness of Ursula. She was rich, full of dangerous power. She was like a strange unconscious bud of powerful womanhood. He was unconsciously drawn to her. She was his future.

Alexander played some Hungarian music, and they all danced, seized by the spirit. Gerald was marvellously exhilarated at finding himself in motion, moving towards Gudrun, dancing with feet that could not yet escape from the waltz and the two-step, but feeling his force stir along his limbs and his body, out of captivity. He did not know yet how to dance their convulsive, rag-time sort of dancing, but he knew how to begin. Birkin, when he could get free from the weight of the people present, whom he disliked, danced rapidly and with a real gaiety. And how Hermione hated him for this irresponsible gaiety.

'Now I see,' cried the Contessa excitedly, watching his purely gay motion, which he had all to himself. 'Mr Birkin, he is a changer.'

Hermione looked at her slowly, and shuddered, knowing that only a foreigner could have seen and have said this.

'Cosa vuol'dire, Palestra?'* she asked, sing-song.

'Look,' said the Contessa, in Italian. 'He is not a man, he is a chameleon, a creature of change.'

'He is not a man, he is treacherous, not one of us,' said itself over in Hermione's consciousness. And her soul writhed in the black subjugation to him, because of his power to escape, to exist, other than she did, because he was not consistent, not a man, less than a man. She hated him in a despair that shattered her and broke her down, so that she suffered sheer dissolution like a corpse, and was unconscious of everything save the horrible sickness of dissolution that was taking place within her, body and soul.

The house being full, Gerald was given the smaller room, really the dressing-room, communicating with Birkin's bedroom. When they all took their candles and mounted the stairs, where the lamps were burning subduedly, Hermione captured Ursula and brought her into her own bedroom, to talk to her. A sort of constraint came over Ursula in the big, strange bedroom. Hermione seemed to be bearing down on her, awful and inchoate, making some appeal. They were looking at some Indian silk shirts, gorgeous and sensual in themselves, their shape, their almost corrupt gorgeousness. And Hermione came near, and her bosom

* (It.) "What do you mean Palestra?"

writhed, and Ursula was for a moment blank with panic. And for a moment Hermione's haggard eyes saw the fear on the face of the other, there was again a sort of crash, a crashing down. And Ursula picked up a shirt of rich red and blue silk, made for a young princess of fourteen, and was crying mechanically:

'Isn't it wonderful – who would dare to put those two strong colours together – '

Then Hermione's maid entered silently and Ursula, overcome with dread, escaped, carried away by powerful impulse.

Birkin went straight to bed. He was feeling happy, and sleepy. Since he had danced he was happy. But Gerald would talk to him. Gerald, in evening dress, sat on Birkin's bed when the other lay down, and must talk.

'Who are those two Brangwens?' Gerald asked.

'They live in Beldover.'

'In Beldover! Who are they then?'

'Teachers in the Grammar School.'

There was a pause.

'They are!' exclaimed Gerald at length. 'I thought I had seen them before.'

'It disappoints you?' said Birkin.

'Disappoints me! No – but how is it Hermione has them here?'

'She knew Gudrun in London – that's the younger one, the one with the darker hair – she's an artist – does sculpture and modelling.'

'She's not a teacher in the Grammar School, then – only the other?'

'Both – Gudrun art mistress, Ursula a class mistress.'

'And what's the father?'

'Handicraft instructor in the schools.'

'Really!'

'Class-barriers are breaking down!'

Gerald was always uneasy under the slightly jeering tone of the other.

'That their father is handicraft instructor in a school! What does it matter to me?'

Birkin laughed. Gerald looked at his face, as it lay there laughing and bitter and indifferent on the pillow, and he could not go away.

'I don't suppose you will see very much more of Gudrun, at least. She is a restless bird she'll be gone in a week or two,' said Birkin.

'Where will she go?'

'London, Paris, Rome – heaven knows. I always expect her to sheer off to Damascus or San Francisco; she's a bird of paradise. God knows what she's got to do with Beldover. It goes by contraries, like dreams.'

Gerald pondered for a few moments.

'How do you know her so well?' he asked.

'I knew her in London,' he replied, 'in the Algernon Strange set. She'll know about Pussum and Libidnikov and the rest – even if she doesn't know them personally. She was never quite that set – more conventional, in a way. I've known her for two years, I suppose.'

'And she makes money, apart from her teaching?' asked Gerald.

'Some – irregularly. She can sell her models. She has a certain réclame.'

'How much for?'

'A guinea, ten guineas.'

'And are they good? What are they?'

'I think sometimes they are marvellously good. That is hers, those two wagtails in Hermione's boudoir – you've seen them – they are carved in wood and painted.'

'I thought it was savage carving again.'

'No, hers. That's what they are – animals and birds, sometimes odd small people in everyday dress, really rather wonderful when they come off. They have a sort of funniness that is quite unconscious and subtle.'

'She might be a well-known artist one day?' mused Gerald.

'She might. But I think she won't. She drops her art if anything else catches her. Her contrariness prevents her taking it seriously – she must never be too serious, she feels she might give herself away. And she won't give herself away – she's always on the defensive. That's what I can't stand about her type. By the way, how did things go off with Pussum after I left you? I haven't heard anything.'

'Oh, rather disgusting. Halliday turned objectionable, and I only just saved myself from jumping in his stomach, in a real old-fashioned row.'

Birkin was silent.

'Of course,' he said, 'Julius is somewhat insane. On the one hand he's had religious mania, and on the other, he is fascinated by obscenity. Either he is a pure servant, washing the feet of Christ, or else he is making obscene drawings of Jesus – action and reaction – and between the two, nothing. He is really insane. He wants a pure lily, another girl, with a baby face, on the one hand, and on the other, he *must* have the Pussum, just to defile himself with her.'

'That's what I can't make out,' said Gerald. 'Does he love her, the Pussum, or doesn't he?'

'He neither does nor doesn't. She is the harlot; the actual harlot of adultery to him. And he's got a craving to throw himself into the filth of her. Then he gets up and calls on the name of the lily of purity, the baby-faced girl, and so enjoys himself all round. It's the old story action and reaction, and nothing between.'

'I don't know,' said Gerald, after a pause, 'that he does insult the Pussum so very much. She strikes me as being rather foul.'

'But I thought you liked her,' exclaimed Birkin. 'I always felt fond of her. I never had anything to do with her, personally, that's true.'

'I liked her all right, for a couple of days,' said Gerald. 'But a week of her would have turned me over. There's a certain smell about the skin of those women, that in the end is sickening beyond words – even if you like it at first.'

'I know,' said Birkin. Then he added, rather fretfully, 'But go to bed, Gerald. God knows what time it is.'

Gerald looked at his watch, and at length rose off the bed, and went to his room. But he returned in a few minutes, in his shirt.

'One thing,' he said, seating himself on the bed again. 'We finished up rather stormily, and I never had time to give her anything.'

'Money?' said Birkin. 'She'll get what she wants from Halliday or from one of her acquaintances.'

'But then,' said Gerald, 'I'd rather give her, her dues and settle the account.'

'She doesn't care.'

'No, perhaps not. But one feels the account is left open, and one would rather it were closed.'

'Would you?' said Birkin. He was looking at the white legs of Gerald, as the latter sat on the side of the bed in his shirt. They were white-skinned, full, muscular legs, handsome and decided. Yet they moved Birkin with a sort of pathos, tenderness, as if they were childish.

'I think I'd rather close the account,' said Gerald, repeating himself vaguely.

'It doesn't matter one way or another,' said Birkin.

'You always say it doesn't matter,' said Gerald, a little puzzled, looking down at the face of the other man affectionately.

'Neither does it,' said Birkin.

'But she was a decent sort, really – '

'Render unto Caesarian the things that are Caesarian's,' said Birkin, turning aside. It seemed to him Gerald was talking for the sake of talking. 'Go away, it wearies me – it's too late at night,' he said.

'I wish you'd tell me something that *did* matter,' said Gerald, looking down all the time at the face of the other man, waiting for something. But Birkin turned his face aside.

'All right then, go to sleep,' said Gerald, and he laid his hand affectionately on the other man's shoulder, and went away.

In the morning when Gerald awoke and heard Birkin move, he called out: 'I still think I ought to give the Pussum ten pounds.'

'Oh God!' said Birkin, 'don't be so matter-of-fact. Close the account in your own soul, if you like. It is there you can't close it.'

'How do you know I can't?'

'Knowing you.'

Gerald meditated for some moments.

'It seems to me the right thing to do, you know, with the Pussums, is to pay them.'

'And the right thing for mistresses: keep them. And the right thing for wives: live under the same roof with them. Integer vitae scelerisque purus* – ' said Birkin.

'There's no need to be nasty about it,' said Gerald.

'It bores me. I'm not interested in your peccadilloes.'

'And I don't care whether you are or not – I am.'

The morning was again sunny. The maid had been in and brought the water, and had drawn the curtains. Birkin, sitting up in bed, looked lazily and pleasantly out on the park, that was so green and deserted, romantic, belonging to the past. He was thinking how lovely, how sure, how formed, how final all the things of the past were – the lovely accomplished past – this house, so still and golden, the park slumbering its centuries of peace. And then, what a snare and a delusion, this beauty of static things – what a horrible, dead prison Breadalby really was, what an intolerable confinement, the peace! Yet it was better than the sordid scrambling conflict of the present. If only one might create the future after one's own heart – for a little pure truth, a little unflinching application of simple truth to life, the heart cried out ceaselessly.

'I can't see what you will leave me at all, to be interested in,' came Gerald's voice from the lower room. 'Neither the Pussums, nor the mines, nor anything else.'

'You be interested in what you can, Gerald. Only I'm not interested myself,' said Birkin.

'What am I to do at all, then?' came Gerald's voice.

* Of unblemished life and clean in reputation.

'What you like. What am I to do myself?'

In the silence Birkin could feel Gerald musing this fact.

'I'm blest if I know,' came the good-humoured answer.

'You see,' said Birkin, 'part of you wants the Pussum, and nothing but the Pussum, part of you wants the mines, the business, and nothing but the business – and there you are – all in bits – '

'And part of me wants something else,' said Gerald, in a queer, quiet, real voice.

'What?' said Birkin, rather surprised.

'That's what I hoped you could tell me,' said Gerald.

There was a silence for some time.

'I can't tell you – I can't find my own way, let alone yours. You might marry,' Birkin replied.

'Who – the Pussum?' asked Gerald.

'Perhaps,' said Birkin. And he rose and went to the window.

'That is your panacea,' said Gerald. 'But you haven't even tried it on yourself yet, and you are sick enough.'

'I am,' said Birkin. 'Still, I shall come right.'

'Through marriage?'

'Yes,' Birkin answered obstinately.

'And no,' added Gerald. 'No, no, no, my boy.'

There was a silence between them, and a strange tension of hostility.

They always kept a gap, a distance between them, they wanted always to be free each of the other. Yet there was a curious heart-straining towards each other.

'Salvator femininus,'* said Gerald, satirically.

'Why not?' said Birkin.

'No reason at all,' said Gerald, 'if it really works. But whom will you marry?'

'A woman,' said Birkin.

'Good,' said Gerald.

Birkin and Gerald were the last to come down to breakfast. Hermione liked everybody to be early. She suffered when she felt

* (Lat.) Female Savior.

her day was diminished, she felt she had missed her life. She seemed to grip the hours by the throat, to force her life from them. She was rather pale and ghastly, as if left behind, in the morning. Yet she had her power, her will was strangely pervasive. With the entrance of the two young men a sudden tension was felt.

She lifted her face, and said, in her amused sing-song:

'Good morning! Did you sleep well? I'm so glad.'

And she turned away, ignoring them. Birkin, who knew her well, saw that she intended to discount his existence.

'Will you take what you want from the sideboard?' said Alexander, in a voice slightly suggesting disapprobation. 'I hope the things aren't cold. Oh no! Do you mind putting out the flame under the chafing-dish, Rupert? Thank you.'

Even Alexander was rather authoritative where Hermione was cool. He took his tone from her, inevitably. Birkin sat down and looked at the table. He was so used to this house, to this room, to this atmosphere, through years of intimacy, and now he felt in complete opposition to it all, it had nothing to do with him. How well he knew Hermione, as she sat there, erect and silent and somewhat bemused, and yet so potent, so powerful! He knew her statically, so finally, that it was almost like a madness. It was difficult to believe one was not mad, that one was not a figure in the hall of kings in some Egyptian tomb, where the dead all sat immemorial and tremendous. How utterly he knew Joshua Mattheson, who was talking in his harsh, yet rather mincing voice, endlessly, endlessly, always with a strong mentality working, always interesting, and yet always known, everything he said known beforehand, however novel it was, and clever. Alexander the up-to-date host, so bloodlessly free-and-easy, Fräulein so prettily chiming in just as she should, the little Italian Countess taking notice of everybody, only playing her little game, objective and cold, like a weasel watching everything, and extracting her own amusement, never giving herself in the slightest; then Miss Bradley, heavy and rather subservient, treated with cool, almost amused contempt by Hermione, and therefore slighted by everybody – how known it all was, like a game with the figures set out, the same figures, the Queen of chess, the knights, the pawns, the same now as they were hundreds of years ago, the same figures moving round in one of the innumerable permutations that make up the game. But the game is known, its going on is like a madness, it is so exhausted.

There was Gerald, an amused look on his face; the game pleased him. There was Gudrun, watching with steady, large, hostile eyes; the game fascinated her, and she loathed it. There was Ursula, with a slightly startled look on her face, as if she were hurt, and the pain were just outside her consciousness.

Suddenly Birkin got up and went out.

'That's enough,' he said to himself involuntarily.

Hermione knew his motion, though not in her consciousness. She lifted her heavy eyes and saw him lapse suddenly away, on a sudden, unknown tide, and the waves broke over her. Only her indomitable will remained static and mechanical, she sat at the table making her musing, stray remarks. But the darkness had covered her, she was like a ship that has gone down. It was finished for her too, she was wrecked in the darkness. Yet the unfailing mechanism of her will worked on, she had that activity.

'Shall we bathe this morning?' she said, suddenly looking at them all. 'Splendid,' said Joshua. 'It is a perfect morning.'

'Oh, it is beautiful,' said Fräulein.

'Yes, let us bathe,' said the Italian woman.

'We have no bathing suits,' said Gerald.

'Have mine,' said Alexander. 'I must go to church and read the lessons. They expect me.'

'Are you a Christian?' asked the Italian Countess, with sudden interest.

'No,' said Alexander. 'I'm not. But I believe in keeping up the old institutions.'

'They are so beautiful,' said Fräulein daintily.

'Oh, they are,' cried Miss Bradley.

They all trailed out on to the lawn. It was a sunny, soft morning in early summer, when life ran in the world subtly, like a reminiscence. The church bells were ringing a little way off, not a cloud was in the sky, the swans were like lilies on the water below, the peacocks walked with long, prancing steps across the shadow and into the sunshine of the grass. One wanted to swoon into the by-gone perfection of it all.

'Good-bye,' called Alexander, waving his gloves cheerily, disappeared behind the bushes, on his way to church.

'Now,' said Hermione, 'Shall we all bathe?'

'I won't,' said Ursula.

'You don't want to?' said Hermione, looking at her slowly.

'No. I don't want to,' said Ursula.

'Nor I,' said Gudrun.

'What about my suit?' asked Gerald.

'I don't know,' laughed Hermione, with an odd, amused intonation. 'Will a handkerchief do – a large handkerchief?'

'That will do,' said Gerald.

'Come along then,' sang Hermione.

The first to run across the lawn was the little Italian, small and like a cat, her white legs twinkling as she went, ducking slightly her head, that was tied in a gold silk kerchief. She tripped through the gate and down the grass, and stood, like a tiny figure of ivory and bronze, at the water's edge, having dropped off her towelling, watching the swans, which came up in surprise. Then out ran Miss Bradley, like a large, soft plum in her dark-blue suit. Then Gerald came, a scarlet silk kerchief round his loins, his towels over his arms. He seemed to flaunt himself a little in the sun, lingering and laughing, strolling easily, looking white but natural in his nakedness. Then came Sir Joshua, in an overcoat, and lastly Hermione, striding with stiff grace from out of a great mantle of purple silk, her head tied up in purple and gold. Handsome was her stiff, long body, her straight-stepping white legs, there was a static magnificence about her as she let the cloak float loosely away from her striding. She crossed the lawn like some strange memory, and passed slowly and statelily towards the water.

There were three ponds, in terraces descending the valley, large and smooth and beautiful, lying in the sun. The water ran over a little stone wall, over small rocks, splashing down from one pond to the level below. The swans had gone out on to the opposite bank, the reeds smelled sweet, a faint breeze touched the skin.

Gerald had dived in, after Sir Joshua, and had swum to the end of the pond. There he climbed out and sat on the wall. There was a dive, and the little Countess was swimming like a rat, to join him. They both sat in the sun, laughing and crossing their arms on their breasts. Sir Joshua swam up to them, and stood near them, up to his arm-pits in the water. Then Hermione and Miss Bradley swam over, and they sat in a row on the embankment.

'Aren't they terrifying? Aren't they really terrifying?' said Gudrun. 'Don't they look saurian? They are just like great lizards. Did you ever see anything like Sir Joshua? But really, Ursula, he belongs to the primeval world, when great lizards crawled about.'

Gudrun looked in dismay on Sir Joshua, who stood up to the breast in the water, his long, greyish hair washed down into his eyes, his neck set into thick, crude shoulders. He was talking to Miss Bradley, who, seated on the bank above, plump and big and wet, looked as if she might roll and slither in the water almost like one of the slithering sea-lions in the Zoo.

Ursula watched in silence. Gerald was laughing happily, between Hermione and the Italian. He reminded her of Dionysos,* because his hair was really yellow, his figure so full and laughing. Hermione, in her large, stiff, sinister grace, leaned near him, frightening, as if she were not responsible for what she might do. He knew a certain danger in her, a convulsive madness. But he only laughed the more, turning often to the little Countess, who was flashing up her face at him.

They all dropped into the water, and were swimming together like a shoal of seals. Hermione was powerful and unconscious in the water, large and slow and powerful. Palestra was quick and silent as a water rat, Gerald wavered and flickered, a white natural

* The Greek god of wine and fertility.

shadow. Then, one after the other, they waded out, and went up to the house.

But Gerald lingered a moment to speak to Gudrun.

'You don't like the water?' he said.

She looked at him with a long, slow inscrutable look, as he stood before her negligently, the water standing in beads all over his skin. 'I like it very much,' she replied.

He paused, expecting some sort of explanation.

'And you swim?'

'Yes, I swim.'

Still he would not ask her why she would not go in then. He could feel something ironic in her. He walked away, piqued for the first time.

'Why wouldn't you bathe?' he asked her again, later, when he was once more the properly-dressed young Englishman.

She hesitated a moment before answering, opposing his persistence.

'Because I didn't like the crowd,' she replied.

He laughed, her phrase seemed to re-echo in his consciousness. The flavour of her slang was' piquant to him. Whether he would or not, she signified the real world to him. He wanted to come up to her standards, fulfil her expectations. He knew that her criterion was the only one that mattered. The others were all outsiders, instinctively, whatever they might be socially. And Gerald could not help it, he was bound to strive to come up to her criterion, fulfil her idea of a man and a human-being.

After lunch, when all the others had withdrawn, Hermione and Gerald and Birkin lingered, finishing their talk. There had been some discussion, on the whole quite intellectual and artificial, about a new state, a new world of man. Supposing this old social state *were* broken and destroyed, then, out of the chaos, what then?

The great social idea, said Sir Joshua, was the *social* equality of man. No, said Gerald, the idea was, that every man was fit for his own little bit of a task – let him do that, and then please himself. The unifying principle was the work in hand. Only work, the business of production, held men together. It was mechanical, but then society *was* a mechanism. Apart from work they were isolated, free to do as they liked.

'Oh!' cried Gudrun. 'Then we shan't have names any more – we shall be like the Germans, nothing but Herr Obermeister and Herr Untermeister. I can imagine it – "I am Mrs Colliery-Manager Crich – I am Mrs Member-of-Parliament Roddice. I am Miss Art-Teacher Brangwen." Very pretty that.'

'Things would work very much better, Miss Art-Teacher Brangwen,' said Gerald.

'What things, Mr Colliery-Manager Crich? The relation between you and me, *par exemple?*'

'Yes, for example,' cried the Italian. 'That which is between men and women – !'

'That is non-social,' said Birkin, sarcastically.

'Exactly,' said Gerald. 'Between me and a woman, the social question does not enter. It is my own affair.'

'A ten-pound note on it,' said Birkin.

'You don't admit that a woman is a social being?' asked Ursula of Gerald.

'She is both,' said Gerald. 'She is a social being, as far as society is concerned. But for her own private self, she is a free agent, it is her own affair, what she does.'

'But won't it be rather difficult to arrange the two halves?' asked Ursula.

'Oh no,' replied Gerald. 'They arrange themselves naturally – we see it now, everywhere.'

'Don't you laugh so pleasantly till you're out of the wood,' said Birkin.

Gerald knitted his brows in momentary irritation.

'Was I laughing?' he said.

'*If,*' said Hermione at last, 'we could only realise, that in the *spirit* we are all one, all equal in the spirit, all brothers there – the rest wouldn't matter, there would be no more of this carping and envy and this struggle for power, which destroys, only destroys.'

This speech was received in silence, and almost immediately the party rose from the table. But when the others had gone, Birkin turned round in bitter declamation, saying:

'It is just the opposite, just the contrary, Hermione. We are all different and unequal in spirit – it is only the *social* differences that are based on accidental material conditions. We are all abstractly or mathematically equal, if you like. Every man has hunger and thirst, two eyes, one nose and two legs. We're all the same in point of number. But spiritually, there is pure difference and neither equality nor inequality counts. It is upon these two bits of knowledge that you must found a state. Your democracy is an absolute lie – your brotherhood of man is a pure falsity, if you apply it further than the mathematical abstraction. We all drank milk first, we all eat bread and meat, we all want to ride in motor-cars – therein lies the beginning and the end of the brotherhood of man. But no equality.

'But I, myself, who am myself, what have I to do with equality with any other man or woman? In the spirit, I am as separate as one star is from another, as different in quality and quantity. Establish a state on *that*. One man isn't any better than another, not because they are equal, but because they are intrinsically *other*, that there is no term of comparison. The minute you begin to compare, one man is seen to be far better than another, all the inequality you can imagine is there by nature. I want every man to have his share in the world's goods, so that I am rid of his importunity, so that I can tell him: "Now you've got what you want – you've got your fair share of the world's gear. Now, you one-mouthed fool, mind yourself and don't obstruct me.'

Hermione was looking at him with leering eyes, along her cheeks. He could feel violent waves of hatred and loathing of all he said, coming out of her. It was dynamic hatred and loathing, coming strong and black out of the unconsciousness. She heard his words in her unconscious self, *consciously* she was as if deafened, she paid no heed to them.

'It *sounds* like megalomania, Rupert,' said Gerald, genially.

Hermione gave a queer, grunting-sound. Birkin stood back.

'Yes, let it,' he said suddenly, the whole tone gone out of his voice, that had been so insistent, bearing everybody down. And he went away.

But he felt, later, a little compunction. He had been violent, cruel with poor Hermione: He wanted to recompense her, to make it up. He had hurt her, he had been vindictive. He wanted to be on good terms with her again.

He went into her boudoir, a remote and very cushiony place. She was sitting at her table writing letters. She lifted her face abstractedly when he entered, watched him go to the sofa, and sit down. Then she looked down at her paper again.

He took up a large volume which he had been reading before, and became minutely attentive to his author. His back was towards Hermione. She could not go on with her writing. Her whole mind was a chaos, darkness breaking in upon it, and herself struggling to gain control with her will, as a swimmer struggles with the swirling water. But in spite of her efforts she was borne down, darkness seemed to break over her, she felt as if her heart was bursting. The terrible tension grew stronger and stronger, it was most fearful agony, like being walled up.

And then she realised that his presence was the wall, his presence was destroying her. Unless she could break out, she must die most fearfully, walled up in horror. And he was the wall. She must break down the wall – she must break him down before her, the awful obstruction of him who obstructed her life to the last. It must be done, or she must perish most horribly.

Terribly shocks ran over her body, like shocks of electricity, as if many volts of electricity suddenly struck her down. She was aware of him sitting silently there, an unthinkable evil obstruction. Only this blotted out her mind, pressed out her very breathing, his silent, stooping back, the back of his head.

A terrible voluptuous thrill ran down her arms – she was going to know her voluptuous consummation. Her arms quivered and were strong, immeasurably and irresistibly strong. What delight, what delight in strength, what delirium of pleasure! She was going to have her consummation of voluptuous ecstasy at last. It was coming! In utmost terror and agony, she knew it was upon her now, in extremity of bliss. Her hand closed on a blue, beautiful ball of lapis lazuli that stood on her desk for a paper-weight. She rolled it round in her hand as she rose silently. Her heart was a pure flame in her breast, she was purely unconscious in ecstasy. She moved towards him and stood behind him for a moment in ecstasy. He, closed within the spell, remained motionless and unconscious.

Then swiftly, in a flame that drenched down her body like fluid lightning and gave her a perfect, unutterable consummation, unutterable satisfaction, she brought down the ball of jewel stone with all her force, crash on his head. But her fingers were in the way and deadened the blow. Nevertheless, down went his head on the table on which his book lay, the stone slid aside and over his ear, it was one convulsion of pure bliss for her, lit up by the crushed pain of her fingers. But it was not somehow complete. She lifted her arm high to aim once more, straight down on the head that lay dazed on the table. She must smash it, it must be smashed before her ecstasy was consummated, fulfilled for ever. A thousand lives, a thousand deaths mattered nothing now, only the fulfilment of this perfect ecstasy.

She was not swift, she could only move slowly. A strong spirit in him woke him and made him lift his face and twist to look at her. Her arm was raised, the hand clasping the ball of lapis lazuli. It was her left hand, he realised again with horror that she was left-handed. Hurriedly, with a burrowing motion, he covered his head under the thick volume of Thucydides, and the blow came down, almost breaking his neck, and shattering his heart.

He was shattered, but he was not afraid. Twisting round to face her he pushed the table over and got away from her. He was like a flask that is smashed to atoms, he seemed to himself that he was all fragments, smashed to bits. Yet his movements were perfectly coherent and clear, his soul was entire and unsurprised.

'No you don't, Hermione,' he said in a low voice. 'I don't let you.'

He saw her standing tall and livid and attentive, the stone clenched tense in her hand.

'Stand away and let me go,' he said, drawing near to her.

As if pressed back by some hand, she stood away, watching him all the time without changing, like a neutralised angel confronting him.

'It is no good,' he said, when he had gone past her. 'It isn't I who will die. You hear?'

He kept his face to her as he went out, lest she should strike again. While he was on his guard, she dared not move. And he was on his guard, she was powerless. So he had gone, and left her standing:

She remained perfectly rigid, standing as she was for a long time. Then she staggered to the couch and lay down, and went heavily to sleep. When she awoke, she remembered what she had done, but it seemed to her, she had only hit him, as any woman might do, because he tortured her. She was perfectly right. She knew that, spiritually, she was right. In her own infallible purity, she had done what must be done. She was right, she was pure. A drugged, almost sinister religious expression became permanent on her face.

Birkin, barely conscious, and yet perfectly direct in his motion, went out of the house and straight across the park, to the open country, to the hills. The brilliant day had become overcast, spots of rain were falling. He wandered on to a wild valley-side, where were thickets of hazel, many flowers, tufts of heather, and little clumps of young fir-trees, budding with soft paws. It was rather wet everywhere, there was a stream running down at the bottom of the valley, which was gloomy, or seemed gloomy. He was aware that he could not regain his consciousness, that he was moving in a sort of darkness.

Yet he wanted something. He was happy in the wet hillside, that was overgrown and obscure with bushes and flowers. He wanted to touch them all, to saturate himself with the touch of them all. He took off his clothes, and sat down naked among the primroses, moving his feet softly among the primroses, his legs, his knees, his arms right up to the arm-pits, lying down and letting them touch his belly, his breasts. It was such a fine, cool, subtle touch all over him, he seemed to saturate himself with their contact.

But they were too soft. He went through the long grass to a clump of young fir-trees, that were no higher than a man. The soft sharp boughs beat upon him, as he moved in keen pangs against them, threw little cold showers of drops on his belly, and beat his loins with their clusters of soft-sharp needles. There was a thistle which pricked him vividly, out not too much, because all his movements were too discriminate and soft. To lie down and roll in the sticky, cool young hyacinths, to lie on one's belly and cover one's back with handfuls of fine wet grass, soft as a breath; soft and more delicate and more beautiful than the touch of any woman; and then to sting one's thigh against the living dark bristles of the fir-boughs; and then to feel the light whip of the hazel on one's shoulders, stinging, and then to clasp the silvery birch-trunk against one's breast, its smoothness, its hardness, its vital knots and ridges – this was good, this was all very good, very satisfying. Nothing else would do, nothing else would satisfy, except this coolness and subtlety of vegetation travelling into one's blood. How fortunate he was, that there was this lovely, subtle, responsive vegetation, waiting for him, as he waited for it; how fulfilled he was, how happy!

As he dried himself a little with his handkerchief, he thought about Hermione and the blow. He could feel a pain on the side of his head. But after all, what did it matter? What did Hermione matter, what did people matter altogether? There was this perfect cool loneliness, so lovely and fresh and unexplored. Really, what a mistake he had made, thinking he wanted people, thinking he wanted a woman. He did not want a woman – not in the least. The leaves and the primroses and the trees, they were really lovely and cool and desirable, they really came into the blood and were added on to him. He was enrichened now immeasurably, and so glad.

It was quite right of Hermione to want to kill him. What had he to do with her? Why should he pretend to have anything to do with human beings at all? Here was his world, he wanted nobody and nothing but the lovely, subtle, responsive vegetation, and himself, his own living self.

It was necessary to go back into the world. That was true. But that did not matter, so one knew where one belonged. He knew now where he belonged. This was his place, his marriage place. The world was extraneous.

He climbed out of the valley, wondering if he were mad. But if so, he preferred his own madness, to the regular sanity. He rejoiced in his own madness, he was free. He did not want that old sanity of the world, which was become so repulsive. He rejoiced in the new-found world of his madness. It was so fresh and delicate and so satisfying.

As for the certain grief he felt at the same time, in his soul, that was only the remains of an old ethic, that bade a human being adhere to humanity. But he was weary of the old ethic, of the human being, and of humanity. He loved now the soft, delicate vegetation, that was so cool and perfect. He would overlook the old grief, he would put away the old ethic, he would be free in his new state.

He was aware of the pain in his head becoming more and more difficult every minute. He was walking now along the road to the nearest station. It was raining and he had no hat. But then plenty of cranks went out nowadays without hats, in the rain.

He wondered again how much of his heaviness of heart, a certain depression, was due to fear, fear lest anybody should have seen him naked lying against the vegetation. What a dread he had of mankind, of other people! It amounted almost to horror, to a sort of dream terror – his horror of being observed by some other people. If he were on an island, like Alexander Selkirk, with only the creatures and the trees, he would be free and glad, there would be none of this heaviness, this misgiving. He could love the vegetation and be quite happy and unquestioned, by himself.

He had better send a note to Hermione: she might trouble about him, and he did not want the onus of this. So at the station, he wrote saying:

> I will go on to town – I don't want to come back to Breadalby for the present. But it is quite all right – I don't want you to mind having biffed me, in the least. Tell the others it is just one

of my moods. You were quite right, to biff me – because I know you wanted to. So there's the end of it.

In the train, however, he felt ill. Every motion was insufferable pain, and he was sick. He dragged himself from the station into a cab, feeling his way step by step, like a blind man, and held up only by a dim will.

For a week or two he was ill, but he did not let Hermione know, and she thought he was sulking; there was a complete estrangement between them. She became rapt, abstracted in her conviction of exclusive righteousness. She lived in and by her own self-esteem, conviction of her own rightness of spirit.

CHAPTER 9

Coaldust

GOING HOME from school in the afternoon, the Brangwen girls descended the hill between the picturesque cottages of Willey Green till they came to the railway crossing. There they found the gate shut, because the colliery train was rumbling nearer. They could hear the small locomotive panting hoarsely as it advanced with caution between the embankments. The one-legged man in the little signal-hut by the road stared out from his security, like a crab from a snail-shell.

Whilst the two girls waited, Gerald Crich trotted up on a red Arab mare. He rode well and softly, pleased with the delicate quivering of the creature between his knees. And he was very picturesque, at least in Gudrun's eyes, sitting soft and close on the slender red mare, whose long tail flowed on the air. He saluted the two girls, and drew up at the crossing to wait for the gate, looking down the railway for the approaching train. In spite of her ironic smile at his picturesqueness, Gudrun liked to look at him. He was well-set and easy, his face with its warm tan showed up his whitish, coarse moustache, and his blue eyes were full of sharp light as he watched the distance.

The locomotive chuffed slowly between the banks, hidden. The mare did not like it. She began to wince away, as if hurt by the unknown noise. But Gerald pulled her back and held her head to the gate. The sharp blasts of the chuffing engine broke with more and more force on her. The repeated sharp blows of unknown, terrifying noise struck through her till she was rocking with terror. She recoiled like a spring let go. But a glistening, half-smiling look came into Gerald's face. He brought her back again, inevitably.

The noise was released, the little locomotive with her clanking steel connecting-rod emerged on the highroad, clanking sharply. The mare rebounded like a drop of water from hot iron. Ursula and Gudrun pressed back into the hedge, in fear. But Gerald was heavy on the mare, and forced her back. It seemed as if he sank into her magnetically, and could thrust her back against herself.

'The fool!' cried Ursula loudly. 'Why doesn't he ride away till it's gone by?'

Gudrun was looking at him with black-dilated, spellbound eyes. But he sat glistening and obstinate, forcing the wheeling mare, which spun and swerved like a wind, and yet could not get out of the grasp of his will, nor escape from the mad clamour of terror that resounded through her, as the trucks thumped slowly, heavily, horrifying, one after the other, one pursuing the other, over the rails of the crossing.

The locomotive, as if wanting to see what could be done, put on the brakes, and back came the trucks rebounding on the iron buffers, striking like horrible cymbals, clashing nearer and nearer in frightful strident concussions. The mare opened her mouth and rose slowly, as if lifted up on a wind of terror. Then suddenly her fore feet struck out, as she convulsed herself utterly away from the horror. Back she went, and the two girls clung to each other, feeling she must fall backwards on top of him. But he leaned forward, his face shining with fixed amusement, and at last he brought her down, sank her down, and was bearing her back to the mark. But as strong as the pressure of his compulsion was the repulsion of her utter terror, throwing her back away from the railway, so that she spun round and round, on two legs, as if she were in the centre of some whirlwind. It made Gudrun faint with poignant dizziness, which seemed to penetrate to her heart.

'No –! No –! Let her go! Let her go, you fool, you *fool* –!' cried Ursula at the top of her voice, completely outside herself. And Gudrun hated her bitterly for being outside herself. It was unendurable that Ursula's voice was so powerful and naked.

A sharpened look came on Gerald's face. He bit himself down on the mare like a keen edge biting home, and *forced* her round. She roared as she breathed, her nostrils were two wide, hot holes, her mouth was apart, her eyes frenzied. It was a repulsive sight. But he held on her unrelaxed, with an almost mechanical relentlessness, keen as a sword pressing in to her. Both man and horse were sweating with violence. Yet he seemed calm as a ray of cold sunshine.

Meanwhile the eternal trucks were rumbling on, very slowly, treading one after the other, one after the other, like a disgusting dream that has no end. The connecting chains were grinding and squeaking as the tension varied, the mare pawed and struck away mechanically now, her terror fulfilled in her, for now the man encompassed her; her paws were blind and pathetic as she beat the air, the man closed round her, and brought her down, almost as if she were part of his own physique.

'And she's bleeding! She's bleeding!' cried Ursula, frantic with opposition and hatred of Gerald. She alone understood him perfectly, in pure opposition.

Gudrun looked and saw the trickles of blood on the sides of the mare, and she turned white. And then on the very wound the bright spurs came down, pressing relentlessly. The world reeled and passed into nothingness for Gudrun, she could not know any more.

When she recovered, her soul was calm and cold, without feeling. The trucks were still rumbling by, and the man and the mare were still fighting. But she herself was cold and separate, she had no more feeling for them. She was quite hard and cold and indifferent.

They could see the top of the hooded guard's-van approaching, the sound of the trucks was diminishing, there was hope of relief from the intolerable noise. The heavy panting of the half-stunned mare sounded automatically, the man seemed to be relaxing confidently, his will bright and unstained. The guard's-van came up, and passed slowly, the guard staring out in his transition on the spectacle in the road. And, through the man in the closed wagon, Gudrun could see the whole scene spectacularly, isolated and momentary, like a vision isolated in eternity.

Lovely, grateful silence seemed to trail behind the receding train. How sweet the silence is! Ursula looked with hatred on the buffers of the diminishing wagon. The gatekeeper stood ready at the door of his hut, to proceed to open the gate. But Gudrun sprang suddenly forward, in front of the struggling horse, threw off the latch and flung the gates asunder, throwing one-half to the keeper, and running with the other half, forwards. Gerald suddenly let go the horse and leaped forwards, almost on to Gudrun. She was not afraid. As he jerked aside the mare's head, Gudrun cried, in a strange, high voice, like a gull, or like a witch screaming out from the side of the road:

'I should think you're proud.'

The words were distinct and formed. The man, twisting aside on his dancing horse, looked at her in some surprise, some wondering interest. Then the mare's hoofs had danced three times on the drum-like sleepers of the crossing, and man and horse were bounding springily, unequally up the road.

The two girls watched them go. The gate-keeper hobbled thudding over the logs of the crossing, with his wooden leg. He had fastened the gate. Then he also turned, and called to the girls:

'A masterful young jockey, that; 'll have his own road, if ever anybody would.'

'Yes,' cried Ursula, in her hot, overbearing voice. 'Why couldn't he take the horse away, till the trucks had gone by? He's a fool, and a bully. Does he think it's manly, torture a horse? It's a living thing, why should he bully it and torture it?'

There was a pause, then the gate-keeper shook his head, and replied:

'Yes, it's as nice a little mare as you could set eyes on – beautiful little thing, beautiful. Now you couldn't see his father treat any animal like that – not you. They're as different as they welly can be, Gerald Crich and his father – two different men, different made.'

Then there was a pause.

'But why does he do it?' cried Ursula, 'why does he? Does he think he's grand, when he's bullied a sensitive creature, ten times as sensitive as himself?'

Again there was a cautious pause. Then again the man shook his head, as if he would say nothing, but would think the more.

'I expect he's got to train the mare to stand to anything,' he replied. 'A pure-bred Harab – not the sort of breed as is used to round here different sort from our sort altogether. They say as he got her from Constantinople.

'He would!' said Ursula. 'He'd better have left her to the Turks, I'm sure they would have had more decency towards her.'

The man went in to drink his can of tea, the girls went on down the lane, that was deep in soft black dust. Gudrun was as if numbed in her mind by the sense of indomitable soft weight of the man, bearing down into the living body of the horse: the strong, indomitable thighs of the blond man clenching the palpitating body of the mare into pure control; a sort of soft white magnetic domination from the loins and thighs and calves, enclosing and encompassing the mare heavily into unutterable subordination, soft blood-subordination, terrible.

On the left, as the girls walked silently, the coal-mine lifted its great mounds and its patterned head-stocks, the black railway with the trucks at rest looked like a harbour just below, a large bay of railroad with anchored wagons.

Near the second level-crossing, that went over many bright rails, was a farm belonging to the collieries, and a great round globe of iron, a disused boiler, huge and rusty and perfectly round, stood silently in a paddock by the road. The hens were pecking round it, some chickens were balanced on the drinking trough, wagtails flew away in among trucks, from the water.

On the other side of the wide crossing, by the road-side, was a heap of pale-grey stones for mending the roads, and a cart standing, and a middle-aged man with whiskers round his face was leaning on his shovel, talking to a young man in gaiters, who stood by the horse's head. Both men were facing the crossing.

They saw the two girls appear, small, brilliant figures in the near distance, in the strong light of the late afternoon. Both wore light, gay summer dresses, Ursula had an orange-coloured knitted coat, Gudrun a pale yellow, Ursula wore canary yellow stockings, Gudrun bright rose, the figures of the two women seemed to glitter in progress over the wide bay of the railway crossing, white and orange and yellow and rose glittering in motion across a hot world silted with coaldust.

The two men stood quite still in the heat, watching. The elder was a short, hard-faced energetic man of middle age, the younger a labourer of twenty-three or so. They stood in silence watching the advance of the sisters. They watched whilst the girls drew near, and whilst they passed, and whilst they receded down the dusty road, that had dwellings on one side, and dusty young corn on the other.

Then the elder man, with the whiskers round his face, said in a prurient manner to the young man:

'What price that, eh? She'll do, won't she?'

'Which?' asked the young man, eagerly, with laugh.

'Her with the red stockings. What d'you say? I'd give my week's wages for five minutes; what! – just for five minutes.'

Again the young man laughed.

'Your missis 'ud have summat to say to you,' he replied.

Gudrun had turned round and looked at the two men. They were to her sinister creatures, standing watching after her, by the heap of pale grey slag. She loathed the man with whiskers round his face.

'You're first class, you are,' the man said to her, and to the distance. 'Do you think it would be worth a week's wages?' said the younger man, musing.

'Do I? I'd put 'em bloody-well down this second – '

The younger man looked after Gudrun and Ursula objectively, as if he wished to calculate what there might be, that was worth his week's wages. He shook his head with fatal misgiving.

'No,' he said. 'It's not worth that to me.'

'Isn't?' said the old man. 'By God, if it isn't to me!'

And he went on shovelling his stones.

The girls descended between the houses with slate roofs and blackish brick walls. The heavy gold glamour of approaching sunset layover all the colliery district, and the ugliness overlaid with beauty was like a narcotic to the senses. On the roads silted with black dust, the rich light fell more warmly, more heavily, over all the amorphous squalor a kind of magic was cast, from the glowing close of day.

'It has a foul kind of beauty, this place,' said Gudrun, evidently suffering from fascination. 'Can't you feel in some way, a thick, hot attraction in it? I can. And it quite stupifies me.'

They were passing between blocks of miners' dwellings. In the back yards of several dwellings, a miner could be seen washing himself in the open on this hot evening, naked down to the loins, his great trousers of moleskin slipping almost away. Miners already cleaned were sitting on their heels, with their backs near the walls, talking and silent in pure physical well-being, tired, and taking physical rest. Their voices sounded out with strong intonation, and the broad dialect was curiously caressing to the blood. It seemed to envelop Gudrun in a labourer's caress, there was in the whole atmosphere a resonance of physical men, a glamorous thickness of labour and maleness, surcharged in the air. But it was universal in the district, and therefore unnoticed by the inhabitants.

To Gudrun, however, it was potent and half-repulsive. She could never tell why Beldover was so utterly different from London and the south, why one's whole feelings were different, why one seemed to live in another sphere. Now she realised that this was the world of powerful, underworld men who spent most of their time in the darkness. In their voices she could hear the voluptuous resonance of darkness, the strong, dangerous underworld, mindless, inhuman. They sounded also like strange machines, heavy, oiled. The voluptuousness was like that of machinery, cold and iron.

It was the same every evening when she came home, she seemed to move through a wave of disruptive force, that was given off from the presence of thousands of vigorous, underworld, half-automatised colliers, and which went to the brain and the heart, awaking a fatal desire, and a fatal callousness.

There came over her a nostalgia for the place. She hated it, she knew how utterly cut off it was, how hideous and how sickeningly mindless. Sometimes she beat her wings like a new Daphne, turning not into a tree but a machine. And yet, she was overcome by the nostalgia. She struggled to get more and more into accord with the atmosphere of the place, she craved to get her satisfaction of it.

She felt herself drawn out at evening into the main street of the town, that was uncreated and ugly, and yet surcharged with this same potent atmosphere of intense, dark callousness. There were always miners about. They moved with their strange, distorted dignity, a certain beauty, and unnatural stillness in their bearing, a look of abstraction and half resignation in their pale, often gaunt faces. They belonged to another world, they had a strange glamour, their voices were full of an intolerable deep resonance, like a machine's burring, a music more maddening than the siren's long ago.

She found herself, with the rest of the common women, drawn out on Friday evenings to the little market. Friday was pay-day for the colliers, and Friday night was market night. Every woman was abroad, every man was out, shopping with his wife, or gathering with his pals. The pavements were dark for miles around with people coming in, the little market-place on the crown of the hill, and the main street of Beldover were black with thickly-crowded men and women.

It was dark, the market-place was hot with kerosene flares, which threw a ruddy light on the grave faces of the purchasing wives, and on the pale abstract faces of the men. The air was full of the sound of criers and of people talking, thick streams of people moved on the pavements towards the solid crowd of the market. The shops were blazing and packed with women, in the streets were men, mostly men, miners of all ages. Money was spent with almost lavish freedom.

The carts that came could not pass through. They had to wait, the driver calling and shouting, till the dense crowd would make way. Everywhere, young fellows from the outlying districts were making conversation with the girls, standing in the road and at the corners. The doors of the public-houses were open and full of light, men passed in and out in a continual stream, everywhere men were calling out to one another, or crossing to meet one another, or standing in little gangs and circles, discussing, endlessly discussing. The sense of talk, buzzing, jarring, half-secret, the endless mining and political wrangling, vibrated in the air like discordant machinery. And it was their voices which affected Gudrun almost to swooning. They aroused a strange, nostalgic ache of desire, something almost demoniacal, never to be fulfilled.

Like any other common girl of the district, Gudrun strolled up and down, up and down the length of the brilliant two hundred paces of the pavement nearest the market-place. She knew it was a vulgar thing to do; her father and mother could not bear it; but the nostalgia came over her, she must be among the people. Sometimes she sat among the louts in the cinema: rakish-looking, unattractive louts they were. Yet she must be among them.

And, like any other common lass, she found her 'boy.' It was an electrician, one of the electricians introduced according to Gerald's new scheme. He was an earnest, clever man, a scientist with a passion for sociology. He lived alone in a cottage, in lodgings, in Willey Green. He was a gentleman, and sufficiently well-to-do. His landlady spread the reports about him; he *would* have a large wooden tub in his bedroom, and every time he came in from work, he *would* have pails and pails of water brought up, to bathe in, then he put on clean shirt and under-clothing *every* day, and clean silk socks; fastidious and exacting he was in these respects, but in every other way, most ordinary and unassuming.

Gudrun knew all these things. The Brangwen's house was one to which the gossip came naturally and inevitably. Palmer was in the first place a friend of Ursula's. But in his pale, elegant, serious face there showed the same nostalgia that Gudrun felt. He too must walk up and down the street on Friday evening. So he walked with Gudrun, and a friendship was struck up between them. But he was not in love with Gudrun; he *really* wanted Ursula, but for some strange reason, nothing could happen between her and him. He liked to have Gudrun about, as a fellow-mind – but that was all. And she had no real feeling for him. He was a scientist, he had to have a woman to back him. But he was really impersonal, he had the fineness of an elegant piece of machinery. He was too cold, too destructive to care really for women, too great an egoist. He was polarised by the men. Individually he detested and despised them. In the mass they fascinated him, as machinery fascinated him. They were a new sort of machinery to him – but incalculable, incalculable.

So Gudrun strolled the streets with Palmer, or went to the cinema with him. And his long, pale, rather elegant face flickered as he made his sarcastic remarks. There they were, the two of them: two elegants in one sense: in the other sense, two units, absolutely adhering to the people, teeming with the distorted colliers. The same secret seemed to be working in the souls of all alike, Gudrun, Palmer, the rakish young bloods, the gaunt, middle-aged men. All had a secret sense of power, and of inexpressible destructiveness, and of fatal half-heartedness, a sort of rottenness in the will.

Sometimes Gudrun would start aside, see it all, see how she was sinking in. And then she was filled with a fury of contempt and anger. She felt she was sinking into one mass with the rest – all so close and intermingled and breathless. It was horrible. She stifled. She prepared for flight, feverishly she flew to her work. But soon she let go. She started off into the country – the darkish, glamorous country. The spell was beginning to work again.

CHAPTER 10

Sketchbook

ONE MORNING the sisters were sketching by the side of Willey Water, at the remote end of the lake. Gudrun had waded out to a gravelly shoal, and was seated like a Buddhist, staring fixedly at the water-plants that rose succulent from the mud of the low shores. What she could see was mud, soft, oozy, watery mud, and from its festering chill, water-plants rose up, thick and cool and fleshy, very straight and turgid, thrusting out their leaves at right angles, and having dark lurid colours, dark green and blotches of black-purple and bronze. But she could feel their turgid fleshy structure as in a sensuous vision, she *knew* how they rose out of the mud, she *knew* how they thrust out from themselves, how they stood stiff and succulent against the air.

Ursula was watching the butterflies, of which there were dozens near the water, little blue ones suddenly snapping out of nothingness into a jewel-life, a large black-and-red one standing upon a flower and breathing with his soft wings, intoxicatingly, breathing pure, ethereal sunshine; two white ones wrestling in the low air; there was a halo round them; ah, when they came tumbling nearer they were orange-tips, and it was the orange that had made the halo. Ursula rose and drifted away, unconscious like the butterflies.

Gudrun, absorbed in a stupor of apprehension of surging water-plants, sat crouched on the shoal, drawing, not looking up for a long time, and then staring unconsciously, absorbedly at the rigid, naked, succulent stems. Her feet were bare, her hat lay on the bank opposite.

She started out of her trance, hearing the knocking of oars. She looked round. There was a boat with a gaudy Japanese parasol, and a man in white, rowing. The woman was Hermione, and the man was Gerald. She knew it instantly. And instantly she perished in the keen *frisson* of anticipation, an electric vibration in her veins, intense, much more intense than that which was always humming low in the atmosphere of Beldover; Gerald was her escape from the heavy slough of the pale, underworld, automatic colliers. He started out of the mud. He was master. She saw his back, the movement of his white loins. But not that – it was the whiteness he seemed to enclose as he bent forwards, rowing. He seemed to stoop to something. His glistening, whitish hair seemed like the electricity of the sky.

'There's Gudrun,' came Hermione's voice floating distinct over the water. 'We will go and speak to her. Do you mind?'

Gerald looked round and saw the girl standing by the water's edge, looking at him. He pulled the boat towards her, magnetically, without thinking of her. In his world, his conscious world, she was still nobody. He knew that Hermione had a curious pleasure in treading down all the social differences, at least apparently, and he left it to her.

'How do you do, Gudrun?' sang Hermione, using the Christian name in the fashionable manner. 'What are you doing?'

'How do you do, Hermione? I *was* sketching.'

'Were you?' The boat drifted nearer, till the keel ground on the bank. 'May we see? I should like to *so* much.'

It was no use resisting Hermione's deliberate intention.

'Well – ' said Gudrun reluctantly, for she always hated to have her unfinished work exposed – 'there's nothing in the least interesting.'

'Isn't there? But let me see, will you?'

Gudrun reached out the sketchbook, Gerald stretched from the boat to take it. And as he did so, he remembered Gudrun's last words to him, and her face lifted up to him as he sat on the swerving horse. An intensification of pride went over his nerves, because he felt, in some way she was compelled by him. The exchange of feeling between them was strong and apart from their consciousness.

And as if in a spell, Gudrun was aware of his body, stretching and surging like the marsh-fire, stretching towards her, his hand coming straight forward like a stem. Her voluptuous, acute apprehension of him made the blood faint in her veins, her mind went dim and unconscious. And he rocked on the water perfectly, like the rocking of phosphorescence. He looked round at the boat. It was drifting off a little. He lifted the oar to bring it back. And the exquisite pleasure of slowly arresting the boat, in the heavy-soft water, was complete as a swoon.

'*That's* what you have done,' said Hermione, looking searchingly at the plants on the shore, and comparing with Gudrun's drawing. Gudrun looked round in the direction of Hermione's long, pointing finger. 'That is it, isn't it?' repeated Hermione, needing confirmation.

'Yes,' said Gudrun automatically, taking no real heed.

'Let me look,' said Gerald, reaching forward for the book. But Hermione ignored him, he must not presume, before she had finished. But he, his will as unthwarted and as unflinching as hers, stretched forward till he touched the book. A little shock, a storm of revulsion against him, shook Hermione unconsciously. She released the book when he had not properly got it, and it tumbled against the side of the boat and bounced into the water.

'There!' sang Hermione, with a strange ring of malevolent victory.

'I'm so sorry, so awfully sorry. Can't you get it, Gerald?'

This last was said in a note of anxious sneering that made Gerald's veins tingle with fine hate for her. He leaned far out of the boat, reaching down into the water. He could feel his position was ridiculous, his loins exposed behind him.

'It is of no importance,' came the strong, clanging voice of Gudrun. She seemed to touch him. But he reached further, the boat swayed violently. Hermione, however, remained unperturbed. He grasped the book, under the water, and brought it up, dripping.

'I'm so dreadfully sorry – dreadfully sorry,' repeated Hermione. 'I'm afraid it was all my fault.'

'It's of no importance – really, I assure you – it doesn't matter in the least,' said Gudrun loudly, with emphasis, her face flushed scarlet. And she held out her hand impatiently for the wet book, to have done with the scene. Gerald gave it to her. He was not quite himself.

'I'm so dreadfully sorry,' repeated Hermione, till both Gerald and Gudrun were exasperated. 'Is there nothing that can be done?'

'In what way?' asked Gudrun, with cool irony.

'Can't we save the drawings?'

There was a moment's pause, wherein Gudrun made evident all her refutation of Hermione's persistence.

'I assure you,' said Gudrun, with cutting distinctness, 'the drawings are quite as good as ever they were, for my purpose. I want them only for reference.'

'But can't I give you a new book? I wish you'd let me do that. I feel so truly sorry. I feel it was all my fault.'

'As far as I saw,' said Gudrun, 'it wasn't your fault at all. If there was any *fault,* it was Mr Crich's. But the whole thing is *entirely* trivial, and it really is ridiculous to take any notice of it.'

Gerald watched Gudrun closely, whilst she repulsed Hermione. There was a body of cold power in her. He watched her with an insight that amounted to clairvoyance. He saw her a dangerous, hostile spirit, that could stand undiminished and unabated. It was so finished, and of such perfect gesture, moreover.

'I'm awfully glad if it doesn't matter,' he said; 'if there's no real harm done.'

She looked back at him, with her fine blue eyes, and signalled full into his spirit, as she said, her voice ringing with intimacy almost caressive now it was addressed to him:

'Of course, it doesn't matter in the *least.'*

The bond was established between them, in that look, in her tone. In her tone, she made the understanding clear – they were of the same kind, he and she, a sort of diabolic freemasonry subsisted between them. Henceforward, she knew, she had her power over him. Wherever they met, they would be secretly associated. And he would be helpless in the association with her. Her soul exulted.

'Good-bye! I'm so glad you forgive me. Gooood-bye!'

Hermione sang her farewell, and waved her hand. Gerald automatically took the oar and pushed off. But he was looking all the time, with a glimmering, subtly-smiling admiration in his eyes, at Gudrun, who stood on the shoal shaking the wet book in her hand. She turned away and ignored the receding boat. But Gerald looked back as he rowed, beholding her, forgetting what he was doing.

'Aren't we going too much to the left?' sang Hermione, as she sat ignored under her coloured parasol.

Gerald looked round without replying, the oars balanced and glancing in the sun.

'I think it's all right,' he said good-humouredly, beginning to row again without thinking of what he was doing. And Hermione disliked him extremely for his good-humoured obliviousness, she was nullified, she could not regain ascendancy.

CHAPTER 11

An Island

MEANWHILE URSULA had wandered on from Willey Water along the course of the bright little stream. The afternoon was full of larks' singing. On the bright hill-sides was a subdued smoulder of gorse. A few forget-me-nots flowered by the water. There was a rousedness and a glancing everywhere.

She strayed absorbedly on, over the brooks. She wanted to go to the mill-pond above. The big mill-house was deserted, save for a labourer and his wife who lived in the kitchen. So she passed through the empty farm-yard and through the wilderness of a garden, and mounted the bank by the sluice. When she got to the top, to see the old, velvety surface of the pond before her, she noticed a man on the bank, tinkering with a punt. It was Birkin sawing and hammering away.

She stood at the head of the sluice, looking at him. He was unaware of anybody's presence. He looked very busy, like a wild animal, active and intent. She felt she ought to go away, he would not want her. He seemed to be so much occupied. But she did not want to go away. Therefore she moved along the bank till he would look up.

Which he soon did. The moment he saw her, he dropped his tools and came forward, saying:

'How do you do? I'm making the punt water-tight. Tell me if you think it is right.'

She went along with him.

'You are your father's daughter, so you can tell me if it will do,' he said.

She bent to look at the patched punt.

'I am sure I am my father's daughter,' she said, fearful of having to judge. 'But I don't know anything about carpentry. It *looks* right, don't you think?'

'Yes, I think. I hope it won't let me to the bottom, that's all. Though even so, it isn't a great matter, I should come up again. Help me to get it into the water, will you?'

With combined efforts they turned over the heavy punt and set it afloat.

'Now,' he said, 'I'll try it and you can watch what happens. Then if it carries, I'll take you over to the island.'

'Do,' she cried, watching anxiously.

The pond was large, and had that perfect stillness and the dark lustre of very deep water. There were two small islands overgrown with bushes and a few trees, towards the middle. Birkin pushed himself off, and veered clumsily in the pond. Luckily the punt drifted so that he could catch hold of a willow bough, and pull it to the island.

'Rather overgrown,' he said, looking into the interior, 'but very nice. I'll come and fetch you. The boat leaks a little.'

In a moment he was with her again, and she stepped into the wet punt.

'It'll float us all right,' he said, and manoeuvred again to the island.

They landed under a willow tree. She shrank from the little jungle of rank plants before her, evil-smelling figwort and hemlock. But he explored into it.

'I shall mow this down,' he said, 'and then it will be romantic – like Paul et Virginie.'

'Yes, one could have lovely Watteau picnics here,' cried Ursula with enthusiasm.

His face darkened.

'I don't want Watteau picnics here,' he said.

'Only your Virginie,' she laughed.

'Virginie enough;' he smiled Wryly. 'No, I don't want her either.'

Ursula looked at him closely. She had not seen him since Breadalby. He was very thin and hollow, with a ghastly look in his face.

'You have been ill; haven't you?' she asked, rather repulsed.

'Yes,' he replied coldly.

They had sat down under the willow tree, and were looking at the pond, from their retreat on the island.

'Has it made you frightened?' she asked.

'What of?' he asked, turning his eyes to look at her. Something in him, inhuman and unmitigated, disturbed her, and shook her out of her ordinary self.

'It *is* frightening to be very ill, isn't it?' she said.

'It isn't pleasant,' he said. 'Whether one is really afraid of death, or not, I have never decided. In one mood, not a bit, in another, very much.'

'But doesn't it make you feel ashamed? I think it makes one so ashamed, to be ill – illness is so terribly humiliating, don't you think?'

He considered for some minutes.

'May-be,' he said. 'Though one knows all the time one's life isn't really right, at the source. That's the humiliation. I don't see that the illness counts so much, after that. One is ill because one doesn't live properly – can't. It's the failure to live that makes one ill, and humiliates one.'

'But do you fail to live?' she asked, almost jeering.

'Why yes – I don't make much of a success of my days. One seems always to be bumping one's nose against the blank wall ahead.'

Ursula laughed. She was frightened, and when she was frightened she always laughed and pretended to be jaunty.

'Your poor nose!' she said, looking at that feature of his face.

'No wonder it's ugly,' he replied.

She was silent for some minutes, struggling with her own self deception. It was an instinct in her, to deceive herself.

'But *I'm* happy – I think life is *awfully* jolly,' she said.

'Good,' he answered, with a certain cold indifference.

She reached for a bit of paper which had wrapped a small piece of chocolate she had found in her pocket, and began making a boat. He watched her without heeding her. There was something strangely pathetic and tender in her moving, unconscious finger-tips, that were agitated and hurt, really.

'I *do* enjoy things – don't you?' she asked.

'Oh yes! But it infuriates me that I can't get right, at the really growing part of me. I feel all tangled and messed up, and I *can't* get straight anyhow. I don't know what really to *do*. One must do something somewhere.'

'Why should you always be *doing?*' she retorted. 'It is so plebeian. I think it is much better to be really patrician, and to do nothing but just be oneself, like a walking flower.'

'I quite agree,' he said, 'if one has burst into blossom. But I can't get my flower to blossom anyhow. Either it is blighted in the bud, or has got the smother-fly, or it isn't nourished. Curse it, it isn't even a bud. It is a contravened knot.'

Again she laughed. He was so very fretful and exasperated. But she was anxious and puzzled. How was one to get out, anyhow. There must be a way out somewhere.

There was a silence, wherein she wanted to cry. She reached for another bit of chocolate paper, and began to fold another boat.

'And why is it,' she asked at length, 'that there is no flowering, no dignity of human life now?'

'The whole idea is dead. Humanity itself is dry-rotten, really. There are myriads of human beings hanging on the bush – and they look very nice and rosy, your healthy young men and women. But they are apples of Sodom*, as a matter of fact, Dead Sea Fruit, gall-apples. It isn't true that they have any significance – their insides are full of bitter, corrupt ash.'

'But there *are* good people,' protested Ursula.

'Good enough for the life of today. But mankind is a dead tree, covered with fine brilliant galls of people.'

Ursula could not help stiffening herself against this, it was too picturesque and final. But neither could she help making him go on.

'And if it is so, *why* is it?' she asked, hostile. They were rousing each other to a fine passion of opposition.

'Why, why are people all balls of bitter dust? Because they won't fall off the tree when they're ripe. They hang on to their old positions when the position is over-past, till they become infested with little worms and dry-rot.'

There was a long pause. His voice had become hot and very sarcastic. Ursula was troubled and bewildered, they were both oblivious of everything but their own immersion.

'But even if everybody is wrong – where are you right?' she cried, 'where are you any better?'

'I? – I'm not right,' he cried back. 'At least my only rightness lies in the fact that I know it. I detest what I am, outwardly. I loathe myself as a human being. Humanity is a huge aggregate lie, and a huge lie is less than a small truth. Humanity is less, far less than the individual, because the individual may sometimes be capable of truth, and humanity is a tree of lies. And they say that love is the greatest thing; they persist in *saying* this, the foul liars, and just look at what they do! Look at all the millions of people who repeat every minute that love is the greatest, and charity is

* Attractive externally, but rotten inside.

the greatest – and see what they are doing all the time. By their works ye shall know them, for dirty liars and cowards, who daren't stand by their own actions, much less by their own words.'

'But,' said Ursula sadly, 'that doesn't alter the fact that love is the greatest, does it? What they *do* doesn't alter the truth of what they say, does it?'

'Completely, because if what they say *were* true, then they couldn't help fulfilling it. But they maintain a lie, and so they run amok at last. It's a lie to say that love is the greatest. You might as well say that hate is the greatest, since the opposite of everything balances. What people want is hate – hate and nothing but hate. And in the name of righteousness and love, they get it. They distil themselves with nitroglycerine, all the lot of them, out of very love. It's the lie that kills. If we want hate, let us have it – death, murder, torture, violent destruction let us have it: but not in the name of love. But I abhor humanity, I wish it was swept away. It could go, and there would be no *absolute* loss, if every human being perished tomorrow. The reality would be untouched. Nay, it would be better. The real tree of life would then be rid of the most ghastly, heavy crop of Dead Sea Fruit, the intolerable burden of myriad simulacra of people, an infinite weight of mortal lies.'

'So you'd like everybody in the world destroyed?' said Ursula.

'I should indeed.'

'And the world empty of people?'

'Yes truly. You yourself, don't you find it a beautiful clean thought, a world empty of people, just uninterrupted grass, and a hare sitting up?'

The pleasant sincerity of his voice made Ursula pause to consider her own proposition. And really it *was* attractive: a clean, lovely, human-less world. It was the *really* desirable. Her heart hesitated, and exulted. But still, she was dissatisfied with *him*.

'But,' she objected, 'you'd be dead yourself, so what good would it do you?'

'I would die like a shot, to know that the earth would really be cleaned of all the people. It is the most beautiful and freeing thought. Then there would *never* be another foul humanity created, for a universal defilement.'

'No,' said Ursula, 'there would be nothing.'

'What! Nothing? Just because humanity was wiped out? You flatter yourself. There'd be everything:'

'But how, if there were no people?'

'Do you think that creation depends on *man!* It merely doesn't. There are the trees and the grass and birds. I much prefer to think of the lark rising up in the morning upon a human-less world. Man is a mistake, he must go. There is the grass, and hares and adders, and the unseen hosts, actual angels that go about freely when a dirty humanity doesn't interrupt them – and good pure-tissued demons: very nice.'

It pleased Ursula, what he said, pleased her very much, as a phantasy. Of course it was only a pleasant fancy. She herself knew too well the actuality of humanity, its hideous actuality. She knew' it could not disappear so cleanly and conveniently. It had a long way to go yet, a long and hideous way. Her subtle, feminine, demoniacal soul knew it well.

'If only man was swept off the face of the earth, creation would go on so marvellously, with a new start, non-human. Man is one of the mistakes of creation – like the ichthyosauri. If only he were gone again, think what lovely things would come out of the liberated days; – things straight out of the fire.'

'But man will never be gone,' she said, with insidious, diabolical knowledge of the horrors of persistence. 'The world will go with him.'

'Ah no,' he answered, 'not so. I believe in the proud angels and the demons that are our fore-runners. They will destroy us, because we are not proud enough. The ichthyosauri were not proud: they crawled and floundered as we do. And besides, look at elder-flowers and bluebells they are a sign that pure creation takes place – even the butterfly. But humanity never gets beyond the caterpillar stage – it rots in the chrysalis, it never will have wings. It is anti-creation, like monkeys and baboons.'

Ursula watched him as he talked. There seemed a certain impatient fury in him, all the while, and at the same time a great amusement in everything, and a final tolerance. And it was this tolerance she mistrusted, not the fury. She saw that, all the while, in spite of himself, he would have to be trying to save the world. And this knowledge, whilst it comforted her heart somewhere with a little self-satisfaction, stability, yet filled her with a certain sharp contempt and hate of him. She wanted him to herself, she hated the Salvator Mundi* touch. It was something diffuse and generalised about him, which she could not stand. He would behave in the same way, say the same things, give himself as completely to anybody who came along, anybody and everybody who liked to appeal to him. It was despicable, a very insidious form of prostitution.

'But,' she said, 'you believe in individual love, even if you don't believe in loving humanity –?'

'I don't believe in love at all – that is, any more than I believe in hate, or in grief. Love is one of the emotions like all the others – and so it is all right whilst you feel it. But I can't see how it becomes an absolute. It is just part of human relationships, no more. And it is only part of *any* human relationship. And why one should be required *always* to feel it, any more than one always feels sorrow or distant joy, I cannot conceive. Love isn't a desideratum [desired as essential] – it is an emotion you feel or you don't feel, according to circumstance.'

'Then why do you care about people at all?' she asked, 'if you don't believe in love? Why do you bother about humanity?'

'Why do I? Because I can't get away from it.'

'Because you love it,' she persisted.

It irritated him.

'If I do love it,' he said, 'it is my disease.'

'But it is a disease you don't want to be cured of,' she said, with some cold sneering.

He was silent now, feeling she wanted to insult him.

'And if you don't believe in love, what *do* you believe in?' she asked mocking. 'Simply in the end of the world, and grass?'

* The purported savior of the world.

He was beginning to feel a fool.

'I believe in the unseen hosts,' he said.

'And nothing else? You believe in nothing visible, except grass and birds? Your world is a poor show.'

'Perhaps it is,' he said, cool and superior now he was offended, assuming a certain insufferable aloof superiority, and withdrawing into his distance.

Ursula disliked him. But also she felt she had lost something. She looked at him as he sat crouched on the bank. There was a certain priggish Sunday-school stiffness over him, priggish and detestable. And yet, at the same time, the moulding of him was so quick and attractive, it gave such a great sense of freedom: the moulding of his brows, his chin, his whole physique, something so alive, somewhere, in spite of the look of sickness.

And it was this duality in feeling which he created in her, that made a fine hate of him quicken in her bowels. There was his wonderful, desirable life-rapidity, the rare quality of an utterly desirable man: and there was at the same time this ridiculous, mean effacement into a Salvator Mundi and a Sunday-school teacher, a prig of the stiffest type.

He looked up at her. He saw her face strangely enkindled, as if suffused from within by a powerful sweet fire. His soul was arrested in wonder. She was enkindled in her own living fire. Arrested in wonder and in pure, perfect attraction, he moved towards her. She sat like a strange queen, almost supernatural in her glowing smiling richness.

'The point about love,' he said, his consciousness quickly adjusting itself, 'is that we hate the word because we have vulgarised it. It ought to be proscribed, tabooed from utterance, for many years, till we get a new, better idea.'

There was a beam of understanding between them.

'But it always means the same thing,' she said.

'Ah God, no, let it not mean that any more,' he cried. 'let the old meanings go.'

'But still it is love,' she persisted. A strange, wicked yellow light shone at him in her eyes.

He hesitated, baffled, withdrawing.

'No,' he said, 'it isn't. Spoken like that, never in the world. You've no business to utter the word.'

'I must leave it to you, to take it out of the Ark of the Covenant* at the right moment,' she mocked.

Again they looked at each other. She suddenly sprang up, turned her back to him, and walked away. He too rose slowly and went to the water's edge, where, crouching, he began to amuse himself unconsciously. Picking a daisy he dropped it on the pond, so that the stem was a keel, the flower floated like a little water lily, staring with its open face up to the sky. It turned slowly round, in a slow, slow Dervish dance as it veered away.

He watched it, then dropped another daisy into the water, and after that another, and sat watching them with bright, absolved eyes, crouching near on the bank. Ursula turned to look. A strange feeling possessed her, as if something were taking place. But it was all intangible. And some sort of control was being put on her. She could not know. She could only watch the brilliant little discs of the daisies veering slowly in travel on the dark, lustrous water. The little flotilla was drifting into the light, a company of white specks in the distance.

'Do let us go to the shore, to follow them,' she said, afraid of being any longer imprisoned on the island. And they pushed off in the punt.

She was glad to be on the free land again. She went along the bank towards the sluice. The daisies were scattered broadcast on the pond, tiny radiant things, like an exaltation, points of exaltation here and there. Why did they move her so strongly and mystically?

'Look,' he said, 'your boat of purple paper is escorting them, and they are a convoy of rafts.'

Some of the daisies came slowly towards her, hesitating, making a shy bright little cotillion on the dark clear water. Their gay bright candour moved her so much as they carne near; that she was almost in tears.

'Why are they so lovely,' she cried. 'Why do I think them so lovely?'

---

* Holy box of the Hebrews containing the parchments of the Ten Commandments.

'They are nice flowers,' he said, her emotional tones putting a constraint on him.

'You know that a daisy is a company of florets, a concourse, become individual. Don't the botanists put it highest in the line of development? I believe they do.'

'The compositae, yes, I think so,' said Ursula, who was never very sure of anything. Things she knew perfectly well, at one moment, seemed to become doubtful the next.

'Explain it so, then,' he said. 'The daisy is a perfect little democracy, so it's the highest of flowers, hence its charm.'

'No,' she cried, 'no – never. It isn't democratic.'

'No,' he admitted. 'It's the golden mob of the proletariat, surrounded by a showy white fence of the idle rich.'

'How hateful – your hateful social orders!' she cried.

'Quite! It's a daisy – we'll leave it alone.'

'Do. Let it be a dark horse for once,' she said: 'if anything can be a dark horse to you,' she added satirically.

They stood aside, forgetful. As if a little stunned, they both were motionless, barely conscious. The little conflict into which they had fallen had torn their consciousness and left them like two impersonal forces, there in contact.

He became aware of the lapse. He wanted to say something, to get on to a new more ordinary footing.

'You know,' he said, 'that I am having rooms here at the mill? Don't you think we can have some good times?'

'Oh are you?' she said, ignoring all his implication of admitted intimacy.

He adjusted himself at once, became normally distant.

'If I find I can live sufficiently by myself,' he continued, 'I shall give up my work altogether. It has become dead to me. I don't believe in the humanity I pretend to be part of, I don't care a straw for the social ideals I live by, I hate the dying organic form of social mankind – so it can't be anything but trumpery, to work at education. I shall drop it as soon as I am clear enough – tomorrow perhaps – and be by myself.'

'Have you enough to live on?' asked Ursula.

'Yes – I've about four hundred a year. That makes it easy for me.' There was a pause.

'And what about Hermione?' asked Ursula.

'That's over, finally – a pure failure, and never could have been anything else.'

'But you still know each other?'

'We could hardly pretend to be strangers, could we?'

There was a stubborn pause.

'But isn't that a half-measure?' asked Ursula at length.

'I don't think so,' he said. 'You'll be able to tell me if it is.'

Again there was a pause of some minutes' duration. He was thinking. 'One must throw everything away, everything – let everything go, to get the one last thing one wants,' he said.

'What thing?' she asked in challenge.

'I don't know – freedom together,' he said.

She had wanted him to say 'love.'

There was heard a loud barking of the dogs below. He seemed disturbed by it. She did not notice. Only she thought he seemed uneasy.

'As a matter of fact,' he said, in rather a small voice, 'I believe that is Hermione come now, with Gerald Crich. She wanted to see the rooms before they are furnished.'

'I know;' said Ursula. 'She will superintend the furnishing for you.'

'Probably. Does it matter?'

'Oh no, I should think not,' said Ursula. 'Though personally, I can't bear her. I think she is a lie, if you like, you who are always talking about lies.' Then she ruminated for a moment, when she broke out: 'Yes, and I do mind if she furnishes your rooms – I do mind. I mind that you keep her hanging on at all.'

He was silent now, frowning.

'Perhaps,' he said. 'I don't *want* her to furnish the rooms here – and I don't keep her hanging on. Only, I needn't be churlish to her, need I? At any rate, I shall have to go down and see them now. You'll come, won't you?'

'I don't think so,' she said coldly and irresolutely.

'Won't you? Yes do. Come and see the rooms as well. Do come.'

CHAPTER 12

Carpeting

HE SET off down the bank, and she went unwillingly with him. Yet she would not have stayed away, either.

'We know each other well, you and I, already,' he said. She did not answer.

In the large darkish kitchen of the mill, the labourer's wife was talking shrilly to Hermione and Gerald, who stood, he in white and she in a glistening bluish foulard, strangely luminous in the dusk of the room; whilst from the cages on the walls, a dozen or more canaries sang at the top of their voices. The cages were all placed round a small square window at the back, where the sunshine came in, a beautiful beam, filtering through green leaves of a tree. The voice of Mrs Salmon shrilled against the noise of the birds, which rose ever more wild and triumphant, and the woman's voice went up and up against them, and the birds replied with wild animation.

'Here's Rupert!' shouted Gerald in the midst of the din. He was suffering badly, being very sensitive in the ear.

'O-o-h them birds, they won't let you speak –!' shrilled the labourer's wife in disgust. 'I'll cover them up.'

And she darted here and there, throwing a duster, an apron, a towel, a table-cloth over the cages of the birds.

'Now will you stop it, and let a body speak for your row,' she said, still in a voice that was too high.

The party watched her. Soon the cages were covered, they had a strange funereal look. But from under the towels odd defiant trills and bubblings still shook out.

'Oh, they won't go on,' said Mrs Salmon reassuringly. 'They'll go to sleep now.'

'Really,' said Hermione, politely.

'They will,' said Gerald. 'They will go to sleep automatically, now the impression of evening is produced.'

'Are they so easily deceived?' cried Ursula.

'Oh, yes,' replied Gerald. 'Don't you know the story of Fabre, who, when he was a boy, put a hen's head under her wing, and she straight away went to sleep? It's quite true.'

'And did that make him a naturalist?' asked Birkin.

'Probably,' said Gerald.

Meanwhile Ursula was peeping under one of the cloths. There sat the canary in a corner, bunched and fluffed up for sleep.

'How ridiculous!' she cried. 'It really thinks the night has come! How absurd! Really, how can one have any respect for a creature that is so easily taken in!'

'Yes,' sang Hermione, coming also to look. She put her hand on Ursula's arm and chuckled a low laugh. 'Yes, doesn't he look comical?' she chuckled. 'Like a stupid husband.'

Then, with her hand still on Ursula's arm, she drew her away, saying, in her mild sing-song:

'How did you come here? We saw Gudrun too.'

'I came to look at the pond,' said Ursula, 'and I found Mr Birkin there.'

'Did you? This is quite a Brangwen land, isn't it!'

'I'm afraid I hoped so,' said Ursula. 'I ran here for refuge, when I saw you down the lake, just putting off.'

'Did you! And now we've run you to earth.'

Hermione's eyelids lifted with an uncanny movement, amused but overwrought. She had always her strange, rapt look, unnatural and irresponsible.

'I was going on,' said Ursula. 'Mr Birkin wanted me to see the rooms. Isn't it delightful to live here? It is perfect.'

'Yes,' said Hermione, abstractedly. Then she turned right away from Ursula, ceased to know her existence.

'How do you feel, Rupert?' she sang in a new, affectionate tone, to Birkin.

'Very well,' he replied.

'Were you quite comfortable?' The curious, sinister, rapt look was on Hermione's face, she shrugged her bosom in a convulsed movement, and seemed like one half in a trance.

'Quite comfortable,' he replied.

There was a long pause, whilst Hermione looked at him for a long time, from under her heavy, drugged eyelids.

'And you think you'll be happy here?' she said at last.

'I'm sure I shall.'

'I'm sure I shall do anything for him as I can,' said the labourer's wife. 'And I'm sure our master will; so I *hope* he'll find himself comfortable.'

Hermione turned and looked at her slowly.

'Thank you so much,' she said, and then she turned completely away again. She recovered her position, and lifting her face towards him, and addressing him exclusively, she said:

'Have you measured the rooms?'

'No,' he said, 'I've been mending the punt.'

'Shall we do it now?' she said slowly, balanced and dispassionate.

'Have you got a tape measure, Mrs Salmon?' he said, turning to the woman.

'Yes sir, I think I can find one,' replied the woman, bustling immediately to a basket. 'This is the only one I've got, if it will do.'

Hermione took it, though it was offered to him.

'Thank you so much,' she said. 'It will do very nicely. Thank you so much.' Then she turned to Birkin, saying with a little gay movement: 'Shall we do it now, Rupert?'

'What about the others, they'll be bored,' he said reluctantly.

'Do you mind?' said Hermione, turning to Ursula and Gerald vaguely.

'Not in the least,' they replied.

'Which room shall we do first?' she said, turning again to Birkin, with the same gaiety, now she was going to *do* something with him.

'We'll take them as they come,' he said.

'Should I be getting your teas ready, while you do that?' said the labourer's wife, also gay because *she* had something to do.

'Would you?' said Hermione, turning to her with the curious motion of intimacy that seemed to envelop the woman, draw her almost to Hermione's breast, and which left the others standing apart. 'I should be so glad. Where shall we have it?'

'Where would you like it? Shall it be in here, or out on the grass?'

'Where shall we have tea?' sang Hermione to the company at large.

'On the bank by the pond. And *we'll* carry the things up, if you'll just get them ready, Mrs Salmon,' said Birkin.

'All right,' said the pleased woman.

The party moved down the passage into the front room. It was empty, but clean and sunny. There was a window looking on to the tangled front garden.

'This is the dining room,' said Hermione. 'We'll measure it this way, Rupert – you go down there – '

'Can't I do it for you,' said Gerald, coming to take the end of the tape.

'No, thank you,' cried Hermione, stooping to the ground in her bluish, brilliant foulard. It was a great joy to her to *do* things, and to have the ordering of the job, with Birkin. He obeyed her subduedly. Ursula and Gerald looked on. It was a peculiarity of Hermione's, that at every moment, she had one intimate, and turned all the rest of those present into onlookers. This raised her into a state of triumph.

They measured and discussed in the dining-room, and Hermione decided what the floor coverings must be. It sent her into a strange, convulsed anger, to be thwarted. Birkin always let her have her way, for the moment.

Then they moved across, through the hall, to the other front room, that was a little smaller than the first.

'This is the study,' said Hermione. 'Rupert, I have a rug that I want you to have for here. Will you let me give it to you? Do – I want to give it you.'

'What is it like?' he asked ungraciously.

'You haven't seen it. It is chiefly rose red, then blue, a metallic, mid blue, and a very soft dark blue. I think you would like it. Do you think you would?'

'It sounds very nice,' he replied. 'What is it? Oriental? With a pile?'

'Yes. Persian! It is made of camel's hair, silky. I think it is called Bergamos – twelve feet by seven – Do you think it will do?'

'It would *do,*' he said. 'But why should you give me an expensive rug? I can manage perfectly well with my old Oxford Turkish.'

'But may I give it to you? Do let me.'

'How much did it cost?'

She looked at him, and said:

'I don't remember. It was quite cheap.'

He looked at her, his face set.

'I don't want to take it, Hermione,' he said.

'Do let me give it to the rooms,' she said, going up to him and putting her hand on his arm lightly, pleadingly. 'I shall be so disappointed.'

'You know I don't want you to give me things,' he repeated helplessly.

'I don't want to give you *things,*' she said teasingly. 'But will you have this?'

'All right,' he said, defeated, and she triumphed.

They went upstairs. There were two bedrooms to correspond with the rooms downstairs. One of them was half furnished, and

Birkin had evidently slept there. Hermione went round the room carefully, taking in every detail, as if absorbing the evidence of his presence, in all the inanimate things. She felt the bed and examined the coverings.

'Are you *sure* you were quite comfortable?' she said, pressing the pillow.

'Perfectly,' he replied coldly.

'And were you warm? There is no down quilt. I am sure you need one. You mustn't have a great pressure of clothes.'

'I've got one,' he said. 'It is coming down.'

They measured the rooms, and lingered over every consideration. Ursula stood at the window and watched the woman carrying the tea up the bank to the pond. She hated the palaver Hermione made, she wanted to drink tea, she wanted anything but this fuss and business.

At last they all mounted the grassy bank, to the picnic. Hermione poured out tea. She ignored now Ursula's presence. And Ursula, recovering from her ill-humour, turned to Gerald saying:

'Oh, I hated you so much the other day, Mr Crich.'

'What for?' said Gerald, wincing slightly away.

'For treating your horse so badly. Oh, I hated you so much!'

'What did he do?' sang Hermione.

'He made his lovely sensitive Arab horse stand with him at the railway-crossing whilst a horrible lot of trucks went by; and the poor thing, she was in a perfect frenzy, a perfect agony. It was the most horrible sight you can imagine.'

'Why did you do it, Gerald?' asked Hermione, calm and interrogative. 'She must learn to stand – what use is she to me in this country, if she shies and goes off every time an engine whistles.'

'But why inflict unnecessary torture?' said Ursula. 'Why make her stand all that time at the crossing? You might just as well have ridden back up the road, and saved all that horror. Her sides were bleeding where you had spurred her. It was too horrible!'

Gerald stiffened.

'I have to use her,' he replied. 'And if I'm going to be sure of her at *all*, she'll have to learn to stand noises.'

'Why should she?' cried Ursula in a passion. 'She is a living creature, why should she stand anything, just because you choose to make her? She has as much right to her own being, as you have to yours.'

'There I disagree,' said Gerald. 'I consider that mare is there for my use. Not because I bought her, but because that is the natural order. It is more natural for a man to take a horse and use it as he likes, than for him to go down on his knees to it, begging it to do as it wishes, and to fulfil its own marvellous nature.'

Ursula was just breaking out, when Hermione lifted her face and began, in her musing sing-song:

'I do think – I do really think we must have the *courage* to use the lower animal life for our needs. I do think there is something wrong, when we look on every living creature as if it were ourselves. I do feel, that it is false to project our own feelings on every animate creature. It is a lack of discrimination, a lack of criticism.'

'Quite,' said Birkin sharply. 'Nothing is so detestable as the maudlin attributing of human feelings and consciousness to animals.'

'Yes,' said Hermione, wearily, 'we must really take a position. Either we are going to use the animals, or they will use us.'

'That's a fact,' said Gerald. 'A horse has got a will like a man, though it has no *mind* strictly. And if your will isn't master, then the horse is master of you. And this is a thing I can't help. I can't help being master of the horse.'

'If only we could learn how to use our will,' said Hermione, 'we could do anything. The will can cure anything, and put anything right. That I am convinced of – if only we use the will properly, intelligibly.'

'What do you mean by using the will properly?' said Birkin.

'A very great doctor taught me,' she said, addressing Ursula and Gerald vaguely. 'He told me for instance, that to cure oneself of a bad habit, one should *force* oneself to do it, when one would not do it make oneself do it – and then the habit would disappear.'

'How do you mean?' said Gerald.

'If you bite your nails, for example. Then, when you don't want to bite your nails, bite them, make yourself bite them. And you would find the habit was broken.'

'Is that so?' said Gerald.

'Yes. And in. so many things, I have *made* myself well. I was a very queer and nervous girl. And by learning to use my will, simply by using my will, I *made* myself right.'

Ursula looked all the while at Hermione, as she spoke in her slow, dispassionate, and yet strangely tense voice. A curious thrill went over the younger woman. Some strange, dark, convulsive power was in Hermione, fascinating and repelling.

'It is fatal to use the will like that,' cried Birkin harshly, 'disgusting. Such a will is an obscenity.'

Hermione looked at him for a long time, with her shadowed, heavy eyes. Her face was soft and pale and thin, almost phosphorescent, her jaw was lean.

'I'm sure it isn't,' she said at length. There always seemed an interval, a strange split between what she seemed to feel and experience, and what she actually said and thought. She seemed to catch her thoughts at length from off the surface of a maelstrom of chaotic black emotions and reactions, and Birkin was always filled with repulsion, she caught so infallibly, her will never failed her. Her voice was always dispassionate and tense, and perfectly confident. Yet she shuddered with a sense of nausea, a sort of seasickness that always threatened to overwhelm her mind. But her mind remained unbroken, her will was still perfect. It almost sent Birkin mad. But he would never, never dare to break her will, and let loose the maelstrom of her subconsciousness, and see her in her ultimate madness. Yet he was always striking at her.

'And of course,' he said to Gerald, 'horses *haven't* got a complete will, like human beings. A horse has no *one* will. Every horse, strictly, has two wills. With one will, it wants to put itself in the human power completely – and with the other, it wants to be free, wild. The two wills sometimes lock – you know that, if ever you've felt a horse bolt, while you've been driving it.'

'I have felt a horse bolt while I was driving it,' said Gerald, 'but it didn't make me know it had two wills. I only knew it was frightened.'

Hermione had ceased to listen. She simply became oblivious when these subjects were started.

'Why should a horse want to put itself in the human power?' asked Ursula. 'That is quite incomprehensible to me. I don't believe it ever wanted it.'

'Yes it did. It's the last, perhaps highest, love-impulse: resign your will to the higher being,' said Birkin.

'What curious notions you have of love,' jeered Ursula.

'And woman is the same as horses: two wills act in opposition inside her. With one will, she wants to subject herself utterly. With the other she wants to bolt, and pitch her rider to perdition.'

'Then I'm a bolter,' said Ursula, with a burst of laughter.

'It's a dangerous thing to domesticate even horses, let alone women,' said Birkin. 'The dominant principle has some rare antagonists.'

'Good thing too,' said Ursula.

'Quite,' said Gerald, with a faint smile. 'There's more fun.' Hermione could bear no more. She rose, saying in her easy sing song:

'Isn't the evening beautiful! I get filled sometimes with such a great sense of beauty, that I feel I can hardly bear it.'

Ursula, to whom she had appealed, rose with her, moved to the last impersonal depths. And Birkin seemed to her almost a monster of hateful arrogance. She went with Hermione along the bank of the pond, talking of beautiful, soothing things, picking the gentle cowslips.

'Wouldn't you like a dress,' said Ursula to Hermione, 'of this yellow spotted with orange – a cotton dress?'

'Yes,' said Hermione, stopping and looking at the flower, letting the thought come home to her and soothe her. 'Wouldn't it be pretty? I should *love* it.'

And she turned smiling to Ursula, in a feeling of real affection.

But Gerald remained with Birkin, wanting to probe him to the bottom, to know what he meant by the dual will in horses. A flicker of excitement danced on Gerald's face.

Hermione and Ursula strayed on together, united in a sudden bond of deep affection and closeness.

'I really do not want to be forced into all this criticism and analysis of life. I really *do* want to see things in their entirety, with their beauty left to them, and their wholeness, their natural holiness. Don't you feel it, don't you feel you *can't* be tortured into any more knowledge?' said Hermione, stopping in front of Ursula, and turning to her with clenched fists thrust downwards.

'Yes,' said Ursula. 'I do. I am sick of all this poking and prying.'

'I'm so glad you are. Sometimes,' said Hermione, again stopping arrested in her progress and turning to Ursula, 'Sometimes I wonder if I *ought* to submit to all this realisation, if I am not being weak in rejecting it. But I feel I *can't – I can't*. It seems to destroy *everything*. All the beauty and the – and the true holiness is destroyed – and I feel I can't live without them.'

'And it would be simply wrong to live without them,' cried Ursula. 'No, it is so *irreverent* to think that everything must be realised in the head. Really, something must be left to the Lord, there always is and always will be.'

'Yes,' said Hermione, reassured like a child, 'it should, shouldn't it? And Rupert – ' she lifted her face to the sky, in a muse – 'he *can* only tear things to pieces. He really *is* like a boy who must pull everything to pieces to see how it is made. And I can't think it is right – it does seem so irreverent, as you say.'

'Like tearing open a bud to see what the flower will be like,' said Ursula.

'Yes. And that kills everything, doesn't it? It doesn't allow any possibility of flowering.'

'Of course not,' said Ursula. 'It is purely destructive.'

'It is, isn't it!

Hermione looked long and slow at Ursula, seeming to accept confirmation from her. Then the two women were silent. As soon as they were in accord, they began mutually to mistrust each other. In spite of herself, Ursula felt herself recoiling from Hermione. It was all she could do to restrain her revulsion.

They returned to the men, like two conspirators who have withdrawn to come to an agreement. Birkin looked up at them. Ursula hated him for his cold watchfulness. But he said nothing.

'Shall we be going?' said Hermione. 'Rupert, you are coming to Shortlands to dinner? Will you come at once, will you come now, with us?'

'I'm not dressed,' replied Birkin. 'And you know Gerald stickles for convention. '

'I don't stickle for it,' said Gerald. 'But if you' d got as sick as I have of rowdy go-as-you-please in the house, you'd prefer it if people were peaceful and conventional, at least at meals.'

'All right,' said Birkin.

'But can't we wait for you while you dress?' persisted Hermione.

'If you like.'

He rose to go indoors. Ursula said she would take her leave.

'Only,' she said, turning to Gerald, 'I must say that, however man is lord of the beast and the fowl, I still don't think he has any right to violate the feelings of the inferior creation. I still think it would have been much more sensible and nice of you if you'd trotted back up the road while the train went by, and been considerate.'

'I see,' said Gerald, smiling, but somewhat annoyed. 'I must remember another time.'

'They all think I'm an interfering female,' thought Ursula to herself, as she went away. But she was in arms against them.

She ran home plunged in thought. She had been very much moved by Hermione, she had really come into contact with her, so that there was a sort of league between the two women. And yet she could not bear her. But she put the thought away. 'She's really good,' she said to herself. 'She really wants what is right.' And she tried to feel at one with Hermione, and to shut off from Birkin. She was strictly hostile to him. But she was held to him by some bond, some deep principle. This at once irritated her and saved her.

Only now and again, violent little shudders would come over her, out of her subconsciousness, and she knew it was the fact that she had stated her challenge to Birkin, and he had, consciously or unconsciously, accepted. It was a fight to the death between them – or to new life: though in what the conflict lay, no one could say.

CHAPTER 13

Mino

THE DAYS went by, and she received no sign. Was he going to ignore her, was he going to take no further notice of her secret? A dreary weight of anxiety and acrid bitterness settled on her. And yet Ursula knew she was only deceiving herself, and that he would proceed. She said no word to anybody.

Then, sure enough, there came a note from him, asking if she would come to tea with Gudrun, to his rooms in town.

'Why does he ask Gudrun as well?' she asked herself at once. 'Does he want to protect himself, or does he think I would not go alone?'

She was tormented by the thought that he wanted to protect himself.

But at the end of all, she only said to herself:

'I don't want Gudrun to be there, because I want him to say something more to me. So I shan't tell Gudrun anything about it, and I shall go alone. Then I shall know.'

She found herself sitting on the tram-car, mounting up the hill going out of the town, to the place where he had his lodging. She seemed to have passed into a kind of dream world, absolved from the conditions of actuality. She watched the sordid streets of the town go by beneath her, as if she were a spirit disconnected from the material universe. What had it all to do with her? She was palpitating and formless within the flux of the ghost life. She could not consider any more, what anybody would say of her or think about her. People had passed out of her range, she was absolved. She had fallen strange and dim, out of the sheath of the material life, as a berry falls from the only world it has ever known, down out of the sheath on to the real unknown.

Birkin was standing in the middle of the room, when she was shown in by the landlady. He too was moved outside himself. She saw him agitated and shaken, a frail, unsubstantial body silent like the node of some violent force, that came out from him and shook her almost into a swoon.

'You are alone?' he said.

'Yes – Gudrun could not come.'

He instantly guessed why.

And they were both seated in silence, in the terrible tension of the room. She was aware that it was a pleasant room, full of light and very restful in its form – aware also of a fuchsia tree, with dangling scarlet and purple flowers.

'How nice the fuchsias are!' she said, to break the silence.

'Aren't they! Did you think I had forgotten what I said?'

A swoon went over Ursula's mind.

'I don't want you to remember it – if you don't want to,' she struggled to say, through the dark mist that covered her.

There was silence for some moments.

'No,' he said. 'It isn't that. Only – if we are going to know each other, we must pledge ourselves for ever. If we are going to make a relationship, even of friendship, there must be something final and infallible about it.'

There was a clang of mistrust and almost anger in his voice. She did not answer. Her heart was too much contracted. She

could not have spoken. Seeing she was not going to reply, he
continued, almost bitterly, giving himself away:

'I can't say it is love I have to offer – and it isn't love I want.
It is something much more impersonal and harder – and rarer.'

There was a silence, out of which she said:

'You mean you don't love me?'

She suffered furiously, saying that.

'Yes, if you like to put it like that. Though perhaps that isn't
true. I don't know. At any rate, I don't feel the emotion of love for
you – no, and I don't want to. Because it gives out in the last issues.'

'Love gives out in the last issues?' she asked, feeling numb
to the lips.

'Yes, it does. At the very last, one is alone, beyond the
influence of love. There is a real impersonal me, that is beyond
love, beyond any emotional relationship. So it is with you. But we
want to delude ourselves that love is the root. It isn't. It is only
the branches. The root is beyond love, a naked kind of isolation,
an isolated me, that does *not* meet and mingle, and never can.'

She watched him with wide, troubled eyes. His face was
incandescent in its abstract earnestness.

'And you mean you can't love?' she asked, in trepidation.

'Yes, if you like. I have loved. But there is a beyond, where
there is not love.'

She could not submit to this. She felt it swooning over her.
But she could not submit.

'But how do you know – if you have never *really* loved?' she
asked.

'It is true, what I say; there is a beyond, in you, in me, which
is further than love, beyond the scope, as stars are beyond the
scope of vision, some of them.'

'Then there is no love,' cried Ursula.

'Ultimately, no, there is something else. But, ultimately, there
if no love.'

Ursula was given over to this statement for some moments.
Then she half rose from her chair, saying, in a final, repellent voice:

'Then let me go home – what am I doing here?'

'There is the door,' he said. 'You are a free agent.'

He was suspended finely and perfectly in this extremity. She hung motionless for some seconds, then she sat down again.

'If there is no love, what is there?' she cried, almost jeering.

'Something,' he said, looking at her, battling with his soul, with all his might.

'What?'

He was silent for a long time, unable to be in communication with her while she was in this state of opposition.

'There is,' he said, in a voice of pure abstraction; 'a final me which is stark and impersonal and beyond responsibility. So there is a final you. And it is there I would want to meet you – not in the emotional, loving plane – but there beyond, where there is no speech and no terms of agreement. There we are two stark, unknown beings, two utterly strange creatures, I would want to approach you, and you me. And there could be no obligation, because there is no standard for action there, because no understanding has been reaped from that plane. It is quite inhuman, – so there can be no calling to book, in any form whatsoever – because one is outside the pale of all that is accepted, and nothing known applies. One can only follow the impulse, taking that which lies in front, and responsible for nothing, asked for nothing, giving nothing, only each taking according to the primal desire.'

Ursula listened to this speech, her mind dumb and almost senseless, what he said was so unexpected and so untoward.

'It is just purely selfish,' she said.

'If it is pure, yes. But it isn't selfish at all. Because I don't *know* what I want of you. I deliver *myself* over to the unknown, in coming to you, I am without reserves or defences, stripped entirely, into the unknown. Only, there needs the pledge between us, that we will both cast off everything, cast off ourselves even, and cease to be, so that that which is perfectly ourselves can take place in us.'

She pondered along her own line of thought.

'But it is because you love me, that you want me?' she persisted.

'No it isn't. It is because I believe in you – if I *do* believe in you.'

'Aren't you sure?' she laughed, suddenly hurt.

He was looking at her steadfastly, scarcely heeding what she said.

'Yes, I must believe in you, or else I shouldn't be here saying this,' he replied. 'But that is all the proof I have. I don't feel any very strong belief at this particular moment.'

She disliked him for this sudden relapse into weariness and faithlessness.

'But don't you think me good-looking?' she persisted, in a mocking voice.

He looked at her, to see if he felt that she was good-looking.

'I don't *feel* that you're good-looking,' he said.

'Not even attractive?' she mocked, bitingly.

He knitted his brows in sudden exasperation.

'Don't you see that it's not a question of visual appreciation in the least,' he cried. 'I don't *want* to see you. I've seen plenty of women, I'm sick and weary of seeing them. I want a woman I don't see.'

'I'm sorry I can't oblige you by being invisible,' she laughed.

'Yes, "he said, 'you are invisible to me, if you don't force me to be visually aware of you. But I don't want to see you or hear you.'

'What did you ask me to tea for, then?' she mocked.

But he would take no notice of her. He was talking to himself.

'I want to find you, where you don't know your own existence, the you that your common self denies utterly. But I don't want your good looks, and I don't want your womanly feelings, and I don't want your thoughts nor opinions nor your ideas – they are all bagatelles to me.'

'You are very conceited, Monsieur,' she mocked. 'How do you know what my womanly feelings are, or my thoughts or my ideas? You don't even know what I think of you now.'

'Nor do I care in the slightest.'

'I think you are very silly. I think you want to tell me you love me, and you go all this way round to do it.'

'All right,' he said, looking up with sudden exasperation. 'Now go away then, and leave me alone. I don't want any more of your meretricious persiflage.'

'Is it really persiflage?' she mocked, her face really relaxing into laughter. She interpreted it, that he had made a deep confession of love to her. But he was so absurd in his words, also.

They were silent for many minutes, she was pleased and elated like a child. His concentration broke, he began to look at her simply and naturally.

'What I want is a strange conjunction with you – ' he said quietly; 'not meeting and mingling – you are quite right – but an equilibrium, a pure balance of two single beings – as the stars balance each other.'

She looked at him. He was very earnest, and earnestness was always rather ridiculous, commonplace, to her. It made her feel unfree and uncomfortable. Yet she liked him so much. But why drag in the stars.

'Isn't this rather sudden?' she mocked.

He began to laugh.

'Best to read the terms of the contract, before we sign,' he said.

A young grey cat that had been sleeping on the sofa jumped down and stretched, rising on its long legs, and arching its slim back. Then it sat considering for a moment, erect and kingly. And then, like a dart, it had shot out of the room, through the open window-doors, and into the garden.

'What's he after?' said Birkin, rising.

The young cat trotted lordly down the path, waving his tail. He was an ordinary tabby with white paws, a slender young gentleman. A crouching, fluffy, brownish-grey cat was stealing up the side of the fence. The Mino walked statelily up to her, with manly nonchalance. She crouched before him and pressed herself on the ground in humility, a fluffy soft outcast, looking up at him with wild eyes that were green and lovely as great jewels. He looked casually down on her. So she crept a few inches further, proceeding on her way to the back door, crouching in a wonderful, soft, self-obliterating manner, and moving like a shadow.

He, going statelily on his slim legs, walked after her, then suddenly, for pure excess, he gave her a light cuff with his paw on the side of her face. She ran off a few steps, like a blown leaf along the ground, then crouched unobtrusively, in submissive, wild patience. The Mino pretended to take no notice of her. He blinked his eyes superbly at the landscape. In a minute she drew herself together and moved softly, a fleecy brown-grey shadow, a few paces forward. She began to quicken her pace, in a moment she would be gone like a dream, when the young grey lord sprang before her, and gave her a light handsome cuff. She subsided at once, submissively.

'She is a wild cat,' said Birkin. 'She has come in from the woods.'

The eyes of the stray cat flared round for a moment, like great green fires staring at Birkin. Then she had rushed in a soft swift rush, half way down the garden. There she paused to look round. The Mino turned his face in pure superiority to his master, and slowly closed his eyes, standing in statuesque young perfection. The wild cat's round, green, wondering eyes were staring all the while like uncanny fires. Then again, like a shadow, she slid towards the kitchen.

In a lovely springing leap, like a wind, the Mino was upon her, and had boxed her twice, very definitely, with a white, delicate fist. She sank and slid back, unquestioning. He walked after her, and cuffed her once or twice, leisurely, with sudden little blows of his magic white paws.

'Now why does he do that?' cried Ursula in indignation.

'They are on intimate terms,' said Birkin.

'And is that why he hits her?'

'Yes,' laughed Birkin, 'I think he wants to make it quite obvious to her.'

'Isn't it horrid of him!' she cried; and going out into the garden she called to the Mino:

'Stop it, don't bully. Stop hitting her.'

The stray cat vanished like a swift, invisible shadow. The Mino glanced at Ursula, then looked from her disdainfully to his master.

'Are you a bully, Mino?' Birkin asked.

The young slim cat looked at him, and slowly narrowed its eyes.

Then it glanced away at the landscape, looking into the distance as if completely oblivious of the two human beings.

'Mino,' said Ursula; 'I don't like you. You are a bully like all males.'

'No,' said Birkin, 'he is justified. He is not a bully. He is only insisting to the poor stray that she shall acknowledge him as a sort of fate, her own fate: because you can see she is fluffy and promiscuous as the wind. I am with him entirely. He wants superfine stability.'

'Yes, I know!' cried Ursula. 'He wants his own way – I know what your fine words work down to – bossiness, I call it, bossiness.'

The young cat again glanced at Birkin in disdain of the noisy woman.

'I quite agree with you, Miciotto,' said Birkin to the cat. 'Keep your male dignity, and your higher understanding.'

Again the Mino narrowed his eyes as if he were looking at the sun. Then, suddenly affecting to have no connection at all with the two people, he went trotting off, with assumed spontaneity and gaiety, his tail erect, his white feet blithe.

'Now he will find the belle sauvage once more, and entertain her with his superior wisdom,' laughed Birkin.

Ursula looked at the man who stood in the garden with his hair blowing and his eyes smiling ironically, and she cried:

'Oh it makes me so cross, this assumption of male superiority! And it is such a lie! One wouldn't mind if there were any justification for it.'

'The wild cat,' said Birkin, 'doesn't mind. She perceives that it is justified.'

'Does she!' cried Ursula. 'And tell it to the Horse Marines.'

'To them also.'

'It is just like Gerald Crich with his horse – a lust for bullying – a real Wille zur Macht* – so base, so petty.'

'I agree that the Wille zur Macht is a base and petty thing. But with the Mino, it is the desire to bring this female cat into a pure stable equilibrium, a transcendent and abiding *rapport* with the single male. Whereas without him, as you see, she is a mere stray, a fluffy sporadic bit of chaos. It is a volonté de pouvoir, if you like, a will to ability, taking pouvoir as a verb.'

'Ah –! Sophistries! It's the old Adam.'

'Oh yes. Adam kept Eve in the indestructible paradise, when he kept her single with himself, like a star in its orbit.'

'Yes – yes – ' cried Ursula, pointing her finger at him. 'There you are a star in its orbit! A satellite – a satellite of Mars – that's what she is to be! There – there – you've given yourself away! You want a satellite, Mars and his satellite! You've said it – you've said it – you've dished yourself!'

He stood smiling in frustration and amusement and irritation and admiration and love. She was so quick, and so lambent, like discernible fire, and so vindictive, and so rich in her dangerous flamy sensitiveness.

'I've not said it at all,' he replied, 'if you will give me a chance to speak.'

'No, no!' she cried. 'I won't let you speak. You've said it, a satellite, you're not going to wriggle out of it. You've said it.'

'You'll never believe now that I *haven't* said it,' he answered. 'I neither implied nor indicated nor mentioned a satellite, nor intended a satellite, never.'

'*You prevaricator!*' she cried, in real indignation.

'Tea is ready, sir,' said the landlady from the doorway.

They both looked at her, very much as the cats had looked at them, a little while before.

'Thank you, Mrs Daykin.'

An interrupted silence fell over the two of them, a moment of breach.

'Come and have tea,' he said.

* The title of Friedrich Nietzsche's work *The Will to Power.*

'Yes, I should love it,' she replied, gathering herself together.

They sat facing each other across the tea table.

'I did not say, nor imply, a satellite. I meant two single equal stars balanced in conjunction – '

'You gave yourself away, you gave away your little game completely,' she cried, beginning at once to eat. He saw that she would take no further heed of his expostulation, so he began to pour the tea.

'What *good* things to eat!' she cried.

'Take your own sugar,' he said.

He handed her her cup. He had everything so nice, such pretty cups and plates, painted with mauve-lustre and green, also shapely bowls and glass plates, and old spoons, on a woven cloth of pale grey and black and purple. It was very rich and fine. But Ursula could see Hermione's influence.

'Your things are so lovely!' she said, almost angrily.

'I like them. It gives me real pleasure to use things that are attractive in themselves – pleasant things. And Mrs Daykin is good. She thinks everything is wonderful, for my sake.'

'Really,' said Ursula, 'landladies are better than wives, nowadays. They certainly *care* a great deal more. It is much more beautiful and complete here now, than if you were married.'

'But think of the emptiness within,' he laughed.

'No,' she said. 'I am jealous that men have such perfect landladies and such beautiful lodgings. There is nothing left them to desire.'

'In the house-keeping way, we'll hope not. It is disgusting, people marrying for a home.'

'Still,' said Ursula, 'a man has very little need for a woman now, has he?'

'In outer things, maybe – except to share his bed and bear his children. But essentially, there is just the same need as there ever was.

Only nobody takes the trouble to be essential.'

'How essential?' she said.

'I do think,' he said, 'that the world is only held together by the mystic conjunction, the ultimate unison between people – a bond. And the immediate bond is between man and woman.'

'But it's such old hat,' said Ursula. 'Why should love be a bond? No, I'm not having any.'

'If you are walking westward,' he said, 'you forfeit the northern and eastward and southern direction. If you admit a unison, you forfeit all the possibilities of chaos.'

'But love is freedom,' she declared.

'Don't cant to me,' he replied. 'Love is a direction which excludes all other directions. It's a freedom *together*, if you like.'

'No,' she said, 'love includes everything.'

'Sentimental cant,' he replied. 'You want the state of chaos, that's all.

It is ultimate nihilism, this freedom-in-love business, this freedom which is love and love which is freedom. As a matter of fact, if you enter into a pure unison, it is irrevocable, and it is never pure till it is irrevocable. And when it is irrevocable, it is one way, like the path of a star.'

'Ha!' she cried bitterly. 'It is the old dead morality.'

'No,' he said, 'it is the law of creation. One is committed. One must commit oneself to a conjunction with the other – forever. But it is not selfless – it is a maintaining of the self in mystic balance and integrity like a star balanced with another star.'

'I don't trust you when you drag in the stars,' she said. 'If you were quite true, it wouldn't be necessary to be so far-fetched.'

'Don't trust me then,' he said, angry. 'It is enough that I trust myself.'

'And that is where you make another mistake,' she replied. 'You *don't* trust yourself. You don't fully believe yourself what you are saying. You don't really want this conjunction, otherwise you wouldn't talk so much about it, you'd get it.'

He was suspended for a moment, arrested.

'How?' he said.

'By just loving,' she retorted in defiance.

He was still a moment, in anger. Then he said:

'I tell you, I don't believe in love like that. I tell you, you want love to administer to your egoism, to subserve you. Love is a process of subservience with you – and with everybody. I hate it.'

'No,' she cried, pressing back her head like a cobra, her eyes flashing. 'It is a process of pride – I want to be proud – '

'Proud and subservient, proud and subservient, I know you,' he retorted dryly. 'Proud and subservient, then subservient to the proud I know you and your love. It is a tick-tack, tick-tack, a dance of opposites.'

'Are you sure?' she mocked wickedly, 'what my love is?'

'Yes, I am,' he retorted.

'So cocksure!' she said. 'How can anybody ever be right, who is so cocksure? It shows you are wrong.'

He was silent in chagrin.

They had talked and struggled till they were both wearied out.

'Tell me about yourself and your people,' he said.

And she told him about the Brangwens, and about her mother, and about Skrebensky, her first love, and about her later experiences. He sat very still, watching her as she talked. And he seemed to listen with reverence. Her face was beautiful and full of baffled light as she told him all the things that had hurt her or perplexed her so deeply. He seemed to warm and comfort his soul at the beautiful light of her nature.

'If she *really* could pledge herself,' he thought to himself, with passionate insistence but hardly any hope. Yet a curious little irresponsible laughter appeared in his heart.

'We have all suffered so much,' he mocked, ironically.

She looked up at him, and a flash of wild gaiety went over her face, a strange flash of yellow light coming from her eyes.

'Haven't we!' she cried, in a high, reckless cry. 'It is almost absurd, isn't it?'

'Quite absurd,' he said. 'Suffering bores me, any more.'

'So it does me.'

He was almost afraid of the mocking recklessness of her splendid face. Here was one who would go to the whole lengths of heaven or hell, whichever she had to go. And he mistrusted her, he was afraid of a woman capable of such abandon, such dangerous thoroughness of destructivity. Yet he chuckled within himself also.

She came over to him and put her hand on his shoulder, looking down at him with strange golden-lighted eyes, very tender, but with a curious devilish look lurking underneath.

'Say you love me, say "my love" to me,' she pleaded

He looked back into her eyes, and saw. His face flickered with sardonic comprehension.

'I love you right enough,' he said, grimly. 'But I want it to be something else.'

'But why? But why?' she insisted, bending her wonderful luminous face to him. 'Why isn't it enough?'

'Because we can go one better,' he said, putting his arms round her.

'No, we can't,' she said, in a strong, voluptuous voice of yielding. 'We can only love each other. Say "my love" to me, say it, say it.'

She put her arms round his neck. He enfolded her, and kissed her subtly, murmuring in a subtle voice of love, and irony, and submission:

'Yes, – my love, yes, – my love. Let love be enough then. I love you then. I love you. I'm bored by the rest.'

'Yes,' she murmured, nestling very sweet and close to him.

CHAPTER 14

Water-party

EVERY YEAR Mr Crich gave a more or less public water-party on the lake. There was a little pleasure-launch on Willey Water and several rowing boats, and guests could take tea either in the marquee that was set up in the grounds of the house, or they could picnic in the shade of the great walnut tree at the boat-house by the lake. This year the staff of the Grammar-School was invited, along with the chief officials of the firm. Gerald and the younger Criches did not care for this party, but it had become customary now, and it pleased the father, as being the only occasion when he could gather some people of the district together in festivity with him. For he loved to give pleasures to his dependents and to those poorer than himself. But his children preferred the company of their own equals in wealth. They hated their inferiors' humility or gratitude or awkwardness.

Nevertheless they were willing to attend at this festival, as they had done almost since they were children, the more so, as they all felt a little guilty now, and unwilling to thwart their father any more, since he was so ill in health. Therefore, quite cheerfully Laura prepared to take her mother's place as hostess, and Gerald assumed responsibility for the amusements on the water.

Birkin had written to Ursula saying he expected to see her at the party, and Gudrun, although she scorned the patronage of the Criches, would nevertheless accompany her mother and father if the weather were fine.

The day came blue and full of sunshine, with little wafts of wind. The sisters both wore dresses of white crepe, and hats of soft grass. But Gudrun had a sash of brilliant black and pink and yellow colour wound broadly round her waist, and she had pink silk stockings, and black and pink and yellow decoration on the brim of her hat, weighing it down a little. She carried also a yellow silk coat over her arm, so that she looked remarkable, like a painting from the Salon. Her appearance was a sore trial to her father, who said angrily:

'Don't you think you might as well get yourself up for a Christmas cracker, an' ha' done with it?'

But Gudrun looked handsome and brilliant, and she wore her clothes in pure defiance. When people stared at her, and giggled after her, she made a point of saying loudly, to Ursula:

'Regarde, regarde ces gens-lá! Ne sont-ils pas des hiboux incroyables?'* And with the words of French in her mouth, she would look over her shoulder at the giggling party.

'No, really, it's impossible!' Ursula would reply distinctly. And so the two girls took it out of their universal enemy. But their father became more and more enraged.

Ursula was all snowy white, save that her hat was pink, and entirely without trimming, and her shoes were dark red, and she carried an orange-coloured coat. And in this guise they were walking all the way to Shortlands, their father and mother going in front.

They were laughing at their mother, who, dressed in a summer material of black and purple stripes, and wearing a hat of purple straw, was setting forth with much more of the shyness and trepidation of a young girl than her daughters ever felt, walking demurely beside her husband, who, as usual, looked rather crumpled in his best suit, as if he were the father of a young family and had been holding the baby whilst his wife got dressed.

'Look at the young couple in front,' said Gudrun calmly. Ursula looked at her mother and father, and was suddenly seized with uncontrollable laughter. The two girls stood in the road and laughed till the tears ran down their faces, as they caught sight again of the shy, unworldly couple of their parents going on ahead.

'We are roaring at you, mother,' called Ursula, helplessly following after her parents.

Mrs Brangwen turned round with a slightly puzzled, exasperated look. 'Oh indeed!' she said. 'What is there so very funny about *me,* I should like to know?'

---

* (Fr.) "Look, look at these people, are they not the unbelievable owls?"

She could not understand that there could be anything amiss with her appearance. She had a perfect calm sufficiency, an easy indifference to any criticism whatsoever, as if she were beyond it. Her clothes were always rather odd, and as a rule slip-shod, yet she wore them with a perfect ease and satisfaction. Whatever she had on, so long as she was barely tidy, she was right, beyond remark; such an aristocrat she was by instinct.

'You look so stately, like a country Baroness,' said Ursula, laughing with a little tenderness at her mother's naive puzzled air.

'*Just* like a country Baroness!' chimed in Gudrun. Now the mother's natural hauteur became self-conscious, and the girls shrieked again.

'Go home, you pair of idiots, great giggling idiots!' cried the father inflamed with irritation.

'Mm-m-er!' booed Ursula, pulling a face at his crossness.

The yellow lights danced in his eyes, he leaned forward in real rage. 'Don't be so silly as to take any notice of the great gabies,' said Mrs Brangwen, turning on her way.

'I'll see if I'm going to be followed by a pair of giggling yelling jackanapes – ' he cried vengefully.

The girls stood still, laughing helplessly at his fury, upon the path beside the hedge.

'Why you're as silly as they are, to take any notice,' said Mrs Brangwen also becoming angry now he was really enraged.

'There are some people coming, father,' cried Ursula, with mocking warning. He glanced round quickly, and went on to join his wife, walking stiff with rage. And the girls followed, weak with laughter.

When the people had passed by, Brangwen cried in a loud, stupid voice:

'I'm going back home if there's any more of this. I'm damned if I'm going to be made a fool of in this fashion, in the public road.'

He was really out of temper. At the sound of his blind, vindictive voice, the laughter suddenly left the girls, and their hearts contracted with contempt. They hated his words 'in the public road.' What did they care for the public road? But Gudrun was conciliatory.

'But we weren't laughing to *hurt* you,' she cried, with an uncouth gentleness which made her parents uncomfortable. 'We were laughing because we're fond of you.'

'We'll walk on in front, if they are *so* touchy,' said Ursula, angry. And in this wise they arrived at Willey Water. The lake was blue and fair, the meadows sloped down in sunshine on one side, the thick dark woods dropped steeply on the other. The little pleasure-launch was fussing out from the shore, twanging its music, crowded with people, flapping its paddles. Near the boat-house was a throng of gaily-dressed persons, small in the distance. And on the high-road, some of the common people were standing along the hedge, looking at the festivity beyond, enviously, like souls not admitted to paradise.

'My eye!' said Gudrun, sotto voce, looking at the motley of guests, 'there's a pretty crowd if you like! Imagine yourself in the midst of that, my dear.'

Gudrun's apprehensive horror of people in the mass unnerved Ursula. 'It looks rather awful,' she said anxiously.

'And imagine what they'll be like – *imagine!*' said Gudrun, still in that unnerving, subdued voice. Yet she advanced determinedly.

'I suppose we can get away from them,' said Ursula anxiously.

'We're in a pretty fix if we can't,' said Gudrun. Her extreme ironic loathing and apprehension was very trying to Ursula.

'We needn't stay,' she said.

'I certainly shan't stay five minutes among that little lot,' said Gudrun. They advanced nearer, till they saw policemen at the gates.

'Policemen to keep you in, too!' said Gudrun. 'My word, this is a beautiful affair.'

'We'd better look after father and mother,' said Ursula anxiously.

'Mother's *perfectly* capable of getting through this little celebration,' said Gudrun with some contempt.

But Ursula knew that her father felt uncouth and angry and unhappy, so she was far from her ease. They waited outside the gate till their parents came up. The tall, thin man in his crumpled clothes was unnerved and irritable as a boy, finding himself on the brink of this social function. He did not feel a gentleman, he did not feel anything except pure exasperation.

Ursula took her place at his side, they gave their tickets to the policeman, and passed in on to the grass, four abreast; the tall, hot, ruddy-dark man with his narrow boyish brow drawn with irritation, the fresh-faced, easy woman, perfectly collected though her hair was slipping on one side, then Gudrun, her eyes round and dark and staring, her full soft face impassive, almost sulky, so that she seemed to be backing away in antagonism even whilst she was advancing; and then Ursula, with the odd, brilliant, dazzled look on her face, that always came when she was in some false situation.

Birkin was the good angel. He came smiling to them with his affected social grace, that somehow was never *quite* right. But he took off his hat and smiled at them with a real smile in his eyes, so that Brangwen cried out heartily in relief:

'How do you do? You're better, are you?'

'Yes, I'm better. How do you do, Mrs Brangwen? I know Gudrun and Ursula very well.'

His eyes smiled full of natural warmth. He had a soft, flattering manner with women, particularly with women who were not young.

'Yes,' said Mrs Brangwen, cool but yet gratified. 'I have heard them speak of you often enough.'

He laughed. Gudrun looked aside, feeling she was being belittled. People were standing about in groups, some women were sitting in the shade of the walnut tree, with cups of tea in their hands, a waiter in evening dress was hurrying round, some girls were simpering with parasols, some young men, who had just come in from rowing, were sitting cross-legged on the grass, coatless, their shirt-sleeves rolled up in manly fashion, their hands resting on their white flannel trousers, their gaudy ties floating about, as they laughed and tried to be witty with the young damsels.

'Why,' thought Gudrun churlishly, 'don't they have the manners to put their coats on, and not to assume such intimacy in their appearance.'

She abhorred the ordinary young man, with his hair plastered back, and his easy-going chumminess.

Hermione Roddice came up, in a handsome gown of white lace, trailing an enormous silk shawl blotched with great embroidered flowers, and balancing an enormous plain hat on her head. She looked striking, astonishing, almost macabre, so tall, with the fringe of her great cream-coloured vividly-blotched shawl trailing on the ground after her, her thick hair coming low over her eyes, her face strange and long and pale, and the blotches of brilliant colour drawn round her.

'Doesn't she look *weird!*' Gudrun heard some girls titter behind her. And she could have killed them.

'How do you do!' sang Hermione, coming up very kindly, and glancing slowly over Gudrun's father and mother. It was a trying moment, exasperating for Gudrun. Hermione was really so strongly entrenched in her class superiority, she could come up and know people out of simple curiosity, as if they were creatures on exhibition. Gudrun would do the same herself. But she resented being in the position when somebody might do it to her.

Hermione, very remarkable, and distinguishing the Brangwens very much, led them along to where Laura Crich stood receiving the guests.

'This is Mrs Brangwen,' sang Hermione, and Laura, who wore a stiff embroidered linen dress, shook hands and said she was glad to see her. Then Gerald came up, dressed in white, with a black and brown blazer, and looking handsome. He too was introduced to the Brangwen parents, and immediately he spoke to Mrs Brangwen as if she were a lady, and to Brangwen as if he were *not* a gentleman. Gerald was so obvious in his demeanour. He had to shake hands with his left hand, because he had hurt his right, and carried it, bandaged up, in the pocket of his jacket. Gudrun was *very* thankful that none of her party asked him what was the matter with the hand.

The steam launch was fussing in, all its music jingling, people calling excitedly from on board. Gerald went to see to the debarkation, Birkin was getting tea for Mrs Brangwen, Brangwen had joined a Grammar-School group, Hermione was sitting down by their mother, the girls went to the landing-stage to watch the launch come in.

She hooted and tooted gaily, then her paddles were silent, the ropes were thrown ashore, she drifted in with a little bump. Immediately the passengers crowded excitedly to come ashore.

'Wait a minute, wait a minute,' shouted Gerald in sharp command.

They must wait till the boat was tight on the ropes, till the small gangway was put out. Then they streamed ashore, clamouring as if they had come from America.

'Oh it's *so* nice!' the young girls were crying. 'It's quite lovely.'

The waiters from on board ran out to the boat-house with baskets, the captain lounged on the little bridge. Seeing all safe, Gerald came to Gudrun and Ursula.

'You wouldn't care to go on board for the next trip, and have tea there?' he asked.

'No thanks,' said Gudrun coldly.

'You don't care for the water?'

'For the water? Yes, I like it very much.'

He looked at her, his eyes searching.

'You don't care for going on a launch, then?'

She was slow in answering, and then she spoke slowly.

'No,' she said. 'I can't say that I do.' Her colour was high, she seemed angry about something.

'Un peu trop de monde,'* said Ursula, explaining.

'Eh? *Trop de monde!*' He laughed shortly. 'Yes there's a fair number of 'em.'

Gudrun turned on him brilliantly.

'Have you ever been from Westminster Bridge to Richmond on one of the Thames steamers?' she cried.

'No,' he said, 'I can't say I have.'

* A bit large number of people.

'Well, it's one of the most *vile* experiences I've ever had.'
She spoke rapidly and excitedly, the colour high in her cheeks.
'There was absolutely nowhere to sit down, nowhere, a man just
above sang "Rocked in the Cradle of the Deep" the *whole* way;
he was blind and he had a small organ, one of those portable
organs, and he expected money; so you can imagine what *that*
was like; there came a constant smell of luncheon from below,
and puffs of hot oily machinery; the journey took hours and hours
and hours; and for miles, literally for miles, dreadful boys ran
with us on the shore, in that *awful* Thames mud, going in *up to
the waist* – they had their trousers turned back, and they went up
to their hips in that indescribable Thames mud, their faces always
turned to us, and screaming, exactly like carrion creatures,
screaming " 'Ere yare sir, 'ere y'are sir, 'ere y'are sir," exactly
like some foul carrion objects, perfectly obscene; and paterfamilias
on board, laughing when the boys went right down in that awful
mud, occasionally throwing them a ha'penny. And if you'd seen
the intent look on the faces of these boys, and the way they
darted in the filth when a coin was flung – really, no vulture or
jackal could dream of approaching them, for foulness. I *never*
would go on a pleasure boat again – never.'

Gerald watched her all the time she spoke, his eyes glittering
with faint rousedness. It was not so much what she said; it was
she herself who roused him, roused him with a small, vivid pricking.

'Of course,' he said, 'every civilised body is bound to have
its vermin.'

'Why?' cried Ursula. '*I* don't have vermin.'

'And it's not that – it's the *quality* of the whole thing –
paterfamilias laughing and thinking it sport, and throwing the
ha'pennies, and materfamilias spreading her fat little knees and
eating, continually eating – ' replied Gudrun.

'Yes,' said Ursula. 'It isn't the boys so much who are vermin;
it's the people themselves, the whole body politic, as you call it.'

Gerald laughed.

'Never mind,' he said. 'You shan't go on the launch.'

Gudrun flushed quickly at his rebuke.

There were a few moments of silence. Gerald, like a sentinel, was watching the people who were going on to the boat. He was very good looking and self-contained, but his air of soldierly alertness was rather irritating.

'Will you have tea here then, or go across to the house, where there's a tent on the lawn?' he asked.

'Can't we have a rowing boat, and get out?' asked Ursula, who was always rushing in too fast.

'To get out?' smiled Gerald.

'You see,' cried Gudrun, flushing at Ursula's outspoken rudeness, 'we don't know the people, we are almost *complete* strangers here.'

'Oh, I can soon set you up with a few acquaintances,' he said easily.

Gudrun looked at him, to see if it were ill-meant. Then she smiled at him.

'Ah,' she said, 'you know what we mean. Can't we go up there, and explore that coast?' She pointed to a grove on the hillock of the meadow-side, near the shore half way down the lake. 'That looks perfectly lovely. We might even bathe. Isn't it beautiful in this light. Really, it's like one of the reaches of the Nile – as one imagines the Nile.'

Gerald smiled at her factitious enthusiasm for the distant spot.

'You're sure it's far enough off?' he asked ironically, adding at once: 'Yes, you might go there, if we could get a boat. They seem to be all out.'

He looked round the lake and counted the rowing boats on its surface.

'How lovely it would be!' cried Ursula wistfully.

'And don't you want tea?' he said.

'Oh,' said Gudrun, 'we could just drink a cup, and be off.'

He looked from one to the other, smiling. He was somewhat offended – yet sporting.

'Can you manage a boat pretty well?' he asked.

'Yes,' replied Gudrun, coldly, 'pretty well.'

'Oh yes,' cried Ursula. 'We can both of us row like water-spiders.'

'You can? There's a light little canoe of mine, that I didn't take out for fear somebody should drown themselves. Do you think you'd be safe in that?'

'Oh perfectly,' said Gudrun.

'What an angel!' cried Ursula.

'Don't, for *my* sake, have an accident – because I'm responsible for the water.'

'Sure,' pledged Gudrun.

'Besides, we can both swim quite well,' said Ursula.

"Well – then I'll get them to put you up a tea-basket, and you can picnic all to yourselves, – that's the idea, isn't it?'

'How fearfully good! How frightfully nice if you could!' cried Gudrun warmly, her colour flushing up again. It made the blood stir in his veins, the subtle way she turned to him and infused her gratitude into his body.

'Where's Birkin?' he said, his eyes twinkling. 'He might help me to get it down.'

'But what about your hand? Isn't it hurt?' asked Gudrun, rather muted, as if avoiding the intimacy. This was the first time the hurt had been mentioned. The curious way she skirted round the subject sent a new, subtle caress through his veins. He took his hand out of his pocket. It was bandaged. He looked at it, then put it in his pocket again. Gudrun quivered at the sight of the wrapped up paw.

'Oh I can manage with one hand. The canoe is as light as a feather,' he said. 'There's Rupert! – Rupert!'

Birkin turned from his social duties and came towards them.

'What have you done to it?' asked Ursula, who had been aching to put the question for the last half hour.

'To my hand?' said Gerald. 'I trapped it in some machinery.'

'Ugh!' said Ursula. 'And did it hurt much?'

'Yes,' he said. 'It did at the time. It's getting better now. It crushed the fingers.'

'Oh,' cried Ursula, as if in pain, 'I hate people who hurt themselves. I can *feel* it.' And she shook her hand.

'What do you want?' said Birkin.

The two men carried down the slim brown boat, and set it on the water.

'You're quite sure you'll be safe in it?' Gerald asked.

'Quite sure,' said Gudrun. 'I wouldn't be so mean as to take it, if there was the slightest doubt. But I've had a canoe at Arundel, and I assure you I'm perfectly safe.'

So saying, having given her word like a man, she and Ursula entered the frail craft, and pushed gently off. The two men stood watching them. Gudrun was paddling. She knew the men were watching her, and it made her slow and rather clumsy. The colour flew in her face like a flag.

'Thanks awfully,' she called back to him, from the water, as the boat slid away. 'It's lovely – like sitting in a leaf.'

He laughed at the fancy. Her voice was shrill and strange, calling from the distance. He watched her as she paddled away. There was something childlike about her, trustful and deferential, like a child. He watched her all the while, as she rowed. And to Gudrun it was a real delight, in make-belief, to be the childlike, clinging woman to the man who stood there on the quay, so good-looking and efficient in his white clothes, and moreover the most important man she knew at the moment. She did not take any notice of the wavering, indistinct, lambent Birkin, who stood at his side. One figure at a time occupied the field of her attention.

The boat rustled lightly along the water. They passed the bathers whose striped tents stood between the willows of the meadow's edge, and drew along the open shore, past the meadows that sloped golden in the light of the already late afternoon. Other boats were stealing under the wooded shore opposite, they could hear people's laughter and voices. But Gudrun rowed on towards the dump of trees that balanced perfect in the distance, in the golden light.

The sisters found a little place where a tiny stream flowed into the lake, with reeds and flowery marsh of pink willow herb, and a gravelly bank to the side. Here they ran delicately ashore, with their frail boat, the two girls took off their shoes and stockings and went through the water's edge to the grass. The tiny ripples of the lake were warm and clear, they lifted their boat on to the bank, and looked round with joy. They were quite alone in a forsaken little stream-mouth, and on the knoll just behind was the clump of trees.

'We will bathe just for a moment,' said Ursula, 'and then we'll have tea.'

They looked round. Nobody could notice them, or could come up in time to see them. In less than a minute Ursula had thrown off her clothes and had slipped naked into the water, and was swimming out. Quickly, Gudrun joined her. They swam silently and blissfully for a few minutes, circling round their little stream-mouth. Then they slipped ashore and ran into the grove again, like nymphs.

'How lovely it is to be free,' said Ursula, running swiftly here and there between the tree trunks, quite naked, her hair blowing loose. The grove was of beech-trees, big and splendid, a steel-grey scaffolding of trunks and boughs, with level sprays of strong green here and there, whilst through the northern side the distance glimmered open as through a window.

When they had run and danced themselves dry, the girls quickly dressed and sat down to the fragrant tea. They sat on the northern side of the grove, in the yellow sunshine facing the slope of the grassy hill, alone in a little wild world of their own. The tea was hot and aromatic, there were delicious little sandwiches of cucumber and of caviare, and winy cakes.

'Are you happy, Prune?' cried Ursula in delight, looking at her sister.

'Ursula, I'm perfectly happy,' replied Gudrun gravely, looking at the westering sun.

'So am I.'

When they were together, doing the things they enjoyed, the two sisters were quite complete in a perfect world of their own.

And this was one of the perfect moments of freedom and delight, such as children alone know, when all seems a perfect and blissful adventure.

When they had finished tea, the two girls sat on, silent and serene. Then Ursula, who had a beautiful strong voice, began to sing to herself, softly: 'Annchen von Tharau.'[1] Gudrun listened, as she sat beneath the trees, and the yearning came into her heart. Ursula seemed so peaceful and sufficient unto herself, sitting there unconsciously crooning her song, strong and unquestioned at the centre of her own universe. And Gudrun felt herself outside. Always this desolating, agonised feeling, that she was outside of life, an onlooker, whilst Ursula was a partaker, caused Gudrun to suffer from a sense of her own negation, and made her, that she must always demand the other to be aware of her, to be in connection with her.

'Do you mind if I do Dalcroze[2] to that tune, Hurtler?' she asked in a curious muted tone, scarce moving her lips.

'What did you say?' asked Ursula, looking up in peaceful surprise.

'Will you sing while I do Dalcroze?' said Gudrun, suffering at having to repeat herself.

Ursula thought a moment, gathering her straying wits together.

'While you do –?' she asked vaguely.

'Dalcroze movements,' said Gudrun, suffering tortures of self consciousness, even because of her sister.

'Oh Dalcroze! I couldn't catch the name. *Do* – I should love to see you,' cried Ursula, with childish surprised brightness. 'What shall I sing?'

'Sing anything you like, and I'll take the rhythm from it.'

But Ursula could not for her life think of anything to sing. However, she suddenly began, in a laughing, teasing voice:

'My love – is a high-born lady – '

Gudrun, looking as if some invisible chain weighed on her hands and feet, began slowly to dance in the eurythmic manner, pulsing and fluttering rhythmically with her feet, making slower,

1 A German folk song.
2 Eurythmic style of learning music through expressive dancing, founded by Emile Dalcroze (1865-1950).

regular gestures with her hands and arms, now spreading her arms wide, now raising them above her head, now flinging them softly apart, and lifting her face, her feet all the time beating and running to the measure of the song, as if it were some strange incantation, her white, rapt form drifting here and there in a strange impulsive rhapsody, seeming to be lifted on a breeze of incantation, shuddering with strange little runs. Ursula sat on the grass, her mouth open in her singing, her eyes laughing as if she thought it was a great joke, but a yellow light flashing up in them, as she caught some of the 'unconscious ritualistic suggestion of the complex shuddering and waving and drifting of her sister's white form, that was clutched in pure, mindless, tossing rhythm, and a will set powerful in a kind of hypnotic influence.

'My love is a high-born lady – She is-s-s – rather dark than shady – ' rang out Ursula's laughing, satiric song, and quicker, fiercer went Gudrun in the dance, stamping as if she were trying to throw off some bond, flinging her hands suddenly and stamping again, then rushing with face uplifted and throat full and beautiful, and eyes half closed, sightless. The sun was low and yellow, sinking down, and in the sky floated a thin, ineffectual moon.

Ursula was quite absorbed in her song, when suddenly Gudrun stopped and said mildly, ironically:

'Ursula!'

'Yes?' said Ursula, opening her eyes out of the trance.

Gudrun was standing still and pointing, a mocking smile on her face, towards the side.

'Ugh!' cried Ursula in sudden panic, starting to her feet.

'They're quite all right,' rang out Gudrun's sardonic voice.

On the left stood a little cluster of Highland cattle, vividly coloured and fleecy in the evening light, – their horns branching into the sky, pushing forward their muzzles inquisitively, to know what it was all about. Their eyes glittered through their tangle of hair, their naked nostrils were full of shadow.

'Won't they do anything?' cried Ursula in fear.

Gudrun, who was usually frightened of cattle, now shook

her head in a queer, half-doubtful, half-sardonic motion, a faint smile round her mouth.

'Don't they look charming, Ursula?' cried Gudrun, in a high, strident voice, something like the scream of a seagull.

'Charming,' cried Ursula in trepidation. 'But won't they do anything to us?'

Again Gudrun looked back at her sister with an enigmatic smile, and shook her head.

'I'm sure they won't,' she said, as if she had to convince herself also, and yet, as if she were confident of some secret power in herself, and had to put it to the test. 'Sit down and sing again,' she called in her high, strident voice.

'I'm frightened,' cried Ursula, in a pathetic voice, watching the group of sturdy short cattle, that stood with their knees planted, and watched with their dark, wicked eyes, through the matted fringe of their hair. Nevertheless, she sank down again, in her former posture.

'They are quite safe,' came Gudrun's high call. 'Sing something, you've only to sing something.'

It was evident she had a strange passion to dance before the sturdy, handsome cattle.

Ursula began to sing, in a false quavering voice:

'Way down in Tennessee – '

She sounded purely anxious. Nevertheless, Gudrun, with her arms outspread and her face uplifted, went in a strange palpitating dance towards the cattle, lifting her body towards them as if in a spell, her feet pulsing as if in some little frenzy of unconscious sensation, her arms, her wrists, her hands stretching and heaving and falling and reaching and reaching and falling, her breasts lifted and shaken towards the cattle, her throat exposed as in some voluptuous ecstasy towards them, whilst she drifted imperceptibly nearer, an uncanny white figure, towards them, carried away in its own rapt trance, ebbing in strange fluctuations upon the cattle, that waited, and ducked their heads a little in sudden contraction from her, watching all the time as if hypnotised, their bare horns branching in the clear light, as the white figure of the woman ebbed upon them, in the slow, hypnotising convulsion of the dance. She could feel them just in front of her, it was as if she had the electric pulse from their breasts running into her hands. Soon she would touch them, actually touch them. A terrible shiver of fear and pleasure went through her. And all the while, Ursula, spell-bound, kept up her high-pitched thin, irrelevant song, which pierced the fading evening like an incantation.

Gudrun could hear the cattle breathing heavily with helpless fear and fascination. Oh, they were brave little beasts, these wild Scotch bullocks, wild and fleecy. Suddenly one of them snorted, ducked its head, and backed.

'Hue! Hi-eee!' came a sudden loud shout from the edge of the grove. The cattle broke and fell back quite spontaneously, went running up the hill, their fleece waving like fire to their motion. Gudrun stood suspended out on the grass, Ursula rose to her feet.

It was Gerald and Birkin come to find them, and Gerald had cried out to frighten off the cattle.

'What do you think you're doing?' he now called, in a high, wondering vexed tone.

'Why have you come?' came back Gudrun's strident cry of anger.

'What do you think you were doing?' Gerald repeated, automatically.

'We were doing eurythmics,' laughed Ursula, in a shaken voice.

Gudrun stood aloof looking at them with large dark eyes of resentment, suspended for a few moments. Then she walked away up the hill, after the cattle, which had gathered in a little, spell-bound cluster higher up.

'Where are you going?' Gerald called after her. And he followed her up the hill-side. The sun had gone behind the hill, and shadows were clinging to the earth, the sky above was full of travelling light.

'A poor song for a dance,' said Birkin to Ursula, standing before her with a sardonic, flickering laugh on his face. And in another second, he was singing softly to himself, and dancing a grotesque step-dance in front of her, his limbs and body shaking loose, his face flickering palely, a constant thing, whilst his feet beat a rapid mocking tattoo, and his body seemed to hang all loose and quaking in between, like a shadow.

'I think we've all gone mad,' she said, laughing rather frightened.

'Pity we aren't madder,' he answered, as he kept up the incessant shaking dance. Then suddenly he leaned up to her and kissed her fingers lightly, putting his face to hers and looking into her eyes with a pale grin. She stepped back, affronted.

'Offended –?' he asked ironically, suddenly going quite still and reserved again. 'I thought you liked the light fantastic.'

'Not like that,' she said, confused and bewildered, almost affronted. Yet somewhere inside her she was fascinated by the sight of his loose, vibrating body, perfectly abandoned to its own dropping and swinging, and by the pallid, sardonic-smiling face above. Yet automatically she stiffened herself away, and disapproved. It seemed almost an obscenity, in a man who talked as a rule so very seriously.

'Why not like that?' he mocked. And immediately he dropped again into the incredibly rapid, slack-waggling dance, watching her malevolently. And moving in the rapid, stationary dance, he came a little nearer, and reached forward with an incredibly mocking, satiric gleam on his face, and would have kissed her again, had she not started back.

'No, don't!' she cried, really afraid.

'Cordelia* after all,' he said satirically. She was stung, as if this were an insult. She knew he intended it as such, and it bewildered her.

'And you,' she cried in retort, 'why do you always take your soul in your mouth, so frightfully full?'

'So that I can spit it out the more readily,' he said, pleased by his own retort.

Gerald Crich, his face narrowing to an intent gleam, followed up the hill with quick strides, straight after Gudrun. The cattle

---

* The daughter of (Shakespeare's) King Lear, who loves her father but is mute in expressing it.

stood with their noses together on the brow of a slope, watching the scene below, the men in white hovering about the white forms of the women, watching above all Gudrun, who was advancing slowly towards them. She stood a moment, glancing back at Gerald, and then at the cattle.

Then in a sudden motion, she lifted her arms and rushed sheer upon the long-horned bullocks, in shuddering irregular runs, pausing for a second and looking at them, then lifting her hands and running forward with a flash, till they ceased pawing the ground, and gave way, snorting with terror, lifting their heads from the ground and flinging themselves away, galloping off into the evening, becoming tiny in the distance, and still not stopping.

Gudrun remained staring after them, with a mask-like defiant face.

'Why do you want to drive them mad?' asked Gerald, coming up with her.

She took no notice of him, only averted her face from him. 'It's not safe, you know,' he persisted. 'They're nasty, when they do turn.'

'Turn where? Turn away?' she mocked loudly.

'No,' he said, 'Turn against you.'

'Turn against *me?*' she mocked.

He could make nothing of this.

'Anyway, they gored one of the farmer's cows to death, the other day,' he said.

'What do I care?' she said.

'*I* cared though,' he replied, 'Seeing that they're my cattle.'

'How are they yours! You haven't swallowed them. Give me one of them now,' she said, holding out her hand.

'You know where they are,' he said, pointing over the hill. 'You can have one if you'd like it sent to you later on.'

She looked at him inscrutably.

'You think I'm afraid of you and your cattle, don't you?' she asked.

His eyes narrowed dangerously. There was a faint domineering smile on his face.

'Why should I think that?' he said.

She was watching him all the time with her dark, dilated, inchoate eyes. She leaned forward and swung round her arm, catching him a light blow on the face with the back of her hand.

'That's why,' she said, mocking.

And she felt in her soul an unconquerable desire for deep violence against him. She shut off the fear and dismay that filled her conscious mind. She wanted to do as she did, she was not going to be afraid.

He recoiled from the slight blow on his face. He became deadly pale, and a dangerous flame darkened his eyes. For some seconds he could not speak, his lungs were so suffused with blood, his heart stretched almost to bursting with a great gush of ungovernable emotion. It was as if some reservoir of black emotion had burst within him, and swamped him.

'You have struck the first blow,' he said at last, forcing the words from his lungs, in a voice so soft and low, it sounded like a dream within her, not spoken in the outer air.

'And I shall strike the last,' she retorted involuntarily, with confident assurance. He was silent, he did not contradict her.

She stood negligently, staring away from him, into the distance. On the edge of her consciousness the question was asking itself, automatically:

'Why *are* you behaving in this *impossible* and ridiculous fashion.' But she was sullen, she half shoved the question out of herself. She could not get it clean away, so she felt self-conscious.

Gerald, very pale, was watching her closely. His eyes were lit up with intent lights, absorbed and gleaming. She turned suddenly on him.

'It's you who make me behave like this, you know,' she said, almost suggestive.

'I? How?' he said.

But she turned away, and set off towards the lake. Below, on the water, lanterns were coming alight, faint ghosts of warm flame floating in the pallor of the first twilight. The earth was spread with darkness, like lacquer, overhead was a pale sky, all primrose, and the lake was pale as milk in one part. Away at the landing stage, tiniest points of coloured rays were stringing themselves in the dusk. The launch was being illuminated. All round, shadow was gathering from the trees.

Gerald, white like a presence in his summer clothes, was following down the open grassy slope. Gudrun waited for him to come up. Then she softly put out her hand and touched him, saying softly:

'Don't be angry with me.'

A flame flew over him, and he was unconscious. Yet he stammered:

'I'm not angry with you. I'm in love with you.'

His mind was gone, he grasped for sufficient mechanical control, to save himself. She laughed a silvery little mockery, yet intolerably caressive.

'That's one way of putting it,' she said.

The terrible swooning burden on his mind, the awful swooning, the loss of all his control, was too much for him. He grasped her arm in his one hand, as if his hand were iron.

'It's all right, then, is it?' he said, holding her arrested.

She looked at the face with the fixed eyes, set before her, and her blood ran cold.

'Yes, it's all right,' she said softly, as if drugged, her voice crooning and witch-like.

He walked on beside her, a striding, mindless body. But he recovered a little as he went. He suffered badly. He had killed his brother when a boy, and was set apart, like Cain.

They found Birkin and Ursula sitting together by the boats, talking and laughing. Birkin had been teasing Ursula.

'Do you smell this little marsh?' he said, sniffing the air. He was very sensitive to scents, and quick in understanding them.

'It's rather nice,' she said.

'No,' he replied, 'alarming.'

'Why alarming?' she laughed.

'It seethes and seethes, a river of darkness,' he said, 'putting forth lilies and snakes, and the ignis fatuus, and rolling all the time onward.

That's what we never take into count – that it rolls onwards.'

'What does?'

'The other river, the black river. We always consider the silver river of life, rolling on and quickening all the world to a brightness, on and on to heaven, flowing into a bright eternal sea, a heaven of angels thronging. But the other is our real reality – '

'But what other? I don't see any other,' said Ursula.

'It is your reality, nevertheless,' he said; 'that dark river of dissolution. You see it rolls in us just as the other rolls – the black river of corruption. And our flowers are of this – our sea-born Aphrodite, all our white phosphorescent flowers of sensuous perfection, all our reality, nowadays.'

'You mean that Aphrodite is really deathly?' asked Ursula.

'I mean she is the flowering mystery of the death-process, yes,' he replied. 'When the stream of synthetic creation lapses, we find ourselves part of the inverse process, the blood of destructive creation. Aphrodite is born in the first spasm of universal dissolution – then the snakes and swans and lotus – marsh-flowers – and Gudrun and Gerald – born in the process of destructive creation.'

'And you and me –?' she asked.

'Probably,' he replied. 'In part, certainly. Whether we are that, in toto, I don't yet know.'

'You mean we are flowers of dissolution – fleurs du mal?[1] I don't feel as if I were,' she protested.

He was silent for a time.

'I don't feel as if we were, *altogether,*' he replied. 'Some people are pure flowers of dark corruption – lilies. But there ought to be some roses, warm and flamy. You know Herakleitos[2] says: "a dry soul is best." I know so well what that means. Do you?'

---

1 French poet Bauldelaire's 'Les fleures du mal'.
2 Ancient Greek philosopher.

'I'm not sure,' Ursula replied. 'But what if people *are* all flowers of dissolution – when they're flowers at all – what difference does it make?'

'No difference – and all the difference. Dissolution rolls on, just as production does,' he said. 'It is a progressive process – and it ends in universal nothing – the end of the world, if you like. But why isn't the end of the world as good as the beginning?'

'I suppose it isn't,' said Ursula, rather angry.

'Oh yes, ultimately,' he said. 'It means a new cycle of creation after but not for us. If it is the end, then we are of the end – fleurs du mal if you like. If we are fleurs du mal, we are not roses of happiness, and there you are.'

'But I think I am,' said Ursula. 'I think I am a rose of happiness.'

'Ready-made?' he asked ironically.

'No – real,' she said, hurt.

'If we are the end, we are not the beginning,' he said.

'Yes we are,' she said. 'The beginning comes out of the end.'

'After it, not out of it. After us, not out of us.'

'You are a devil, you know, really,' she said. 'You want to destroy our hope. You *want us* to be deathly.'

'No,' he said, 'I only want us to *know* what we are.'

'Ha!' she cried in anger. 'You only want us to know death.'

'You're quite right,' said the soft voice of Gerald, out of the dusk behind.

Birkin rose. Gerald and Gudrun came up. They all began to smoke, in the moments of silence. One after another, Birkin lighted their cigarettes. The match flickered in the twilight, and they were all smoking peacefully by the water-side. The lake was dim, the light dying from off it, in the midst of the dark land. The air all round was intangible, neither here nor there, and there was an unreal noise of banjoes, or suchlike music.

As the golden swim of light overhead died out, the moon gained brightness, and seemed to begin to smile forth her ascendancy. The dark woods on the opposite shore melted into

universal shadow. And amid this universal under-shadow, there
was a scattered intrusion of lights. Far down the lake were fantastic
pale strings of colour, like beads of wan fire, green and red and
yellow. The music came out in a little puff, as the launch, all
illuminated, veered into the great shadow, stirring her outlines of
half-living lights, puffing out her music in little drifts.

All were lighting up, Here and there, close against the faint
water, and at the far end of the lake, where the water lay milky in
the last whiteness of the sky, and there was no shadow, solitary,
frail flames of lanterns floated from the unseen boats. There was
a sound of oars, and a boat passed from the pallor into the darkness
under the wood, where her lanterns seemed to kindle into fire,
hanging in ruddy lovely globes. And again, in the lake, shadowy
red gleams hovered in reflection about the boat. Everywhere were
these noiseless ruddy creatures of fire drifting near the surface
of the water, caught at by the rarest, scarce visible reflections.

Birkin brought the lanterns from the bigger boat, and the four
shadowy white figures gathered round, to light them. Ursula held
up the first, Birkin lowered the light from the rosy, glowing cup
of his hands, into the depths of the lantern. It was kindled, and
they all stood back to look at the great blue moon of light that
hung from Ursula's hand, casting a strange gleam on her face. It
flickered, and Birkin went bending over the well of light. His face
shone out like an apparition, so unconscious, and again, something
demoniacal. Ursula was dim and veiled, looming over him.

'That is all right,' said his voice softly.

She held up the lantern. It had a flight of storks streaming
through a turquoise sky of light, over a dark earth.

'This is beautiful,' she said.

'Lovely,' echoed Gudrun, who wanted to hold one also, and
lift it up full of beauty.

'Light one for me,' she said. Gerald stood by her,
incapacitated. Birkin lit the lantern she held up. Her heart beat
with anxiety, to see how beautiful it would be: It was primrose
yellow, with tall straight flowers growing darkly from their dark

leaves, lifting their heads into the primrose day, while butterflies hovered about them, in the pure clear light.

Gudrun gave a little cry of excitement, as if pierced with delight.

'Isn't it beautiful, oh, isn't it beautiful!'

Her soul was really pierced with beauty, she was translated beyond herself. Gerald leaned near to her, into her zone of light, as if to see. He came close to her, and stood touching her, looking with her at the primrose-shining globe. And she turned her face to his, that was faintly bright in the light of the lantern, and they stood together in one luminous union, close together and ringed round with light, all the rest excluded.

Birkin looked away, and went to light Ursula's second lantern. It had a pale ruddy sea-bottom, with black crabs and sea-weed moving sinuously under a transparent sea, that passed into flamy ruddiness above.

'You've got the heavens above, and the waters under the earth,' said Birkin to her.

'Anything but the earth itself,' she laughed, watching his live hands that hovered to attend to the light.

'I'm dying to see what my second one is,' cried Gudrun, in a vibrating rather strident voice, that seemed to repel the others from her.

Birkin went and kindled it. It was of a lovely deep blue colour, with a red floor, and a great white cuttle-fish flowing in white soft streams all over it. The cuttle-fish had a face that stared straight from the heart of the light, very fixed and coldly intent.

'How truly terrifying!' exclaimed Gudrun, in a voice of horror. Gerald, at her side, gave a low laugh.

'But isn't it really fearful!' she cried in dismay.

Again he laughed, and said:

'Change it with Ursula, for the crabs.'

Gudrun was silent for a moment.

'Ursula,' she said, 'could you bear to have this fearful thing?'

'I think the colouring is *lovely,*' said Ursula.

'So do I,' said Gudrun. 'But could you *bear* to have it swinging to your boat? Don't you want to destroy it at *once?*'

'Oh no,' said Ursula. 'I don't want to destroy it.'

'Well do you mind having it instead of the crabs? Are you sure you don't mind?'

Gudrun came forward to exchange lanterns.

'No,' said Ursula, yielding up the crabs and receiving the cuttle-fish.

Yet she could not help feeling rather resentful at the way in which Gudrun and Gerald should assume a right over her, a precedence.

'Come then,' said Birkin. 'I'll put them on the boats.'

He and Ursula were moving away to the big boat.

'I suppose you'll row me back, Rupert,' said Gerald, out of the pale shadow of the evening.

'Won't you go with Gudrun in the canoe?' said Birkin. 'It'll be more interesting.'

There was a moment's pause. Birkin and Ursula stood dimly, with their swinging lanterns, by the water's edge. The world was all illusive.

'Is that all right?' said Gudrun to him.

'It'll suit *me* very well,' he said. 'But what about you, and the rowing? I don't see why you should pull me.'

'Why not?' she said. 'I can pull you as well as I could pull Ursula.'

By her tone he could tell she wanted to have him in the boat to herself, and that she was subtly gratified that she should have power over them both. He gave himself, in a strange, electric submission.

She handed him the lanterns, whilst she went to fix the cane at the end of the canoe. He followed after her, and stood with the lanterns dangling against his white-flannelled thighs, emphasising the shadow around.

'Kiss me before we go,' came his voice softly from out of the shadow above.

She stopped her work in real, momentary astonishment.

'But why?' she exclaimed, in pure surprise.

'Why?' he echoed, ironically.

And she looked at him fixedly for some moments. Then she leaned forward and kissed him, with a slow, luxurious kiss, lingering on the mouth. And then she took the lanterns from him, while he stood swooning with the perfect fire that burned in all his joints.

They lifted the canoe into the water, Gudrun took her place, and Gerald pushed off.

'Are you sure you don't hurt your hand, doing that?' she asked, solicitous. 'Because I could have done it *perfectly.*'

'I don't hurt myself,' he said in a low, soft voice, that caressed her with inexpressible beauty.

And she watched him as he sat near her, very near to her, in the stem of the canoe, his legs coming towards hers, his feet touching hers. And she paddled softly, lingeringly, longing for him to say something meaningful to her. But he remained silent.

'You like this, do you?' she said, in a gentle, solicitous voice. He laughed shortly.

'There is a space between us,' he said, in the same low, unconscious voice, as if something were speaking out of him. And she was as if magically aware of their being balanced in separation, in the boat. She swooned with acute comprehension and pleasure.

'But I'm very near,' she said caressively, gaily.

'Yet distant, distant,' he said.

Again she was silent with pleasure, before she answered, speaking, with a reedy, thrilled voice:

'Yet we cannot very well change, whilst we are on the water.' She caressed him subtly and strangely, having him completely at her mercy.

A dozen or more boats on the lake swung their rosy and moon-like lanterns low on the water, that reflected as from a fire. In the distance, the steamer twanged and thrummed and washed

with her faintly-splashing paddles, trailing her strings of coloured
lights, and occasionally lighting up the whole scene luridly with
an effusion of fireworks, Roman candles and sheafs of stars and
other simple effects, illuminating the surface of the water, and
showing the boats creeping round, low down. Then the lovely
darkness fell again, the lanterns and the little threaded lights
glimmered softly, there was a muffled knocking of oars and a
waving of music.

Gudrun paddled almost imperceptibly. Gerald could see, not
far ahead, the rich blue and the rose globes of Ursula's lanterns
swaying softly cheek to cheek as Birkin rowed, and iridescent,
evanescent gleams chasing in the wake. He was aware, too, of his
own delicately coloured lights casting their softness behind him.

Gudrun rested her paddle and looked round. The canoe lifted
with the lightest ebbing of the water. Gerald's white knees were
very near to her.

'Isn't it beautiful!' she said softly, as if reverently.

She looked at him, as he leaned back against the faint crystal
of the lantern-light. She could see his face, although it was a pure
shadow. But it was a piece of twilight. And her breast was keen
with passion for him, he was so beautiful in his male stillness and
mystery. It was a certain pure effluence of maleness, like an
aroma from his softly, firmly moulded contours, a certain rich
perfection of his presence, that touched her with an ecstasy, a
thrill of pure intoxication. She loved to look at him. For the present
she did not want to touch him, to know the further, satisfying
substance of his living body. He was purely intangible, yet so
near. Her hands lay on the paddle like slumber, she only wanted
to see him, like a crystal shadow, to feel his essential presence.

'Yes,' he said vaguely. 'It is very beautiful.'

He was listening to the faint near sounds, the dropping of
water-drops from the oar-blades, the slight drumming of the
lanterns behind him, as they rubbed against one another, the
occasional rustling of Gudrun's full skirt, an alien land noise. His
mind was almost submerged, he was almost transfused, lapsed
out for the first time in his life, into the things about him. For he

always kept such a keen attentiveness, concentrated and unyielding in himself. Now he had let go, imperceptibly he was melting into oneness with the whole. It was like pure, perfect sleep, his first great sleep of life. He had been so insistent, so guarded, all his life. But here was sleep, and peace, and perfect lapsing out.

'Shall I row to the landing-stage?' asked Gudrun wistfully.

'Anywhere,' he answered. 'Let it drift.'

'Tell me then, if we are running into anything,' she replied, in that very quiet, toneless voice of sheer intimacy.

'The lights will show,' he said.

So they drifted almost motionless, in silence. He wanted silence, pure and whole. But she was uneasy yet for some word, for some assurance.

'Nobody will miss you?' she asked, anxious for some communication.

'Miss me?' he echoed. 'No! Why?'

'I wondered if anybody would be looking for you.'

'Why should they look for me?' And then he remembered his manners. 'But perhaps you want to get back,' he said, in a changed voice.

'No, I don't want to get back,' she replied. 'No, I assure you.'

'You're quite sure it's all right for you?'

'Perfectly all right.'

And again they were still. The launch twanged and hooted, somebody was singing. Then as if the night smashed, suddenly there was a great shout, a confusion of shouting; warring on the water, then the horrid noise of paddles reversed and churned violently.

Gerald sat up, and Gudrun looked at him in fear.

'Somebody in the water,' he said, angrily, and desperately, looking keenly across the dusk. 'Can you row up?'

'Where, to the launch?' asked Gudrun, in nervous panic.

'Yes.'

'You'll tell me if I don't steer straight,' she said, in nervous apprehension.

'You keep pretty level,' he said, and the canoe hastened forward.

The shouting and the noise continued, sounding horrid through the dusk, over the surface of the water.

'Wasn't this *bound* to happen?' said Gudrun, with heavy hateful irony. But he hardly heard, and she glanced over her shoulder to see her way. The half-dark waters were sprinkled with lovely bubbles of swaying lights, the launch did not look far off. She was rocking her lights in the early night. Gudrun rowed as hard as she could. But now that it was a serious matter, she seemed uncertain and clumsy in her stroke, it was difficult to paddle swiftly. She glanced at his face. He was looking fixedly into the darkness, very keen and alert and single in himself, instrumental. Her heart sank, she seemed to die a death. 'Of course,' she said to herself, 'nobody will be drowned. Of course they won't. It would be too extravagant and sensational.' But her heart was cold, because of his sharp impersonal face. It was as if he belonged naturally to dread and catastrophe, as if he were himself again.

Then there came a child's voice, a girl's high, piercing shriek:

'Di – Di – Di – Di – Oh Di – Oh Di – Oh Di!'

The blood ran cold in Gudrun's veins.

'It's Diana, is it,' muttered Gerald. 'The young monkey, she'd have to be up to some of her tricks.'

And he glanced again at the paddle, the boat was not going quickly enough for him. It made Gudrun almost helpless at the rowing, this nervous stress. She kept up with all her might. Still the voices were calling and answering.

'Where, where? There you are – that's it. Which? No – No-o-o. Damn it all, here, *here* –' Boats were hurrying from all directions to the scene, coloured lanterns could be seen waving close to the surface of the lake, reflections swaying after them in uneven haste. The steamer hooted again, for some unknown reason. Gudrun's boat was travelling quickly, the lanterns were swinging behind Gerald.

And then again came the child's high, screaming voice, with a note of weeping and impatience in it now:

'Di – Oh Di – Oh Di – Di –!'

It was a terrible sound, coming through the obscure air of the evening.

'You'd be better if you were in bed, Winnie,' Gerald muttered to himself.

He was stooping unlacing his shoes, pushing them off with the foot. Then he threw his soft hat into the bottom of the boat.

'You can't go into the water with your hurt hand,' said Gudrun, panting, in a low voice of horror.

'What? It won't hurt.'

He had struggled out of his jacket, and had dropped it between his feet. He sat bare-headed, all in white now. He felt the belt at his waist.

They were nearing the launch, which stood still big above them, her myriad lamps making lovely darts, and sinuous running tongues of ugly red and green and yellow light on the lustrous dark water, under the shadow.

'Oh get her out! Oh Di, *darling!* Oh get her out! Oh Daddy, Oh Daddy!' moaned the child's voice, in distraction. Somebody was in the water, with a life belt. Two boats paddled near, their lanterns swinging ineffectually, the boats nosing round.

'Hi there – Rockley! – hi there!'

'Mr Gerald!' came the captain's terrified voice. 'Miss Diana's in the water.'

'Anybody gone in for her?' came Gerald's sharp voice.

'Young Doctor Brindell, sir.'

'Where?'

'Can't see no signs of them, sir. Everybody's looking, but there's nothing so far.'

There was a moment's ominous pause.

'Where did she go in?'

'I think – about where that boat is,' came the uncertain answer, 'That one with red and green lights.'

'Row there,' said Gerald quietly to Gudrun.

'Get her out, Gerald, oh get her out,' the child's voice was crying anxiously. He took no heed.

'Lean back that way,' said Gerald to Gudrun, as he stood up in the frail boat. 'She won't upset.'

In another moment, he had dropped clean down, soft and plumb, into the water. Gudrun was swaying violently in her boat, the agitated water shook with transient lights, she realised that it was faintly moonlight, and that he was gone. So it was possible to be gone. A terrible sense of fatality robbed her of all feeling and thought. She knew he was gone out of the world, there was merely the same world, and absence, his absence. The night seemed large and vacuous. Lanterns swayed here and there, people were talking in an undertone on the launch and in the boats. She could hear Winifred moaning: '*Oh do find her Gerald, do find her,*' and someone trying to comfort the child. Gudrun paddled aimlessly here and there. The terrible, massive, cold, boundless surface of the water terrified her beyond words. Would he never come back? She felt she must jump into the water too, to know the horror also.

She started, hearing someone say: 'There he is.' She saw the movement of his swimming, like a water-rat. And she rowed involuntarily to him. But he was near another boat, a bigger one. Still she rowed towards him. She must be very near. She saw him – he looked like a seal. He looked like a seal as he took hold of the side of the boat. His fair hair was washed down on his round head, his face seemed to glisten suavely. She could hear him panting.

Then he clambered into the boat. Oh, and the beauty of the subjection of his loins, white and dimly luminous as he climbed over the side of the boat, made her want to die, to die. The beauty of his dim and luminous loins as he climbed into the boat, his back rounded and soft – ah, this was too much for her, too final a vision. She knew it, and it was fatal. The terrible hopelessness of fate, and of beauty, such beauty!

He was not like a man to her, he was an incarnation, a great phase of life. She saw him press the water out of his face, and look at the bandage on his hand. And she knew it was all no good, and that she would never go beyond him, he was the final approximation of life to her.

'Put the lights out, we shall see better,' came his voice, sudden and mechanical and belonging to the world of man. She could scarcely believe there was a world of man. She leaned round and blew out her lanterns. They were difficult to blow out. Everywhere the lights were gone save the coloured points on the sides of the launch. The bluey-grey, early night spread level around, the moon was overhead, there were shadows of boats here and there.

Again there was a splash, and he was gone under. Gudrun sat, sick at heart, frightened of the great, level surface of the water, so heavy and deadly. She was so alone, with the level, unliving field of the water stretching beneath her. It was not a good isolation, it was a terrible, cold separation of suspense. She was suspended upon the surface of the insidious reality until such time as she also should disappear beneath it.

Then she knew, by a stirring of voices, that he had climbed out again, into a boat. She sat wanting connection with him. Strenuously she claimed her connection with him, across the invisible space of the water. But round her heart was an isolation unbearable, through which nothing would penetrate.

'Take the launch in. It's no use keeping her there. Get lines for the dragging,' came the decisive, instrumental voice, that was full of the sound of the world.

The launch began gradually to beat the waters.

'Gerald! Gerald!' came the wild crying voice of Winifred. He did not answer. Slowly the launch drifted round in a pathetic, clumsy circle, and slunk away to the land, retreating into the dimness. The wash of her paddles grew duller. Gudrun rocked in her light boat, and dipped the paddle automatically to steady herself.

'Gudrun?' called Ursula's voice.

'Ursula!'

The boats of the two sisters pulled together.

'Where is Gerald?' said Gudrun.

'He's dived again,' said Ursula plaintively. 'And I know he ought not, with his hurt hand and everything.'

'I'll take him in home this time,' said Birkin.

The boats swayed again from the wash of steamer. Gudrun and Ursula kept a look-out for Gerald.

'There he is!' cried Ursula, who had the sharpest eyes. He had not been long under. Birkin pulled towards him, Gudrun following. He swam slowly, and caught hold of the boat with his wounded hand. It slipped, and he sank back.

'Why don't you help him?' cried Ursula sharply.

He came again, and Birkin leaned to help him in to the boat. Gudrun again watched Gerald climb out of the water, but this time slowly, heavily, with the blind clambering motions of an amphibious beast, clumsy. Again the moon shone with faint luminosity on his white wet figure, on the stooping back and the rounded loins. But it looked defeated now, his body, it clambered and fell with slow clumsiness. He was breathing hoarsely too, like an animal that is suffering. He sat slack and motionless in the boat, his head blunt and blind like a seal's, his whole appearance inhuman, unknowing. Gudrun shuddered as she mechanically followed his boat. Birkin rowed without speaking to the landing-stage.

'Where are you going?' Gerald asked suddenly, as if just waking up.

'Home,' said Birkin.

'Oh no!' said Gerald imperiously. 'We can't go home while they're in the water. Turn back again, I'm going to find them.' The women were frightened, his voice was so imperative and dangerous, almost mad, not to be opposed.

'No!' said Birkin. 'You can't.' There was a strange fluid compulsion in his voice. Gerald was silent in a battle of wills. It was as if he would kill the other man. But Birkin rowed evenly and unswerving, with an inhuman inevitability.

'Why should you interfere?' said Gerald, in hate.

Birkin did not answer. He rowed towards the land. And Gerald sat mute, like a dumb beast, panting, his teeth chattering, his arms inert, his head like a seal's head.

They came to the landing-stage. Wet and naked-looking, Gerald climbed up the few steps. There stood his father, in the night.

'Father!' he said.

'Yes my boy? Go home and get those things off.'

'We shan't save them, father,' said Gerald.

'There's hope yet, my boy.'

'I'm afraid not. There's no knowing where they are. You can't find them. And there's a current, as cold as hell.'

'We'll let the water out,' said the father. 'Go home you and look to yourself. See that he's looked after, Rupert,' he added in a neutral voice.

'Well father, I'm sorry. I'm sorry. I'm afraid it's my fault. But it can't be helped; I've done what I could for the moment. I could go on diving, of course – not much, though – and not much use – '

He moved away barefoot, on the planks of the platform. Then he trod on something sharp.

'Of course, you've got no shoes on,' said Birkin.

'His shoes are here!' cried Gudrun from below. She was making fast her boat.

Gerald waited for them to be brought to him. Gudrun came with them. He pulled them on his feet.

'If you once die,' he said, 'Then when it's over, it's finished. Why come to life again? There's room under that water there for thousands.'

'Two is enough,' she said murmuring.

He dragged on his second shoe. He was shivering violently, and his jaw shook as he spoke.

'That's true,' he said, 'maybe. But it's curious how much room there seems, a whole universe under there; and as cold as hell, you're as helpless as if your head was cut off.' He could scarcely speak, he shook so violently. 'There's one thing about our family, you know,' he continued. 'Once anything goes wrong, it can never be put right again not with us. I've noticed it all my life – you can't put a thing right, once it has gone wrong.'

They were walking across the high-road to the house.

'And do you know, when you are down there, it is so cold, actually, and so endless, so different really from what it is on top, so endless you wonder how it is so many are alive, why we're up here. Are you going? I shall see you again, shan't I? Good-night, and thank you. Thank you very much!'

The two girls waited a while, to see if there were any hope. The moon shone clearly overhead, with almost impertinent brightness, the small dark boats clustered on the water, there were voices and subdued shouts. But it was all to no purpose. Gudrun went home when Birkin returned.

He was commissioned to open the sluice that let out the water from the lake, which was pierced at one end, near the high-road, thus serving as a reservoir to supply with water the distant mines, in case of necessity. 'Come with me,' he said to Ursula, 'and then I will walk home with you, when I've done this.'

He called at the water-keeper's cottage and took the key of the sluice. They went through a little gate from the high-road, to the head of the water, where was a great stone basin which received the overflow, and a flight of stone steps descended into the depths of the water itself. At the head of the steps was the lock of the sluice-gate.

The night was silver-grey and perfect, save for the scattered restless sound of voices. The grey sheen of the moonlight caught the stretch of water, dark boats plashed and moved. But Ursula's mind ceased to be receptive, everything was unimportant and unreal.

Birkin fixed the iron handle of the sluice, and turned it with a wrench. The cogs began slowly to rise. He turned and turned, like a slave, his white figure became distinct. Ursula looked away. She could not bear to see him winding heavily and laboriously, bending and rising mechanically like a slave, turning the handle.

Then, a real shock to her, there came a loud splashing of water from out of the dark, tree-filled hollow beyond the road, a splashing that deepened rapidly to a harsh roar, and then became a heavy, booming noise of a great body of water falling solidly all the time. It occupied the whole of the night, this great steady booming of water, everything was drowned within it, drowned and lost. Ursula seemed to have to struggle for her life. She put her hands over her ears, and looked at the high bland moon.

'Can't we go now?' she cried to Birkin, who was watching the water on the steps, to see if it would get any lower. It seemed to fascinate him. He looked at her and nodded.

The little dark boats had moved nearer, people were crowding curiously along the hedge by the high-road, to see what was to be seen. Birkin and Ursula went to the cottage with the key, then turned their backs on the lake. She was in great haste. She could not bear the terrible crushing boom of the escaping water.

'Do you think they are dead?' she cried in a high voice, to make herself heard.

'Yes,' he replied.

'Isn't it horrible!'

He paid no heed. They walked up the hill, further and further away from the noise.

'Do you mind very much?' she asked him.

'I don't mind about the dead,' he said, 'once they are dead. The worst of it is, they cling on to the living, and won't let go.'

She pondered for a time.

'Yes,' she said. 'The *fact* of death doesn't really seem to matter much, does it?'

'No,' he said. 'What does it matter if Diana Crich is alive or dead?'

'Doesn't it?' she said, shocked.

'No, why should it? Better she were dead – she'll be much more real.

She'll be positive in death. In life she was a fretting, negated thing.'

'You are rather horrible,' murmured Ursula.

'No! I'd rather Diana Crich were dead. Her living somehow, was all wrong. As for the young man, poor devil – he'll find his way out quickly instead of slowly. Death is all right – nothing better.'

'Yet you don't want to die,' she challenged him.

He was silent for a time. Then he said, in a voice that was frightening to her in its change:

'I should like to be through with it – I should like to be through with the death process.'

'And aren't you?' asked Ursula nervously.

They walked on for some way in silence, under the trees. Then he said, slowly, as if afraid:

'There is life which belongs to death, and there is life which isn't death. One is tired of the life that belongs to death – our kind of life. But whether it is finished, God knows. I want love that is like sleep, like being born again, vulnerable as a baby that just comes into the world.'

Ursula listened, half attentive, half avoiding what he said. She seemed to catch the drift of his statement, and then she drew away. She wanted to hear, but she did not want to be implicated. She was reluctant to yield there, where he wanted her, to yield as it were her very identity.

'Why should love be like sleep?' she asked sadly.

'I don't know. So that it is like death – I *do* want to die from this life and yet it is more than life itself. One is delivered over like a naked infant from the womb, all the old defences and the old body gone, and new air around one, that has never been breathed before.'

She listened, making out what he said. She knew, as well as he knew, that words themselves do not convey meaning, that they are but a gesture we make, a dumb show like any other. And she seemed to feel his gesture through her blood, and she drew back, even though her desire sent her forward.

'But,' she said gravely, 'didn't you say you wanted something that was *not* love – something beyond love?'

He turned in confusion. There was always confusion in speech. Yet it must be spoken. Whichever way one moved, if one were to move forwards, one must break a way through. And to know, to give utterance, was to break a way through the walls of the prison as the infant in labour strives through the walls of the womb: There is no new movement now, without the breaking through of the old body, deliberately, in knowledge, in the struggle to get out.

'I don't want love,' he said. 'I don't want to know you. I want to be gone out of myself, and you to be lost to yourself, so we are found different. One shouldn't talk when one is tired and wretched. One Hamletises, and it seems a lie. Only believe me when I show you a bit of healthy pride and insouciance. I hate myself serious.'

'Why shouldn't you be serious?' she said.

He thought for a minute, then he said, sulkily:

'I don't know.' Then they walked on in silence, at outs. He was vague and lost.

'Isn't it strange,' she said, suddenly putting her hand on his arm, with a loving impulse, 'how we always talk like this! I suppose we do love each other, in some way.'

'Oh yes,' he said; 'Too much.'

She laughed almost gaily.

'You'd have to have it your own way, wouldn't you?' she teased. 'You could never take it on trust.'

He changed, laughed softly, and turned and took her in his arms, in the middle of the road.

'Yes,' he said softly.

And he kissed her face and brow, slowly, gently, with a sort of delicate happiness which surprised her extremely, and to which she could not respond. They were soft, blind kisses, perfect in their stillness. Yet she held back from them. It was like strange moths, very soft and silent, settling on her from the darkness of her soul. She was uneasy. She drew away.

'Isn't somebody coming?' she said.

So they looked down the dark road, then set off again walking towards Beldover. Then suddenly, to show him she was no shallow prude, she stopped and held him tight, hard against her, and covered his face with hard, fierce kisses of passion. In spite of his otherness, the old blood beat up in him.

'Not this, not this,' he whimpered to himself, as the first perfect mood of softness and sleep-loveliness ebbed back away from the rushing of passion that came up to his limbs and over his face as she drew him. And soon he was a perfect hard flame of passionate desire for her. Yet in the small core of the flame was an unyielding anguish of another thing. But this also was lost; he only wanted her, with an extreme desire that seemed inevitable as death, beyond question.

Then, satisfied and shattered, fulfilled and destroyed, he went home away from her, drifting vaguely through the darkness, lapsed into the old fire of burning passion. Far away, far away, there seemed to be a small lament in the darkness. But what did it matter? What did it matter, what did anything matter save this ultimate and triumphant experience of physical passion, that had blazed up anew like a new spell of life. 'I was becoming quite dead-alive, nothing but a word-bag,' he said in triumph, scorning his other self. Yet somewhere far off and small, the other hovered.

The men were still dragging the lake when he got back. He stood on the bank and heard Gerald's voice. The water was still booming in the night, the moon was fair, the hills beyond were elusive. The lake was sinking. There came the raw smell of the banks, in the night air.

Up at Shortlands there were lights in the windows, as if nobody had gone to bed. On the landing-stage was the old doctor, the father of the young man who was lost. He stood quite silent, waiting. Birkin also stood and watched, Gerald came up in a boat.

'You still here, Rupert?' he said. 'We can't get them. The bottom slopes, you know, very steep. The water lies between two very sharp slopes, with little branch valleys, and God knows where the drift will take you. It isn't as if it was a level bottom. You never know where you are, with the dragging.'

'Is there any need for you to be working?' said Birkin. 'Wouldn't it be much better if you went to bed?'

'To bed! Good God, do you think I should sleep? We'll find 'em, before I go away from here.'

'But the men would find them just the same without you – why should you insist?'

Gerald looked up at him. Then he put his hand affectionately on Birkin's shoulder, saying:

'Don't you bother about me, Rupert. If there's anybody's health to think about, it's yours, not mine. How do you feel yourself?'

'Very well. But you, you spoil your own chance of life – you waste your best self.'

Gerald was silent for a moment. Then he said:

'Waste it? What else is there to do with it?'

'But leave this, won't you? You force yourself into horrors, and put a mill-stone of beastly memories round your neck. Come away now.'

'A mill-stone of beastly memories!' Gerald repeated. Then he put his hand again affectionately on Birkin's shoulder. 'God, you've got such a telling way of putting things, Rupert, you have.'

Birkin's heart sank. He was irritated and weary of having a telling way of putting things.

'Won't you leave it? Come over to my place' – he urged as one urges a drunken man.

'No,' said Gerald coaxingly, his arm across the other man's shoulder. 'Thanks very much, Rupert – I shall be glad to come tomorrow, if that'll do. You understand, don't you? I want to see this job through. But I'll come tomorrow, right enough. Oh, I'd rather come and have a chat with you than – than do anything else, I verily believe. Yes, I would. You mean a lot to me, Rupert, more than you know.'

'What do I mean, more than I know?' asked Birkin irritably. He was acutely aware of Gerald's hand on his shoulder. And he did not want this altercation. He wanted the other man to come out of the ugly misery.

'I'll tell you another time,' said Gerald coaxingly.

'Come along with me now – I want you to come,' said Birkin.

There was a pause, intense and real. Birkin wondered why his own heart beat so heavily. Then Gerald's fingers gripped hard and communicative into Birkin's shoulder, as he said:

'No, I'll see this job through, Rupert. Thank you – I know what you mean. We're all right, you know, you and me.'

'I may be all right, but I'm sure you're not, mucking about here,' said Birkin. And he went away.

The bodies of the dead were not recovered till towards dawn. Diana had her arms tight round the neck of the young man, choking him.

'She killed him,' said Gerald.

The moon sloped down the sky and sank at last. The lake was sunk to quarter size, it had horrible raw banks of clay, that smelled of raw rottenish water. Dawn roused faintly behind the eastern hill. The water still boomed through the sluice.

As the birds were whistling for the first morning, and the hills at the back of the desolate lake stood radiant with the new mists, there was a straggling procession up to Shortlands, men bearing the bodies on a stretcher, Gerald going beside them, the two grey-bearded fathers following in silence. Indoors the family was all sitting up, waiting. Somebody must go to tell the mother, in her room. The doctor in secret struggled to bring back his son, till he himself was exhausted.

Over all the outlying district was a hush of dreadful excitement on that Sunday morning. The colliery people felt as if this catastrophe had happened directly to themselves, indeed they were more shocked and frightened than if their own men had been killed. Such a tragedy in Shortlands, the high home of the district! One of the young mistresses, persisting in dancing on the cabin roof of the launch, wilful young madam, drowned in the midst of the festival, with the young doctor! Everywhere on the Sunday morning, the colliers wandered about, discussing the calamity. At all the Sunday dinners of the people, there seemed a strange presence. It was as if the angel of death were very near, there was a sense of the supernatural in the air. The men had excited, startled faces, the women looked solemn, some of them had been crying. The children enjoyed the excitement at first. There was an intensity in the air, almost magical. Did all enjoy it? Did all enjoy the thrill?

Gudrun had wild ideas of rushing to comfort Gerald. She was thinking all the time of the perfect comforting, reassuring thing to say to him. She was shocked and frightened, but she put that away, thinking of how she should deport herself with Gerald: act her part. That was the real thrill: how she should act her part.

Ursula was deeply and passionately in love with Birkin, and she was capable of nothing. She was perfectly callous about all the talk of the accident, but her estranged air looked like trouble. She merely sat by herself, whenever she could, and longed to see him again. She wanted him to come to the house, – she would not have it otherwise, he must come at once. She was waiting for him. She stayed indoors all day, waiting for him to knock at the door. Every minute, she glanced automatically at the window. He would be there.

CHAPTER 15

Sunday Evening

As THE day wore on, the life-blood seemed to ebb away from Ursula, and within the emptiness a heavy despair gathered. Her passion seemed to bleed to death, and there was nothing. She sat suspended in a state of complete nullity, harder to bear than death.

'Unless something happens,' she said to herself, in the perfect lucidity of final suffering, 'I shall die. I am at the end of my line of life.'

She sat crushed and obliterated in a darkness that was the border of death. She realised how all her life she had been drawing nearer and nearer to this brink, where there was no beyond, from which one had to leap like Sappho* into the unknown. The knowledge of the imminence of death was like a drug. Darkly, without thinking at all, she knew that she was near to death. She had travelled all her life along the line of fulfilment, and it was

---

* Ancient Greek poet, some 600 BC, who drowned himself into the sea when rejected by a beautiful youth Phaon.

nearly concluded. She knew all she had to know, she had experienced all she had to experience, she was fulfilled in a kind of bitter ripeness, there remained only to fall from the tree into death. And one must fulfil one's development to the end, must carry the adventure to its conclusion. And the next step was over the border into death. So it was then! There was a certain peace in the knowledge.

After all, when one was fulfilled, one as happiest in falling into death, as a bitter fruit plunges in its ripeness downwards. Death is a great consummation, a consummating experience. It is a development from life. That we know, while we are yet living. What then need we think for further? One can never see beyond the consummation. It is enough that death is a great and conclusive experience. Why should we ask what comes after the experience, when the experience is still unknown to us? Let us die, since the great experience is the one that follows now upon all the rest, death, which is the next great crisis in front of which we have arrived. If we wait, if we baulk the issue, we do but hang about the gates in undignified uneasiness. There it is, in front of us, as in front of Sappho, the illimitable space. Thereinto goes the journey. Have we not the courage to go on with our journey, must we cry 'I daren't'? On ahead we will go, into death, and whatever death may mean. If a man can see the next step to be taken, why should he fear the next but one? Why ask about the next but one? Of the next step we are certain. It is the step into death.

'I shall die – I shall quickly die,' said Ursula to herself, clear as if in a trance, clear, calm, and certain beyond human certainty. But somewhere behind, in the twilight, there was a bitter weeping and a hopelessness. That must not be attended to. One must go where the unfaltering spirit goes, there must be no baulking the issue, because of fear. No baulking the issue, no listening to the lesser voices. If the deepest desire be now, to go on into the unknown of death, shall one forfeit the deepest truth for one more shallow?

'Then let it end,' she said to herself. It was a decision. It was not a question of taking one's life – she would *never* kill herself,

that was repulsive and violent. It was a question of *knowing* the
next step. And the next step led into the space of death. Did it? –
or was there –?

Her thoughts drifted into unconsciousness, she sat as if
asleep beside the fire. And then the thought came back. The
space o' death! Could she give herself to it? Ah yes – it was a
sleep. She had had enough. So long she had held out; and resisted.
Now was the time to relinquish, not to resist any more.

In a kind of spiritual trance, she yielded, she gave way; and
all was dark. She could feel; within the darkness, the terrible
assertion of her body, the unutterable anguish of dissolution, the
only anguish that is too much, the far-off, awful nausea of
dissolution set in within the body.

'Does the body correspond so immediately with the spirit?'
she asked herself. And she knew, with the clarity of ultimate
knowledge, that the body is only one of the manifestations of the
spirit, the transmutation of the integral spirit is the transmutation
of the physical body as well. Unless I set my will, unless I absolve
myself from the rhythm of life, fix myself and remain static, cut
off from living, absolved within my own will. But better die than
live mechanically a life that is a repetition of repetitions. To die is
to move on with the invisible. To die is also a joy, a joy of
submitting to that which is greater than the known, namely, the
pure unknown. That is a joy. But to live mechanised and cut off
within the motion of the will, to live as an entity absolved from
the unknown, that is shameful and ignominious. There is no
ignominy in death. There is complete ignominy in an unreplenished,
mechanised life. Life indeed may be ignominious, shameful to the
soul. But death is never a shame. Death itself, like the illimitable
space, is beyond our sullying.

Tomorrow was Monday. Monday, the beginning of another
schoolweek! Another shameful, barren school-week, mere routine
and mechanical activity. Was not the adventure of death infinitely
preferable? Was not death infinitely more lovely and noble than
such a life? A life of barren routine, without inner meaning, without
any real significance. How sordid life was, how it was a terrible

shame to the soul, to live now! How much cleaner and more
dignified to be dead! One could not bear any more of this shame
of sordid routine and mechanical nullity. One might come to fruit
in death. She had had enough. For where was life to be found?
No flowers grow upon busy machinery, there is no sky to a
routine, there is no space to a rotary motion. And all life was a
rotary motion, mechanised, cut off from reality. There was nothing
to look for from life – it was the same in all countries and all
peoples. The only window was death. One could look out on to
the great dark sky of death with elation, as one had looked out of
the classroom window as a child, and seen perfect freedom in
the outside. Now one was not a child, and one knew that the soul
was a prisoner within this sordid vast edifice of life, and there
was no escape, save in death.

But what a joy! What a gladness to think that whatever
humanity did, it could not seize hold of the kingdom of death, to
nullify that. The sea they turned into a murderous alley and a
soiled road of commerce, disputed like the dirty land of a city
every inch of it. The air they claimed too, shared it up, parcelled
it out to certain owners, they trespassed in the air to fight for it.
Everything was gone, walled in, with spikes on top of the walls,
and one must ignominiously creep between the spiky walls through
a labyrinth of life.

But the great, dark, illimitable kingdom of death, there
humanity was put to scorn. So much they could do upon earth,
the multifarious little gods that they were. But the kingdom of
death put them all to scorn, they dwindled into their true vulgar
silliness in face of it.

How beautiful, how grand and perfect death was, how good
to look forward to. There one would wash off all the lies and
ignominy and dirt that had been put upon one here, a perfect bath
of cleanness and glad refreshment, and go unknown,
unquestioned, unabased. After all, one was rich, if only in the
promise of perfect death. It was a gladness above all, that this
remained to look forward to, the pure inhuman otherness of death.

Whatever life might be, it could not take away death, the
inhuman transcendent death. Oh, let us ask no question of it,

what it is or is not. To know is human, and in death we do not know, we are not human. And the joy of this compensates for all the bitterness of knowledge and the sordidness of our humanity. In death we shall not be human, and we shall not know. The promise of this is our heritage, we look forward like heirs to their majority.

Ursula sat quite still and quite forgotten, alone by the fire in the drawing-room. The children were playing in the kitchen, all the others were gone to church. And she was gone into the ultimate darkness of her own soul.

She was startled by hearing the bell ring, away in the kitchen, the children came scudding along the passage in delicious alarm.

'Ursula, there's somebody.'

'I know. Don't be silly,' she replied. She too was startled, almost frightened. She dared hardly go to the door.

Birkin stood on the threshold, his rain-coat turned up to his ears. He had come now, now she was gone far away. She was aware of the rainy night behind him.

'Oh is it you?' she said.

'I am glad you are at home,' he said in a low voice, entering the house.

'They are all gone to church.'

He took off his coat and hung it up. The children were peeping at him round the corner.

'Go and get undressed now, Billy and Dora,' said Ursula. 'Mother will be back soon, and she'll be disappointed if you're not in bed.'

The children, in a sudden angelic mood, retired without a word. Birkin and Ursula went into the drawing-room.

The fire burned low. He looked at her and wondered at the luminous delicacy of her beauty, and the wide shining of her eyes. He watched from a distance, with wonder in his heart, she seemed transfigured with light.

'What have you been doing all day?' he asked her.

'Only sitting about,' she said.

He looked at her. There was a change in her. But she was separate from him. She remained apart, in a kind of brightness. They both sat silent in the soft light of the lamp. He felt he ought to go away again, he ought not to have come. Still he did not gather enough resolution to move. But he was *de trop*, her mood was absent and separate.

Then there came the voices of the two children calling shyly outside the door, softly, with self-excited timidity:

'Ursula! Ursula!'

She rose and opened the door. On the threshold stood the two children in their long nightgowns, with wide-eyed, angelic faces. They were being very good for the moment, playing the role perfectly of two obedient children.

'Shall you take us to bed!' said Billy, in a loud whisper.

'Why you *are* angels tonight,' she said softly. 'Won't you come and say good-night to Mr Birkin?'

The children merged shyly into the room, on bare feet. Billy's face was wide and grinning, but there was great solemnity of being good in his round blue eyes. Dora, peeping from the floss of her fair hair, hung back like some tiny Dryad, that has no soul.

'Will you say good-night to me?' asked Birkin, in a voice that was strangely soft and smooth. Dora drifted away at once, like a leaf lifted on a breath of wind. But Billy went softly forward, slow and willing, lifting his pinched-up mouth implicitly to be kissed. Ursula watched the full, gathered lips of the man gently touch those of the boy, so gently. Then Birkin lifted his fingers and touched the boy's round, confiding cheek, with a faint touch of love. Neither spoke. Billy seemed angelic like a cherub boy, or like an acolyte, Birkin was a tall, grave angel looking down to him.

'Are you going to be kissed?' Ursula broke in, speaking to the little girl. But Dora edged away like a tiny Dryad that will not be touched.

'Won't you say good-night to Mr Birkin? Go, he's waiting for you,' said Ursula. But the girl-child only made a little motion away from him.

'Silly Dora, silly Dora!' said Ursula.

Birkin felt some mistrust and antagonism in the small child. He could not understand it.

'Come then,' said Ursula. 'Let us go before mother comes.'

'Who'll hear us say our prayers?' asked Billy anxiously.

'Whom you like.'

'Won't you?'

'Yes, I will.'

'Ursula?'

'Well Billy?'

'Is it *whom* you like?'

'That's it.'

'Well what is *whom?*'

'It's the accusative of who.'

There was a moment's contemplative silence, then the confiding:

'Is it?'

Birkin smiled to himself as he sat by the fire. When Ursula came down he sat motionless, with his arms on his knees. She saw him, how he was motionless and ageless, like some crouching idol, some image of a deathly religion. He looked round at her, and his face, very pale and unreal, seemed to gleam with a whiteness almost phosphorescent.

'Don't you feel well?' she asked, in indefinable repulsion.

'I hadn't thought about it.'

'But don't you know without thinking about it?'

He looked at her, his eyes dark and swift, and he saw her revulsion. He did not answer per question.

'Don't you know whether you are unwell or not, without thinking about it?' she persisted.

'Not always,' he said coldly.

'But don't you think that's very wicked?'

'Wicked?'

'Yes. I think it's *criminal* to have so little connection with your own body that you don't even know when you are ill.'

He looked at her darkly.

'Yes,' he said.

'Why don't you stay in bed when you are seedy? You look perfectly ghastly.'

'Offensively so?' he asked ironically.

'Yes, quite offensive. Quite repelling.'

'Ah!! Well that's unfortunate.'

'And it's raining, and it's a horrible night. Really, you shouldn't be forgiven for treating your body like it – you *ought* to suffer, a man who takes as little notice of his body as that.'

' – takes as little notice of his body as that,' he echoed mechanically.

This cut her short, and there was silence.

The others came in from church, and the two had the girls to face, then the mother and Gudrun, and then the father and the boy.

'Good-evening,' said Brangwen, faintly surprised. 'Came to see me, did you?'

'No,' said Birkin, 'not about anything, in particular, that is. The day was dismal, and I thought you wouldn't mind if I called in.'

'It *has* been a depressing day,' said Mrs Brangwen sympathetically. At that moment the voices of the children were heard calling from upstairs: 'Mother! Mother!' She lifted her face and answered mildly into the distance: 'I shall come up to you in a minute, Doysie.' Then to Birkin: 'there is nothing fresh at Shortlands, I suppose? Ah,' she sighed, 'no, poor things, I should think not.'

'You've been over there today, I suppose?' asked the father.

'Gerald came round to tea with me, and I walked back with him. The house is overexcited and unwholesome, I thought.'

'I should think they were people who hadn't much restraint,' said Gudrun.

'Or too much,' Birkin answered.

'Oh yes, I'm sure,' said Gudrun, almost vindictively, 'one or the other.'

'They all feel they ought to behave in some unnatural fashion,' said Birkin. 'When people are in grief, they would do better to cover their faces and keep in retirement, as in the old days.'

'Certainly!' cried Gudrun, flushed and inflammable. 'What can be worse than this public grief – what is more horrible, more false! If *grief* is not private, and hidden, what is?'

'Exactly,' he said. 'I felt ashamed when I was there and they were all going about in a lugubrious false way, feeling they must not be natural or ordinary.'

'Well – ' said Mrs Brangwen, offended at this criticism, 'it isn't so easy to bear a trouble like that.'

And she went upstairs to the children.

He remained only a few minutes longer, then took his leave. When he was gone Ursula felt such a poignant hatred of him, that all her brain seemed turned into a sharp crystal of fine hatred. Her whole nature seemed sharpened and intensified into a pure dart of hate. She could not imagine what it was. It merely took hold of her, the most poignant and ultimate hatred, pure and clear and beyond thought. She could not think of it at all, she was translated beyond herself. It was like a possession. She felt she was possessed. And for several days she went about possessed by this exquisite force of hatred against him. It surpassed anything she had ever known before, it seemed to throw her out of the world into some terrible region where nothing of her old life held good. She was quite lost and dazed, really dead to her own life.

It was so completely incomprehensible and irrational. She did not know *why* she hated him, her hate was quite abstract. She had only realised with a shock that stunned her, that she was overcome by this pure transportation. He was the enemy, fine as a diamond, and as hard and jewel-like, the quintessence of all that was inimical.

She thought of his face, white and purely wrought, and of his eyes that had such a dark, constant will of assertion, and she touched her own forehead, to feel if she were mad, she was so transfigured in white flame of essential hate.

It was not temporal, her hatred, she did not hate him for this or for that; she did not want to do anything to him, to have any connection with him. Her relation was ultimate and utterly beyond words, the hate was so pure and gemlike. It was as if he were a beam of essential enmity, a beam of light that did not only destroy her, but denied her altogether, revoked her whole world. She saw him as a clear stroke of uttermost contradiction, a strange gem-like being whose existence defined her own non-existence. When she heard he was ill again, her hatred only intensified itself a few degrees, if that were possible. It stunned her and annihilated her, but she could not escape it. She could not escape this transfiguration of hatred that had come upon her.

CHAPTER 16

Man to Man

HE LAY sick and unmoved, in pure opposition to everything. He knew how near to breaking was the vessel that held his life. He knew also how strong and durable it was. And he did not care. Better a thousand times take one's chance with death, than accept a life one did not want. But best of all to persist and persist and persist for ever, till one were satisfied in life.

He knew that Ursula was referred back to him. He knew his life rested with her. But he would rather not live than accept the love she proffered. The old way of love seemed a dreadful bondage, a sort of conscription. What it was in him he did not know, but the thought of love, marriage, and children, and a life lived together, in the horrible privacy of domestic and connubial satisfaction, was repulsive. He wanted something clearer, more open, cooler, as it were. The hot narrow intimacy between man and wife was abhorrent. The way they shut their doors, these married people, and shut themselves in to their own exclusive alliance with each other, even in love, disgusted him. It was a whole community of mistrustful couples insulated in private houses or private rooms, always in couples, and no further life, no further immediate, no disinterested relationship admitted: a kaleidoscope of couples, disjoined, separatist, meaningless entities of married couples. True, he hated promiscuity even worse than marriage, and a liaison was only another kind of coupling, reactionary from the legal marriage. Reaction was a greater bore than action.

On the whole, he hated sex, it was such a limitation. It was sex that turned a man into a broken half of a couple, the woman into the other broken half. And he wanted to be single in himself, the woman single in herself. He wanted sex to revert to the level of the other appetites, to be regarded as a functional process, not as a fulfilment. He believed in sex marriage. But beyond this, he wanted a further conjunction, where man had being and woman had being, two pure beings, each constituting the freedom of the other, balancing each other like two poles of one force, like two angels, or two demons.

He wanted so much to be free, not under the compulsion of any need for unification, or tortured by unsatisfied desire. Desire and aspiration should find their object without all this torture, as now, in a world of plenty of water, simple thirst is inconsiderable, satisfied almost unconsciously. And he wanted to be with Ursula as free as with himself, single and clear and cool, yet balanced, polarised with her. The merging, the clutching, the mingling of love was become madly abhorrent to him.

But it seemed to him, woman was always so horrible and clutching, she had such a lust for possession, a greed of self-importance in love. She wanted to have, to own, to control, to be dominant. Everything must be referred back to her, to Woman, the Great Mother of everything, out of whom proceeded everything and to whom everything must finally be rendered up.

It filled him with almost insane fury, this calm assumption of the Magna Mater, that all was hers, because she had borne it. Man was hers because she had borne him. A Mater Dolorosa, she had borne him, a Magna Mater, she now claimed him again, soul and body, sex, meaning, and all. He had a horror of the Magna Mater, she was detestable.

She was on a very high horse again, was woman, the Great Mother. Did he not know it in Hermione. Hermione, the humble, the subservient, what was she all the while but the Mater Dolorosa, in her subservience, claiming with horrible, insidious arrogance and female tyranny, her own again, claiming back the man she had borne in suffering. By her very suffering and humility she bound her son with chains, she held him her everlasting prisoner.

And Ursula, Ursula was the same – or the inverse. She too was the awful, arrogant queen of life, as if she were a queen bee on whom all the rest depended. He saw the yellow flare in her eyes, he knew the unthinkable overweening assumption of primacy in her. She was unconscious of it herself. She was only too ready to knock her head on the ground before a man. But this was only when she was so certain of her man, that she could worship him as a woman worships her own infant, with a worship of perfect possession.

It was intolerable, this possession at the hands of woman. Always a man must be considered as the broken off fragment of a woman, and the sex was the still aching scar of the laceration. Man must be added on to a woman, before he had any real place or wholeness.

And why? Why should we consider ourselves, men and women, as broken fragments of one whole? It is not true. We are not broken fragments of one whole. Rather we are the singling away into purity and clear being, of things that were mixed. Rather the sex is that which remains in us of the mixed, the unresolved. And passion is the further separating of this mixture, that which is manly being taken into the being of the man, that which is womanly passing to the woman, till the two are clear and whole as angels, the admixture of sex in the highest sense surpassed, leaving two single beings constellated together like two stars.

In the old age, before sex was, we were mixed, each one a mixture. The process of singling into individuality resulted into the great polarisation of sex. The womanly drew to one side, the manly to the other. But the separation was imperfect even them. And so our world-cycle passes. There is now to come the new day, when we are beings each of us, fulfilled in difference. The man is pure man, the woman pure woman, they are perfectly polarised. But there is no longer any of the horrible merging, mingling self-abnegation of love. There is only the pure duality of polarisation, each one free from any contamination of the other. In each, the individual is primal, sex is subordinate, but perfectly polarised. Each has a single, separate being, with its own laws. The man has his pure freedom, the woman hers. Each acknowledges the perfection of the polarised sex-circuit. Each admits the different nature in the other.

So Birkin meditated whilst he was ill. He liked sometimes to be ill enough to take to his bed. For then he got better very quickly, and things came to him clear and sure.

Whilst he was laid up, Gerald came to see him. The two men had a deep, uneasy feeling for each other. Gerald's eyes were quick and restless, his whole manner tense and impatient, he seemed strung up to some activity. According to conventionality, he wore black clothes, he looked formal, handsome and *comme il faut*. His hair was fair almost to whiteness, sharp like splinters of light, his face was keen and ruddy, his body seemed full of northern energy. Gerald really loved Birkin, though he never quite believed in him. Birkin was too unreal; – clever, whimsical, wonderful, but not practical enough. Gerald felt that his own understanding was much sounder and safer. Birkin was delightful, a wonderful spirit, but after all, not to be taken seriously, not quite to be counted as a man among men.

Why are you laid up again?' he asked kindly, taking the sick man's hand. It was always Gerald who was protective, offering the warm shelter of his physical strength.

'For my sins, I suppose,' Birkin said, smiling a little ironically.

'For your sins? Yes, probably that is so. You should sin less, and keep better in health?'

'You'd better teach me.'

He looked at Gerald with ironic eyes.

'How are things with you?' asked Birkin.

With me?' Gerald looked at Birkin, saw he was serious, and a warm light came into his eyes.

'I don't know that they're any different. I don't see how they could be. There's nothing to change.'

'I suppose you are conducting the business as successfully as ever, and ignoring the demand of the soul.'

'That's it,' said Gerald. 'At least as far as the business is concerned. I couldn't say about the soul, I'm sure.'

'No.'

'Surely you don't expect me to?' laughed Gerald.

'No. How are the rest of your affairs progressing, apart from the business?'

'The rest of my affairs? What are those? I couldn't say; I don't know what you refer to.'

'Yes, you do,' said Birkin. 'Are you gloomy or cheerful? And what about Gudrun Brangwen?'

'What about her?' A confused look came over Gerald. 'Well,' he added, 'I don't know. I can only tell you she gave me a hit over the face last time I saw her.'

'A hit over the face! What for?'

'That I couldn't tell you, either.'

'Really! But when?'

'The night of the party – when Diana was drowned. She was driving the cattle up the hill, and I went after her – you remember.'

'Yes, I remember. But what made her do that? You didn't definitely ask her for it, I suppose?'

'I? No, not that I know of. I merely said to her, that it was dangerous to drive those Highland bullocks – as it *is*. She turned in such a way, and said – "I suppose you think I'm afraid of you and your cattle, don't you?" So I asked her "why," and for answer she flung me a back-hander across the face.'

Birkin laughed quickly, as if it pleased him. Gerald looked at him, wondering, and began to laugh as well, saying:

'I didn't laugh at the time, I assure you. I was never so taken aback in my life.'

'And weren't you furious?'

'Furious? I should think I was. I'd have murdered her for two pins.'

'H'm!' ejaculated Birkin. 'Poor Gudrun, wouldn't she suffer afterwards for having given herself away!' He was hugely delighted.

'Would she suffer?' asked Gerald, also amused now.

Both men smiled in malice and amusement.

'Badly, I should think; seeing how self-conscious she is.'

'She is self-conscious, is she? Then what made her do it? For I certainly think it was quite uncalled-for, and quite unjustified.'

'I suppose it was a sudden impulse.'

'Yes, but how do you account for her having such an impulse? I'd done her no harm.'

Birkin shook his head.

'The Amazon suddenly came up in her, I suppose,' he said.

'Well,' replied Gerald, 'I'd rather it had been the Orinoco.'

They both laughed at the poor joke. Gerald was thinking how Gudrun had said she would strike the last blow too. But some reserve made him keep this back from Birkin.

'And you resent it?' Birkin asked.

'I don't resent it. I don't care a tinker's curse about it.' He was silent a moment, then he added, laughing, 'No, I'll see it through, that's all. She seemed sorry afterwards.'

'Did she? You've not met since that night?'

Gerald's face clouded.

'No,' he said. 'We've been – you can imagine how it's been, since the accident.'

'Yes. Is it calming down?'

'I don't know. It's a shock, of course. But I don't believe mother minds. I really don't believe she takes any notice. And what's so funny, she used to be all for the children – nothing mattered, nothing whatever mattered but the children. And now, she doesn't take any more notice than if it was one of the servants.'

'No? Did it upset *you* very much?'

'It's a shock. But I don't feel it very much, really. I don't feel any different. We've all got to die, and it doesn't seem to make any great difference, anyhow, whether you die or not. I can't feel any *grief* you know. It leaves me cold. I can't quite account for it.'

'You don't care if you die or not?' asked Birkin.

Gerald looked at him with eyes blue as the blue-fibred steel of a weapon. He felt awkward, but indifferent. As a matter of fact, he did care terribly, with a great fear.

'Oh,' he said, 'I don't want to die, why should I? But I never trouble. The question doesn't seem to be on the carpet for me at all. It doesn't interest me, you know.'

'*Timor mortis conturbat me,*'* quoted Birkin, adding – 'No, death doesn't really seem the point any more. It curiously doesn't concern one. It's like an ordinary tomorrow.'

Gerald looked closely at his friend. The eyes of the two men met, and an unspoken understanding was exchanged.

Gerald narrowed his eyes, his face was cool and unscrupulous as he looked at Birkin, impersonally, with a vision that ended in a point in space, strangely keen-eyed and yet blind.

'If death isn't the point,' he said, in a strangely abstract, cold, fine voice – 'what is?' He sounded as if he had been found out.

'What is?' re-echoed Birkin. And there was a mocking silence.

'There's a long way to go, after the point of intrinsic death, before we disappear,' said Birkin.

'There is,' said Gerald. 'But what sort of way?' He seemed to press the other man for knowledge which he himself knew far better than Birkin did.

'Right down the slopes of degeneration – mystic, universal degeneration. There are many stages of pure degradation to go through: agelong. We live on long after our death, and progressively, in progressive devolution.'

Gerald listened with a faint, fine smile on his face, all the time, as if, somewhere, he knew so much better than Birkin, all about this: as if his own knowledge were direct and personal, whereas Birkin's was a matter of observation and inference, not quite hitting the nail on the head: – though aiming near enough at

* I am disturbed by the fear of death.

it. But he was not going to give himself away. If Birkin could get at the secrets, let him. Gerald would never help him. Gerald would be a dark horse to the end.

'Of course,' he said, with a startling change of conversation, 'it is father who really feels it. It will finish him. For him the world collapses. All his care now is for Winnie – he must save Winnie. He says she ought to be sent away to school, but she won't hear of it, and he'll never do it. Of course she *is* in rather a queer way. We're all of us curiously bad at living. We can do things – but we can't get on with life at all. It's curious – a family failing.'

'She oughtn't to be sent away to school,' said Birkin, who was considering a new proposition.

'She oughtn't. Why?'

'She's a queer child – a special child, more special even than you. And in my opinion special children should never be sent away to school. Only moderately ordinary children should be sent to school – so it seems to me.'

'I'm inclined to think just the opposite. I think it would probably make her more normal if she went away and mixed with other children.'

'She wouldn't mix, you see. *You* never really mixed, did you? And she wouldn't be willing even to pretend to. She's proud, and solitary, and naturally apart. If she has a single nature, why do you want to make her gregarious?'

'No, I don't want to make her anything. But I think school would be good for her.'

'Was it good for you?'

Gerald's eyes narrowed uglily. School had been torture to him. Yet he had not questioned whether one should go through this torture. He seemed to believe in education through subjection and torment.

'I hated it at the time, but I can see it was necessary,' he said. 'It brought me into line a bit – and you can't live unless you do come into line somewhere.'

'Well,' said Birkin, 'I begin to think that you can't live unless you keep entirely out of the line. It's no good trying to toe the line, when your one impulse is to smash up the line. Winnie is a special nature, and for special natures you must give a special world.'

'Yes, but where's your special world?' said Gerald.

'Make it. Instead of chopping yourself down to fit the world, chop the world down to fit yourself. As a matter of fact, two exceptional people make another world. You and I, we make another, separate world. You don't *want* a world same as your brothers-in-law. It's just the special quality you value. Do you *want* to be normal or ordinary! It's a lie. You want to be free and extraordinary, in an extraordinary world of liberty.'

Gerald looked at Birkin with subtle eyes of knowledge. But he would never openly admit what he felt. He knew more than Birkin, in one direction – much more. And this gave him his gentle love for the other man, as if Birkin were in some way young, innocent, child-like: so amazingly clever, but incurably innocent.

'Yet you are so banal as to consider me chiefly a freak,' said Birkin pointedly.

'A freak!' exclaimed Gerald, startled. And his face opened suddenly, as if lighted with simplicity, as when a flower opens out of the cunning bud. 'No – I never consider you a freak.' And he watched the other man with strange eyes, that Birkin could not understand. 'I feel,' Gerald continued, 'that there is always an element of uncertainty about you – perhaps you are uncertain about yourself. But I'm never sure of you. You can go away and change as easily as if you had no soul.'

He looked at Birkin with penetrating eyes. Birkin was amazed. He thought he had all the soul in the world. He stared in amazement. And Gerald, watching, saw the amazing attractive goodliness of his eyes, a young, spontaneous goodness that attracted the other man infinitely, yet filled him with bitter chagrin, because he mistrusted it so much. He knew Birkin could do without him – could forget, and not suffer. This was always present in Gerald's consciousness, filling him with bitter unbelief: this consciousness of the young, animal-like spontaneity of detachment. It seemed almost like hypocrisy and lying, sometimes, oh, often, on Birkin's part, to talk so deeply and importantly.

Quite other things were going through Birkin's mind. Suddenly he saw himself confronted with another problem – the problem of love and eternal conjunction between two men. Of course this was necessary – it had been a necessity inside himself all his life – to love a man purely and fully. Of course he had been loving Gerald all along, and all along denying it.

He lay in the bed and wondered, whilst his friend sat beside him, lost in brooding. Each man was gone in his own thoughts.

'You know how the old German knights used to swear a *Blutbruderschaft*,'* he said to Gerald, with quite a new happy activity in his eyes.

'Make a little wound in their arms, and rub each other's blood into the cut?' said Gerald.

'Yes – and swear to be true to each other, of one blood, all their lives. That is what we ought to do. No wounds, that is obsolete. But we ought to swear to love each other, you and I, implicitly, and perfectly, finally, without any possibility of going back on it.'

He looked at Gerald with clear, happy eyes of discovery. Gerald looked down at him, attracted, so deeply bondaged in fascinated attraction, that he was mistrustful, resenting the bondage, hating the attraction.

'We will swear to each other, one day, shall we?' pleaded Birkin. 'We will swear to stand by each other – be true to each other – ultimately – infallibly – given to each other, organically – without possibility of taking back.'

Birkin sought hard to express himself. But Gerald hardly listened. His face shone with a certain luminous pleasure. He was pleased. But he kept his reserve. He held himself back.

'Shall we swear to each other, one day?' said Birkin, putting out his hand towards Gerald.

Gerald just touched the extended fine, living hand, as if withheld and afraid.

'We'll leave it till I understand it better,' he said, in a voice of excuse.

* (Ger.) Blood-brotherhood.

Birkin watched him. A little sharp disappointment, perhaps a touch of contempt came into his heart.

'Yes,' he said. 'You must tell me what you think, later. You know what I mean? Not sloppy emotionalism. An impersonal union that leaves one free.'

They lapsed both into silence. Birkin was looking at Gerald all the time. He seemed now to see, not the physical, animal man, which he usually saw in Gerald, and which usually he liked so much, but the man himself, complete, and as if fated, doomed, limited. This strange sense of fatality in Gerald, as if he were limited to one form of existence, one knowledge, one activity, a sort of fatal halfness, which to himself seemed wholeness, always overcame Birkin after their moments of passionate approach, and filled him with a sort of contempt, or boredom. It was the insistence on the limitation which so bored Birkin in Gerald. Gerald could never fly away from himself, in real indifferent gaiety. He had a clog, a sort of monomania.

There was silence for a time. Then Birkin said, in a lighter tone, letting the stress of the contact pass:

'Can't you get a good governess for Winifred? – somebody exceptional? '

'Hermione Roddice suggested we should ask Gudrun to teach her to draw and to model in clay. You know Winnie is astonishingly clever with that plasticine stuff. Hermione declares she is an artist.' Gerald spoke in the usual animated, chatty manner, as if nothing unusual had passed. But Birkin's manner was full of reminder.

'Really! I didn't know that. Oh well then, if Gudrun *would* teach her, it would be perfect – couldn't be anything better – if Winifred is an artist. Because Gudrun somewhere is one. And every true artist is the salvation of every other.'

'I thought they got on so badly, as a rule.'

'Perhaps. But only artists produce for each other the world that is fit to live in. If you can arrange *that* for Winifred, it is perfect.'

'But you think she wouldn't come?'

'I don't know. Gudrun is rather self-opinionated. She won't go cheap anywhere. Or if she does, she'll pretty soon take herself back. So whether she would condescend to do private teaching, particularly here, in Beldover, I don't know. But it would be just the thing. Winfred has got a special nature. And if you can put into her way the means of being self-sufficient, that is the best thing possible. She'll never get on with the ordinary life. You find it difficult enough yourself, and she is several skins thinner than you are. It is awful to think what her life will be like unless she does find a means of expression, some way of fulfilment. You can see what mere leaving it to fate brings. You can see how much marriage is to be trusted to – look at your own mother.'

'Do you think mother is abnormal?'

'No! I think she only wanted something more, or other than the common run of life. And not getting it, she has gone wrong perhaps.'

'After producing a brood of wrong children,' said Gerald gloomily.

'No more wrong than any of the rest of us,' Birkin replied. 'The most normal people have the worst subterranean selves, take them one by one.'

'Sometimes I think it is a curse to be alive,' said Gerald with sudden impotent anger.

'Well,' said Birkin, 'why not! Let it be a curse sometimes to be alive at other times it is anything but a curse. You've got plenty of zest in it really.'

'Less than you'd think,' said Gerald, revealing a strange poverty in his look at the other man.

There was silence, each thinking his own thoughts.

'I don't see what she has to distinguish between teaching at the Grammar School, and coming to teach Win,' said Gerald.

'The difference between a public servant and a private one. The only nobleman today, king and only aristocrat, is the public, the public. You are quite willing to serve the public – but to be a private tutor – '

'I don't want to serve either – '

'No! And Gudrun will probably feel the same.'

Gerald thought for a few minutes. Then he said:

'At all events, father won't make her feel like a private servant. He will be fussy and grateful enough.'

'So he ought. And so ought all of you. Do you think you can hire a woman like Gudrun Brangwen with money? She is your equal like anything – probably your superior.'

'Is she?' said Gerald.

'Yes, and if you haven't the guts to know it, I hope she'll leave you to your own devices.'

'Nevertheless,' said Gerald, 'if she is my equal, I wish she weren't a teacher, because I don't think teachers as a rule are my equal.'

'Nor do I, damn them. But am I a teacher because I teach, or a parson because I preach?'

Gerald laughed. He was always uneasy on this score. He did not *want* to claim social superiority, yet he *would* not claim intrinsic personal superiority, because he would never base his standard of values on pure being. So he wobbled upon a tacit assumption of social standing. No, Birkin wanted him to accept the fact of intrinsic difference between human beings, which he did not intend to accept. It was against his social honour, his principle. He rose to go.

'I've been neglecting my business all this while,' he said smiling.

'I ought to have reminded you before,' Birkin replied, laughing and mocking.

'I knew you'd say something like that,' laughed Gerald, rather uneasily.

'Did you?'

'Yes, Rupert. It wouldn't do for us all to be like you are – we should soon be in the cart. When I am above the world, I shall ignore all businesses.'

'Of course, we're not in the cart now,' said Birkin, satirically.

'Not as much as you make out. At any rate, we have enough to eat and drink – '

'And be satisfied,' added Birkin.

Gerald came near the bed and stood looking down at Birkin whose throat was exposed, whose tossed hair fell attractively on the warm brow, above the eyes that were so unchallenged and still in the satirical face. Gerald, full-limbed and turgid with energy, stood unwilling to go, he was held by the presence of the other man. He had not the power to go away.

'So,' said Birkin. 'Good-bye.' And he reached out his hand from under the bed-clothes, smiling with a glimmering look.

'Good-bye,' said Gerald, taking the warm hand of his friend in a firm grasp. 'I shall come again. I miss you down at the mill.'

'I'll be there in a few days,' said Birkin.

The eyes of the two men met again. Gerald's, that were keen as a hawk's, were suffused now with warm light and with unadmitted love, Birkin looked back as out of a darkness, unsounded and unknown, yet with a kind of warmth, that seemed to flow over Gerald's brain like a fertile sleep.

'Good-bye then. There's nothing I can do for you?'

'Nothing, thanks.'

Birkin watched the black-clothed form of the other man move out of the door, the bright head was gone, he turned over to sleep.

CHAPTER 17

The Industrial Magnate

IN BELDOVER, there was both for Ursula and for Gudrun an interval. It seemed to Ursula as if Birkin had gone out of her for the time, he had lost his significance, he scarcely mattered in her world. She had her own friends, her own activities, her own life. She turned back to the old ways with zest, away from him.

And Gudrun, after feeling every moment in all her veins conscious of Gerald Crich, connected even physically with him, was now almost indifferent to the thought of him. She was nursing new schemes for going away and trying a new form of life. All the time, there was something in her urging her to avoid the final establishing of a relationship with Gerald. She felt it would be wiser and better to have no more than a casual acquaintance with him.

She had a scheme for going to St Petersburg, where she had a friend who was a sculptor like herself, and who lived with a wealthy Russian whose hobby was jewel-making. The emotional, rather rootless life of the Russians appealed to her. She did not want to go to Paris. Paris was dry, and essentially boring. She would like to go to Rome, Munich, Vienna, or to St Petersburg or Moscow. She had a friend in St Petersburg and a friend in Munich. To each of these she wrote, asking about rooms.

She had a certain amount of money. She had come home partly to save, and now she had sold several pieces of work, she had been praised in various shows. She knew she could become quite the 'go' if she went to London. But she knew London, she wanted something else. She had seventy pounds, of which nobody knew anything. She would move soon, as soon as she heard from her friends. Her nature, in spite of her apparent placidity and calm, was profoundly restless.

The sisters happened to call in a cottage in Willey Green to buy honey. Mrs Kirk, a stout, pale, sharp-nosed woman, sly, honied, with something shrewish and cat-like beneath, asked the girls into her too-cosy, too tidy kitchen. There was a cat-like comfort and cleanliness everywhere.

'Yes, Miss Brangwen,' she said, in her slightly whining, insinuating voice, 'and how do you like being back in the old place, then?' Gudrun, whom she addressed, hated her at once.

'I don't care for it,' she replied abruptly.

'You don't? Ay, well, I suppose you found a difference from London.

You like life, and big, grand places. Some of us has to be content with Willey Green and Beldover. And what do you think of our Grammar School, as there's so much talk about?'

'What do I think of it?' Gudrun looked round at her slowly. 'Do you mean, do I think it's a good school?'

'Yes. What is your opinion of it?'

"I *do* think it's a good school.'

Gudrun was very cold and repelling. She knew the common people hated the school.

'Ay, you do, then! I've heard so much, one way and the other. It's nice to know what those that's in it feel. But opinions vary, don't they? Mr Crich up at Highclose is all for it. Ay, poor man, I'm afraid he's not long for this world. He's very poorly.'

'Is he worse?' asked Ursula.

'Eh, yes – since they lost Miss Diana. He's gone off to a shadow. Poor man, he's had a world of trouble.'

'Has he?' asked Gudrun, faintly ironic.

'He has, a world of trouble. And as nice and kind a gentleman as ever you could wish to meet. His children don't take after him.'

'I suppose they take after their mother?' said Ursula.

'In many ways.' Mrs Kirk lowered her voice a little. 'She was a proud haughty lady when she came into these parts – my word, she was that! She mustn't be looked at, and it was worth your life to speak to her.' The woman made a dry, sly face.

'Did you know her when she was first married?'

'Yes, I knew her. I nursed three of her children. And proper little terrors they were, little fiends – that Gerald was a demon if ever there was one, a proper demon, ay, at six months old.' A curious malicious, sly tone came into the woman's voice.

'Really,' said Gudrun.

'That wilful, masterful – he'd mastered one nurse at six months. Kick, and scream, and struggle like a demon. Many's the time I've pinched his little bottom for him, when he was a child in arms. Ay, and he'd have been better if he'd had it pinched oftener. But she wouldn't have them corrected – no-o, wouldn't hear of it. I can remember the rows she had with Mr Crich, my word. When he'd got worked up, properly worked up till he could stand no more, he'd lock the study door and whip them. But she paced up and down all the while like a tiger outside, like a tiger, with very murder in her face. She had a face that could *look* death. And when the door was opened, she'd go in with her hands lifted – "What have you been doing to *my* children, you coward." She was like one out of her mind. I believe he was frightened of her; he had to be driven mad before he'd lift a finger. Didn't the servants have a life of it! And didn't we used to be thankful when one of them caught it. They were the torment of your life.'

'Really!' said Gudrun.

'In every possible way. If you wouldn't let them smash their pots on the table, if you wouldn't let them drag the kitten about with a string round its neck, if you wouldn't give them whatever they asked for, every mortal thing – then there was a shine on, and their mother coming in asking – "What's the matter with him? What have you done to him? What is it, Darling?" And then she'd turn on you as if she'd trample you under her feet. But she didn't trample on me. I was the only one that could do anything with her demons – for she wasn't going to be bothered with them herself. No, *she* took no trouble for them. But they must just have their way, they mustn't be spoken to. And Master Gerald was the beauty. I left when he was a year and a half, I could stand no more. But I pinched his little bottom for him when he was in arms, I did, when there was no holding him, and I'm not sorry I did – '

Gudrun went away in fury and loathing. The phrase, 'I pinched his little bottom for him,' sent her into a white, stony fury. She could not bear it, she wanted to have the woman taken out at once and strangled. And yet there the phrase was lodged in her mind for ever, beyond escape. She felt, one day, she would *have* to tell him, to see how he took it. And she loathed herself for the thought.

But at Shortlands the life-long struggle was coming to a close. The father was ill and was going to die. He had bad internal pains, which took away all his attentive life, and left him with only a vestige of his consciousness. More and more a silence came over him, he was less and less acutely aware of his surroundings. The pain seemed to absorb his activity. He knew it was there, he knew it would come again. It was like something lurking in the darkness within him. And he had not the power, or the will, to seek it out and to know it. There it remained in the darkness, the great pain, tearing him at times, and then being silent. And when it tore him he crouched in silent subjection under it, and when it left him alone again, he refused to know of it. It was within the darkness, let it remain unknown. So he never admitted it, except in a secret corner of himself, where all his never-revealed fears and secrets were accumulated. For the rest, he had a pain, it went away, it made no difference. It even stimulated him, excited him.

But it gradually absorbed his life. Gradually it drew away all his potentiality, it bled him into the dark, it weaned him of life and drew him away into the darkness. And in this twilight of his life little remained visible to him. The business, his work, that was gone entirely. His public interests had disappeared as if they had never been. Even his family had become extraneous to him, he could only remember, in some slight non-essential part of himself, that such and such were his children. But it was historical fact, not vital to him. He had to make an effort to know their relation to him. Even his wife barely existed. She indeed was like the darkness, like the pain within him. By some strange association, the darkness that contained the pain and the darkness that contained his wife were identical. All his thoughts and understandings became blurred and fused, and now his wife and the consuming pain were the same dark secret power against him, that he never faced. He never drove the dread out of its lair within him. He only knew that there was a dark place, and something inhabiting this darkness which issued from time to time and rent him. But he dared not penetrate and drive the beast into the open. He had rather ignore its existence. Only, in his vague way, the dread was his wife, the destroyer, and it was the pain, the destruction, a darkness which was one and both.

He very rarely saw his wife. She kept her room. Only occasionally she came forth, with her head stretched forward, and in her low, possessed voice, she asked him how he was. And he answered her, in the habit of more than thirty years: 'Well, I don't think I'm any the worse, dear.' But he was frightened of her, underneath this safeguard of habit, frightened almost to the verge of death.

But all his life, he had been so constant to his lights, he had never broken down. He would die even now without breaking down, without knowing what his feelings were, towards her. All his life, he had said: 'Poor Christiana, she has such a strong temper.' With unbroken will, he had stood by this position with regard to her, he had substituted pity for all his hostility, pity had been his shield and his safeguard, and his infallible weapon. And still, in his consciousness, he was sorry for her, her nature was so violent and so impatient.

But now his pity, with his life, was wearing thin, and the dread almost amounting to horror, was rising into being. But before the armour of his pity really broke, he would die, as an insect when its shell is cracked. This was his final resource. Others would live on, and know the living death, the ensuing process of hopeless chaos. He would not. He denied death its victory.

He had been so constant to his lights, so constant to charity, and to his love for his neighbour. Perhaps he had loved his neighbour even better than himself – which is going one further than the commandment. Always, this flame had burned in his heart, sustaining him through everything, the welfare of the people. He was a large employer overlabor, he was a great mine-owner. And he had never lost this from his heart, that in Christ he was one with his workmen. Nay, he had felt inferior to them, as if they through poverty and labour were nearer to God than he. He had always the unacknowledged belief, that it was his workmen, the miners, who held in their hands the means of salvation. To move nearer to God, he must move towards his miners, his life must gravitate towards theirs. They were, unconsciously, his idol, his God made manifest. In them he worshipped the highest, the great, sympathetic, mindless Godhead of humanity.

And all the while, his wife had opposed him like one of the great demons of hell. Strange, like a bird of prey, with the fascinating beauty and abstraction of a hawk, she had beat against the bars of his philanthropy, and like a hawk in a cage, she had sunk into silence. By force of circumstance, because all the world combined to make the cage unbreakable, he had been too strong for her, he had kept her prisoner. And because she was his prisoner, his passion for her had always remained keen as death. He had always loved her, loved her with intensity. Within the cage, she was denied nothing, she was given all licence.

But she had gone almost mad. Of wild and overweening temper, she could not bear the humiliation of her husband's soft, half-appealing kindness to everybody. He was not deceived by the poor. He knew they came and sponged on him, and whined to him, the worse sort; the majority, luckily for him, were much too proud to ask for anything, much too independent to come knocking at his door. But in Beldover, as everywhere else, there were the whining, parasitic, foul human beings who come crawling after charity, and feeding on the living body of the public like lice. A kind of fire would go over Christiana Crich's brain, as she saw two more pale-faced, creeping women in objectionable black clothes, cringing lugubriously up the drive to the door. She wanted to set the dogs on them, 'Hi Rip! Hi Ring! Ranger! At 'em boys, set 'em off.' But Crowther, the butler, with all the rest of the servants, was Mr Crich's man. Nevertheless, when her husband was away, she would come down like a wolf on the crawling supplicants; 'What do you people want? There is nothing for you here. You have no business on the drive at all. Simpson, drive them away and let no more of them through the gate.'

The servants had to obey her. And she would stand watching with an eye like the eagle's, whilst the groom in clumsy confusion drove the lugubrious persons down the drive, as if they were rusty fowls, scuttling before him.

But they learned to know, from the lodge-keeper, when Mrs Crich was away, and they timed their visits. How many times, in the first years, would Crowther knock softly at the door: 'Person to see you, sir.'

'What name?'

'Grocock, sir.'

'What do they want?' The question was half impatient, half gratified. He liked hearing appeals to his charity.

'About a child, sir.'

'Show them into the library, and tell them they shouldn't come after eleven o'clock in the morning.'

'Why do you get up from dinner? – send them off,' his wife would say abruptly.

'Oh, I can't do that. It's no trouble just to hear what they have to say.'

'How many more have been here today? Why don't you establish open house for them? They would soon oust me and the children.'

'You know dear, it doesn't hurt me to hear what they have to say. And if they really are in trouble – well, it is my duty to help them out of it.'

'It's your duty to invite all the rats in the world to gnaw at your bones.'

'Come, Christiana, it isn't like that. Don't be uncharitable.'

But she suddenly swept out of the room, and out to the study. There sat the meagre charity-seekers, looking as if they were at the doctor's.

'Mr Crich can't see you. He can't see you at this hour. Do you think he is your property, that you can come whenever you like? You must go away, there is nothing for you here.'

The poor people rose in confusion. But Mr Crich, pale and black bearded and deprecating, came behind her, saying:

'Yes, I don't like you coming as late as this. I'll hear any of you in the morning part of the day, but I can't really do with you after. What's amiss then, Gittens. How is your Missis?'

'Why, she's sunk very low, Mester Crich, she's a'most gone, she is – '

Sometimes, it seemed to Mrs Crich as if her husband were some subtle funeral bird, feeding on the miseries of the people. It seemed to her he was never satisfied unless there was some sordid tale being poured out to him, which he drank in with a sort of mournful, sympathetic satisfaction. He would have no *raison d'être* if there were no lugubrious miseries in the world, as an undertaker would have no meaning if there were no funerals.

Mrs Crich recoiled back upon herself, she recoiled away from this world of creeping democracy. A band of tight, bâleful exclusion fastened round her heart, her isolation was fierce and hard, her antagonism was passive but terribly pure, like that of a hawk in a cage. As the years went on, she lost more and more count of the world, she seemed rapt in some glittering abstraction, almost purely unconscious. She would wander about the house and about the surrounding country, staring keenly and seeing nothing. She rarely spoke, she had no connection with the world. And she did not even think. She was consumed in a fierce tension of opposition, like the negative pole of a magnet.

And she bore many children. For, as time went on, she never opposed her husband in word or deed. She took no notice of him, externally. She submitted to him, let him take what he wanted and do as he wanted with her. She was like a hawk that sullenly submits to everything. The relation between her and her husband was wordless and unknown, but it was deep, awful, a relation of utter inter-destruction. And he, who triumphed in the world, he became more and more hollow in his vitality, the vitality was bled from within him, as by some haemorrhage. She was hulked like a hawk in a cage, but her heart was fierce and undiminished within her, though her mind was destroyed.

So to the last he would go to her and hold her in his arms sometimes, before his strength was all gone. The terrible white, destructive light that burned in her eyes only excited and roused him. Till he was bled to death, and then he dreaded her more than anything. But he always said to himself, how happy he had been, how he had loved her with a pure and consuming love ever since he had known her. And he thought of her as pure, chaste; the white flame which was known to him alone, the flame of her sex, was a white flower of snow to his mind. She was a wonderful white snow-flower, which he had desired infinitely. And now he was dying with all his ideas and interpretations intact. They would only collapse when the breath left his body. Till then they would be pure truths for him. Only death would show the perfect completeness of the lie. Till death, she was his white snow-flower. He had subdued her, and her subjugation was to him an infinite chastity in her, a virginity which he could never break, and which dominated him as by a spell.

She had let go the outer world, but within herself she was unbroken and unimpaired. She only sat in her room like a moping, dishevelled hawk, motionless, mindless. Her children, for whom she had been so fierce in her youth, now meant scarcely anything to her. She had lost all that, she was quite by herself. Only Gerald, the gleaming, had some existence for her. But of late years, since he had become head of the business, he too was forgotten. Whereas the father, now he was dying, turned for compassion to Gerald. There had always been opposition between the two of them. Gerald had feared and despised his father, and to a great extent had avoided him all through boyhood and young manhood. And the father had felt very often a real dislike of his eldest son, which, never wanting to give way to, he had refused to acknowledge. He had ignored Gerald as much as possible, leaving him alone.

Since, however, Gerald had come home and assumed responsibility in the firm, and had proved such a wonderful director, the father, tired and weary of all outside concerns, had put all his trust of these things in his son, implicitly, leaving everything to him, and assuming a rather touching dependence on the young enemy. This immediately roused a poignant pity and allegiance in Gerald's heart, always shadowed by contempt and by unadmitted enmity. For Gerald was in reaction against Charity; and yet he was dominated by it, it assumed supremacy in the inner life, and he could not confute it. So he was partly subject to that which his father stood for, but he was in reaction against it. Now he could not save himself. A certain pity and grief and tenderness for his father overcame him, in spite of the deeper, more sullen hostility.

The father won shelter from Gerald through compassion. But for love he had Winifred. She was his youngest child, she was the only one of his children whom he had ever closely loved. And her he loved with all the great, overweening, sheltering love of a dying man. He wanted to shelter her infinitely, infinitely, to wrap her in warmth and love and shelter, perfectly. If he could save her she should never know one pain, one grief, one hurt. He had been so right all his life, so constant in his kindness and his goodness. And this was his last passionate righteousness, his love for the child Winifred. Some things troubled him yet. The world had passed away from him, as his strength ebbed. There were no more poor and injured and humble to protect and succour. These were all lost to him. There were no more sons and daughters to trouble him, and to weigh on him as an unnatural responsibility. These too had faded out of reality All these things had fallen out of his hands, and left him free.

There remained the covert fear and horror of his wife, as she sat mindless and strange in her room, or as she came forth with slow, prowling step, her head bent forward. But this he put away. Even his life-long righteousness, however, would not quite deliver him from the inner horror. Still, he could keep it sufficiently at bay. It would never break forth openly. Death would come first.

Then there was Winifred! If only he could be sure about her, if only he could be sure. Since the death of Diana, and the development of his illness, his craving for surety with regard to Winifred amounted almost to obsession. It was as if, even dying, he must have some anxiety, some responsibility of love, of Charity, upon his heart.

She was an odd, sensitive, inflammable child, having her father's dark hair and quiet bearing, but being quite detached, momentaneous. She was like a changeling indeed, as if her feelings did not matter to her, really. She often seemed to be talking and playing like the gayest and most childish of children, she was full of the warmest, most delightful affection for a few things – for her father, and for her animals in particular. But if she heard that her beloved kitten Leo had been run over by the motor-car she put her head on one side, and replied, with a faint contraction like resentment on her face: 'Has he?' Then she took no more notice.

She only disliked the servant who would force bad news on her, and wanted her to be sorry. She wished not to know, and that seemed her chief motive. She avoided her mother, and most of the members of her family. She *loved* her Daddy, because he wanted her always to be happy, and because he seemed to become young again, and irresponsible in her presence. She liked Gerald, because he was so self-contained. She loved people who would make life a game for her. She had an amazing instinctive critical faculty, and was a pure anarchist, a pure aristocrat at once. For she accepted her equals wherever she found them, and she ignored with blithe indifference her inferiors, whether they were her brothers and sisters, or whether they were wealthy guests of the house, or whether they were the common people or the servants. She was quite single and by herself, deriving from nobody. It was as if she were cut off from all purpose or continuity, and existed simply moment by moment.

The father, as by some strange final illusion, felt as if all his fate depended on his ensuring to Winfred her happiness. She who could never suffer, because she never formed vital connections, she who could lose the dearest things of her life and be just the same the next day, the whole memory dropped out, as if deliberately, she whose will was so strangely and easily free, anarchistic, almost nihilistic, who like a soulless bird flits on its own will, without attachment or responsibility beyond the moment, who in her every motion snapped the threads of serious relationship with blithe, free hands, really nihilistic, because never troubled, she must be the object of her father's final passionate solicitude.

When Mr Crich heard that Gudrun Brangwen might come to help Winfred with her drawing and modelling he saw a road to salvation for his child. He believed that Winifred had talent, he had seen Gudrun, he knew that she was an exceptional person. He could give Winifred into her hands as into the hands of a right being. Here was a direction and a positive force to be lent to his child, he need not leave her directionless and defenceless. If he could but graft the girl on to some tree of utterance before he died, he would have fulfilled his responsibility. And here it could be done. He did not hesitate to appeal to Gudrun.

Meanwhile, as the father drifted more and more out of life, Gerald experienced more and more a sense of exposure. His father after all had stood for the living world to him. Whilst his father lived Gerald was not responsible for the world. But now his father was passing away, Gerald found himself left exposed and unready before the storm of living, like the mutinous first mate of a ship that has lost his captain, and who sees only a terrible chaos in front of him. He did not inherit an established order and a living idea. The whole unifying idea of mankind seemed to be dying with his father, the centralising force that had held the whole together seemed to collapse with his father, the parts were ready to go asunder in terrible disintegration. Gerald was as if left on board of a ship that was going asunder beneath his feet, he was in charge of a vessel whose timbers were all coming apart.

He knew that all his life he had been wrenching at the frame of life to break it apart. And now, with something of the terror of a destructive child, he saw himself on the point of inheriting his own destruction. And during the last months, under the influence of death, and of Birkin's talk, and of Gudrun's penetrating being, he had lost entirely that mechanical certainty that had been his triumph. Sometimes spasms of hatred came over him, against Birkin and Gudrun and that whole set. He wanted to go back to the dullest conservatism, to the most stupid of conventional people. He wanted to revert to the strictest Toryism. But the desire did not last long enough to carry him into action.

During his childhood and his boyhood he had wanted a sort of savagedom. The days of Homer were his ideal, when a man was chief of an army of heroes, or spent his years in wonderful Odyssey. He hated remorselessly the circumstances of his own life, so much that he never really saw Beldover and the colliery valley. He turned his face entirely away from the blackened mining region that stretched away on the right hand of Shortlands, he turned entirely to the country and the woods beyond Willey Water. It was true that the panting and rattling of the coal mines could always be heard at Shortlands. But from his earliest childhood, Gerald had paid no heed to this. He had ignored the whole of the industrial sea which surged in coal-blackened tides against the grounds of the house. The world was really a wilderness where one hunted and swam and rode. He rebelled against all authority. Life was a condition of savage freedom.

Then he had been sent away to school, which was so much death to him. He refused to go to Oxford, choosing a German university. He had spent a certain time at Bonn, at Berlin, and at Frankfurt. There, a curiosity had been aroused in his mind. He wanted to see and to know, in a curious objective fashion, as if it were an amusement to him. Then he must try war. Then he must travel into the savage regions that had so attracted him.

The result was, he found humanity very much alike everywhere, and to a mind like his, curious and cold, the savage was duller, less exciting than the European. So he took hold of all kinds of sociological ideas, and ideas of reform. But they never went more than skin-deep, they were never more than a mental amusement. Their interest lay chiefly in the reaction against the positive order, the destructive reaction.

He discovered at last a real adventure in the coal-mines. His father asked him to help in the firm. Gerald had been educated in the science of mining, and it had never interested him. Now, suddenly, with a sort of exultation, he laid hold of the world.

There was impressed photographically on his consciousness the great industry. Suddenly, it was real, he was part of it. Down the valley ran the colliery railway, linking mine with mine. Down the railway ran the trains, short trains of heavily laden trucks, long trains of empty wagons, each one bearing in big white letters the initials:

'C.B.&Co.'

These white letters on all the wagons he had seen since his first childhood, and it was as if he had never seen them, they were so familiar, and so ignored. Now at last he saw his own name written on the wall. Now he had a vision of power.

So many wagons, bearing his initial, running all over the country. He saw them as he entered London in the train, he saw them at Dover. So far his power ramified. He looked at Beldover, at Selby, at Whatmore, at Lethley Bank, the great colliery villages which depended entirely on his mines. They were hideous and sordid, during his childhood they had been sores in his consciousness. And now he saw them with pride. Four raw new towns, and many ugly industrial hamlets were crowded under his dependence. He saw the stream of miners flowing along the causeways from the mines at the end of the afternoon, thousands of blackened, slightly distorted human beings with red mouths, all moving subjugate to his will. He pushed slowly in his motor-car through the little market-top on Friday nights in Beldover, through a solid mass of human beings that were making their purchases and doing their weekly spending. They were all subordinate to him. They were ugly and uncouth, but they were his instruments. He was the God of the machine. They made way for his motor-car automatically, slowly.

He did not care whether they made way with alacrity, or grudgingly. He did not care what they thought of him. His vision had suddenly crystallised. Suddenly he had conceived the pure instrumentality of mankind. There had been so much humanitarianism, so much talk of sufferings and feelings. It was ridiculous. The sufferings and feelings of individuals did not matter in the least. They were mere conditions, like the weather. What mattered was the pure instrumentality of the individual. As a man as of a knife: does it cut well? Nothing else mattered.

Everything in the world has its function, and is good or not good in so far as it fulfils this function more or less perfectly. Was a miner a good miner? Then he was complete. Was a manager a good manager? That was enough. Gerald himself, who was responsible for all this industry, was he a good director? If he were, he had fulfilled his life. The rest was by-play.

The mines were there, they were old. They were giving out, it did not pay to work the seams. There was talk of closing down two of them. It was at this point that Gerald arrived on the scene.

He looked around. There lay the mines. They were old, obsolete. They were like old lions, no more good. He looked again. Pah! the mines were nothing but the clumsy efforts of impure minds. There they lay, abortions of a half-trained mind. Let the idea of them be swept away. He cleared his brain of them, and thought only of the coal in the under earth. How much was there?

There was plenty of coal. The old workings could not get at it, that was all. Then break the neck of the old workings. The coal lay there in its seams, even though the seams were thin. There it lay, inert matter, as it had always lain, since the beginning of time, subject to the will of man. The will of man was the determining factor. Man was the arch-god of earth. His mind was obedient to serve his will. Man's will was the absolute, the only absolute.

And it was his will to subjugate Matter to his own ends. The subjugation itself was the point, the fight was the be-all, the fruits of victory were mere results. It was not for the sake of money that Gerald took over the mines. He did not care about money, fundamentally. He was neither ostentatious nor luxurious, neither did he care about social position, not finally. What he wanted was the pure fulfilment of his own will in the struggle with the natural conditions. His will was now, to take the coal out of the earth, profitably. The profit was merely the condition of victory, but the victory itself lay in the feat achieved. He vibrated with zest before the challenge. Every day he was in the mines, examining, testing, he consulted experts, he gradually gathered the whole situation into his mind, as a general grasps the plan of his campaign.

Then there was need for a complete break. The mines were run on an old system, an obsolete idea. The initial idea had been, to obtain as much money from the earth as would make the owners comfortably rich, would allow the workmen sufficient wages and good conditions, and would increase the wealth of the country altogether. Gerald's father, following in the second generation, having a sufficient fortune, had thought only of the men. The mines, for him, were primarily great fields to produce bread and plenty for all the hundreds of human beings gathered about them. He had lived and striven with his fellow owners to benefit the men every time. And the men had been benefited in their fashion. There were few poor, and few needy. All was plenty, because the mines were good and easy to work. And the miners, in those days, finding themselves richer than they might have expected, felt glad and triumphant. They thought themselves well-off, they congratulated themselves on their good-fortune, they remembered how their fathers had starved and suffered, and they felt that better times had come. They were grateful to those others, the pioneers, the new owners, who had opened out the pits, and let forth this stream of plenty.

But man is never satisfied, and so the miners, from gratitude to their owners, passed on to murmuring. Their sufficiency decreased with knowledge, they wanted more. Why should the master be so out-of-all-proportion rich?

There was a crisis when Gerald was a boy, when the Masters' Federation closed down the mines because the men would not accept a reduction. This lock-out had forced home the new conditions to Thomas Crich. Belonging to the Federation, he had been compelled by his honour to close the pits against his men. He, the father, the Patriarch, was forced to deny the means of life to his sons, his people. He, the rich man who would hardly enter heaven because of his possessions, must now turn upon the poor, upon those who were nearer Christ than himself, those who were humble and despised and closer to perfection, those who were manly and noble in their labours, and must say to them: 'Ye shall neither labour nor eat bread.'

It was this recognition of the state of war which really broke his heart. He wanted his industry to be run on love. Oh, he wanted love to be the directing power even of the mines. And now, from under the cloak of love, the sword was cynically drawn, the sword of mechanical necessity.

This really broke his heart. He must have the illusion and now the illusion was destroyed. The men were not against *him*, but they were against the masters. It was war, and willy nilly he found himself on the wrong side, in his own conscience. Seething masses of miners met daily, carried away by a new religious impulse. The idea flew through them: 'All men are equal on earth,' and they would carry the idea to its material fulfilment. After all, is it not the teaching of Christ? And what is an idea, if not the germ of action in the material world. 'All men are equal in spirit, they are all sons of God. Whence then this obvious *disquality?'* It was a religious creed pushed to its material conclusion. Thomas Crich at least had no answer. He could but admit, according to his sincere tenets, that the disquality was wrong. But he could not give up his goods, which were the stuff of disquality. So the men would fight for their rights. The last impulses of the last religious passion left on earth, the passion for equality, inspired them.

Seething mobs of men marched about, their faces lighted up as for holy war, with a smoke of cupidity. How disentangle the passion for equality from the passion of cupidity, when begins the fight for equality of possessions? But the God was the machine. Each man claimed equality in the Godhead of the great productive machine. Every man equally was part of this Godhead. But somehow, somewhere, Thomas Crich knew this was false. When the machine is the Godhead, and production or work is worship, then the most mechanical mind is purest and highest, the representative of God on earth. And the rest are subordinate, each according to his degree.

Riots broke out, Whatmore pit-head was in flames. This was the pit furthest in the country, near the woods. Soldiers came. From the windows of Shortlands, on that fatal day, could be seen the flare of fire in the sky not far off, and now the little colliery train, with the workmen's carriages which were used to convey the miners to the distant Whatmore, was crossing the valley full of soldiers, full of redcoats. Then there was the far-off sound of firing, then the later news that the mob was dispersed, one man was shot dead, the fire was put out.

Gerald, who was a boy, was filled with the wildest excitement and delight. He longed to go with the soldiers to shoot the men. But he was not allowed to go out of the lodge gates. At the gates were stationed sentries with guns. Gerald stood near them in delight, whilst gangs of derisive miners strolled up and down the lanes, calling and jeering:

'Now then, three ha'porth o' coppers, let's see thee shoot thy gun.' Insults were chalked on the walls and the fences, the servants left.

And all this while Thomas Crich was breaking his heart, and giving away hundreds of pounds in charity. Everywhere there was free food, a surfeit of free food. Anybody could have bread for asking, and a loaf cost only three-ha'pence. Every day there was a free tea somewhere, the children had never had so many treats in their lives. On Friday afternoon great basketfuls of buns and cakes were taken into the schools, and great pitchers of milk, the school children had what they wanted. They were sick with eating too much cake and milk.

And then it came to an end, and the men went back to work. But it was never the same as before. There was a new situation created, a new idea reigned. Even in the machine, there should be equality. No part' should be subordinate to any other part: all should be equal. The instinct for chaos had entered. Mystic equality lies in abstraction, not in having or in doing, which are processes. In function and process, one man, one part, must of necessity be subordinate to another. It is a condition of being. But the desire for chaos had risen, and the idea of mechanical equality was the weapon of disruption which should execute the will of man, the will for chaos.

Gerald was a boy at the time of the strike, but he longed to be a man, to fight the colliers. The father however was trapped between two half-truths, and broken. He wanted to be a pure Christian, one and equal with all men. He even wanted to give away all he had, to the poor. Yet he was a great promoter of industry, and he knew perfectly that he must keep his goods and keep his authority. This was as divine a necessity in him, as the need to give away all he possessed – more divine, even, since this was the necessity he acted upon. Yet because he did *not* act on the other ideal, it dominated him, he was dying of chagrin because he must forfeit it. He wanted to be a father of loving kindness and sacrificial benevolence. The colliers shouted to him about his thousands a year. They would not be deceived.

meaningless it was, confronted with the reality of him. Birkin could see only a strange, inexplicable, almost patternless collection of passions and desires and suppressions and traditions and mechanical ideas, all cast unfused and disunited into this slender, bright-faced man of nearly fifty, who was as unresolved now as he was at twenty, and as uncreated. How could he be the parent of Ursula, when he was not created himself. He was not a parent. A slip of living flesh had been transmitted through him, but the spirit had not come from him. The spirit had not come from any ancestor, it had come out of the unknown. A child is the child of the mystery, or it is uncreated.

'The weather's not so bad as it has been,' said Brangwen, after waiting a moment. There was no connection between the two men.

'No,' said Birkin. 'It was full moon two days ago.'

'Oh! You believe in the moon then, affecting the weather?'

'No, I don't think I do. I don't really know enough about it.'

'You know what they say? The moon and the weather may change together, but the change of the moon won't change the weather.'

'Is that it?' said Birkin. 'I hadn't heard it.'

There was a pause. Then Birkin said:

'Am I hindering you? I called to see Ursula, really. Is she at home?'

'I don't believe she is. I believe she's gone to the library. I'll just see.'

Birkin could hear him enquiring in the dining-room.

'No,' he said, coming back. 'But she won't be long. You wanted to speak to her?'

Birkin looked across at the other man with curious calm, clear eyes. 'As a matter of fact,' he said, 'I wanted to ask her to marry me.'

A point of light came on the golden-brown eyes of the elder man.

'O-oh?' he said, looking at Birkin, then dropping his eyes before the calm, steadily watching look of the other: 'Was she expecting you then?'

'No,' said Birkin.

'No? I didn't know anything of this sort was on foot – ' Brangwen smiled awkwardly.

Birkin looked back at him, and said to himself: 'I wonder why it should be "on foot"!' Aloud he said:

'No, it's perhaps rather sudden.' At which, thinking of his relationship with Ursula, he added – 'but I don't know – '

'Quite sudden, is it? Oh!' said Brangwen, rather baffled and annoyed.

'In one way,' replied Birkin, ' – not in another.'

There was a moment's pause, after which Brangwen said:

'Well, she pleases herself – '

'Oh yes!' said Birkin, calmly.

A vibration came into Brangwen's strong voice, as he replied:

'Though I shouldn't want her to be in too big a hurry, either. It's no good looking round afterwards, when it's too late.'

'Oh, it need never be too late,' said Birkin, 'as far as that goes.'

'How do you mean?' asked the father.

'If one repents being married, the marriage is at an end,' said Birkin.

'You think so?'

'Yes.'

'Ay, well that may be your way of looking at it.'

Birkin, in silence, thought to himself: 'so it may. As for *your* way of looking at it, William Brangwen, it needs a little explaining.'

'I suppose,' said Brangwen, 'you know what sort of people we are? What sort of a bringing-up she's had?'

' "She",' thought Birkin to himself, remembering his childhood's corrections, 'is the cat's mother.'

'Do I know what sort of a bringing-up she's had?' he said aloud.

He seemed to annoy Brangwen intentionally.

'Well,' he said, 'she's had everything that's right for a girl to have – as far as possible, as far as we could give it her.'

'I'm sure she has,' said Birkin, which caused a perilous full-stop. The father was becoming exasperated. There was something naturally irritant to him in Birkin's mere presence.

'And I don't want to see her going back on it all,' he said, in a clanging voice.

'Why?' said Birkin.

This monosyllable exploded in Brangwen's brain like a shot.

'Why! *I* don't believe in your new-fangled ways and new-fangled ideas – in and out like a frog in a gallipot. It would never do for me.'

Birkin watched him with steady emotionless eyes. The radical antagonism in the two men was rousing.

'Yes, but are my ways and ideas new-fangled?' asked Birkin.

'Are they?' Brangwen caught himself up. 'I'm not speaking of you in particular,' he said. 'What I mean is that my children have been brought up to think and do according to the religion I was brought up in myself, and I don't want to see them going away from *that.*'

There was a dangerous pause.

'And beyond that –?' asked Birkin.

The father hesitated, he was in a nasty position.

'Eh? What do you mean? All I want to say is that my daughter' – he tailed off into silence, overcome by futility. He knew that in some way he was off the track.

'Of course,' said Birkin, 'I don't want to hurt anybody or influence anybody. Ursula does exactly as she pleases.'

There was a complete silence, because of the utter failure in mutual understanding. Birkin felt bored. Her father was not a coherent human being, he was a roomful of old echoes. The eyes of the younger man rested on the face of the elder. Brangwen looked up, and saw Birkin looking at him. His face was covered with inarticulate anger and humiliation and sense of inferiority in strength.

'And as for beliefs, that's one thing,' he said. 'But I'd rather see my daughters dead tomorrow than that they should be at the beck and call of the first man that likes to come and whistle for them.'

A queer painful light came into Birkin's eyes.

'As to that,' he said, 'I only know that it's much more likely that it's I who am at the beck and call of the woman, than she at mine.'

Again there was a pause. The father was somewhat bewildered.

'I know,' he said, 'she'll please herself – she always has done. I've done my best for them, but that doesn't matter. They've got themselves to please, and if they can help it they'll please nobody *but* themselves. But she's a right to consider her mother, and me as well – ' Brangwen was thinking his own thoughts.

'And I tell you this much, I would rather bury them, than see them getting into a lot of loose ways such as you see everywhere nowadays. I'd rather bury them – '

'Yes but, you see,' said Birkin slowly, rather wearily, bored again by this new turn, 'they won't give either you or me the chance to bury them, because they're not to be buried.'

Brangwen looked at him in a sudden flare of impotent anger.

'Now, Mr Birkin,' he said, 'I don't know what you've come here for, and I don't know what you're asking for. But my daughters are my daughters – and it's my business to look after them while I can.'

Birkin's brows knitted suddenly, his eyes concentrated in mockery. But he remained perfectly stiff and still. There was a pause.

'I've nothing against your marrying Ursula,' Brangwen began at length. 'It's got nothing to do with me, she'll do as she likes, me or no me.'

Birkin turned away, looking out of the window and letting go his consciousness. After all, what good was this? It was hopeless to keep it up. He would sit on till Ursula came home, then speak to her, then go away. He would not accept trouble at the hands of her father. It was all unnecessary, and he himself need not have provoked it.

The two men sat in complete silence, Birkin almost unconscious of his own whereabouts. He had come to ask her to marry him – well then he would wait on, and ask her. As for what she said, whether she accepted or not, he did not think about it. He would say what he had come to say, and that was all he was conscious of. He accepted the complete insignificance of this household, for him. But everything now was as if fated. He could see one thing ahead, and no more. From the rest, he was absolved entirely for the time being. It had to be left to fate and chance to resolve the issues.

At length they heard the gate. They saw her coming up the steps with a bundle of books under her arm. Her face was bright and abstracted as usual, with the abstraction, that look of being not quite *there,* not quite present to the facts of reality, that galled her father so much. She had a maddening faculty of assuming a light of her own, which excluded the reality, and within which she looked radiant as if in sunshine.

They heard her go into the dining-room, and drop her armful of books on the table.

'Did you bring me that Girl's Own?' cried Rosalind.

'Yes, I brought it. But I forgot which one it was you wanted.'

'You would,' cried Rosalind angrily. 'It's right for a wonder.'

Then they heard her say something in a lowered tone.

'Where?' cried Ursula.

Again her sister's voice was muffled.

Brangwen opened the door, and called, in his strong, brazen voice:

'Ursula.'

She appeared in a moment, wearing her hat.

'Oh how do you do!' she cried, seeing Birkin, and all dazzled as if taken by surprise. He wondered at her, knowing she was aware of his presence. She had her queer, radiant, breathless manner, as if confused by the actual world, unreal to it, having a complete bright world of herself alone.

'Have I interrupted a conversation?' she asked.

'No, only a complete silence,' said Birkin.

'Oh,' said Ursula, vaguely, absent. Their presence was not vital to her, she was withheld, she did not take them in. It was a subtle insult that never failed to exasperate her father.

'Mr Birkin came to speak to *you*, not to me,' said her father.

'Oh, did he!' she exclaimed vaguely, as if it did not concern her. Then, recollecting herself, she turned to him rather radiantly, but still quite superficially, and said: 'Was it anything special?'

'I hope so,' he said, ironically.

' – To propose to you, according to all accounts,' said her father.

'Oh,' said Ursula.

'Oh,' mocked her father, imitating her. 'Have you nothing more to say?'

She winced as if violated.

'Did you really come to propose to me?' she asked of Birkin, as if it were a joke.

'Yes,' he said. 'I suppose I came to propose.' He seemed to fight shy of the last word.

'Did you?' she cried, with her vague radiance. He might have been saying anything whatsoever. She seemed pleased.

'Yes,' he answered. 'I wanted to – I wanted you to agree to marry me.'

She looked at him. His eyes were flickering with mixed lights, wanting something of her, yet not wanting it. She shrank a little, as if she were exposed to his eyes, and as if it were a pain to her. She darkened, her soul clouded over, she turned aside. She had been driven out of her own radiant, single world. And she dreaded contact, it was almost unnatural to her at these times.

'Yes,' she said vaguely, in a doubting, absent voice.

Birkin's heart contracted swiftly, in a sudden fire of bitterness. It all meant nothing to her. He had been mistaken again. She was in some self-satisfied world of her own. He and his hopes were accidentals, violations to her. It drove her father to a pitch of mad exasperation. He had had to put up with this all his life, from her.

'Well, what do you say?' he cried.

She winced. Then she glanced down at her father, half-frightened, and she said:

'I didn't speak, did I?' as if she were afraid she might have committed herself.

'No,' said her father, exasperated. 'But you needn't look like an idiot. You've got your wits, haven't you?'

She ebbed away in silent hostility.

'I've got my wits, what does that mean?' she repeated, in a sullen voice of antagonism.

'You heard what was asked you, didn't you?' cried her father in anger.

'Of course I heard.'

'Well then, can't you answer?' thundered her father.

'Why should I?'

At the impertinence of this retort, he went stiff. But he said nothing.

'No,' said Birkin, to help out the occasion, 'there's no need to answer at once. You can say when you like.'

Her eyes flashed with a powerful light.

'Why should I say anything?' she cried. 'You do this off your *own* bat, it has nothing to do with me. Why do you both want to bully me?

'Bully you! Bully you!' cried her father, in bitter, rancorous anger. 'Bully you! Why, it's a pity you can't be bullied into some sense and decency. Bully you! *You'll* see to that, you self-willed creature.'

She stood suspended in the middle of the room, her face glimmering and dangerous. She was set in satisfied defiance. Birkin looked up at her. He too was angry.

'But none is bullying you,' he said, in a very soft dangerous voice also.

'Oh yes,' she cried. 'You both want to force me into something.'

'That is an illusion of yours,' he said ironically.

'Illusion!' cried her father. 'A self-opinionated fool, that's what she is.'

Birkin rose, saying:

'However, we'll leave it for the time being.'

And without another word, he walked out of the house.

'You fool! You fool!' her father cried to her, with extreme bitterness. She left the room, and went upstairs, singing to herself. But she was terribly fluttered, as after some dreadful fight. From her window, she could see Birkin going up the road. He went in such a blithe drift of rage, that her mind wondered over him. He was ridiculous, but she was afraid of him. She was as if escaped from some danger.

Her father sat below, powerless in humiliation and chagrin. It was as if he were possessed with all the devils, after one of these unaccountable conflicts with Ursula. He hated her as if his only reality were in hating her to the last degree. He had all hell in his heart. But he went away, to escape himself. He knew he must despair, yield, give in to despair, and have done.

Ursula's face closed, she completed herself against them all. Recoiling upon herself, she became hard and self-completed, like a jewel. She was bright and invulnerable, quite free and happy, perfectly liberated in her self-possession. Her father had to learn not to see her blithe obliviousness, or it would have sent him mad. She was so radiant with all things, in her possession of perfect hostility.

She would go on now for days like this, in this bright frank state of seemingly pure spontaneity, so essentially oblivious of the existence of anything but herself, but so ready and facile in her interest. Ah it was a bitter thing for a man to be near her, and her father cursed his fatherhood. But he must learn not to see her, not to know.

She was perfectly stable in resistance when she was in this state: so bright and radiant and attractive in her pure opposition, so very pure, and yet mistrusted by everybody, disliked on every hand. It was her voice, curiously clear and repellent, that gave her away. Only Gudrun was in accord with her. It was at these times that the intimacy between the two sisters was most complete, as if their intelligence were one. They felt a strong, bright bond of understanding between them, surpassing everything else. And during all these days of blind bright abstraction and intimacy of his two daughters, the father seemed to breathe an air of death, as if he were destroyed in his very being. He was irritable to madness, he could not rest, his daughters seemed to be destroying him. But he was inarticulate and helpless against them. He was forced to breathe the air of his own death. He cursed them in his soul, and only wanted, that they should be removed from him.

They continued radiant in their easy female transcendancy, beautiful to look at. They exchanged confidences, they were intimate in their revelations to the last degree, giving each other at last every secret. They withheld nothing, they told everything, till they were over the border of evil. And they armed each other with knowledge, they extracted the subtlest flavours from the apple of knowledge. It was curious how their knowledge was complementary, that of each to that of the other.

Ursula saw her men as sons, pitied their yearning and admired their courage, and wondered over them as a mother wonders over her child, with a certain delight in their novelty. But to Gudrun, they were the opposite camp. She feared them and despised them, and respected their activities even overmuch.

'Of course,' she said easily, 'there is a quality of life in Birkin which is quite remarkable. There is an extraordinary rich spring of life in him, really amazing, the way he can give himself to things. But there are so many things in life that he simply doesn't know. Either he is not aware of their existence at all, or he dismisses them as merely negligible things which are vital to the other person. In a way, he is not clever enough, he is too intense in spots.'

'Yes,' cried Ursula, 'too much of a preacher. He is really a priest.'

'Exactly! He can't hear what anybody else has to say – he simply cannot hear. His own voice is so loud.'

'Yes. He cries you down.'

'He cries you down,' repeated Gudrun. 'And by mere force of violence. And of course it is hopeless. Nobody is convinced by violence. It makes talking to him impossible – and living with him I should think would be more than impossible.'

'You don't think one could live with him' asked Ursula.

'I think it would be too wearing, too exhausting. One would be shouted down every time, and rushed into his way without any choice.

He would want to control you entirely. He cannot allow that there is any other mind than his own. And then the real clumsiness of his mind is its lack of self-criticism. No, I think it would be perfectly intolerable.'

'Yes,' assented Ursula vaguely. She only half agreed with Gudrun. 'The nuisance is,' she said, 'that one would find almost any man intolerable after a fortnight.'

'It's perfectly dreadful,' said Gudrun. 'But Birkin – he is too positive. He couldn't bear it if you called your soul your own. Of him that is strictly true.'

'Yes,' said Ursula. 'You must have *his* soul.'

'Exactly! And what can you conceive more deadly?' This was all so true, that Ursula felt jarred to the bottom of her soul with ugly distaste.

She went on, with the discord jarring and jolting through her, in the most barren of misery.

Then there started a revulsion from Gudrun. She finished life off so thoroughly, she made things so ugly and so final. As a matter of fact, even if it were as Gudrun said, about Birkin, other things were true as well. But Gudrun would draw two lines tinder him and cross him out like an account that is settled. There he was, summed up, paid for, settled, done with. And it was such a lie. This finality of Gudrun's, this dispatching of people and things in a sentence, it was all such a lie. Ursula began to revolt from her sister.

One day as they were walking along the lane, they saw a robin sitting on the top twig of a bush, singing shrilly. The sisters stood to look at him. An ironical smile flickered on Gudrun's face.

'Doesn't he feel important?' smiled Gudrun.

'Doesn't he!' exclaimed Ursula, with a little ironical grimace. 'Isn't he a little Lloyd George of the air!'

'Isn't he! Little Lloyd George of the air! That's just what they are,' cried Gudrun in delight. Then for days, Ursula saw the persistent, obtrusive birds as stout, short politicians lifting up their voices from the platform, little men who must make themselves heard at any cost.

But even from this there came the revulsion. Some yellowhammers suddenly shot along the road in front of her. And they looked to her so uncanny and inhuman, like flaring yellow barbs shooting through the air on some weird, living errand, that she said to herself: 'After all, it is impudence to call them little Lloyd Georges. They are really unknown to us, they are the unknown forces. It is impudence to look at them as if they were the same as human beings. They are of another world. How stupid anthropomorphism is! Gudrun is really impudent, insolent, making herself the measure of everything, making everything come down to human standards. Rupert is quite right, human beings are boring, painting the universe with their own image. The universe is non-human, thank God.' It seemed to her irreverence, destructive of all true life, to make little Lloyd Georges of the birds. It was such a lie towards the robins, and such a defamation. Yet she had done it herself. But under Gudrun's influence: so she exonerated herself.

So she withdrew away from Gudrun and from that which she stood for, she turned in spirit towards Birkin again. She had not seen him since the fiasco of his proposal. She did not want to, because she did not want the question of her acceptance thrust upon her. She knew what Birkin meant when he asked her to marry him; vaguely, without putting it into speech, she knew. She knew what kind of love, what kind of surrender he wanted. And she was not at all sure that this was the kind of love that she herself wanted. She was not at all sure that it was this mutual unison in separateness that she wanted. She wanted unspeakable intimacies. She wanted to have him, utterly, finally to have him as her own, oh, so unspeakably, in intimacy. To drink him down – ah, like a life-draught. She made great professions, to herself, of her willingness to warm his foot-soles between her breasts, after the fashion of the nauseous Meredith poem. But only on condition that he, her lover, loved her absolutely, with complete self-abandon. And subtly enough, she knew he would never abandon himself *finally* to her. He did not believe in final self-abandonment. He said it openly. It was his challenge. She was prepared to fight him for it. For she believed in an absolute surrender to love. She believed that love far surpassed the individual. He said the individual was *more* than love, or than any relationship. For him, the bright, single soul accepted love as one of its conditions, a condition of its own equilibrium. She believed that love was *everything*. Man must render himself up to her. He must be quaffed to the dregs by her. Let him be *her man* utterly, and she in return would be his humble slave – whether she wanted it or not.

CHAPTER 20

Gladiatorial

AFTER THE fiasco of the proposal, Birkin had hurried blindly away from Beldover, in a whirl of fury. He felt he had been a complete fool, that the whole scene had been a farce of the first water. But that did not trouble him at all. He was deeply, mockingly angry that Ursula persisted always in this old cry: 'Why do you want to bully me?' and in her bright, insolent abstraction.

He went straight to Shortlands. There he found Gerald standing with his back to the fire, in the library, as motionless as a man is, who is completely and emptily restless, utterly hollow. He had done all the work he wanted to do – and now there was nothing. He could go out in the car, he could run to town. But he did not want to go out in the car, he did not want to run to town, he did not want to call on the Thirlbys. He was suspended motionless, in an agony of inertia, like a machine that is without power.

This was very bitter to Gerald, who had never known what boredom was, who had gone from activity to activity, never at a loss. Now, gradually, everything seemed to be stopping in him. He did not want any more to do the things that offered. Something dead within him just refused to respond to any suggestion. He cast over in his mind, what it would be possible to do, to save himself from this misery of nothingness, relieve the stress of this hollowness. And there were only three things left, that would rouse him, make him live. One was to drink or smoke hashish, the other was to be soothed by Birkin, and the third was women. And there was no-one for the moment to drink with. Nor was there a woman. And he knew Birkin was out. So there was nothing to do but to bear the stress of his own emptiness.

When he saw Birkin his face lit up in a sudden, wonderful smile.

'By God, Rupert,' he said, 'I'd just come to the conclusion that nothing in the world mattered except somebody to take the edge off one's being alone: the right somebody.'

The smile in his eyes was very astonishing, as he looked at the other man. It was the pure gleam of relief. His face was pallid and even haggard.

'The right woman, I suppose you mean,' said Birkin spitefully.

'Of course, for choice. Failing that, an amusing man.'

He laughed as he said it. Birkin sat down near the fire.

'What were you doing?' he asked.

'I? Nothing. I'm in a bad way just now, everything's on edge, and I can neither work nor play. I don't know whether it's a sign of old age, I'm sure.'

'You mean you are bored?'

'Bored, I don't know. I can't apply myself. And I feel the devil is either very present inside me, or dead.'

Birkin glanced up and looked in his eyes.

'You should try hitting something,' he said.

Gerald smiled.

'Perhaps,' he said. 'so long as it was something worth hitting.'

'Quite!' said Birkin, in his soft voice. There was a long pause during which each could feel the presence of the other.

'One has to wait,' said Birkin.

'Ah God! Waiting! What are we waiting for?'

'Some old Johnny says there are three cures for *ennui,* sleep, drink, and travel,' said Birkin.

'All cold eggs,' said Gerald. 'In sleep, you dream, in drink you curse, and in travel you yell at a porter. No, work and love are the two. When you're not at work you should be in love.'

'Be it then,' said Birkin.

'Give me the object,' said Gerald. 'The possibilities of love exhaust themselves.'

'Do they? And then what?'

'Then you die,' said Gerald.

'So you ought,' said Birkin.

'I don't see it,' replied Gerald. He took his hands out of his trousers pockets, and reached for a cigarette. He was tense and nervous. He lit the cigarette over a lamp, reaching forward and drawing steadily. He was dressed for dinner, as usual in the evening, although he was alone.

'There's a third one even to your two,' said Birkin. 'Work, love, and fighting. You forget the fight.'

'I suppose I do,' said Gerald. 'Did you ever do any boxing –?'

'No, I don't think I did,' said Birkin.

'Ay – ' Gerald lifted his head and blew the smoke slowly into the air.

'Why?' said Birkin.

'Nothing. I thought we might have a round. It is perhaps true, that I want something to hit. It's a suggestion.'

'So you think you might as well hit me?' said Birkin.

'You? Well! Perhaps –! In a friendly kind of way, of course.'

'Quite!' said Birkin, bitingly.

Gerald stood leaning back against the mantel-piece. He looked down at Birkin, and his eyes flashed with a sort of terror like the eyes of a stallion, that are bloodshot and overwrought, turned glancing back wards in a stiff terror.

'I feel that if I don't watch myself, I shall find myself doing something silly,' he said.

'Why not do it?' said Birkin coldly.

Gerald listened with quick impatience. He kept glancing down at Birkin, as if looking for something from the other man.

'I used to do some Japanese wrestling,' said Birkin. 'A Jap lived in the same house with me in Heidelberg, and he taught me a little. But I was never much good at it.'

'You did!' exclaimed Gerald. 'That's one of the things I've never ever seen done. You mean jiu-jitsu, I suppose?'

'Yes. But I am no good at those things – they don't interest me.'

'They don't? They do me. What's the start?'

'I'll show you what I can, if you like,' said Birkin.

'You will?' A queer, smiling look tightened Gerald's face for a moment, as he said, 'Well, I'd like it very much.'

'Then we'll try jiu-jitsu. Only you can't do much in a starched shirt.'

'Then let us strip, and do it properly: Hold a minute – ' He rang the bell, and waited for the butler.

'Bring a couple of sandwiches and a syphon,' he said, 'and then don't trouble me any more tonight – or let anybody else.'

The man went. Gerald turned to Birkin with his eyes lighted.

'And you used to wrestle with a Jap?' he said. 'Did you strip?'

'Sometimes.'

'You did! What was he like then, as a wrestler?'

'Good, I believe. I am no judge. He was very quick and slippery and full of electric fire. It is a remarkable thing, what a curious sort of fluid force they seem to have in them, those people – not like a human grip like a polyp – '

Gerald nodded.

'I should imagine so,' he said, 'to look at them. They repel me, rather.'

'Repel and attract, both. They are very repulsive when they are cold, and they look grey. But when they are hot and roused, there is a definite attraction – a curious kind of full electric fluid-like eels.'

'Well – yes – probably.'

The man brought in the tray and set it down.

'Don't come in any more,' said Gerald.

The door closed.

'Well then,' said Gerald; 'shall we strip and begin? Will you have a drink first?'

'No, I don't want one.'

'Neither do I.'

Gerald fastened the door and pushed the furniture aside. The room was large, there was plenty of space, it was thickly carpeted. Then he quickly threw off his clothes, and waited for Birkin. The latter, white and thin, came over to him. Birkin was more a presence than a visible object, Gerald was aware of him completely, but not really visually. Whereas Gerald himself was concrete and noticeable, a piece of pure final substance.

'Now,' said Birkin, 'I will show you what I learned, and what I remember. You let me take you so – ' And his hands closed on the naked body of the other man. In another moment, he had Gerald swung over lightly and balanced against his knee, head downwards. Relaxed, Gerald sprang to his feet with eyes glittering.

'That's smart,' he said. 'Now try again.'

So the two men began to struggle together. They were very dissimilar. Birkin was tall and narrow, his bones were very thin and fine. Gerald was much heavier and more plastic. His bones were strong and round, his limbs were rounded, all his contours were beautifully and fully moulded. He seemed to stand with a proper, rich weight on the face of the earth, whilst Birkin seemed to have the centre of gravitation in his own middle. And Gerald had a rich, frictional kind of strength, rather mechanical, but sudden and invincible, whereas Birkin was abstract as to be almost intangible. He impinged invisibly upon the other man, scarcely seeming to touch him, like a garment, and then suddenly piercing in a tense fine grip that seemed to penetrate into the very quick of Gerald's being.

They stopped, they discussed methods, they practised grips and throws, they became accustomed to each other, to each other's rhythm, they got a kind of mutual physical understanding. And then again they had a real struggle. They seemed to drive their white flesh deeper and deeper against each other, as if they would break into a oneness. Birkin had a great subtle energy, that would press upon the other man with an uncanny force, weigh him like a spell put upon him. Then it would pass, and Gerald would, heave free, with white, heaving, dazzling movements.

So the two men entwined and wrestled with each other, working nearer and nearer. Both were white and clear, but Gerald flushed smart red where he was touched, and Birkin remained white and tense. He seemed to penetrate into Gerald's more solid, more diffuse bulk, to interfuse his body through the body of the other, as if to bring it subtly into subjection, always seizing with some rapid necromantic foreknowledge every motion of the other flesh, converting and counteracting it, playing upon the limbs and trunk of Gerald like some hard wind. It was as if Birkin's whole physical intelligence interpenetrated into Gerald's body, as if his fine, sublimated energy entered into the flesh of the fuller man, like some potency, casting a fine net, a prison, through the muscles into the very depths of Gerald's physical being.

So they wrestled swiftly, rapturously, intent and mindless at last, two essential white figures working into a tighter closer oneness of struggle, with a strange, octopus-like knotting and flashing of limbs in the subdued light of the room; a tense white knot of flesh gripped in silence between the walls of old brown books. Now and again came a sharp gasp of breath, or a sound like a sigh, then the rapid thudding of movement on the thickly-carpeted floor, then the strange sound of flesh escaping under flesh. Often, in the white interlaced knot of violent living being that swayed silently, there was no head to be seen, only the swift, tight limbs, the solid white backs, the physical junction of two bodies clinched Into oneness. Then would appear the gleaming, ruffled head of Gerald, as the struggle changed, then for a moment the dun-coloured, shadow-like head of the other man would lift up from the conflict, the eyes wide and dreadful and sightless.

At length Gerald lay back inert on the carpet, his breast rising in great slow panting, whilst Birkin kneeled over him, almost unconscious. Birkin was much more exhausted. He caught little, short breaths, he could scarcely breathe any more. The earth seemed to tilt and sway, and a complete darkness was coming over his mind. He did not know what happened. He slid forward quite unconscious, over Gerald, and Gerald did not notice. Then he was half-conscious again, aware only of the strange tilting and sliding of the world. The world was sliding, everything was sliding off into the darkness. And he was sliding, endlessly, endlessly away.

He came to consciousness again, hearing an immense knocking outside. What could be happening, what was it, the great hammer-stroke resounding through the house? He did not know. And then it came to him that it was his own heart beating. But that seemed impossible, the noise was outside. No, it was inside himself, it was his own heart. And the beating was painful, so strained, surcharged. He wondered if Gerald heard it. He did not know whether he were standing or lying or falling.

When he realised that he had fallen prostrate upon Gerald's body he wondered, he was surprised. But he sat up, steadying himself with his hand and waiting for his heart to become stiller and less painful. It hurt very much, and took away his consciousness.

Gerald however was still less conscious than Birkin. They waited dimly, in a sort of not-being, for many uncounted, unknown minutes.

'Of course – ' panted Gerald, 'I didn't have to be rough – with you – I had to keep back – my force – '

Birkin heard the sound as if his own spirit stood behind him, outside him, and listened to it. His body was in a trance of exhaustion, his spirit heard thinly. His body could not answer. Only he knew his heart was getting quieter. He was divided entirely between his spirit, which stood outside, and knew, and his body, that was a plunging, unconscious stroke of blood.

'I could have thrown you – using violence – ' panted Gerald. 'But you beat roe right enough.'

'Yes,' said Birkin, hardening his throat and producing the words in the tension there, 'you're much stronger than I – you could beat me – easily.'

Then he relaxed again to the terrible plunging of his heart and his blood.

'It surprised me,' panted Gerald, 'what strength you've got. Almost supernatural.'

'For a moment,' said Birkin.

He still heard as if it were his own disembodied spirit hearing, standing at some distance behind him. It drew nearer however, his spirit. And the violent striking of blood in his chest was sinking quieter, allowing his mind to come back. He realised that he was leaning with all his weight on the soft body of the other man. It startled him, because he thought he had withdrawn. He recovered himself, and sat up. But he was still vague and unestablished. He put out his hand to steady himself. It touched the hand of Gerald, that was lying out on the floor. And Gerald's hand closed warm and sudden over Birkin's, they remained exhausted and breathless, the one hand clasped closely over the other. It was Birkin whose hand, in swift response; had closed in a strong, warm clasp over the hand of the other. Gerald's clasp had been sudden and momentaneous.

The normal consciousness however was returning, ebbing back. Birkin could breathe almost naturally again. Gerald's hand slowly withdrew, Birkin slowly, dazedly rose to his feet and went towards the table. He poured out a whiskey and soda. Gerald also came for a drink.

'It was a real set-to, wasn't it?' said Birkin, looking at Gerald with darkened eyes.

'God, yes,' said Gerald. He looked at the delicate body of the other man, and added: 'It wasn't too much for you, was it?'

'No. One ought to wrestle and strive and be physically close. It makes one sane.'

'You do think so?'

'I do. Don't you?'

'Yes,' said Gerald.

There were long spaces of silence between their words. The wrestling had some deep meaning to them – an unfinished meaning.

'We are mentally, spiritually intimate, therefore we should be more or less physically intimate too – it is more whole.'

'Certainly it is,' said Gerald. Then he laughed pleasantly, adding:

'It's rather wonderful to me.' He stretched out his arms handsomely.

'Yes,' said Birkin. 'I don't know why one should have to justify oneself.'

'No.'

The two men began to dress.

'I think also that you are beautiful,' said Birkin to Gerald, 'and that is enjoyable too. One should enjoy what is given.'

'You think I am beautiful – how do you mean, physically?' asked Gerald, his eyes glistening.

'Yes. You have a northern kind of beauty, like light refracted from snow – and a beautiful, plastic form. Yes, that is there to enjoy as well. We should enjoy everything.'

Gerald laughed in his throat, and said:

'That's certainly one way of looking at it. I can say this much, I feel better. It has certainly helped me. Is this the Bruderschaft you wanted?'

'Perhaps. Do you think this pledges anything?'

'I don't know,' laughed Gerald.

'At any rate, one feels freer and more open now – and that is what we want.'

'Certainly,' said Gerald.

They drew to the fire, with the decanters and the glasses and the food.

'I always eat a little before I go to bed,' said Gerald. 'I sleep better.'

'I should not sleep so well,' said Birkin.

'No? There you are, we are not alike. I'll put a dressing-gown on.' Birkin remained alone, looking at the fire. His mind had reverted to Ursula. She seemed to return again into his consciousness. Gerald came down wearing a gown of broad-barred, thick black-and-green silk, brilliant and striking.

'You are very fine,' said Birkin, looking at the full robe.

'It was a caftan in Bokhara,' said Gerald. 'I like it.'

'I like it too.'

Birkin was silent, thinking how scrupulous Gerald was in his attire, how expensive too. He wore silk socks, and studs of fine workmanship, and silk underclothing, and silk braces. Curious! This was another of the differences between them. Birkin was careless and unimaginative about his own appearance.

'Of course you,' said Gerald, as if he had been thinking; 'there's something curious about you. You're curiously strong. One doesn't expect it, it is rather surprising.'

Birkin laughed. He was looking at the handsome figure of the other man, blond and comely in the rich robe, and he was half thinking of the difference between it and himself – so different; as far, perhaps, apart as man from woman, yet in another direction. But really it was Ursula, it was the woman who was gaining ascendance over Birkin's being, at this moment. Gerald was becoming aim again, lapsing out of him.

'Do you know,' he said suddenly, 'I went and proposed to Ursula Brangwen tonight, that she should marry me.'

He saw the blank shining wonder come over Gerald's face. 'You did?'

'Yes. Almost formally – speaking first to her father, as it should be, in the world – though that was accident – or mischief.'

Gerald only stared in wonder, as if he did not grasp.

'You don't mean to say that you seriously went and asked her father to let you marry her?'

'Yes,' said Birkin, 'I did.'

'What, had you spoken to her before about it, then?'

'No, not a word. I suddenly thought I would go there and ask her and her father happened to come instead of her – so I asked him first.'

'If you could have her?' concluded Gerald.

'Ye-es, that.'

'And you didn't speak to her?'

'Yes. She came in afterwards. So it was put to her as well.'

'It was! And what did she say then? You're an engaged man?'

'No, – she only said she didn't want to be bullied into answering.'

'She what?'

'Said she didn't want to be bullied into answering.'

' "Said she didn't want to be bullied into answering!" Why, what did she mean by that?'

Birkin raised his shoulders. 'Can't say,' he answered. 'Didn't want to be bothered just then, I suppose.'

'But is this really so? And what did you do then?'

'I walked out of the house and came here.'

'You came straight here?'

'Yes.'

Gerald stared in amazement and amusement. Be could not take it in.

'But is this really true, as you say it now?'

'Word for word.'

'It is?'

He leaned back in his chair, filled with delight and amusement.

'Well, that's good,' he said. 'And so you came here to wrestle with your good angel, did you?'

'Did I?' said Birkin.

'Well, it looks like it. Isn't that what you did?'

Now Birkin could not follow Gerald's meaning.

'And what's going to happen?' said Gerald. 'You're going to keep open the proposition, so to speak?'

'I suppose so. I vowed to myself I would see them all to the devil. But I suppose I shall ask her again, in a little while.'

Gerald watched him steadily.

'So you're fond of her then?' he asked.

'I think – I love her,' said Birkin, his face going very still and fixed. Gerald glistened for a moment with pleasure, as if it were something done specially to please him. Then his face assumed a fitting gravity, and he nodded his head slowly.

'You know,' he said, 'I always believed in love – true love. But where does one find it nowadays?'

'I don't know,' said Birkin.

'Very rarely,' said Gerald. Then, after a pause, 'I've never felt it myself – not what I should call love. I've gone after women – and been keen enough over some of them. But I've never felt *love*. I don't believe I've ever felt as much *love* for a woman, as I have for you – not *love*. You understand what I mean?'

'Yes. I'm sure you've never loved a woman.'

'You feel that, do you? And do you, think I ever shall? You understand what I mean?' He put his hand to his breast, closing his fist there, as if he would draw something out. 'I mean that – that I can't express what it is, but I know it.'

'What is it, then?' asked Birkin.

'You see, I can't put it into words. I mean, at any rate, something abiding, something that can't change – '

His eyes were bright and puzzled.

'Now do you think I shall ever feel that for a woman?' he said, anxiously.

Birkin looked at him, and shook his head.

'I don't know,' he said. 'I could not say.'

Gerald had been on the *qui vive,* as awaiting his fate. Now he drew back in his chair.

'No,' he said, 'and neither do I, and neither do I.'

'We are different, you and I,' said Birkin. 'I can't tell your life.'

'No,' said Gerald, 'no more can I. But I tell you – I begin to doubt it!'

'That you will ever love a woman?'

'Well – yes – what you would truly call love – '

'You doubt it?'

'Well – I begin to.'

There was a long pause.

'Life has all kinds of things,' said Birkin. 'There isn't only one road.'

'Yes, I believe that too. I believe it. And mind you, I don't care how it is with me – I don't care how it is – so long as I don't feel – ' he paused, and a blank, barren look passed over his face, to express his feeling – 'so long as I feel I've *lived,* somehow – and I don't care how it is – but I want to feel that – '

'Fulfilled,' said Birkin.

'We-ell, perhaps it is fulfilled; I don't use the same words as you.'

'It is the same.'

CHAPTER 21

Threshold

GUDRUN WAS away in London, having a little show of her work, with a friend, and looking round, preparing for flight from Beldover. Come what might she would be on the wing in a very short time. She received a letter from Winifred Crich, ornamented with drawings.

'Father also has been to London, to be examined by the doctors. It made him very tired. They say he must rest a very great deal, so he is mostly in bed. He brought me a lovely topical parrot in faience,* of Dresden ware, also a man ploughing, and two mice climbing up a stalk, also in faience. The mice were

---

* Delicate chinaware.

Copenhagen ware. They are the best, but mice don't shine so much, otherwise they are very good, their tails are slim and long. They all shine nearly like glass. Of course it is the glaze, but I don't like it. Gerald likes the man ploughing the best, his trousers are torn, he is ploughing with an ox, being I suppose a German peasant. It is all grey and white, white shirt and grey trousers, but very shiny and clean. Mr Birkin likes the girl best, under the hawthorn blossom, with a lamb, and with daffodils painted on her skirts, in the drawing room. But that is silly, because the lamb is not a real lamb, and she is silly too.

'Dear Miss Brangwen, are you coming back soon, you are very much missed here. I enclose a drawing of father sitting up in bed. He says he hopes you are not going to forsake us. Oh dear Miss Brangwen, I am sure you won't. Do come back and draw the ferrets, they are the most lovely noble darlings in the world. We might carve them in Hollywood, playing against a background of green leaves. Oh do let us, for they are most beautiful.

'Father says we might have a studio. Gerald says we could easily have a beautiful one over the stables, it would only need windows to be put in the slant of the roof, which is a simple matter. Then you could stay here all day and work, and we could live in the studio, like two real artists, like the man in the picture in the hall, with the frying-pan and the walls all covered with drawings. I long to be free, to live the free life of an artist. Even Gerald told father that only an artist is free, because he lives in a creative world of his own – '

Gudrun caught the drift of the family intentions, in this letter. Gerald wanted her to be attached to the household at Shortlands, he was using Winifred as his stalking-horse. The father thought only of his child, he saw a rock of salvation in Gudrun. And Gudrun admired him for his perspicacity. The child, moreover, was really exceptional. Gudrun was quite content. She was quite willing, given a studio, to spend her days at Shortlands. She disliked the Grammar School already throughway, she wanted to be free. If a studio were provided, she would be free to go on with her work, she would await the turn of events with complete serenity. And she was really interested in Winifred, she would be quite glad to understand the girl.

So there was quite a little festivity on Winifred's account, the day Gudrun returned to Shortlands.

'You should make a bunch of flowers to give to Miss Brangwen when she arrives,' Gerald said smiling to his sister.

'Oh no,' cried Winfred, 'it's silly.'

'Not at all. It is a very charming and ordinary attention.'

'Oh, it is silly,' protested Winifred, with all the extreme *mauvaise honte** of her years. Nevertheless, the idea appealed to her. She wanted very much to carry it out. She flitted round the green-houses and the conservatory looking wistfully at the flowers on their stems. And the more she looked, the more she *longed* to have a bunch of the blossoms she saw, the more fascinated she became with her little vision of ceremony, and the more consumedly shy and self-conscious she grew, till she was almost beside herself. She could not get the idea out of her mind. It was as if some haunting challenge prompted her, and she had not enough courage to take it up. So again she drifted into the green houses, looking at the lovely roses in their pots, and at the virginal cyclamens, and at the mystic white clusters of a creeper. The beauty, oh the beauty of them, and oh the paradisal bliss, if she should have a perfect bouquet and could give it to Gudrun the next day. Her passion and her complete indecision almost made her ill.

At last she slid to her father's side.

'Daddie – ' she said.

'What, my precious?'

But she hung back, the tears almost coming to her eyes, in her sensitive confusion. Her father looked at her, and his heart ran hot with tenderness, an anguish of poignant love.

'What do you want to say to me, my love?'

'Daddie –!' her eyes smiled laconically – 'isn't it silly if I give Miss Brangwen some flowers when she comes?'

The sick man looked at the bright, knowing eyes of his child, and his heart burned with love.

---

* (Ger.) Demure and modest.

'No, darling, that's not silly. It's what they do to queens.'

This was not very reassuring to Winifred. She half suspected that queens in themselves were a silliness. Yet she so wanted her little romantic occasion.

'Shall I then?' she asked.

'Give Miss Brangwen some flowers? Do, Birdie. Tell Wilson I say you are to have what you want.'

The child smiled a small, subtle, unconscious smile to herself, in anticipation of her way.

'But I won't get them till tomorrow,' she said.

'Not till tomorrow, Birdie. Give me a kiss then – '

Winifred silently kissed the sick man, and drifted out of the room. She again went the round of the green-houses and the conservatory, informing the gardener, in her high, peremptory, simple fashion, of what she wanted, telling him all the blooms she had selected.

'What do you want these for?' Wilson asked.

'I want them,' she said. She wished servants did not ask questions.

'Ay, you've said as much. But what do you want them for, for decoration, or to send away, or what?'

'I want them for a presentation bouquet.'

'A presentation bouquet! Who's coming then? – the Duchess of Portland?'

'No.'

'Oh, not her? Well you'll have a rare poppy-show if you put all the things you've mentioned into your bouquet.'

'Yes, I want a rare poppy-show.'

'You do! Then there's no more to be said.'

The next day Winifred, in a dress of silvery velvet, and holding a gaudy bunch of flowers in her hand, waited with keen impatience in the schoolroom, looking down the drive for Gudrun's arrival. It was a wet morning. Under her nose was the strange fragrance of hot-house flowers, the bunch was like a little fire to her, she seemed to have a strange new fire in her heart. This slight sense of romance stirred her like an intoxicant.

At last she saw Gudrun coming, and she ran downstairs to warn her father and Gerald. They, laughing at her anxiety and gravity, came with her into the hall. The man-servant came hastening to the door, and there he was, relieving Gudrun of her umbrella, and then of her raincoat. The welcoming party hung back till their visitor entered the hall.

Gudrun was flushed with the rain, her hair was blown in loose little curls she was like a flower just opened in the rain, the heart of the blossom just newly visible, seeming to emit a warmth of retained sunshine. Gerald winced in spirit, seeing her so beautiful and unknown. She was wearing a soft blue dress, and her stockings were of dark red.

Winifred advanced with odd, stately formality.

'We are so glad you've come back,' she said. 'These are your flowers.' She presented the bouquet.

'Mine!' cried Gudrun. She was suspended for a moment, then a vivid flush went over her, she was as if blinded for a moment with a flame of pleasure. Then her eyes, strange and flaming, lifted and looked at the father, and at Gerald. And again Gerald shrank in spirit, as if it would be more than he could bear, as her hot, exposed eyes rested on him. There was something so revealed, she was revealed beyond bearing, to his eyes. He turned his face aside. And he felt he would not be able to avert her. And he writhed under the imprisonment.

Gudrun put her face into the flowers.

'But how beautiful they are!' she said, in a muffled voice. Then, with a strange, suddenly revealed passion, she stooped and kissed Winifred.

Mr Crich went forward with his hand held out to her.

'I was afraid you were going to run away from us,' he said, playfully.

Gudrun looked up at him with a luminous, roguish, unknown face.

'Really!' she replied. 'No, I didn't want to stay in London.' Her voice seemed to imply that she was glad to get back to Shortlands, her tone was warm and subtly caressing.

'That is a good thing,' smiled the father. 'You see you are very welcome here among us.'

Gudrun only looked into his face with dark-blue, warm, shy eyes. She was unconsciously carried away by her own power.

'And you look as if you came home in every possible triumph,' Mr Crich continued, holding her hand.

'No,' she said, glowing strangely. 'I haven't had any triumph till I came here.'

'Ah, come, come! We're not going to hear any of those tales. Haven't we read notices in the newspaper, Gerald?'

'You came off pretty well,' said Gerald to her, shaking hands. 'Did you sell anything?'

'No,' she said, 'not much.'

'Just as well,' he said.

She wondered what he meant. But she was all aglow with her reception, carried away by this little flattering ceremonial on her behalf.

'Winifred,' said the father, 'have you a pair of shoes for Miss Brangwen? You had better change at once – '

Gudrun went out with her bouquet in her hand.

'Quite a remarkable young woman,' said the father to Gerald, when she had gone.

'Yes,' replied Gerald briefly, as if he did not like the observation.

Mr Crich liked Gudrun to sit with him for half an hour. Usually he was ashy and wretched, with all the life gnawed out of him. But as soon as he rallied, he liked to make believe that he was just as before, quite well and in the midst of life – not of the outer world, but in the midst of a strong essential life. And to this belief, Gudrun contributed perfectly. With her, he could get by stimulation those precious half-hours of strength and exaltation and pure freedom, when he seemed to live more than he had ever lived.

She came to him as he lay propped up in the library. His face was like yellow wax, his eyes darkened, as it were sightless. His black beard, now streaked with grey, seemed to spring out of the

waxy flesh of a corpse. Yet the atmosphere about him was
energetic and playful. Gudrun subscribed to this, perfectly. To
her fancy, he was just an ordinary man. Only his rather terrible
appearance was photographed upon her soul, away beneath her
consciousness. She knew that, in spite of his playfulness, his
eyes could not change from their darkened vacancy, they were
the eyes of a man who is dead.

'Ah, this is Miss Brangwen,' he said, suddenly rousing as
she entered, announced by the man-servant. 'Thomas, put Miss
Brangwen a chair here – that's right.' He looked at her soft, fresh
face with pleasure. It gave him the illusion of life. 'Now, you will
have a glass of sherry and a little piece of cake. Thomas – '

'No thank you,' said Gudrun. And as soon as she had said
it, her heart sank horribly. The sick man seemed to fall into a
gap of death, at her contradiction. She ought to play up to him,
not to contravene him. In an instant she was smiling her rather
roguish smile.

'I don't like sherry very much,' she said. 'But I like almost
anything else.'

The sick man caught at this straw instantly.

'Not sherry! No! Something else! What then? What is there, Thomas?'

'Port wine – curaçao – '

'I would love some curaçao – ' said Gudrun, looking at the
sick man confidingly.

'You would. Well then Thomas, curaçao – and a little cake,
or a biscuit?'

'A biscuit,' said Gudrun. She did not want anything, but she
was wise.

'Yes.'

He waited till she was settled with her little glass and her
biscuit Then he was satisfied.

'You have heard the plan,' he said with some excitement,
'for a studio for Winifred, over the tables?'

'No!' exclaimed Gudrun, in mock wonder.

'Oh! – I thought Winnie wrote it to you, in her letter!'

'Oh – yes – of course. But I thought perhaps it was only her own little idea – ' Gudrun smiled subtly, indulgently. The sick man smiled also, elated.

'Oh no. It is a real project. There is a good room under the roof of the stables – with sloping rafters. We had thought of converting it into a studio.'

'How *very* nice that would be!' cried Gudrun, with excited warmth.

The thought' of the rafters stirred her.

'You think it would? Well, it can be done.'

'But how perfectly splendid for Winfred! Of course, it is just what is needed, if she is to work at all seriously. One must have one's workshop, otherwise one never ceases to be an amateur.'

'Is that so? Yes. Of course, I should like you to share it with Winifred.

'Thank you *so* much.'

Gudrun knew all these things already, but she must look shy and very grateful, as if overcome.

'Of course, what I should like best, would be if you could give up your work at the Grammar School, and just avail yourself of the studio, and work there – well, as much or as little as you liked – '

He looked at Gudrun with dark, vacant eyes. She looked back at him as if full of gratitude. These phrases of a dying man were so complete and natural, coming like echoes through his dead mouth.

'And as to your earnings – you don't mind taking from me what you have taken from the Education Committee, do you? I don't want you to be a loser.'

'Oh,' said Gudrun, 'if I can have the studio and work there, I can earn money enough, really I can.'

'Well,' he said, pleased to be the benefactor, 'we can see about all that. You wouldn't mind spending your days here?'

If there were a studio to work in,' said Gudrun, 'I could ask for nothing better.'

'Is that so?'

He was really very pleased. But already he was getting tired. She could see the grey, awful semi-consciousness of mere pain and dissolution coming over him again, the torture coming into the vacancy of his darkened eyes. It was not over yet, this process of death. She rose softly saying:

'Perhaps you will sleep. I must look for Winifred.'

She went out, telling the nurse that she had left him. Day by day the tissue of the sick man was further and further reduced, nearer and nearer the process came, towards the last knot which held the human being in its unity. But this knot was hard and unrelaxed, the will of the dying man never gave way. He might be dead in nine-tenths, yet the remaining tenth remained unchanged, till it too was torn apart. With his will he held the unit of himself firm, but the circle of his power was ever and ever reduced, it would be reduced to a point at last, then swept away.

To adhere to life, he must adhere to human relationships, and he caught at every straw. Winifred, the butler, the nurse, Gudrun, these were the people who meant all to him, in these last resources. Gerald, in his father's presence, stiffened with repulsion. It was so, to a less degree, with all the other children except Winifred. They could not see anything but the death, when they looked at their father. It was as if some subterranean dislike overcame them. They could not see the familiar face, hear the familiar voice. They were overwhelmed by the antipathy of visible and audible death. Gerald could not breathe in his father's presence. He must get out at once. And so, in the same way, the father could not bear the presence of his son. It sent a final irritation through the soul of the dying man.

The studio was made ready, Gudrun and Winifred moved in. They enjoyed so much the ordering and the appointing of it. And now they need hardly be in the house at all. They had their meals in the studio, they lived there safely. For the house was becoming dreadful. There were two nurses in white, flitting silently about, like heralds of death. The father was confined to his bed, there was a come and go of *sotto-voce* sisters and brothers and children.

Winifred was her father's constant visitor. Every morning, after breakfast, she went into his room when he was washed and propped up in bed, to spend half an hour with him,

'Are you better, Daddie?' she asked him invariably.

And invariably he answered:

'Yes, I think I'm a little better, pet.'

She held his hand in both her own, lovingly and protectively. And this was very dear to him,

She ran in again as a rule at lunchtime, to tell him the course of events and every evening, when the curtains were drawn, and his room was cosy, she spent a long time with him. Gudrun was gone home, Winifred was alone in the house: she liked best to be with her father. They talked and prattled at random, he always as if he were well, just the same as when he was going about, So that Winifred, with a child's subtle instinct for avoiding the painful things, behaved as if nothing serious was the matter. Instinctively, she withheld her attention, and was happy. Yet in her remoter soul, she knew as well as the adults knew: perhaps better.

Her father was quite well in his make-belief with her. But when she went away, he relapsed under the misery of his dissolution. But still there were these bright moments, though as his strength waned, his faculty for attention grew weaker, and the nurse had to send Winifred away, to save him from exhaustion.

He never admitted that he was going to die. He knew it was so, he knew it was the end. Yet even to himself he did not admit it. He hated the fact, mortally. His will was rigid. He could not bear being overcome by death. For him, there was no death. And yet, at times, he felt a great need to cry out and to wail and complain. He would have liked to cry aloud to Gerald, so that his son should be horrified out of his composure. Gerald was instinctively aware of this, and he recoiled, to avoid any such thing. This uncleanness of death repelled him too much. One should die quickly, like the Romans, one should be master of one's fate in dying as in living. He was convulsed in the clasp of this death of his father's, as in the coils of the great serpent of Laocoön.* The great serpent had got the father, and the son was

* The Trojan priest Laocoön and his two sons were trampled to death by snakes for fore-warning the Trojans against the Greek wooden horse.

dragged into the embrace of horrifying death along with him, He resisted always. And in some strange way, he was a tower of strength to his father.

The last time the dying man asked to see Gudrun he was grey with near death. Yet he must see someone, he must, in the intervals of consciousness, catch into connection with the living world, lest he should have to accept his own situation. Fortunately he was most of his time dazed and half gone. And he spent many hours dimly thinking of the past, as it were, dimly re-living his old experiences. But there were times even to the end when he was capable of realising what was happening to him in the present, the death that was on him. And these were the times when he called in outside help, no matter whose. For to realise this death that he was dying was a death beyond death, never to be borne. It was an admission never to be made.

Gudrun was shocked by his appearance, and by the darkened, almost disintegrated eyes, that still were unconquered and firm.

'Well,' he said in his weakened voice, 'and how are you and Winifred getting on?'

'Oh, very well indeed,' replied Gudrun.

There were slight dead gaps in the conversation, as if the ideas called up were only elusive straws floating on the dark chaos of the sick man's dying.

'The studio answers all right?' he said.

'Splendid. It couldn't be more beautiful and perfect,' said Gudrun. She waited for what he would say next.

'And you think Winifred has the makings of a sculptor?'

It was strange how hollow the words were, meaningless.

'I'm sure she has. She will do good things one day.'

'Ah! Then her life won't be altogether wasted, you think?'

Gudrun was rather surprised.

'Sure it won't!' she exclaimed softly.

'That's right.'

Again Gudrun waited for what he would say.

'You find life pleasant, it is good to live, isn't it?' he asked, with a pitiful faint smile that was almost too much for Gudrun.

'Yes,' she smiled – she would lie at random – 'I get a pretty good time
I believe.'

'That's right. A happy nature is a great asset.'

Again Gudrun smiled, though her soul was dry with repulsion. Did one have to die like this – having the life extracted forcibly from one, whilst one smiled and made conversation to the end? Was there no other way? Must one go through all the horror of this victory over death, the triumph of the integral will, that would not be broken till it disappeared utterly? One must, it was the only way. She admired the self-possession and the control of the dying man exceedingly. But she loathed the death itself. She was glad the everyday world held good, and she need not recognise anything beyond.

'You are quite all right here? – nothing we can do for you? – nothing you find wrong in your position?'

'Except that you are too good to me,' said Gudrun:

'Ah, well, the fault of that lies with yourself,' he said, and he felt a little exultation, that he had made this speech.

He was still so strong and living! But the nausea of death began to creep back on him, in reaction.

Gudrun went away, back to Winfred. Mademoiselle had left, Gudrun stayed a good deal at Shortlands, and a tutor came in to carry on Winifred's education. But he did not live in the house, he was connected with the Grammar School.

One day, Gudrun was to drive with Winifred and Gerald and Birkin town, in the car. It was a dark, showery day. Winifred and Gudrun were ready and waiting at the door. Winifred was very quiet, but Gudrun had not noticed. Suddenly the child asked, in a voice of unconcern:

'Do you think my father's going to die, Miss Brangwen?'

Gudrun started.

'I don't know,' she replied.

'Don't you truly?'

'Nobody knows for certain. He *may* die, of course.'

The child pondered a few moments, then she asked:

'But do you *think* he will die?'

It was put almost like a question in geography or science, insistent, as if she would force an admission from the adult. The watchful, slightly triumphant child was almost diabolical.

'Do I think he will die?' repeated Gudrun. 'Yes, I do.'

But Winifred's large eyes were fixed on her, and the girl did not move.

'He is very ill,' said Gudrun.

A small smile came over Winifred's face, subtle and sceptical.

'*I* don't believe he will,' the child asserted, mockingly, and she moved away into the drive. Gudrun watched the isolated figure, and her heart stood still. Winifred was playing with a little rivulet of water, absorbedly as if nothing had been said.

'I've made a proper dam,' she said, out of the moist distance. Gerald came to the door from out of the hall behind.

'It is just as well she doesn't choose to believe it,' he said.

Gudrun looked at him. Their eyes met; and they exchanged a sardonic understanding.

'Just as well,' said Gudrun.

He looked at her again, and a fire flickered up in his eyes.

'Best to dance while Rome bums, since it must bum, don't you think?' he said.

She was rather taken aback. But, gathering herself together, she replied:

'Oh – better dance than wail, certainly.'

'So I think.'

And they both felt the subterranean desire to let go, to fling away everything, and lapse into a sheer unrestraint, brutal and licentious. A strange black passion surged up pure in Gudrun. She felt strong. She felt her hands so strong, as if she could tear the world asunder with them. She remembered the abandonments of Roman licence, and her heart grew hot. She knew she wanted this herself also – or something, something equivalent. Ah, if that which was unknown and suppressed in her were once let loose, what an orgiastic and satisfying event it would be. And she wanted it, she trembled slightly from the proximity of the man, who stood just behind her, suggestive of the same black licentiousness that rose in herself. She wanted it with him, this unacknowledged frenzy. For a moment the clear perception of this preoccupied her, distinct and perfect in its final reality. Then she shut it off completely, saying:

'We might as well go down to the lodge after Winifred – we can get in the car there.'

'So we can,' he answered, going with her.

They found Winifred at the lodge admiring the litter of purebred white puppies. The girl looked up, and there was a rather ugly, unseeing cast in her eyes as she turned to Gerald and Gudrun. She did not want to see them.

'Look!' she cried. 'Three new puppies! Marshall says this one seems perfect. Isn't it a sweetling? But it isn't so nice as its mother.' She turned to caress the fine white bull-terrier bitch that stood uneasily near her.

'My dearest Lady Crich,' she said, 'you are beautiful as an angel on earth. Angel – angel – don't you think she's good enough and beautiful enough to go to heaven, Gudrun? They will be in heaven, won't they – and *especially* my darling Lady Crich! Mrs Marshall, I say!'

'Yes, Miss Winifred?' said the woman, appearing at the door.

'Oh do call this one Lady Winifred, if she turns out perfect, will you? Do tell Marshall to call it Lady Winifred.'

'I'll tell him – but I'm afraid that's a gentleman puppy, Miss Winifred.'

'Oh *no!*' There was the sound of a car. 'There's Rupert!' cried the child, and she ran to the gate.

Birkin, driving his car, pulled up outside the lodge gate.

'We're ready!' cried Winifred. 'I want to sit in front with you, Rupert. May I?'

'I'm afraid you'll fidget about and fall out,' he said.

'No I won't. I do want to sit in front next to you. It makes my feet so lovely and warm, from the engines.'

Birkin helped her up, amused at sending Gerald to sit by Gudrun in the body of the car.

'Have you any news, Rupert?' Gerald called, as they rushed along the lanes.

'News?' exclaimed Birkin.

'Yes.' Gerald looked at Gudrun, who sat by his side, and he said, his eyes narrowly laughing, 'I want to know whether I ought to congratulate him, but I can't get anything definite out of him.'

Gudrun flushed deeply.

'Congratulate him on what?' she asked.

'There was some mention of an engagement – at least, he said something to me about it.'

Gudrun flushed darkly.

'You mean with Ursula?' she said, in challenge.

'Yes. That is so, isn't it?'

'I don't think there's any engagement,' said Gudrun, coldly.

'That so? Still no developments, Rupert?' he called.

'Where? Matrimonial? No.'

'How's that?' called Gudrun.

Birkin glanced quickly round. There was irritation in his eyes also.

'Why?' he replied. 'What do you think of it, Gudrun?'

'Oh,' she cried, determined to fling her stone also into the pool, since they had begun, 'I don't think she wants an engagement. Naturally, she's a bird that prefers the bush.' Gudrun's voice was clear and gonglike. It reminded Rupert of her father's, so strong and vibrant.

'And I,' said Birkin, his face playful but yet determined, 'I want a binding contract, and am not keen on love, particularly free love.'

They were both amused. *Why* this public avowal? Gerald seemed suspended a moment, in amusement.

'Love isn't good enough for you?' he called.

'No!' shouted Birkin.

'Ha, well that's being over-refined,' said Gerald, and the car ran through the mud.

'What's the matter, really?' said Gerald, turning to Gudrun.

This was an assumption of a sort of intimacy that irritated Gudrun almost like an affront. It seemed to her that Gerald was deliberately insulting her, and infringing on the decent privacy of them all.

'What is it?' she said, in her high, repellent voice. 'Don't ask me! – I know nothing about *ultimate* marriage, I assure you: or even penultimate.'

'Only the ordinary unwarrantable brand!' replied Gerald. 'Just so – same here. I am no expert on marriage, and degrees of ultimateness. It seems to be a bee that buzzes loudly in Rupert's bonnet.'

'Exactly! But that is his trouble, exactly! Instead of wanting a woman for herself, he wants his *ideas* fulfilled. Which, when it comes to actual practice, is not good enough.'

'Oh no. Best go slap for what's womanly in woman, like a bull at a gate.' Then he seemed to glimmer in himself. 'You think love is the ticket, do you?' he asked.

'Certainly, while it lasts – you only can't insist on permanency,' came

Gudrun's voice, strident above the noise.

'Marriage or no marriage, ultimate or penultimate or just so-so? take the love as you find it.'

'As you please, or as you don't please,' she echoed. 'Marriage is a social arrangement, I take it, and has nothing to do with the question of love.'

His eyes were flickering on her all the time. She felt as is he were kissing her freely and malevolently. It made the colour bum in her cheeks, but her heart was quite firm and unfailing.

'You think Rupert is off his head a bit?' Gerald asked.

Her eyes flashed with acknowledgment.

'As regards a woman, yes,' she said, 'I do. There if such a thing as two people being in love for the whole of their lives – perhaps. But marriage is neither here nor there, even then. If they are in love, well and good. If not – why break eggs about it!'

'Yes,' said Gerald. 'That's how it strikes me. But what about Rupert?'

'I can't make out – neither can he nor anybody. He seems to think that if you marry you can get through marriage into a third heaven, or something – all very vague.'

'Very! And who wants a third heaven? As a matter of fact, Rupert has a great yearning to be *safe* – to tie himself to the mast.'

'Yes. It seems to me he's mistaken there too,' said Gudrun. 'I'm sure a mistress is more likely to be faithful than a wife – just because she is her *own* mistress. No – he says he believes that a man and wife can go further than any other two beings – but *where,* is not explained. They can know each other, heavenly and hellish, but particularly hellish, so perfectly that they go beyond heaven and hell – into – there it all breaks down – into nowhere.'

'Into Paradise, he says,' laughed Gerald.

Gudrun shrugged her shoulders. '*Je m'en fiche* of your Paradise!' she said.

'Not being a Mohammedan,'* said Gerald. Birkin sat motionless, driving the car, quite unconscious of what they said. And Gudrun, sitting immediately behind him, felt a sort of ironic pleasure in thus exposing him.

'He says,' she added, with a grimace of irony, 'that you can find an eternal equilibrium in marriage, if you accept the unison, and still leave yourself separate, don't try to fuse.'

'Doesn't inspire me,' said Gerald.

'That's just it,' said Gudrun.

'I believe in love, in a real *abandon,* if you're capable of it,' said Gerald.

'So do I,' said she.

'And so does Rupert, too – though he is always shouting.'

'No,' said Gudrun. 'He won't abandon himself to the other person.

* Refers to the sensual paradise.

You can't be sure of him. That's the trouble I think.'

'Yet he wants marriage! Marriage – *et puis?*'*

'Le paradis!' mocked Gudrun.

Birkin, as he drove, felt a creeping of the spine, as if somebody was threatening his neck. But he shrugged with indifference. It began to rain. Here was a change. He stopped the car and got down to put up the hood.

CHAPTER 22

Woman to Woman

THEY CAME to the town, and left Gerald at the railway station. Gudrun and Winifred were to come to tea with Birkin, who expected Ursula also. In the afternoon, however, the first person to turn up was Hermione. Birkin was out, so she went in the drawing-room, looking at his books and papers, and playing on the piano. Then Ursula arrived. She was surprised, unpleasantly so, to see Hermione, of whom she had heard nothing for some time.

'It is a surprise to see you,' she said.

'Yes,' said Hermione – 'I've been away at Aix – '

'Oh, for your health?'

'Yes.'

The two women looked at each other. Ursula resented Hermione's long, grave, downward-looking face. There was something of the stupidity and the unenlightened self-esteem of a horse in it. 'She's got a horse-face,' Ursula said to herself, 'she runs between blinkers.' It did seem as if Hermione, like the moon, had only one side to her penny. There was no obverse. She stared out all the time on the narrow, but to her, complete world of the extant consciousness. In the darkness, she did not exist. Like the moon, one half of her was lost to life. Her self was all in her head, she did not know what it was spontaneously to run or move, like a fish in the water, or a weasel on the grass. She must always *know*.

But Ursula only suffered from Hermione's one-sidedness. She only felt Hermione's cool evidence, which seemed to put her down as nothing. Hermione, who brooded and brooded till she was exhausted with the ache of her effort at consciousness, spent and ashen in her body, who gained so slowly and with such effort her final and barren conclusions of knowledge, was apt, in the presence of other women, whom she thought simply female, to wear the conclusions of her bitter assurance like jewels which conferred on her an unquestionable distinction, established her in a higher order of life. She was apt, mentally, to condescend to women such as Ursula, whom she regarded as purely emotional. Poor Hermione, it was her one possession, this aching certainty of hers, it was her only justification. She must be confident here, for God knows, she felt rejected and deficient enough elsewhere. In the life of thought, of the spirit, she was one of the elect. And she wanted to be universal. But there was a devastating cynicism at the bottom of her. She did not believe in her own universals – they were sham. She did not believe in the inner life – it was a trick, not a reality. She did not believe in the spiritual world – it was an affectation. In the last resort, she believed in Mammon,* the flesh, and the devil – these at least were not sham. She was a priestess without belief, without conviction, suckled in a creed outworn, and condemned to the reiteration of mysteries that were not divine to her. Yet there was no escape. She was a leaf upon a dying tree. What help was there then, but to fight still for the old, withered truths, to die for the old, outworn belief, to be a sacred and inviolate priestess of desecrated mysteries? The old great truths *had* been true. And she was a leaf of the old great tree of knowledge that was withering now. To the old and last truth then she must be faithful even though cynicism and mockery took place at the bottom of her soul.

'I am so glad to see you,' she said to Ursula, in her slow voice, that was like an incantation. 'You and Rupert have become quite friends?'

* The spirit of the material world of greed and evil.

'Oh yes,' said Ursula. 'He is always somewhere in the background.'

Hermione paused before she answered. She saw perfectly well the other woman's vaunt: it seemed truly vulgar.

'Is he?' she said slowly, and with perfect equanimity. 'And do you think you will marry?'

The question was so calm and mild, so simple and bare and dispassionate that Ursula was somewhat taken aback, rather attracted. It pleased her almost like a wickedness. There was some delightful naked irony in Hermione.

'Well,' replied Ursula, '*He* wants to, awfully, but I'm not so sure.'

Hermione watched her with slow calm eyes. She noted this new expression of vaunting. How she envied Ursula a certain unconscious positivity! Even her vulgarity!

'Why aren't you sure?' she asked, in her easy sing song. She was perfectly at her ease, perhaps even rather happy in this conversation. 'You don't really love him?'

Ursula flushed a little at the mild impertinence of this question. And yet she could not definitely take offence. Hermione seemed so calmly and sanely candid. After all, it was rather great to be able to be so sane.

'He says it isn't love he wants,' she replied.

'What is it then?' Hermione was slow and level.

'He wants me really to accept him in marriage.'

Hermione was silent for some time, watching Ursula with slow, pensive eyes.

'Does he?' she said at length, without expression. Then, rousing, 'And what is it you don't want? You don't want marriage?'

'No – I don't – not really. I don't want to give the sort of *submission* he insists on. He wants me to give myself up – and I simply don't feel that I *can* do it.'

Again there was a long pause, before Hermione replied:

'Not if you don't want to.' Then again there was silence. Hermione shuddered with a strange desire. Ah, if only he had asked *her* to subserve him, to be his slave! She shuddered with desire.

'You see I can't – '

'But exactly in what does – '

They had both begun at once, they both stopped. Then, Hermione, assuming priority of speech, resumed as if wearily:

'To what does he want you to submit?'

'He says he wants me to accept him non-emotionally, and finally – I really don't know what he means. He says he wants the demon part of himself to be mated – physically – not the human being. You see he says one thing one day, and another the next – and he always contradicts himself – '

'And always thinks about himself, and his own dissatisfaction,' said Hermione slowly.

'Yes,' cried Ursula. 'As if there were no-one but himself concerned. That makes it so impossible.'

But immediately she began to retract.

'He insists on my accepting God knows what in *him,'* she resumed. 'He wants me to accept *him* as – as an absolute – But it seems to me he doesn't want to *give* anything. He doesn't want real warm intimacy – he won't have it – he rejects it. He won't let me think, really, and he won't let me *feel* – he hates feelings.'

There was a long pause, bitter for Hermione. Ah, if only he would have made this demand of her? Her he *drove* into thought, drove inexorably into knowledge – and then execrated her for it.

'He wants me to sink myself,' Ursula resumed, 'not to have any being of my own – '

'Then why doesn't he marry an odalisk?'* said Hermione in her mild sing-song, 'if it is that he wants.' Her long face looked sardonic and amused.

'Yes,' said Ursula vaguely. After all, the tiresome thing was, he did not want an odalisk, he did not want a slave. Hermione would have been his slave – there was in her a horrible desire to prostrate herself before a man – a man who worshipped her, however, and admitted her as the supreme thing. He did not want an odalisk. He wanted a woman to *take* something from him, to

---

* An enslaved woman of a harem.

give herself up so much that she could take the last realities of
him, the last facts, the last physical facts, physical and unbearable.

And if she did, would he acknowledge her? Would he be able
to acknowledge her through everything, or would he use her just
as his instrument, use her for his own private satisfaction, not
admitting her? That was what the other men had done. They had
wanted their own show, and they would not admit her, they turned
all she was into nothingness. Just as Hermione now betrayed
herself as a woman. Hermione was like a man, she believed only
in men's things. She betrayed the woman in herself And Birkin,
would he acknowledge, or would he deny her?

'Yes,' said Hermione, as each woman came out of her own
separate reverie. 'It 'would be a mistake – I think it would be a
mistake – '

'To marry him?' asked Ursula.

'Yes,' said Hermione slowly – 'I think you need a man –
soldierly, strong-willed – ' Hermione held out her hand and
clenched it with rhapsodic intensity. 'You should have a man like
the old heroes – you need to stand behind him as he goes into
battle, you need to *see* his strength, and to *hear* his shout – You
need a man physically strong, and virile in his will, *not* a sensitive
man – ' There was a break, as if the pythoness had uttered the
oracle, and now the woman went on, in a rhapsody wearied voice:
'And you see, Rupert isn't this, he isn't. He is frail in health and
body, he needs great, great care. Then he is so changeable and
unsure of himself – it requires the greatest patience and
understanding to help him. And I don't think you are patient. You
would have to be prepared to suffer – dreadfully. I can't *tell* you
how much suffering it would take to make him happy. He lives
an *intensely* spiritual life, at times – too, too wonderful. And then
come the reactions. I can't speak of what I have been through
with him. We have been together so long, I really do know him,
I *do* know what he is. And I feel I must say it; I feel it would be
perfectly *disastrous* for you to marry him – for you even more
than for him.' Hermione lapsed into bitter reverie. 'He is so
uncertain, so unstable – he wearies, and then reacts. I couldn't

tell you what his re-actions are. I couldn't *tell* you the agony of them. That which he affirms and loves one day – a little later he turns on it in a fury of destruction. He is never constant, always this awful, dreadful reaction. Always the quick change from good to bad, bad to good. And nothing is so devastating, nothing – '

'Yes,' said Ursula humbly, 'you must have suffered.'

An unearthly light came on Hermione's face. She clenched her hand like one inspired.

'And one must be willing to suffer – willing to suffer for him hourly, daily – if you are going to help him, if he is to keep true to anything at all – '

'And I don't *want* to suffer hourly and daily,' said Ursula. 'I don't, I should be ashamed. I think it is degrading not to be happy.'

Hermione stopped and looked at her a long time.

'Do you?' she said at last. And this utterance seemed to her a mark of Ursula's far distance from herself. For to Hermione suffering was the greatest reality, come what might. Yet she too had a creed of happiness.

'Yes,' she said. 'One *should* be happy – ' But it was a matter of will.

'Yes,' said Hermione, listlessly now, 'I can only feel that it would be disastrous, disastrous – at least, to marry in a hurry. Can't you be together without marriage? Can't you go away and live somewhere without marriage? I do feel that marriage would be fatal, for both of you. I think for you even more than for him – and I think of his health – '

'Of course,' said Ursula, '*I* don't care about marriage – it isn't really important to me – it's he who wants it.'

'It is his idea for the moment,' said Hermione, with that weary finality, and a sort of *si jeunesse savait** infallibility.

There was a pause. Then Ursula broke into faltering challenge. 'You think I'm merely a physical woman, don't you?'

'No indeed,' said Hermione. 'No, indeed! But I think you are vital and young – it isn't a question of years, or even of experience – it is almost a question of race. Rupert is race-old, he comes of

* (Fr.) If only the youth *understood*.

an old race and you seem to me so young, you come of a young, inexperienced race.'

'Do I!' said Ursula. 'But I think he is awfully young, on one side.'

'Yes, perhaps childish in many respects. Nevertheless – '

They both lapsed into silence. Ursula was filled with deep resentment and a touch of hopelessness. 'It isn't true,' she said to herself, silently addressing her adversary. 'It isn't true. And it is *you* who want a physically strong, bullying man, not I. It is you who want an unsensitive man, not I. You *don't* know anything about Rupert, not really, in spite of the 'years you have had with him. You don't give him a woman's love, you give him an ideal love, and that is why he reacts away from you. You don't know. You only know the dead things. Any kitchen maid would know something about him, you don't know. What do you think your knowledge is but dead understanding, that doesn't mean a thing. You are so false, and untrue, how could you know anything? What is the good of your talking about love – you untrue spectre of a woman! How can you know anything, when you don't believe? You don't believe in yourself and your own womanhood, so what good is your conceited, shallow cleverness –!'

The two women sat on in antagonistic silence. Hermione felt injured, that all her good intention, all her offering, only left the other woman in vulgar antagonism. But then, Ursula could not understand, never would understand, could never be more than the usual jealous and unreasonable female, with a good deal of powerful female emotion, female attraction, and a fair amount of female understanding, but no mind. Hermione had decided long ago that where there was no mind, it was useless to appeal for reason – one had merely to ignore the ignorant. And Rupert – he had now reacted towards the strongly female, healthy, selfish woman – it was his reaction for the time being there was no helping it all. It was all a foolish backward and forward, a violent oscillation that would at length be too violent for his coherency, and he would smash and be dead. There was no saving him. This violent and directionless reaction between animalism and spiritual truth would go on in him till he tore himself in two between the opposite directions, and disappeared meaninglessly out of life. It was no good – he too was without-unity, without *mind,* in the ultimate stages of living; not quite man enough to make a destiny for a woman.

They sat on till Birkin came in and found them together. He felt at once the antagonism in the atmosphere, something radical and insuperable, and he bit his lip. But he affected a bluff manner.

'Hello, Hermione, are you back again? How do you feel?'

'Oh, better. And how are you – you don't look well – '

'Oh! – I believe Gudrun and Winnie Crich are coming in to tea. At least they said they were. We shall be a tea-party. What train did you come by, Ursula?'

It was rather annoying to see him trying to placate both women at once. Both women watched him, Hermione with deep resentment and pity for him, Ursula very impatient. He was nervous and apparently in quite good spirits, chattering the conventional commonplaces. Ursula was amazed and indignant at the way he made small-talk; he was adept as any *fat* in Christendom. She became quite stiff, she would not answer. It all seemed to her so false and so belittling. And still Gudrun did not appear.

'I think I shall go to Florence for the winter,' said Hermione at length.

'Will you?' he answered. 'But it is so cold there.'

'Yes, but I shall stay with Palestra. It is quite comfortable.'

'What takes you to Florence?'

'I don't know,' said Hermione slowly. Then she looked at him with her slow, heavy gaze. 'Barnes is starting his school of aesthetics, and Olandese is going to give a set of discourses on the Italian national policy – '

'Both rubbish,' he said.

'No, I don't think so,' said Hermione.

'Which do you admire, then?'

'I admire both. Barnes is a pioneer. And then I am interested in Italy, in her coming to national consciousness.'

'I wish she'd come to something different from national consciousness, then,' said Birkin; 'especially as it only means a sort of commercial-industrial consciousness. I hate Italy and her national rant. And I think Barnes is an amateur.'

Hermione was silent for some moments, in a state of hostility. But yet, she had got Birkin back again into her world! How subtle her influence was, she seemed to start his irritable attention into her direction exclusively, in one minute. He was her creature.

'No,' she said, 'you are wrong.' Then a sort of tension carne over her, she raised her face like the pythoness inspired with oracles, and went on, in rhapsodic manner: 'Il Sandro mi scrive che ha accolto il piu grande entusiasmo, tutti i giovani, e fanciulle e ragazzi, sono tutti – '*

She went on in Italian, as if, in thinking of the Italians she thought in their language.

He listened with a shade of distaste to her rhapsody, then he said:

'For all that, I don't like it. Their nationalism is just industrialism that and a shallow jealousy I detest so much.'

'I think you are wrong – I think you are wrong – ' said Hermione. 'It seems to me purely spontaneous and beautiful, the modern Italian's *passion,* for it is a passion, for Italy, L'Italia – '

'Do you know Italy well?' Ursula asked of Hermione. Hermione hated to be broken in upon in this manner. Yet she answered mildly:

'Yes, pretty well. I spent several years of my girlhood there, with my mother. My mother died in Florence.'

'Oh.'

There was a pause, painful to Ursula and to Birkin. Hermione however seemed abstracted and calm. Birkin was white, his eyes glowed as if he were in a fever, he was far too over-wrought. How Ursula suffered in this tense atmosphere of strained wills! Her head seemed bound round by iron bands.

Birkin rang the bell for tea. They could not wait for Gudrun any longer. When the door was opened, the cat walked in.

---

* (Italian) Sandro writes that he has been enthusiastically welcomed. The young boys and girls are passionate for Italy, and wish to learn everything – .

'Micio! Micio!' called Hermione, in her slow, deliberate sing-song. The young cat turned to look at her, then, with his slow and stately walk he advanced to her side.

'Vieni – vieni qua,' Hermione was saying, in her strange caressive, protective voice, as if she were always the elder, the mother superior. 'Vieni dire Buon' Giorno alla zia. Mi ricorde, mi ricorde bene – non he vero, piccolo? E vero che mi ricordi? E vero?' And slowly she rubbed his head, slowly and with ironic indifference.

'Does he understand Italian?' said Ursula, who knew nothing of the language.

'Yes,' said Hermione at length. 'His mother was Italian. She was born in my waste-paper basket in Florence, on the morning of Rupert's birthday. She was his birthday present.'

Tea was brought in. Birkin poured out for them. It was strange how inviolable was the intimacy which existed between him and Hermione. Ursula felt that she was an outsider. The very tea-cups and the old silver was a bond between Hermione and Birkin. It seemed to belong to an old, past world which they had inhabited together, and in which Ursula was a foreigner. She was almost a parvenue in their old cultured milieu. Her convention was not their convention, their standards were not her standards. But theirs were established, they had the sanction and the grace of age. He and she together, Hermione and Birkin, were people of the same old tradition, the same withered deadening culture. And she, Ursula, was an intruder. So they always made her feel.

Hermione poured a little cream into a saucer. The simple way she assumed her rights in Birkin's room maddened and discouraged Ursula. There was a fatality about it, as if it were bound to be. Hermione lifted the cat and put the cream before him. He planted his two paws on the edge of the table and bent his gracious young head to drink.

'Siccuro che capisce italiano,' sang Hermione, 'non l'avrà dimenticato, la lingua della Mamma.'

She lifted the cat's head with her long, slow, white fingers, not letting him drink, holding him in her power. It was always the same, this joy in power she manifested, peculiarly in power over any male being. He blinked forbearingly, with a male, bored expression, licking his whiskers. Hermione laughed in her short, grunting fashion.

'Ecco, il bravo ragazzo, come e superbo, questo!'

She made a vivid picture, so calm and strange with the cat. She had a true static impressiveness, she was a social artist in some ways.

The cat refused to look at her, indifferently avoided her fingers, and began to drink again, his nose down to the cream, perfectly balanced, as he lapped with his odd little click.

'It's bad for him, teaching him to eat at table,' said Birkin.

'Yes,' said Hermione, easily assenting.

Then, looking down at the cat, she resumed her old, mocking, humorous sing-song.

'Ti imparano fare brutte cose, brutte cose – '

She lifted the Mino's white chin on her forefinger, slowly. The young cat looked round with a supremely forbearing air, avoided seeing anything, withdrew his chin, and began to wash his face with his paw. Hermione grunted her laughter, pleased.

'Bel giovanotto – ' she said.

The cat reached forward again and put his fine white paw on the edge of the saucer. Hermione lifted it down with delicate slowness. This deliberate, delicate carefulness of movement reminded Ursula of Gudrun.

'No! Non e permesso di mettere il zampino nel tondinetto. Non piace al babbo. Un signor gatto cosi selvatico –!'*

And she kept her finger on the softly planted paw of the cat, and her voice had the same whimsical, humorous note of bullying.

Ursula had her nose out of joint. She wanted to go away now. It all seemed no good. Hermione was established for ever, she herself was ephemeral and had not yet even arrived.

'I will go now,' she said suddenly.

---

* Addressing the cat, Hermoine here, talks of her intimacy with Berkin, and teasingly says (in It.): "they are asking you to do *bad* things".

Birkin looked at her almost in fear – he so dreaded her anger. 'But there is no need for such hurry,' he said.

'Yes,' she answered. 'I will go.' And turning to Hermione, before there was time to say any more, she held out her hand and said 'Good-bye.'

'Good-bye – ' sang Hermione, detaining the hand. 'Must you really go now?'

'Yes, I think I'll go,' said Ursula, her face set, and averted from Hermione's eyes.

'You think you will – '

But Ursula had got her hand free. She turned to Birkin with a quick, almost jeering: 'Good-bye,' and she was opening the door before he had time to do it for her.

When she got outside the house she ran down the road in fury and agitation. It was strange, the unreasoning rage and violence Hermione roused in her, by her very presence. Ursula knew she gave herself away to the other woman, she knew she looked ill-bred, uncouth, exaggerated. But she did not care. She only ran up the road, lest she should go back and jeer in the faces of the two she had left behind. For they outraged her.

<hr />

CHAPTER 23

Excurse

NEXT DAY Birkin sought Ursula out. It happened to be the half-day at the Grammar School. He appeared towards the end of the morning, and asked her, would she drive with him in the afternoon. She consented. But her face was closed and unresponding, and his heart sank.

The afternoon was fine and dim. He was driving the motor-car, and she sat beside him. But still her face was closed against him, unresponding. When she became like this, like a wall against him, his heart contracted.

His life now seemed so reduced, that he hardly cared any more. At moments it seemed to him he did not care a straw whether Ursula or Hermione or anybody else existed or did not exist. Why bother! Why strive for a coherent, satisfied life? Why not drift on in a series of accidents – like a picaresque novel? Why not? Why bother about human relationships? Why take them seriously – male or female? Why form any serious connections at all? Why not be casual, drifting along, taking all for what it was worth?

And yet, still, he was damned and doomed to the old effort at serious living.

'Look,' he said, 'what I bought.' The car was running along a broad white road, between autumn trees.

He gave her a little bit of screwed-up paper. She took it and opened it.

'How lovely,' she cried.

She examined the gift.

'How perfectly lovely!' she cried again. 'But why do you give them me?' She put the question offensively.

His face flickered with bored irritation. He shrugged his shoulders slightly.

'I wanted to,' he said, coolly.

'But why? Why should you?'

'Am I called on to find reasons?' he asked.

There was a silence, whilst she examined the rings that had been screwed up in the paper.

'I think they are *beautiful*,' she said, 'especially this. This is wonderful – '

It was a round opal, red and fiery, set in a circle of tiny rubies.

'You like that best?' he said.

'I think I do.'

'I like the sapphire,' he said.

'This?'

It was a rose-shaped, beautiful sapphire, with small brilliants.

'Yes,' she said, 'it is lovely.' She held it in the light. 'Yes, perhaps it if the best – '

'The blue – ' he said.

'Yes, wonderful – '

He suddenly swung the car out of the way of a farm-cart. It tilted on the bank. He was a careless driver, yet very quick. But Ursula was frightened. There was always that something regardless in him which terrified her. She suddenly felt he might kill her, by making some dreadful accident with the motor-car. For a moment she was stony with fear.

'Isn't it rather dangerous, the way you drive?' she asked him.

'No, it isn't dangerous,' he said. And then, after a pause: 'Don't you like the yellow ring at all?'

It was a squarish topaz set in a frame of steel, or some other similar mineral, finely wrought.

'Yes,' she said, 'I do like it. But why did you buy these rings?'

'I wanted them. They are second-hand.'

'You bought them for yourself?'

'No. Rings look wrong on my hands.'

'Why did you buy them then?'

'I bought them to give to you.'

'But why? Surely you ought to give them to Hermione! You belong to her.'

He did not answer. She remained with the jewels shut in her hand. She wanted to try them on her fingers, but something in her would not let her. And moreover, she was afraid her hands were too large, she shrank from the mortification of a failure to put them on any but her little finger. They travelled in silence through the empty lanes.

Driving in a motor-car excited her, she forgot his presence even.

'Where are we?' she asked suddenly.

'Not far from Worksop.'

'And where are we going?'

'Anywhere.'

It was the answer she liked.

She opened her hand to look at the rings. They gave her *such* pleasure, as they lay, the three circles, with their knotted jewels, entangled in her palm. She would have to try them on. She did so secretly, unwilling to let him see, so that he should not know her finger was too large for them. But he saw nevertheless. He always saw, if she wanted him not to. It was another of his hateful, watchful characteristics.

Only the opal, with its thin wire loop, would go on her ring finger. And she was superstitious. No, there was ill-portent enough, she would not accept this ring from him in pledge.

'Look,' she said, putting forward her hand, that was half-closed and shrinking. 'The others don't fit me.'

He looked at the red-glinting, soft stone, on her over-sensitive skin.

'Yes,' he said.

'But opals are unlucky, aren't they?' she said wistfully.

'No. I prefer unlucky things. Luck is vulgar. Who wants what *luck* would bring? I don't.'

'But why?' she laughed.

And, consumed with a desire to see how the other rings would look on her hand, she put them on her little finger.

'They can be made a little bigger,' he said.

'Yes,' she replied, doubtfully. And she sighed. She knew that, in accepting the rings, she was accepting a pledge. Yet fate seemed more than herself. She looked again at the jewels. They were very beautiful to her eyes – not as ornament, or wealth, but as tiny fragments of loveliness.

'I'm glad you bought them,' she said, putting her hand, half unwillingly, gently on his arm.

He smiled, slightly. He wanted her to come to him. But he was angry at the bottom of his soul, and indifferent. He knew she had a passion for him, really. But it was not finally interesting. There were depths of passion when one became impersonal and indifferent, unemotional. Whereas Ursula was still at the emotional personal level – always so abominably personal. He had taken her as he had never been taken himself. He had taken her at the roots of her darkness and shame – like a demon, laughing over the fountain of mystic corruption which was one of the sources of her being, laughing, shrugging, accepting, accepting finally. As for her, when would she so much go beyond herself as to accept him at the quick of death?

She now became quite happy. The motor-car ran on, the afternoon was soft and dim. She talked with lively interest, analysing people and their motives – Gudrun, Gerald. He answered vaguely. He was not very much interested any more in personalities and in people – people were all different, but they were all enclosed nowadays in a definite limitation, he said; there were only about two great ideas, two great streams of activity remaining, with various forms of reaction therefrom. The reactions were all varied in various people, but they followed a few great laws, and intrinsically there was no difference. They acted and reacted involuntarily according to a few great laws, and once the laws, the great principles, were known, people were no longer mystically interesting. They were all essentially alike, the differences were only variations on a theme. None of them transcended the given terms.

Ursula did not agree – people were still an adventure to her – but – perhaps not as much as she tried to persuade herself. Perhaps there was something mechanical, now, in her interest. Perhaps also her interest was destructive, her analysing was a real tearing to pieces. There was an under-space in her where she did not care for people and their idiosyncracies, even to destroy them. She seemed to touch for a moment this undersilence in herself, she became still, and she turned for a moment purely to Birkin.

'Won't it be lovely to go home in the dark?' she said. 'We might have tea rather late – shall we? – and have high tea? Wouldn't that be rather nice?'

'I promised to be at Shortlands for dinner,' he said.

'But – it doesn't matter – you can go tomorrow – '

'Hermione is there,' he said, in rather an uneasy voice. 'She is going away in two days. I suppose I ought to say good-bye to her. I shall never see her again.'

Ursula drew away, closed in a violent silence. He knitted his brows, and his eyes began to sparkle again in anger.

'You don't mind, do you?' he asked irritably.

'No, I don't care. Why should I? Why should I mind?' Her tone was jeering and offensive.

'That's what I ask myself,' he said; 'why *should* you mind! But you seem to.' His brows were tense with violent irritation.

'I *assure* you I don't, I don't mind in the least. Go where you belong it's what I want you to do.'

'Ah you fool!' he cried, 'with your "go where you belong." It's finished between Hermione and me. She means much more to *you,* if it comes to that, than she does to me. For you can only revolt in pure reaction from her – and to be her opposite is to be her counterpart.'

'Ah, opposite!' cried Ursula. 'I know your dodges. I am not taken in by your word-twisting. You belong to Hermione and her dead show.

Well, if you do, you do. I don't blame you. But then you've nothing to do with me.

In his inflamed, overwrought exasperation, he stopped the car, and they sat there, in the middle of the country lane, to have it out. It was a crisis of war between them, so they did not see the ridiculousness of their situation.

'If you weren't a fool, if only you weren't a fool,' he cried in bitter despair, 'you'd see that one could be decent, even when one has been wrong. I *was* wrong to go on all those years with Hermione – it was a deathly process. But after all, one can have a little human decency. But no, you would tear my soul out with your jealousy at the very mention of Hermione's name.'

'I jealous! *I* – jealous! You *are* mistaken if you think that. I'm not jealous in the least of Hermione, she is nothing to me, not *that!'* And Ursula snapped her fingers. 'No, it's you who are a liar. It's you who must return, like a dog to his vomit. It is what Hermione *stands for* that I *hate*. I *hate* it. It is lies, it is false, it is death. But you want it, you can't help it, you can't help yourself. You belong to that old, deathly way of living – then go back to it. But don't come to me, for I've nothing to do with it.'

And in the stress of her violent emotion, she got down from the car and went to the hedgerow, picking unconsciously some flesh-pink spindleberries, some of which were burst, showing their orange seeds.

'Ah, you are a fool,' he cried, bitterly, with some contempt.

'Yes, I am. I *am* a fool. And thank God for it. I'm too big a fool to swallow your cleverness. God be praised. You go to your women – go to them – they are your sort – you've always had a string of them trailing after you – and you always will. Go to your spiritual brides but don't come to me as well, because I'm not having any, thank you. You're not satisfied, are you? Your spiritual brides can't give you what you want, they aren't common and fleshy enough for you, aren't they?

So you come to me, and keep them in the background! You will marry me for daily use. But you'll keep yourself well provided with spiritual brides in the background. I know your dirty little game.' Suddenly a flame ran over her, and she stamped her foot madly on the road, and he winced, afraid that she would strike him. 'And *I, I'm* not spiritual enough, *I'm* not as spiritual as that Hermione –!' Her brows knitted, her eyes blazed like a tiger's. 'Then go to her, that's all I say, *go* to her, *go*. Ha, she spiritual – *spiritual,* she! A dirty materialist as she is. *She* spiritual? What does she care for, what is her spirituality? What if it?' Her fury seemed to blaze out and burn his face. He shrank a little. 'I tell you it's *dirt, dirt,* and nothing *but* dirt. And it's dirt you want, you crave for it. Spiritual! Is *that* spiritual, her bullying, her conceit, her sordid materialism? She's a fishwife, a fishwife, she is such a materialist. And all so sordid. What does she work out to, in the end, with all her social passion, as you call it. Social passion – what social passion has she? – show it me! – where is it? She wants petty, immediate *power,* she wants the illusion that she is a great woman, that is all. In her soul she's a devilish unbeliever, common as dirt. That's what she is at the bottom. And all the rest is pretence – but you love it. You love the sham spirituality, it's your food. And why? Because of the dirt underneath. Do you think I don't know the foulness of your sex life – and her's? – I do. And it's that foulness you want, you liar. Then have it, have it. You're such a liar.'

She turned away, spasmodically tearing the twigs of spindleberry from the hedge, and fastening them, with vibrating fingers, in the bosom of her coat.

He stood watching in silence. A wonderful tenderness burned in him, at the sight of her quivering, so sensitive fingers: and at the same time he was full of rage and callousness.

'This is a degrading exhibition,' he said coolly.

'Yes, degrading indeed,' she said. 'But more to me than to you.'

'Since you choose to degrade yourself,' he said. Again the flash came over her face, the yellow lights concentrated in her eyes.

'*You!*' she cried. 'You! You truth-lover! You purity-monger! It *stinks,* your truth and your purity. It stinks of the offal you. feed on, you scavenger dog, you eater of corpses. You are foul, *foul* and you must know it. Your purity, your candour, your goodness – yes, thank you, we've had some. What you are is a foul, deathly thing, obscene, that's what you are, obscene and perverse. You, and love! You may well say, you don't want love. No, you want *yourself,* and dirt, and death – that's what you want. You are so *perverse,* so death-eating. And then – '

'There's a bicycle coming,' he said, writhing under her loud denunciation.

She glanced down the road.

'I don't care,' she cried.

Nevertheless she was silent. The cyclist, having heard the voices raised in altercation, glanced curiously at the man, and the woman, and at the standing motor-car as he passed.

' – Afternoon,' he said, cheerfully.

'Good-afternoon,' replied Birkin coldly.

They were silent as the man passed into the distance.

A clearer look had come over Birkin's face. He knew she was in the main right. He knew he was perverse, so spiritual on the one hand, and in some strange way, degraded, on the other. But was she herself any better? Was anybody any better?

'It may all be true, lies and stink and all,' he said. 'But Hermione's spiritual intimacy is no rottener than your emotional-jealous intimacy. One can preserve the decencies, even to one's enemies: for one's own sake. Hermione is my enemy – to her last breath! That's why I must bow her off the field.'

'You! You and your enemies and your bows! A pretty picture you make of yourself. But it takes nobody in but yourself. I *jealous! I!* What I say,' her voice sprang into flame, 'I say because it is *true,* do you see, because you are *you,* a foul and false liar, a whited sepulchre. That's why I say it. And *you* hear it.'

'And be grateful,' he added, with a satirical grimace.

'Yes,' she cried, 'and if you have a spark of decency in you, be grateful.'

'Not having a spark of decency, however – ' he retorted.

'No,' she cried, 'you haven't a *spark.* And so you can go your way, and I'll go mine. It's no good, not the slightest. So you can leave me now, I don't want to go any further with you – leave me – '

'You don't even know where you are,' he said.

'Oh, don't bother, I assure you I shall be all right. I've got ten shillings in my purse, and that will take me back from anywhere *you* have brought me to.' She hesitated. The rings were still on her fingers, two on her little finger, one on her ring finger. Still she hesitated.

'Very good,' he said. 'The only hopeless thing is a fool.'

'You are quite right,' she said.

Still she hesitated. Then an ugly, malevolent look came over her face, she pulled the rings from her fingers, and tossed them at him. One touched his face, the others hit his coat, and they scattered into the mud.

'And take your rings,' she said, 'and go and buy yourself a female elsewhere – there are plenty to be had, who will be quite glad to share your spiritual mess, – or to have your physical mess, and leave your spiritual mess to Hermione.'

With which she walked away, desultorily, up the road. He stood motionless, watching her sullen, rather ugly walk. She was sullenly picking and pulling at the twigs of the hedge as she passed. She grew smaller, she seemed to pass out of his sight. A darkness came over his mind. Only a small, mechanical speck of consciousness hovered near him.

He felt tired and weak. Yet also he was relieved. He gave up his old position. He went and sat on the bank. No doubt Ursula was right. It was true, really, what she said. He knew that his spirituality was concomitant of a process of depravity, a sort of pleasure in self-destruction. There really *was* a certain stimulant in self-destruction, for him – especially when it was translated spiritually. But then he knew it – he knew it, and had done. And was not Ursula's way of emotional intimacy, emotional and physical, was it not just as dangerous as Hermione's abstract spiritual intimacy? Fusion, fusion, this horrible fusion of two beings, which every woman and most men insisted on, was it not nauseous and horrible anyhow, whether it was a fusion of the spirit or of the emotional body? Hermione saw herself as the perfect Idea, to which all men must come: And Ursula was the perfect Womb, the bath of birth, to which all men must come! And both were horrible. Why could they not remain individuals, limited by their own limits? Why this dreadful all-comprehensiveness, this hateful tyranny? Why not leave the other being free, why try to absorb, or melt, or merge? One might abandon oneself utterly to the *moments,* but not to any other being.

He could not bear to see the rings lying in the pale mud of the road. He picked them up, and wiped them unconsciously on his hands. They were the little tokens of the reality of beauty, the reality of happiness in warm creation. But he had made his hands all dirty and gritty.

There was a darkness over his mind. The terrible knot of consciousness that had persisted there like an obsession was broken, gone, his life was dissolved in darkness over his limbs and his body. But there was a point of anxiety in his heart now. He wanted her to come back. He breathed lightly and regularly like an infant, that breathes innocently, beyond the touch of responsibility.

She was coming back. He saw her drifting desultorily under the high hedge, advancing towards him slowly. He did not move, he did not look again. He was as if asleep, at peace, slumbering and utterly relaxed.

She came up and stood before him, hanging her head.

'See what a flower I found you,' she said, wistfully holding a piece of purple-red bell-heather under his face. He saw the clump of coloured bells, and the tree-like, tiny branch: also her hands, with their over fine, over-sensitive skin.

'Pretty!' he said, looking up at her with a smile, taking the flower. Everything had become simple again, quite simple, the complexity gone into nowhere. But he badly wanted to cry: except that he was weary and bored by emotion.

Then a hot passion of tenderness for her filled his heart. He stood up and looked into her face. It was new and oh, so delicate in its luminous wonder and fear. He put his arms round her, and she hid her face on his shoulder.

It was peace, just simple peace, as he stood folding her quietly there on the open lane. It was peace at last. The old, detestable world of tension had passed away at last, his soul was strong and at ease.

She looked up at him. The wonderful yellow light in her eyes now was soft and yielded, they were at peace with each other. He kissed her, softly, many, many times. A laugh came into her eyes.

'Did I abuse you?' she asked.

He smiled too, and took her hand, that was so soft and given. 'Never mind,' she said, 'it is all for the good.' He kissed her again, softly, many times.

'Isn't it?' she said.

'Certainly,' he replied. 'Wait! I shall have my own back.'

She laughed suddenly, with a wild catch in her voice, and flung her arms around him.

'You are mine, my love, aren't you?' she cried straining him close. 'Yes,' he said, softly.

His voice was so soft and final, she went very still, as if under a fate which had taken her. Yes, she acquiesced – but it was accomplished without her acquiescence. He was kissing her quietly, repeatedly, with a soft, still happiness that almost made her heart stop beating.

'My love!' she cried, lifting her face and looking with frightened, gentle wonder of bliss. Was it all real? But his eyes were beautiful and soft and immune from stress or excitement, beautiful and smiling lightly to her, smiling with her. She hid her face on his shoulder, hiding before him, because he could see her so completely. She knew he loved her, and she was afraid, she was in a strange element, a new heaven round about her. She wished he were passionate, because in passion she was at home. But this was so still and frail, as space is more frightening than force.

Again, quickly, she lifted her head.

'Do you love me?' she said, quickly, impulsively.

'Yes,' he replied, not heeding her motion, only her stillness.

She knew it was true. She broke away.

'So you ought,' she said, turning round to look at the road. 'Did you find the rings?'

'Yes.'

'Where are they?'

'In my pocket.'

She put her hand into his pocket and took them out.

She was restless.

'Shall we go?' she said.

'Yes,' he answered. And they mounted to the car once more, and left behind them this memorable battle-field.

They drifted through the wild, late afternoon, in a beautiful motion that was smiling and transcendent. His mind was sweetly at ease, the life flowed through him as from some new fountain, he was as if born out of the cramp of a womb.

'Are you happy?' she asked him, in her strange, delighted way. 'Yes,' he said.

'So am I,' she cried in sudden ecstasy, putting her arm round him and clutching him violently against her, as he steered the motor-car.

'Don't drive much more,' she said. 'I don't want you to be always doing something.'

'No,' he said. 'We'll finish this little trip, and then we'll be free.'

'We will, my love, we will,' she, cried in delight, kissing him as he turned to her.

He drove on in a strange new wakefulness, the tension of his consciousness broken. He seemed to be conscious all over, all his body awake with a simple, glimmering awareness, as if he had just come awake, like a thing that is born, like a bird when it comes out of an egg, into a new universe.

They dropped down a long hill in the dusk, and suddenly Ursula recognised on her right hand, below in the hollow, the form of Southwell Minster.

'Are we here!' she cried with pleasure.

The rigid, sombre, ugly cathedral was settling under the gloom of the coming night, as they entered the narrow town, the golden lights showed like slabs of revelation, in the shop-windows.

'Father came here with mother,' she said, 'when they first knew each other. He loves it – he loves the Minster. Do you?'

'Yes. It looks like quartz crystals sticking up out of the dark hollow. We'll have our high tea at the Saracen's Head.'

As they descended, they heard the Minster bells playing a hymn, when the hour had struck six.

> Glory to thee my God this night
> For all the blessings of the light –

So, to Ursula's ear, the tune fell out, drop by drop, from the unseen sky on to the dusky town. It was like dim, bygone centuries sounding. It was all so far off. She stood in the old yard of the inn, smelling of straw and stables and petrol. Above, she could see the first stars. What was it all? This was no actual world, it was the dream-world of one's childhood – a great circumscribed reminiscence. The world had become unreal. She herself was a strange, transcendent reality.

They sat together in a little parlour by the fire.

'Is it true?' she said, wondering.

'What?'

'Everything – is everything true?'

'The best is true,' he said, grimacing at her.

'Is it?' she replied, laughing, but unassured.

She looked at him. He seemed still so separate. New eyes were opened in her soul. She saw a strange creature from another world, in him. It was as if she were enchanted, and everything were metamorphosed. She recalled again the old magic of the Book of Genesis, where the sons of God saw the daughters of men, that they were fair. And he was one of these, one of these strange creatures from the beyond, looking down at her, and seeing she was fair.

He stood on the hearth-rug looking at her, at her face that was upturned exactly like a flower, a fresh, luminous flower, glinting faintly golden with the dew of the first light. And he was smiling faintly as if there were no speech in the world, save the silent delight of flowers in each other. Smilingly they delighted in each other's presence, pure presence, not to be thought of, even known. But his eyes had a faintly ironical contraction.

And she was drawn to him strangely, as in a spell. Kneeling on the hearth-rug before him, she put her arms round his loins, and put her face against his thigh. Riches! Riches! She was overwhelmed with a sense of a heavenful of riches.

'We love each other,' she said in delight.

'More than that,' he answered, looking down at her with his glimmering, easy face.

Unconsciously, with her sensitive fingertips, she was tracing the back of his thighs, following some mysterious life-flow there. She had discovered something, something more than wonderful, more wonderful than life itself. It was the strange mystery of his life-motion, there, at the back of the thighs, down the flanks. It was a strange reality of his being, the very stuff of being, there in the straight downflow of the thighs. It was here she discovered him one of the sons of God such as were in the beginning of the world, not a man, something other, something more.

This was release at last. She had had lovers, she had known passion. But this was neither love nor passion. It was the daughters of men coming back to the sons of God, the strange inhuman sons of God who are in the beginning.

Her face was now one dazzle of released, golden light, as she looked up at him, and laid her hands full on his thighs, behind, as he stood before her. He looked down at her with a rich bright brow like a diadem above his eyes. She was beautiful as a new marvellous flower opened at his knees, a paradisal flower she was, beyond womanhood, such a flower of luminousness. Yet something was tight and unfree in him. He did not like this crouching, this radiance – not altogether.

It was all achieved, for her. She had found one of the sons of God from the Beginning, and he had found one of the first most luminous daughters of men.

She traced with her hands the line of his loins and thighs, at the back, and a living fire ran through her, from him, darkly. It was a dark flood of electric passion she released from him, drew into herself. She had established a rich new circuit, a new current of passional electric energy, between the two of them, released from the darkest poles of the body and established in perfect circuit. It was a dark fire of electricity that rushed from him to her, and flooded them both with rich peace, satisfaction.

'My love,' she cried, lifting her face to him, her eyes, her mouth open in transport.

'My love,' he answered, bending and kissing her, always kissing her.

She closed her hands over the full, rounded body of his loins, as he stooped over her, she seemed to touch the quick of the mystery of darkness that was bodily him. She seemed to faint beneath, and he seemed to faint, stooping over her. It was a perfect passing away for both of them, and at the same time the most intolerable accession into being, the marvellous fullness of immediate gratification, overwhelming, out-flooding from the source of the deepest life-force, the darkest, deepest, strangest life-source of the human body, at the back and base of the loins.

After a lapse of stillness, after the rivers of strange dark fluid richness had passed over her, flooding, carrying away her mind and flooding down her spine and down her knees, past her feet, a strange flood, sweeping away everything and leaving her an essential new being, she was left quite free, she was free in complete ease, her complete self. So she rose, stilly and blithe, smiling at him. He stood before her, glimmering, so awfully real, that her heart almost stopped beating. He stood there in his strange, whole body, that had its marvelous fountains, like the bodies of the sons of God who were in the beginning. There were strange fountains of his body, more mysterious and potent than any she had imagined or known, more satisfying, ah, finally, mystically-physically satisfying. She had thought there was no source deeper than the phallic source. And now, behold, from the smitten rock of the man's body, from the strange marvellous flanks and thighs, deeper, further in mystery than the phallic source, came the floods of ineffable darkness and ineffable riches.

They were glad, and they could forget perfectly. They laughed, and went to the meal provided. There was a venison pasty, of all things, a large broad-faced cut ham, eggs and cresses and red beet-root, and medlars and apple-tart, and tea.

'What *good* things!' she cried with pleasure. 'How noble it looks! shall I pour out the tea? – '

She was usually nervous and uncertain at performing these public duties, such as giving tea. But today she forgot, she was at her ease, entirely forgetting to have misgivings. The tea-pot poured beautifully from a proud slender spout. Her eyes were warm with smiles as she gave him his tea. She had learned at last to be still and perfect.

'Everything is ours,' she said to him.

'Everything,' he answered.

She gave a queer little crowing sound of triumph.

'I'm so glad!' she cried, with unspeakable relief.

'So am I,' he said. 'But I'm thinking we'd better get out of our responsibilities as quick as we can.'

'What responsibilities?' she asked, wondering.

'We must drop our jobs, like a shot.'

A new understanding dawned into her face.

'Of course,' she said, 'there's that.'

'We must get out,' he said. 'There's nothing for it but to get out, quick.'

She looked at him doubtfully across the table.

'But where?' she said.

'I don't know,' he said. 'We'll just wander about for a bit.'

Again she looked at him quizzically.

'I should be perfectly happy at the Mill,' she said:

'It's very near the old thing,' he said. 'Let us wander a bit.'

His voice could be so soft and happy-go-lucky, it went through her veins like an exhilaration. Nevertheless she dreamed of a valley, and wild gardens, and peace. She had a desire too for splendour – an aristocratic extravagant splendour. Wandering seemed to her like restlessness, dissatisfaction.

'Where will you wander to?' she asked.

'I don't know. I feel as if I would just meet you and we'd set off – just towards the distance.'

'But where can one go?' she asked anxiously. 'After all, there is only the world, and none of it is very distant.'

'Still,' he said, 'I should like to go with you – nowhere. It would be rather wandering just to nowhere. That's the place to get to – nowhere. One wants to wander away from the world's somewheres, into our own nowhere.'

Still she meditated.

'You see, my love,' she said, 'I'm so afraid that while we are only people, we've got to take the world that's given – because there isn't any other.'

'Yes there is,' he said. 'There's somewhere where we can be free – somewhere where one needn't wear much clothes – none even – where one meets a few people who have gone through enough, and can take things for granted – where you be yourself, without bothering. There is somewhere – there are one or two people – '

'But where –?' she sighed.

'Somewhere – anywhere. Let's wander off. That's the thing to do let's wander off.'

'Yes – ' she said, thrilled at the thought of travel. But to her it was only travel.

'To be free,' he said: 'To be free, in a free place, with a few other people!'

'Yes,' she said wistfully. Those 'few other people' depressed her.

'It isn't really a locality, though,' he said. 'It's a perfected relation between you and me, and others – the perfect relation – so that we are free together.'

'It is, my love, isn't it,' she said. 'It's you and me. It's you and me, isn't it?' She stretched out her arms to him. He went across and stooped to kiss her face. Her arms closed round him again, her hands spread upon his shoulders, moving slowly there, moving slowly on his back, down his back slowly, with a strange recurrent, rhythmic motion, yet moving slowly down, pressing mysteriously over his loins, over his flanks. The sense of the awfulness of riches that could never be impaired flooded her mind like a swoon, a death in most marvellous possession, mystic-sure. She possessed him so utterly and intolerably, that she herself lapsed out. And yet she was only sitting still in the chair, with her hands pressed upon him, and lost.

Again he softly kissed her.

'We shall never go apart again,' he murmured quietly. And she did not speak, but only pressed her hands firmer down upon the source of darkness in him.

They decided, when they woke again from the pure swoon, to write their resignations from the world of work there and then. She wanted this.

He rang the bell, and ordered note-paper without a printed address. The waiter cleared the table.

'Now then,' he said, 'yours first. Put your home address, and the date – then "Director of Education, Town Hall – Sir – " Now then! – I don't know how one really stands – I suppose one could get out of it in less than month – Anyhow "Sir – I beg to resign my post as class-mistress in the Willey Green Grammar School. I should be very grateful if you would liberate me as soon as possible, without waiting for the expiration of the month's notice." That'll do. Have you got it? Let me look. "Ursula Brangwen." Good! Now I'll write mine. I ought to give them three months, but I can plead health. I can arrange it all right.'

He sat and wrote out his formal resignation.

'Now,' he said, when the envelopes were sealed and addressed, 'shall we post them here, both together? I know Jackie will say, "Here's a coincidence!" when he receives them in all their identity. Shall we let him say it, or not?'

'I don't care,' she said.

'No –?' he said, pondering.

'It doesn't matter, does it?' she said.

'Yes,' he replied. 'Their imaginations shall not work on us. I'll post yours here, mine after. I cannot be implicated in their imaginings.'

He looked at her with his strange, non-human singleness.

'Yes, you are right,' she said.

She lifted her face to him, all shining and open. It was as if he might enter straight into the source of her radiance. His face became a little distracted.

'Shall we go?' he said.

'As you like,' she replied.

They were soon out of the little town, and running through the uneven lanes of the country. Ursula nestled near him, into his constant warmth, and watched the pale-lit revelation racing ahead, the visible night. Sometimes it was a wide old road, with grass-spaces on either side, flying magic and elfin in the greenish illumination, sometimes it was trees looming overhead, sometimes it was bramble bushes, sometimes the walls of a crew-yard and the butt of a barn.

'Are you going to Shortlands to dinner?' Ursula asked him suddenly. He started.

'Good God!' he said. 'Shortlands! Never again. Not that. Besides we should be too late.'

'Where are we going then – to the Mill?'

'If you like. Pity to go anywhere on this good dark night. Pity to come out of it, really. Pity we can't stop in the good darkness. It is better than anything ever would be – this good immediate darkness.'

She sat wondering. The car lurched and swayed. She knew there was no leaving him, the darkness held them both and contained them, it was not to be surpassed Besides she had a full mystic knowledge of his suave loins of darkness, dark-clad and suave, and in this knowledge there was some of the inevitability and the beauty of fate, fate which one asks for, which one accepts in full.

He sat still like an Egyptian Pharoah, driving the car. He felt as if he were seated in immemorial potency, like the great carven statues of real Egypt, as real and as fulfilled with subtle strength, as these are, with a vague inscrutable smile on the lips. He knew what it was to have the strange and magical current of force in his back and loins, and down his legs, force so perfect that it stayed him immobile, and left his face subtly, mindlessly smiling. He knew what it was to be awake and potent in that other basic mind, the deepest physical mind. And from this source he had a pure and magic control, magical, mystical, a force in darkness, like electricity.

It was very difficult to speak, it was so perfect to sit in this pure living silence, subtle, full of unthinkable knowledge and unthinkable force, upheld immemorially in timeless force, like the immobile, supremely potent Egyptians, seated forever in their living, subtle silence.

'We need not go home,' he said. 'This car has seats that let down and make a bed, and we can lift the hood.'

She was glad and frightened. She cowered near to him.

'But what about them at home?' she said.

'Send a telegram.'

Nothing more was said. They ran on in silence. But with a sort of second consciousness he steered the car towards a destination. For he had the free intelligence to direct his own ends. His arms and his breast and his head were rounded and living like those of the Greek, he had not the unawakened straight arms of the Egyptian, nor the sealed; slumbering head. A lambent intelligence played secondarily above his pure Egyptian concentration in darkness.

They came to a village that lined along the road. The car crept slowly along, until he saw the post-office. Then he pulled up.

'I will send a telegram to your father,' he said. 'I will merely say "spending the night in town," shall I?'

'Yes,' she answered. She did not want to be disturbed into taking thought.

She watched him move into the post-office. It was also a shop, she saw. Strange, he was. Even as he went into the lighted, public place he remained dark and magic, the living silence seemed the body of reality in him, subtle, potent, indiscoverable. There he was! In a strange uplift of elation she saw him, the being never to be revealed, awful in its potency, mystic and real. This dark, subtle reality of him, never to be translated, liberated her into perfection, her own perfected being. She too was dark and fulfilled in silence.

He came out, throwing some packages into the car.

'There is some bread, and cheese, and raisins, and apples, and hard chocolate,' he said, in his voice that was as if laughing, because of the unblemished stillness and force which was the reality in him. She would have to touch him. To speak, to see, was nothing. It was a travesty to look and to comprehend the man there. Darkness and silence must fall perfectly on her, then she could know mystically, in unrevealed touch. She must lightly, mindlessly connect with him, have the knowledge which is death of knowledge, the reality of surety in not-knowing;

Soon they had run on again into the darkness. She did not ask where they were going, she did not care. She sat in a fullness and a pure potency that was like apathy, mindless and immobile. She was next to him, and hung in a pure rest, as a star is hung, balanced unthinkably. Still there remained a dark lambency of anticipation. She would touch him. With perfect fine finger-tips of reality she would touch the reality in him, the suave, pure, untranslatable reality of his loins of darkness. To touch, mindlessly in darkness to come in pure touching upon the living reality of him, his suave perfect loins and thighs of darkness, this was her sustaining anticipation.

And he too waited in the magical steadfastness of suspense, for her to take this knowledge of him as he had taken it of her. He knew her darkly, with the fullness of dark knowledge. Now she would know him, and he too would be liberated. He would be night-free, like an Egyptian, steadfast in perfectly suspended equilibrium, pure mystic nodality of physical being. They would give each other this star-equilibrium which alone is freedom.

She saw that they were running among trees – great old trees with dying bracken undergrowth. The palish, gnarled trunks showed ghostly, and like old priests in the hovering distance, the fern rose magical and mysterious. It was a night all darkness, with low cloud. The motor-car advanced slowly.

'Where are we?' she whispered.

'In Sherwood Forest.'

It was evident he knew the place. He drove softly, watching. Then they came to a green road between the trees. They turned cautiously round, and were advancing between the oaks of the forest, down a green lane. The green lane widened into a little circle of grass, where there was a small trickle of water at the bottom of a sloping bank. The car stopped.

'We will stay here,' he said, 'and put out the lights.'

He extinguished the lamps at once, and it was pure night, with shadows of trees like realities of other, nightly being. He threw a rug on to the bracken, and they sat in stillness and mindless silence. There were faint sounds from the wood, but no disturbance, no possible disturbance, the world was under a strange ban, a new mystery had supervened. They threw off their clothes, and he gathered her to him, and found her, found the pure lambent reality of her forever-invisible flesh. Quenched, inhuman, his fingers upon her unrevealed nudity were the fingers of silence upon silence, the body of mysterious night upon the body of mysterious night, the night masculine and feminine, never to be seen with the eye, or known with the mind, only known as a palpable revelation of living otherness.

She had her desire of him, she touched, she received the maximum of unspeakable communication in touch, dark, subtle, positively silent, a magnificent gift and give again, a perfect acceptance and yielding, a mystery, the reality of that which can never be known, vital, sensual reality that can never be transmuted into mind content, but remains outside, living body of darkness and silence and subtlety, the mystic body of reality. She had her desire fulfilled. He had his desire fulfilled. For she was to him what he was to her, the immemorial magnificence of mystic, palpable, real otherness.

They slept the chilly night through under the hood of the car, a night of unbroken sleep. It was already high day when he awoke. They looked at each other and laughed, then looked away, filled with darkness and secrecy. Then they kissed and remembered the magnificence of the night. It was so magnificent, such an inheritance of a universe of dark reality, that they were afraid to seem to remember. They hid away the remembrance and the knowledge.

CHAPTER 24

Death and Love

THOMAS CRICH died slowly, terribly slowly. It seemed impossible to everybody that the thread of life could be drawn out so thin, and yet not break. The sick man lay unutterably weak and spent, kept alive by morphia and by drinks, which he sipped slowly. He was only half conscious – a thin strand of consciousness linking the darkness of death with the light of day. Yet his will was unbroken, he was integral, complete. Only he must have perfect stillness about him.

Any presence but that of the nurses was a strain and an effort to him now. Every morning Gerald went into the room, hoping to find his father passed away at last. Yet always he saw the same transparent face, the same dread dark hair on the waxen forehead, and the awful, inchoate dark eyes, which seemed to be decomposing into formless darkness, having only a tiny grain of vision within them.

And always, as the dark, inchoate eyes turned to him, there passed through Gerald's bowels a burning stroke of revolt, that seemed to resound through his whole being, threatening to break his mind with its clangour, and making him mad.

Every morning, the son stood there, erect and taut with life, gleaming in his blondness. The gleaming blondness of his strange, imminent being put the father into a fever of fretful irritation. He could not bear to meet the uncanny, downward look of Gerald's blue eyes. But it was only for a moment. Each on the brink of departure, the father and son looked at each other, then parted.

For a long time Gerald preserved a perfect sang froid, he remained quite collected. But at last, fear undermined him. He was afraid of some horrible collapse in himself. He had to stay and see this thing through. Some perverse will made him watch his father drawn over the borders of life. And yet, now, every day, the great red-hot stroke of horrified fear through the bowels of the son struck a further inflammation. Gerald went about all day with a tendency to cringe, as if there were the point of a sword of Damocles pricking the nape of his neck.

There was no escape – he was bound up with his father, he had to see him through. And the father's will never relaxed or yielded to death. It would have to snap when death at last snapped it, – if it did not persist after a physical death. In the same way, the will of the son never yielded. He stood firm and immune, he was outside this death and this dying.

It was a trial by ordeal. Could he stand and see his father slowly dissolve and disappear in death, without once yielding his will, without once relenting before the omnipotence of death. Like a Red Indian undergoing torture, Gerald would experience the whole process of slow death without wincing or flinching. He even triumphed in it. He somehow *wanted* this death, even forced it. It was as if he himself were dealing the death, even when he most recoiled in horror. Still, he would deal it, he would triumph through death.

But in the stress of this ordeal, Gerald too lost his hold on the outer, daily life. That which was much to him, came to mean nothing. Work, pleasure – it was all left behind. He went on more or less mechanically with his business, but this activity was all extraneous. The real activity was this ghastly wrestling for death in his own soul. And his own will should triumph. Come what might, he would not bow down or submit or acknowledge a master. He had no master in death.

But as the fight went on, and all that he had been and was continued to be destroyed, so that life was a hollow shell all round him, roaring and clattering like the sound of the sea, a noise in which he participated externally, and inside this hollow shell was all the darkness and fearful space of death, he knew he would have to find reinforcements, otherwise he would collapse inwards upon the great dark void which circled at the centre of his soul. His will held his outer life, his outer mind, his outer being unbroken and unchanged. But the pressure was too great. He would have to find something to make good the equilibrium. Something must come with him into the hollow void of death in his soul, fill it up, and so equalise the pressure within to the pressure without. For day by day he felt more and more like a bubble filled with darkness, round which whirled the iridescence of his consciousness, and upon which the pressure of the outer world, the outer life, roared vastly.

In this extremity his instinct led him to Gudrun. He threw away everything now – he only wanted the relation established with her. He would follow her to the studio, to be near her, to talk to her. He would stand about the room, aimlessly picking up the implements, the lumps of clay, the little figures she had cast – they were whimsical and grotesque-looking at them without perceiving them. And she felt him following her, dogging her heels like a doom. She held away from him, and yet she knew he drew always a little nearer, a little nearer.

'I say,' he said to her one evening, in an odd, unthinking, uncertain way, 'won't you stay to dinner tonight? I wish you would.'

She started slightly. He spoke to her like a man making a request of another man.

'They'll be expecting me at home,' she said.

'Oh, they won't mind, will they?' he said. 'I should be awfully glad if you'd stay.'

Her long silence gave consent at last.

'I'll tell Thomas, shall I?' he said.

'I must go almost immediately after dinner,' she said.

It was a dark, cold evening. There was no fire in the drawing-room, they sat in the library: He was mostly silent, absent, and Winfred talked little. But when Gerald did rouse himself, he smiled and was pleasant and ordinary with her. Then there came over him again the long blanks, of which he was not aware.

She was very much attracted by him. He looked so preoccupied, and his strange, blank silences, which she could not read, moved her and made her wonder over him, made her feel reverential towards him.

But he was very kind. He gave her the best things at the table, he had a bottle of slightly sweet, delicious golden wine brought out for dinner, knowing she would prefer it to the burgundy. She felt herself esteemed, needed almost.

As they took coffee in the library, there was a soft, very soft knocking at the door. He started, and called 'Come in.' The timbre of his voice, like something vibrating at high pitch, unnerved Gudrun. A nurse in white entered, half hovering in the doorway like a shadow. She was very good-looking, but strangely enough, shy and self-mistrusting.

'The doctor would like to speak to you, Mr Crich,' she said, in her low, discreet voice.

'The doctor!' he said, starting up. 'Where is he?'

'He is in the dining-room.'

'Tell him I'm coming.'

He drank up his coffee, and followed the nurse, who had dissolved like a shadow.

'Which nurse was that?' asked Gudrun.

'Miss Inglis – I like her best,' replied Winifred.

After a while Gerald came back, looking absorbed by his own thoughts, and having some of that tension and abstraction which is seen in a slightly drunken man. He did not say what the doctor had wanted him for, but stood before the fire, with his hands behind his back, and his face open and as if rapt. Not that he was really thinking – he was only arrested in pure suspense inside himself, and thoughts wafted through his mind without order.

'I must go now and see Mama,' said Winifred, 'and see Dadda before he goes to sleep.'

She bade them both good-night.

Gudrun also rose to take her leave.

'You needn't go yet, need you?' said Gerald, glancing quickly at the lock.' It is early yet. I'll walk down with you when you go. Sit down, don't hurry away.

Gudrun sat down, as if, absent as he was, his will had power over her. She felt almost mesmerised. He was strange to her, something unknown. What was he thinking, what was he feeling, as he stood there so rapt, saying nothing? He kept her – she could feel that. He would not let her go. She watched him in humble submissiveness.

'Had the doctor anything new to tell you?' she asked, softly, at length, with that gentle, timid sympathy which touched a keen fibre in his heart. He lifted his eyebrows with a negligent, indifferent expression.

'No – nothing new,' he replied, as if the question were quite casual, trivial. 'He says the pulse is very weak indeed, very intermittent – but that doesn't necessarily mean much, you know.'

He looked down at her. Her eyes were dark and soft and unfolded, with a stricken look that roused him.

'No,' she murmured at length. 'I don't understand anything about these things.'

'Just as well not,' he said. 'I say, won't you have a cigarette? – do!' He quickly fetched the box, and held her a light. Then he stood before her on the hearth again.

'No,' he said, 'we've never had much illness in the house, either – not till father.' He seemed to meditate a while. Then looking down at her, with strangely communicative blue eyes, that filled her with dread, he continued: 'It's something you don't reckon with, you know, till it is there. And then you realise that it was there all the time – it was always there – you understand what I mean? – the possibility of this incurable illness, this slow death.'

He moved his. feet uneasily on the marble hearth, and put his cigarette to his mouth, looking up at the ceiling.

'I know,' murmured Gudrun: 'it is dreadful.'

He smoked without knowing. Then he took the cigarette from his lips, bared his teeth, and putting the tip of his tongue between his teeth spat off a grain of tobacco, turning slightly aside, like a man who is alone, or who is lost in thought.

'I don't know what the effect actually if, on one,' he said, and again he looked down at her. Her eyes were dark and stricken with knowledge, looking into his. He saw her submerged, and he turned aside his face. 'But I absolutely am not the same. There's nothing left, if you understand what I mean. You seem to be clutching at the void – and at the same time you are void yourself. And so you don't know what to *do.*'

'No,' she murmured. A heavy thrill ran down her nerves, heavy, almost pleasure, almost pain. 'What can be done?' she added.

He turned, and flipped the ash from his cigarette on to the great marble hearth-stones, that lay bare in the room, without fender or bar.

'I don't know, I'm sure,' he replied. 'But I do think you've got to find some way of resolving the situation – not because you want to, but because you've *got* to, otherwise you're done. The whole of everything, and yourself included, is just on the point of caving in, and you are just holding it up with your hands. Well, it's a situation that obviously can't continue. You can't stand holding the roof up with your hands, for ever. You know that sooner or later you'll *have* to let go. Do you understand what I mean? And so something's got to be done, or there's a universal collapse – as far as you yourself are concerned.'

He shifted slightly on the hearth, crunching a cinder under his heel. He looked down at it. Gudrun was aware of the beautiful old marble panels of the fireplace, swelling softly carved, round him and above him. She felt as if she were caught at last by fate, imprisoned in some horrible and fatal trap.

'But what *can* be done?' she murmured humbly. 'You must use me if I can be of any help at all – but how can I? I don't see how I *can* help you.'

He looked down at her critically.

'I don't want you to *help,*' he said, slightly irritated, 'because there's nothing to be *done.* I only want sympathy, do you see: I want somebody I can talk to sympathetically. That eases the strain. And there *is* nobody to talk to sympathetically. That's the curious thing. There *is* nobody. There's Rupert Birkin. But then he *isn't* sympathetic, he wants to *dictate*. And that is no use whatsoever.'

She was caught in a strange snare. She looked down at her hands.

Then there was the sound of the door softly opening. Gerald started. He was chagrined. It was his starting that really startled Gudrun. Then he went forward, with quick, graceful, intentional courtesy.

'Oh, mother!' he said. 'How nice of you to come down. How are you?'

The elderly woman, loosely and bulkily wrapped in a purple gown, came forward silently, slightly hulked, as usual. Her son was at her side. He pushed her up a chair, saying 'You know Miss Brangwen, don't you?'

The mother glanced at Gudrun indifferently.

'Yes,' she said. Then she turned her wonderful, forget-me-not blue eyes up to her son, as she slowly sat down in the chair he had brought her.

'I came to ask you about your father,' she said, in her rapid, scarcely audible voice. 'I didn't know you had company.'

'No? Didn't Winifred tell you? Miss Brangwen stayed to dinner, to make us a little more lively – '

Mrs Crich turned slowly round to Gudrun, and looked at her, but with unseeing eyes.

'I'm afraid it would be no treat to her.' Then she turned again to her son. 'Winifred tells me the doctor had something to say about your father. What is it?'

'Only that the pulse is very weak – misses altogether a good many times – so that he might not last the night out,' Gerald replied.

Mrs Crich sat perfectly impassive, as if she had not heard. Her bulk seemed hunched in the chair, her fair hair hung slack over her ears. But her skin was clear and fine, her hands, as she sat with them forgotten and folded, were quite beautiful, full of potential energy. A great mass of energy seemed decaying up in that silent, hulking form.

She looked up at her son, as he stood, keen and soldierly, near to her. Her eyes were most wonderfully blue, bluer than forget-me-nots. She seemed to have a certain confidence in Gerald, and to feel a certain motherly mistrust of him.

'How are *you?*' she muttered, in her strangely quiet voice, as if nobody should hear but him. 'You're not getting into a state, are you? You're not letting it make you hysterical?'

The curious challenge in the last words startled Gudrun.

'I don't think so, mother,' he answered, rather coldly cheery. 'Somebody's got to see it through, you know.'

'Have they? Have they?' answered his mother rapidly. 'Why should *you* take it on yourself? What have you got to do, seeing it through. It will see itself through. You are not needed.'

'No, I don't suppose I can do any good,' he answered. 'It's just how it affects us, you see.'

'You like to be affected – don't you? It's quite nuts for you? You would have to be important. You have no need to stop at home. Why don't you go away!'

These sentences, evidently the ripened grain of many dark hours, took Gerald by surprise.

'I don't think it's any good going away now, mother, at the last minute,' he said, coldly.

'You take care,' replied his mother. 'You mind *yourself* – that's your business. You take too much on yourself. You mind *yourself,* or you'll find yourself in Queer Street, that's what will happen to you. You're hysterical, always were.'

'I'm all right, mother,' he said. 'There's no need to worry about *me,* I assure you.'

'Let the dead bury their dead – don't go and bury yourself along with them – that's what I tell you. I know you well enough.'

He did not answer this, not knowing what to say. The mother sat bunched up in silence, her beautiful white hands, that had no rings whatsoever, clasping the pommels of her arm-chair.

'You can't do it,' she said, almost bitterly. 'You haven't the nerve. You're as weak as a cat, really – always were. Is this young woman staying here?'

'No,' said Gerald. 'She is going home tonight.'

'Then she'd better have the dog-cart. Does she go far?'

'Only to Beldover.'

'Ah!' The elderly woman never looked at Gudrun, yet she seemed to take knowledge of her presence.

'You are inclined to take too much on yourself, Gerald,' said the mother, pulling herself to her feet, with a little difficulty.

'Will you go, mother?' he asked, politely.

'Yes, I'll go up again,' she replied. Turning to Gudrun; she bade her

'Good-night.' Then she went slowly to the door, as if she were unaccustomed to walking. At the door she lifted her face to him, implicitly. He kissed her.

'Don't come any further with me,' she said, in her barely audible voice. 'I don't want you any further.'

He bade her good-night, watched her across to the stairs and mount slowly. Then he closed the door and came back to Gudrun. Gudrun rose also, to go.

'A queer being, my mother,' he said.

'Yes,' replied Gudrun.

'She has her own thoughts.'

'Yes,' said Gudrun.

Then they were silent.

'You want to go?' he asked. 'Half a minute, I'll just have a horse put in – '

'No,' said Gudrun. 'I want to walk.'

He had promised to walk with her down the long, lonely mile of drive, and she wanted this.

'You might *just* as well drive,' he said.

'I'd *much rather* walk,' she asserted, with emphasis.

'You would! Then I will come along with you. You know where your things are? I'll put boots on.'

He put on a cap, and an overcoat over his evening dress. They went out into the night.

'Let us light a cigarette,' he said, stopping in a sheltered angle of the porch. 'You have one too.'

So with the scent of tobacco on the night air, they set off down the dark drive that ran between close-cut hedges through sloping meadows.

He wanted to put his arm round her. If he could put his arm round her and draw her against him as they walked, he would equilibriate himself. For now he felt like a pair of scales, the half of which tips down and down into an indefinite void. He must recover some sort of balance. And here was the hope and the perfect recovery.

Blind to her, thinking only of himself, he slipped his arm softly round her waist, and drew her to him. Her heart fainted, feeling herself taken. But then, his arm was so strong, she quailed under its powerful close grasp. She died a little death, and was drawn against him as they walked down the stormy darkness. He seemed to balance her perfectly in opposition to himself, in their dual motion of walking. So, suddenly, he was liberated and perfect, strong, heroic.

He put his hand to his mouth and threw his cigarette away, a gleaming point, into the unseen hedge. Then he was quite free to balance her.

'That's better,' he said, with exultancy.

The exultation in his voice was like a sweetish, poisonous drug to her. Did she then mean so much to him! She sipped the poison.

'Are you happier?' she asked, wistfully.

'Much better,' he said, in the same exultant voice, 'and I was rather far gone.'

She nestled against him. He felt her all soft and warm, she was the rich, lovely substance of his being. The warmth and motion of her walk suffused through him wonderfully.

'I'm *so* glad if I help you,' she said.

'Yes,' he answered. 'There's nobody else could do it, if you wouldn't.'

'That is true,' she said to herself, with a thrill of strange, fatal elation. As they walked, he seemed to lift her nearer and nearer to himself, till she moved upon the firm vehicle of his body.

He was so strong, so sustaining, and he could not be opposed. She drifted along in a wonderful interfusion of physical motion, down the dark, blowy hillside. Far across shone the little yellow lights of Beldover, many of them, spread in a thick patch on another dark hill.

But he and she were walking in perfect, isolated darkness, outside the world.

'But how much do you care for me!' came her voice, almost querulous. 'You see, I don't know, I don't understand!'

'How much!' His voice rang with a painful elation. 'I don't know either – but everything.' He was startled by his own declaration. It was true. So he stripped himself of every safeguard, in making this admission to her. He cared everything for her – she was everything.

'But I can't believe it,' said her low voice, amazed, trembling. She was trembling with doubt and exultance. This was the thing she wanted to hear, only this. Yet now she heard it, heard the strange clapping vibration of truth in his voice as he said it, she could not believe. She could not believe – she did not believe. Yet she believed, triumphantly, with fatal exultance.

'Why not?' he said. 'Why don't you believe it? It's true. It is true, as we stand at this moment – ' he stood still with her in the wind; 'I care for nothing on earth, or in heaven, outside this spot where we are. And it isn't my own presence I care about, it is all yours. I'd sell my soul a hundred times – but I couldn't bear not to have you here. I couldn't bear to be alone. My brain would burst. It is true.' He drew her closer to him, with definite movement.

'No,' she murmured, afraid. Yet this was what she wanted. Why did she so lose courage?

They resumed their strange walk. They were such strangers – and yet they were so frightfully, unthinkably near. It was like a madness. Yet it was what she wanted, it was what she wanted. They had descended the hill, and now they were coming to the square arch where the road passed under the colliery railway. The arch, Gudrun knew, had walls of squared stone, mossy on one side with water that trickled down, dry on the other side. She had stood under it to hear the train rumble thundering over the logs overhead. And she knew that under this dark and lonely bridge the young colliers stood in the darkness with their sweethearts, in rainy weather. And so she wanted to stand under the bridge with *her* sweetheart, and be kissed under the bridge in the invisible darkness. Her steps dragged as she drew near.

So, under the bridge, they came to a standstill, and he lifted her upon his breast. His body vibrated taut and powerful as he closed upon her and crushed her, breathless and dazed and destroyed, crushed her upon his breast. Ah, it was terrible, and perfect. Under this bridge, the colliers pressed their lovers to their breast. And now, under the bridge, the master of them all pressed her to himself! And how much more powerful and terrible was his embrace than theirs, how much more concentrated and supreme his love was, than theirs in the same sort! She felt she would swoon, die, under the vibrating, inhuman tension of his arms and his body – she would pass away. Then the unthinkable high vibration slackened and became more undulating. He slackened and drew her with him to stand with his back to the wall.

She was almost unconscious. So the colliers' lovers would stand with their backs to the walls, holding their sweethearts and kissing them as she was being kissed. Ah, but would their kisses be fine and powerful as the kisses of the firm-mouthed master? Even the keen, short-cut moustache – the colliers would not have that.

And the colliers' sweethearts would, like herself, hang their heads back limp over their shoulder, and look out from the dark archway, at the close patch of yellow lights on the unseen hill in the distance, or at the vague form of trees, and at the buildings of the colliery wood-yard, in the other direction.

His arms were fast around her, he seemed to be gathering her into himself, her warmth, her softness, her adorable weight, drinking in the suffusion of her physical being, avidly. He lifted her, and seemed to pour her into himself, like wine into a cup.

'This is worth everything,' he said, in a strange, penetrating voice.

So she relaxed, and seemed to melt, to flow into him, as if she were some infinitely warm and precious suffusion filling into his veins, like an intoxicant. Her arms were round his neck, he kissed her and held her perfectly suspended, she was all slack and flowing into him, and he was the firm, strong cup that receives the wine of her life. So she lay cast upon him, stranded, lifted up against him, melting and melting under his kisses, melting into his limbs and bones, as if he were soft iron becoming surcharged with hey electric life.

Till she seemed to swoon, gradually her mind went, and she passed away, everything in her was melted down and fluid, and she lay still, become contained by him, sleeping in him as lightning sleeps in a pure, soft stone. So she was passed away and gone in him, and he was perfected.

When she opened her eyes again, and saw the patch of lights in the distance, it seemed to her strange that the world still existed, that she was standing under the bridge resting her head on Gerald's breast. Gerald – who was he? He was the exquisite adventure, the desirable unknown to her.

She looked up, and in the darkness saw his face above her, his shapely, male face. There seemed a faint, white light emitted from him, a white aura, as if he were visitor from the unseen. She reached up, like Eve reaching to the apples on the tree of knowledge, and she kissed him, though her passion was a transcendent fear of the thing he was, touching his face with her infinitely delicate, encroaching wondering fingers. Her fingers went over the mould of his face, over his features. How perfect and foreign he was – ah how dangerous! Her soul thrilled with complete knowledge. This was the glistening, forbidden apple, this face of a man. She kissed him, putting her fingers over his face, his eyes, his nostrils, over his brows and his ears, to his neck, to know him, to gather him in by touch. He was so firm, and shapely, with such satisfying, inconceivable shapeliness, strange, yet unutterably clear. He was such an unutterable enemy, yet glistening with uncanny white fire. She wanted to touch him and touch him and. touch him, till she had him all in her hands, till she had strained him into her knowledge. Ah, if she could have the precious *knowledge* of him, she would be filled, and nothing could deprive her of this. For he was so unsure, so risky in the common world of day.

'You are so *beautiful,*' she murmured in her throat.

He wondered, and was suspended. But she felt him quiver, and she came down involuntarily nearer upon him. He could not help himself. Her fingers had him under their power. The fathomless, fathomless desire they could evoke in him was deeper than death, where he had no choice.

But she knew now, and it was enough. For the time, her soul was destroyed with the exquisite shock of his invisible fluid lightning. She knew. And this knowledge was a death from which she must recover. How much more of him was there to know? Ah much, much, many days harvesting for her large, yet perfectly subtle and intelligent hands upon the field of his living, radio-active body. Ah, her hands were eager, greedy for knowledge. But for the present it was enough, enough, as much as her soul could bear. Too much, and she would shatter herself, she would fill the fine vial of her soul too quickly, and it would break. Enough now – enough for the time being. There were all the after days when her hands, like birds, could feed upon the fields of his mystical plastic form – till then enough.

And even he was glad to be checked, rebuked, held back. For to desire is better than to possess, the finality of the end was dreaded as deeply as it was desired.

They walked on towards the town, towards where the lamps threaded singly, at long intervals down the dark high-road of the valley. They came at length to the gate of the drive.

'Don't come any further,' she said.

'You'd rather I didn't?' he asked, relieved. He did not want to go up the public streets with her, his soul all naked and alight as it was.

'Much rather – good-night.' She held out her hand. He grasped it, then touched the perilous, potent fingers with his lips.

'Good-night,' he said. 'Tomorrow.'

And they parted. He went home full of the strength and the power of living desire.

But the next day, she did not come, she sent a note that she was kept indoors by a cold. Here was a torment! But he possessed his soul in some sort of patience, writing a brief answer, telling her how sorry he was not to see her.

The day after this, he stayed at home – it seemed so futile to go down to the office. His father could not live the week out. And he wanted to be at home, suspended.

Gerald sat on a chair by the window in his father's room. The landscape outside was black and winter-sodden. His father lay grey and ashen on the bed, a nurse moved silently in her white dress, neat and elegant, even beautiful. There was a scent of eau-de-cologne in the room. The nurse went out of the room, Gerald was alone with death, facing the winter-black landscape.

'Is there much more water in Denley?' came the faint voice, determined and querulous, from the bed. The dying man was asking about a leakage from Willey Water into one of the pits.

'Some more – we shall have to run off the lake,' said Gerald.

'Will you?' The faint voice filtered to extinction. There was dead stillness. The grey-faced, sick man lay with eyes closed, more dead than death. Gerald looked away. He felt his heart was seared, it would perish if this went on much longer.

Suddenly he heard a strange noise. Turning round, he saw his father's eyes wide open, strained and rolling in a frenzy of inhuman struggling. Gerald started to his feet, and stood transfixed in horror.

'Wha-a-ah-h-h-' came a horrible choking rattle from his father's throat, the fearful, frenzied eye, rolling awfully in its wild fruitless search for help, passed blindly over Gerald, then up came the dark blood and mess pumping over the face of the agonised being. The tense body relaxed, the head fell aside, down the pillow.

Gerald stood transfixed, his soul echoing in horror. He would move, but he could not. He could not move his limbs. His brain seemed to re-echo, like a pulse.

The nurse in white softly entered. She glanced at Gerald, then at the bed.

'Ah!' came her soft whimpering cry, and she hurried forward to the dead man. 'Ah-h!' came the slight sound of her agitated distress, as she stood bending over the bedside. Then she recovered, turned, and came for towel and sponge. She was wiping the dead face carefully, and murmuring, almost whimpering, very softly: 'Poor Mr Crich! – Poor Mr Crich! Poor Mr Crich!'

'Is he dead?' clanged Gerald's sharp voice.

'Oh yes, he's gone,' replied the soft, moaning voice of the nurse, as she looked up at Gerald's face. She was young and beautiful and quivering. A strange sort of grin went over Gerald's face, over the horror. And he walked out of the room.

He was going to tell his mother. On the landing he met his brother Basil.

'He's gone, Basil,' he said, scarcely able to subdue his voice, not to let an unconscious, frightening exultation sound through.

'What?' cried Basil, going pale.

Gerald nodded. Then he went on to his mother's room.

She was sitting in her purple gown, sewing, very slowly sewing, putting in a stitch then another stitch. She looked up at Gerald with her blue undaunted eyes.

'Father's gone,' he said.

'He's dead? Who says so?'

'Oh, you know, mother, if you see him.'

She put her sewing down, and slowly rose.

'Are you going to see him?' he asked.

'Yes,' she said

By the bedside the children already stood in a weeping group.

'Oh, mother!' cried the daughters, almost in hysterics, weeping loudly.

But the mother went forward. The dead man lay in repose, as if gently asleep, so gently, so peacefully, like a young man sleeping in purity. He was still warm. She stood looking at him in gloomy, heavy silence, for some time.

'Ay,' she said bitterly, at length, speaking as if to the unseen witnesses of the air. 'You're dead.' She stood for some minutes in silence, looking down. 'Beautiful,' she asserted, 'beautiful as if life had never touched you – never touched you. God send I look different. I hope I shall look my years, when I am dead. Beautiful, beautiful,' she crooned over him. 'You can see him in his teens, with his first beard on his face. A beautiful soul, beautiful – ' Then there was a tearing in her voice as she cried: 'None of you look like this, when you are dead! Don't let it happen again.' It was a strange, wild command from out of the unknown. Her children moved unconsciously together, in a nearer group, at the dreadful command in her voice. The colour was flushed bright in her cheek, she looked awful and wonderful. 'Blame me, blame me if you like, that he lies there like a lad in his teens, with his first beard on his face. Blame me if you like. But you none of you know.' She was silent in intense silence.

Then there came, in a low, tense voice: 'If I thought that the children I bore would lie looking like that in death, I'd strangle them when they were infants, yes – '

'No, mother,' came the strange, clarion voice of Gerald from the background, 'we are different, we don't blame you.'

She turned and looked full in his eyes. Then she lifted her hands in a strange half-gesture of mad despair.

'Pray!' she said strongly. 'Pray for yourselves to God, for there's no help for you from your parents.'

'Oh mother!' cried her daughters wildly.

But she had turned and gone, and they all went quickly away from each other.

When Gudrun heard that Mr Crich was dead, she felt rebuked. She had stayed away lest Gerald should think her too easy of winning. And now, he was in the midst of trouble, whilst she was cold.

The following day she went up as usual to Winifred, who was glad to see her, glad to get away into the studio. The girl had wept, and then, too frightened, had turned aside to avoid any more tragic eventuality. She and Gudrun resumed work as usual, in the isolation of the studio, and this seemed an immeasurable happiness, a pure world of freedom, after the aimlessness and misery of the house. Gudrun stayed on till evening. She and Winifred had dinner brought up to the studio, where they ate in freedom, away from all the people in the house.

After dinner Gerald came up. The great high studio was full of shadow and a fragrance of coffee. Gudrun and Winifred had a little table near the fire at the far end, with a white lamp whose light did not travel far. They were a tiny world to themselves, the two girls surrounded by lovely shadows, the beams and rafters shadowy over head, the benches and implements shadowy down the studio.

'You are cosy enough here,' said Gerald, going up to them.

There was a low brick fireplace, full of fire, an old blue Turkish rug, the little oak table with the lamp and the white-and-blue cloth and the dessert, and Gudrun making coffee in an odd brass coffee-maker, and Winifred scalding a little milk in a tiny saucepan.

'Have you had coffee?' said Gudrun.

'I have, but I'll have some more with you,' he replied.

'Then you must have it in a glass – there are only two cups,' said Winifred.

'It is the same to me,' he said, taking a chair and coming into the charmed circle of the girls. How happy they were, how cosy and glamorous it was with them, in a world of lofty shadows! The outside world, in which he had been transacting funeral business all the day was completely wiped out. In an instant he snuffed glamour and magic.

They had all their things very dainty, two odd and lovely little cups, scarlet and solid gilt, and a little black jug with scarlet discs, and the curious coffee-machine, whose spirit-flame flowed steadily, almost invisibly. There was the effect of rather sinister richness, in which Gerald at once escaped himself.

They all sat down, and Gudrun carefully poured out the coffee.

'Will you have milk?' she asked calmly, yet nervously poising the little black jug with its big red dots. She was always so completely controlled, yet so bitterly nervous.

'No, I won't,' he replied.

So, with a curious humility, she placed him the little cup of coffee, and herself took the awkward tumbler. She seemed to want to serve him.

'Why don't you give me the glass – it is so clumsy for you,' he said. He would much rather have had it, and seen her daintily served. But she was silent, pleased with the disparity, with her self-abasement.

'You are quite *en ménage,*'* he said.

'Yes. We aren't really at home to visitors,' said Winifred.

'You're not? Then I'm an intruder?'

For once he felt his conventional dress was out of place, he was an outsider.

Gudrun was very quiet. She did not feel drawn to talk to him. At this stage, silence was best – or mere light words. It was best to leave serious things aside. So they talked gaily and lightly, till they heard the man below lead out the horse, and call it to 'back-back!' into the dog-cart that was to take Gudrun home. So she put on her things, and shook hands with Gerald, without once meeting his eyes. And she was gone.

The funeral was detestable. Afterwards, at the tea-table, the daughters kept saying – 'He was a good father to us – the best father in the world' or else – 'We shan't easily find another man as good as father was.'

Gerald acquiesced in all this. It was the right conventional attitude, and, as far as the world went, he believed in the conventions. He took it as a matter of course. But Winifred hated everything, and hid in the studio, and cried her heart out, and wished Gudrun would come.

Luckily everybody was going away. The Criches never stayed long at home. By dinner-time, Gerald was left quite alone. Even Winifred was carried off to London, for a few days with her sister Laura.

* (Fr.) Like a couple at home.

But when Gerald was really left alone, he could not bear it. One day passed by, and another. And all the time he was like a man hung in chains over the edge of an abyss. Struggle as he might, he could not turn himself to the solid earth, he could not get footing. He was suspended on the edge of a void, writhing. Whatever he thought of, was the abyss – whether it were friends or strangers, or work or play, it all showed him only the same bottomless void, in which his heart swung perishing. There was no escape, there was nothing to grasp hold of. He must writhe on the edge of the chasm, suspended in chains of invisible physical life.

At first he was quiet, he kept still, expecting the extremity to pass away, expecting to find himself released into the world of the living, after this extremity of penance. But it did not pass, and a crisis gained upon him.

As the evening of the third day came on, his heart rang with fear. He could not bear another night. Another night was coming on, for another night he was to be suspended in chain of physical life, over the bottomless pit of nothingness. And he could not bear it. He could hot bear it. He was frightened deeply, and coldly, frightened in his soul. He did not believe in his own strength any more. He could not fall into this infinite void, and rise again. If he fell, he would be gone forever. He must withdraw, he must seek reinforcements. He did not believe in his own single self, any further than this.

After dinner, faced with the ultimate experience of his own nothingness, he turned aside. He pulled on his boots, put on his coat, and set out to walk in the night.

It was dark and misty. He went through the wood, stumbling and feeling his way to the Mill. Birkin was away. 'Good – he was half glad. He turned up the hill, and stumbled blindly over the wild slopes, having lost the path in the complete darkness. It was boring. Where was he going? No matter. He stumbled on till he came to a path again. Then he went on through another wood. His mind became dark, he went on automatically. Without thought or sensation, he stumbled unevenly on, out into the open again, fumbling for stiles, losing the path, and going along the hedges of the fields till he came to the outlet.

And at last he came to the high road. It had distracted him to struggle blindly through the maze of darkness. But now, he must take a direction. And he did not even know where he was. But he must take a direction now. Nothing would be resolved by merely walking, walking away. He had to take a direction.

He stood still on the road, that was high in the utterly dark night, and he did not know where he was. It was a strange sensation, his heart beating, and ringed round with the utterly unknown darkness. So he stood for some time.

Then he heard footsteps, and saw a small, swinging light. He immediately went towards this. It was a miner.

'Can you tell me,' he said, 'where this road goes?'

'Road? Ay, it goes ter Whatmore.'

'Whatmore! Oh thank you, that's right. I thought I was wrong. Good-night.'

'Good-night,' replied the broad voice of the miner.

Gerald guessed where he was. At least when he came to Whatmore, he would know. He was glad to be on a high road. He walked forward as in a sleep of decision.

That was Whatmore Village —? Yes, the King's Head — and there the hall gates. He descended the steep hill almost running. Winding through the hollow, he passed the Grammar School, and came to Willey Green Church. The churchyard! He halted.

Then in another moment he had clambered up the wall and was going among the graves. Even in this darkness he could see the heaped pallor of old white flowers at his feet. This then was the grave. He stooped down. The flowers were cold and clammy. There was a raw scent of chrysanthemums and tube-roses, deadened. He felt the clay beneath, and shrank, it was so horribly cold and sticky. He stood away in revulsion.

Here was one centre then, here in the complete darkness beside the unseen, raw grave. But there was nothing for him here. No, he had nothing to stay here for. He felt as if some of the clay were sticking cold and unclean, on his heart. No, enough of this.

Where then? – home? Never! It was no use going there. That was less than no use. It could not be done. There was somewhere else to go. Where?

A dangerous resolve formed in his heart, like a fixed idea. There was Gudrun – she would be safe in her home. But he could get at her – he would get at her. He would not go back tonight till he had come to her, if it cost him his life. He staked his all on this throw.

He set off walking straight across the fields towards Beldover. It was so dark, nobody could ever see him. His feet were wet and cold, heavy with clay. But he went on persistently, like a wind, straight forward, as if to his fate. There were great gaps in his consciousness. He was conscious that he was at Winthorpe hamlet, but quite unconscious how he had got there. And then, as in a dream, he was in the long street of Beldover, with its street-lamps.

There was a noise of voices, and of a door shutting loudly, and being barred, and of men talking in the night. The 'Lord Nelson' had just closed, and the drinkers were going home. He had better ask one of these where she lived – for he did not know the side streets at all.

'Can you tell me where Somerset Drive is?' he asked of one of the uneven men.

'Where what?' replied the tipsy miner's voice.

'Somerset Drive.'

'Somerset Drive! – I've heard o' such a place, but I couldn't for my life say where it is. Who might you be wanting?'

'Mr Brangwen – William Brangwen.'

'William Brangwen –? –?'

'Who teaches at the Grammar School, at Willey Green – his daughter teaches there too.'

'O-o-o-oh, Brangwen! *Now* I've got you. Of *course*, William Brangwen! Yes, yes, he's got two lasses as teachers, aside hisself. Ay, that's him – that's him! Why certainly I know where he lives, back your life I do! Yi – *what* place do they ca' it?'

'Somerset Drive,' repeated Gerald patiently. He knew his own colliers fairly well.

'Somerset Drive, for certain!' said the collier, swinging his arm as if catching something up. 'Somerset Drive – yi! I couldn't for my life lay hold o' the lercality o' the place. Yis, I know the place, to be sure I do – '

He turned unsteadily on his feet, and pointed up the dark, nigh deserted road.

'You go up theer – an' you ta'e th' first – yi, th' first turnin' on your left – o' that side – past Withamses tuffy shop – '

'*I* know,' said Gerald.

'Ay! You go down a bit, past wheer th' water-man lives – and then Somerset Drive, as they ca' it, branches off on 't right hand side – an' there's nowt but three houses in it, no more than three, I believe, – an' I'm a'most certain as theirs is th' last – th' last o' th' three – you see – '

'Thank you very much,' said Gerald. 'Good-night.'

And he started off, leaving the tipsy man there standing rooted.

Gerald went past the dark shops and houses, most of them sleeping now, and twisted round to the little blind road that ended on a field of darkness. He slowed down, ashen neared his goal, not knowing how he should proceed. What if the house were closed in darkness?

But it was not. He saw a big lighted window, and heard voices, then a gate banged. His quick ears caught the sound of Birkin's voice, his keen eyes made out Birkin, with Ursula standing in a pale dress on the step of the garden path. Then Ursula stepped down, and came along the road, holding Birkin's arm.

Gerald went across into the darkness and they dawdled past him, talking happily, Birkin's voice low, Ursula's high and distinct. Gerald went quickly to the house.

The blinds were drawn before the big, lighted window of the dining-room. Looking up the path at the side he could see the door left open, shedding a soft, coloured light from the hall lamp. He went quickly and silently up the path, and looked up into the hall. There were pictures on the walls, and the antlers of a stag – and the stairs going up on one side – and just near the foot of the stairs the half opened door of the dining-room.

With heart drawn fine, Gerald stepped into the hall, whose floor was of coloured tiles, went quickly and looked into the large, pleasant room. In a chair by the fire, the father sat asleep, his head tilted back against the side of the big oak chimney-piece, his ruddy face seen foreshortened, the nostrils open, the mouth fallen a-little. It would take the merest sound to wake him.

Gerald stood a second suspended. He glanced down the passage behind him. It was all dark. Again he was suspended. Then he went swiftly upstairs. His senses were so finely, almost supernaturally keen, that he seemed to cast his own will over the half-unconscious house.

He came to the first landing. There he stood, scarcely breathing. Again, corresponding to the door below, there was a door again. That would be the mother's room. He could hear her moving about in the candlelight. She would be expecting her husband to come up. He looked along the dark landing.

Then, silently, on infinitely careful feet, he went along the passage, feeling the wall with the extreme tips of his fingers. There was a door. He stood and listened. He could hear two people's breathing. It was not that. He went stealthily forward. There was another door, slightly open. The room was in darkness. Empty. Then there was the bathroom, he could smell the soap and the heat. Then at the end another bedroom – one soft breathing. This was she.

With an almost occult carefulness he turned the door handle, and opened the door an inch. It creaked slightly. Then he opened it another inch – then another. His heart did not beat, he seemed to create a silence about himself, an obliviousness.

He was in the room. Still the sleeper breathed softly. It was very dark. He felt his way forward inch by inch, with his feet and hands. He touched the bed, he could hear the sleeper. He drew nearer, bending close as if his eyes would disclose whatever there was. And then, very near to his face, to his fear, he saw the round, dark head of a boy.

He recovered, turned round, saw the door ajar, a faint light revealed. And he retreated swiftly, drew the door to without fastening it, and passed rapidly down the passage. At the head of the stairs he hesitated. There was still time to flee.

But it was unthinkable. He would maintain his will. He turned past the door of the parental bedroom like a shadow, and was climbing the second flight of stairs. They creaked under his weight – it was exasperating. Ah what disaster, if the mother's door opened just beneath him, and she saw him! It would have to be, if it were so. He held the control still.

He was not quite up these stairs when he heard a quick running of feet below, the outer door was closed and locked, he heard Ursula's voice, then the father's sleepy exclamation. He pressed on swiftly to the upper landing.

Again a door was ajar, a room was empty. Feeling his way forward, with the tips of his fingers, travelling rapidly, like a blind man, anxious lest Ursula should come upstairs, he found another door. There, with his preternaturally fine senses alert, he listened. He heard someone moving in bed. This would be she.

Softly now, like one who has only one sense, the tactile sense, he turned the latch. It clicked. He held still. The bed-clothes rustled. His heart did not beat. Then again he drew the latch back, and very gently pushed the door. It made a sticking noise as it gave.

'Ursula?' said Gudrun's voice, frightened. He quickly opened the door and pushed it behind him.

'Is it you, Ursula?' came Gudrun's frightened voice. He heard her sitting up in bed. In another moment she would scream.

'No, it's me,' he said, feeling his way towards her. 'It is I, Gerald.'

She sat motionless in her bed in sheer astonishment. She was too astonished, too much taken by surprise, even to be afraid.

'Gerald!' she echoed, in blank amazement. He had found his way to the bed, and his outstretched hand touched her warm breast blindly. She shrank away.

'Let me make a light,' she said, springing out.

He stood perfectly motionless. He heard her touch the matchbox, he heard her fingers in their movement. Then he saw her in the light of a match, which she held to the candle. The light rose in the room, then sank to a small dimness, as the flame sank down on the candle, before it mounted again.

She looked at him, as he stood near the other side of the bed. His cap was pulled low over his brow, his black overcoat was buttoned close up to his chin. His face was strange and luminous. He was inevitable as a supernatural being. When she had seen him, she knew. She knew there was something fatal in the situation, and she must accept it. Yet she must challenge him.

'How did you come up?' she asked.

'I walked up the stairs – the door was open.'

She looked at him.

'I haven't closed this door, either,' he said. She walked swiftly across the room, and closed her door, softly, and locked it. Then she came back.

She was wonderful, with startled eyes and flushed cheeks, and her plait of hair rather short and thick down her back, and her long, fine white night-dress falling to her feet.

She saw that his boots were all clayey, even his trousers were plastered with clay. And she wondered if he had made footprints all the way up. He was a very strange figure, standing in her bedroom, near the tossed bed.

'Why have you come?' she asked, almost querulous.

'I wanted to,' he replied.

And this she could see from his face. It was fate.

'You are so muddy,' she said, in distaste, but gently.

He looked down at his feet.

'I was walking in the dark,' he replied. But he felt vividly elated.

There was a pause. He stood on one side of the tumbled bed, she on the other. He did not even take his cap from his brows.

'And what do you want of me,' she challenged.

He looked aside, and did not answer. Save for the extreme beauty and mystic attractiveness of this distinct, strange face, she would have sent him away. But his face was too wonderful and undiscovered to her. It fascinated her with the fascination of pure beauty, cast a spell on her, like nostalgia, an ache.

'What do you want of me?' she repeated in an estranged voice.

He pulled off his cap, in a movement of dream-liberation, and went across to her. But he could not touch her, because she stood barefoot in her night-dress, and he was muddy and damp. Her eyes, wide and large and wondering, watched him, and asked him the ultimate question.

'I came – because I must,' he said. 'Why do you ask?'

She looked at him in doubt and wonder.

'I must ask,' she said.

He shook his head slightly.

'There is no answer,' he replied, with strange vacancy.

There was about him a curious, and almost godlike air of simplicity and naive directness. He reminded her of an apparition, the young Hermes.

'But why did you come to me?' she persisted.

'Because – it has to be so. If there weren't you in the world, then I shouldn't be in the world, either.'

She stood looking at him, with large, wide, wondering, stricken eyes. His eyes were looking steadily into hers all the time, and he seemed fixed in an odd supernatural steadfastness. She sighed. She was lost now. She had no choice.

'Won't you take off your boots,' she said. 'They must be wet.'

He dropped his cap on a chair, unbuttoned his overcoat, lifting up his chin to unfasten the throat buttons. His short, keen hair was ruffled. He was so beautifully blond, like wheat. He pulled off his overcoat.

Quickly he pulled off his jacket, pulled loose his black tie, and was unfastening his studs, which were headed each with a pearl. She listened, watching, hoping no one would hear the starched linen crackle. It seemed to snap like pistol shots.

He had come for vindication. She let him hold her in his arms, clasp her close against him. He found in her an infinite relief. Into her he poured all his pent-up darkness and corrosive death, and he was whole again. It was wonderful, marvellous, it was a miracle. This was the ever recurrent miracle of his life, at the knowledge of which he was lost in an ecstasy of relief and wonder. And she, subject, received him as a vessel filled with his bitter potion of death. She had no power at this crisis to resist. The terrible frictional violence of death filled her, and she received it in an ecstasy of subjection, in throes of acute, violent sensation.

As he drew nearer to her, he plunged deeper into her enveloping soft warmth, a wonderful creative heat that penetrated' his veins and gave him life again. He felt himself dissolving and sinking to rest in the bath of her living strength. It seemed as if her heart in her breast were a second unconquerable sun, into the glow and creative strength of which he plunged further and further. All his veins, that were murdered and – lacerated, healed softly as life came pulsing in, stealing invisibly in to him as if it were the all-powerful effluence of the sun. His blood, which seemed to have been drawn back into death, came ebbing on the return, surely, beautifully, powerfully.

He felt his limbs growing fuller and flexible with life, his body gained an unknown strength. He was a man again, strong and rounded. And he was a child, so soothed and restored and full of gratitude.

And she, she was the great bath of life, he worshipped her. Mother and substance of all life she was. And he, child and man, received of her and was made whole. His pure body was almost killed. But the miraculous, soft effluence of her breast suffused over him, over his seared, damaged brain, like a healing lymph, like a soft, soothing flow of life itself, perfect as if he were bathed in the womb again.

His brain was hurt, seared, the tissue was as if destroyed. He had not known how hurt he was, how his tissue, the very tissue of his brain was damaged by the corrosive flood of death. Now, as the healing lymph of her effluence flowed through him, he knew how destroyed he was, like a plant whose tissue is burst from inwards by a frost.

He buried his small, hard head between her breasts, and pressed her breasts against him with his hands. And she with quivering hands pressed his head against her, as he lay suffused out, and she lay fully conscious. The lovely creative warmth flooded through him like a sleep of fecundity within the womb. Ah, if only she would grant him the flow of this living effluence, he would be restored, he would be complete again. He was afraid she would deny him before it was finished. Like a child at the breast, he cleaved intensely to her, and she could not put him away. And his seared, ruined membrane relaxed, softened, that which was seared and stiff and blasted yielded again, became soft and flexible, palpitating with new life. He was infinitely grateful, as to God, or as an infant is at its mother's breast. He was glad and grateful like a delirium, as he felt his own wholeness come over him again, as he felt the full, unutterable sleep coming over him, the sleep of complete exhaustion and restoration.

But Gudrun lay wide awake, destroyed into perfect consciousness. She lay motionless, with wide eyes staring motionless into the darkness, whilst he was sunk away in sleep, his arms round her.

She seemed to be hearing waves break on a hidden shore, long, slow, gloomy waves, breaking with the rhythm of fate, so monotonously that it seemed eternal. This endless breaking of slow, sullen waves of fate held her life a possession, whilst she lay with dark, wide eyes looking into the darkness. She could see so far, as far as eternity – yet she saw nothing. She was suspended in perfect consciousness – and of what was she conscious?

This mood of extremity, when she lay staring into eternity, utterly suspended, and conscious of everything, to the last limits, passed and left her uneasy. She had lain so long motionless. She moved, she became self-conscious. She wanted to look at him, to see him.

But she dared not make a light, because she knew he would wake, and she did not want to break his perfect sleep, that she knew he had got of her.

She disengaged herself, softly, and rose up a little to look at him. There was a faint light, it seemed to her, in the room. She could just distinguish his features, as he slept the perfect sleep. In this darkness, she seemed to see him so distinctly. But he was far off, in another world. Ah, she could shriek with torment, he was so far off, and perfected, in another world. She seemed to look at him as at a pebble far away under clear dark water. And here was she, left with all the anguish of consciousness, whilst he was sunk deep into the other element of mindless, remote, living shadow-gleam. He was beautiful, far-off, and perfected. They would never be together. Ah, this awful, inhuman distance which would always be interposed between her and the other being!

There was nothing to do but to lie still and endure. She felt an overwhelming tenderness for him, and a dark, under-stirring of jealous hatred, that he should lie so perfect and immune, in an other-world, whilst she was tormented with violent wakefulness, cast out in the outer darkness.

She lay in intense and vivid consciousness, an exhausting superconsciousness. The church clock struck the hours, it seemed to her, in quick succession. She heard them distinctly in the tension of her vivid consciousness. And he slept as if time were one moment, unchanging and unmoving.

She was exhausted, wearied. Yet she must continue in this state of violent active superconsciousness. She was conscious of everything – her childhood, her girlhood, all the forgotten incidents, all the unrealised influences and all the happenings she had not understood, pertaining to herself, to her family, to her friends, her lovers, her acquaintances, everybody. It was as if she drew a glittering rope of knowledge out of the sea of darkness, drew and drew and drew it out of the fathomless depths of the past, and still it did not come to an end, there was no end to it, she must haul and haul at the rope of glittering consciousness, pull it out phosphorescent from the endless depths of the unconsciousness, till she was weary, aching, exhausted, and fit to break, and yet she had not done.

Ah, if only she might wake him! She turned uneasily. When could she rouse him and send him away? When could she disturb him? And she relapsed into her activity of automatic consciousness, that would never end.

But the time was drawing near when she could wake him. It was like a release. The clock had struck four, outside in the night. Thank God the night had passed almost away. At five he must go, and she would be released. Then she could relax and fill her own place. Now she was driven up against his perfect sleeping motion like a knife white-hot on a grindstone. There was something monstrous about him, about his juxtaposition against her.

The last hour was the longest. And yet, at last it passed. Her heart leapt with relief – yes, there was the slow, strong stroke of the church clock – at last, after this night of eternity. She waited to catch each slow, fatal reverberation. 'Three – four – five!' There, it was finished. A weight rolled off her.

She raised herself, leaned over him tenderly, and kissed him. She was sad to wake him. After a few moments, she kissed him again. But he did not stir. The darling, he was so deep in sleep! What a shame to take him out of it. She let him lie a little longer. But he must go – he must really go.

With full over-tenderness she took his face between her hands, and kissed his eyes. The eyes opened, he remained motionless, looking at her. Her heart stood still. To hide her face from his dreadful opened eyes, in the darkness, she bent down and kissed him, whispering:

'You must go, my love.'

But she was sick with terror, sick.

He put his arms round her. Her heart sank.

'But you must go, my love. It's late.'

'What time is it?' he said.

Strange, his man's voice. She quivered. It was an intolerable oppression to her.

'Past five o'clock,' she said.

But he only closed his arms round her again. Her heart cried within her in torture. She disengaged herself firmly.

'You really must go,' she said.

'Not for a minute,' he said.

She lay still, nestling against him, but unyielding.

'Not for a minute,' he repeated, clasping her closer.

'Yes,' she said, unyielding, 'I'm afraid if you stay any longer.'

There was a certain coldness in her voice that made him release her, and she broke away, rose and lit the candle. That then was the end.

He got up. He was warm and full of life and desire. Yet he felt a little bit ashamed, humiliated, putting on his clothes before her, in the candle-light. For he felt revealed, exposed to her, at a time when she was in some way against him. It was all very difficult to understand. He dressed himself quickly, without collar or tie. Still he felt full and complete, perfected. She thought it humiliating to see a man dressing: the ridiculous shirt, the ridiculous trousers and braces. But again an idea saved her.

'It is like a workman getting up to go to work,' thought Gudrun. 'And I am like a workman's wife.' But an ache like nausea was upon her: a nausea of him.

He pushed his collar and tie into his overcoat pocket. Then he sat down and pulled on his boots. They were sodden, as were his socks and trouser-bottoms. But he himself was quick and warm.

'Perhaps you ought to have put your boots on downstairs,' she said.

At once, without answering, he pulled them off again, and stood holding them in his hand. She had thrust her feet into slippers, and flung a loose robe round her. She was ready. She looked at him as he stood waiting, his black coat buttoned to the chin, his cap pulled down, his boots in his hand. And the passionate almost hateful fascination revived in her for a moment. It was not exhausted. His face was so warm-looking, wide-eyed and full of newness, so perfect. She felt old, old. She went to him heavily, to be kissed. He kissed her quickly. She wished his warm, expressionless beauty did not so fatally put a spell on her, compel her and subjugate her. It was a burden upon her, that she resented, but could not escape. Yet when she looked at his straight man's brows, and at his rather small, well-shaped nose, and at his blue, indifferent eyes, she knew her passion for him was not yet satisfied, perhaps never could be satisfied. Only now she was weary, with an ache like nausea. She wanted him gone.

They went downstairs quickly. It seemed they made a prodigious noise. He followed her as, wrapped in her vivid green wrap, she preceded him with the light. She suffered badly with fear, lest her people should be roused. He hardly cared. He did not care now who knew. And she hated this in him. One *must* be cautious. One must preserve oneself.

She led the way to the kitchen. It was neat and tidy, as the woman had left it. He looked up at the clock – twenty minutes past five. Then he sat down on a chair to put on his boots. She waited, watching his every movement. She wanted it to be over, it was a great nervous strain on her.

He stood up – she unbolted the back door, and looked out. A cold, raw night, not yet dawn, with a piece of a moon in the vague sky. She was glad she need not go out.

'Good-bye then,' he murmured.

'I'll come to the gate,' she said.

And again she hurried on in front, to warn him of the steps. And at the gate, once more she stood on the step whilst he stood below her. 'Good-bye,' she whispered.

He kissed her dutifully, and turned away.

She suffered torments hearing his firm tread going so distinctly down the road. Ah, the insensitiveness of that firm tread!

She closed the gate, and crept quickly and noiselessly back to bed. When she was in her room, and the door closed, and all safe, she breathed freely, and a great weight fell off her. She nestled down in bed, in the groove his body had made, in the warmth he had left. And excited, worn-out, yet still satisfied, she fell soon into a deep, heavy sleep.

Gerald walked quickly through the raw darkness of the coming dawn. He met nobody. His mind was beautifully still and thoughtless, like a still pool, and his body full and warm and rich. He went quickly along towards Shortlands, in a grateful self-sufficiency.

CHAPTER 25

Marriage or Not

THE BRANGWEN family was going to move from Beldover. It was necessary now for the father to be in town.

Birkin had taken out a marriage licence, yet Ursula deferred from day to day. She would not fix any definite time – she still wavered. Her month's notice to leave the Grammar School was in its third week. Christmas was not far off.

Gerald waited for the Ursula-Birkin marriage. It was something crucial to him.

'Shall we make it a double-barrelled affair?' he said to Birkin one day.

'Who for the second shot?' asked Birkin.

'Gudrun and me,' said Gerald, the venturesome twinkle in his eyes. Birkin looked at him steadily, as if somewhat taken aback.

'Serious – or joking?' he asked.

'Oh, serious. Shall I? Shall Gudrun and I rush in along with you?'

'Do by all means,' said Birkin. 'I didn't know you'd got that length.'

'What length?' said Gerald, looking at the other man, and laughing.

'Oh yes, we've gone all the lengths.'

'There remains to put it on a broad social basis, and to achieve a high moral purpose,' said Birkin.

'Something like that: the length and breadth and height of it,' replied Gerald, smiling.

'Oh well,' said Birkin,' it's a very admirable step to take, I should say.' Gerald looked at him closely.

'Why aren't you enthusiastic?' he asked. 'I thought you were such dead nuts on marriage.'

Birkin lifted his shoulders.

'One might as well be dead nuts on noses. There are all sorts of noses, snub and otherwise – '

Gerald laughed.

'And all sorts of marriage, also snub and otherwise?' he said.

'That's it.'

'And you think if I marry, it will be snub?' asked Gerald quizzically, his head a little on one side.

Birkin laughed quickly.

'How do I know what it will be!' he said. 'Don't lambaste me with my own parallels – '

Gerald pondered a while.

'But I should like to know your opinion, exactly,' he said.

'On your marriage? – or marrying? Why should you want my opinion? I've got no opinions. I'm not interested in legal marriage, one way or another. It's a mere question of convenience.'

Still Gerald watched him closely.

'More than that, I think,' he said seriously. 'However you may be bored by the ethics of marriage, yet really to marry, in one's own personal case, is something critical, final – '

'You mean there is something final in going to the registrar with a woman?'

'If you're coming back with her, I do,' said Gerald. 'It is in some way irrevocable.'

'Yes, I agree,' said Birkin.

'No matter how one regards legal marriage, yet to enter into the married state, in one's own personal instance, is final – '

'I believe it is,' said Birkin, 'somewhere.'

'The question remains then, should one do it,' said Gerald.

Birkin watched him narrowly, with amused eyes.

'You are like Lord Bacon, Gerald,' he said. 'You argue it like a lawyer – or like Hamlet's to-be-or-not-to-be. If I were you I would *not* marry: but ask Gudrun, not me. You're not marrying me, are you?'

Gerald did not heed the latter part of this speech.

'Yes,' he said, 'one must consider it coldly. It is something critical. One comes to the point where one must take a step in one direction or another. And marriage is one direction – '

'And what is the other?' asked Birkin quickly.

Gerald looked up at him with hot, strangely-conscious eyes, that tile other man could not understand.

'I can't say,' he replied. 'If I knew *that* – ' He moved uneasily on his feet, and did not finish.

'You mean if you knew the alternative?' asked Birkin. 'And since you don't know it, marriage is a *pis aller*.'[1]

Gerald looked up at Birkin with the same hot, constrained eyes.

'One does have the feeling that marriage is a *pis aller,*' he admitted.

'Then don't do it,' said Birkin. 'I tell you,' he went on, 'the same as I've said before, marriage in the old sense seems to me repulsive. *Egoisme a deux*[2] is nothing to it. It's a sort of tacit hunting in couples: the world all in couples, each couple in its own little house, watching its own little interests, and stewing in its own little privacy – it's the most repulsive thing on earth.'

'I quite agree,' said Gerald. 'There's something inferior about it. But as I say, what's the alternative.'

'One should avoid this *home* instinct. It's not an instinct, it's a habit of cowardliness. One should never have a *home.*'

'I agree really,' said Gerald. 'But there's no alternative.'

'We've got to find one. I do believe in a permanent union between a man and a woman. Chopping about is merely an exhaustive process. But a permanent relation between a man and a woman isn't the last word – it certainly isn't.'

'Quite,' said Gerald.

'In fact,' said Birkin, 'because the relation between man and woman is made the supreme and exclusive relationship, that's where all the tightness and meanness and insufficiency comes in.'

'Yes, I believe you,' said Gerald.

'You've got to take down the love-and-marriage ideal from its pedestal. We want something broader. I believe in the *additional* perfect relationship between man and man – additional to marriage.'

'I can never see how they can be the same,' said Gerald.

1 A make-shift arrangement.
2 Attributed to French-Swiss writer Germaine de Staël's 'Egoism for two'.

'Not the same – but equally important, equally creative, equally sacred, if you like.'

'I know,' said Gerald, 'you believe something like that. Only I can't *feel* it, you see.' He put his hand on Birkin's arm, with a sort of deprecating affection. And he smiled as if triumphantly.

He was ready to be doomed. Marriage was like a doom to him. He was willing to condemn himself in marriage, to become like a convict condemned to the mines of the underworld, living no life in the sun, but having a dreadful subterranean activity. He was willing to accept this. And marriage was the seal of his condemnation. He was willing to be sealed thus in the underworld, like a soul damned but living forever in damnation. But he would not make any pure relationship with any other soul. He could not. Marriage was not the committing of himself into a relationship with Gudrun. It was a committing of himself in acceptance of the established world, he would accept the established order, in which he did not livingly believe, and then he would retreat to the underworld for his life. This he would do.

The other way was to accept Rupert's offer of alliance, to enter into the bond of pure trust and love with the other man, and then subsequently with the woman. If he pledged himself with the man he would later be able to pledge himself with the woman: not merely in legal marriage, but in absolute, mystic marriage.

Yet he could not accept the offer. There was a numbness upon him, a numbness either of unborn, absent volition, or of atrophy. Perhaps it was the absence of volition. For he was strangely elated at Rupert's offer. Yet he was still more glad to reject it, not to be committed.

———————◆————————◆———————

CHAPTER 26

A Chair

THERE WAS a jumble market every Monday afternoon in the old market-place in town. Ursula and Birkin strayed down there one afternoon. They had been talking of furniture, and they wanted to see if there was any fragment they would like to buy, amid the heaps of rubbish collected on the cobble-stones.

The old market-square was not very large, a mere bare patch of granite setts, usually with a few fruit-stalls under a wall. It was in a poor quarter of the town. Meagre houses stood down one side, there was a hosiery factory, a great blank with myriad oblong windows, at the end, a street of little shops with flagstone pavement down the other side, and, for a crowning monument, the public baths, of new red brick, with a clock-tower. The people who moved about seemed stumpy and sordid, the air seemed to smell rather dirty, there was a sense of many mean streets ramifying off into warrens of meanness. Now and again a great chocolate-and-yellow tramcar ground round a difficult bend under the hosiery factory.

Ursula was superficially thrilled when she found herself out among the common people, in the jumbled place piled with old bedding, heaps of old iron, shabby crockery in pale lots, muffled lots of unthinkable clothing. She and Birkin went unwillingly down the narrow aisle between the rusty wares. He was looking at the goods, she at the people.

She excitedly watched a young woman, who was going to have a baby, and who was turning over a mattress and making a young man, down-at-heel and dejected, feel it also. So secretive and active and anxious the young woman seemed, so reluctant, slinking, the young man. He was going to marry her because she was having a child.

When they had felt the mattress, the young woman asked the old man seated on a stool among his wares, how much it was. He told her, and she turned to the young man. The latter was ashamed, and self-conscious. He turned his face away, though he left his body standing there, and muttered aside. And again the woman anxiously and actively fingered the mattress and added up in her mind and bargained with the old, unclean man. All the while, the young man stood by, shamefaced and down-at-heel, submitting.

'Look,' said Birkin, 'there is a pretty chair.'

'Charming!' cried Ursula. 'Oh, charming.'

It was an arm-chair of simple wood, probably birch, but of such fine delicacy of grace, standing there on the sordid stones, it almost brought tears to the eyes. It was square in shape, of the purest, slender lines, and four short lines of wood in the back, that reminded Ursula of harp-strings.

'It was once,' said Birkin, 'gilded – and it had a cane seat. Somebody has nailed this wooden seat in. Look, here is a trifle of the red that underlay the gilt. The rest is all black, except where the wood is worn pure and glossy. It is the fine unity of the lines that is so attractive. Look, how they run and meet and counteract. But of course the wooden seat is wrong – it destroys the perfect lightness and unity in tension the cane gave. I like it though – '

'Ah yes,' said Ursula, 'so do I.'

'How much is it?' Birkin asked the man.

'Ten shillings.'

'And you will send it –?'

It was bought.

'So beautiful, so pure!' Birkin said. 'It almost breaks my heart.' They walked along between the heaps of rubbish. 'My beloved country – it had something to express even when it made that chair.'

'And hasn't it now?' asked Ursula. She was always angry when he took this tone.

'No, it hasn't. When I see that clear, beautiful chair, and I think of England, even Jane Austen's England – it had living thoughts to unfold even then, and pure happiness in unfolding them. And now, we can only fish among the rubbish heaps for the remnants of their old expression. There is no production in us now, only sordid and foul mechanicalness.'

'It isn't true,' cried Ursula. 'Why must you always praise the past, at the expense of the present? *Really,* I don't think so much of Jane Austen's England. It was materialistic enough, if you like – '

'It could afford to be materialistic,' said Birkin, 'because it had the power to be something other – which we haven't. We are materialistic because we haven't the power to be anything else – try as we may, we can't bring off anything but materialism: mechanism, the very soul of materialism.'

Ursula was subdued into angry silence. She did not heed what he said. She was rebelling against something else.

'And I hate your past. I'm sick of it,' she cried. 'I believe I even hate that old chair, though it *is* beautiful. It isn't *my* sort of beauty. I wish it had been smashed up when its day was over, not left to preach the beloved past to us. I'm sick of the beloved past.'

'Not so sick as I am of the accursed present,' he said.

'Yes, just the same. I hate the present – but I don't want the past to take its place – I don't want that old chair.'

He was rather angry for à moment. Then he looked at the sky shining beyond the tower of the public baths, and he seemed to get over it all. He laughed.

'All right,' he said, 'then let us not have it. I'm sick of it all, too. At any rate one can't go on living on the old bones of beauty.'

'One can't,' she cried. 'I *don't* want old things.'

'The truth is, we don't want things at all,' he replied. 'The thought of a house and furniture of my own is hateful to me.'

This startled her for a moment. Then she replied:

'So it is to me. But one must live somewhere.'

'Not somewhere – anywhere,' he said. 'One should just live any where – not have a definite place. I don't want a definite place. As soon as you get a room, and it is *complete,* you want to run from it. Now my rooms at the Mill are quite complete, I want them at the bottom of the sea. It is a horrible tyranny of a fixed milieu, where each piece of furniture is a commandment-stone.'

She clung to his arm as they walked away from the market.

'But what are we going to do?' she said. 'We must live somehow. And I do want some beauty in my surroundings. I want a sort of natural *grandeur* even, *splendour.*'

'You'll never get it in houses and furniture – or even clothes. Houses and furniture and clothes, they are all terms of an old base world, a detestable society of man. And if you have a Tudor house and old, beautiful furniture, it is only the past perpetuated on top of you, horrible. And if you have a perfect modern house done for you by Poiret, it is something else perpetuated on top of you. It is all horrible. It is all possessions, possessions, bullying you and turning you into a generalisation. You have to be like Rodin, Michelangelo, and leave a piece of raw rock unfinished to your figure. You must leave your surroundings sketchy, unfinished, so that you are never contained, never confined, never dominated from the outside.'

She stood in the street contemplating.

'And we are never to have a complete place of our own – never a home?' she said.

'Pray God, in this world, no,' he answered.

'But there's only this world,' she objected.

He spread out his hands with a gesture of indifference.

'Meanwhile, then, we'll avoid having things of our own,' he said.

'But you've just bought a chair,' she said.

'I can tell the man I don't want it,' he replied.

She pondered again. Then a queer little movement twitched her face.

'No,' she said, 'we don't want it. I'm sick of old things.'

'New ones as well,' he said.

They retraced their steps.

There – in front of some furniture, stood the young couple, the woman who was going to have a baby, and the narrow-faced youth. She was fair, rather short, stout. He was of medium height, attractively built. His dark hair fell sideways over his brow, from under his cap, he stood strangely aloof, like one of the damned.

'Let us give it to *them*,' whispered Ursula. 'Look they are getting a home together.'

'*I* won't aid and abet them in it,' he said petulantly, instantly sympathising with the aloof, furtive youth, against the active, procreant female.

'Oh yes,' cried Ursula. 'It's right for them – there's nothing else for them.'

'Very well,' said Birkin, 'you offer it to them. I'll watch.'

Ursula went rather nervously to the young couple, who were discussing an iron washstand – or rather, the man was glancing furtively and wonderingly, like a prisoner, at the abominable article, whilst the woman was arguing.

'We bought a chair,' said Ursula, 'and we don't want it. Would you have it? We should be glad if you would.'

The young couple looked round at her, not believing that she could be addressing them.

'Would you care for it?' repeated Ursula. 'It's really *very* pretty – but but – 'she smiled rather dazzlingly.

The young couple only stared at her, and looked significantly at each other, to know what to do. And the man curiously obliterated himself, as if he could make himself invisible, as a rat can.

'We wanted to *give* it to you,' explained Ursula, now overcome with confusion and dread of them. She was attracted by the young man. He was a still, mindless creature, hardly a man at all, a creature that the towns have produced, strangely pure-bred and fine in one sense, furtive, quick, subtle. His lashes were dark and long and fine over his eyes, that had no mind in them, only a dreadful kind of subject, inward consciousness, glazed and dark. His dark brows and all his lines, were finely drawn. He would be a dreadful, but wonderful lover to a woman, so marvellously contributed. His legs would be marvellously subtle and alive, under the shapeless trousers; he had some of the fineness and stillness and silkiness of a dark-eyed, silent rat.

Ursula had apprehended him with a fine *frisson* of attraction. The full-built woman was staring offensively. Again Ursula forgot him.

'Won't you have the chair?' she said.

The man looked at her with a sideways look of appreciation, yet far off, almost insolent. The woman drew herself up. There was a certain costermonger richness about her. She did not know what Ursula was after, she was on her guard, hostile. Birkin approached, smiling wickedly at seeing Ursula so nonplussed and frightened.

'What's the matter?' he said, smiling. His eyelids had dropped slightly, there was about him the same suggestive, mocking secrecy that was in the bearing of the two city creatures. The man jerked his head a little on one side, indicating Ursula, and said, with curious amiable, jeering warmth:

'What she warnt? – eh?' An odd smile writhed his lips.

Birkin looked at him from under his slack, ironical eyelids.

'To give you a chair – that – with the label on it,' he said, pointing. The man looked at the object indicated. There was a curious hostility in male, outlawed understanding between the two men.

'What's she warnt to give it *us* for, guvnor,' he replied, in a tone of free intimacy that insulted Ursula.

'Thought you'd like it – it's a pretty chair. We bought it and don't want it. No need for you to have it, don't be frightened,' said Birkin, with a wry smile.

The man glanced up at him, half inimical, half recognising.

'Why don't you want it for yourselves, if you've just bought it?' asked the woman coolly. ' 'Taint good enough for you, now you've had a look at it. Frightened it's got something in it, eh?'

She was looking at Ursula, admiringly, but with some resentment.

'I'd never thought of that,' said Birkin. 'But no, the wood's too thin everywhere.'

'You see,' said Ursula, her face luminous and pleased. '*We* are just going to get married, and we thought we'd buy things. Then we decided, just now, that we wouldn't have furniture, we'd go abroad.'

The full-built, slightly blowsy city girl looked at the fine face of the other woman, with appreciation. They appreciated each other. The youth stood aside, his face expressionless and timeless, the thin line of the black moustache drawn strangely suggestive over his rather wide, closed mouth. He was impassive, abstract, like some dark suggestive presence, a gutter-presence.

'It's all right to be some folks,' said the city girl, turning to her own young man. He did not look at her, but he smiled with the lower part of his face, putting his head aside in an odd gesture of assent. His eyes were unchanging, glazed with darkness.

'Cawsts something to change your mind,' he said, in an incredibly low accent.

'Only ten shillings this time,' said Birkin.

The man looked up at him with a grimace of a smile, furtive, unsure.

'Cheap at 'arf a quid, guvnor,' he said. 'Not like getting divawced.'

'We're not married yet,' said Birkin.

'No, no more aren't we,' said the young woman loudly. 'But we shall be, a Saturday.'

Again she looked at the young man with a determined, protective look, at once overbearing and very gentle. He grinned sicklily, turning away his head. She had got his manhood, but Lord, what did he care! He had a strange furtive pride and slinking singleness.

'Good luck to you,' said Birkin.

'Same to you,' said the young woman. Then, rather tentatively: 'When's yours coming off, then?'

Birkin looked round at Ursula.

'It's for the lady to say,' he replied. 'We go to the registrar the moment she's ready.'

Ursula laughed, covered with confusion and bewilderment.

'No 'urry,' said the young man, grinning suggestive.

'Oh, don't break your neck to get there,' said the young woman. ' 'Slike when you're dead – you're a long time married.'

The young man turned aside as if this hit him.

'The longer the better, let us hope,' said Birkin.

'That's it, guvnor,' said the young man admiringly. 'Enjoy it while it larsts – niver whip a dead donkey.'

'Only when he's shamming dead,' said the young woman, looking at her young man with caressive tenderness of authority.

'Aw, there's a difference,' he said satirically.

'What about the chair?' said Birkin.

'Ycs, all right,' said the woman.

They trailed off to the dealer, the handsome but abject young fellow hanging a little aside.

'That's it,' said Birkin. 'Will you take it with you, or have the address altered.'

'Oh, Fred can carry it. Make him do what he can for the dear old 'ome.'

'Mike use of 'im,' said Fred, grimly humorous, as he took the chair from the dealer. His movements were graceful, yet curiously abject, slinking.

' 'Erc's mother's cosy chair,' he said. 'Warnts a cushion.' And he stood it down on the market stones.

'Don't you think it's pretty?' laughed Ursula.

'Oh, I do,' said the young woman.

'Ave a sit in it, you'll wish you'd kept it,' said the young man.

Ursula promptly sat down in the middle of the market-place.

'Awfully comfortable,' she said. 'But rather hard. You try it.' She invited the young man to a seat. But he turned uncouthly, awkwardly aside, glancing up at her with quick bright eyes, oddly suggestive, like a quick, live rat.

'Don't spoil him,' said the young woman. 'He's not used to arm chairs, 'e isn't.'

The young man turned away, and said, with averted grin:

'Only warnts legs on 'is.'

The four parted. The young woman thanked them.

'Thank you for the chair – it'll last till it gives way.'

'Keep it for an ornyment,' said the young man.

'Good afternoon – good afternoon,' said Ursula and Birkin.

'Goo'-luck to you,' said the young man, glancing and avoiding Birkin's eyes, as he turned aside his head.

The two couples went asunder, Ursula clinging to Birkin's arm. When they had gone some distance, she glanced back and saw the young man going beside the full, easy young woman. His trousers sank over his heels, he moved with a sort of slinking evasion, more crushed with odd self-consciousness now he had the slim old arm-chair to carry, his arm over the back, the four fine, square tapering legs swaying perilously near the granite setts of the pavement. And yet he was somewhere indomitable and separate, like a quick, vital rat. He had a queer, subterranean beauty, repulsive too.

'How strange they are!' said Ursula.

'Children of men,' he said. 'They remind me of Jesus: "The meek shall inherit the earth."'

'But they aren't the meek,' said Ursula.

'Yes, I don't know why, but they are,' he replied.

They waited for the tramcar. Ursula sat on top and looked out on the town. The dusk was just dimming the hollows of crowded houses. 'And are they going to inherit the earth?' she said.

'Yes – they.'

'Then what are we going to do?' she asked. 'We're not like them are we? We're not the meek?'

'No. We've got to live in the chinks they leave us.'

'How horrible!' cried Ursula. 'I don't want to live in chinks.'

'Don't worry,' he said. 'They are' the children of men, they like market-places and street-corners best. That leaves plenty of chinks.'

'All the world,' she said.

'Ah no – but some room.'

The tramcar mounted slowly up the hill, where the ugly winter-grey masses of houses looked like a vision of hell that is cold and angular. They sat and looked. Away in the distance was an angry redness of sunset. It was all cold, somehow small, crowded, and like the end of the world.

'I don't mind it even then,' said Ursula, looking at the repulsiveness of it all. 'It doesn't concern me.'

'No more it does,' he replied, holding her hand. 'One needn't see. One goes one's way. In my world it is sunny and spacious – '

'It is, my love, isn't it?' she cried, hugging near to him on the top of the tramcar, so that the other passengers stared at them.

'And we will wander about on the face of the earth,' he said, 'and we'll look at the world beyond just this bit.'

There was a long silence. Her face was radiant like gold, as she sat thinking.

'I don't want to inherit the earth,' she said. 'I don't want to inherit anything.'

He closed his hand over hers.

'Neither do I. I want to be disinherited.'

She clasped his fingers closely.

'We won't care about *anything*,' she said.

He sat still, and laughed.

'And we'll be married, and have done with them,' she added.

Again he laughed.

'It's one way of getting rid of everything,' she said, 'to get married.'

'And one way of accepting the whole world,' he added.

'A whole other world, yes,' she said happily.

'Perhaps there's Gerald – and Gudrun – ' he said.

'If there is there is, you see,' she said. 'It's no good our worrying. We can't really alter them, can we?'

'No,' he said. 'One has no right to try – not with the best intentions in the world.'

'Do you try to force them?' she asked.

'Perhaps,' he said. 'Why should I want him to be free, if it isn't his business?'

She paused for a time.

'We can't *make* him happy, anyhow,' she said. 'He'd have to be it of himself.'

'I know,' he said. 'But we want other people with us, don't we?'

'Why should we?' she asked.

'I don't know,' he said uneasily. 'One has a hankering after a sort of further fellowship.'

'But why?' she insisted. 'Why should you hanker after other people? Why should you need them?'

This hit him right on the quick. His brows knitted.

'Does it end with just our two selves?' he asked, tense.

'Yes – what more do you want? If anybody likes to come along, let them. But why must you run after them?'

His face was tense and unsatisfied.

'You see,' he said, 'I always imagine our being really happy with some few other people – a little freedom with people.'

She pondered for a moment.

'Yes, one does want that. But it must *happen*. You can't do anything for it with your will. You always seem to think you can *force* the flowers to come out. People must love us because they love us – you can't *make* them.'

'I know,' he said. 'But must one take no steps at all? Must one just go as if one were alone in the world – the only creature in the world?'

'You've got me,' she said. 'Why should you *need* others? Why must you force people to agree with you? Why can't you be single by yourself, as you are always saying? You try to bully Gerald – as you tried to bully Hermione. You must learn to be alone. And it's so horrid of you. You've got me. And yet you want to force other people to love you as well. You do try to bully them to love you. And even then, you don't want their love.'

His face was full of real perplexity.

'Don't I?' he said. 'It's the problem I can't solve. I *know* I want a perfect and complete relationship with you: and we've nearly got it we really have. But beyond that. *Do* I want a real, ultimate relationship with Gerald? Do I want a final, almost extra-human relationship with him – a relationship in the ultimate of me and him – or don't I?'

She looked at him for a long time, with strange bright eyes, but she did not answer.

CHAPTER 27

Flitting

THAT EVENING Ursula returned home very bright-eyed and wondrous – which irritated her people. Her father came home at suppertime, tired after the evening class, and the long journey home. Gudrun was reading, the mother sat in silence.

Suddenly Ursula said to the company at large, in a bright voice, 'Rupert and I are going to be married tomorrow.'

Her father turned round, stiffly.

'You what?' he said.

'Tomorrow!' echoed Gudrun.

'Indeed!' said the mother.

But Ursula only smiled wonderfully, and did not reply.

'Married tomorrow!' cried her father harshly. 'What are you talking about.'

'Yes,' said Ursula. 'Why not?' Those two words, from her, always drove him mad. 'Everything is all right – we shall go to the registrar's office – '

There was a second's hush in the room, after Ursula's blithe vagueness.

'*Really*, Ursula!' said Gudrun.

'Might we ask why there has been all this secrecy?' demanded the mother, rather superbly.

'But there hasn't,' said Ursula. 'You knew.'

'Who knew?' now cried the father. 'Who knew? What do you mean by your "you knew"?'

He was in one of his stupid rages, she instantly closed against him.

'Of course you knew,' she said coolly. 'You knew we were going to get married.'

There was a dangerous pause.

'We knew you were going to get married, did we? Knew! Why, does anybody know anything about you, you shifty bitch!'

'Father!' cried Gudrun, flushing deep in violent remonstrance. Then, in a cold, but gentle voice, as if to remind her sister to be tractable: 'But isn't it a *fearfully* sudden decision, Ursula?' she asked.

'No, not really,' replied Ursula, with the same maddening cheerfulness. 'He's been *wanting* me to agree for weeks – he's had the licence ready. Only I – I wasn't ready in myself. Now I am ready – is there anything to be disagreeable about?'

'Certainly not,' said Gudrun, but in a tone of cold reproof. 'You are perfectly free to do as you like.'

' "Ready in yourself" – *yourself,* that's all that matters, isn't it! "I wasn't ready in myself," ' he mimicked her phrase offensively. 'You and *yourself,* you're of some importance, aren't you?'

She drew herself up and set back her throat, her eyes shining yellow and dangerous.

'I am to myself,' she said, wounded and mortified. 'I know I am not to anybody else. You only wanted to *bully* me – you never cared for my happiness.'

He was leaning forward watching her, his face intense like a spark.

'Ursula, what are you saying? Keep your tongue still;' cried her mother.

Ursula swung round, and the lights in her eyes flashed.

'No, I won't,' she cried. 'I won't hold my tongue and be bullied. What does it matter which day I get married – what does it *matter!* It doesn't affect anybody but myself.'

Her father was tense and gathered together like a cat about to spring.

'Doesn't it?' he cried, coming nearer to her. She shrank away.

'No, how can it?' she replied, shrinking but stubborn.

'It doesn't matter to *me* then, what you do – what becomes of you?' he cried, in a strange voice like a cry.

The mother and Gudrun stood back as if hypnotised.

'No,' stammered Ursula. Her father was very near to her. 'You only want to – '

She knew it was dangerous, and she stopped. He was gathered together, every muscle ready.

'What?' he challenged.

'Bully me,' she muttered, and even as her lips were moving, his hand had caught her smack at the side of the face and she was sent up against the door.

'Father!' cried Gudrun in a high voice, 'it is impossible!'

He stood unmoving. Ursula recovered, her hand was on the door handle. She slowly drew herself up. He seemed doubtful now.

'It's true,' she declared, with brilliant tears in her eyes, her head lifted up in defiance. 'What has your love meant, what did it ever mean? bullying, and denial – it did – '

He was advancing again with strange, tense movements, and clenched fist, and the face of a murderer. But swift as lightning she had flashed out of the door, and they heard her running upstairs.

He stood for a moment looking at the door. Then, like a defeated animal, he turned and went back to his seat by the fire.

Gudrun was very white. Out of the intense silence, the mother's voice was heard saying, cold and angry:

'Well, you shouldn't take so much notice of her.'

Again the silence fell, each followed a separate set of emotions and thoughts.

Suddenly the door opened again: Ursula, dressed in hat and furs, with a small valise in her hand:

'Good-bye!' she said, in her maddening, bright, almost mocking tone. 'I'm going.'

And in the next instant the door was closed, they heard the outer door, then her quick steps down the garden path, then the gate banged, and her light footfall was gone. There was a silence like death in the house.

Ursula went straight to the station, hastening heedlessly on winged feet. There was no train, she must walk on to the junction. As she went through the darkness, she began to cry, and she wept bitterly, with a dumb, heart-broken, child's anguish, all the way on the road, and in the train. Time passed unheeded and unknown, she did not know where she was, nor what was taking place. Only she wept from fathomless depths of hopeless, hopeless grief, the terrible grief of a child, that knows no extenuation.

Yet her voice had the same defensive brightness as she spoke to Birkin's landlady at the door.

'Good evening! Is Mr Birkin in? Can I see him?'

'Yes, he's in. He's in his study.'

Ursula slipped past the woman. His door opened. He had heard her voice.

'Hello!' he exclaimed in surprise, seeing her standing there with the valise in her hand, and marks of tears on her face. She was one who wept without showing many traces, like a child.

'Do I look a sight?' she said, shrinking.

'No – why? Come in,' he took the bag from her hand and they went into the study.

There – immediately, her lips began to tremble like those of a child that remembers again, and the tears came rushing up.

'What's the matter?' he asked, taking her in his arms. She sobbed violently on his shoulder, whilst he held her still, waiting.

'What's the matter?' he said again, when she was quieter. But she only pressed her face further into his shoulder, in pain, like a child that cannot tell.

'What is it, then?' he asked.

Suddenly she broke away, wiped her eyes, regained her composure, and went and sat in a chair.

'Father hit me,' she announced, sitting bunched up, rather like a ruffled bird, her eyes very bright.

'What for?' he said.

She looked away, and would not answer. There was a pitiful redness about her sensitive nostrils, and her quivering lips.

'Why?' he repeated, in his strange, soft, penetrating voice.

She looked round at him, rather defiantly.

'Because I said I was going to be married tomorrow, and he bullied me.'

'Why did he bully you?'

Her mouth dropped again, she remembered the scene once more, the tears came up.

'Because I said he didn't care – and he doesn't, it's only his domineeringness that's hurt – ' she said, her mouth pulled awry by her weeping, all the time she spoke, so that he almost smiled, it seemed so childish. Yet it was not childish, it was a mortal conflict, a deep wound.

'It isn't quite true,' he said. 'And even so, you shouldn't *say* it.'

'It *is* true – it *is* true,' she wept, 'and I won't be bullied by his pretending it's love – when it *isn't* – he doesn't care, how can he – no, he can't – '

He sat in silence. She moved him beyond himself.

'Then you shouldn't rouse him, if he can't,' replied Birkin quietly.

'And I *have* loved him, I have,' she wept. 'I've loved him always, and he's always done this to me, he has – '

'It's been a love of opposition, then,' he said. 'Never mind – it will be all right. It's nothing desperate.'

'Yes,' she wept, 'it is, it is.'

'Why?'

'I shall never see him again – '

'Not immediately. Don't cry, you had to break with him, it had to be – don't cry.'

He went over to her and kissed her fine, fragile hair, touching her wet cheeks gently.

'Don't cry,' he repeated, 'don't cry any more.'

He held her head close against him, very close and quiet.

At last she was still. Then she looked up, her eyes wide and frightened.

'Don't you want me?' she asked.

'Want you?' His darkened, steady eyes puzzled her and did not give her play.

'Do you wish I hadn't come?' she asked, anxious now again for fear she might be out of place.

'No,' he said. 'I wish there hadn't been the violence – so much ugliness – but perhaps it was inevitable.'

She watched him in silence. He seemed deadened.

'But where shall I stay?' she asked, feeling humiliated.

He thought for a moment.

'Here, with me,' he said. 'We're married as much today as we shall be tomorrow.'

'But – '

'I'll tell Mrs Varley,' he said. 'Never mind now.'

He sat looking at her. She could feel his darkened steady eyes looking at her all the time. It made her a little bit frightened. She pushed her hair off her forehead nervously.

'Do I look ugly?' she said.

And she blew her nose again.

A small smile came round his eyes.

'No,' he said, 'fortunately.'

And he went across to her, and gathered her like a belonging in his arms. She was so tenderly beautiful, he could not bear to see her, he could only bear to hide her against himself. Now, washed all clean by her tears, she was new and frail like a flower just unfolded, a flower so new, so tender, so made perfect by inner light, that he could not bear to look at her, he must hide her against himself, cover his eyes against her. She had the perfect candour of creation, something translucent and simple, like a radiant, shining flower that moment unfolded in primal blessedness. She was so new, so wonder-clear, so undimmed. And he was so old, so steeped in heavy memories. Her soul was new, undefined and glimmering with the unseen. And his soul was dark and gloomy, it had only one grain of living hope, like a grain of mustard seed. But this one living grain in him matched the perfect youth in her.

'I love you,' he whispered as he kissed her, and trembled with pure hope, like a man who is born again to a wonderful, lively hope far exceeding the bounds of death.

They were married by law on the next day, and she did as he bade her, she wrote to her father and mother. Her mother replied, not her father.

She did not go back to school. She stayed with Birkin in his rooms, or at the Mill, moving with him as he moved. But she did not see anybody, save Gudrun and Gerald. She was all strange and wondering as yet, but relieved as by dawn.

Gerald sat talking to her one afternoon in the warm study down at the Mill. Rupert had not yet come home.

'You are happy?' Gerald asked her, with a smile.

'Very happy!' she cried, shrinking a little in her brightness.

'Yes, one can see it.'

'Can one?' cried Ursula in surprise.

He looked up at her with a communicative smile.

'Oh yes, plainly.'

She was pleased. She meditated a moment.

'And can you see that Rupert is happy as well?'

He lowered his eyelids, and looked aside.

'Oh yes,' he said.

'Really!'

'Oh yes.'

He was very quiet, as if it were something not to be talked about by him. He seemed sad.

She was very sensitive to suggestion. She asked the question he wanted her to ask.

'Why don't you be happy as well?' she said. 'You could be just the same.'

He paused a moment.

'With Gudrun?' he asked.

'Yes!' she cried, her eyes glowing. But there was a strange tension, an emphasis, as if they were asserting their wishes, against the truth.

'You think Gudrun would have me, and we should be happy?' he said.

She could not know how much it meant to him, how much he meant by the few words. Almost childish, she wanted proof and statement, even over-statement, for everything seemed so uncertain, unfixed to her.

But the passion of gratitude with which he received her into his soul, the extreme, unthinkable gladness of knowing himself living and fit to unite with her, he, who was so nearly dead, who was so near to being gone with the rest of his race down the slope of mechanical death, could never be understood by her. He worshipped her as age worships youth, he gloried in her, because, in his one grain of faith, he was young as she, he was her proper mate. This marriage with her was his resurrection and his life.

All this she could not know. She wanted to be made much of, to be adored. There were infinite distances of silence between them. How could he tell her of the immanence of her beauty, that was not form, or weight, or colour, but something like a strange, golden light! How could he know himself what her beauty lay in, for him. He said 'Your nose is beautiful, your chin is adorable.' But it sounded like lies, and she was disappointed, hurt. Even when he said, whispering with truth, 'I love you, I love you,' it was not the real truth. It was something beyond love, such a gladness of having surpassed oneself, of having transcended the old existence. How could he say "I" when he was something new and unknown, not himself at all? This I, this old formula of the age, was a dead letter.

In the new, superfine bliss, a peace superseding knowledge, there was no I and you, there was only the third, unrealised wonder, the wonder of existing not as oneself, but in a consummation of my being and of her being in a new one, a new, paradisal unit regained from the duality. Nor can I say 'I love you,' when I have ceased to be, and you have ceased to be: we are both caught up and transcended into a new oneness where everything is silent, because there is nothing to answer, all is perfect and at one. Speech travels between the separate parts. But in the perfect One there is perfect silence of bliss.

'Yes, I'm *sure!*' she cried.

Her eyes were round with delight. Yet underneath she was constrained, she knew her own insistence.

'Oh, I'm *so* glad,' she added.

He smiled.

'What makes you glad?' he said.

'For *her* sake,' she replied. 'I'm sure you'd – you're the right man for her.'

'You are?' he said. 'And do you think she would agree with you?'

'Oh yes!' she exclaimed hastily. Then, upon reconsideration, very uneasy: 'Though Gudrun isn't so very simple, is she? One doesn't know her in five minutes, does one? She's not like me in that.' She laughed at him with her strange, open, dazzled face.

'You think she's not much like you?' Gerald asked.

She knitted her brows.

'Oh, in many ways she is. But I never know what she will do when anything new comes.'

'You don't?' said Gerald. He was silent for some moments. Then he moved tentatively. 'I was going to ask her, in any case, to go away with me at Christmas,' he said, in a very small, cautious voice.

'Go away with you? For a time, you mean?'

'As long as she likes,' he said, with a deprecating movement.

They were both silent for some minutes.

'Of course,' said Ursula at last, 'she *might* just be willing to rush into marriage. You can see.'

'Yes,' smiled Gerald. 'I can see. But in case she won't – do you think she would go abroad with me for a few days – or for a fortnight?'

'Oh yes,' said Ursula. 'I'd ask her.'

'Do you think we might all go together?'

'All of us?' Again Ursula's face lighted up. 'It would be rather fun, don't you think?'

'Great fun,' he said.

'And then you could see,' said Ursula.

'What?'

'How things went. I think it is best to take the honeymoon before the wedding – don't you?'

She was pleased with this *mot*.[1] He laughed.

'In certain cases,' he said. 'I'd rather it were so in my own case.'

'Would you!' exclaimed Ursula. Then doubtingly, 'Yes, perhaps you're right. One should please oneself.'

Birkin came in a little later, and Ursula told him what had been said.

'Gudrun!' exclaimed Birkin. 'She's a born mistress, just as Gerald is a born lover – *amant en titre*.[2] If as somebody says all women are either wives or mistresses, then Gudrun is a mistress.'

'And all men either lovers or husbands,' cried Ursula. 'But why not both?'

'The one excludes the other,' he laughed.

'Then I want a lover,' cried Ursula.

'No you don't,' he said.

'But I do,' she wailed.

He kissed her, and laughed.

It was two days after this that Ursula was to go to fetch her things from the house in Beldover. The removal had taken place, the family had gone. Gudrun had rooms in Willey Green.

Ursula had not seen her parents since her marriage. She wept over the rupture, yet what was the good of making it up! Good or not good, she could not go to them. So her things had been left behind and she and Gudrun were to walk over for them, in the afternoon.

It was a wintry afternoon, with red in the sky, when they arrived at the house. The windows were dark and blank, already the place was frightening. A stark, void entrance-hall struck a chill to the hearts of the girls.

'I don't believe I dare have come in alone,' said Ursula. 'It frightens me.'

'Ursula!' cried Gudrun. 'Isn't it amazing! Can you believe

1 (Fr. *bon mot*) – wit.
2 (Fr.) established lover.

you lived in this place and never felt it? How I lived here a day without dying of terror, I cannot conceive!'

They looked in the big dining-room. It was a good-sized room, but now a cell would have been lovelier. The large bay windows were naked, the floor was stripped, and a border of dark polish went round the tract of pale boarding.

In the faded wallpaper were dark patches where furniture had stood, where pictures had hung. The sense of walls, dry, thin, flimsy-seeming walls, and a flimsy flooring, pale with its artificial black edges, was neutralising to the mind. Everything was null to the senses, there was enclosure without substance, for the walls were dry and papery. Where were they standing, on earth, or suspended in some cardboard box? In the hearth was burnt paper, and scraps of half-burnt paper.

'Imagine that we passed our days here!' said Ursula.

'I know,' cried Gudrun. 'It is too appalling. What must we be like, if we are the contents of *this!*'

'Vile!' said Ursula. 'It really is.'

And she recognised half-burnt covers of 'Vogue' – half-burnt representations of women in gowns – lying under the grate.

They went to the drawing-room. Another piece of shut-in air; without weight or substance, only a sense of intolerable papery imprisonment in nothingness. The kitchen did look more substantial, because of the red-tiled floor and the stove, but it was cold and horrid.

The two girls tramped hollowly up the bare stairs. Every sound reechoed under their hearts. They tramped down the bare corridor. Against the wall of Ursula's bedroom were her things – a trunk, a work-basket, some books, loose coats, a hat-box, standing desolate in the universal emptiness of the dusk.

'A cheerful sight, aren't they?' said Ursula, looking down at her forsaken possessions.

'Very cheerful,' said Gudrun.

The two girls set to, carrying everything down to the front door. Again and again they made the hollow, re-echoing transit.

The whole place seemed to resound about them with a noise of hollow, empty futility. In the distance the empty, invisible rooms sent forth a vibration almost of obscenity. They almost fled with the last articles, into the out-of-door.

But it was cold. They were waiting for Birkin, who was coming with the car. They went indoors again, and upstairs to their parents' front bedroom, whose windows looked down on the road, and across the country at the black-barred sunset, black and red barred, without light.

They sat down in the window-seat, to wait. Both girls were looking over the room. It was void, with a meaninglessness that was almost dreadful.

'Really,' said Ursula, 'this room *couldn't* be sacred, could it?'

Gudrun looked over it with slow eyes.

'Impossible,' she replied.

'When I think of their lives – father's and mother's, their love, and their marriage, and all of us children, and our bringing-up – would you have such a life, Prune?'

'I wouldn't, Ursula.'

'It all seems so *nothing* – their two lives – there's no meaning in it. Really, if they had *not* met, and *not* married, and not lived together – it wouldn't have mattered, would it?'

'Of course – you can't tell,' said Gudrun.

'No. But if I thought my life was going to be like it – Prune,' she caught Gudrun's arm, 'I should run.'

Gudrun was silent for a few moments.

'As a matter of fact, one cannot contemplate the ordinary life – one cannot contemplate it,' replied Gudrun. 'With you, Ursula, it is quite different. You will be out of it all, with Birkin. He's a special case. But with the ordinary man, who has his life fixed in one place, marriage is just impossible. There may be, and there *are,* thousands of women who want it, and could conceive of nothing else. But the very thought of it sends me *mad*. One must be free, above all, one must be free. One may forfeit everything else, but one must be free – one must not become 7, Pinchbeck

Street – or Somerset Drive – or Shortlands. No man will be
sufficient to make that good – no man! To marry, one must have
a free lance, or nothing, a comrade-in-arms, a Glücksritter. A
man with a position in the social world – well, ids just impossible,
impossible!'

'What a lovely word – a Glücksritter!' said Ursula. 'So much
nicer than a soldier of fortune.'

'Yes, isn't it?' said Gudrun. 'I'd tilt the world with a
Glücksritter. But a home, an establishment! Ursula, what would
it mean? – think!'

'I know,' said Ursula. 'We've had one home – that's enough
for me.'

'Quite enough,' said Gudrun.

'The little grey home in the west,' quoted Ursula ironically.

'Doesn't it sound grey, too,' said Gudrun grimly.

They were interrupted by the sound of the car. There was
Birkin. Ursula was surprised that she felt so lit up, that she became
suddenly so free from the problems of grey homes in the west.

They heard his heels click on the hall pavement below.

'Hello!' he called, his voice echoing alive through the house.
Ursula smiled to herself. *He* was frightened of the place too.

'Hello! Here we are,' she called downstairs. And they heard
him quickly running up.

'This is a ghostly situation,' he said.

'These houses don't have ghosts – they've never had any
personality, and only a place with personality can have a ghost,'
said Gudrun.

'I suppose so. Are you both weeping over the past?'

'We are,' said Gudrun, grimly.

Ursula laughed.

'Not weeping that it's gone, but weeping that it ever *was*,'
she said. 'Oh,' he replied, relieved.

He sat down for a moment. There was something in his
presence, Ursula thought, lambent and alive. It made even the
impertinent structure of this null house disappear.

'Gudrun says she could not bear to be married and put into a house,' said Ursula meaningful – they knew this referred to Gerald.

He was silent for some moments.

'Well,' he said, 'if you know beforehand you couldn't stand it, you're safe.'

'Quite!' said Gudrun.

'Why *does* every woman think her aim in life is to have a hubby and a little grey home in the west? Why is this the goal of life? Why should it be?' said Ursula.

'Il faut avoir le respect de ses betises,' said Birkin.

'But you needn't have the respect for the *bêtise* before you've committed it,' laughed Ursula.

'Ah then, des betises du papa?'

'Et de la maman,' added Gudrun satirically.

'Et des voisins,' said Ursula.*

They all laughed, and rose. It was getting dark. They carried the things to the car. Gudrun locked the door of the empty house. Birkin had lighted the lamps of the automobile. It all seemed very happy, as if they were setting out.

'Do you mind stopping at Coulsons. I have to leave the key there,' said Gudrun.

'Right,' said Birkin, and they moved off.

They stopped in the main street. The shops were just lighted, the last miners were passing home along the causeways, half-visible shadows in their grey pit-dirt, moving through the blue air. But their feet rang harshly in manifold sound, along the pavement.

How pleased Gudrun was to come out of the shop, and enter the car, and be borne swiftly away into the downhill of palpable dusk, with Ursula and Birkin! What an adventure life seemed at this moment! How deeply, how suddenly she envied Ursula! Life for her was so quick, and an open door – so reckless as if not only this world, but the world that was gone and the world to come were nothing to her. Ah, if she could be *just like that,* it would be perfect.

---

* These French phrases mean: one must respect one's own follies; those of Daddy, Mummy, and the neighbours.

For always, except in her moments of excitement, she felt a want within herself. She was unsure. She had felt that now, at last, in Gerald's strong and violent love, she was living fully and finally. But when she compared herself with Ursula, already her soul was jealous, unsatisfied. She was not satisfied – she was never to be satisfied.

What was she short of now? It was marriage – it was the wonderful stability of marriage. She did want it, let her say what she might. She had been lying. The old idea of marriage was right even now marriage and the home. Yet her mouth gave a little grimace at the words. She thought of Gerald and Shortlands – marriage and the home! Ah well, let it rest! He meant a great deal to her – but –! Perhaps it was not in her to marry. She was one of life's outcasts, one of the drifting lives that have no root. No, no it could not be so. She suddenly conjured up a rosy room, with herself in a beautiful gown, and a handsome man in evening dress who held her in his arms in the firelight, and kissed her. This picture she entitled 'Home.' It would have done for the Royal Academy.

'Come with us to tea – *do,*' said Ursula, as they ran nearer to the cottage of Willey Green.

'Thanks awfully – but I *must* go in – ' said Gudrun. She wanted very much to go on with Ursula and Birkin.

That seemed like life indeed to her. Yet a certain perversity would not let her.

'Do come – yes, it would be so nice,' pleaded Ursula.

'I'm awfully sorry – I should love to – but I can't – really – '
She descended from the car in trembling haste.

'Can't you really!' came Ursula's regretful voice.

'No, really I can't,' responded Gudrun's pathetic, chagrined words out of the dusk.

'All right, are you?' called Birkin.

'Quite!' said Gudrun. 'Good-night!'

'Good-night,' they called.

'Come whenever you like, we shall be glad,' called Birkin.

'Thank you very much,' called Gudrun, in the strange, twanging voice of lonely chagrin that was very puzzling to him. She turned away to her cottage gate, and they drove on. But immediately she stood to watch them, as the car ran vague into the distance. And as she went up the path to her strange house, her heart was full of incomprehensible bitterness.

In her parlour was a long-case clock, and inserted into its dial was a ruddy, round, slant-eyed, joyous-painted face, that wagged over with the most ridiculous ogle when the clock ticked, and back again with the same absurd glad-eye at the next tick. All the time the absurd smooth, brown-ruddy face gave her an obtrusive 'glad-eye.' She stood for minutes, watching it, till a sort of maddened disgust overcame her, and she laughed at herself hollowly. And still it rocked, and gave her the glad-eye from one side, then from the other, from one side, then from the other. Ah, how unhappy she was! In the midst of her most active happiness, ah, how unhappy she was! She glanced at the table. Gooseberry jam, and the same home-made cake with too much soda in it! Still, gooseberry jam was good, and one so rarely got it.

All the evening she wanted to go to the Mill. But she coldly refused to allow herself. She went the next afternoon instead. She was happy to find Ursula alone. It was a lovely, intimate secluded atmosphere. They talked endlessly and delightedly. 'Aren't you *fearfully* happy here?' said Gudrun to her sister glancing at her own bright eyes in the mirror. She always envied, almost with resentment, the strange positive fullness that subsisted in the atmosphere around Ursula and Birkin.

'How really beautifully this room is done,' she said aloud. 'This hard plaited matting – what a lovely colour it is, the colour of cool light!'

And it seemed to her perfect.

'Ursula,' she said at length, in a voice of question and detachment, 'did you know that Gerald Crich had suggested our going away all together at Christmas?'

'Yes, he's spoken to Rupert.'

A deep flush dyed Gudrun's cheek. She was silent a moment, as if taken aback, and not knowing what to say.

'But don't you think,' she said at last, 'it is *amazingly cool!*'
Ursula laughed.

'I like him for it,' she said.

Gudrun was silent. It was evident that, whilst she was almost
mortified by Gerald's taking the liberty of making such a
suggestion to Birkin, yet the idea itself attracted her strongly.

'There's a rather lovely simplicity about Gerald, I think,' said
Ursula, 'so defiant, somehow! Oh, I think he's *very* lovable.'

Gudrun did not reply for some moments. She had still to get
over the feeling of insult at the liberty taken with her freedom.

'What did Rupert say – do you know?' she asked.

'He said it would be most awfully jolly,' said Ursula.

Again Gudrun looked down, and was silent.

'Don't you think it would?' said Ursula, tentatively. She was
never quite sure how many defences Gudrun was having round
herself.

Gudrun raised her face with difficulty and held it averted.

'I think it *might* be awfully jolly, as you say,' she replied.
'But don't you think it was an unpardonable liberty to take – to
talk of such things to Rupert – who after all – you see what I
mean, Ursula – they might have been two men arranging an outing
with some little *type* they'd picked up. Oh, I think it's unforgivable,
quite!' She used the French word '*type.*'

Her eyes flashed, her soft face was flushed and sullen. Ursula
looked on, rather frightened, frightened most of all because she
thought Gudrun seemed rather common, really like a little *type*.
But she had not the courage quite to think this – not right out.

'Oh no,' she cried, stammering. 'Oh no – not at all like that –
oh no! No, I think it's rather beautiful, the friendship between
Rupert and Gerald. They just are simple – they say anything to
each other, like brothers.'

Gudrun flushed deeper. She could not *bear* it that Gerald
gave her away – even to Birkin.

'But do you think even brothers have any right to exchange
confidences of that sort?' she asked, with deep anger.

'Oh yes,' said Ursula. 'There's never anything said that isn't perfectly straightforward. No, the thing that's amazed me most in Gerald – how perfectly simple and direct he can be! And you know, it takes rather a big man. Most of them *must* be indirect, they are such cowards.'

But Gudrun was still silent with anger. She wanted the absolute secrecy kept, with regard to her movements.

'Won't you go?' said Ursula. 'Do, we might all be so happy! There is something I *love* about Gerald – he's *much* more lovable than I thought him. He's free, Gudrun, he really is.'

Gudrun's mouth was still closed, sullen and ugly. She opened it at length.

'Do you know where he proposes to go?' she asked.

'Yes – to the Tyrol, where he used to go when he was in Germany – a lovely place where students go, small and rough and lovely, for winter sport!'

Through Gudrun's mind went the angry thought – 'they know everything.'

'Yes,' she said aloud, 'about forty kilometres from Innsbruck, isn't it?'

'I don't know exactly where – but it would be lovely, don't you think, high in the perfect snow –?'

'Very lovely!' said Gudrun, sarcastically.

Ursula was put out.

'Of course,' she said, 'I think Gerald spoke to Rupert so that it shouldn't seem like an outing with a *type* – '

'I know, of course,' said Gudrun, 'that he quite commonly does take up with that sort.'

'Does he!' said Ursula. 'Why how do you know?'

'I know of a model in Chelsea,' said Gudrun coldly. Now Ursula was silent. 'Well,' she said at last, with a doubtful laugh, 'I hope he has a good time with her.' At which Gudrun looked more glum.

CHAPTER 28

Gudrun in the Pompadour

CHRISTMAS DREW near, all four prepared for flight. Birkin and Ursula were busy packing their few personal things, making them ready to be sent off, to whatever country and whatever place they might choose at last. Gudrun was very much excited. She loved to be on the wing.

She and Gerald, being ready first, set off via London and Paris to Innsbruck, where they would meet Ursula and Birkin. In London they stayed one night. They went to the music-hall, and afterwards to the Pompadour Café.

Gudrun hated the Café, yet she always went back to it, as did most of the artists of her acquaintance. She loathed its atmosphere of petty vice and petty jealousy and petty art. Yet she always called in again, when she was in town. It was as if she *had* to return to this small, slow, central whirlpool of disintegration and dissolution: just give it a look.

She sat with Gerald drinking some sweetish liqueur, and staring with black, sullen looks at the various groups of people at the tables. She would greet nobody, but young men nodded to her frequently, with a kind of sneering familiarity. She cut them all. And it gave her pleasure to sit there, cheeks flushed, eyes black and sullen, seeing them all objectively, as put away from her, like creatures in some menagerie of apish degraded souls. God, what a foul crew they were! Her blood beat black and thick in her veins with rage and loathing. Yet she must sit and watch, watch. One or two people came to speak to her. From every side of the Café, eyes turned half furtively, half jeeringly at her, men looking over their shoulders, women under their hats.

The old crowd was there, Carlyon in his corner with his pupils and his girl, Halliday and Libidnikov and the Pussum – they were all there. Gudrun watched Gerald. She watched his eyes linger a moment on Halliday, on Halliday's party. These last were on the look-out – they nodded to him, he nodded again. They giggled and whispered among themselves. Gerald watched them with the steady twinkle in his eyes. They were urging the Pussum to something.

She at last rose. She was wearing a curious dress of dark silk splashed and spattered with different colours, a curious motley effect. She was thinner, her eyes were perhaps hotter, more disintegrated. Otherwise she was just the same. Gerald watched her with the same steady twinkle in his eyes as she came across. She held out her thin brown hand to him.

'How are you?' she said.

He shook hands with her, but remained seated, and let her stand near him, against the table. She nodded blackly to Gudrun, whom she did not know to speak to, but well enough by sight and reputation.

'I am very well,' said Gerald. 'And you?'

'Oh I'm all wight. What about Wupert?'

'Rupert? He's very well, too.'

'Yes, I don't mean that. What about him being married?'

'Oh – yes, he is married.'

The Pussum's eyes had a hot flash.

'Oh, he's weally bwought it off then, has he? When was he married?'

'A week or two ago.'

'Weally! He's never written.'

'No.'

'No. Don't you think it's too bad?'

This last was in a tone of challenge. The Pussum let it be known by her tone, that she was aware of Gudrun's listening.

'I suppose he didn't feel like it,' replied Gerald.

'But why didn't he?' pursued the Pussum.

This was received in silence. There was an ugly, mocking persistence in the small, beautiful figure of the short-haired girl, as she stood near Gerald.

'Are you staying in town long?' she asked.

'Tonight only.'

'Oh, only tonight. Are you coming over to speak to Julius?'

'Not tonight.'

'Oh very well. I'll tell him then.' Then came her touch of diablerie. 'You're looking awf'lly fit'

'Yes – I feel it.' Gerald was quite calm and easy, a spark of satiric amusement in his eye.

'Are you having a good time?'

This was a direct blow for Gudrun, spoken in a level, toneless voice of callous ease.

'Yes,' he replied, quite colourlessly.

'I'm awf'lly sorry you aren't coming round to the flat. You aren't very faithful to your fwiends.'

'Not very,' he said.

She nodded them both! Good-night', and went back slowly to her own set. Gudrun watched her curious walk, stiff and jerking at the loins. They heard her level, toneless voice distinctly.

'He won't come over; – he is otherwise engaged,' it said. There was more laughter and lowered voices and mockery at the table.

'Is she a friend of yours?' said Gudrun, looking calmly at Gerald.

'I've stayed at Halliday's flat with Birkin,' he said, meeting her slow, calm eyes. And she knew that the Pussum was one of his mistresses and he knew she knew.

She looked round, and called for the waiter. She wanted an iced cocktail, of all things. This amused Gerald – he wondered what was up.

The Halliday party was tipsy, and malicious. They were talking out loudly about Birkin, ridiculing him on every point, particularly on his marriage.

'Oh, *don't* make me think of Birkin,' Halliday was squealing. 'He makes me perfectly sick. He is as bad as Jesus. "Lord, *what* must I do to be saved!" '

He giggled to himself tipsily.

'Do you remember,' came the quick voice of the Russian, 'the letters he used to send. "Desire is holy – " '

'Oh yes!' cried Halliday. 'Oh, how perfectly splendid. Why, I've got one in my pocket. I'm sure I have.'

He took out various papers from his pocket book.

'I'm sure I've – *hic! Oh dear!* – got one.'

Gerald and Gudrun were watching absorbedly.

'Oh yes, how perfectly – *hic!* – splendid! Don't make me laugh, Pussum, it gives me the hiccup. Hic! – ' They all giggled.

'What did he say in that one?' the Pussum asked, leaning forward, her dark, soft hair falling and swinging against her face. There was something curiously indecent, obscene, about her small, longish, dark skull, particularly when the ears showed.

'Wait – oh do wait! *No-o*, I won't give it to you, I'll read it aloud. I'll read you the choice bits, – hic! Oh dear! Do you think if I drink water it would take off this hiccup? *Hic!* Oh, I feel perfectly helpless.'

'Isn't that the letter about uniting the dark and the light – and the Flux of Corruption?' asked Maxim, in his precise, quick voice.

'I believe so,' said the Pussum.

'Oh is it? I'd forgotten – *hic!* – it was that one,' Halliday said, opening the letter. '*Hic!* Oh yes. How perfectly splendid! This is one of the best. "There is a phase in every race – " ' he read in the sing-song, slow, distinct voice of a clergyman reading the Scriptures, ' "when the desire for destruction overcomes every other desire. In the individual, this desire is ultimately a desire for destruction in the self" – *hic!* – ' he paused and looked up.

'I hope he's going ahead with the destruction of himself,' said the quick voice of the Russian. Halliday giggled, and lolled his head back, vaguely.

'There's not much to destroy in him,' said the Pussum. 'He's so thin already, there's only a fag-end to start on.'

'Oh, isn't it beautiful! I love reading it! I believe it has cured my hiccup!' squealed Halliday. 'Do let me go on. "It is a desire for the reduction process in oneself, a reducing back to the origin, a return along the Flux of Corruption, to the original rudimentary conditions of being –!" Oh, but I *do* think it is wonderful. It almost supersedes the Bible – '

'Yes – Flux of Corruption,' said the Russian, 'I remember that phrase.'

'Oh, he was always talking about Corruption,' said the Pussum. 'He must be corrupt himself, to have it so much on his mind.'

'Exactly!' said the Russian.

'Do let me go on! Oh, this is a perfectly wonderful piece! But do listen to this. "And in the great retrogression, the reducing back of the created body of life, we get knowledge, and beyond knowledge, the phosphorescent ecstasy of acute sensation." Oh, I do think these phrases are too absurdly wonderful. Oh but don't you think they *are* they're nearly as good as Jesus. "And if, Julius, you want this ecstasy of reduction with the Pussum, you must go on till it is fulfilled. But surely there is in you also, somewhere, the living desire for positive creation, relationships in ultimate faith, when all this process of active corruption, with all its flowers of mud, is transcended, and more or less finished – " I do wonder what the flowers of mud are. Pussum, you are a flower of mud.'

'Thank you – and what are you?'

'Oh, I'm another, surely, according to this letter! We're all flowers of mud – *Fleurs – hic! du mal!* It's perfectly wonderful, Birkin harrowing Hell – harrowing the Pompadour – *Hic!'*

'Go on – go on,' said Maxim. 'What comes next? It's really very interesting.'

'I think it's awful cheek to write like that,' said the Pussum.

'Yes – yes, so do I,' said the Russian. 'He is a megalomaniac, of course, it is a form of religious mania. He thinks he is the Saviour of man – go on reading.'

'Surely,' Halliday intoned, ' "surely goodness and mercy hath followed me all the days of my life – " ' he broke off and giggled. The he began again, intoning like a clergyman. ' "Surely there will come an end in Us to this desire – for the constant going apart, – this passion for putting asunder – everything – ourselves, reducing ourselves part from part – reacting in intimacy only for destruction, – using sex as a great reducing agent, reducing the two great elements of male' and female from their highly complex unity – reducing the old ideas, going back to the savages for our sensations, – always seeking to *lose* ourselves in some ultimate black sensation, mindless and infinite – burning only with destructive fires, raging on with the hope of being burnt out utterly – " '

'I want to go,' said Gudrun to Gerald, as she signalled the waiter. Her eyes were flashing, her cheeks were flushed. The strange effect of Birkin's letter read aloud in a perfect clerical sing-song, clear and resonant, phrase by phrase, made the blood mount into her head as if she were mad.

She rose, whilst Gerald was paying the bill, and walked over to Halliday's table. They all glanced up at her.

'Excuse me,' she said. 'Is that a genuine letter you are reading?'

'Oh yes,' said Halliday. 'Quite genuine.'

'May I see?'

Smiling foolishly he handed it to her, as if hypnotised.

'Thank you,' she said.

And she turned and walked out of the Café with the letter, all down the brilliant room, between the tables, in her measured fashion. It was some moments before anybody realised what was happening.

From Halliday's table came half articulate cries, then somebody booed, then all the far end of the place began booing after Gudrun's retreating form. She was fashionably dressed in blackish-green and silver, her hat was brilliant green, like the sheen on an insect, but the brim was soft dark green, a falling edge with fine silver, her coat was dark green, lustrous, with a high collar of grey fur, and great fur cuffs, the edge of her dress showed silver and black velvet, her stockings and shoes were silver grey. She moved with slow, fashionable indifference to the door. The porter opened obsequiously for her, and, at her nod, hurried to the edge of the pavement and whistled for a taxi. The two lights of a vehicle almost immediately curved round towards her, like two eyes.

Gerald had followed in wonder, amid all the booing, not having caught her misdeed. He heard the Pussum's voice saying:

'Go and get it back from her. I never heard of such a thing! Go and get it back from her. Tell Gerald Crich – there he goes – go and make him give it up.'

Gudrun stood at the door of the taxi, which the man held open for her.

'To the hotel?' she asked, as Gerald came out, hurriedly.

'Where you like,' he answered.

'Right!' she said. Then to the driver, 'Wagstaff's – Barton Street.'

The driver bowed his head, and put down the flag.

Gudrun entered the taxi, with the deliberate cold movement of a woman who is well-dressed and contemptuous in her soul. Yet she was frozen with overwrought feelings. Gerald followed her.

'You've forgotten the man,' she said coolly, with a slight nod of her hat. Gerald gave the porter a shilling. The man saluted. They were in motion.

'What was all the row about?' asked Gerald, in wondering excitement.

'I walked away with Birkin's letter,' she said, and he saw the crushed paper in her hand.

His eyes glittered with satisfaction.

'Ah!' he said. 'Splendid! A set of jackasses!'

'I could have *killed* them!' she cried in passion. '*Dogs!* – they are dogs! Why is Rupert such a *fool* as to write such letters to them? Why does he give himself away to such canaille?* It's a thing that *cannot be borne.*'

Gerald wondered over her strange passion.

And she could not rest any longer in London. They must go by the morning train from Charing Cross. As they drew over the bridge, in the train, having glimpses of the river between the great iron girders, she cried:

'I feel I could *never* see this foul town again – I couldn't *bear* to come back to it.'

---

* (Fr.) riff-raff.

CHAPTER 29

Continental

URSULA WENT on in an unreal suspense, the last weeks before going away. She was not herself, – she was not anything. She was something that is going to be – soon – soon – very soon. But as yet, she was only imminent.

She went to see her parents. It was a rather stiff, sad meeting, more like a verification of separateness than a reunion. But they were all vague and indefinite with one another, stiffened in the fate that moved them apart.

She did not really come to until she was on the ship crossing from Dover to Ostend. Dimly she had come down to London with Birkin, London had been a vagueness, so had the train-journey to Dover. It was all like a sleep.

And now, at last, as she stood in the stem of the ship, in a pitch-dark, rather blowy night, feeling the motion of the sea, and watching the small, rather desolate little lights that twinkled on the shores of England, as on the shores of nowhere, watched them sinking smaller and smaller on the profound and living darkness, she felt her soul stirring to awake from its anaesthetic sleep.

'Let us go forward, shall we?' said Birkin. He wanted to be at the tip of their projection. So they left off looking at the faint sparks that glimmered out of nowhere, in the far distance, called England, and turned their faces to the unfathomed night in front.

They went right to the bows of the softly plunging vessel. In the complete obscurity, Birkin found a comparatively sheltered nook, where a great rope was coiled up. It was quite near the very point of the ship, near the black, unpierced space ahead. There they sat down, folded together, folded round with the same rug, creeping in nearer and ever nearer to one another, till it seemed they had crept right into each other, and become one substance. It was very cold, and the darkness was palpable.

One of the ship's crew carne along the deck, dark as the darkness, not really visible. They then made out the faintest pallor of his face. He felt their presence, and stopped, unsure – then bent forward. When his face was near them, he saw the faint pallor of their faces. Then he withdrew like a phantom. And they watched him without making any sound.

They seemed to fall away into the profound darkness. There was no sky, no earth, only one unbroken darkness, into which, with a soft, sleeping motion, they seemed to fall like one closed seed of life falling through dark, fathomless space.

They had forgotten where they were, forgotten all that was and all that had been, conscious only in their heart, and there conscious only of this pure trajectory through the surpassing darkness. The ship's prow cleaved on, with a faint noise of cleavage, into the complete night, without knowing, without seeing, only surging on.

In Ursula the sense of the unrealised world ahead triumphed over everything. In the midst of this profound darkness, there seemed to glow on her heart the effulgence of a paradise unknown and unrealised. Her heart was full of the most wonderful light, golden like honey of darkness, sweet like the warmth of day, a light which was not shed on the world, only on the unknown paradise towards which she was going, a sweetness of habitation, a delight of living quite unknown, but hers infallibly. In her transport she lifted her face suddenly to him, and he touched it with his lips. So cold, so fresh, so sea-clear her face was, it was like kissing a flower that grows near the surf.

But he did not know the ecstasy of bliss in fore-knowledge that she knew. To him, the wonder of this transit was overwhelming. He was falling through a gulf of infinite darkness, like a meteorite plunging across the chasm between the worlds. The world was torn in two, and he was plunging like an unlit star through the ineffable rift. What was beyond was not yet for him. He was overcome by the trajectory.

In a trance he lay enfolding Ursula round about. His face was against her fine, fragile hair, he breathed its fragrance with the

sea and the profound night. And his soul was at peace; yielded,
as he fell into the unknown. This was the first time that an utter
and absolute peace had entered his heart, now, in this final transit
out of life.

When there carne some stir on the deck, they roused. They
stood up. How stiff and cramped they were, in the night-time!
And yet the paradisal glow on her heart, and the unutterable peace
of darkness in his, this was the all-in-all.

They stood up and looked ahead. Low lights were seen down
the darkness. This was the world again. It was not the bliss of
her heart, nor the peace of his. It was the superficial unreal world
of fact. Yet not quite the old world. For the peace and the bliss in
their hearts was enduring.

Strange, and desolate above all things, like disembarking from
the Styx into the desolated underworld, was this landing at night.
There was the raw, half-lighted, covered-in vastness of the dark
place, boarded and hollow underfoot, with only desolation
everywhere. Ursula had caught sight of the big, pallid, mystic
letters 'OSTEND,' standing in the darkness. Everybody was
hurrying with a blind, insect-like intentness through the dark grey
air, porters were calling in un-English English, then trotting with
heavy bags, their colourless blouses looking ghostly as they
disappeared; Ursula stood at a long, low, zinc-covered barrier,
along with hundreds of other spectral people, and all the way
down the vast, raw darkness was this low stretch of open bags
and spectral people, whilst, on the other side of the barrier, pallid
officials in peaked caps and. moustaches were turning the
underclothing in the bags, then scrawling a chalk-mark.

It was done. Birkin snapped the hand bags, off they went,
the porter corning behind. They were through a great doorway,
and in the open night again – ah, a railway platform! Voices were
still calling in inhuman agitation through the dark-grey air, spectres
were running along the darkness between the train.

'Köln – Berlin – ' Ursula made out on the boards hung on the
high train on one side.

'Here we are,' said Birkin. And on her side she saw: 'Elsass
– Lothringen – Luxembourg, Metz – Basle.'

'That was it, Basle!'

The porter came up.

'A Bâle – deuxieme classe? – Voila!' And he clambered into the high train. They followed. The compartments were already some of them taken. But many were dim and empty. The luggage was stowed, the porter was tipped.

'Nous avons encore –?' said Birkin, looking at his watch and at the porter.

'Encore une demi-heure.'* With which, in his blue blouse, he disappeared. He was ugly and insolent.

'Come,' said Birkin. 'It is cold. Let us eat.'

There was a coffee-wagon on the platform. They drank hot, watery coffee, and ate the long rolls, split, with ham between, which were such a wide bite that it almost dislocated Ursula's jaw; and they walked beside the high trains. It was all so strange, so extremely desolate, like the underworld, grey, grey, dirt grey, desolate, forlorn, nowhere grey, dreary nowhere.

At last they were moving through the night. In the darkness Ursula made out the flat fields, the wet flat dreary darkness of the Continent. They pulled up surprisingly soon – Bruges! Then on through the level darkness, with glimpses of sleeping farms and thin poplar trees and deserted high-roads. She sat dismayed, hand in hand with Birkin. He pale, immobile like a *revenant* himself, looked sometimes out of the window, sometimes closed his eyes. Then his eyes opened again, dark as the darkness outside.

A flash of a few lights on the darkness – Ghent station! A few more spectres moving outside on the platform – then the bell – then motion again through the level darkness. Ursula saw a man with a lantern come out of a farm by the railway, and cross to the dark farm-buildings. She thought of the Marsh, the old, intimate farm-life at Cossethay. My God, how far was she projected from her childhood, how far was she still to go! In one life-time one travelled through aeons. The great chasm of memory from her childhood in the intimate country surroundings of Cossethay and the Marsh Farm – she remembered the servant

---

* In the conversation in French above, a porter shows the second class seats and says that the train would leave after half an hour.

Tilly, who used to give her bread and butter sprinkled with brown sugar, in the old living-room where the grandfather clock had two pink roses in a basket painted above the figures on the face – and now when she was travelling into the unknown with Birkin, an utter stranger – was so great, that it seemed she had no identity, that the child she had been, playing in Cossethay churchyard, was a little creature of history, not really herself.

They were at Brussels – half an hour for breakfast. They got down. On the great station clock it said six o'clock. They had coffee and rolls and honey in the vast desert refreshment room, so dreary, always so dreary, dirty, so spacious, such desolation of space. But she washed her face and hands in hot water, and combed her hair – that was a blessing.

Soon they were in the train again and moving on. The greyness of dawn began. There were several people in the compartment, large florid Belgian business-men with long brown beards, talking incessantly in an ugly French she was too tired to follow.

It seemed the train ran by degrees out of the darkness into a faint light, then beat after beat into the day. Ah, how weary it was! Faintly, the trees showed, like shadows. Then a house, white, had a curious distinctness. How was it? Then she saw a village – there were always houses passing.

This was an old world she was still journeying through, winter-heavy and dreary. There was plough-land and pasture, and copses of bare trees; copses of bushes, and homesteads naked and work-bare. No new earth had come to pass.

She looked at Birkin's face. It was white and still and eternal, too eternal. She linked her fingers imploringly in his, under the cover of her rug. His fingers responded, his eyes looked back at her. How dark, like a night, his eyes were, like another world beyond! Oh, if he were the world as well, if only the world were he! If only he could call a world into being, that should be their own world!

The Belgians left, the train ran on, through Luxembourg, through Alsace-Lorraine, through Metz. But she was blind, she could see no more. Her soul did not look out.

They came at last to Basle, to the hotel. It was all a drifting trance, from which she never came to. They went out in the morning, before the train departed. She saw the street, the river, she stood on the bridge. But it all meant nothing. She remembered some shops – one full of pictures, one with orange velvet and ermine. But what did these signify? – nothing.

She was not at ease till they were in the train again. Then she was relieved. So long as they were moving onwards, she was satisfied. They came to Zürich, then, before very long, ran under the mountains, that were deep in snow. At last she was drawing near. This was the other world now.

Innsbruck was wonderful, deep in snow, and evening. They drove in an open sledge over the snow: the train had been so hot and stifling. And the hotel, with the golden light glowing under the porch, seemed like a home.

They laughed with pleasure when they were in the hall. The place seemed full and busy.

'Do you know if Mr and Mrs Crich – English – from Paris, have arrived?' Birkin asked in German.

The porter reflected a moment, and was just going to answer, when Ursula caught sight of Gudrun sauntering down the stairs, wearing her dark glossy coat, with grey fur.

'Gudrun! Gudrun!' she called, waving up the well of the staircase. 'Shu-hu!'

Gudrun looked over the rail, and immediately lost her sauntering, diffident air. Her eyes flashed.

'Really – Ursula!' she cried. And she began to move downstairs as Ursula ran up. They met at a turn and kissed with laughter and exclamations inarticulate and stirring.

'But!' cried Gudrun, mortified. 'We thought it was *tomorrow* you were coming! I wanted to come to the station.'

'No, we've come today!' cried Ursula. 'Isn't it lovely here!'

'Adorable!' said Gudrun. 'Gerald's just gone out to get something. Ursula, aren't you *fearfully* tired?'

'No, not so very. But I look a filthy sight, don't I!'

'No, you don't. You look almost perfectly fresh. I like that
fur cap *immensely!*' She glanced over Ursula, who wore a big
soft coat with a collar of deep, soft, blond fur, and a soft blond
cap of fur.

'And you!' cried Ursula. 'What do you think *you* look like!'

Gudrun assumed an unconcerned, expressionless face.

'Do you like it?' she said.

'It's *very* fine!' cried Ursula, perhaps with a touch of satire.

'Go up – or come down,' said Birkin. For there the sisters
stood, Gudrun with her hand on Ursula's arm, on the turn of the
stairs half way to the first landing, blocking the way and affording
full entertainment to the whole of the hall below, from the door
porter to the plump Jew in black clothes.

The two young women slowly mounted, followed by Birkin
and the waiter.

'First floor?' asked Gudrun, looking back over her shoulder.

'Second Madam – the lift!' the waiter replied. And he darted
to the elevator to forestall the two women. But they ignored him,
as, chattering without heed, they set to mount the second flight.
Rather chagrined, the waiter followed.

It was curious, the delight of the sisters in each other, at this
meeting. It was as if they met in exile, and united their solitary
forces against all the world. Birkin looked on with some mistrust
and wonder.

When they had bathed and changed, Gerald came in. He looked
shining like the sun on frost.

'Go with Gerald and smoke,' said Ursula to Birkin. 'Gudrun
and I want to talk.'

Then the sisters sat in Gudrun's bedroom, and talked clothes,
and experiences. Gudrun told Ursula the experience of the Birkin
letter in the café. Ursula was shocked and frightened.

'Where is the letter?' she asked.

'I kept it,' said Gudrun.

'You'll give it me, won't you?' she said.

But Gudrun was silent for some moments, before she replied:

'Do you really want it, Ursula?'

'I want to read it,' said Ursula.

'Certainly,' said Gudrun.

Even now, she could not admit, to Ursula, that she wanted to keep it, as a memento, or a symbol. But Ursula knew, and was not pleased. So the subject was switched off.

'What did you do in Paris?' asked Ursula.

'Oh,' said Gudrun laconically – 'the usual things. We had a *fine* party one night in Fanny Bath's studio.'

'Did you? And you and Gerald were there! Who else? Tell me about it.'

'Well,' said Gudrun. 'There's nothing particular to tell. You know Fanny is *frightfully* in love with that painter, Billy Macfarlane. He was there – so Fanny spared nothing, she spent *very* freely. It was really remarkable! Of course, everybody got fearfully drunk – but in an interesting way, not like that filthy London crowd. The fact is these were all people that matter, which makes all the difference. There was a Roumanian, a fine chap. He got completely drunk, and climbed to the top of a high studio ladder, and gave the most marvellous address really, Ursula, it was wonderful! He began in French – La vie, c'est une affaire d'âmes impériales* – in a most beautiful voice – he was a fine-looking chap – but he had got into Roumanian before he had finished, and not a soul understood. But Donald Gilchrist was worked to a frenzy. He dashed his glass to the ground, and declared, by God, he was glad he had been born, by God, it was a miracle to be alive. And do you know, Ursula, so it was – ' Gudrun laughed rather hollowly.

'But how was Gerald among them all?' asked Ursula.

'Gerald! Oh, my word, he came out like a dandelion in the sun! *He's* a whole saturnalia in himself, once he is roused. I shouldn't like to say whose waist his arm did not go round. Really, Ursula, he seems to reap the women like a harvest. There wasn't one that would have resisted him. It was too amazing! Can you understand it?'

Ursula reflected, and a dancing light came into her eyes.

* (Fr.) Life is an affair of Imperial souls.

'Yes,' she said. 'I can. He is such a whole-hogger.'

'Whole-hogger! I should think so!' exclaimed Gudrun. 'But it is true, Ursula, every woman in the room was ready to surrender to him. Chanticleer isn't in it – even Fanny Bath, who is *genuinely* in love with Billy Macfarlane! I never was more amazed in my life! And you know, afterwards – I felt I was a whole *roomful* of women. I was no more myself to him, than I was Queen Victoria. I was a whole roomful of women at once. It was most astounding! But my eye, I'd caught a Sultan that time – '

Gudrun's eyes were flashing, her cheek was hot, she looked strange, exotic, satiric. Ursula was fascinated at once – and yet uneasy.

They had to get ready for dinner. Gudrun came down in a daring gown of vivid green silk and tissue of gold, with green velvet bodice and a strange black-and-white band round her hair. She was really brilliantly beautiful and everybody noticed her. Gerald was in that full-blooded, gleaming state when he was most handsome. Birkin watched them with quick, laughing, half-sinister eyes, Ursula quite lost her head. There seemed a spell, almost a blinding spell, cast round their table, as if they were lighted up more strongly than the rest of the dining-room.

'Don't you love to be in this place?' cried Gudrun. 'Isn't the snow wonderful! Do you notice how it exalts everything? It is simply marvellous. One really does feel *übermenschlich** – more than human.'

'One does,' cried Ursula. 'But isn't that partly the being out of England?'

'Oh, of course,' cried Gudrun. 'One could never feel like this in England, for the simple reason that the damper is *never* lifted off one, there. It is quite impossible really to let go, in England, of that I am assured.'

And she turned again to the food she was eating. She was fluttering with vivid intensity.

'It's quite true,' said Gerald, 'it never is quite the same in England. But perhaps we don't want it to be – perhaps it's like

* (Ger.) Superman.

bringing the light a little too near the powder-magazine, to let go altogether, in England. One is afraid what might happen, if *everybody else* let go.'

'My God!' cried Gudrun. 'But wouldn't it be wonderful, if all England did suddenly go off like a display of fireworks.'

'It couldn't,' said Ursula. 'They are all too damp, the powder is damp in them.'

'I'm not so sure of that,' said Gerald.

'Nor I,' said Birkin. 'When the English really begin to go off, *en masse,* it'll be time to shut your ears and run.'

'They never will,' said Ursula.

'We'll see,' he replied.

'Isn't it marvellous,' said Gudrun, 'how thankful one can be, to be out of one's country. I cannot believe myself, I am so transported, the moment I set foot on a foreign shore. I say to myself "Here steps a new creature into life." '

'Don't be too hard on poor old England,' said Gerald. 'Though we curse it, we love it really.'

To Ursula, there seemed a fund of cynicism in these words.

'We may,' said Birkin. 'But it's a damnably uncomfortable love: like a love for an aged parent who suffers horribly from a complication of diseases, for which there is no hope.'

Gudrun looked at him with dilated dark eyes.

'You think there is no hope?' she asked, in her pertinent fashion.

But Birkin backed away. He would not answer such a question.

'Any hope of England's becoming real? God knows. It's a great actual unreality now, an aggregation into unreality. It might be real, if there were no Englishmen.'

'You think the English will have to disappear?' persisted Gudrun. It was strange, her pointed interest in his answer. It might have been her own fate she was inquiring after. Her dark, dilated eyes rested on Birkin, as if she could conjure the truth of the future out of him, as out of some instrument of divination.

He was pale. Then, reluctantly, he answered:

'Well – what else is in front of them, but disappearance? They've got to disappear from their own special brand of Englishness, anyhow.'

Gudrun watched him as if in a hypnotic state, her eyes wide and fixed on him.

'But in what way do you mean, disappear? – ' she persisted.

'Yes, do you mean a change of heart?' put in Gerald.

'I don't mean anything, why should I?' said Birkin. 'I'm an Englishman, and I've paid the price of it. I can't talk about England – I can only speak for myself.'

'Yes,' said Gudrun slowly, 'you love England immensely, *immensely,* Rupert.'

'And leave her,' he replied.

'No, not for good. You'll come back,' said Gerald, nodding sagely.

'They say the lice crawl off a dying body,' said Birkin, with a glare of bitterness. 'So I leave England.'

'Ah, but you'll come back,' said Gudrun, with a sardonic smile.

'Tant pis pour moi,'* he replied.

'Isn't he angry with his mother country!' laughed Gerald, amused.

'Ah, a patriot!' said Gudrun, with something like a sneer.

Birkin refused to answer any more.

Gudrun watched him still for a few seconds. Then she turned away. It was finished, her spell of divination in him. She felt already purely cynical. She looked at Gerald. He was wonderful like a piece of radium to her. She felt she could consume herself and know *all,* by means of this fatal, living metal. She smiled to herself at her fancy. And what would she do with herself, when she had destroyed herself? For if spirit, if integral being is destructible, Matter is indestructible.

He was looking bright and abstracted, puzzled, for the moment. She stretched out her beautiful arm, with its fluff of green tulle, – and touched his chin with her subtle, artist's fingers.

'What are they then?' she asked, with a strange, knowing smile.

'What?' he replied, his eyes suddenly dilating with wonder.

---

* (Fr.) So much the worse for me.

'Your thoughts.'

Gerald looked like a man coming awake.

'I think I had none,' he said.

'Really!' she said, with grave laughter in her voice.

And to Birkin it was as if she killed Gerald, with that touch.

'Ah but,' cried Gudrun, 'let us drink to Britannia – let us drink to Britannia.'

It seemed there was wild despair in her voice. Gerald laughed, and filled the glasses.

'I think Rupert means,' he said, 'that *nationally* all Englishmen must die, so that they can exist individually and – '

'Super-nationally – ' put in Gudrun, with a slight ironic grimace, raising her glass.

The next day, they descended at the tiny railway station of Hohenhausen, at the end of the tiny valley railway. It was snow everywhere, a white, perfect cradle of snow, new and frozen, sweeping up an either side, black crags, and white sweeps of silver towards the blue pale heavens.

As they stepped out on the naked platform, with only snow around and above, Gudrun shrank as if it chilled her heart.

'My God, Jerry,' she said, turning to Gerald with sudden intimacy, 'you've done it now.'

'What?'

She made a faint gesture, indicating the world on either hand.

'Look at it!'

She seemed afraid to go on. He laughed.

They were in the heart of the mountains. From high above, on either side, swept down the white fold of snow, so that one seemed small and tiny in a valley of pure concrete heaven, all strangely radiant and changeless and silent.

'It makes one feel so small and alone,' said Ursula, turning to Birkin and laying her hand on his arm.

'You're not sorry you've come, are you?' said Gerald to Gudrun.

She looked doubtful. They went out of the station between banks of snow.

'Ah,' said Gerald, sniffing the air in elation, 'this is perfect. There's our sledge. We'll walk a bit – we'll run up the road.'

Gudrun, always doubtful, dropped her heavy coat on the sledge, as he did his, and they setoff. Suddenly she threw up her head and set off scudding along the road of snow, pulling her cap down over her ears. Her blue, bright dress fluttered in the wind, her thick scarlet stockings were brilliant above the whiteness. Gerald watched her: she seemed to be rushing towards her fate, and leaving him behind. He let her get some distance, then, loosening his limbs, he went after her.

Everywhere was deep and silent snow. Great snow-eaves weighed down the broad-roofed Tyrolese houses, that were sunk to the window-sashes in snow. Peasant-women, full-skirted, wearing each a cross-over shawl, and thick snow-boots, turned in the way to look at the soft, determined girl running with such heavy fleetness from the man, who was overtaking her, but not gaining any power over her.

They passed the inn with its painted shutters and balcony, a few cottages, half buried in the snow; then the snow-buried silent sawmill by the roofed bridge, which crossed the hidden stream, over which they ran into the very depth of the untouched sheets of snow. It was a silence and a sheer whiteness exhilarating to madness. But the perfect silence was most terrifying, isolating the soul, surrounding the heart with frozen air.

'It's a marvellous place, for all that,' said Gudrun, looking into his eyes with a strange, meaning look. His soul leapt.

'Good,' he said.

A fierce electric energy seemed to flow over all his limbs, his muscles were surcharged, his hands felt hard with strength. They walked along rapidly up the snow-road, that was marked by withered branches of trees stuck in at intervals. He and she were separate, like opposite poles of one fierce energy. But they felt powerful enough to leap over the confines of life into the forbidden places, and back again.

Birkin and Ursula were running along also, over the snow. He had disposed of the luggage, and they had a little start of the sledges. Ursula was excited and happy, but she kept turning suddenly to catch hold of Birkin's arm, to make sure of him.

'This is something I never expected,' she said. 'It is a different world, here.'

They went on into a snow meadow. There they were overtaken by the sledge, that came tinkling through the silence. It was another mile before they came upon Gudrun and Gerald on the steep up-climb, beside the pink, half-buried shrine.

Then they passed into a gulley, where were walls of black rock and a river filled with snow, and a still blue sky above. Through a covered bridge they went, drumming roughly over the boards, crossing the snow-bed once more, then slowly up and up, the horses walking swiftly, the driver cracking his long whip as he walked beside, and calling his strange wild *hue-hue!,* the walls of rock passing slowly by, till they emerged again between slopes and masses of snow. Up and up, gradually they went, through the cold shadow-radiance of the afternoon, silenced by the imminence of the mountains, the luminous, dazing sides of snow that rose above them and fell away beneath.

They came forth at last in a little high table-land of snow, where stood the last peaks of snow like the heart petals of an open rose. In the midst of the last deserted valleys of heaven stood a lonely building with brown wooden walls and white heavy roof, deep and deserted in the waste of snow, like a dream. It stood like a rock that had rolled down from the last steep slopes, a rock that had taken the form of a house, and was now half-buried. It was unbelievable that one could live there uncrushed by all this terrible waste of whiteness and silence and clear, upper, ringing cold.

Yet the sledges ran up in fine style, people came to the door laughing and excited, the floor of the hostel rang hollow, the passage was wet with snow, it was a real, warm interior.

The new-comers tramped up the bare wooden stairs, following the serving woman. Gudrun and Gerald took the first bedroom. In a moment they found themselves alone in a bare, smallish, close-shut room that was all of golden-coloured wood, floor, walls, ceiling, door, all of the same warm gold panelling of oiled pine. There was a window opposite the door, but low down, because the roof sloped. Under the slope of the ceiling were the table with wash-hand bowl and jug, and across, another table with mirror. On either side the door were two beds piled high with an enormous blue-checked overbolster, enormous.

This was all – no cupboard, none of the amenities of life. Here they ere shut up together in this cell of golden-coloured wood, with two blue checked beds. They looked at each other and laughed, frightened by this naked nearness of isolation.

A man knocked and came in with the luggage. He was a sturdy fellow with flattish cheek-bones, rather pale, and with coarse fair moustache. Gudrun watched him put down the bags, in silence, then tramp heavily out.

'It isn't too rough, is it?' Gerald asked.

The bedroom was not very warm, and she shivered slightly.

'It is wonderful,' she equivocated. 'Look at the colour of this panelling – it's wonderful, like being inside a nut.'

He was standing watching her, feeling his short-cut moustache, leaning back slightly and watching her with his keen, undaunted eyes, dominated by the constant passion, that was like a doom upon him.

She went and crouched down in front of the window, curious.

'Oh, but this –!' she cried involuntarily, almost in pain.

In front was a valley shut in under the sky, the last huge slopes of snow and black rock, and at the end, like the navel of the earth, a white-folded wall, and two peaks glimmering in the late light. Straight in front ran the cradle of silent snow, between the great slopes that were fringed with a little roughness of pine-trees, like hair, round the base. But the cradle of snow ran on to the eternal closing-in, where the walls of snow and rock rose impenetrable, and the mountain peaks above were in heaven immediate. This was the centre, the knot, the navel of the world, where the earth belonged to the skies, pure, unapproachable, impassable.

It filled Gudrun with a strange rapture. She crouched in front of the window, clenching her face in her hands, in a sort of trance. At last she had arrived, she had reached her place. Here at last she folded her venture and settled down like a crystal in the navel of snow, and was gone.

Gerald bent above her and was looking out over her shoulder. Already he felt he was alone. She was gone. She was completely gone, and there was icy vapour round his heart. He saw the blind valley, the great cul-de-sac of snow and mountain peaks, under the heaven. And there was no way out. The terrible silence and cold and the glamorous whiteness of the dusk wrapped him round, and she remained crouching before the window, as at a shrine, a shadow.

'Do you like it?' he asked, in a voice that sounded detached and foreign. At least she might acknowledge he was with her. But she only averted her soft, mute face a little from his gaze. And he knew that there were tears in her eyes, her own tears, tears of her strange religion, that put him to nought.

Quite suddenly, he put his hand under her chin and lifted up her face to him. Her dark blue eyes, in their wetness of tears, dilated as if she was startled in her very soul. They looked at him through their tears in terror and a little horror. His light blue eyes were keen, small-pupilled and unnatural in their vision. Her lips parted, as she breathed with difficulty.

The passion came up in him, stroke after stroke, like the ringing of a bronze bell, so strong and unflawed and indomitable. His knees tightened to bronze as he hung above her soft face, whose lips parted and whose eyes dilated in a strange violation. In the grasp of his hand her chin was unutterably soft and silken. He felt strong as winter, his hands were living metal, invincible and not to be turned aside. His heart rang like a bell clanging inside him.

He took her up in his arms. She was soft and inert, motionless. All the while her eyes, in which the tears had not yet dried, were dilated as if in a kind of swoon of fascination and helplessness.

He was superhumanly strong, and unflawed, as if invested with supernatural force.

He lifted her close and folded 'her against him. Her softness, her inert, relaxed weight lay against his own surcharged, bronze-like limbs in a heaviness of desirability that would destroy him, if he were not fulfilled. She moved convulsively, recoiling away from him. His heart went up like a flame of ice, he closed over her like steel. He would destroy her rather than be denied.

But the overweening power of his body was too much for her. She relaxed again, and lay loose and soft, panting in a little delirium. And to him, she was so sweet, she was such bliss of release, that he would have suffered a whole eternity of torture rather than forego one second of this pang of unsurpassable bliss.

'My God,' he said to her, his face drawn and strange, transfigured, 'what next?'

She lay perfectly still, with a still, child-like face and dark eyes, looking at him. She was lost, fallen right away.

'I shall always love you,' he said, looking at her.

But she did not hear. She lay, looking at him as at something she could never understand, never: as a child looks at a grown-up person, without hope of understanding, only submitting.

He kissed her, kissed her eyes shut, so that she could not look any more. He wanted something now, some recognition, some sign, some admission. But she only lay silent and child-like and remote, like a child that is overcome and cannot understand, only feels lost. He kissed her again, giving up.

'Shall we go down and have coffee and Kuchen?' he asked.

The twilight was falling slate-blue at the window. She closed her eyes, closed away the monotonous level of dead wonder, and opened them again to the every-day world.

'Yes,' she said briefly, regaining her will with a click. She went again to the window. Blue evening had fallen over the cradle of snow and over the great pallid slopes. But in the heaven the peaks of snow were rosy, glistening like transcendent, radiant spikes of blossom in the heavenly upper-world, so lovely and beyond.

Gudrun saw all their loveliness, she *knew* how immortally beautiful they were, great pistils of rose-coloured, snow-fed fire in the blue twilight of the heaven. She could *see* it, she knew it, but she was not of it. She was divorced, debarred, a soul shut out.

With a last look of remorse, she turned away, and was doing her hair. He had unstrapped the luggage, and was waiting, watching her. She knew he was watching her. It made her a little hasty and feverish in her precipitation.

They went downstairs, both with a strange other-world look on their faces, and with a glow in their eyes. They saw Birkin and Ursula sitting at the long table in a corner, waiting for them.

'How good and simple they look together,' Gudrun thought, jealously. She envied them some spontaneity, a childish sufficiency to which she herself could never approach. They seemed such children to her.

'Such good Kranzkuchen!' cried Ursula greedily. 'So good!'

'Right,' said Gudrun. 'Can we have Kaffee mit Kranzkuchen?' she added to the waiter.

And she seated herself on the bench beside Gerald. Birkin, looking at them, felt a pain of tenderness for them.

'I think the place is really wonderful, Gerald,' he said; 'prachtvoll and wunderbar and wunderschon and unbeschreiblich and all the other German adjectives.'*

Gerald broke into a slight smile.

'*I* like it,' he said.

The tables, of white scrubbed wood, were placed round three sides of the room, as in a Gasthaus. Birkin and Ursula sat with their backs to the wall, which was of oiled wood, and Gerald and Gudrun sat in the corner next them, near to the stove. It was a fairly large place, with a tiny bar, just like a country inn, but quite simple and bare, and all of oiled wood, ceilings and walls and floor, the only furniture being the tables and benches going round three sides, the great green stove, and the bar and the doors on the fourth side. The windows were double, and quite un-curtained. It was early evening.

---

* Splendid, wonderful, beautiful, indescribable.

The coffee came – hot and good – and a whole ring of cake.

'A whole Kuchen!' cried Ursula. 'They give you more than us! I want some of yours.'

There were other people in the place, ten altogether, so Birkin had found out: two artists, three students, a man and wife, and a Professor and two daughters – all Germans. The four English people, being newcomers, sat in their coign of vantage to watch. The Germans peeped in at the door, called a word to the waiter, and went away again. It was not meal-time, so they did not come into this dining-room, but betook themselves, when their boots were changed, to the Reunionsaal.

The English visitors could hear the occasional twanging of a zither, the strumming of a piano, snatches of laughter and shouting and singing, a faint vibration of voices. The whole building being of wood, it seemed to carry every sound, like 'a drum, but instead of increasing each particular noise, it decreased it, so that the sound of the zither seemed tiny, as if a diminutive zither were playing somewhere, and it seemed the piano must be a small one, like a little spinet.

The host came when the coffee was finished. He was a Tyrolese, broad, rather flat-cheeked, with a pale, pock-marked skin and flourishing moustaches.

'Would you like to go to the Reunionsaal to be introduced to the other ladies and gentlemen?' he asked, bending forward and smiling, showing his large, strong teeth. His blue eyes went quickly from one to the other – he was not quite sure of his ground with these English people. He was unhappy too because he spoke no English and he was not sure whether to try his French.

'Shall we go to the Reunionsaal, and be introduced to the other people?' repeated Gerald, laughing.

There was a moment's hesitation.

'I suppose we'd better – better break the ice,' said Birkin.

The women rose, rather flushed. And the Wirt's black, beetle-like, broad-shouldered figure went on ignominiously in front, towards the noise. He opened the door and ushered the four strangers into the play-room.

Instantly a silence fell, a slight embarrassment came over the company. The newcomers had a sense of many blond faces looking their way. Then, the host was bowing to a short, energetic-looking man with large moustaches, and saying in a low voice:

'Herr Professor, darf ich vorstellen – '

The Herr Professor was prompt and energetic. He bowed low to the English people, smiling, and began to be a comrade at once.

'Nehmen die Herrschaften teil an unserer Unterhaltung?'[1] said, with a vigorous suavity, his voice curling up in the question.

The four English people smiled, lounging with an attentive uneasiness in the middle of the room. Gerald, who was spokesman, said that they would willingly take part in the entertainment. Gudrun and Ursula, laughing, excited, felt the eyes of all the men upon them, and they lifted their heads and looked nowhere, and felt royal.

The Professor announced the names of those present, *sans cérémonie*.[2] There was a bowing to the wrong people and to the right people. Everybody was there, except the man and wife. The two tall, clear-skinned, athletic daughters of the professor, with their plain-cut, dark blue blouses and loden skirts, their rather long, strong necks, their clear blue eyes and carefully banded hair, and their blushes, bowed and stood back; the three students bowed very low, in the humble hope of making an impression of extreme good-breeding; then there was a thin, dark-skinned man with full eyes, an odd creature, like a child, and like a troll, quick, detached; he bowed slightly; his companion, a large fair young man, stylishly dressed, blushed to the eyes and bowed very low.

It was over.

'Herr Loerke was giving us a recitation in the Cologne dialect,' said the Professor.

'He must forgive us for interrupting him,' said Gerald, 'we should

like very much to hear it.'

There was instantly a bowing and an offering of seats. Gudrun and Ursula, Gerald and Birkin sat in the deep sofas against the

1 Spoken in German, the host invites the guests to join the entertainment.
2 (Fr.) Without ceremony.

wall. The room was of naked oiled panelling, like the rest of the house. It had a piano, sofas and chairs, and a couple of tables with books and magazines. In its complete absence of decoration, save for the big, blue stove, it was cosy and pleasant.

Herr Loerke was the little man with the boyish figure, and the round, full, sensitive-looking head, and the quick, full eyes, like a mouse's. He glanced swiftly from one to the other of the strangers, and held himself aloof.

'Please go on with the recitation,' said the Professor, suavely, with his slight authority. Loerke, who was sitting hunched on the piano stool, blinked and did not answer.

'It would be a great pleasure,' said Ursula, who had been getting the sentence ready, in German, for some minutes.

Then, suddenly, the small, unresponding man swung aside, towards his previous audience and broke forth, exactly as he had broken off; in a controlled, mocking voice, giving an imitation of a quarrel between an old Cologne woman and a railway guard.

His body was slight and unformed, like boy's, but his voice was mature, sardonic, its movement had the flexibility of essential energy, and of a mocking penetrating understanding. Gudrun could not understand a word of his monologue, but she was spellbound, watching him. He must be an artist, nobody else could have such fine adjustment and singleness. The Germans were doubled up with laughter, hearing his strange droll words, his droll phrases of dialect. And in the midst of their paroxysms, they glanced with deference at the four English strangers, the elect. Gudrun and Ursula were forced to laugh. The room rang with shouts of laughter. The blue eyes of the Professor's daughters were swimming over with laughter-tears, their clear cheeks were flushed crimson with mirth, their father broke out in the most astonishing peals of hilarity, the students bowed their heads on their knees in excess of joy. Ursula looked round amazed, the laughter was bubbling out of her involuntarily. She looked at Gudrun. Gudrun looked at her, and the two sisters burst out laughing, carried away. Loerke glanced at them swiftly, with his full eyes. Birkin was sniggering involuntarily. Gerald Crich sat erect, with a glistening look of amusement on his face. And the laughter crashed out again, in wild paroxysms, the Professor's daughters were reduced to shaking helplessness, the veins of the Professor's neck were swollen, his face was purple, he was strangled in ultimate, silent spasms of laughter. The students were shouting half-articulated words that tailed off in helpless explosions. Then suddenly the rapid patter of the artist ceased, there were little whoops of subsiding mirth, Ursula and Gudrun were wiping their eyes, and the Professor was crying loudly.

'Das war ausgezeichnet, das war famos – '

'Wirklich famos,' echoed his exhausted daughters, faintly.

'And we couldn't understand it,' cried Ursula.

'Oh leider, leider!' cried the Professor.

'You couldn't understand it?' cried the Students, let loose at last in speech with the newcomers. 'Ja, das ist wirklich schade, das ist schade, gnädige Fräu. Wissen Sie – '*

The mixture was made, the newcomers were stirred into the party, like new ingredients, the whole room was alive. Gerald was in his element, he talked freely and excitedly, his face glistened with a strange amusement. Perhaps even Birkin, in the end, would break forth. He was shy and withheld, though full of attention.

Ursula was prevailed upon to sing 'Annie Lowrie,' as the Professor called it. There was a hush of *extreme* deference. She had never been so flattered in her life. Gudrun accompanied her on the piano, playing from memory.

Ursula had a beautiful ringing voice, but usually no confidence, she spoiled everything. This evening she felt conceited and untrammelled. Birkin was well in the background, she shone almost in reaction, the Germans made her feel fine and infallible, she was liberated into overweening self-confidence. She felt like a bird flying in the air, as her voice soared out, enjoying herself extremely in the balance and flight of the song, like the motion of a bird's wings that is up in the wind, sliding and playing on the air, she played with sentimentality, supported by rapturous attention. She was very happy, singing that song by herself, full

---

* (Ger.) The 'remarkable' and 'great' adjectives spoken by Loerke are, as per the regret expressed here, not understood by the English.

of a conceit of emotion and power, working upon all those people, and upon herself, exerting herself with gratification, giving immeasurable gratification to the Germans.

At the end, the Germans were all touched with admiring, delicious melancholy, they praised her in soft, reverent voices, they could not say too much.

'Wie schon, wie ruhrend! Ach, die Schottischen Lieder, sie haben so viel Stimmung! Aber die gnädige Fräu hat eine *wunderbare* Stimme; die gnädige Fräu ist wirklich eine Kunstlerin, aber wirklich!'*

She was dilated and brilliant, like a flower in the morning sun. She felt Birkin looking at her, as if he were jealous of her, and her breasts thrilled, her veins were all golden. She was as happy as the sun that has just opened above clouds. And everybody seemed so admiring and radiant, it was perfect.

After dinner she wanted to go out for a minute, to look at the world. The company tried to dissuade her – it was so terribly cold. But just to look, she said.

They all four wrapped up warmly, and found themselves in a vague, unsubstantial outdoors of dim snow and ghosts of an upper-world, that made strange shadows before the stars. It was indeed cold, bruisingly, frighteningly, unnaturally cold. Ursula could not believe the air in her nostrils. It seemed conscious, malevolent, purposive in its intense murderous coldness.

Yet it was wonderful, an intoxication, a silence of dim, unrealised snow, of the invisible intervening between her and the visible, between her and the flashing stars. She could see Orion sloping up. How wonderful he was, wonderful enough to make one cry aloud.

And all around was this cradle of snow, and there was firm snow underfoot, that struck with heavy cold through her boot-soles. It was night, and silence. She imagined she could hear the stars. She imagined distinctly she could hear the celestial, musical motion of the stars, quite near at hand. She seemed like a bird flying amongst their harmonious motion.

---

* (Ger.) How beautiful and moving! Ah! The Scottish songs have such a feeling! And the gracious lady has such a captivating voice! She is really an artist!

And she clung close to Birkin. Suddenly she realised she did not know what he was thinking. She did not know where he was ranging.

'My love!' she said, stopping to look at him.

His face was pale, his eyes dark, there was a faint spark of starlight on them. And he saw her face soft and upturned to him, very near. He kissed her softly.

'What then?' he asked.

'Do you love me?' she asked.

'Too much,' he answered quietly.

She clung a little closer.

'Not too much,' she pleaded.

'Far too much,' he said, almost sadly.

'And does it make you sad, that I am everything to you?' she asked, wistful. He held her close to him, kissing her, and saying, scarcely audible:

'No, but I feel like a beggar – I feel poor.'

She was silent, looking at the stars now. Then she kissed him. 'Don't be a beggar,' she pleaded, wistfully. 'It isn't ignominious that you love me.'

'It is ignominious to feel poor, isn't it?' he replied.

'Why? Why should it be?' she asked. He only stood still, in the terribly cold air that moved invisibly over the mountain tops, folding her round with his arms.

'I couldn't bear this cold, eternal place without you,' he said. 'I couldn't bear it, it would kill the quick of my life.'

She kissed him again, suddenly.

'Do you hate it?' she asked, puzzled, wondering.

'If I couldn't come near to you, if you weren't here, I should hate it. I couldn't bear it,' he answered.

'But the people are nice,' she said.

'I mean the stillness, the cold, the frozen eternality,' he said.

She wondered. Then her spirit came home to him, nestling unconscious in him.

'Yes, it is good we are warm and together,' she said.

And they turned home again. They saw the golden lights of the hotel glowing out in the night of snow-silence, small in the hollow, like a cluster of yellow berries. It seemed like a bunch of sun-sparks, tiny and orange in. the midst of the snow-darkness. Behind, was a high shadow of a peak, blotting out the stars, like a ghost.

They drew near to their home. They saw a man come from the dark building, with a lighted lantern which swung golden, and made that his dark feet walked in a halo of snow. He was a small, dark figure in the darkened snow. He unlatched the door of an outhouse. A smell of cows, hot, animal, almost like beef, came out on the heavily cold air. There was a glimpse of two cattle in their dark stalls, then the door was shut again, and not a chink of light showed. It had reminded Ursula again of home, of the Marsh, of her childhood, and of the journey to Brussels, and, strangely, of Anton Skrebensky.

Oh, God, could one bear it, this past which was gone down the abyss? Could she bear, that it ever had been! She looked round this silent, upper world of snow and stars and powerful cold. There was another world, like views on a magic lantern; The Marsh, Cossethay, Ilkeston, lit up with a common, unreal light. There was a shadowy unreal Ursula, a whole shadow-play of an unreal life. It was as unreal, and circumscribed, as a magic-lantern show. She wished the slides could all be broken. She wished it could be gone for ever, like a lantern-slide which was broken. She wanted to have no past. She wanted to have come down from the slopes of heaven to this place, with Birkin, not to have toiled out of the murk of her childhood and her upbringing, slowly, all soiled. She felt that memory was a dirty trick played upon her. What was this decree, that she should 'remember'! Why not a bath of pure oblivion, a new birth, without any recollections or blemish of a past life. She was with Birkin, she had just come into life, here in the high snow, against the stars. What had she to do with parents and antecedents? She knew herself new and unbegotten, she had no father, no mother, no anterior connections, she was herself, pure and silvery, she belonged only to the oneness with Birkin, a oneness that struck deeper notes, sounding into the heart of the universe, the heart of reality, where she had never existed before.

Even Gudrun was a separate unit, separate, separate, having nothing to do with this self, this Ursula, in her new world of reality. That old shadow-world, the actuality of the past – ah, let it go! She rose free on the wings of her new condition.

Gudrun and Gerald had not come in. They had walked up the valley straight in front of the house, not like Ursula and Birkin, on to the little hill at the right. Gudrun was driven by a strange desire. She wanted to plunge on and on, till she came to the end of the valley of snow. Then she wanted to climb the wall of white finality, climb over, into the peaks that sprang up like sharp petals in the heart of the frozen, mysterious navel of the world. She felt that there, over the strange blind, terrible wall of rocky snow, there in the navel of the mystic world, among the final cluster of peaks, there, in the infolded navel of it all, was her consummation. If she could but come there, alone, and pass into the infolded navel of eternal snow and of uprising, immortal peaks of snow and rock, she would be a oneness with all, she would be herself the eternal, infinite silence, the sleeping, timeless, frozen centre of the All.

They went back to the house, to the Reunionsaal. She was curious to see what was going on. The men there made her alert, roused her curiosity. It was a new taste of life for her, they were so prostrate before her, yet so full of life.

The party was boisterous; they were dancing all together, dancing the Schuhplatteln, the Tyrolese dance of the clapping hands and tossing the partner in the air at the crisis. The Germans were all proficient – they were from Munich chiefly. Gerald also was quite passable. There were three zithers twanging away in a corner. It was a scene of great animation and confusion. The Professor was initiating Ursula into the dance, stamping, clapping, and swinging her high, with amazing force and zest. When the crisis came even Birkin was behaving manfully with one of the Professor's fresh, strong daughters, who was exceedingly happy. Everybody was dancing, there was the most boisterous turmoil.

Gudrun looked on with delight. The solid wooden floor resounded to the knocking heels of the men, the air quivered with the clapping hands and the zither music, there was a golden dust about the hanging lamps.

Suddenly the dance finished, Loerke and the students rushed out to bring in drinks. There was an excited clamour of voices, a clinking of mug-lids, a great crying of 'Prosit – Prosit!'* Loerke was everywhere at once, like a gnome, suggesting drinks for the women, making an obscure, slightly risky joke with the men, confusing and mystifying the waiter.

He wanted very much to dance with Gudrun. From the first moment he had seen her, he wanted to make a connection with her. Instinctively she felt this, and she waited for him to come up. But a kind of sulkiness kept him away from her, so she thought he disliked her.

'Will you schuhplatteln, gnädige Fräu?' said the large, fair youth, Loerke's companion. He was too soft, too humble for Gudrun's taste. But she wanted to dance, and the fair youth, who was called Leitner, was handsome enough in his uneasy, slightly abject fashion, a humility that covered a certain fear. She accepted him as a partner.

The zithers sounded out again, the dance began. Gerald led them, laughing, with one of the Professor's daughters. Ursula danced with one of the students, Birkin with the other daughter of the Professor, the Professor with Fräu Kramer, and the rest of the men danced together, with quite as much zest as if they had had women partners.

Because Gudrun had danced with the well-built, soft youth, his companion, Loerke, was more pettish and exasperated than ever, and would not even notice her existence in the room. This piqued her, but she made up to herself by dancing with the Professor, who was strong as a mature, well-seasoned bull, and as full of coarse energy. She could not bear him, critically, and yet she enjoyed being rushed through the dance, and tossed up into the air, on his

* To your health!

coarse, powerful impetus. The Professor enjoyed it too, he eyed her with strange, large blue eyes, full of galvanic fire. She hated him for the seasoned, semi-paternal animalism with which he regarded her, but she admired his weight of strength.

The room was charged with excitement and strong, animal emotion. Loerke was kept away from Gudrun, to whom he wanted to speak, as by a hedge of thorns, and he felt a sardonic ruthless hatred for this young love-companion, Leitner, who was his penniless dependent. He mocked the youth, with an acid ridicule, that made Leitner red in the face and impotent with resentment.

Gerald, who had now got the dance perfectly, was dancing again with the younger of the Professor's daughters, who was almost dying of virgin excitement, because she thought Gerald so handsome, so superb. He had her in his power, as if she were a palpitating bird, a fluttering, flushing, bewildered creature. And it made him smile, as she shrank convulsively between his hands, violently, when he must throw her into the air. At the end, she was so overcome with prostrate love for him, that she could scarcely speak sensibly at all.

Birkin was dancing with Ursula. There were odd little fires playing in his eyes, he seemed to have turned into something wicked and flickering, mocking, suggestive, quite impossible. Ursula was frightened of him, and fascinated. Clear, before her eyes, as in a vision, she could see the sardonic, licentious mockery of his eyes, he moved towards her with subtle, animal, indifferent approach. The strangeness of his hands, which came quick and cunning, inevitably to the vital place beneath her breasts, and, lifting with mocking, suggestive impulse, carried her through the air as if without strength, through black-magic, made her swoon with fear. For a moment she revolted, it was horrible. She would break the spell. But before the resolution had formed she had submitted again, yielded to her fear. He knew all the time what he was doing, she could see it in his smiling, concentrated eyes. It was his responsibility, she would leave it to him.

When they were alone in the darkness, she felt the strange, licentiousness of him hovering upon her. She was troubled and repelled. Why should he turn like this?

'What is it?' she asked in dread.

But his face only glistened on her, unknown, horrible. And yet she was fascinated. Her impulse was to repel him violently, break from this spell of mocking brutishness. But she was too fascinated, she wanted to submit, she wanted to know. What would he do to her?

He was so attractive, and so repulsive at once. The sardonic suggestivity that flickered over his face and looked from his narrowed eyes, made her want to hide, to hide herself away from him and watch him from somewhere unseen.

'Why are you like this?' she demanded again, rousing against him with sudden force and animosity. The flickering fires in his eyes concentrated as he looked into her eyes. Then the lids drooped with a faint motion of satiric contempt. Then they rose again to the same remorseless suggestivity. And she gave way, he might do as he would. His licentiousness was repulsively attractive. But he was self-responsible, she would see what it was.

They might do as they liked – this she realised as she went to sleep. How could anything that gave one satisfaction be excluded? What was degrading? Who cared? Degrading things were real, with a different reality. And he was so unabashed and unrestrained. Wasn't it rather horrible, a man who could be so soulful and spiritual, now to be so she balked at her own thoughts and memories: then she added – so bestial? So bestial, they two! – so degraded! She winced. But after all, why not? She exulted as well. Why not be bestial, and go the whole round of experience? She exulted in it. She was bestial. How good it was to be really shameful! There would be no shameful thing she had not experienced. Yet she was unabashed, she was herself. Why not? She was free, when she knew everything, and no dark shameful things were denied her.

Gudrun, who had been watching Gerald in the Reunionsaal, suddenly thought:

'He should have all the women he can – it is his nature. It is absurd to call him monogamous – he is naturally promiscuous. That is his nature.'

The thought came to her involuntarily. It shocked her somewhat. It was as if she had seen some new *Mene! Mene!* upon the wall.[1] Yet it was merely true. A voice seemed to have spoken it to her so clearly, that for the moment she believed in inspiration.

'It is really true,' she said to herself again. She knew quite well she had believed it all along. She knew it implicitly. But she must keep it dark – almost from herself. She must keep it completely secret. It was knowledge for her alone, and scarcely even to be admitted to herself.

The deep resolve formed in her, to combat him. One of them must triumph over the other. Which should it be? Her soul steeled itself with strength. Almost she laughed within herself, at her confidence. It woke a certain keen, half contemptuous pity, tenderness for him: she was so ruthless.

Everybody retired early. The Professor and Loerke went into a small lounge to drink. They both watched Gudrun go along the landing by the railing upstairs.

'Ein schönes Fräuenzimmer,'[2] said the Professor.

'Ja!'[3] asserted Loerke, shortly.

Gerald walked with his queer, long wolf-steps across the bedroom to the window, stooped and looked out, then rose again, and turned to Gudrun, his eyes sharp with an abstract smile. He seemed very tall to her, she saw the glisten of his whitish eyebrows, that met between his brows.

'How do you like it?' he said.

He seemed to be laughing inside himself, quite unconsciously. She looked at him. He was a phenomenon to her, not a human being: a sort of creature, greedy.

'I like it very much,' she replied.

'Who do you like best downstairs?' he asked, standing tall and glistening above her, with his glistening stiff hair erect.

'Who do I like best?' she repeated, wanting to answer his question, and finding it difficult to collect herself. 'Why I don't

1 These words were seen being written on a wall by the king of Babylon whose doom they forecast. (Daniel: 5:25).
2 (Ger.) A beautiful lady!
3 (Ger.) Yes.

know, I don't know enough about them yet, to be able to say. Who do *you* like best?'

'Oh, I don't care — I don't like or dislike any of them. It doesn't matter about me. I wanted to know about you.'

'But why?' she asked, going rather pale. The abstract, unconscious smile in his eyes was intensified.

'I wanted to know,' he said.

She turned aside, breaking the spell. In some strange way, she felt he was getting power over her.

'Well, I can't tell you already,' she said.

She went to the mirror to take out the hairpins from her hair. She stood before the mirror every night for some minutes, brushing her fine dark hair. It was part of the inevitable ritual of her life.

He followed her, and stood behind her. She was busy with bent head, taking out the pins and shaking her warm hair loose. When she looked up, she saw him in the glass standing behind her, watching unconsciously, not consciously seeing her, and yet watching, with fine-pupilled eyes that *seemed* to smile, and which were not really smiling.

She started. It took all her courage for her to continue brushing her hair, as usual, for her to pretend she was at her ease. She was far, far from being at her ease with him. She beat her brains wildly for something to say to him.

'What are your plans for tomorrow?' she asked nonchalantly, whilst her heart was beating so furiously, her eyes were so bright with strange nervousness, she felt he could not but observe. But she knew also that he was completely blind, blind as a wolf looking at her. It was a strange battle between her ordinary consciousness and his uncanny, black-art consciousness.

'I don't know,' he replied, 'what would you like to do?'

He spoke emptily, his mind was sunk away.

'Oh,' she said, with easy protestation, 'I'm ready for anything — anything — will be fine for *me,* I'm sure.'

And to herself she was saying: 'God, why am I so nervous — why are you so nervous, you fool. If he sees it I'm done for forever – you *know* you're done for forever, if he sees the absurd state you're in.'

And she smiled to herself as if it were all child's play. Meanwhile her heart was plunging, she was almost fainting. She could see him, in the mirror, as he stood there behind her, tall and over-arching – blond and terribly frightening. She glanced at his reflection with furtive eyes, willing to give anything to save him from knowing she could see him. He did not know she could see his reflection. He was looking unconsciously, glisteningly down at her head, from which the hair fell loose, as she brushed it with wild, nervous hand. She held her head aside and brushed and brushed her hair madly. For her life, she could not turn round and face him. For her life, *she could not*. And the knowledge made her almost sink to the ground in a faint, helpless, spent. She was aware of his frightening, impending figure standing close behind her, she was aware of his hard, strong, unyielding chest, close upon her back. And she felt she could not bear it any more, in a few minutes she would fall down at his feet, grovelling at his feet, and letting him destroy her.

The thought pricked up all her sharp intelligence and presence of mind. She dared not turn round to him – and there he stood motionless, unbroken. Summoning all her strength, she said, in a full, resonant, nonchalant voice, that was forced out with all her remaining self-control:

'Oh, would you mind looking in that bag behind there and giving me my – '

Here her power fell inert. 'My what – my what –?' she screamed in silence to herself.

But he had started round, surprised and startled that she should ask him to look in her bag, which she always kept so *very* private to herself. She turned now, her face white, her dark eyes blazing with uncanny, overwrought excitement. She saw him stooping to the bag, undoing the loosely buckled strap, unattentive.

'Your what?' he asked.

'Oh, a little enamel box – yellow – with a design of a cormorant plucking her breast – '

She went towards him, stooping her beautiful, bare arm, and deftly turned some of her things, disclosing the box, which was exquisitely painted.

'That is it, see,' she said, taking it from under his eyes.

And he was baffled now. He was left to fasten up the bag, whilst she swiftly did up her hair for the night, and sat down to unfasten her shoes. She would not turn her back to him any more.

He was baffled, frustrated, but unconscious. She had the whip hand over him now. She knew he had not realised her terrible panic. Her heart was beating heavily still. Fool, fool that she was, to get into such a state! How she thanked God for Gerald's obtuse blindness. Thank God he could see nothing.

She sat slowly unlacing her shoes, and he too commenced to undress. Thank God that crisis was over. She felt almost fond of him now, almost in love with him.

'Ah, Gerald,' she laughed, caressively, teasingly, 'Ah, what a fine game you played with the Professor's daughter – didn't you now?'

'What game?' he asked, looking round.

'*Isn't* she in love with you – oh *dear,* isn't she in love with you!' said Gudrun, in her gayest, most attractive mood.

'I shouldn't think so,' he said.

'Shouldn't think so!' she teased. 'Why the poor girl is lying at this moment overwhelmed, dying with love for you. She thinks you're *wonderful* – oh marvellous, beyond what man has ever been. *Really,* isn't it funny?'

'Why funny, what is funny?' he asked.

'Why to see you working it on her,' she said, with a half reproach that confused the male conceit in him. 'Really Gerald, the poor girl –!'

'I did nothing to her,' he said.

'Oh, it was too shameful, the way you simply swept her off her feet.'

'That was Schuhplatteln,' he replied, with a bright grin.

'Ha – ha – ha!' laughed Gudrun.

Her mockery quivered through his muscles with curious re-echoes.

When he slept he seemed to crouch down in the bed, lapped up in his own strength, that yet was hollow.

And Gudrun slept strongly, a victorious sleep. Suddenly, she was almost fiercely awake. The small timber room glowed with the dawn, that came upwards from the low window. She could see down the valley when she lifted her head: the snow with a pinkish, half-revealed magic, the fringe of pine-trees at the bottom of the slope. And one tiny figure moved over the vaguely-illuminated space.

She glanced at his watch; it was seven o'clock. He was still completely asleep. And she was so hard awake, it was almost frightening – a hard, metallic wakefulness. She lay looking at him.

He slept in the subjection of his own health and defeat. She was overcome by a sincere regard for him. Till now, she was afraid before him. She lay and thought about him, what he was, what he represented in the world. A fine, independent will, he had. She thought of the revolution he had worked in the mines, in so short a time. She knew that, if he were confronted with any problem, any hard actual difficulty, he would overcome it. If he laid hold of any idea, he would carry it through. He had the faculty of making order out of confusion. Only let him grip hold of a situation, and he would bring to pass an inevitable conclusion.

For a few moments she was borne away on the wild wings of ambition. Gerald, with his force of will and his power for comprehending the actual world, should be set to solve the problems of the day, the problem of industrialism in the modern world. She knew he would, in the course of time, effect the changes he desired, he could re-organise the industrial system. She knew he could do it. As an instrument, in these things, he was marvellous, she had never seen any man with his potentiality. He was unaware of it, but she knew.

He only needed to be hitched on, he needed that his hand should be set to the task, because he was so unconscious. And this she could do. She would marry him, he would go into

Parliament in the Conservative interest, he would clear up the great muddle of labour and industry. He was so superbly fearless, masterful, he knew that every problem could be worked out, in life as in geometry. And he would care neither about himself nor about anything but the pure working out of the problem. He was very pure, really.

Her heart beat fast, she flew away on wings of elation, imagining a future. He would be a Napoleon of peace, or a Bismarck – and she the woman behind him. She had read Bismarck's letters, and had been deeply moved by them. And Gerald would be freer, more dauntless than Bismarck.

But even as she lay in fictitious transport, bathed in the strange, false sunshine of hope in life, something seemed to snap in her, and a terrible cynicism began to gain upon her, blowing in like a wind. Everything turned to irony with her: the last flavour of everything was ironical. When she felt her pang of undeniable reality, this was when she knew the hard irony of hopes and ideas.

She lay and looked at him, as he slept. He was sheerly beautiful, he was a perfect instrument. To her mind, he was a pure, inhuman, almost superhuman instrument. His instrumentality appealed so strongly to her, she wished she were God, to use him as a tool.

And at the same instant, came the ironical question: 'What for?' She thought of the colliers' wives, with their linoleum and their lace curtains and their little girls in high-laced boots. She thought of the wives and daughters of the pit-managers, their tennis-parties, and their terrible struggles to be superior each to the other, in the social scale. There was Shortlands with its meaningless distinction, the meaningless crowd of the Criches. There was London, the House of Commons, the extant social world. My God!

Young as she was, Gudrun had touched the whole pulse of social England. She had no ideas of rising in the world. She knew, with the perfect cynicism of cruel youth, that to rise in the world meant to have one outside show instead of another, the advance was like having a spurious half-crown instead of a spurious penny. The whole coinage of valuation was spurious. Yet of course, her cynicism knew well enough that, in a world where spurious coin was current, a bad sovereign was better than a bad farthing. But rich and poor, she despised both alike.

Already she mocked at herself for her dreams. They could be fulfilled easily enough. But she recognised too well, in her spirit, the mockery of her own impulses. What did she care, that Gerald had created a richly paying industry out of an old worn-out concern? What did she care? The worn-out concern and the rapid, splendidly organised industry, they were bad money. Yet of course, she cared a great deal, outwardly and outwardly was all that mattered, for inwardly was a bad joke.

Everything was intrinsically a piece of irony to her. She leaned over Gerald and said in her heart, with compassion:

'Oh, my dear, my dear, the game isn't worth even you. You are a fine thing really – why should you be used on such a poor show!'

Her heart was breaking with pity and grief for him. And at the same moment, a grimace came over her mouth, of mocking irony at her own unspoken tirade. All, what a farce it was! She thought of Parnell and Katherine O'Shea. Parnell! After all, who can take the nationalisation of Ireland seriously? Who can take political Ireland really seriously, Whatever it does? And who can take political England seriously? Who can? Who can care a straw, really, how the old patched-up Constitution is tinkered at any more? Who cares a button for our national ideas, any more than for our national bowler hat? Aha, it is all old hat, it is all old bowler hat!

That's all it is, Gerald, my young hero. At any rate we'll spare ourselves the nausea of stirring the old broth any more. You be beautiful, my Gerald, and reckless. There *are* perfect moments. Wake up, Gerald, wake up, convince me of the perfect moments. Oh, convince me, I need it.

He opened his eyes, and looked at her. She greeted him with a mocking, enigmatic smile in which was a poignant gaiety. Over his face went the reflection of the smile, he smiled, too, purely unconsciously.

That filled her with extraordinary delight, to see the smile cross his face, reflected from her face. She remembered that was how a baby smiled. It filled her with extraordinary radiant delight.

'You've done it,' she said. 'What?' he asked, dazed. 'Convinced me.'

And she bent down, kissing him passionately, passionately, so that he was bewildered. He did not ask her of what he had convinced her, though he meant to. He was glad she was kissing him. She seemed to be feeling for his very heart to touch the quick of him. And he wanted her to touch the quick of his being, he wanted that most of all.

Outside, somebody was singing, in a manly, reckless handsome voice:

> 'Mach mir auf, mach mir auf, du Stolze,
> Mach mir ein Feuer von Holze.
> Vom Regen bin ich nass
> Vom Regen bin ich nass – '*

Gudrun knew that that song would sound through her eternity, sung in a manly, reckless, mocking voice. It marked one of her supreme moments, the supreme pangs of her nervous gratification. There it was, fixed in eternity for her.

The day came fine and bluish. There was a light wind blowing among the mountain-tops, keen as a rapier where it touched, carrying with it a fine dust of snow-powder. Gerald went out with the fine, blind face of a man who is in his state of fulfilment. Gudrun and he were in perfect static unity this morning, but unseeing and unwitting. They went out with a toboggan, leaving Ursula and Birkin to follow.

Gudrun was all scarlet and royal blue – a scarlet jersey and cap, and a royal blue skirt and stockings. She went gaily over the white snow, with Gerald beside her, in white and grey, pulling the little toboggan. They grew small in the distance of snow, climbing the steep slope.

---

* German folk song:
    Allow me inside, you proud woman;
    Light a fire of wood,
    for, I am soaked in the rain.

For Gudrun herself, she seemed to pass altogether into the whiteness of the snow, she became a pure, thoughtless crystal. When she reached the top of the slope, in the wind, she looked round, and saw peak beyond peak of rock and snow, bluish, transcendent in heaven. And it seemed to her like a garden, with the peaks for pure flowers, and her heart gathering them. She had no separate consciousness for Gerald.

She held on to him as they went sheering down over the keen slope. She felt as if her senses were being whetted on some fine grindstone, that was keen as flame. The snow sprinted on either side, like sparks from a blade that is being sharpened, the whiteness round about ran swifter, swifter, in pure flame the white slope flew against her, and she fused like one molten, dancing globule, rushed through a white intensity. Then there was a great swerve at the bottom, when they swung as it were in a fall to earth, in the diminishing motion.

They came to rest. But when she rose to her feet, she could not stand. She gave a strange cry, turned and clung to him, sinking her face on his breast, fainting in him. Utter oblivion came over her, as she lay for a few moments abandoned against him.

'What is it?' he was saying. 'Was it too much for you?'

But she heard nothing.

When she came to, she stood up and looked round, astonished. Her face was white, her eyes brilliant and large.

'What is it?' he repeated. 'Did it upset you?'

She looked at him with her brilliant eyes that seemed to have undergone some transfiguration, and she laughed, with a terrible merriment.

'No,' she cried, with triumphant joy. 'It was the complete moment of my life.'

And she looked at him with her dazzling, overweening laughter, like one possessed. A fine blade seemed to enter his heart, but he did not care, or take any notice.

But they climbed up the slope again, and they flew down through the white flame again, splendidly, splendidly. Gudrun was laughing and flashing, powdered with snow-crystals, Gerald worked perfectly. He felt he could guide the toboggan to a hair-breadth, almost he could make it pierce into the air and right into the very heart of the sky. It seemed to him the flying sledge was but his strength spread out, he had but to move his arms, the motion was his own. They explored the great slopes, to find another slide. He felt there must be something better than they had known. And he found what he desired, a perfect long, fierce sweep, sheering past the foot of a rock and into the trees at the base. It was dangerous, he knew. But then he knew also he would direct the sledge between his fingers.

The first days passed in an ecstasy of physical motion, sleighing, skiing, skating, moving in an intensity of speed and white light that surpassed life itself, and carried the souls of the human beings beyond into an inhuman abstraction of velocity and weight and eternal, frozen snow.

Gerald's eyes became hard and strange, and as he went by on his skis he was more like some powerful, fateful sigh than a man, his muscles elastic in a perfect, soaring trajectory, his body projected in pure flight, mindless, soulless, whirling along one perfect line of force.

Luckily there came a day of snow, when they must all stay indoors: otherwise Birkin said, they would all lose their faculties, and begin to utter themselves in cries and shrieks, like some strange, unknown species of snow-creatures.

It happened in the afternoon that Ursula sat in the Reunionsaal talking to Loerke. The latter had seemed unhappy lately. He was lively and full of mischievous humour, as usual.

But Ursula had thought he was sulky about something. His partner, too, the big, fair, good-looking youth, was ill at ease, going about as if he belonged to nowhere, and was kept in some sort of subjection, against which he was rebelling.

Loerke had hardly talked to Gudrun. His associate, on the other hand, had paid her constantly a soft, over-deferential attention. Gudrun wanted to talk to Loerke. He was a sculptor, and she wanted to hear his view of his art. And his figure attracted her. There was the look of a little wastrel about him, that intrigued her, and an old man's look, that interested her, and then, beside this, an uncanny singleness, a quality of being by himself, not in contact with anybody else, that marked out an artist to her. He was a chatterer, a magpie, a maker of mischievous word-jokes, that were sometimes very clever, but which often were not. And she could see in his brown, gnome's eyes, the black look of inorganic misery, which lay behind all his small buffoonery.

His figure interested her – the figure of a boy, almost a street arab. He made no attempt to conceal it. He always wore a simple loden suit, with knee breeches. His legs were thin, and he made no attempt to disguise the fact: which was of itself remarkable, in a German. And he never ingratiated himself anywhere, not in the slightest, but kept to himself, for all his apparent playfulness.

Leitner, his companion, was a great sportsman, very handsome with his big limbs and his blue eyes. Loerke would go toboganning or skating, in little snatches, but he was indifferent. And his fine, thin nostrils, the nostrils of a pure-bred street arab, would quiver with contempt at Leitner's splotchering gymnastic displays. It was evident that the two men who had travelled and lived together, sharing the same bedroom, had now reached the stage of loathing. Leitner hated Loerke with an injured, writhing, impotent hatred, and Loerke treated Leitner with a fine quivering contempt and sarcasm. Soon the two would have to go apart.

Already they were rarely together. Leitner ran attaching himself to somebody or other, always deferring, Loerke was a good deal alone. Out of doors he wore a Westphalian cap, a close brown-velvet head with big brown velvet flaps down over his ears, so that he looked like a lop-eared rabbit, or a troll. His face was brown-red, with a dry, bright skin, that seemed to crinkle with his mobile expressions. His eyes were arresting – brown, full, like a rabbit's, or like a troll's, or like the eyes of a lost being, having a strange, dumb, depraved look of knowledge, and a quick spark of uncanny fire. Whenever Gudrun had tried to talk to him he had shied away unresponsive, looking at her with his watchful dark eyes, but entering into no relation with her. He had made her feel that her slow French and her slower German, were hateful to him. As for his own inadequate English, he was much too awkward to try it at all. But he understood a good deal of what was said, nevertheless. And Gudrun, piqued, left him alone.

This afternoon, however, she came into the lounge as he was talking to Ursula. His fine, black hair somehow reminded her of a bat, thin as it was on his full, sensitive-looking head, and worn away at the temples. He sat hunched up, as if his spirit were bat-like. And Gudrun could see he was making some slow confidence to Ursula, unwilling, a slow, grudging, scanty self-revelation. She went and sat by her sister.

He looked at her, then looked away again, as if he took no notice of her. But as a matter of fact, she interested him deeply.

'Isn't it interesting, Prune,' said Ursula, turning to her sister, 'Herr Loerke is doing a great frieze for a factory in Cologne, for the outside, the street.'

She looked at him, at his thin, brown, nervous hands, that were prehensile, and somehow like talons, like 'griffes,'[1] inhuman.

'What *in?*' she asked.

'*Aus was?*' repeated Ursula.

'*Granit,*' he replied.

It had become immediately a laconic series of question and answer between fellow craftsmen.

'What is the relief?' asked Gudrun.

'Alto relievo.'[2]

'And at what height?'

It was very interesting to Gudrun to think of his making the great granite frieze for a great granite factory in Cologne. She got from him some notion of the design. It was a representation of a fair, with peasants and artisans in an orgy of enjoyment, drunk and absurd in their modem dress, whirling ridiculously in roundabouts, gaping at shows, kissing and staggering and rolling in knots, swinging in swingboats, and firing down shooting galleries, a frenzy of chaotic motion.

1 Claws.
2 (It.) High relief.

There was a swift discussion of technicalities. Gudrun was very much impressed.

'But how wonderful, to have such a factory!' cried Ursula. 'Is the whole building fine?'

'Oh yes,' he replied. 'The frieze is part of the whole architecture. Yes, it is a colossal thing.'

Then he seemed to stiffen, shrugged his shoulders, and went on:

'Sculpture and architecture must go together. The day for irrelevant statues, as for wall pictures, is over. As a matter of fact sculpture is always part of an architectural conception. And since churches are all museum stuff, since industry is our business, now, then let us make our places of industry our art – our factory-area our Parthenon, *ecco!*'

Ursula pondered.

'I suppose,' she said, 'there is no *need* for our great works to be so hideous.'

Instantly he broke into motion.

'There you are!' he cried, 'there you are! There is not only *no need* for our places of work to be ugly, but their ugliness ruins the work, in the end. Men will not go on submitting to such intolerable ugliness. In the end it will hurt too much, and they will wither because of it. And this will wither the *work* as well. They will think the work itself is ugly: the machines, the very act of labour. Whereas the machinery and the acts of labour are extremely, maddeningly beautiful. But this will be the end of our civilisation, when people will not work because work has become so intolerable to their senses, it nauseates them too much, they would rather starve. *Then* we shall see, the hammer used only for smashing, then we shall see it. Yet here we are – we have the opportunity to make beautiful factories, beautiful machine-houses we have the opportunity – '

Gudrun could only partly understand. She could have cried with vexation.

'What does he say?' she asked Ursula. And Ursula translated, stammering and brief. Loerke watched Gudrun's face, to see her judgment.

'And do you think then,' said Gudrun, 'that art should serve industry?'

'Art should *interpret* industry, as art once interpreted religion,' he said.

'But does your fair interpret industry?' she asked him.

'Certainly. What is man doing, when he is at a fair like this? He is fulfilling the counterpart of labour – the machine works him, instead of he the machine. He enjoys the mechanical motion, in his own body.'

'But is there nothing but work – mechanical work?' said Gudrun.

'Nothing but work!' he repeated, leaning forward, his eyes two darknesses, with needle-points of light. 'No, it is nothing but this, serving a machine, or enjoying the motion of a machine – motion, that is all. You have never worked for hunger, or you would know what god governs us.'

Gudrun quivered and flushed. For some reason she was almost in tears.

'No, I have not worked for hunger,' she replied, 'but I have worked!'

'Travaillé – lavorato?' he asked. 'E che lavoro – che lavoro? Quel travail est-ce que vous avez fait?'*

He broke into a mixture of Italian and French, instinctively using a foreign language when he spoke to her.

'You have never worked as the world works,' he said to her, with sarcasm.

'Yes,' she said. 'I have. And I do – I work now for my daily bread.'

He paused, looked at her steadily, then dropped the subject entirely. She seemed to him to be trifling.

'But have *you* ever worked as the world works?' Ursula asked him.

He looked at her untrustful.

'Yes,' he replied, with a surly bark. 'I have known what it was to lie in bed for three days, because I had nothing to eat.'

Gudrun was looking at him with large, grave eyes, that seemed to draw the confession from him as the marrow from his bones. All his nature held him back from confessing. And yet her large,

---

* (Mix of It. and Fr.) Worked! What work? What work have you done?

grave eyes upon him seemed to open some valve in his veins, and
involuntarily he was telling.

'My father was a man who did not like work, and we had no
mother. We lived in Austria, Polish Austria. How did we live? Ha!
– somehow! Mostly in a room with three other families – one set
in each corner and the W.C. in the middle of the room – a pan
with a plank on it – ha! I had two brothers and a sister – and there
might be a woman with my father. He was a free being, in his
way – would fight with any man in the town – a garrison town –
and was a little man too. But he wouldn't work for anybody – set
his heart against it, and wouldn't.'

'And how did you live then?' asked Ursula.

He looked at her – then, suddenly, at Gudrun.

'Do you understand?' he asked.

'Enough,' she replied.

Their eyes met for a moment. Then he looked away. He would
say no more.

'And how did you become a sculptor?' asked Ursula.

'How did I become a sculptor – ' he paused. 'Dunque – ' he
resumed, in a changed manner, and beginning to speak French –
'I became old enough – I used to steal from the market-place.
Later I went to work-imprinted the stamp on clay bottles, before
they were baked. It was an earthenware-bottle factory. There I
began making models. One day, I had had enough. I lay in the
sun and did not go to work. Then I walked to Munich – then I
walked to Italy – begging, begging everything.'

'The Italians were very good to me – they were good and
honourable to me. From Bozen to Rome, almost every night I
had a meal and a bed, perhaps of straw, with some peasant. I
love the Italian people, with all my heart.

'Dunque, adesso – maintenant* – I earn a thousand pounds
in a year, or I earn two thousand – '

He looked down at the ground, his voice tailing off into silence.

Gudrun looked at his fine, thin, shiny skin, reddish-brown
from the sun, drawn tight over his full temples; and at his thin

---

* So, now!

hair – and at the thick, coarse, brush-like moustache, cut short about his mobile, rather shapeless mouth.

'How old are you?' she asked.

He looked up at her with his full, elfin eyes startled.

'*Wie alt?*' he repeated. And he hesitated. It was evidently one of his reticencies.

'How old are *you?*' he replied, without answering.

'I am twenty-six,' she answered.

'Twenty-six,' he repeated, looking into her eyes. He paused. Then he said:

'*Und Ihr Herr Gemahl, wie alt is er?*'

'Who?' asked Gudrun.

'Your husband,' said Ursula, with a certain irony.

'I haven't got a husband,' said Gudrun in English. In German she answered,

'He is thirty-one.'

But Loerke was watching closely, with his uncanny, full, suspicious eyes. Something in Gudrun seemed to accord with him. He was really like one of the 'little people' who have no soul, who has found his mate in a human being. But he suffered in his discovery. She too was fascinated by him, fascinated, as if some strange creature, a rabbit or a bat, or a brown seal, had begun to talk to her. But also, she knew what he was unconscious of, his tremendous power of understanding, of apprehending her living motion. He did not know his own power. He did not know how, with his full, submerged, watchful eyes, he could look into her and see her, what she was, see her secrets. He would only want her to be herself – he knew her verily, with a subconscious, sinister knowledge, devoid of illusions and hopes.

To Gudrun, there was in Loerke the rock-bottom of all life. Everybody else had their illusion, must have their illusion, their before and after. But he, with a perfect stoicism, did without any before and after, dispensed with all illusion. He did not deceive himself in the last issue. In the last issue he cared about nothing, he was troubled about nothing, he made not the slightest attempt to be at one with anything. He existed a pure, unconnected will, stoical and momentaneous. There was only his work.

It was curious too, how his poverty, the degradation of his earlier life, attracted her. There was something insipid and tasteless to her, in the idea of a gentleman, a man who had gone the usual course through school and university. A certain violent sympathy, however, came up in her for this mud-child. He seemed to be the very stuff of the underworld of life. There was no going beyond him.

Ursula too was attracted by Loerke. In both sisters he commanded a certain homage. But there were moments when to Ursula he seemed indescribably inferior, false, a vulgarism.

Both Birkin and Gerald disliked him, Gerald ignoring him with some contempt, Birkin exasperated.

'What do the women find so impressive in that little brat?' Gerald asked.

'God alone knows,' replied Birkin, 'unless it's some sort of appeal he makes to them, which flatters them and has such a power over them.' Gerald looked up in surprise.

'*Does* he make an appeal to them?' he asked.

'Oh yes,' replied Birkin. 'He is the perfectly subjected being, existing almost like a criminal. And the women rush towards that, like a current of air towards a vacuum.'

'Funny they should rush to that,' said Gerald.

'Makes one mad, too,' said Birkin. 'But he has the fascination of pity and repulsion for them, a little obscene monster of the darkness that he is.'

Gerald stood still, suspended in thought.

'What *do* women want, at the bottom?' he asked.

Birkin shrugged his shoulders.

'God knows,' he said. 'Some satisfaction in basic repulsion, it seems to me. They seem to creep down some ghastly tunnel of darkness, and will never be satisfied till they've come to the end.'

Gerald looked out into the mist of fine snow that was blowing by. Everywhere was blind today, horribly blind.

'And what is the end?' he asked.

Birkin shook his head.

'I've not got there yet, so I don't know. Ask Loerke, he's pretty near. He is a good many stages further than either you or I can go.'

'Yes, but stages further in what?' cried Gerald, irritated.

Birkin sighed, and gathered his brows into a knot of anger.

'Stages further in social hatred,' he said. 'He lives like a rat, in the river of corruption, just where it falls over into the bottomless pit. He's further on than we are. He hates the ideal more acutely. He *hates* the ideal utterly, yet it still dominates him. I expect he is a Jew – or part Jewish.'

'Probably,' said Gerald.

'He is a gnawing little negation, gnawing at the roots of life.'

'But why does anybody care about him?' cried Gerald.

'Because they hate the ideal also, in their souls. They want to explore the sewers, and he's the wizard rat that swims ahead.'

Still Gerald stood and stared at the blind haze of snow outside.

'I don't understand your terms, really,' he said, in a flat, doomed voice. 'But it sounds a rum sort of desire.'

'I suppose we want the same,' said Birkin. 'Only we want to take a quick jump downwards, in a sort of ecstasy – and he ebbs with the stream, the sewer stream.'

Meanwhile Gudrun and Ursula waited for the next opportunity to talk to Loerke. It was no use beginning when the men were there. Then they could get into no touch with the isolated little sculptor. He had to be alone with them. And he preferred Ursula to be there, as a sort of transmitter to Gudrun.

'Do you do nothing but architectural sculpture?' Gudrun asked him one evening.

'Not now,' he replied. 'I have done all sorts – except portraits – I never did portraits. But other things – '

'What kind of things?' asked Gudrun.

He paused a moment, then rose, and went out of the room. He returned almost immediately with a little roll of paper, which he handed to her. She unrolled it. It was a photogravure reproduction of a statuette, signed F. Loerke.

'That is quite an early thing – *not* mechanical,' he said, 'more popular.'

The statuette was of a naked girl, small, finely made, sitting on a great naked horse. The girl was young and tender, a mere bud. She was sitting sideways on the horse, her face in her hands, as if in shame and grief, in a little abandon. Her hair, which was short and must be flaxen, fell forward, divided, half covering her hands.

Her limbs were young and tender. Her legs, scarcely formed yet, the legs of a maiden just passing towards cruel womanhood, dangled childishly over the side of the powerful horse, pathetically, the small feet folded one over the other, as if to hide. But there was no hiding. There she was exposed naked on the naked flank of the horse.

The horse stood stock still, stretched in a kind of start. It was a massive, magnificent stallion, rigid with pent-up power. Its neck was arched and terrible, like a sickle, its flanks were pressed back, rigid with power.

Gudrun went pale, and a darkness came over her eyes, like shame, she looked up with a certain supplication, almost slave-like. He glanced at her, and jerked his head a little.

'How big is it?' she asked, in a toneless voice, persisting in appearing casual and unaffected.

'How big?' he replied, glancing again at her. 'Without pedestal – so high – ' he measured with his hand – 'with pedestal, so – '

He looked at her steadily. There was a little brusque, turgid contempt for her in his swift gesture, and she seemed to cringe a little.

'And what is it done in?' she asked, throwing back her head and looking at him with affected coldness.

He still gazed at her steadily, and his dominance was not shaken.

'Bronze – green bronze.'

'Green bronze!' repeated Gudrun, coldly accepting his challenge: She was thinking of the slender, immature, tender limbs of the girl, smooth and cold in green bronze.

'Yes, beautiful,' she murmured, looking up at him with a certain dark homage.

He closed his eyes and looked aside, triumphant.

'Why,' said Ursula, 'did you make the horse so stiff? It is as stiff as a block.'

'Stiff?' he repeated, in arms at once.

'Yes. *Look* how stock and stupid and brutal it is. Horses are sensitive, quite delicate and sensitive, really.'

He raised his shoulders, spread his hands in a shrug of slow indifference, as much as to inform her she was an amateur and an impertinent nobody.

'Wissen Sie,'[1] he said, with an insulting patience and condescension in his voice, 'that horse is a certain *form,* part of a whole form. It is part of a work of art, a piece of form. It is not a picture of a friendly horse to which you give a lump of sugar, do you see – it is part of a work of art, it has no relation to anything outside that work of art.'

Ursula, angry at being treated quite so insultingly *de haut en bas,*[2] from the height of esoteric art to the depth of general exoteric amateurism, replied, hotly, flushing and lifting her face.

'But it *is* a picture of a horse, nevertheless.'

He lifted his shoulders in another shrug.

'As you like – it is not a picture of a cow, certainly.'

Here Gudrun broke in, flushed and brilliant, anxious to avoid any more of this, any more of Ursula's foolish persistence in giving herself away.

'What do you mean by "it is a picture of a horse?" ' she cried at her sister. 'What do you mean by a horse? You mean an idea you have in *your* head, and which you want to see represented. There is another idea altogether, quite another idea. Call it a horse if you like, or say it is not a horse. I have just as much right to say that *your* horse isn't a horse, that it is a falsity of your own make-up.'

Ursula wavered, baffled. Then her words came.

'But why does he have this idea of a horse?' she said. 'I know it is his idea. I know it is a picture of himself, really – '

Loerke snorted with rage.

1 (Ger.) You know.
2 (Fr.) Relegated to a less dignified level.

'A picture of myself!' he repeated, in derision. 'Wissen sie, gnädige Fräu, that is a Kunstwerk, a work of art. It is a work of art, it is a picture of nothing, of absolutely nothing. It has nothing to do with anything but itself, it has no relation with the everyday world of this and other, there is no connection between them, absolutely none, they are two different and distinct planes of existence, and to translate one into the other is worse than foolish, it is a darkening of all counsel, a making confusion everywhere. Do you see, you *must not* confuse the relative work of action, with the absolute world of art. That you *must not do.*'

'That is quite true,' cried Gudrun, let loose in a sort of rhapsody. 'The two things are quite and permanently apart, they have *nothing* to do with one another. *I* and my art, they have nothing to do with each other. My art stands in another world, I am in this world.'

Her face was flushed and transfigured. Loerke who was sitting with his head ducked, like some creature at bay, looked up at her, swiftly, almost furtively, and murmured,

'Ja – so ist es, so ist es.'*

Ursula was silent after this outburst. She was furious. She wanted to poke a hole into them both.

'It isn't a word of it true, of all this harangue you have made me,' she replied flatly. 'The horse is a picture of your own stock, stupid brutality, and the girl was a girl you loved and tortured and then ignored.'

He looked up at her with a small smile of contempt in his eyes. He would not trouble to answer this last charge.

Gudrun too was silent in exasperated contempt. Ursula *was* such an insufferable outsider, rushing in where angels would fear to tread. But then – fools must be suffered, if not gladly.

But Ursula was persistent too.

'As for your world of art and your world of reality,' she replied, 'you have to separate the two, because you can't bear to know what you are.

You can't bear to realise what a stock, stiff, hide-bound brutality you *are* really, so you say "it's the world of art." The

* (Ger.) Yes, so it is!

world of art is only the truth about the real world, that's all – but you are too far gone to see it.'

She was white and trembling, intent. Gudrun and Loerke sat in stiff dislike of her. Gerald too, who had come up in the beginning of the speech, stood looking at her in complete disapproval and opposition. He felt she was undignified, she put a sort of vulgarity over the esotericism which gave man his last distinction. He joined his forces with the other two. They all three wanted her to go away. But she sat on in silence, her soul weeping, throbbing violently, her fingers twisting her handkerchief.

The others maintained a dead silence, letting the display of Ursula's obtrusiveness pass by. Then Gudrun asked, in a voice that was quite cool and casual, as if resuming a casual conversation:

'Was the girl a model?'

'Nein, sie war kein Modell. Sie war eine kleine Malschülerin.'*

'An art-student!' replied Gudrun.

And how the situation revealed itself to her! She saw the girl art-student, unformed and of pernicious recklessness, too young, her straight flaxen hair cut short, hanging just into her neck, curving inwards slightly, because it was rather thick; and Loerke, the well known master-sculptor, and the girl, probably well-brought-up, and of good family, thinking herself so great to be his mistress. Oh how well she knew the common callousness of it all. Dresden, Paris, or London, what did it matter? She knew it.

'Where is she now?' Ursula asked.

Loerke raised his shoulders, to convey his complete ignorance and indifference.

'That is already six years ago,' he said; 'she will be twenty-three years old, no more good.'

Gerald had picked up the picture and was looking at it. It attracted him also. He saw on the pedestal, that the piece was called 'Lady Godiva.

'But this isn't Lady Godiva,' he said, smiling good-humouredly. 'She was the middle-aged wife of some Earl or other, who covered herself with her long hair.'

* (Ger.) "No. She was not a model, but an Art student."

'A la Maud Allan,' said Gudrun with a mocking grimace.

'Why Maud Allan?' he replied. 'Isn't it so? I always thought the legend was that.'

'Yes, Gerald dear, I'm quite *sure* you've got the legend perfectly.'

She was laughing at him, with a little, mock-caressive contempt.

'To be sure, I'd rather see the woman than the hair,' he laughed in return.

'Wouldn't you just!' mocked Gudrun.

Ursula rose and went away, leaving the three together.

Gudrun took the picture again from Gerald, and sat looking at it closely.

'Of course,' she said, turning to tease Loerke now, 'you *understood* your little Malschülerin.'

He raised his eyebrows and his shoulders in a complacent shrug.

'The little girl?' asked Gerald, pointing to the figure.

Gudrun was sitting with the picture in her lap. She looked up at Gerald, full into his eyes, so that he seemed to be blinded.

'*Didn't* he understand her!' she said to Gerald, in a slightly mocking, humorous playfulness. 'You've only to look at the feet – *aren't* they darling, so pretty and tender – oh, they're really wonderful, they are really – '

She lifted her eyes slowly, with a hot, flaming look into Loerke's eyes. His soul was filled with her burning recognition, he seemed to grow more uppish and lordly.

Gerald looked at the small, sculptured feet. They were turned together, half covering each other in pathetic shyness and fear. He looked at them a long time, fascinated. Then, in some pain, he put the picture away from him. He felt full of barrenness.

'What was her name?' Gudrun asked Loerke.

'Annette von Weck,' Loerke replied reminiscent. 'Ja, sie war hübsch – She was pretty – but she was tiresome. She was a nuisance, – not for a minute would she keep still – not until I'd slapped her hard and made her cry – then she'd sit for five minutes.'

He was thinking over the work, his work, the all important to him.

'Did you really slap her?' asked Gudrun, coolly.

He glanced back at her, reading her challenge.

'Yes, I did,' he said, nonchalant, 'harder than I have ever beat anything in my life. I had to, I had to. It was the only way I got the work done.'

Gudrun watched him with large, dark-filled eyes, for some moments. She seemed to be considering his very soul. Then she looked down, in silence.

'Why did you have such a young Godiva then?' asked Gerald. 'She is so small, besides, on the horse – not big enough for it – such a child.'

A queer spasm went over Loerke's face.

'Yes,' he said. 'I don't like them any bigger, any older. Then they are beautiful, at sixteen, seventeen, eighteen – after that, they are no use tome.'

There was a moment's pause.

'Why not?' asked Gerald.

Loerke shrugged his shoulders.

'I don't find them interesting – or beautiful – they are no good to me, for my work.'

'Do you mean to say a woman isn't beautiful after she is twenty?' asked Gerald.

'For me, no. Before twenty, she is small and fresh and tender and slight. After that – let her be what she likes, she has nothing for me. The Venus of Milo is a bourgeoise – so are they all.'

'And you don't care for women at all after twenty?' asked Gerald.

'They are no good to me, they are of no use in my art,' Loerke repeated impatiently. 'I don't find them beautiful.'

'You are an epicure,' said Gerald, with a slight sarcastic laugh. 'And what about men?' asked Gudrun suddenly.

'Yes, they are good at all ages,' replied Loerke. 'A man should be big and powerful – whether he is old or young is of no account, so he has the size, something of massiveness and – and stupid form.'

Ursula went out alone into the world of pure, new snow. But the dazzling whiteness seemed to beat upon her till it hurt her, she felt the cold was slowly strangling her soul. Her head felt dazed and numb.

Suddenly she wanted to go away. It occurred to her, like a miracle, that she might go away into another world. She had felt so doomed up here in the eternal snow, as if there were no beyond.

Now suddenly, as by a miracle she remembered that away beyond, below her, lay the dark fruitful earth, that towards the south there were stretches of land dark with orange trees and cypress, grey with olives, that ilex trees lifted wonderful plumy tufts in shadow against a blue sky. Miracle of miracles! – this utterly silent, frozen world of the mountain-tops was not universal! One might leave it and have done with it. One might go away.

She wanted to realise the miracle at once. She wanted at this instant to have done with the snow-world, the terrible, static ice-built mountain tops. She wanted to see the dark earth, to smell its earthy fecundity, to see the patient wintry vegetation, to feel the sunshine touch a response in the buds.

She went back gladly to the house, full of hope. Birkin was reading, lying in bed.

'Rupert,' she said, bursting in on him. 'I want to go away.'

He looked up at her slowly.

'Do you?' he replied mildly.

She sat by him und put her arms round his neck. It surprised her that he was so little surprised.

'Don't *you?*' she asked troubled.

'I hadn't thought about it,' he said. 'But I'm sure I do.'

She sat up, suddenly erect.

'I hate it,' she said. 'I hate the snow, and the unnaturalness of it, the unnatural light it throws on everybody, the ghastly glamour, the unnatural feelings it makes everybody have.'

He lay still and laughed, meditating.

'Well,' he said, 'we can go away – we can go tomorrow. We'll go tomorrow to Verona, and find Romeo and Juliet, and sit in the amphitheatre – shall we?'

Suddenly she hid her face against his shoulder with perplexity and shyness. He lay so untrammelled.

'Yes,' she said softly, filled with relief. She felt her soul had new wings, now he was so uncaring. 'I shall love to be Romeo and Juliet,' she said. 'My love!'

'Though a fearfully cold wind blows in Verona,' he said, 'from out of the Alps. We shall have the smell of the snow in our noses.'

She sat up and looked at him.

'Are you glad to go?' she asked, troubled.

His eyes were inscrutable and laughing. She hid her face against his neck, clinging close to him, pleading:

'Don't laugh at me – don't laugh at me.'

'Why how's that?' he laughed, putting his arms round her.

'Because I don't want to be laughed at,' she whispered.

He laughed more, as he kissed her delicate, finely perfumed hair.

'Do you love me?' she whispered, in wild seriousness.

'Yes,' he answered, laughing.

Suddenly she lifted her mouth to be kissed. Her lips were taut and quivering and strenuous, his were soft, deep and delicate. He waited a few moments in the kiss. Then a shade of sadness went over his soul.

'Your mouth is so hard,' he said, in faint reproach.

'And yours is so soft and nice,' she said gladly.

'But why do you always grip your lips?' he asked, regretful.

'Never mind,' she said swiftly. 'It is my way.'

She knew he loved her; she was sure of him. Yet she could not let go a certain hold over herself, she could not bear him to question her. She gave herself up in delight to being loved by him. She knew that, in spite of his joy when she abandoned herself, he was a little bit saddened too. She could give herself up to his activity. But she could not be herself, she *dared* not come forth quite nakedly to his nakedness, abandoning all adjustment, lapsing in pure faith with him. She abandoned herself to *him*, or she took hold of him and gathered her joy of him. And she enjoyed him fully. But they were never *quite* together, at the same moment, one was always a little left out. Nevertheless she was glad in hope, glorious and free, full of life and liberty. And he was still and soft and patient, for the time.

They made their preparations to leave the next day. First they went to Gudrun's room, where she and Gerald were just dressed ready for the evening indoors.

'Prune,' said Ursula, 'I think we shall go away tomorrow. I can't stand the snow any more. It hurts my skin and my soul.'

'Does it really hurt your soul, Ursula?' asked Gudrun, in some surprise. 'I can believe quite it hurts your skin – it is *terrible*. But I thought it was *admirable* for the soul.'

'No, not for mine. It just injures it,' said Ursula.

'Really!' cried Gudrun.

There was a silence in the room. And Ursula and Birkin could feel that Gudrun and Gerald were relieved by their going.

'You will go south?' said Gerald, a little ring of uneasiness in his voice.

'Yes,' said Birkin, turning away. There was a queer, indefinable hostility between the two men, lately. Birkin was on the whole dim and indifferent, drifting along in a dim, easy flow, unnoticing and patient, since he came abroad, whilst Gerald on the other hand, was intense and gripped into white light, agonistes. The two men revoked one another.

Gerald and Gudrun were very kind to the two who were departing, solicitous for their welfare as if they were two children. Gudrun came to Ursula's bedroom with three pairs of the coloured stockings for which she was notorious, and she threw them on the bed. But these were thick silk stockings, vermilion, cornflower blue, and grey, bought in Paris. The grey ones were knitted, seamless and heavy. Ursula was in raptures. She knew Gudrun must be feeling *very* loving, to give away such treasures.

'I can't take them from you, Prune,' she cried. 'I can't possibly deprive you of them – the jewels.'

'*Aren't* they jewels!' cried Gudrun, eyeing her gifts with an envious eye. '*Aren't* they real lambs!'

'Yes, you *must* keep them,' said Ursula.

'I don't *want* them, I've got three more pairs. I *want* you to keep them – I want you to have them. They're yours, there – '

And with trembling, excited hands she put the coveted stockings under Ursula's pillow.

'One gets the greatest joy of all out of really lovely stockings,' said Ursula.

'One does,' replied Gudrun; 'the greatest joy of all.'

And she sat down in the chair. It was evident she had come for a last talk. Ursula, not knowing what she wanted, waited in silence.

'Do you *feel,* Ursula,' Gudrun began, rather sceptically, 'that you are going-away-for-ever, never-to-return, sort of thing?'

'Oh, we shall come back,' said Ursula. 'It isn't a question of train journeys.

'Yes, I know. But spiritually, so to speak, you are going away from us all?'

Ursula quivered.

'I don't know a bit what is going to happen,' she said. 'I only know we are going somewhere.'

Gudrun waited.

'And you are glad?' she asked.

Ursula meditated for a moment.

'I believe I am *very* glad,' she replied.

But Gudrun read the unconscious brightness on her sister's face, rather than the uncertain tones of her speech.

'But don't you think you'll *want* the old connection with the world father and the rest of us, and all that it means, England and the world of thought – don't you think you'll *need* that, really to make a world?'

Ursula was silent, trying to imagine.

'I think,' she said at length, involuntarily, 'that Rupert is right – one wants a new space to be in, and one falls away from the old.'

Gudrun watched her sister with impassive face and steady eyes.

'One wants a new space to be in, I quite agree,' she said. 'But *I* think that a new world is a development from this world, and that to isolate oneself with one other person, isn't to find a new world at all, but only to secure oneself in one's illusions.'

Ursula looked out of the window. In her soul she began to wrestle, and she was frightened. She was always frightened of words, because she knew that mere word-force could always make her believe what she did not believe.

'Perhaps,' she said, full of mistrust, of herself and everybody. 'But,' she added, 'I do think that one can't have anything new whilst one cares for the old – do you know what I mean? – even fighting the old is belonging to it. I know, one is tempted to stop with the world, just to fight it. But then it isn't worth it.'

Gudrun considered herself.

'Yes,' she said. 'In a way, one is of the world if one lives in it. But isn't it really an illusion to think you can get out of it? After all, a cottage in the Abruzzi, or wherever it may be, isn't a new world. No, the only thing to do with the world, is to see it through.'

Ursula looked away. She was so frightened of argument.

'But there *can* be something else, can't there?' she said. 'One can see it through in one's soul, long enough before it sees itself through in actuality. And then, when one has seen one's soul, one is something else.'

'*Can* one see it through in one's soul?' asked Gudrun. 'If you mean that you can see to the end of what will happen, I don't agree. I really can't agree. And anyhow, you can't suddenly fly off on to a new planet, because you think you can see to the end of this.'

Ursula suddenly straightened herself.

'Yes,' she said. 'Yes – one knows. One has no more connections here.

One has a sort of other self, that belongs to a new planet, not to this. You've got to hop off.'

Gudrun reflected for a few moments. Then a smile of ridicule, almost of contempt, came over her face.

'And what will happen when you find yourself in space?' she cried in derision. 'After all, the great ideas of the world are the same there. You above everybody can't get away from the fact that love, for instance, is the supreme thing, in space as well as on earth.'

'No,' said Ursula, 'it isn't. Love is too human and little. I believe in something inhuman, of which love is only a little part. I believe what we must fulfil comes out of the unknown to us, and it is something infinitely more than love. It isn't so merely *human*.'

Gudrun looked at Ursula with steady, balancing eyes. She admired and despised her sister so much, both! Then, suddenly she averted her face, saying coldly, uglily:

'Well, I've got no further than love, yet.'

Over Ursula's mind flashed the thought: 'Because you never *have* loved, you can't get beyond it.'

Gudrun rose, came over to Ursula and put her arm round her neck.

'Go and find your new world, dear,' she said, her voice clanging with false benignity. 'After all, the happiest voyage is the quest of Rupert's Blessed Isles.'

Her arm rested round Ursula's neck, her fingers on Ursula's cheek for a few moments. Ursula was supremely uncomfortable meanwhile. There was an insult in Gudrun's protective patronage that was really too hurting. Feeling her sister's resistance, Gudrun drew awkwardly away, turned over the pillow, and disclosed the stockings again.

'Ha – ha!' she laughed, rather hollowly. 'How we do talk indeed new worlds and old –!'

And they passed to the familiar worldly subjects.

Gerald and Birkin had walked on ahead, waiting for the sledge to overtake them, conveying the departing guests.

'How much longer will you stay here?' asked Birkin, glancing up at Gerald's very red, almost blank face.

'Oh, I can't say,' Gerald replied. 'Till we get tired of it.'

'You're not afraid of the snow melting first?' asked Birkin.

Gerald laughed.

'Does it melt?' he said.

'Things are all right with you then?' said Birkin.

Gerald screwed up his eyes a little.

'All right?' he said. 'I never know what those common words mean. All right and all wrong, don't they become synonymous, somewhere?'

'Yes, I suppose. How about going back?' asked Birkin.

'Oh, I don't know. We may never get back. I don't look before and after,' said Gerald.

'*Nor* pine for what is not,' said Birkin.

Gerald looked into the distance, with the small-pupilled, abstract eyes of a hawk.

'No. There's something final about this. And Gudrun seems like the end, to me. I don't know – but she seems so soft, her skin like silk, her arms heavy and soft. And it withers my consciousness, somehow, it burns the pith of my mind.' He went on a few paces, staring ahead, his eyes fixed, looking like a mask used in ghastly religions of the barbarians. 'It blasts your soul's eye,' he said, 'and leaves you sightless. Yet you *want* to be sightless, you *want* to be blasted, you don't want it any different.'

He was speaking as if in a trance, verbal and blank. Then suddenly he braced himself up with a kind of rhapsody, and looked at Birkin with vindictive, cowed eyes, saying:

'Do you know what it is to suffer when you are with a woman? She's so beautiful, so perfect, you find her *so good*, it tears you like a silk, and every stroke and bit cuts hot – ha, that perfection, when you blast yourself, you blast yourself! And then – ' he stopped on the snow and suddenly opened his clenched hands – 'it's nothing – your brain might have gone charred as rags – and – ' he looked round into the air with a queer histrionic movement 'it's blasting – you understand what I mean – it is a great experience, something final – and then – you're shrivelled as if struck by electricity.' He walked on in silence. It seemed like bragging, but like a man in extremity bragging truthfully.

'Of course,' he resumed, 'I wouldn't *not* have had it! It's a complete experience. And she's a wonderful woman. But – how I hate her somewhere! It's curious – '

Birkin looked at him, at his strange, scarcely conscious face. Gerald seemed blank before his own words.

'But you've had enough now?' said Birkin. 'You have had your experience. Why work on an old wound?'

'Oh,' said Gerald, 'I don't know. It's not finished – '

And the two walked on.

'I've loved you, as well as Gudrun, don't forget,' said Birkin bitterly. Gerald looked at him strangely, abstractedly.

'Have you?' he said, with icy scepticism. 'Or do you think you have?' He was hardly responsible for what he said.

The sledge came. Gudrun dismounted and they all made their farewell. They wanted to go apart, all of them. Birkin took his place, and the sledge drove away leaving Gudrun and Gerald standing on the snow, waving. Something froze Birkin's heart, seeing them standing there in the isolation of the snow, growing smaller and more isolated.

<hr/>

CHAPTER 30

Snowed Up

WHEN URSULA and Birkin were gone, Gudrun felt herself free in her contest with Gerald. As they grew more used to each other, he seemed to press upon her more and more. At first she could manage him, so that her own will was always left free. But very soon, he began to ignore her female tactics, he dropped his respect for her whims and her privacies, he began to exert his own will blindly, without submitting to hers.

Already a vital conflict had set in, which frightened them

both. But he was alone, whilst already she had begun to cast round for external resource.

When Ursula had gone, Gudrun felt her own existence had become stark and elemental. She went and crouched alone in her bedroom, looking out of the window at the big, flashing stars. In front was the faint shadow of the mountain-knot. That was the pivot. She felt strange and inevitable, as if she were centred upon the pivot of all existence, there was no further reality.

Presently Gerald opened the door. She knew he would not be long before he came. She was rarely alone, he pressed upon her like a frost, deadening her.

'Are you alone in the dark?' he said. And she could tell by his tone he resented it, he resented this isolation she had drawn round herself. Yet, feeling static and inevitable, she was kind towards him.

'Would you like to light the candle?' she asked.

He did not answer, but came and stood behind her, in the darkness.

'Look,' she said, 'at that lovely star up there. Do you know its name?'

He crouched beside her, to look through the low window.

'No,' he said. 'It is very fine.'

'*Isn't* it beautiful! Do you notice how it darts different coloured fires – it flashes really superbly – '

They remained in silence. With a mute, heavy gesture she put her hand on his knee, and took his hand.

'Are you regretting Ursula?' he asked.

'No, not at all,' she said. Then, in a slow mood, she asked:

'How much do you love me?'

He stiffened himself further against her.

'How much do you think I do?' he asked.

'I don't know,' she replied.

'But what is your opinion?' he asked.

There was a pause. At length, in the darkness, came her voice, hard and indifferent:

'Very little indeed,' she said coldly, almost flippant.

His heart went icy at the sound of her voice.

'Why don't I love you?' he asked, as if admitting the truth of her accusation, yet hating her for it.

'I don't know why you don't – I've been good to you. You were in a *fearful* state when you came to me.'

Her heart was beating to suffocate her, yet she was strong and unrelenting.

'When was I in a fearful state?' he asked.

'When you first came to me. I *had* to take pity on you. But it was never love.'

It was that statement 'It was never love,' which sounded in his ears with madness.

'Why must you repeat it so often, that there is no love?' he said in a voice strangled with rage.

'Well you don't *think* you love, do you?' she asked.

He was silent with cold passion of anger.

'You don't think you *can* love me, do you?' she repeated almost with a sneer.

'No,' he said.

'You know you never *have* loved me, don't you?'

'I don't know what you mean by the word 'love,'' he replied.

'Yes, you do. You know all right that you have never loved me. Have you, do you think?'

'No,' he said, prompted by some barren spirit of truthfulness and obstinacy.

'And you never *will* love me,' she said finally, 'will you?'

There was a diabolic coldness in her, too much to bear.

'No,' he said.

'Then,' she replied, 'what have you against me!'

He was silent in cold, frightened rage and despair. 'If only I could kill her,' his heart was whispering repeatedly. 'If only I could kill her – I should be free.'

It seemed to him that death was the only severing of this Gordian knot.

'Why do you torture me?' he said.

She flung her arms round his neck.

'Ah, I don't want to torture you,' she said pityingly, as if she were comforting a child. The impertinence made his veins go cold, he was insensible. She held her arms round his neck, in a triumph of pity. And her pity for him was as cold as stone, its deepest motive was hate of him, and fear of his power over her, which she must always counterfoil.

'Say you love me,' she pleaded. 'Say you will love me for ever – won't you – won't you?'

But it was her voice only that coaxed him. Her senses were entirely apart from him, cold and destructive of him. It was her overbearing *will* that insisted.

'Won't you say you'll love me always?' she coaxed. 'Say it, even if it isn't true – say it Gerald, do.'

'I will love you always,' he repeated, in real agony, forcing the words out.

She gave him a quick kiss.

'Fancy your actually having said it,' she said with a touch of raillery.

He stood as if he had been beaten.

'Try to love me a little more, and to want me a little less,' she said, in a half contemptuous, half coaxing tone.

The darkness seemed to be swaying in waves across his mind, great waves of darkness plunging across his mind. It seemed to him he was degraded at the very quick, made of no account.

'You mean you don't want me?' he said.

'You are so insistent, and there is so little grace in you, so little fineness. You are so crude. You break me – you only waste me – it is horrible to me.'

'Horrible to you?' he repeated.

'Yes. Don't you think I might have a room to myself, now Ursula has gone? You can say you want a dressing room.'

'You do as you like – you can leave altogether if you like,' he managed to articulate.

'Yes, I know that,' she replied. 'So can you. You can leave me whenever you like – without notice even.'

The great tides of darkness were swinging across his mind, he could hardly stand upright. A terrible weariness overcame him, he felt he must lie on the floor. Dropping off his clothes, he got into bed, and lay like a man suddenly overcome by drunkenness, the darkness lifting and plunging as if he were lying upon a black, giddy sea. He lay still in this strange, horrific reeling for some time, purely unconscious.

At length she slipped from her own bed and came over to him. He remained rigid, his back to her. He was all but unconscious.

She put her arms round his terrifying, insentient body, and laid her cheek against his hard shoulder.

'Gerald,' she whispered. 'Gerald.'

There was no change in him. She caught him against her. She pressed her breasts against his shoulders, she kissed his shoulder, through the sleeping jacket. Her mind wondered, over his rigid, unliving body. She was bewildered, and insistent, only her will was set for him to speak to her.

'Gerald, my dear!' she whispered, bending over him, kissing his ear.

Her warm breath playing, flying rhythmically over his ear, seemed to relax the tension. She could feel his body gradually relaxing a little, losing its terrifying, unnatural rigidity. Her hands clutched his limbs, his muscles, going over him spasmodically.

The hot blood began to flow again through his veins, his limbs relaxed.

'Turn round to me,' she whispered, forlorn with insistence and triumph.

So at last he was given again, warm and flexible. He turned and gathered her in his arms. And feeling her soft against him, so perfectly and wondrously soft and recipient, his arms tightened on her. She was as if crushed, powerless in him. His brain seemed hard and invincible now like a jewel, there was no resisting him.

His passion was awful to her, tense and ghastly, and impersonal, like a destruction, ultimate. She felt it would kill her. She was being killed.

'My God, my God,' she cried, in anguish, in his embrace, feeling her life being killed within her. And when he was kissing her, soothing her, her breath came slowly, as if she were really spent, dying.

'Shall I die, shall I die?' she repeated to herself.

And in the night, and in him, there was no answer to the question.

And yet, next day, the fragment of her which was not destroyed remained intact and hostile, she did not go away, she remained to finish the holiday, admitting nothing. He scarcely ever left her alone, but followed her like a shadow, he was like a doom upon her, a continual 'thou shalt,' 'thou shalt not.' Sometimes it was he who seemed strongest, whilst she was almost gone, creeping near the earth like a spent wind; sometimes it was the reverse. But always it was this eternal see-saw, one destroyed that the other might exist, one ratified because the other was nulled.

'In the end,' she said to herself, 'I shall go away from him.'

'I can be free of her,' he said to himself in his paroxysms of suffering. And he set himself to be free. He even prepared to go away, to leave her in the lurch. But for the first time there was a flaw in his will.

'Where shall I go?' he asked himself.

'Can't you be self-sufficient?' he replied to himself, putting himself upon his pride.

'Self-sufficient!' he repeated.

It seemed to him that Gudrun was sufficient unto herself, closed round and completed, like a thing in a case. In the calm, static reason of his soul, he recognised this, and admitted it was her right, to be closed round upon herself, self-complete, without desire. He realised it, he admitted it, it only needed one last effort on his own part, to win for himself the same completeness. He knew that it only needed one convulsion of his will for him to be able to turn upon himself also, to close upon himself as a stone fixes upon itself, and is impervious, self-completed, a thing isolated.

This knowledge threw him into a terrible chaos. Because, however much he might mentally *will* to be immune and self-complete, the desire for this state was lacking, and he could not create it. He could see that, to exist at all, he must be perfectly free of Gudrun, leave her if she wanted to be left, demand nothing of her, have no claim upon her.

But then, to have no claim upon her, he must stand by himself, in sheer nothingness. And his brain turned to nought at the idea. It was a state of nothingness. On the other hand, he might give in, and fawn to her. Or, finally, he might kill her. Or he might become just indifferent, purposeless, dissipated, momentaneous. But his nature was too serious, not gay enough or subtle enough for mocking licentiousness.

A strange rent had been torn in him; like a victim that is torn open and given to the heavens, so he had been torn apart and given to Gudrun. How should he close again? This wound, this strange, infinitely-sensitive opening of his soul, where he was exposed, like an open flower, to all the universe, and in which he was given to his complement, the other, the unknown, this wound, this disclosure, this unfolding of his own covering, leaving him incomplete, limited, unfinished, like an open flower under the sky, this was his cruellest joy. Why then should he forego it? Why should he close up and become impervious, immune, like a partial thing in a sheath, when he had broken forth, like a seed that has germinated, to issue forth in being, embracing the unrealised heavens.

He would keep the unfinished bliss of his own yearning even through the torture she inflicted upon him. A strange obstinacy possessed him. He would not go away from her whatever she said or did. A strange, deathly yearning carried him along with her. She was the determinating influence of his very being, though she treated him with contempt, repeated rebuffs, and denials, still he would never be gone, since in being near her, even, he felt the quickening, the going forth in him, the release, the knowledge of his own limitation and the magic of the promise, as well as the mystery of his own destruction and annihilation.

She tortured the open heart of him even as he turned to her. And she was tortured herself. It may have been her will was stronger. She felt, with horror, as if he tore at the bud of her heart, tore it open, like an irreverent persistent being. Like a boy who pulls off a fly's wings, or tears open a bud to see what is in the flower, he tore at her privacy, at her very life, he would destroy her as an immature bud, torn open, is destroyed.

She might open towards him, a long while hence, in her dreams, when she was a pure spirit. But now she was not to be violated and ruined. She closed against him fiercely.

They climbed together, at evening, up the high slope, to see the sunset. In the finely breathing, keen wind they stood and watched the yellow sun sink in crimson and disappear. Then in the east the peaks and ridges glowed with living rose, incandescent like immortal flowers against a brown-purple sky, a miracle, whilst down below the world was a bluish shadow, and above, like an annunciation, hovered a rosy transport in mid-air.

To her it was so beautiful, it was a delirium, she wanted to gather the glowing, eternal peaks to her breast, and die. He saw them, saw they were beautiful. But there arose no clamour in his breast, only a bitterness that was visionary in itself. He wished the peaks were grey and unbeautiful, so that she should not get her support from them. Why did she betray the two of them so terribly, in embracing the glow of the evening? Why did she leave him standing there, with the ice-wind blowing through his heart, like death, to gratify herself among the rosy snow-tips?

'What does the twilight matter?' he said. 'Why do you grovel before it? Is it so important to you?'

She winced in violation and in fury.

'Go away,' she cried, 'and leave me to it. It is beautiful, beautiful,' she sang in strange, rhapsodic tones. 'It is the most beautiful thing I have ever seen in my life. Don't try to come between it and me. Take yourself away, you are out of place – '

He stood back a little, and left her standing there, statue-like, transported into the mystic glowing east. Already the rose was fading, large white stars were flashing out. He waited. He would forego everything but the yearning.

'That was the most perfect thing I have ever seen,' she said in cold, brutal tones, when at last she turned round to him. 'It amazes me that you should want to destroy it. If you can't see it yourself, why try to debar me?' But in reality, he had destroyed it for her, she was straining after a dead effect.

'One day,' he said, softly, looking up at her, 'I shall destroy *you,* as you stand looking at the sunset; because you are such a liar.'

There was a soft, voluptuous promise to himself in the words. She was chilled but arrogant.

'Ha!' she said. 'I am not afraid of your threats!' She denied herself to him, she kept her room rigidly private to herself. But he waited on, in a curious patience, belonging to his yearning for her.

'In the end,' he said to himself with real voluptuous promise, 'when it reaches that point, I shall do away with her.' And he trembled delicately in every limb, in anticipation, as he trembled in his most violent accesses of passionate approach to her trembling with too much desire.

She had a curious sort of allegiance with Loerke, all the while, now, something insidious and traitorous. Gerald knew of it. But in the unnatural state of patience, and the unwillingness to harden himself against her, in which he found himself, he took no notice, although her soft kindliness to the other man, whom he hated as a noxious insect, made him shiver again with an access of the strange shuddering that came over him repeatedly.

He left her alone only when he went skiing, a sport he loved, and which she did not practise. Then he seemed to sweep out of life, to be a projectile into the beyond. And often, when he went away, she talked to the little German sculptor. They had an invariable topic, in their art.

They were almost of the same ideas. He hated Mestrovic,* was not satisfied with the Futurists, he liked the West African wooden figures, the Aztec art, Mexican and Central American. He saw the grotesque, and a curious sort of mechanical motion intoxicated him, a confusion in nature. They had a curious game with each other, Gudrun and Loerke, of infinite suggestivity, strange and leering, as if they had some esoteric understanding

---

* Sculptor Ivan Mestrovic (1883-1962) of Yugoslavia.

of life, that they alone were initiated into the fearful central secrets, that the world dared not know. Their whole correspondence was in a strange, barely comprehensible suggestivity, they kindled themselves at the subtle lust of the Egyptians or the Mexicans. The whole game was one of subtle inter-suggestivity, and they wanted to keep it on the plane of suggestion. From their verbal and physical nuances they got the highest satisfaction in the nerves, from a queer interchange of half-suggested ideas, looks, expressions and gestures, which were quite intolerable, though incomprehensible, to Gerald. He had no terms in which to think of their commerce, his terms were much too gross.

The suggestion of primitive art was their refuge, and the inner mysteries of sensation their object of worship. Art and Life were to them the Reality and the Unreality.

'Of course,' said Gudrun, 'life doesn't *really* matter – it is one's art which is central. What one does in one's life has *peu de rapport,*[1] it doesn't signify much.'

'Yes, that is so, exactly,' replied the sculptor. 'What one does in one's art, that is the breath of one's being. What one does in one's life, that is a bagatelle for the outsiders to fuss about.'

It was curious what a sense of elation and freedom Gudrun found in this communication. She felt established for ever. Of course Gerald was *bagatelle.*[2] Love was one of the temporal things in her life, except in so far as she was an artist. She thought of Cleopatra – Cleopatra must have been an artist; she reaped the essential from a man, she harvested the ultimate sensation, and threw away the husk; and Mary Stuart, and the great Rachel, panting with her lovers after the theatre, these were the exoteric exponents of love. After all, what was the lover but fuel for the transport of this subtle knowledge, for a female art, the art of pure, perfect knowledge in sensuous understanding.

One evening Gerald was arguing with Loerke about Italy and Tripoli. The Englishman was in a strange, inflammable state, the German was excited. It was a contest of words, but it meant a conflict of spirit between the two men. And all the while Gudrun could see in Gerald an arrogant English contempt for a foreigner.

1 Of minor relationship.
2 (Fr.) Trifle.

Although Gerald was quivering, his eyes flashing, his face flushed, in his argument there was a brusqueness, a savage contempt in his manner, that made Gudrun's blood flare up, and made Loerke keen and mortified. For Gerald came down like a sledge-hammer with his assertions, anything the little German said was merely contemptible rubbish.

At last Loerke turned to Gudrun, raising his hands in helpless irony, a shrug of ironical dismissal, something appealing and child-like.

'Sehen sie, gnädige Fräu – ' he began.

'Bitte sagen Sie nicht immer, gnädige Fräu,' cried Gudrun, her eyes flashing, her cheeks burning. She looked like a vivid Medusa.[1] Her voice was loud and clamorous, the other people in the room were startled.

'Please don't call me Mrs Crich,' she cried aloud.

The name, in Loerke's mouth particularly, had been an intolerable humiliation and constraint upon her, these many days.

The two men looked at her in amazement. Gerald went white at the cheek-bones.

'What shall I say, then?' asked Loerke, with soft, mocking insinuation.

'Sagen Sie nur nicht das,' she muttered, her cheeks flushed crimson. 'Not that, at least.'

She saw, by the dawning look on Loerke's face, that he had understood. She was *not* Mrs Crich! So – o – , that explained a great deal.

'Soll ich Fräulein sagen?'[2] he asked, malevolently.

'I am not married,' she said, with some hauteur.

Her heart was fluttering now, beating like a bewildered bird. She knew she had dealt a cruel wound, and she could not bear it.

Gerald sat erect, perfectly still, his face pale and calm, like the face of a statue. He was unaware of her, or of Loerke or anybody. He sat perfectly still, in an unalterable calm. Loerke, meanwhile, was crouching and glancing up from under his ducked head.

---

1 The principle Gorgon empowered with claws, and snakes for hair. Her ferocious face instantly turned an onlooker into a stone.
2 In this curt dialogue, Gudrun wants that she should not be addressed as 'gracious lady' or 'Mrs. Crich'. Loerke inquires whether he should call her 'Miss'?

Gudrun was tortured for something to say, to relieve the suspense. She twisted her face in a smile, and glanced knowingly, almost sneering, at Gerald.

'Truth is best,' she said to him, with a grimace.

But now again she was under his domination; now, because she had dealt him this blow; because she had destroyed him, and she did not know how he had taken it. She watched him. He was interesting to her. She had lost her interest in Loerke.

Gerald rose at length, and went over in a leisurely still movement, to the Professor. The two began a conversation on Goethe.*

She was rather piqued by the simplicity of Gerald's demeanour this evening. He did not seem angry or disgusted, only he looked curiously innocent and pure, really beautiful. Sometimes it came upon him, this look of clear distance, and it always fascinated her.

She waited, troubled, throughout the evening. She thought he would avoid her, or give some sign. But he spoke to her simply and unemotionally, as he would to anyone else in the room. A certain peace, an abstraction possessed his soul.

She went to his room, hotly, violently in love with him. He was so beautiful and inaccessible. He kissed her, he was a lover to her. And she had extreme pleasure of him. But he did not come to, he remained remote and candid, unconscious. She wanted to speak to him. But this innocent, beautiful state of unconsciousness that had come upon him prevented her. She felt tormented and dark.

In the morning, however, he looked at her with a little aversion, some horror and some hatred darkening into his eyes. She withdrew on to her old ground. But still he would not gather himself together, against her.

Loerke was waiting for her now. The little artist, isolated in his own complete envelope, felt that here at last was a woman from whom he could get something. He was uneasy all the while, waiting to talk with her, subtly contriving to be near her. Her presence filled him with keenness and excitement, he gravitated

---

* Von Goethe (1749-1832). German scientist, poet, novelist, and a famed personality that played a great role in German Romanticism.

cunningly towards her, as if she had some unseen force of attraction.

He was not in the least doubtful of himself, as regards Gerald. Gerald was one of the outsiders. Loerke only hated him for being rich and proud and of fine appearance. All these things, however, riches, pride of social standing, handsome physique, were externals. When it came to the relation with a woman such as Gudrun, he, Loerke, had an approach and a power that Gerald never dreamed of.

How should Gerald hope to satisfy a woman of Gudrun's calibre? Did he think that pride or masterful will or physical strength would help him? Loerke knew a secret beyond these things. The greatest power is the one that is subtle 'and adjusts itself, not one which blindly attacks. And he, Loerke, had understanding where Gerald was a calf.

He, Loerke, could penetrate into depths far out of Gerald's knowledge. Gerald was left behind like a postulant in the ante-room of this temple of mysteries, this woman. But he Loerke, could he not penetrate into the inner darkness, find the spirit of the woman in its inner recess, and wrestle with it there, the central serpent that is coiled at the core of life.

What was it, after all, that a woman wanted? Was it mere social effect, fulfilment of ambition in the social world, in the community of mankind? 'Vas it even a union in love and goodness? Did she want 'goodness'? Who but a fool would accept this of Gudrun? This was but the street view of her wants. Cross the threshold, and you found her completely, completely cynical about the social world and its advantages. Once inside the house of her soul and there was a pungent atmosphere of corrosion, an inflamed darkness of sensation, and a vivid, subtle, critical consciousness, that saw the world distorted, horrific.

What then, what next? Was it sheer blind force of passion that would satisfy her now? Not this, but the subtle thrills of extreme sensation in reduction. It was an unbroken will reacting against her unbroken will in a myriad subtle thrills of reduction, the last subtle activities of analysis and breaking down, carried out in the darkness of her, whilst the outside form, the individual, was utterly unchanged, even sentimental in its poses.

But between two particular people, any two people on earth, the range of pure sensational experience is limited. The climax of sensual reaction, once reached in any direction, is reached finally, there is no going on. There is only repetition possible, or the going apart of the two protagonists, or the subjugating of the one will to the other, or death.

Gerald had penetrated all the outer places of Gudrun's soul. He was to her the most crucial instance of the existing world, the *ne plus ultra* of the world of man as it existed for her. In him she knew the world, and. had done with it. Knowing him finally she was the Alexander seeking new worlds. But there *were* no new worlds, there were no more *men,* there were only creatures, little, ultimate *creatures* like Loerke. The world was finished now, for her. There was only the inner, individual darkness, sensation within the ego, the obscene religious mystery of ultimate reduction, the mystic frictional activities of diabolic reducing down, disintegrating the vital organic body of life.

All this Gudrun knew in her subconsciousness, not in her mind. She knew her next step – she knew what she should move on to, when she left Gerald. She was afraid of Gerald, that he might kill her. But she did not intend to be killed. A fine thread still united her to him. It should not be *her* death which broke it. She had further to go, a further, slow exquisite experience to reap, unthinkable subtleties of sensation to know, before she was finished.

Of the last series of subtleties, Gerald was not capable. He could not touch the quick of her. But where his ruder blows could not penetrate, the fine, insinuating blade of Loerke's insect-like comprehension could. At least, it was time for her now to pass over to the other, the creature, the final craftsman. She knew that Loerke, in his innermost soul, was detached from everything, for him there was neither heaven nor earth nor hell. He admitted no allegiance, he gave no adherence anywhere. He was single and, by abstraction from the rest, absolute in himself.

Whereas in Gerald's soul there still lingered some attachment to the rest, to the whole. And this was his limitation. He was limited, *borné,* subject to his necessity, in the last issue, for goodness, for righteousness, for oneness with the ultimate purpose. That the ultimate purpose might be the perfect and subtle experience of the process of death, the will being kept unimpaired, that was not allowed in him. And this was his limitation.

There was a hovering triumph in Loerke, since Gudrun had denied her marriage with Gerald. The artist seemed to hover like a creature on the wing, waiting to settle. He did not approach Gudrun violently, he was never ill-timed. But carried on by a sure instinct in the complete darkness of his soul, he corresponded mystically with her, imperceptibly, but palpably.

For two days, he talked to her, continued the discussions of art, of life, in which they both found such pleasure. They praised the by-gone things, they took a sentimental, childish delight in the achieved perfections of the past. Particularly they liked the late eighteenth century, the period of Goethe and of Shelley, and Mozart.

They played with the past, and with the great figures of the past, a sort of little game of chess, or marionettes, all to please themselves. They had all the great men for their marionettes, and they two were the God of the show, working it all. As for the future, that they never mentioned except one laughed out some mocking dream of the destruction of the world by a ridiculous catastrophe of man's invention: a man invented such a perfect explosive that it blew the earth in two, and the two halves set off in different directions through space, to the dismay of the inhabitants: or else the people of the world divided into two halves, and each half decided *it* was perfect and right, the other half was wrong and must be destroyed; so another end of the world. Or else, Loerke's dream of fear, the world went cold, and snow fell everywhere, and only white creatures, polar-bears, white foxes, and men like awful white snow-birds, persisted in ice cruelty.

Apart from these stories, they never talked of the future. They delighted most either in mocking imaginations of destruction, or in sentimental, fine marionette-shows of the past. It was a sentimental delight to reconstruct the world of Goethe at Weimar, or of Schiller and poverty and faithful love, or to see again Jean

Jacques in his quakings, or Voltaire at Ferney, or Frederick the Great reading his own poetry.

They talked together for hours, of literature and sculpture and painting, amusing themselves with Flaxman and Blake and Fuseli, with tenderness, and with Feuerbach and Böcklin. It would take them a life-time, they felt to live again, *in petto,* the lives of the great artists. But they preferred to stay in the eighteenth and the nineteenth centuries.

They talked in a mixture of languages. The ground-work was French, in either case. But he ended most of his sentences in a stumble of English and a conclusion of German, she skilfully wove herself to her end in whatever phrase came to her. She took a peculiar delight in this conversation. It was full of odd, fantastic expression, of double meanings, of evasions, of suggestive vagueness. It was a real physical pleasure to her to make this thread of conversation out of the different-coloured strands of three languages.

And all the while they two were hovering, hesitating round the flame of some invisible declaration. He wanted it, but was held back by some inevitable reluctance. She wanted it also, but she wanted to put it off, to put it off indefinitely, she still had some pity for Gerald, some connection with him. And the most fatal of all, she had the reminiscent sentimental compassion for herself in connection with him. Because of what *had* been, she felt herself held to him by immortal, invisible threads – because of what *had* been, because of his coming to her that first night, into her own house, in his extremity, because

Gerald was gradually overcome with a revulsion of loathing for Loerke. He did not take the man seriously, he despised him merely, except as he felt in Gudrun's veins the influence of the little creature. It was this that drove Gerald wild, the feeling in Gudrun's veins of Loerke's presence, Loerke's being, flowing dominant through her.

'What makes you so smitten with that little vermin?' he asked, really puzzled, For he, man-like, could not see anything attractive or important *at all* in Loerke. Gerald expected to find some handsomeness or nobleness, to account for a woman's subjection. But he saw none here, only an insect-like repulsiveness.

Gudrun flushed deeply. It was these attacks she would never forgive.

'What do you mean?' she replied. 'My God, what a mercy I am *not* married to you!'

Her voice of flouting and contempt scotched him. He was brought up short. But he recovered himself

'Tell me, only tell me,' he reiterated in a dangerous narrowed voice 'tell me what it is that fascinates you in him.'

'I am not fascinated,' she said, with cold repelling innocence.

'Yes, you are. You are fascinated by that little dry snake, like a bird gaping ready to fall down its throat.'

She looked at him with black fury.

'I don't choose to be discussed by you,' she said.

'It doesn't matter whether you choose or not,' he replied, 'that doesn't alter the fact that you are ready to fall down and kiss the feet of that little insect. And I don't want to prevent you – do it, fall down and kiss his feet. But I want to know, what it is that fascinates you – what is it?'

She was silent, suffused with black rage.

'How *dare* you come brow-beating me,' she cried, 'how dare you, you little squire, you bully. What right have you over me, do you think?'

His face was white and gleaming, she knew by the light in his eyes that she was in his power – the wolf. And because she was in his power, she hated him with a power that she wondered did not kill him. In her will she killed him as he stood, effaced him.

'It is not a question of right,' said Gerald, sitting down on a chair. She watched the change in his body. She saw his clenched, mechanical body moving there like an obsession. Her hatred of him was tinged with fatal contempt.

'It's not a question of my right over you – though I *have* some right, remember. I want to know, I only want to know what it is that subjugates you to that little scum of a sculptor downstairs, what it is that brings you down like a humble maggot, in worship of him. I want to know what you creep after.'

She stood over against the window, listening. Then she turned round.

'Do you?' she said, in her most easy, most cutting voice. 'Do you want to know what it is in him? It's because he has some understanding of a woman, because he is not stupid. That's why it is.'

A queer, sinister, animal-like smile came over Gerald's face.

'But what understanding is it?' he said. 'The understanding of a flea, a hopping flea with a proboscis. Why should you crawl abject before the understanding of a flea?'

There passed through Gudrun's mind Blake's representation of the soul of a flea. She wanted to fit it to Loerke. Blake was a clown too. But it was necessary to answer Gerald.

'Don't you think the understanding of a flea is more interesting than the understanding of a fool?' she asked.

'A fool!' he repeated.

'A fool, a conceited fool – a Dummkopf,' she replied, adding the German word.

'Do you call me a fool?' he replied. 'Well, wouldn't I rather be the fool I am, than that flea downstairs?'

She looked at him. A certain blunt, blind stupidity in him palled on her soul, limiting her.

'You give yourself away by that last,' she said.

He sat and wondered.

'I shall go away soon,' he said.

She turned on him.

'Remember,' she said, 'I am completely independent of you completely. You make your arrangements, I make mine.'

He pondered this.

'You mean we are strangers from this minute?' he asked.

She halted and flushed. He was putting her in a trap, forcing her hand. She turned round on him.

'Strangers,' she said, 'we can never be. But if you *want* to make any movement apart from me, then I wish you to know you are perfectly free to do so. Do not consider me in the slightest.'

Even so slight an implication that she needed him and was depending on him still was sufficient to rouse his passion. As he sat a change came over his body, the hot, molten stream mounted involuntarily through his veins. He groaned inwardly, under its bondage, but he loved it. He looked at her with clear eyes, waiting for her.

She knew at once, and was shaken with cold revulsion. *How* could he look at her with those clear, warm, waiting eyes, waiting for her, even now? What had been said between them, was it not enough to put them worlds asunder, to freeze them forever apart! And yet he was all transfused and roused, waiting for her.

It confused her. Turning her head aside, she said:

'I shall always *tell* you, whenever I am going to make any change – '

And with this she moved out of the room.

He sat suspended in a fine recoil of disappointment, that seemed gradually to be destroying his understanding. But the unconscious state of patience persisted in him. He remained motionless, without thought or knowledge, for a long time. Then he rose, and went downstairs, to play at chess with one of the students. His face was open and clear, with a certain innocent *laisser-aller*** that troubled Gudrun most, made her almost afraid of him, whilst she disliked him deeply for it.

It was after this that Loerke, who had never yet spoken to her personally, began to ask her of her state.

'You are not married at all, are you?' he asked.

She looked full at him.

'Not in the least,' she replied, in her measured way. Loerke laughed, wrinkling up his face oddly. There was a thin wisp of his hair straying on his forehead, she noticed that his skin was of a clear brown colour, his hands, his wrists. And his hands seemed closely prehensile. He seemed like topaz, so strangely brownish and pellucid.

---

* (Fr.) of easy and free manner.

'Good,' he said.

Still it needed some courage for him to go on.

'Was Mrs Birkin your sister?' he asked.

'Yes.'

'And was *she* married?'

'She was married.'

'Have you parents, then?'

'Yes,' said Gudrun, 'we have parents.'

And she told him, briefly, laconically, her position. He watched her closely, curiously all the while.

'So!' he exclaimed, with some surprise. 'And the Herr Crich, is he rich?'

'Yes, he is rich, a coal owner.'

'How long has your friendship with him lasted?'

'Some months.'

There was a pause.

'Yes, I am surprised,' he said at length. 'The English, I thought they were so – cold. And what do you think to do when you leave here?'

'What do I think to do?' she repeated.

'Yes. You cannot go back to the teaching. No – ' he shrugged his shoulders – 'that is impossible. Leave that to the *canaille* who can do nothing else. You, for your part – you know, you are a remarkable woman, eine seltsame Fräu. Why deny it – why make any question of it? You are an extraordinary woman, why should you follow the ordinary course, the ordinary life?'

Gudrun sat looking at her hands, flushed. She was pleased that he said, so simply, that she was a remarkable woman. He would not say that to flatter her – he was far too self-opinionated and objective by nature. He said it as he would say a piece of sculpture was remarkable, because he knew it was so.

And it gratified her to hear it from him. Other people had such a passion to make everything of one degree, of one pattern. In England it was chic to be perfectly ordinary. And it was a relief to her to be acknowledged extraordinary. Then she need not fret about the common standards.

'You see,' she said, 'I have no money whatsoever.'

'Ach, money!' he cried, lifting his shoulders. 'When one is grown up, money is lying about at one's service. It is only when one is young that it is rare. Take no thought for money – that always lies to hand.'

'Does it?' she said, laughing.

'Always. The Gerald will give you a sum, if you ask him for it – '

She flushed deeply.

'I will ask anybody else,' she said, with some difficulty – 'but not him.'

Loerke looked closely at her.

'Good,' he said. 'Then let it be somebody else. Only don't go back to that England, that school. No, that is stupid.'

Again there was a pause. He was afraid to ask her outright to go with him, he was not even quite sure he wanted her; and she was afraid to be asked. He begrudged his own isolation, was *very* chary of sharing his life, even for a day.

'The only other place I know is Paris,' she said, 'and I can't stand that.'

She looked with her wide, steady eyes full at Loerke. He lowered his head and averted his face.

'Paris, no!' he said. 'Between the *réligion d'amour,** and the latest 'ism, and the new turning to Jesus, one had better ride on a carrousel all day. But come to Dresden. I have a studio there – I can give you work, – oh, that would be easy enough. I haven't seen any of your things, but I believe in you. Come to Dresden – that is a fine town to be in, and as good a life as you can expect of a town. You have everything there, without the foolishness of Paris or the beer of Munich.'

He sat and looked at her, coldly. What she liked about him was that he spoke to her simple and flat, as to himself. He was a fellow craftsman, a fellow being to her, first.

_____

* The religion of Love.

'No – Paris,' he resumed, 'it makes me sick. Pah – l'amour.
I detest it. L'amour, l'amore, die Liebe – I detest it in every
language. Women and love, there is no greater tedium,' he cried.

She was slightly offended. And yet, this was her own basic
feeling. Men, and love – there was no greater tedium.

'I think the same,' she said.

'A bore,' he repeated. 'What does it matter whether I wear
this hat or another. So love. I needn't wear a hat at all, only for
convenience. Neither need I love except for convenience. I tell
you what, gnädige Fräu – ' and he leaned towards her – then he
made a quick, odd gesture, as of striking something aside –
'gnädige Fräulein, never mind – I tell you what, I would give
everything, everything, all your love, for a little companionship in
intelligence – ' his eyes flickered darkly, evilly at her. 'You
understand?' he asked, with a faint smile. 'It wouldn't matter if
she were a hundred years old, a thousand – it would be all the
same to me, so that she can *understand.*' He shut his eyes with a
little snap.

Again Gudrun was rather offended. Did he not think her good
looking, then? Suddenly she laughed.

'I shall have to wait about eighty years to suit you, at that!'
she said. 'I am ugly enough, aren't I?'

He looked at her with an artist's sudden, critical, estimating eye.

'You are beautiful,' he said, 'and I am glad of it. But it isn't
that – it isn't that,' he cried, with emphasis that flattered her. 'It
is that you have a certain wit, it is the kind of understanding. For
me, I am little, chétif, insignificant. Good! Do not ask me to be
strong and handsome, then. But it is the *me* – ' he put his fingers
to his mouth, oddly – 'it is the *me* that is looking for a mistress,
and my *me* is waiting for the *thee* of the mistress, for the match
to my particular intelligence. You understand?'

'Yes,' she said, 'I understand.'

'As for the other, this amour – ' he made a gesture, dashing
his hand aside, as if to dash away something troublesome – 'it is
unimportant, unimportant. Does it matter, whether I drink white
wine this evening, or whether I drink nothing? *It does not matter,*

it does not matter. So this love, this amour, this *baiser.* Yes or no,
soit ou soit pas, today, tomorrow, or never, it is all the same, it
does not matter – no more than the white wine.'

He ended with an odd dropping of the head in a desperate
negation. Gudrun watched him steadily. She had gone pale.

Suddenly she stretched over and seized his hand in her own.

'That is true,' she said, in rather a high, vehement voice,
'that is true for me too. It is the understanding that matters.'

He looked up at her almost frightened, furtive. Then he
nodded, a little sullenly. She let go his hand: he had made not the
lightest response. And they sat in silence.

'Do you know,' he said, suddenly looking at her with dark,
self-important; prophetic eyes, 'your fate and mine, they will run
together, till – ' and he broke off in a little grimace.

'Till when?' she asked, blanched, her lips going white. She
was terribly susceptible to these evil prognostications, but he
only shook his head.

'I don't know,' he said, 'I don't know.'

Gerald did not come in from his skiing until nightfall, he missed
the coffee and cake that she took at four o'clock. The snow was
in perfect condition, he had travelled a long way, by himself,
among the snow ridges, on his skis, he had climbed high, so high
that he could see over the top of the pass, five miles distant,
could see the Marienhütte, the hostel on the crest of the pass,
half buried in snow, and over into the deep valley beyond, to the
dusk of the pine trees. One could go that way home; but he
shuddered with nausea at the thought of home; – one could travel
on skis down there, and come to the old imperial road, below the
pass. But why come to any road? He revolted at the thought of
finding himself in the world again. He must stay up there in the
snow forever. He had been happy by himself, high up there alone,
travelling swiftly on skis, taking far flights, and skimming past
the dark rocks veined with brilliant snow.

But he felt something icy gathering at his heart. This strange
mood of patience and innocence which had persisted in him for

some days, was passing away, he would be left again a prey to the horrible passions and tortures.

So he came down reluctantly, snow-burned, snow-estranged, to the house in the hollow, between the knuckles of the mountain tops. He saw its lights shining yellow, and he held back, wishing he need not go in, to confront those people, to hear the turmoil of voices and to feel the confusion of other presences. He was isolated as if there were a vacuum round his heart, or a sheath of pure ice.

The moment he saw Gudrun something jolted in his soul. She was looking rather lofty and superb, smiling slowly and graciously to the Germans. A sudden desire leapt in his heart, to kill her. He thought, what a perfect voluptuous fulfilment it would be, to kill her. His mind was absent all the evening, estranged by the snow and his passion. But he kept the idea constant within him, what a perfect voluptuous consummation it would be to strangle her, to strangle every spark of life out of her, till she lay completely inert, soft, relaxed for ever, a soft heap lying dead between his hands, utterly dead. Then he would have had her finally and for ever; there would be such a perfect voluptuous finality.

Gudrun was unaware of what he was feeling, he seemed so quiet and amiable, as usual. His amiability even made her feel brutal towards him.

She went into his room when he was partially undressed. She did not notice the curious, glad gleam of pure hatred, with which he looked at her. She stood near the door, with her hand behind her.

'I have been thinking, Gerald,' she said, with an insulting nonchalance, 'that I shall not go back to England.'

'Oh,' he said, 'where will you go then?'

But she ignored his question. She had her own logical statement to make, and it must be made as she had thought it.

'I can't see the use of going back,' she continued. 'It is over between me and you – '

She paused for him to speak. But he said 'nothing. He was only talking to himself, saying' Over, is it? I believe it is over. But

it isn't finished. Remember, it isn't finished. We must put some
sort of a finish on it. There must be a conclusion, there must be
finality.'

So he talked to' himself, but aloud he said nothing whatever.
'What has been, has been,' she continued. 'There is nothing that
I regret. I hope you regret nothing – '

She waited for him to speak.

'Oh, I regret nothing,' he said, accommodatingly.

'Good then,' she answered, 'good then. Then neither of us
cherishes any regrets, which is as it should be.'

'Quite as it should be,' he said aimlessly.

She paused to gather up her thread again.

'Our attempt has been a failure,' she said. 'But we can try
again, elsewhere.'

A little flicker of rage ran through his blood. It was as if she
were rousing him, goading him. Why must she do it?

'Attempt at what?' he asked.

'At being lovers, I suppose,' she said, a little baffled, yet so
trivial she made it all seem.

'Our attempt at being lovers has been a failure?' he repeated aloud.

To himself he was saying, 'I ought to kill her here. There is
only this left, for me to kill her.' A heavy, overcharged desire to
bring about her death possessed him. She was unaware.

'Hasn't it?' she asked. 'Do you think it has been a success?'

Again the insult of the flippant question ran through his blood
like a current of fire.

'It had some of the elements of success, our relationship,'
he replied.

'It – might have come off.'

But he paused before concluding the last phrase. Even as he
began the sentence, he did not believe in what he was going to
say. He knew it never could have been a success.

'No,' she replied. 'You cannot love.'

'And you?' he asked.

Her wide, dark-filled eyes were fixed on him, like two moons of darkness.

'I couldn't love *you*,' she said, with stark cold truth.

A blinding flash went over his brain, his body jolted. His heart had burst into flame. His consciousness was gone into his wrists, into his hands. He was one blind, incontinent desire, to kill her. His wrists were bursting, there would be no satisfaction till his hands had closed on her.

But even before his body swerved forward on her, a sudden, cunning comprehension was expressed on her face, and in a flash she was out of the door. She ran in one flash to her room and locked herself in. She was afraid, but confident. She knew her life trembled on the edge of an abyss. But she was curiously sure of her footing. She knew her cunning could outwit him.

She trembled, as she stood in her room, with excitement and awful exhilaration. She knew she could outwit him. She could depend on her presence of mind, and on her wits. But it was a fight to the death, she knew it now. One slip, and she was lost. She had a strange, tense, exhilarated sickness in her body, as one who is in peril of falling from a great height, but who does not look down, does not admit the fear.

'I will go away the day after tomorrow,' she said.

She only did not want Gerald to think that she was afraid of him, that she was running away because she was afraid of him. She was not afraid of him, fundamentally. She knew it was her safeguard to avoid his physical violence. But even physically she was not afraid of him. She wanted to prove it to him. When she had proved it, that, whatever he was, she was not afraid of him; when she had proved *that*, she could leave him forever. But meanwhile the fight between them, terrible as she knew it to be, was inconclusive. And she wanted to be confident in herself. However many terrors she might have, she would be unafraid, uncowed by him. He could never cow her, nor dominate her, nor have any right over her; this she would maintain until she had proved it. Once it was proved, she was free of him forever.

But she had not proved it yet, neither to him nor to herself. And this was what still bound her to him. She was bound to him, she could not live beyond him. She sat up in bed, closely wrapped up, for many hours, thinking endlessly to herself. It was as if she would never have done weaving the great provision of her thoughts.

'It isn't as if he really loved me,' she said to herself. 'He doesn't. Every woman he comes across he wants to make her in love with him. He doesn't even know that he is doing it. But there he is, before every woman he unfurls his male attractiveness, displays his great desirability, he tries to make every woman think how wonderful it would be to have him for a lover. His very ignoring of the women is part of the game. He is never *unconscious* of them. He should have been a cockerel, so he could strut before fifty females, all his subjects. But really, his Don Juan does *not* interest me. I could play Dona Juanita a million times better than he plays Juan. He bores me, you know. His maleness bores me. Nothing is so boring, so inherently stupid and stupidly conceited.' Really, the fathomless conceit of these men, it is ridiculous – the little strutters.

'They are all alike. Look at Birkin. Built out of the limitation of conceit they are, and nothing else. Really, nothing but their ridiculous limitation and intrinsic insignificance could make them so conceited.

'As for Loerke, there is a thousand times more in him than in a Gerald. Gerald is so limited, there is a dead end to him. He would grind on at the old mills forever. And really, there is no corn between the millstones any more. They grind on and on, when there is nothing to grind – saying the same things, believing the same things, acting the same things. Oh, my God, it would wear out the patience of a stone.

'I don't worship Loerke, but at any rate, he is a free individual. He is not stiff with conceit of his own maleness. He is not grinding dutifully at the old mills. Oh God, when I think of Gerald, and his work – those offices at Beldover, and the mines – it makes my heart sick. What *have* I to do with it – and him thinking he can be a lover to a woman! One might as well ask it of a self-satisfied lamp-post. These men, with their eternal jobs – and their eternal mills of God that keep on grinding at nothing! It is too boring, just boring. However did I come to take him seriously at all!

'At least in Dresden, one will have one's back to it all. And there will be amusing things to do. It will be amusing to go to these eurythmic displays, and the German opera, the German theatre. It *will* be amusing to take part in German Bohemian life. And Loerke is an artist, he is a free individual. One will escape from so much, that is the chief thing, escape so much hideous boring repetition of vulgar actions, vulgar phrases, vulgar postures. I don't delude myself that I shall find an elixir of life in Dresden. I know I shan't. But I shall get away from people who have their own homes and their own children and their own acquaintances and their own this and their own that. I shall be among people who *don't* own things and who *haven't* got a home and a domestic servant in the background, who haven't got a standing and a status and a degree and a circle of friends of the same. Oh God, the wheels within wheels of people, it makes one's head tick like a clock, with a very madness of dead mechanical monotony and meaninglessness. How I *hate* life, how I hate it. How I hate the Geralds, that they can offer one nothing else.

'Shortlands! – Heavens! Think of living there, one week, then the next, and *then the third* –

'No, I won't think of it – it is too much.'

And she broke off, really terrified, really unable to bear any more.

The thought of the mechanical succession of day following day, day following day, *ad infinitum,* was one of the things that made her heart palpitate with a real approach of madness. The terrible bondage of this tick-tack of time, this twitching of the hands of the clock, this eternal repetition of hours and days – oh God, it was too awful to contemplate. And there was no escape from it, no escape.

She almost wished Gerald were with her to save her from the terror of her own thoughts. Oh, how she suffered, lying there alone, confronted by the terrible clock, with its eternal tick-tack. All life, all life resolved itself into this: tick-tack, tick-tack, tick-tack; then the striking of the hour; then the tick-tack, tick-tack, and the twitching of the clock-fingers.

Gerald could not save her from it. He, his body, his motion, his life it was the same ticking, the same twitching across the dial, a horrible mechanical twitching forward over the face of the hours. What were his kisses, his embraces. She could hear their tick-tack, tick-tack.

Ha – ha – she laughed to herself, so frightened that she was trying to laugh it off – ha – ha, how maddening it was, to be sure, to be sure!

Then, with a fleeting self-conscious motion, she wondered if she would be very much surprised, on rising in the morning, to realise that her hair had turned white. She had *felt* it turning white so often, under the intolerable burden of her thoughts, und her sensations. Yet there it remained, brown as ever, and there she was herself, looking a picture of health.

Perhaps she was healthy. Perhaps it was only her unabateable health that left her so exposed to the truth. If she were sickly she would have her illusions, imaginations. As it was, there was no escape. She must always see and know and never escape. She could never escape. There she was, placed before the clock-face of life. And if she turned round as in a railway station, to look at the bookstall, still she could see, with her very spine, she could see the clock, always the great white clock-face. In vain she fluttered the leaves of books, or made statuettes in clay. She knew she was not *really* reading. She was not *really* working. She was watching the fingers twitch across the eternal, mechanical, monotonous clock-face of time. She never really lived, she only watched. Indeed, she was like a little, twelve-hour clock, vis-à-vis with the enormous clock of eternity – there she was, like Dignity and Impudence, or Impudence and Dignity.

The picture pleased her. Didn't her face really look like a clock dial – rather roundish and often pale, and impassive. She would have got up to look, in the mirror, but the thought of the sight of her own face, that was like a twelve-hour clock-dial, filled her with such deep terror, that she hastened to think of something else.

Oh, why wasn't somebody kind to her? Why wasn't there somebody who would take her in their arms, and hold her to their breast, and give her rest, pure, deep, healing rest. Oh, why wasn't there somebody to take her in their arms and fold her safe and perfect, for sleep. She wanted so much this perfect enfolded sleep. She lay always so unsheathed in sleep. She would lie always unsheathed in sleep, unrelieved, unsaved. Oh, how could she bear it, this endless unrelief, this eternal unrelief.

Gerald! Could he fold her in his arms and sheathe her in sleep? Ha! He needed putting to sleep himself – poor Gerald. That was all he needed. What did he do, he made the burden for her greater, the burden of her sleep was the more intolerable, when he was there. He was an added weariness upon her unripening nights, her unfruitful slumbers. Perhaps he got some repose from her. Perhaps he did. Perhaps this was what he was always dogging her for, like a child that is famished, crying for the breast. Perhaps this was the secret of his passion, his forever unquenched desire for her – that he needed her to put him to sleep, to give him repose.

What then! Was she his mother? Had she asked for a child, whom she must nurse through the nights, for her lover. She despised him, she despised him, she hardened her heart. An infant crying in the night, this Don Juan.

Ooh, but how she hated the infant crying in the night. She would murder it gladly. She would stifle it and bury it, as Hetty Sorrell did. No doubt Hetty Sorrell's infant cried in the night – no doubt Arthur Donnithorne's infant would. Ha – the Arthur Donnithornes, the Geralds of this world. So manly by day, yet all the while, such a crying of infants in the night. Let them turn into mechanisms, let them. Let them become instruments, pure machines, pure wills, that work like clock-work, in perpetual repetition. Let them be this, let them be taken up entirely in their work, let them be perfect parts of a great machine, having a slumber of constant repetition. Let Gerald manage his firm. There he would be satisfied, as satisfied as a wheelbarrow that goes backwards and forwards along a plank all day – she had seen it.

The wheel-barrow – the one humble wheel – the unit of the firm. Then the cart, with two wheels; then the truck, with four; then the donkey-engine, with eight, then the winding-engine, with sixteen, and so on, till it came to the miner, with a thousand wheels, and then the electrician, with three thousand, and the underground manager, with twenty thousand, and the general manager with a hundred thousand little wheels working away to complete his make-up, and then Gerald, with a million wheels and cogs and axles.

Poor Gerald, such a lot of little wheels to his make-up! He was more intricate than a chronometer-watch. But oh heavens, what weariness! What weariness, God above! A chronometer-watch – a beetle – her soul fainted with utter ennui, from the thought. So many wheels to count and consider and calculate! Enough, enough – there was an end to man's capacity for complications, even. Or perhaps there was no end.

Meanwhile Gerald sat in his room, reading. When Gudrun was gone, he was left stupefied with arrested desire. He sat on the side of the bed for an hour, stupefied, little strands of consciousness appearing and reappearing. But he did not move, for a long time he remained inert, his head dropped on his breast.

Then he looked up and realised that he was going to bed. He was cold. Soon he was lying down in the dark.

But what he could not bear was the darkness. The solid darkness confronting him drove him mad. So he rose, and made a light. He remained seated for a while, staring in front. He did not think of Gudrun, he did not think of anything.

Then suddenly he went downstairs for a book. He had all his life been in terror of the nights that should come, when he could not sleep. He knew that this would be too much for him, to have to face nights of sleeplessness and of horrified watching the hours.

So he sat for hours in bed, like a statue, reading. His mind, hard and acute, read on rapidly, his body understood nothing. In a state of rigid unconsciousness, he read on through the night, till morning, when, weary and disgusted in spirit, disgusted most of all with himself, he slept for two hours.

Then he got up, hard and full of energy. Gudrun scarcely spoke to him, except at coffee when she said:

'I shall be leaving tomorrow.'

'We will go together as far as Innsbruck, for appearance's sake?' he asked.

'Perhaps,' she said.

She said 'Perhaps' between the sips of her coffee. And the sound of her taking her breath in the word, was nauseous to him. He rose quickly to be away from her.

He went and made arrangements for the departure on the morrow. Then, taking some food, he set out for the day on the skis. Perhaps, he said to the Wirt, he would go up to the Marienhütte, perhaps to the village below.

To Gudrun this day was full of a promise like spring. She felt an approaching release, a new fountain of life rising up in her. It gave her pleasure to dawdle through her packing, it gave her pleasure to dip into books, to try on her different garments, to look at herself in the glass. She felt a new lease of life was come upon her, and she was happy like a child, very attractive and beautiful to everybody, with her soft, luxuriant figure, and her happiness. Yet underneath was death itself.

In the afternoon she had to go out with Loerke. Her tomorrow was perfectly vague before her. This was what gave her pleasure. She might be going to England with Gerald, she might be going to Dresden with Loerke, she might be going to Munich, to a girl-friend she had there. Anything might come to pass on the morrow. And today was the white, snowy iridescent threshold of all possibility. All possibility – that was the charm to her, the lovely, iridescent, indefinite charm, – pure illusion. All possibility – because death was inevitable, and *nothing* was possible but death.

She did not want things to materialise, to take any definite shape. She wanted, suddenly, at one moment of the journey tomorrow, to be wafted into an utterly new course, by some utterly unforeseen event, or motion. So that, although she wanted to go out with Loerke for the lást time into the snow, she did not want to be serious or businesslike.

And Loerke was not a serious figure. In his brown velvet cap, that made his head as round as a chestnut, with the brown-velvet flaps loose and wild over his ears, and a wisp of elf-like, thin black hair 'blowing above his full, elf-like dark eyes, the shiny, transparent brown skin crinkling up into odd grimaces on his small-featured face, he looked an odd little boy-man, a bat. But in his figure, in the greeny loden suit, he looked *chétif** and puny, still strangely different from the rest.

He had taken a little toboggan, for the two of them, and they trudged between the blinding slopes of snow, that burned their now hardening faces, laughing in an endless sequence of quips and jests and polyglot fancies. The fancies were the reality to both of them, they were both so happy, tossing about the little coloured balls of verbal humour and whimsicality. Their natures seemed to sparkle in full interplay, they were enjoying a pure game. And they wanted to keep it on the level of a game, their relationship: *such* a fine game.

Loerke did not take the toboganning very seriously. He put no fire and intensity into it, as Gerald did. Which pleased Gudrun. She was weary, oh so weary of Gerald's gripped intensity of physical motion. Loerke let the sledge go wildly, and gaily, like a flying leaf, and when, at a bend, he pitched both her and him out into the snow, he only waited for them both to pick themselves up unhurt off the keen white ground, to be laughing and pert as a pixie. She knew he would be making ironical, playful remarks as he wandered in hell – if he were in the humour. And that pleased her immensely. It seemed like a rising above the dreariness of actuality, the monotony of contingencies.

They played till the sun went down, in pure amusement, careless and timeless. Then, as the little sledge twirled riskily to rest at the bottom of the slope, 'Wait!' he said suddenly, and he produced from somewhere a large thermos flask, a packet of Keks, and a bottle of Schnapps.

* (Fr.) Sickly.

'Oh Loerke,' she cried. 'What an inspiration! What a *comble de joie indeed!* What is the Schnapps?'

He looked at it, and laughed.

'Heidelbeer!' he said.

'No! From the bilberries under the snow. Doesn't it look as if it were distilled from snow. Can you – ' she sniffed, and sniffed at the bottle 'can you smell bilberries? Isn't it wonderful? It is exactly as if one could smell them through the snow.'

She stamped her foot lightly on the ground. He kneeled down and whistled, and put his ear to the snow. As he did so his black eyes twinkled up.

'Ha! Ha!' she laughed, warmed by the whimsical way in which he mocked at her verbal extravagances. He was always teasing her, mocking her ways. But as he in his mockery was even more absurd than she in her extravagances, what could one do but laugh and feel liberated.

She could feel their voices, hers and his, ringing silvery like bells in the frozen, motionless air of the first twilight. How perfect it was, how *very* perfect it was, this silvery isolation and interplay.

She sipped the hot coffee, whose fragrance flew around them like bees murmuring around flowers, in the snowy air, she drank tiny sips of the Heidelbeerwasser, she ate the cold, sweet, creamy wafers. How good everything was! How perfect everything tasted and smelled and sounded, here in this utter stillness of snow and falling twilight.

'You are going away tomorrow?' his voice came at last.

'Yes.'

There was a pause, when the evening seemed to rise in its silent, ringing pallor infinitely high, to the infinite which was near at hand.

'*Wohin?*'

That was the question – *wohin?* Whither? *Wohin?* What a lovely word! She *never* wanted it answered. Let it chime for ever.

'I don't know,' she said, smiling at him.

He caught the smile from her.

'One never does,' he said.

'One never does,' she repeated.

There was a silence, wherein he ate biscuits rapidly, as a rabbit eats leaves.

'But,' he laughed, 'where will you take a ticket to?'

'Oh heaven!' she cried. 'One must take a ticket.'

Here was a blow. She saw herself at the wicket, at the railway station. Then a relieving thought came to her. She breathed freely.

'But one needn't go,' she cried.

'Certainly not,' he said.

'I mean one needn't go where one's ticket says.'

That struck him. One might take a ticket, so as not to travel to the destination it indicated. One might break off, and avoid the destination. A point located. That was an idea!

'Then take a ticket to London,' he said. 'One should never go there.'

'Right,' she answered.

He poured a little coffee into a tin can.

'You won't tell me where you will go?' he asked.

'Really and truly,' she said, 'I don't know. It depends which way the wind blows.'

He looked at her quizzically, then he pursed up his lips, like Zephyrus,* blowing across the snow.

'It goes towards Germany,' he said.

'I believe so,' she laughed.

Suddenly, they were aware of a vague white figure near them. It was Gerald. Gudrun's heart leapt in sudden terror, profound terror. She rose to her feet.

'They told me where you were,' came Gerald's voice, like a judgment in the whitish air of twilight.

'*Maria!* You come like a ghost,' exclaimed Loerke.

Gerald did not answer. His presence was unnatural and ghostly to them.

* The Greek God of wind.

Loerke shook the flask – then he held it inverted over the snow. Only a few brown drops trickled out.

'All gone!' he said.

To Gerald, the smallish, odd figure of the German was distinct and objective, as if seen through field glasses. And he disliked the small figure exceedingly, he wanted it removed.

Then Loerke rattled the box which held the biscuits.

'Biscuits there are still,' he said.

And reaching from his seated posture in the sledge, he handed them to Gudrun. She fumbled, and took one. He would have held them to Gerald, but Gerald so definitely did not want to be offered a biscuit, that Loerke, rather vaguely, put the box aside. Then he took up the small bottle, and held it to the light.

'Also there is some Schnapps,' he said to himself.

Then suddenly, he elevated the bottle gallantly in the air, a strange, grotesque figure leaning towards Gudrun, and said:

'Gnädiges Fräulein,' he said, 'wohl – '

There was a crack, the bottle was flying, Loerke had started back, the three stood quivering in violent emotion.

Loerke turned to Gerald, a devilish leer on his bright-skinned face.

'Well done!' he said, in a satirical demoniac frenzy. 'C'est le sport, sans doute.'

The next instant he was sitting ludicrously in the snow, Gerald's fist having rung against the side of his head. But Loerke pulled himself together, rose, quivering, looking full at Gerald, his body weak and furtive, but his eyes demoniacal with satire.

'Vive le héros, vive – '*

But he flinched, as, in a black flash Gerald's fist came upon him, banged into the other side of his head, and sent him aside like a broken straw.

But Gudrun moved forward. She raised her clenched hand high, and brought it down, with a great downward stroke on to the face and on to the breast of Gerald.

A great astonishment burst upon him, as if the air had broken.

* Long live the Hero!

Wide, wide his soul opened, in wonder, feeling the pain. Then it laughed, turning, with strong hands outstretched, at last to take the apple of his desire. At last he could finish his desire.

He took the throat of Gudrun between his hands, that were hard and indomitably powerful. And her throat was beautifully, so beautifully soft, save that, within, he could feel the slippery chords of her life. And this he crushed, this he could crush. What bliss! Oh what bliss, at last, what satisfaction, at last! The pure zest of satisfaction filled his soul. He was watching the unconsciousness come unto her swollen face, watching the eyes roll back. How ugly she was! What a fulfilment, what a satisfaction! How good this was, oh how good it was, what a God-given gratification, at last! He was unconscious of her fighting and struggling. The struggling was her reciprocal lustful passion in this embrace, the more violent it became, the greater the frenzy of delight, till the zenith was reached, the crisis, the struggle was overborne, her movement became softer, appeased.

Loerke roused himself on the snow, too dazed and hurt to get up. Only his eyes were conscious.

'Monsieur!' he said, in his thin, roused voice: 'Quand vous aurez fini – '*

A revulsion of contempt and disgust came over Gerald's soul. The disgust went to the very bottom of him, a nausea. Ah, what was he doing, to what depths was he letting himself go! As if he cared about her enough to kill her, to have her life on his hands!

A weakness ran over his body, a terrible relaxing, a thaw, a decay of strength. Without knowing, he had let go his grip, and Gudrun had fallen to her knees. Must he see, must he know?

A fearful weakness possessed him, his joints were turned to water. He drifted, as on a wind, veered, and went drifting away.

'I didn't want it, really,' was the last confession of disgust in his soul, as he drifted up the slope, weak, finished, only sheering off unconsciously from any further contact. 'I've had enough – I want to go to sleep. I've had enough.' He was sunk under a sense of nausea.

* (Fr.) "When you've quite finished – ."

He was weak, but he did not want to rest, he wanted to go on and on, to the end. Never again to stay, till he came to the end, that was all the desire that remained to him. So he drifted on and on, unconscious and weak, not thinking of anything, so long as he could keep in action.

The twilight spread a weird, unearthly light overhead, bluish-rose in colour, the cold blue night sank on the snow. In the valley below, behind, in the great bed of snow, were two small figures: Gudrun dropped on her knees, like one executed, and Loerke sitting propped up near her. That was all.

Gerald stumbled on up the slope of snow, in the bluish darkness, always climbing, always unconsciously climbing, weary though he was. On his left was a steep slope with black rocks and fallen masses of rock and veins of snow slashing in and about the blackness of rock, veins of snow slashing vaguely in and about the blackness of rock. Yet there was no sound, all this made no noise.

To add to his difficulty, a small bright moon shone brilliantly just ahead, on the right, a painful brilliant thing that was always there, unremitting, from which there was no escape. He wanted so to come to the end – he had had enough. Yet he did not sleep.

He surged painfully up, sometimes having to cross a slope of black rock, that was blown bare of snow. Here he was afraid of falling, very much afraid of falling. And high up here, on the crest, moved a wind that almost overpowered him with a sleep-heavy iciness. Only it was not here, the end, and he must still go on. His indefinite nausea would not let him stay.

Having gained one ridge, he saw the vague shadow of something higher in front. Always higher, always higher. He knew he was following the track towards the summit of the slopes, where was the Marienhütte, and the descent on the other side. But he was not really conscious. He only wanted to go on, to go on whilst he could, to move, to keep going, that was all, to keep going, until it was finished. He had lost all his sense of place. And yet in the remaining instinct of life, his feet sought the track where the skis had gone.

He slithered down a sheer snow slope. That frightened him. He had no alpenstock, nothing. But having come safely to rest, he began to walk on, in the illuminated darkness. It was as cold as sleep. He was between two ridges, in a hollow. So he swerved. Should he climb the other ridge, or wander along the hollow? How frail the thread of his being was stretched! He would perhaps climb the ridge. The snow was firm and simple. He went along. There was something standing out of the snow. He approached, with dimmest curiosity.

It was a half-buried Crucifix, a little Christ under a little sloping hood, at the top of a pole. He sheered away. Somebody was going to murder him. He had a great dread of being murdered. But it was a dread which stood outside him, like his own ghost.

Yet why be afraid? It was bound to happen. To be murdered! He looked round in terror at the snow, the rocking, pale, shadowy slopes of the upper world. He was bound to be murdered, he could see it. This was the moment when the death was uplifted, and there was no escape.

Lord Jesus, was it then bound to be – Lord Jesus! He could feel the blow descending, he knew he was murdered. Vaguely wandering forward, his hands lifted as if to feel what would happen, he was waiting for the moment when he would stop, when it would cease. It was not over yet.

He had come to the hollow basin of snow, surrounded by sheer slopes and precipices, out of which rose a track that brought one to the top of the mountain. But he wandered unconsciously, till he slipped and fell down, and as he fell something broke in his soul, and immediately he went to sleep.

CHAPTER 31

Exeunt

WHEN THEY brought the body home, the next morning, Gudrun was shut up in her room. From her window she saw men coming along with a burden, over the snow. She sat still and let the minutes go by.

There came a tap at her door. She opened. There stood a woman, saying softly, oh, far too reverently:

'They have found him, madam!'

'Il est mort?'*

'Yes – hours ago.'

Gudrun did not know what to say. What should she say? What should she feel? What should she do? What did they expect of her? She was coldly at a loss.

'Thank you,' she said, and she shut the door of her room. The woman went away mortified. Not a word, not a tear – ha! Gudrun was cold, a cold woman.

Gudrun sat on in her room, her face pale and impassive. What was she to do? She could not weep and make a scene. She could not alter herself. She sat motionless, hiding from people. Her one motive was to avoid actual contact with events. She only wrote out a long telegram to Ursula and Birkin.

In the afternoon, however, she rose suddenly to look for Loerke. She glanced with apprehension at the door of the room that had been Gerald's. Not for worlds would she enter there.

She found Loerke sitting alone in the lounge. She went straight up to him.

'It isn't true, is it?' she said.

He looked up at her. A small smile of misery twisted his face. He shrugged his shoulders.

'True?' he echoed.

'We haven't killed him?' she asked.

* Is he dead?

He disliked her coming to him in such a manner. He raised his shoulders wearily.

'It has happened,' he said.

She looked at him. He sat crushed and frustrated for the rime being, quite as emotionless and barren as herself. My God! this was a barren tragedy, barren, barren.

She returned to her room to wait for Ursula and Birkin. She wanted to get away, only to get away. She could not think or feel until she had got away, till she was loosed from this position.

The day passed, the next day came. She heard the sledge, saw Ursula and Birkin alight, and she shrank from these also.

Ursula came straight up to her.

'Gudrun!' she cried, the tears running down her cheeks. And she took her sister in her arms. Gudrun hid her face on Ursula's shoulder, but still she could not escape the cold devil of irony that froze her soul.

'Ha, ha!' she thought, 'this is the right behaviour.'

But she could not weep, and the sight of her cold, pale, impassive face soon stopped the fountain of Ursula's tears. In a few moments, the sisters had nothing to say to each other.

'Was it very vile to be dragged back here again?' Gudrun asked at length.

Ursula looked up in some bewilderment.

'I never thought of it,' she said.

'I felt a beast, fetching you,' said Gudrun. 'But I simply couldn't see people. That is too much for me.'

'Yes,' said Ursula, chilled.

Birkin tapped and entered. His face was white and expressionless. She knew he knew. He gave her his hand, saying:

'The end of *this* trip, at any rate.'

Gudrun glanced at him, afraid.

There was silence between the three of them, nothing to be said. At length Ursula asked in a small voice:

'Have you seen him?'

He looked back at Ursula with a hard, cold look, and did not trouble to answer.

'Have you seen him?' she repeated.

'I have,' he said, coldly.

Then he looked at Gudrun.

'Have you done anything?' he said.

'Nothing,' she replied, 'nothing.'

She shrank in cold disgust from making any statement.

'Locrke says that Gerald came to you, when you were sitting on the sledge at the bottom of the Rudelbahn, that you had words, and Gerald walked away. What were the words about? I had better know, so that I can satisfy the authorities, if necessary.'

Gudrun looked up at him, white, childlike, mute with trouble. 'There weren't even any words,' she said. 'He knocked Loerke down and stunned him, he half strangled me, then he went away.'

To herself she was saying:

'A pretty little sample of the eternal triangle!' And she turned ironically away, because she knew that the fight had been between Gerald and herself and that the presence of the third party was a mere contingency – an inevitable contingency perhaps, but a contingency none the less. But let them have it as an example of the eternal triangle, the trinity of hate. It would be simpler for them.

Birkin went away, his manner cold and abstracted. But she knew he would do things for her, nevertheless, he would see her through. She smiled slightly to herself, with contempt. Let him do the work, since he was so extremely *good* at looking after other people.

Birkin went again to Gerald. He had loved him. And yet he felt chiefly disgust at the inert body lying there. It was so inert, so coldly dead, a carcase, Birkin's bowels seemed to turn to ice. He had to stand and look at the frozen dead body that had been Gerald.

It was the frozen carcase of a dead male. Birkin remembered a rabbit which he had once found frozen like a board on the snow. It had been rigid like a dried board when he picked it up.

And now this was Gerald, stiff as a board, curled up as if for sleep, yet with the horrible hardness somehow evident. It filled him with horror. The room must be made warm, the body must be thawed. The limbs would break like glass or like wood if they had to be straightened.

He reached and touched the dead face. And the sharp, heavy bruise of ice bruised his living bowels. He wondered if he himself were freezing too, freezing from the inside. In the short blond moustache the life-breath was frozen into a block of ice, beneath the silent nostrils. 'And this was Gerald!

Again he touched the sharp, almost glittering fair hair of the frozen body. It was icy-cold, hair icy-cold, almost venomous. Birkin's heart began to freeze. He had loved Gerald. Now he looked at the shapely, strange-coloured face, with the small, fine, pinched nose and the manly cheeks, saw it frozen like an ice-pebble – yet he had loved it. What was one to think or feel? His brain was beginning to freeze, his blood was turning to ice-water. So cold, so cold, a heavy, bruising cold pressing on his arms from outside, and a heavier cold congealing within him, in his heart and in his bowels.

He went over the snow slopes, to see where the death had been. At last he came to the great shallow among the precipices and slopes, near the summit of the pass. It was a grey day, the third day of greyness and stillness. All was white, icy, pallid, save for the scoring of black rocks that jutted like roots sometimes, and sometimes were in naked faces. In the distance a slope sheered down from a peak, with many black rock-slides.

It was like a shallow pot lying among the stone and snow of the upper world. In this pot Gerald had gone to sleep. At the far end, the guides had driven iron stakes deep into the snow-wall, so that, by means of the great rope attached, they could haul themselves up the massive snow-front, out on to the jagged summit of the pass, naked to heaven, where the Marienhütte hid among the naked rocks. Round about, spiked, slashed snow-peaks pricked the heaven.

Gerald might have found this rope. He might have hauled himself up to the crest. He might have heard the dogs in the

Marienhütte, and found shelter. He might have gone on, down the steep, steep fall of the south-side, down into the dark valley with its pines, on to the great Imperial road leading south to Italy.

He might! And what then? The Imperial road! The south? Italy? What then? Was it a way out? It was only a way in again. Birkin stood high in the painful air, looking at the peaks, and the way south. Was it any good going south, to Italy? Down the old, old Imperial road?

He turned away. Either the heart would break, or cease to care. Best cease to care. Whatever the mystery which has brought forth man and the universe, it is a non-human mystery, it has its own great ends, man is not the criterion. Best leave it all to the vast, creative, non-human mystery. Best strive with oneself only, not with the universe.

'God cannot do without man.' It was a saying of some great French religious teacher. But surely this is false. God can do without man. God could do without the ichthyosauri and the mastodon. These monsters failed creatively to develop, so God, the creative mystery, dispensed with them. In the same way the mystery could dispense with man, should he too fail creatively to change and develop. The eternal creative mystery could dispose of man, and replace him with a finer created being. Just as the horse has taken the place of the mastodon.

It was very consoling to Birkin, to think this. If humanity ran into a *cul de sac* and expended itself, the timeless creative mystery would bring forth some other being, finer, more wonderful, some new, more lovely race, to carry on the embodiment of creation. The game was never up. The mystery of creation was fathomless, infallible, inexhaustible, forever. Races came and went, species passed away, but ever new species arose, more lovely, or equally lovely, always surpassing wonder. The fountain-head was incorruptible and unsearchable. It' had no limits. It could bring forth miracles, create utter new races and new species, in its own hour, new forms of consciousness, new forms of body, new units of being. To be man was as nothing compared to the possibilities of the creative mystery. To have one's pulse beating direct from the mystery, this was perfection, unutterable satisfaction. Human or inhuman mattered nothing. The perfect pulse throbbed with indescribable being, miraculous unborn species.

Birkin went home again to Gerald. He went into the room, and sat down on the bed. Dead, dead and cold!

> Imperial Caesar dead, and turned to clay
> Would stop a hole to keep the wind away.[1]

There was no response from that which had been Gerald. Strange, congealed, icy substance – no more. No more!

Terribly weary, Birkin went away, about the day's business. He did it all quietly, without bother. To rant, to rave, to be tragic, to make situations – it was all too late. Best be quiet, and bear one's soul in patience and in fullness.

But when he went in again, at evening, to look at Gerald between the candles, because of his heart's hunger, suddenly his heart contracted, his own candle all but fell from his hand, as, with a strange whimpering cry, the tears broke out. He sat down in a chair, shaken by a sudden access. Ursula who had followed him, recoiled aghast from him, as he sat with sunken head and body convulsively shaken, making a strange, horrible sound of tears.

'I didn't want it to be like this – I didn't want it to be like this,' he cried to himself. Ursula could but think of the Kaiser's: 'Ich habe as nicht gewollt.'[2] She looked almost with horror on Birkin.

Suddenly he was silent. But he sat with his head dropped, to hide his face. Then furtively he wiped his face with his fingers. Then suddenly he lifted his head, and looked straight at Ursula, with dark, almost vengeful eyes.

'He should have loved me,' he said. 'I offered him.' She, afraid, white, with mute lips answered: 'What difference would it have made!'

'It would!' he said. 'It would.'

He forgot her, and turned to look at Gerald. With head oddly lifted, like a man who draws his head back from an insult, half haughtily, he watched the cold, mute, material face. It had a bluish

1 Lines from Shakespeare's *Hamlet*.
2 (Ger.) "I didn't want it." (as purportedly said by the Kaiser, on war.)

cast. It sent a shaft like ice through the heart of the living man. Cold, mute, material! Birkin remembered how once Gerald had clutched his hand, with a warm, momentaneous grip of final love. For one second – then let go again, let go for ever. If he had kept true to that clasp, death would not have mattered. Those who die, and dying still can love, still believe, do not die. They live still in the beloved. Gerald might still have been living in the spirit with Birkin, even after death. He might have lived with his friend, a further life.

But now he was dead, like clay, like bluish, corruptible ice. Birkin looked at the pale fingers, the inert mass. He remembered a dead stallion he had seen: a dead mass of maleness, repugnant. He remembered also the beautiful face of one whom he had loved, and who had died still having the faith to yield to the mystery. That dead face was beautiful, no one could call it cold, mute, material. No one could remember it without gaining faith in the mystery, without the soul's warming with new, deep life-trust.

And Gerald! The denier! He left the heart cold, frozen, hardly able to beat. Gerald's father had looked wistful, to break the heart: but not this last terrible look of cold, mute Matter. Birkin watched and watched.

Ursula stood aside watching the living man stare at the frozen face of the dead man. Both faces were unmoved and unmoving. The candle-flames flickered in the frozen air, in the intense silence.

'Haven't you seen enough?' she said.

He got up.

'It's a bitter thing to me,' he said.

'What – that he's dead?' she said.

His eyes just met hers. He did not answer.

'You've got me,' she said.

He smiled and kissed her.

'If I die,' he said, 'you'll know I haven't left you.'

'And me?' she cried.

'And you won't have left me,' he said. 'We shan't have any need to despair, in death.'

She took hold of his hand.

'But need you despair over Gerald?' she said.

'Yes,' he answered.

They went away. Gerald was taken to England, to be buried. Birkin and Ursula accompanied the body, along with one of Gerald's brothers. It was the Crich brothers and sisters who insisted on the burial in England. Birkin wanted to leave the dead man in the Alps, near the snow. But the family was strident, loudly insistent.

Gudrun went to Dresden. She wrote no particulars of herself. Ursula stayed at the Mill with Birkin for a week or two. They were both very quiet.

'Did you need Gerald?' she asked one evening.

'Yes,' he said.

'Aren't I enough for you?' she asked.

'No,' he said. 'You are enough for me, as far as a woman is concerned. You are all women to me. But I wanted a man friend, as eternal as you and I are eternal.'

'Why aren't I enough?' she said. 'You are enough for me. I don't want anybody else but you. Why isn't it the same with you?'

'Having you, I can live all my life without anybody else, any other sheer intimacy. But to make it complete, really happy, I wanted eternal union with a man too: another kind of love,' he said.

'I don't believe it,' she said. 'It's an obstinacy, a theory, a perversity.'

'Well – ' he said.

'You can't have two kinds of love. Why should you!'

It seems as if I can't,' he said. 'Yet I wanted it.'

'You can't have it, because it's false, impossible,' she said.

'I don't believe that,' he answered.

THE END